Praise for *The Tây Sơn Rebellion*

"David Lindsay's novel gives us an entertaining and instructive account of the dramatic events that created the Nguyen dynasty of Vietnam in the late eighteenth century. In this critical period of modern Vietnamese history, rebel soldiers, court officials, French soldiers of fortune and missionaries fought and negotiated with each other, until the Nguyen army (fights repeatedly) the band of rebel brothers who launched the Tay Son rebellion.

The author stays close to the historical facts, but he enlivens his account with characters drawn from famous works of Vietnamese literature. There are enough political intrigues, sex scenes, love affairs, and rowdy behavior by sailors, soldiers, and missionaries to satisfy any modern reader. At the same time, readers will gain insights into one of the most formative periods of modern Vietnamese history.

Highly recommended for anyone seeking greater understanding of modern Vietnam in the form of a riveting adventure story."

Peter C. Perdue
Professor of Chinese History, Yale University
Author of two widely acclaimed books: *Exhausting the Earth: State and Peasant in Hunan 1500-1850 A.D.* (Council on East Asian Studies, Harvard University, 1987) and *China Marches West: The Qing Conquest of Central Eurasia* (Harvard University Press, 2005), winner of the 2006 Joseph Levenson Book Prize.

"David Lindsay's *The Tay Son Rebellion* does for Vietnam what Clavell's *Shogun* did for Japan in creating a meticulously researched history of a much misunderstood and under-recognized country. Most Americans have little or incorrect knowledge of Vietnam. Lindsay integrates his very plausible story with a vivid clarification of the history and culture of a society continuously challenged by other countries, large and small throughout the last two thousand years.

His characters give us much to consider when we learn of the country's ability to preserve and value the fundamentals of their culture and history while absorbing nourishing aspects of foreign invaders.

Like Jade River, the Vietnamese have learned to survive, accepting fate as a way of life, yet holding true to their beliefs rooted in Confucianism and filial piety. For this reader, it was more than a good read, it was an epiphany."

Sandra Greer
Senior Human Resource Specialist, Yale University, Retired.

Praise for *The Tây Sơn Rebellion,* continued

"This work of historical fiction takes the reader to three continents to reveal the global connections behind the life and times of late eighteenth-century Vietnam. Although a product of Lindsay's imagination, it is informed by the author's diligent historical research, his knowledge of local customs, and many imagined, but plausible, conversations. The work climaxes in the step-by-step story of the Tayson Rebellion. Lindsay has created a suspenseful and unforgettable account, which results in a pleasing introduction to an important period."

Beatrice "Betsy" Bartlett
Professor Emeritus, Chinese History, Yale University. Author of *Monarchs and Ministers, The Grand Council in Mid-Ch'ing China, 1723-1820* (University of California Press, 1991).

"*The Tay Son Rebellion* was enjoyable reading, bringing back many good memories of my grandmother telling us such stories. It was also eerie as well as sometimes, it was confusing what is fiction and what was real. Sometimes it felt like I was listening to my Grandmother again. As a historical novel, it is great providing so much information. I like that at times, it has a martial art feel to it and at times romantic.

The book is not only about the Tay Son period, it is also about the history of Vietnam. The author finds every opportunity to tell about other important historical events as well. I really liked how even in the conversations of your characters, you inserted bits of Vietnamese history, so I learned a lot while enjoying the story.

The first time I read the manuscript was very slow, because I am Vietnamese, and I wanted to check on your facts on history I didn't know well, which repeatedly turned out to be correct. Thank you for letting me read it."

Kimanh Nguyen
Bookkeeper and Office Manager, New Haven, Connecticut.

Praise for *The Tây Sơn Rebellion,* continued

"What a great book! It is truly powerful storytelling that conveys fascinating history. Your storytelling shows so much respect for the different cultures and people. ... What I most loved was having the historical perspective between the three continents. Your knowledge of martial arts and music add enormously to the story. I appreciate how you handle the different cultural perceptions of sex and prostitution."

Marney Morrison
Retired teacher, English for Speakers of Other Languages (ESOL), Albemarle County, Virginia.

"Your writing gives the reader an opening to see eighteenth-century 'Vietnam.' *The Tay Son Rebellion* dislodges twentieth-century media images of Vietnam by offering a glimpse of the Vietnamese spirit alive on the land with a depth of field in time and temperament. People, with humility and reverence, or with duplicity and greed, stand in their own struggle in their unique natural and political landscapes.

I share in the lingering psychic guilt from my generation's part in the saga of the Vietnam War, and in our nation's collective sense of 'failure to win.' Somehow, *The Tay Son Rebellion* delivers a respite to confusion with greater understanding as a healing balm. Thank you for this book."

Kathleen Schomaker
Executive Director, Gray Is Green, Hamden, Connecticut.

My language tutor and consultant, the extraordinary Huỳnh Sanh Thông, who passed away in 2008, was a Lecturer at Yale in Vietnamese Studies and the Director of Yale's Southeast Asian Refugee Project. Around 1986, he read an earlier draft of this book. To my great relief, he found my portrayals of Vietnamese acceptable and enjoyable. He said, "It is a good book, and well written. But it is too much like James Michener, and not enough like James Clavell." I was relieved and delighted. I never forgot his help or advice, and I hope he would be charmed by the changes.

David Lindsay, Jr.
From "Acknowledgements and Gratitude"
The Tây Sơn Rebellion

Praise for *The Tây Sơn Rebellion,* continued

"This book is a very engaging read, and I thoroughly enjoyed it. Having had the opportunity to read a much earlier draft some twenty years ago I can say the novel has reached a very pleasing level of maturity in the interim. I felt educated, entertained and appreciative at the close. Incorporating material from different corners of the world during the same time period gave added depth and context to the story. And it also reminded me never to go into politics. This novel would make a great audiobook.

The martial arts scenes and the marine battles provided yet another dimension to the novel, adding to its already high quality. Clearly the author has had first hand experience in both these areas and has generously leaned on those experiences in order to produce such realistic details. He has struck a good balance in the level of detail—enough to allow one to develop a vivid mental picture of the scenes, yet not so much as to prompt one to skip passages."

Raymond S. Farinato
Aikido Shihan (6th Dan master teacher**)**, PhD physical chemist, Adjunct Professor at Columbia University, Earth & Environmental Engineering.

Short Summary from the back cover of the book

The Tây Sơn Rebellion covers a major civil war in Vietnam, 1770-1802. The country had been divided into north and south for 150 years: the Trịnh dynasty in the north, and the Nguyễn dynasty in the South. Both dynasties allowed corruption to grow, and their people suffered. The three Hồ brothers started a peasant uprising in the center, in Tây Sơn, and eventually defeated both warlords. They let a young Nguyễn prince escape, and he is helped by a French Catholic Bishop, who raises a small French Navy in India to help the young Prince Nguyễn Ánh attack the Ho brothers. The outcome helps to determine important parameters of modern Vietnam.

The Tây Sơn Rebellion

Historical Fiction of Eighteenth-Century Vietnam

by David Lindsay, Jr.

A hundred years—in this life span on earth,
talent and destiny how apt to feud.
You must go through a play of ebb and flow
and watch such things as make you sick at heart.
Is it so strange that losses balance gains?
Blue Heaven's wont to strike a rose from spite.

> —Nguyễn Du, *The Tale of Kiều*
> translation by Huỳnh Sanh Thông

Diamonds are found only in the dark places of the
earth, truths are found only in the depths of thought.

> —Victor Hugo, *Les Misérables*

When you know you do not yet have the means to conquer,
you guard your energy and wait.
When you know that an opponent is vulnerable, then you
attack the heart and take it.

> —Sun Tzu, *The Art of War*

The Tây Sơn Rebellion

Historical Fiction of Eighteenth-Century Vietnam

Published by
Footmad & Cherry Blossom Press
37 Hepburn Rd., Hamden, CT 06517

Cover Design by CSA
Interior Design by Alex Wheelwright

For more information about
The Tây Sơn Rebellion, please visit either (www):
TheTaysonRebellion.com
or, DavidLindsayJr.com

Copies of this book can be purchased
almost anywhere books are sold.

For bulk purchases or promotions,
contact: footmad.cbpress@gmail.com

The Tây Sơn Rebellion
Historical Fiction of Eighteenth-Century Vietnam
Library of Congress Control Number: 2017914762
ISBN-13: 978-0-692-95443-0
ISBN-10:   0-692-95443-0

BISAC: Fiction / Historical / General

170925.11

Contents

14. Le Dai Viet en 1790

Map of Đại Việt in 1790 from Alexis Faure,
Les Français en Cochinchine au XVIIIe siècle.
Mgr. Pigneau de Béhaine Évêque d'Adran

i

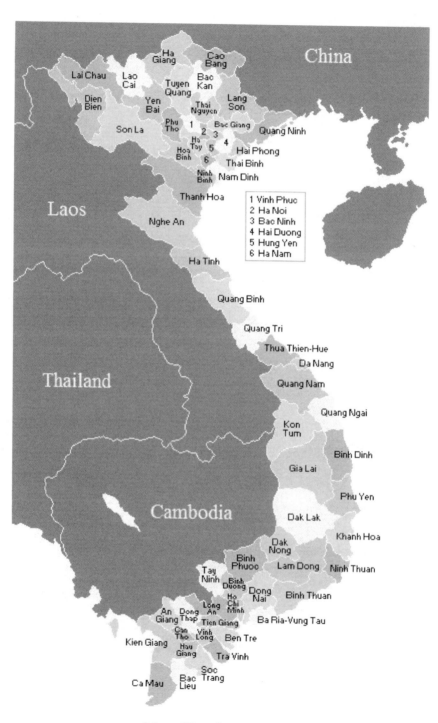

China

Laos

Thailand

Cambodia

Ha Giang

Cao Bang

Lai Chau

Lao Cai

Bac Kan

Tuyen Quang

Dien Bien

Yen Bai

Thai Nguyen

Lang Son

Son La

Phu Tho

1 Bac Giang

2 3

4 Quang Ninh

Hoa Binh

Ha Tay

5

6

Hai Phong

Ninh Binh

Thai Binh

Nam Dinh

Thanh Hoa

Nghe An

1	Vinh Phuc
2	Ha Noi
3	Bac Ninh
4	Hai Duong
5	Hung Yen
6	Ha Nam

Ha Tinh

Quang Binh

Quang Tri

Thua Thien-Hue

Da Nang

Quang Nam

Quang Ngai

Kon Tum

Binh Dinh

Gia Lai

Phu Yen

Dak Lak

Khanh Hoa

Dak Nong

Binh Phuoc

Lam Dong

Ninh Thuan

Tay Ninh

Binh Duong

Dong Nai

Binh Thuan

Ho Chi Minh

An Giang

Dong Thap

Long An

Tien Giang

Kien Giang

Can Tho

Vinh Long

Ben Tre

Ba Ria-Vung Tau

Hau Giang

Tra Vinh

Ca Mau

Bac Lieu

Soc Trang

Map of Provinces of Vietnam

After the war with the U.S., from Wikipedia, "Vietnam shaded relief."
Licensed under Public Domain

Dedication

It is appropriate before a novel about the history
and culture of Confucian Vietnam, to offer a
respectful and loving bow to the ancestors.

Therefore, I dedicate this effort
to my esteemed ancestors: my grandparents;
Edwin Charles Austin and Marion Roberts Austin, and
George Nelson Lindsay and F. Eleanor Vliet Lindsay,
and my parents;
Elizabeth Austin Lindsay and David Alexander Lindsay.

David A. Lindsay, Jr.

For your convenience there is a
List of Characters at the end, page 403.

Huệ is pronounced *Whey*.
Nguyễn is pronounced *Win*.
Tây Sơn is pronounced *Tey Shun*.
Benoit is pronounced *Ben-wha*.
Guillaume is pronounced *Gee-yome*
Tao is pronounced *Dow*.
Palanquin is pronounced *pallen-keen*.

Prologue
Historical Background of Vietnam

Vietnam is a land of sea coast and mountains with a long and distinguished history. This historical fiction unfolds near the end of the eighteenth century. At that time, as at the present, the political environment had evolved from events preceding it. Just as mountains are made over millennia, societies are created over many centuries.

Two of the venerable and ancient civilizations of the Far East, China and India, are held apart by the once impenetrable walls of Tibet. The Tibetan Plateau hides behind the Himalayas to the south, the Kunlun to the north, and the Tanglha Mountains to the east. The Tanglha Mountains are composed of many chains, which drift south like the fingers of a giant hand, providing natural boundaries between Burma (now Myanmar), Siam (now Thailand), Laos, Vietnam, and China. Without those long, finger-like mountain ranges coming from the great palm of Tibet, these little countries might never have gained or preserved their autonomy from the giants to the north and west.

Both cultural titans, China and India, were slowly expanding, and this great drooping hand of mountains forced them to grow toward each other via the sea. With the patience of mountain glaciers, the two cultures inched closer together. They clashed and crushed and mingled blood along the long coast that became known in the West as Indo-China, or Indochina—the land of blended cultures between India and China.

Vietnam has had many names. Long ago Vietnam was an ancient land called Văn Lang. This minor kingdom on the Red River became Âu Lạc, which begat Nam Việt, or Southern Việt Kingdom, which a Chinese army, in 111 B.C., conquered and turned into An Nam, or Pacified South. Việt refers to the Chinese word yüeh, meaning many. The Chinese called the Việt. the Yüeh tribes: the one hundred tribes of non-Chinese ethnic groups in southern China and northern Vietnam.

The Chinese conquerors from the north established colonies in An Nam. They kept their Việt slaves and lackeys in line for 1,000 years with whips, swords, and thumbscrews. They tried hard to teach the Việt to think of themselves as Chinese, or like the civilized people of *Zhongguo*, meaning Middle or Central Kingdom. They introduced the Vietnamese to many Chinese educational and organizational structures, such as advancement through government exams. Over time, intermarriage blurred the lines of social and racial separation. Soon the Việt aristocracy contained a mixture of Chinese and Vietnamese lords and ladies. Many of the Chinese colonists adopted the Việt perspective that the land was separate and unique from China. The new generations of the scholar class wrote in Chinese, but thought and spoke in Vietnamese.

After a number of brave attempts, the scholars and peasants of An Nam successfully rebelled against Chinese military rule and colonial occupation. They overthrew their Chinese overlords, and defeated a Chinese army sent to restore order. Once again, a local Việt aristocracy ruled the land. In A.D. 937, An Nam, the Pacified South, became Đại Cồ Việt, or Great Việt. The Chinese were never far away from Đại Cồ Việt, which from its inception to the 1500s was just the northern Tonkin of modern Vietnam. The Chinese remained eager to reconquer their old colony to the south.

In the fifteenth century the great cities of Hà Nội, Sài Gòn, and Huế did not exist in name; Sài Gòn, renamed Hồ Chí Minh City in 1975, did not exist at all. Hà Nội in the north was called Thăng Long, meaning Ascending Dragon. The dragon stood for kingship and sovereignty. Thăng Long was the capital of the Kingdom of Đại Cồ Việt. The Sài Gòn area and the huge Mekong Delta in the south were mostly unpopulated. Near the present site of Đà Nẵng (Tourane) stood Indrapura, the capital city of the expanding Cham Empire, which ruled hundreds of miles of narrow coastland. The Chams were merchants and seafarers, hardy fighters whose ancestors came from India and the Malay and Polynesian islands. They worshiped the gods of India: Brahma, Vishnu, and Shiva, the Gods of Creation, Preservation, and Destruction. They offered for sacrifice food and drink, especially soma stalks, soma beverages (an intoxicating drink prepared from the plant and used in Vedic rituals), and animal meats. The Chams practiced the cult of idol worship, believed in reincarnation, and that each individual must sing and dance for the Gods, and take individual responsibility for his or her own salvation, or liberation.

While the Indic Chams were idol worshippers, the Chinese-oriented or Sinic Việt were Ancestor worshippers. For this and other reasons, the two peoples were not compatible, and both cultures were expanding over the rich littoral, the coastline near the shore, and populating the adjacent bottom lands. The Chams attacked the Việt in the eleventh century from their base at Indrapura and were defeated. The two cultures fought each other periodically and ruthlessly until 1471, when the Việts finally annihilated the Chams as a military power. The destruction of the Chams made possible the colonization of Champa, today's central Vietnam, and then the rich Mekong Delta in the south over the next 400 years. The surviving Chams fled up into the mountains.

The Mekong Delta had ostensibly belonged to the Indic Khmers of Cambodia and a variety of local tribes, but the Khmer Empire had risen like a giant, grown old, and declined centuries before. Also significant, the Khmer people of Kampuchea (later called Cambodia) had never seriously settled the wide delta area or cleared its jungles.

As units of Việt soldier-colonists pushed south out of the narrow coastal plains of the central part of the country, they emerged into the rich and wide plains of the

Mekong wilderness, a wilderness that was as large and as promising as the densely populated Red River Delta to the north. Poor peasants from the north streamed south to join the expansion units. These peasant-soldiers were motivated by the promise that most of the land that they cleared would become their own. By the seventeenth century, Sài Gòn had become the new commercial center for the pioneers of the Mekong Delta frontier.

Of small concern to the Việt mandarins at the time, around 1516 there appeared long-nosed and bearded barbarians in square-rigged ships bristling with cannon and transporting priests. First came the Portuguese, then the Dutch, then the English, followed soon after by the French. In some ways the Western barbarians were all alike. They all had long noses and body hair on their arms and legs. They were all keenly interested in trade, and they all believed in the Lord God Jesus Christ, the Son of God, true God from true God. They insisted unabashedly that their God, the Father, Son, and Holy Ghost, was the only God; their trinity, was the only trinity.

Chapter 1
Tây Sơn, a Village in Đại Việt
1770

Dawn began with a dark purple sky and a red glimmer of light. As light spread behind the plain to the east, it illuminated a ridge of mountains to the west. Morning birdsong and insect noise made a vibrating racket.

Five men, four side by side in a row behind the first, faced the blue-red firmament in the east, a cool northeast breeze in their faces. They executed an exercise called the Salutation to the Sun. Their hands moved up together very slowly, five souls in physical synchrony with one another, searching for harmony within themselves and with the awakening world around them. As coordinated as a school of fish underwater, and as silent as reflections of bamboo on a lake, they arched their backs backward, then bent down, touching their fingertips to the ground. After a slow lunge to stretch the groin, they executed a martial push-up into the cobra position, a body wave that inverted their backs like the bow of a boat. As they uncoiled to the forward arch, not a groan could be heard through their deep exhalations of breath. The sounds of birds and insects were muffled by the rustle of the constant monsoon breeze through the tall pines and the thickets of tangled banyan with its many trunks.

Young Hồ Huệ's right foot came forward for the second groin stretch of the ancient yoga exercise. His mind was still sleepy, and his concentration was weak as his body went through the motions. He was aware of the rising sun, a God flying on the back of a dragon, as it sailed up through the distant hilltops. Huệ and the others finished their Salutation to the Sun, arms slowly rising over their heads to acknowledge the God of Heaven and to strengthen the whole body.

What beautiful light, Huệ thought, as the glow haloed the black hills. His mind felt calm and in unison with his body, and with the greater universe of Heaven above. *I love this place, my home,* he thought. *It has bottom land, and that's good. Bottom land is scarce—but it is the only land you want. Land has to be flat and open for the rice to grow. Grandfather and Grandmother cleared it; their bones are nearby. They were such an imposing couple, as tough as bamboo, which grows in the north. I must never disappoint them.*

Hồ Huệ and his family lived outside the village of Tây Sơn by the highlands of Central Vietnam. Like the Chinese, the Vietnamese give their surname or family name first, and their given or personal name second. Huệ began to meditate. He became open and receptive. He simply absorbed the beauty of his surroundings while he tested the stiffness and flexibility of his muscular, seventeen-year-old frame after a good night of sleep on a reed mat.

Huệ's father, Physician Hồ Danh, was leading the exercises as usual. He too was thinking of his father and mother, their newest Great Ancestors. *Today I feel closer to them than I did as a child,* thought Physician Hồ. *I have spent many years stooped over this field, and I know it like my wife; both are ever-changing and yet familiar. Year after year the Gods are generous, and the land makes enough rice for the whole family and even a surplus.* Physician Hồ was a rugged, square-jawed man with laugh lines around his eyes. He was a *kung-fu,* or master, of both medicine and Võ thuật Bình Định, the martial arts of Bình Định Province. Hồ Danh led the four young men behind him in a long T'ai chi exercise. The moves were slow and distinct, but their meaning was obscure. The men danced slowly and gracefully through the dawn.

The Hồ boys were studying one of the mysteries of the East—*T'ai chi chuan,* or Supreme ultimate fist, the art of moving naturally with mind and body in unison to unleash extraordinary strength. Physician Hồ indicated this morning that he wanted to do the toughening exercises with Huệ. The five then split up into two and three for arm rubbing and body pounding.

Huệ looked straight into his father's dark, penetrating eyes and began to push against him. Huệ dropped his center deeper and deeper into the ground. *I am honored,* he thought, *to be chosen first. Nhạc and Lữ won't like it, since I'm the youngest. It could be a rough workout. I must concentrate harder. Look at nothing and see everything. Concentrate on the big picture, and not every little distraction. Watch the body and not the weapon to know where the weapon will attack from. I must tell Father soon that I want to study law, not medicine. I wish to study the Classics and take the government exams. I can't do all that and study medicine.*

Physician Hồ Danh's eldest son, Nhạc, took up a strong stance between his brother Lữ and their friend and neighbor, Lương Hoàng, both nineteen years old. Nhạc was two years older than Lữ, and four years older than Huệ—he had always been the leader. Nhạc already had some success in business, trading betel leaves and areca nuts, both required as essential wedding gifts for every Việt marriage. Nhạc stared straight ahead, while his two partners stood on either side. He tried to open the aperture of his circle of vision so he could see both opponents by not staring at either one.

Nhạc addressed the neighbor Lương Hoàng, "You appear tired this morning. Have you been smelling flowers in the moonlight?"

Lương Hoàng grinned. "I went last night to Diem's Wine Shop and played dominoes with Võ Văn Nhậm till very late."

"Did you win anything from the frog?"

"Yes, it was an extremely profitable night."

Lữ said under his breath, "That frog-faced buffalo herder couldn't win at dominoes to save his grandfather's tablet."

Nhạc said smiling, "If I recall, he won money from you the last time you played with him."

"Oh, that was a trivial amount," said Lữ with a grimace, pulling down the corners of his mouth.

The Hồ brothers were strong and healthy, with sharp brown eyes and bushy shocks of black hair. Hồ Nhạc was not only the eldest of the three sons, but the strongest as well. Nhạc had a hard, square face. He was neither handsome nor ugly, just plain and tough looking. His squat nose seemed too small on his wide face. The top half of his large ears stuck out beyond his wide cheekbones, especially where the cheeks indented sharply at the eyes. He loosely resembled a ferocious temple guardian. Nhạc turned handsome when he smiled, but that was not his way. He thought it unmanly to smile too much. Nhạc had grown up throwing his younger brothers around, so Lữ's and Huệ's nicknames for him were Brute and Pond Monster.

Second Son Lữ thought, *Father shouldn't favor Huệ like this; he will just become more pompous. Oww! Arm rubbing is all right, but I hate this arm pounding that follows. Oww! I never like the pain, I don't care how useful the training is supposed to be. Fornicating duck—against weapons boxing is a waste of time!*

Lữ hit his fist against Nhạc's bare forearm. He was a poor copy of his elder brother, and a little less successful at everything. His face was flat and rough like a poorly mortared wall and his expression usually one of disinterest. His ears also stuck out. His face seemed bland until he smiled, and even then he seemed shy and hesitant. Lữ wiped his nose with his free hand, felt his balance was off, and moved his feet.

Third Son Huệ and his father switched from arm pounding to leg kicking. Huệ was not only the youngest and the brightest, he was also the most appealing. Huệ had a more graceful chin and thinner lips than his brothers. The bridge of his nose was finer. His eyes and face were quick to smile with confidence. It was as if the Gods had made Nhạc, decided to soften the look for the next face, Lữ's, but did not find the right balance of lines until the third attempt, with Huệ. To the annoyance of Nhạc and Lữ, two girls they spoke to at the market referred teasingly to Huệ as the handsome one.

To make matters worse, Huệ was also the most successful of the three in poetry and calligraphy. He was not as big as Nhạc or as fat as Lữ, but he made up for his smaller size with wit and coordination. Of course, he had been picked on for years, particularly by Lữ, so he was naturally more attached to Nhạc, whom he had worshipped and looked to as his protector when he was very young.

Physician Hồ Danh began to vigorously rub his lightly bruised forearms, signaling the end of the toughening exercise to Huệ and the others. Hồ Danh said, "Line up for *Sanchin*." The young men made a line of uneven heights behind him.

All bowed to the golden sun and then tightened their bodies in preparation for the arduous training exercise of the Kata of Three Conflicts in the hourglass stance. After three times through the strenuous drill of fingertip strikes and short circular blocks, and a short rest for breath, they practiced prearranged fighting exercises.

Demons and Genie, Lữ thought, *I am tired. Luckily, no one realizes how late I came home last night. I can't wait to tell Nhạc and Hoàng that I went to the Fragrant Flower House of Bliss to see Wondrous Blossom. If only the wind-breaking trollop wasn't as costly as jade.*

Wincing in pain as he blocked a volley of furious punches from Nhạc, Huệ said, "Not so hard."

"I'm so sorry," said Nhạc, and thought, *You'd better be quick or I'll bruise you good.* In some ways it was a typical workout. Nhạc was often full of anger, while Lữ was frequently tired. Huệ was usually the alert student. Between brief daydreams, he managed to glean the most from the instructor.

Near the end of the workout, Hồ Danh said, "Pair off for sparring." He bowed to his eldest, Nhạc. Lữ bowed to Lương Hoàng. Huệ watched the others trade combinations of punches and kicks, all controlled so as not to cause any serious damage. Huệ admired his father's fluid technique. He thought, *Father is a master of his art. His movements are all simple and natural; they appear effortless.*

Huệ rubbed his arms; they hurt from the arm pounding. He comforted himself by remembering some of his father's favorite words: *To become tolerant of pain is one of the great benefits of boxing. In a fight, you know that you can take a punch and still think. It is useful in many other applications as well.*

This is true, Huệ thought. *When is life ever completely free of pain?*

Physician Hồ and Nhạc began to spar. Huệ carefully watched Nhạc and their father trade hard punches and kicks. With admiration he thought, *Their conditioning is so good, they are not in pain or in danger of hurting each other.* Repeatedly Hồ Danh made blocks that created openings for his attacks. He was scoring most of the points, but every year Nhạc came closer to being his father's equal.

"You must recover from your attack much faster," Hồ Danh said to Nhạc, though he was breathing hard. "Every attack must end in a block, because every time you attack, you leave yourself open somewhere." Then Physician Hồ chuckled and smiled kindly at his eldest son. "It is a very simple idea, and yet hard to execute. And from the other side, every block offers an effective time to attack. The openings are always created by the attacker."

Nhạc bowed stiffly to his father. *I wasn't just passing wind,* he thought. *It wasn't that bad.* He was embarrassed at being corrected in front of his younger brothers. Nhạc put on his mask of calm to hide his inability to comprehend the full meaning of the advice. Huệ could see that his brother looked frustrated and irritated.

The sharp-eyed neighbor Lương Hoàng had no trouble controlling Lữ, for Hoàng was better. Before long Hồ Danh said, "That's enough. Now Nhạc and Huệ spar together." The eldest and the youngest sons bowed to each other, and put up their hands. In wrestling and throwing, Nhạc was hard to beat because of his size and strength. But in boxing, Huệ could usually outscore his elder brother with superior strategy. At the age of seventeen, he was already an outstanding boxer. He had speed and cunning. His toughest opponent besides his father was his best friend, Lương Hoàng.

Nhạc and Huệ began to circle, exchanging kicks and punches. Nhạc kicked Huệ hard in the stomach. Huệ winced. Trying to make light of his bruise, he said, "Remember that filial piety is the highest virtue, and that the ancients said, of the thirty-six ways to escape, the best is to run away." He then retreated, deftly using wrist blocks before a flurry of punches. Nhạc punched right again. Huệ moved in with a right wrist block and an immediate left punch to the open side. He pulled the punch well before it hit Nhạc's face. Huệ did not touch his older brother, who missed what had happened, but the point was clear to their father and to Lương Hoàng, both careful observers compared to Lữ, who was admiring some striped squirrels at play.

Huệ made a few more points, some of them obvious. *This wind maker thinks he knows everything,* Nhạc thought angrily. He attacked the younger Huệ again with punches and kicks, drove him back, then let Huệ drive him back again. Suddenly Nhạc's head bobbed before he leapt up into the air and sent off a flying jump-kick. The reaction was instantaneous.

Huệ jumped back and automatically executed fast circular blocks with each hand. The blocks were instinctive and powerful. A vicious strike requires a lightning counter. Huệ's right hand caught Nhạc's foot before it penetrated to the chest, and by the time Huệ's block was finished, Nhạc had lost his balance and center. As he was flying through the air, his whole body tilted back until it was horizontal to the ground, as if he were now a table and Huệ was the leg. Huệ held his block as Nhạc's larger body poised in the air and then crashed to the ground. Nhạc slapped the grass to cushion the blow. Their father, Hồ Danh, laughed heartily, and so did the others. Huệ, proud as a peacock, offered his brother a hand and helped him stand up. Nhạc pulled himself up, his pride the only injured party, and he bowed correctly to his brother. *Damn that little bastard,* he thought. *I'll get him yet.* Nhạc could hide his fury at his brother, but he shook his head and muttered, showing disgust with himself.

Chapter 2
The Tết Thanh Minh Festival
1770

It was the morning of the Tết Thanh Minh, or Pure and Bright Moon Festival, also called Tomb Sweeping Day, in the year of 342 in the Later Lê Dynasty, or Năm Canh Mùi, the Year of the Goat, or 4468 by the old Chinese calendar. Tomb Sweeping Day occurred every year in the third month, the magical month of the Dragon, usually April in the calendar of Pope Gregory XIII. After vegetable and noodle soup and tea for breakfast, the Hồ family visited the ancestral graveyard, a small plot of their own land between two green rice paddies. The graves had some shade from a few gnarled pine trees.

A small canal ran along the property, and other rice paddies lay on both sides of the Hồ plot, but there were no other solitary thatched houses nearby. Most of the other families of the village of Tây Sơn chose to live in the closed quarters of the village compound, almost a stockade, protected by high, impenetrable hedges, a mile away from the Hồ farmhouse and thirty miles northwest of Quy Nhơn, the capital of Bình Định Province.

The enclosed hamlet was how the Việt had lived for centuries. Although it was designed for protection, it also provided for a cohesive, tightly knit community. The Hồ family house was east of the village, and acted as a kind of sentinel. Another family lived on the road on the western side of the village, guarding that approach. There the road went up into the less traveled mountains, and was used mostly by the Degar—the highlanders.

The wide emerald paddy fields, which ran on both sides of the irrigation canal, were hemmed in by green, forested hills to the north and south. Patches of trees grew densely at the base of steep-sloped hills where the cultivated paddies ended. The jungle foliage climbed up the hillsides in ragged tentacles; the upper slopes were often too steep and rocky for many trees to take hold. Large, leafy palm trees and pine thickets made the base of the hills seem especially dense and green, except where cut down and cleared. The poorer farmers—mostly Cham, Gia Rai, and Ê Đê highlanders—had to cultivate the more gradual hillsides for lack of better lands. Here and there copses of trees were interspersed with carefully terraced vegetable gardens.

The Hồ family members helped weed the ancestral grave site and tended the flowers planted beside the mounds. Physician Hồ Danh, wearing a blue silk, four-panel tunic, made offerings of incense to the dead. He and his family knelt and kow-towed, or knocked their heads to the ground, to honor the graves of their Ancestors, as he solemnly intoned, "We have our Ancestors to thank for our land and our lives, our position and good standing in the village of Tây Sơn.

"My father, your Great Ancestor, was drafted by the Trịnh. He fought for those cutthroats as a medic and archer against the Nguyễn for many years, till he was captured after a battle. He was sent to a brutal Nguyễn prison camp that had the responsibility of cutting back and clearing the jungle for the village of Tây Sơn. After surviving six years of hard labor and near starvation, he was allowed to clear his own farm. He apprenticed under a physician to study medicine, married, and settled down. Their poverty during those first years of freedom is hard to imagine for any of us who have not lived on the edge of starvation, living on insects, weeds, and small creatures. It took years of apprenticeship before he practiced medicine and healing. The Great Ancestor continued to labor on the public work projects to buy rice until his own fields were cleared, planted, and harvested. His wife raised vegetables, and when she wasn't selling them, she was sewing, weaving, or spinning from sunup to sundown."

Physician Hồ observed his three sons, his daughter, and the few others listening in silence. "We still hate our rulers the Nguyễn and have no love for the Trịnh. Let us pray that they continue the peace, until a worthy emperor under Heaven may reign over all our people. Our people are tenacious, and they will rally behind a worthy leader."

Physician Hồ stood up and started back toward the house. The rite was over, and the family slowly filed down the path surrounded on all sides by brimming rice fields. They were accompanied by Lương Hoàng, whose parents were away tending a sick relative.

Third son Huệ's mind was full of familiar questions. *How can I best serve such a noble ancestor? The old goat is a hard act to follow. My father has chosen me as the next physician. He has tried to teach the medical texts to both of my older brothers, but neither seemed interested or able to apply themselves to the enormous task of memorizing the chapters of knowledge, the anatomy, medicines, diseases, and concordant rites. Nhạc prefers being a trader. And yet I am attracted more to government. Will the old man think me ungrateful?*

After they quietly walked back to the main house, Lữ captured a chicken and stretched its neck out for Nhạc, who decapitated it with a meat cleaver. The red blood spurted into a wok. After the pulsations stopped, they gave the warm carcass to Nhạc's capable young wife, Spring Flower (Xuân Hoa), who plucked, gutted, and then boiled it whole.

Autumn Moon (Thu Nguyệt), Physician Hồ's small-bodied wife, creased from many years and from bearing six children, with two lost at childbirth, had changed out of her red and green silk four-panel tunic. Jade River (Ngọc Hà), their slender daughter, had her mother's high cheekbones. She had changed out of her new blue and green tunic. The women, including the daughter-in-law Spring Flower, now again wore their plain flaxen work clothes, and they spent the rest of the morning making ceremonial dishes. Spring Flower said, "Mistress, would you season the chicken for me? I want to watch, because your chicken tastes so good."

"I would be happy to show you," said Autumn Moon. She quickly made a marinade of garlic, ginger, soy, parsley, and fish sauce, which she handed to her daughter-in-law. "Those are the amounts, but I never measure. Now take the big brush and paint the bird with the sauce till it's gone. Jade River, go out front and cut a chrysanthemum flower."

"Yes, Mother," she said taking up a small knife. The women left the bird unstuffed, as tradition demanded. Minutes later, Jade River carefully placed the chrysanthemum in the fowl's beak. She placed the chicken on the altar, next to the clay pot of glutinous rice with waxy beans.

Father, mother, the three brothers, their sister, and Nhạc's wife all kowtowed to their ancestral tablets at the family altar, while Lương Hoàng politely watched. They knelt, clapped their hands above their heads to signal the spirits for their attention, and bowed their heads toward the floor three times out of respect for the living spirits of their beloved Ancestors. The essence of the fine foods with the offerings of burning incense rose up to Heaven, where the Ancestors could feast on the spiritual nectar. The leftovers, or that part of each dish that did not rise to Heaven after the ritual feeding of the Ancestors, the family cheerfully consumed themselves.

After the offerings of kowtows, prayers, and food to the Great Ancestors at the family altar, the men of the Hồ family sat down at the benches and stools of the long table in the main room. The house was fragrant with the incense sticks that still burned slowly on the altar alcove. Physician Hồ, his back to the altar, sat with his three strong sons, Nhạc, Lữ, and Huệ, and their friend Hoàng. While one could see Nhạc's square head came from his father, Huệ's handsome lines echoed his mother. Autumn Moon's face was wide at the eyes and narrow in the jaw. Her tawny face was lined like fine driftwood. A weathered beauty, Autumn Moon was cheerful and apparently serene, content to serve her family as she worked quietly in the background. Women, not equal to men under Việt law or custom, learned to accept their lot, or grew bitter as a bad melon.

By the stove, Jade River said, "Ma, I do not like that we do all the housework. I wish to wander outdoors like my brothers and play in the fields." Autumn Moon, her rich black hair streaked with gray, looked fondly at her smooth-faced daughter.

"Child, my mother told me that once long ago we were the masters. Grandma said, 'We will not be servants to the men forever. But we were cruel masters, so now we are paying for sins in many previous lives.' We are not so unlucky, my darling. At least we are not Han Chinese; our feet are not folded in two and bound into painful little *Penjing* lilies. We can run and dance like the Hindu God Shiva on the head of ignorance."

Autumn Moon, Spring Flower, and Jade River carried ceremonial offerings from the altar to the red-lacquered food table. Autumn Moon was concealing certain worries even from her daughter. *I wonder,* she thought, as she moved to the altar, *if the Great Ancestor was a philanderer the way I suspect my husband is. I don't know for certain, but I'm almost sure that he's lying about the widow Cao's bouts of fever. To add insult to injury, she's simple and dull both to look at and to talk to. She's a skinny bit of skirt. Yhek, if Merciful Heaven hadn't given her a nose, you couldn't tell her front from her behind.*

Jade River sang as she worked. She was an unblemished beauty of fifteen, a child who was almost a woman, and the jewel of her father's heart. Her face was more delicate than Huệ's. She had large, sensuous lips floating between her delicate chin and her dancing eyes, framed by half-moon eyebrows. Her hands moved quickly, cutting vegetables. *I hope I will be allowed to go to the fair today,* she thought. *The needlepoint I made for Hoàng has been ready for months. If Father knew of it, he would never let me go. I know it is my duty not to lie to my father, but I heard it is an old tradition that women are allowed to have their secrets from men.*

Jade River remembered the day her smiling mother called her away from her chores and said in a careful voice, "Daughter, I have a gift for you today." Autumn Moon had a gleam in her eye. Her mother handed her a small packet in colored paper, which Jade River carefully opened to discover her mother's favorite silver hair pins.

"Ma , how soon can I wear them?" she asked, her eyes aglow. Once those metal pins caught the folds of her long black hair, she was officially no longer a child but a woman, ready to have the parents of suitors approach her own parents discreetly through a go-between, or vice versa.

"Let's see how they look," her mother said laughing, and placed them carefully on the young maiden's head, pulling the tresses up into glamorous folds. After several starts, the hairdo had the classical air, and mother presented daughter to her father.

Physician Hồ was in his study going over accounts between patients when his wife entered and announced their daughter. Jade River walked in, as if in a dream, terrified that her father would disapprove, and she gracefully knelt before him and kowtowed, placing her delicate hands on the floor, making a diamond-triangle space between forefingers and thumbs, and then touching her forehead to the hands.

"You look beautiful my darling, and it amazes me, you are almost sixteen," said Physician Hồ. "Time is an invincible dragon. I am not surprised that you appear like a woman. What did we expect, for you to stop growing? Now please come here." She got up and he kissed her forehead. He embraced his daughter and murmured to her, "Heaven offers no gain without a loss." Jade River was proud and excited, but she noticed her father was sad and her joy turned to sadness for them both.

Jade River's attention was forced back to the table. "The Gods have blessed me with a wonderful family," Physician Hồ said warmly, his olive skin rough with age. The men all picked up their chopsticks, bowed their heads slightly to Physician Hồ, and began to sample the fragrant dishes while Nhạc's wife, Spring Flower, served tea. Lương Hoàng was delighted to be invited to the physician's table. His handsome round head was topped with straight black hair, and his forehead was creased with a long childhood scar, where Huệ had accidently struck him with an over-enthusiastic backswing of a hoe. He tried ever so hard not to look at Jade River, but nevertheless managed to see her every time she walked behind her brothers Lữ and Huệ. He admired her profile; she moved with the grace of a muntjac doe.

Huệ quietly observed the romance growing between his sister and his friend, and he wondered when his father would become alarmed. *Father has to be aware of it, but he doesn't appear to notice. Perhaps Father likes Hoàng for the same reasons that I do. He's thoughtful, hardworking, and dependable.*

In fact, Physician Hồ was observing his daughter though trying to conceal his concern. Physician Hồ remembered neighbor Trai's recent poetry party at the Stream of Bliss Tea Garden. Each guest had had to compose a poem and read it. Three judges chose the best verse, and its author had to drink a cup of rice wine, small cups of which he found placed on leaf-rafts floating down the little stream meandering through the center of the garden. Hồ had written a melancholy verse about farewells:

Most animals follow the way of nature.
They mate and have offspring,
that they feed and succor,
till the cub is strong enough
to leave the den.
Does the crane, the tiger, or the snake
cry in his heart, as do I,
when my daughter departs?

After it was chosen as one of the best, and he had drunk a cup of wine, his thoughts went to the image of his daughter, dreading her departure. None of the wives his sons would bring into the household would make up for the loss of Jade River. He took his poem, placed it on the leaf, and released both to go down the stream to the River God. *Oh mighty Gods of Heaven and Earth, Spirits and Genie, protect my daughter and my wife, my sons, and their families.*

Physician Hồ now beheld the beautiful young girl before him, his own flesh and blood, a reminder of his wife's early beauty, and realized that the time would soon come to launch his precious flower on a boat-leaf down the garden stream. In his heart, he was saying goodbye to his little girl. She would soon leave them. He shuddered as sadness swept over him.

Huệ noticed that his father was daydreaming like an old man, and wondered if he was oblivious to his sister and Lương Hoàng. Huệ returned his attention to the meal, which he relished, especially the pickled vegetables and the lemongrass soup. "It is wonderful to have such great food and a good appetite," he said cheerfully. Autumn Moon smiled and nodded her thanks. The variety of dishes testified to the success of the doctor and the hard work of the whole family.

There were wooden and ceramic platters and bowls of vegetable spring rolls, fresh lettuce with mint and parsley, cold pickled vegetables—including bamboo shoots—diced carrots and cucumbers, boiled pork with peapods and cabbage, a pond-raised fish from the fishmonger's stall, and onions, yams, and squash. Brightly lacquered wooden platters were full of bananas, oranges, and papaya. The papaya was a traditional holiday food and a tacit prayer. The word for papaya was đu đủ, which also meant enough. You reached for the papaya to say you were đu đủ, quite full. There was plenty; times were good for the Hồ family.

Huệ said, "Mother, you have stunned the Ancestors again! I am sure that we are not deserving of all this good fortune and all your attention."

"You're right about that, as far as you are concerned," Nhạc said jovially, with his mouth full. Lữ laughed with agreement.

"Thank you Huệ," she said, ignoring her eldest. "Are you flattering me again? What are you after this time?" Everyone laughed. "I have only done my duty," she said grinning, displaying her black-lacquered teeth. "I like cooking to honor the Ancestors, especially on Tomb Sweeping Day. It is so quiet. It is a pleasure to serve such hearty eaters."

As Nhạc served himself from the plates, Second Son Lữ admonished him, "Please leave some for all the minor members of the family."

Nhạc took more spring rolls and passed the dish to Lữ, saying, "If we divide them, Little Brother won't get any," and both chuckled.

"Father," Huệ said, ignoring the bait and changing the subject, "would it be possible for Lương Hoàng and his father to borrow our water buffalo, Mandarin, and then later we in exchange could use Hoàng's water buffalo, Fatso? Nhạc, Lữ, and I could help the Lương family transplant their rice seedlings, since our rice paddies are not quite ready. Then when the Lương family finishes transplanting their paddies, they could help us finish transplanting ours. What do you think of this arrangement; can we propose it to Hoàng's father?

"What do you think, Nhạc?" asked the physician.

"It is a good plan," said Nhạc, "as long as we aren't late with our own crops. The bargain is of course subject to the approval of Hoàng's father, and it allows me to spend more time in my store."

"Then go ahead, Hoàng," said Hồ Danh, "and make this proposal to your father. I see it as beneficial to both families."

After the meal, the family got out instruments and played music together. Jade River was trained by her mother to sing and play the lute. Huệ and Lương Hoàng played flutes, while Lữ and Nhạc played two- and four-string guitars. After a few good tunes and a song, Physician Hồ put down his two-string fiddle and said, "I have patients to visit on the other side of the village. Since today is a festival day, perhaps you would like to see the performances. There should be some boxing." This suggestion won hearty and open approval from the young men, ready to abandon their instruments. "I only ask that you stay out of any competitions in which people are already getting hurt. Use your common sense."

After the women finished their own meal in the kitchen, Jade River asked her mother, "Ma-ma, do you think I dare ask Father if I could go to the festival today?"

Autumn Moon looked at her beautiful daughter and smiled. "Child, it won't hurt to try," she said laughing, as Jade River skipped out of the room.

"Father," Jade River said innocently, "it is such a lovely day. May I go with my three brothers to the market festival today? I would especially like to see how they do in the boxing."

Physician Hồ viewed his lovely daughter keenly and with concern, and chose to conceal his doubts. "It is fine day, and I see no harm in your visiting the market, on your best behavior. You can tell me about the boxing if I miss it."

"Oh thank you Papa," she responded with a smile, and she joined her brothers and Hoàng for the walk into town. Autumn Moon and Spring Flower stayed behind, for it was the custom that married women did not leave the property often except to go food shopping in the morning, or occasionally to visit other wives in the afternoon.

ֆ ֆ

There were hundreds of brightly clothed people at the commons outside the village compound. People came from all the surrounding villages, in myriad shapes and colors. Hawkers sang out their wares, and the market was full of buyers and sellers, beggars and sightseers.

The Hồ boys, Jade River, and Hoàng moved slowly through the crowds, past the food stalls and the lane of silk booths. They moved over to the storyteller. He was an old and wrinkled blind man who was familiar to them, and renowned in the area for his memory and wit.

There was a crowd around the old man, as usual, but the young people pushed close. Hoàng's pulse increased as he felt the warmth of Jade River next to him. She looked straight into his handsome round face under straight black hair and then blushed, her light brown skin glowing. The blind man was singing to his large and respectful audience about the value of their own village marketplace. He sang,

"The market of Tây Sơn is a fine market.
Tis held at the end of the wooden bridge,
by the banks of the earthen water canal.
There the seller of soup is pretty, and the cleanser of ears adroit.
All along the clear river and the earthen water canal,
the women of other villages bring their poles and baskets filled with vegetables.
When they return they have strings of coins
round their necks and round their shoulders.
There they marry the Đại Việt maidens to Chinamen greedy and fat;
but at the market of Tây Sơn they sell not the daughters of Đại Việt.
There, the plighted lovers alone may walk in the shadow of their beloved ones,
and carry the over-heavy baskets."

"I do not care for this old man, he's just passing wind." Lữ said. "Let's go see the fighting."

"Shush," Huệ said. "Wait till he has finished. Listen, he sings beautifully and he loves our people." The blind man was chanting poetry that had been preserved and improved by generations of bards and minstrels.

"At the market of Tây Sơn both they who buy and they who sell
give alms to the blind, and for their generosity the Gods do love them.
May the all-powerful Genie of the village of Tây Sơn
bless its happy inhabitants!
May old men behold the sons of their sons!
May the maidens be beautiful and good!
May the students be numerous, and diligent and successful in the examinations!
May the father of the family have rice for his children,
and the mother be able to suckle the lesser ones!
May the harvest be abundant!
The blind man says: To all the Gods give thanks!
The market of Tây Sơn is held at the end of the wooden bridge,
by the banks of the earthen water canal.
The market of Tây Sơn is a fine market!"

The old man was finished with his song; the audience clapped and stomped hard as a monsoon rain. A servant man sprang up with a basket to collect money and food for his master and himself. Nhạc said, "That's enough of this old man. It's time we move over to the boxing matches."

"Hoàng and I want to hear the old man some more," said Jade River.

Huệ was torn between the two activities. He said to his sister and his best friend, "I too want to hear more of this old man. His stories inspire his listeners. He makes them fiercely proud of the simple things that they already have. I like rhetoric, but don't we also like boxing? I promised Nhạc and Lữ," nodding at his brothers, "that I would box today, and I would hate not to test myself against the visiting master. Let's listen to another tale. But," addressing Nhạc and Lữ, "we will join you at the boxing ring after one more story."

Nhạc gave Hoàng a serious glance, as if to say, *You realize that I am the official chaperone,* but then conceded, "All right, but hurry over with Huệ when you are done." Nhạc and Lữ, swinging their forearms, strode across the grounds to the fighting ring.

The old blind man stood surrounded by respectful villagers, who sat or squatted on three sides of him. He held his arms up to Heaven for silence, which he quickly received, and then folded his arms ceremoniously in his old robe and said, "Have you heard the story of the Rival Genie?" There were murmurs of approval. Many had in fact heard it before. The bard's eyes were dull, but his voice was strong and resonant from years of outdoor performance.

"You do well to tremble, my sons, when the typhoon breaks like a rice stalk the mightiest trees of the forest. When the stream, canal, and ditch overflow, when the river forsakes its bed, then the Genie are fighting for their loved one."

The storyteller, his teeth stained red from chewing the betel leaf, and surrounded by the royal splendor of lush green hills of a paradise that he couldn't see, and which he often sang that he would defend with his life, stood erect, and his voice rang out.

"King Văn Lang had a beautiful daughter. Both the Genie of the Mountain and the Genie of the Sea sought her hand in marriage. Dressed in precious stones, they arrived at the Palace of the King at the same time, each filled with hatred for the other. They each petitioned the King, who knew not how to chose between them, so he summoned his daughter and ordered her to choose. The Genie of the Mountain hid his evil mood with an agreeable smile, while the Genie of the Sea guilelessly retained the sour looks of his angry heart. Ordered to decide then and there, the princess chose the smiling, two-faced Genie of the Mountain.

"Anyone who has been unhappy in love will feel a part of the Sea Genie's despair. After the daughter married the Mountain Genie, the Sea Genie wanted to tear and rend his enemy. He made war against him, with great rains and tidal waves. Tens of thousands of innocent peasants and animals drowned. Brave men, dutiful women, and darling children—they all drowned.

"The Mountain Genie beat back the rising waters with a great wind. More innocents were killed. The Mountain Genie made thunder and lightning; the flames of Heaven set the earth on fire. The earth shook and was rent asunder.

"Peace-bringing Time has not assuaged the Sea Genie's eternal hate.

"You know his anguish, my sons, whose love has been luckless. As ye dream of your 'beloved sister,' torn from you by one deceitful or over-bold, so are there days and nights when the Sea Genie dreams of the beautiful princess. Then he goes to war with his smug rival.

"You do well to tremble, my sons, when the typhoon breaks like a rice stalk the mightiest trees of the forest. When the stream, canal, and ditch overflow, when the river forsakes its bed, then the Genie are fighting for their loved-one.

"Tis not for me, poor blind mortal, to sit in judgment on the conduct of two powerful Genies; but think you, my sons, that it becomes them thus to strew the earth with ruins for a lady's lovely eyes?

"Does your 'beloved sister' disdain you? Condemn her, forget her, replace her and peace shall be yours."

After the old man finished there was enthusiastic applause. Huệ was electrified by the story and the skill of the artist. He clapped his hands and stamped his feet like those around him. He joined in the admiration of the villagers for the storyteller. He said to Hoàng and Jade River, "This man can really move people. It is small wonder that he, like Father, who also tells a good story, is sought out by others for counsel, and to solve disputes. More than any of Father's herbal remedies, these stories are cures in their own right for many heavy woes that we carry in our hearts, be it guilt, jealousy, or hatred. Free of such weights, our village is more united and strengthened against the threat of intruders."

Hoàng smiled and said, "Perhaps, but you read a lot into what seems like just an entertaining story." Jade River giggled with appreciation.

Huệ turned to his sister and said cheerfully, "I'm glad I stayed. His stories are as rich as the sound of his voice. Now I want to see the boxing. Come with me!"

"The storyteller is very good," said Jade River, testing her brother. "Let's wait and hear one more."

"Enough, Rivulet of Jade!" Huệ said firmly. "I might miss all the matches. It's time we joined the others."

"Oh Bodhisattva's temptation, all right. Lead the way."

Huệ smiled awkwardly at his chastened sister and his friend, and led them away, feeling suddenly lonely. *This is a bad sign,* he thought. *Hoàng is more interested in my sister than in a good boxing contest. I had no idea it was this serious.*

The blind man started to tell the story of "The Betel and the Areca Tree." Huệ did not turn around till he reached the edge of the crowd by the boxing ring. When he did, his sister and Hoàng were nowhere to be seen. They had given him the slip. He had not seen who initiated the escape. Was it his sister or his best friend? Maybe he didn't want to know the answer to that.

Now aren't they both a disgrace to their Ancestors? he thought, somewhat amused and impressed by his sister's audacity. He was about to go hunt them down when Nhạc and Lữ found him. "Huệ, you must come and see this boxer," Nhạc said.

"He is very good," said Lữ. "Demons of Hell, he'll squash us like insects."

"Let's have a peek at him," said Huệ. *Hoàng, you'd better behave yourself,* he thought, and he turned his attention to the boxing.

"Let me buy you a bowl of tea," Hoàng said.

"I would like that, thank you," said Jade River, trying to keep her voice sounding calm. For a few copper pennies Hoàng purchased two teas and little cakes from a gray-haired woman in a tidy stall. They ate the little sugar cakes and drank in silence, standing by the stall under the scrutiny of the nosey old lady. They looked out at the crowd of villagers milling about between the stalls and stations. There were farmers, artisans, beggars, and traders. Amid the browsers many shoppers were inspecting goods and haggling over prices.

That afternoon Jade River wore her hair like a young girl, but already she had the curves of a young woman. She could feel the eyes of men upon her as they walked by and it made her aware of new powers. She couldn't help but worry that her brothers or someone she knew would run up and reproach them.

Hoàng realized that they were being quite reckless. Too many people of the village knew them both by name and that they shouldn't be alone together. His frustration made him laugh. Looking at all the people before them he said, "No one can say that we are alone and without chaperones." The tea woman wiped her clean counter, pretending not to be listening to every word.

They strolled as casually as possible up to a shade tree on a knoll and sat on the wild grass together. Hoàng, his face clear and his eyes bright, spoke first. "Do you remember last year, in this same month, your father had the flood in the rice paddy? Your mother and I walked you home from the Temple of Lao Tzu." Jade River smiled shyly and nodded. Hoàng tried to ignore the bulge of her breasts suggested under her silk tunic as she straightened her neck.

Jade River was so aware of her physical proximity to Hoàng that she blushed. She remembered that day Scholar Trương Văn Hiến at the temple was teaching Hoàng and her brothers and her to read and write. On the day of the flooding, her mother, Autumn Moon, had hurried at Hồ Danh's order to tell her three brothers to run home and help him rebuild the dike.

"Of course I remember," she said. "That was before my mother gave me her silver hair pins. It certainly was easier to talk to you before I wore them." She made a face and they both laughed to hide their fear of their own foolishness, their ardent desire, and some unknown but serious danger should they defy their parents and Ancestors and anger the Gods.

A heavy peasant with an old cart covered with religious paraphernalia for sale, such as fruit, incense sticks, and paper animal and trinket offerings to burn, pushed past the spot where the two young people sat watching the market at Tây Sơn.

Now Jade River gazed at Hoàng's powerful features, his bushy hair and eyebrows, his jutting nose and chin, and prayed silently to the man in the moon, Chú Cuội, that he tie them together with his red string. She prayed to fate that they would wed and neither wander, and that Hoàng would be successful, but not, like so many men in their success, want a second or a third wife, or concubines.

"Words cannot express how I feel for you," Hoàng said. "I have spent months waiting for another chance to talk with you." He took a small scroll from his poem bag, carefully untied the red string, and unrolled the thin paper. Holding the paper poem gift, he read:

"I am like Wei Sheng.
I am ready to hug the pillar
under the bridge as the river rises,
waiting for you to meet me,
until I drown with the high tide.
I must know,
Will your warmth and beauty
Shine on my worthless self?"

Jade River was quiet. She averted her eyes to the ground. She said quietly, "That was beautiful. If it were only up to me, I would say yes. With all my heart. But you know that it is for my parents to decide such important matters; our customs demand that I should defer to them."

"Your sentiments are noble," said Hoàng carefully. "But if you care for me, at least, let's pledge ourselves secretly to do all within our power to wake up the moon, so that the old man will tie the thread, with or without our parents."

Hoàng's voice was strong and sincere, but subversive. She bowed to him deeply, unsure whether she dared commit to join in his proposed pact of revolt. He handed her the scroll, which he had painted months before in his own calligraphy, and a small gold bracelet. She accepted both, and she painstakingly read the Chinese characters of the poem. Hoàng had waited several months for this moment.

"Your calligraphy is clean and strong," she said admiringly, and met his gaze. "Here, Hoàng, these are for you." And she gave him a handkerchief that she had embroidered with blue cranes and yellow clouds, and her fan, painted with sunflowers, a symbol of constancy.

He took her hands in his, looked her in the eyes, and said carefully, "With these magic gifts, let us engage our troth in stone and bronze."

She smiled, but with a tear in her eye. She squeezed Hoàng's hand, nodded, almost kissed him, and said, "Now I am bound to you for life." He squeezed her hands in return. Jade River then shyly cast her eyes away. She added, "Gods and Genie protect us. Let us hurry now and join the others at the boxing stage."

"Yes," said Hoàng, "let's join them before they start looking for us."

As they walked through the bustling market, Jade River fought off a terrible sense of dread. *I've acted rashly,* she thought. *Haven't I disobeyed my parents and dishonored my Ancestors? A woman is not permitted to make her own alliances. But I have been fond of Hoàng for so long, and I do love and admire him, I know it. If Father insists on another man for my husband, what choice has honor left me then but to obey him, or become a nun? Oh Buddha, protect me from the loneliness and tedium of that!*

Chapter 3
The Boxing Match
1770

The three brothers, Nhạc, Lữ, and Huệ, were standing by the boxing ring, watching the Mountain of Fire fight with another opponent. "He has an ugly square face," said Nhạc.

"His nose is too flat," added Lữ. "He's too good, we'll wet ourselves, we're doomed."

"This won't be easy," Huệ observed. "He's quick, and look at those muscles on his thighs and chest."

The challenger wrapped his arms around the Mountain's arms, and then they moved their weight from side to side, testing for an opening. When he thought he had the Mountain in a counter-rhythm, the challenger reversed himself and entered with a low body spiral for a hip throw. The Mountain sank his weight, and the challenger spun free. Then the challenger threw a series of punches.

Blocking a punch with both hands, the Mountain grabbed the challenger's wrist, then stepped away as his opponent shot off a sharp kick, which struck the Mountain's hard stomach without effect. Still holding the challenger's wrist, the Mountain then pivoted next to his attacker so they were almost back to back. As the challenger curved around, the Mountain, using both his hands, twisted the challenger's wrist to the outside. The challenger, screaming a "Ki-yai," sailed over his own arm and crashed into the grass mats that covered the stage.

Lữ squeezed Nhạc's arm. "Did you see that! He makes the wrist throw look like child's play."

The Mountain then stood beside his opponent and applied the auger pin. Bending the challenger's arm at the elbow, so the challenger's fingers pointed at his own face, the Mountain turned the man's body around by forcing the arm into a lever. As if holding a hand drill, he rotated the bent elbow in a circle. The shoulder became the fulcrum of the lever, and the shoulder joint became excruciatingly painful. The challenger had to roll onto his stomach to save his arm. The Mountain gracefully slid to a kneeling position and applied pressure on the trapped arm, slowly dislocating the shoulder until the challenger slapped the mat loudly in surrender.

The crowd roared approval. The Mountain was not only strong, he was beautifully trained, especially in *Qinna*, the art of seizing, and *Ts'o-ku shu*, twisting skill, also called Devil's Hand. The challenger stood up humbled, dismayed, but unharmed, and both men bowed. The challenger had lost his hope of victory, and the string of cash, a roll of copper coins he'd given to the promoter. Huệ turned to Nhạc, made an unhappy grimace, then pretended to cry on his shoulder. Then, playfully, the two began to tussle, testing each other's center and rootedness.

The odds were ten to one. Another man placed his string of coppers on the judge's table, and removed his shirt and sandals. He stretched out as the crowd waited and the Mountain rested. Then the new opponent entered the ring and bowed.

This man was a good boxer. He threw fast punches and kicks at the permissible targets on the Mountain while dancing away from those powerful hands. Head, spine, and groin strikes and deliberate limb breaking were not allowed. The Mountain moved onto his back leg into the classical cat stance, the front leg ready to block or kick. "Those are good wrist blocks he has," said Nhạc.

"His counter-punches are so fast," added Lữ in a defeated tone.

"Look at how his opponent grows anxious," said Huệ.

As the opponent sallied again with a punching, feint-feint strike combination, the Mountain caught the man's foot in a smooth but solid leg sweep and sent him down. A quick kick to the ribs, followed by another wrist lock and auger pin, finished the match. The fighter turned over onto his stomach; resistance was futile. The auger pin brought more roars of approval from the throng.

Huệ watched quietly, studying the Mountain and taking his measure. *Nhạc could get the better of him if he's lucky,* he thought. *And as Father likes to say, you can always change your luck with preparation.* Huệ signaled his brothers to follow him, and they withdrew from the ringside briefly for a discussion of strategies.

"Did you see how little he moves?" Huệ said. "I think he is afraid of tiring."

"When he does move, he's very fast," said Nhạc.

"Maybe we should fight some other day," Lữ said hopefully.

Huệ said, "Walk with me and listen to this idea. ..."

❧　❦

Soon the Hồ brothers reappeared to view the next contest. After dispatching two more locals with no serious injuries, the promoter announced new odds, seven to one. The odds went down because, presumably, the professional was growing tired. However, to second son Lữ the Mountain looked untouched.

Out of sight behind the crowd, all three brothers began limbering up. After several more short matches, the reward was reduced to six to one. Huệ put down his string of cash, his lunch and spending money for the day. The little coins were perforated in the center, and tied into a roll with an oiled hemp line.

The lightweight Huệ and the Mountain both bowed, and then began to box. At first, Huệ was frightened. *Good heavens, this brute could hurt someone,* he realized. Huệ danced around a lot, and when it became obvious that he was avoiding his opponent, the Mountain grew impatient and spectators began to make taunts. A spectator yelled, "We came to see a fight. Catch the little coward and break his arms."

The Mountain didn't seen worried, but a long fight meant less income, and a bad show was bad business, especially when they passed the rice basket, so he chased after the kid, trying to avoid all the possible weight traps—to avoid getting thrown by his own attack. In boxing and wrestling, as in jujitsu in Japan, one uses the attacker's momentum to throw him in the direction he has committed his weight. The Mountain could not attack too aggressively, or he would get thrown with his own momentum. Minute after minute, the swift-footed local evaded the increasingly angry Mountain. When he finally grabbed one of Huệ's quick blocks, the Mountain was so mad that he had to suppress the urge to break the youngster's arm. Injuring an opponent unnecessarily was also bad for business.

He held Huệ's wrist out, threw a hard punch that Huệ blocked, and then slid under Huệ's extended arm. Huệ's wrist now was locked in the Mountain's two hands, and he simply lifted them. Huệ slapped his body, while his wrist burned with pain. With two steps and a lunge the Mountain cut down and forward, but then executed a leading circle so that Huệ's arm locked behind him. The Mountain then sent Huệ flying through the air. Huệ saved his face by rolling like an acrobat.

The crowd applauded, stamped, and cheered, mostly for Huệ, the local youngster, who was checking himself for bruises and broken parts, and Lữ was already bowing to the Mountain. Lữ fought for time as well. He managed to connect a few hardy, straight punches and even a kick or two. He withstood a considerable beating, before crashing down after the Mountain's lightning leg sweep. The crowd applauded and yelled, as Lữ quickly bowed out and Nhạc entered the ring.

Nhạc was not nearly as big as the unbeaten Mountain. The Mountain was, however, out of breath. He bowed, and immediately saw the resemblance between this man and the last two opponents. They all had the same square faces with wide eyes and sturdy noses. His experienced eye warned him that he was winded, and he'd just been set up for this new opponent. He looked at Huệ and Lữ standing together in the crowd. They both bowed to him, confirming his suspicion. A hint of concern crossed his face. The Mountain focused on Nhạc; losing was expensive.

The boxing began, and neither fellow hurried. Nhạc was just warming up. The Mountain was catching his breath. He played a defensive game, waiting for Nhạc to make an error.

"Go get him now!" Huệ yelled. Nhạc entered with a volley of fast punches and off-rhythm kicks. The first time the Mountain returned the volley, Nhạc sensed correctly that the second punch was full and avoided it with a spin. He grabbed his opponent's wrist while pivoting on his own forward foot, so they met back to back. Nhạc lunged, sending the Mountain forward and off-balance. Nhạc now pivoted and twisted the Mountain's wrist down. The giant flew over his own arm so that it wouldn't break, and slapped the mat with a bang. Nhạc pressed finger to face, and rotated wrist against elbow, and forced the Mountain to his belly with the auger pin. The Mountain went limp in defeat, but then tried once to withdraw his arm. Nhạc instantly sped up his move, and twisted the locked arm past the opponent's head, till it felt as if about to rip out at the shoulder socket. The Mountain slapped in pain and surrender, and Huệ, Lữ and the crowd cheered with delight.

Nhạc raised his hands above his head and the crowd went wild. An attendant handed him a purse with the prize money. As he moved away, men crowded around him to bow in respect and congratulate him. The three brothers embraced in a hearty, three-way hug. Lữ lost his balance and they all fell to the ground laughing. Nhạc jumped up, shook the prize purse in one fist over his head, and the crowd cheered again.

☙ ❧

Only a week later, Jade River carefully approached her mother about her interest in marrying Lương Hoàng. After thinking it over, Autumn Moon brought her daughter's request to her husband to consider. Autumn Moon noted with some amusement that her husband was not surprised. Physician Hồ Danh agreed to his daughter's bold request to seek a marital alliance with the son named Hoàng of the neighbor Lương. Quietly, Hồ Danh was delighted. Jade River would get a good match that she favored, and after she moved to her husband's parent's house, as a neighbor, he would be able to see her and watch her children grow up.

Old Lương and his wife were also delighted by the idea. They had only the highest opinion of their neighbors, the Hồ family, and liked the girl as a wife for their boy too. Hoàng was overjoyed when his father told him, and it was on that same day that Physician Hồ informed his daughter that her marriage to Hoàng had been agreed upon.

Jade River was so happy that she thought she would need extra protection from the local Genie, and made an offering of incense and paper money and a paper pig at the Đình, the village temple and community center. She realized that her father was pleased, but also that her departure would make him sad, which tethered her soaring spirit. She held herself still to listen with all of her attention and energy as her father told her, "I will miss you after you have moved to your future father-in-law and mother-in-law's house, but you will be happy. When the time comes, you will begin with your husband to build your own apartment."

"Oh Father, thank you so much," she said. "I will miss you too. I'm sorry that Hoàng cannot come here to live with us instead."

"It is hard," he said, "but you will not be far away!"

☙ ❧

Hoàng was so happy that, as soon as he could sneak away, he found some pretense to visit the house of Physician Hồ. He found Jade River alone by the well in front of the house. His grin reflected her own feeling of excitement. Their eyes met.

Hoàng gave Jade River a bouquet of wild red roses and white lotus blossoms. She was so excited that the flowers shook in her hand.

After their very brief meeting, Jade River skipped across the fields and through the woods to the clean stream of the Cầu River. Keeping on her tunic, she waded into the water. She swam upstream till her limbs were cool and her mind was once again calm, then she let the current slowly carry her back to where she had started. She was so happy that she prayed to the Gods that they not feel jealous of her. "I promise," she said to the river God, "to burn two incense sticks in the Tây Sơn Temple, to the Genie of our village, Quán Thế Âm, the Goddess of Mercy.

Chapter 4
The Pawnbroker and the Marriage Broker
1770

Physician Hồ Danh, still trim and robust though forty-five, found his way to the pawn shop on Market Street. He was greeted by the pawnbroker's wife, Quách Nu Xấu Xí, a square lady with bulbous features. She was of the Quách clan, and her name, Nu Xấu Xí, everyone knew, meant Ugly Female, though most of her friends called her either Tidbit or Peach. Her parents had lost her older brother, Nam Nhiều Lắm, or Male of Abundance, to the coughing demons. Whatever demon it was, the boy suffered several days of spasmodic pains, and died from an inability to breathe.

It was well known that it was dangerous to name a child too propitiously. Lurking demons might take an unhealthy interest, or develop a jealousy, and then attempt to kidnap or destroy the child. It was common therefore, after losing a well-named child, to name others with ugly or vulgar names so as to fool any lurking demons.

Ugly Female, or Tidbit, had been such a child, but now she was forty, and at any rate, her several nicknames were another good way to keep the demons confused or disinterested. Her face tensed when Physician Hồ entered her shop; she did not like doctors. Physician Hồ noted her apprehension. After brief greetings she took him to her husband. They walked to the back of the store, past bins and shelves of shiny new items and miscellaneous junk, through the bead curtain to the dark living room and kitchen behind the shop.

Mister Quách Văn Thọ lay reclining against pillows on his wooden bed, his bald head and gray beard giving him the look of a man of distinction, even if a very sick one. Physician Hồ carefully examined the patient, whose skin had a taupe hue, a ghastly brown-gray, and his pulse was weak.

"My heart suddenly beats very fast," Quách Văn Thọ said, "and then I feel these jabs of pain across my chest." The doctor studied the nine pulses in his wrist, and then checked the pressure points and nerve endings on his hands and feet. Satisfied that he could probably help, Physician Hồ asked Quách Văn Thọ, "What do you think is the matter?"

"This wretched slave doesn't know," Quách Văn Thọ answered. "I have not abused my duties to my Ancestors, or my household altar. Furthermore, I make at least annual donations to the Shrines for Buddha, the great Chinese Warrior Quan Công, and the Goddess of Mercy Quán Thế Âm, as well as pray to the Guardian Deity of Men of Honor Hộ Pháp. Who could be angry at me?" he asked.

"Who might be angry with you?" the doctor asked. Quách Văn Thọ's face grew tight with concentration.

"Maybe Hộ Pháp, who upholds men of honor, or the warrior Quan Công." He lowered his voice and added confidentially, "Business has been very good for several years, but I did not increase my contribution to the village temple."

Physician Hồ said, "I have an amulet that might be just the thing you need." He held up a simply woven, silk cord necklace with a green stone pendant. "Unfortunately, one has to chant many hours when one makes even such a simple piece, so it is expensive, though not overpriced at three silver coins. At any rate, you probably won't need it and shouldn't bother with it. However, you had better increase your donations to the temples. That should improve your karma, and will definitely improve your reputation." The old man examined the necklace, and then after weighing it in his hand, placed it on the side table, deferring his decision. Physician Hồ then said, "Let me treat you now with my North People needles."

He opened his large medicine bag and picked out a silk cloth that held his long Chinese acupuncture needles. He carefully probed with his fingers down Quách Văn Thọ's arm along the entire heart meridian. He could feel the little knots of muscle and tissue that lay near the locations of the eight pressure points from the inside of the armpit to the end of the little finger.

Noting that the patient was truly uncomfortable, and that his whole back was stiff, the muscles taut, he began with massage. Physician Hồ asked Quách Văn Thọ to roll onto his stomach and massaged his back, concentrating on the two meridians that ran along the spinal column. He probed deftly with his strong fingers into the jammed fiber areas and loosened obvious knots in Văn Thọ's shoulders and neck. After relocating point number seven in the left arm, he inserted his needle as far as the length of his thumbnail. He pierced the arm, hands, chest, and feet in numerous places with individual needles and left the needles in place.

He told the man to lie still, took a cup of tea from Tidbit, and chatted with her about the vagrants on the road who were escaping the famine just to the north. "These poor people," she said, pressing her stubby hands together at her breast in the prayer position. "They must be paying for terrible crimes in a previous life. I certainly can't feed all of Bình Định Province," she said, and forced a mechanical laugh, "and so I say no to every single bedraggled one—man woman or child. Of course I do direct them to the temples, which as Heaven knows, we, like most everyone else of stature, support more than generously."

After the half-hour glass drained empty, Physician Hồ removed his needles and woke up Quách Văn Thọ, who already felt like a new man. Văn Thọ smiled and said, "The pain is gone. Your reputation is well deserved; you must possess some secrets of the Gods."

"The pain will probably come back," Physician Hồ said calmly, "but if I keep treating you with the needles, you should enjoy a full recovery. I am freeing energy meridians or paths in your own body's chakras, the energy centers."

Hồ would accept only his usual fee of five strings of cash for the visit, but he also accepted three silver coins for the neck amulet, and when Tidbit insisted, a lovely silk robe from the North Country as well.

Physician Hồ accepted the tunic gratefully. If you could afford it, silk was one of the great gifts of the Gods. It kept you warm in the cold, and cool and dry in the heat. Could you ask more of any garment? He picked up his wide-brimmed wicker hat, which offered protection from the sun and rain, and bowed to his patient. The pawnbroker and his wife saw the renowned doctor to the door. They thanked him profusely. Quách Văn Thọ's transformation was remarkable, and they agreed to repeat the needle treatment if needed in ten days.

ಞ ೂ

The next day, physician Hồ Danh had an unexpected visitor. It was highly unusual for a palanquin with four porters to arrive at the Hồ family compound. A man in a brilliant green and red silk four-piece tunic approached the house, and struck it three times with his cane. Physician Hồ opened his door, exchanged greetings and salutations, and invited the man to sit at his table. Hồ Danh scrutinized the notorious commodities and marriage broker and said, "Well, Amiable Son, to what do I owe the honor of your exalted visit to my humble cottage?"

Amiable Son smiled benignly, showing a mouth with just a few red-stained teeth remaining. He folded the arms of his tunic. "Most famous and successful doctor," the old man began, "I represent a distinguished party who would like a rare flower for his garden. He has gone so far as to procure my time to inquire after your own extraordinary little blossom."

"My daughter is a delicate flower, and I do not part from her easily," Physician Hồ replied carefully, as he tried not to stare at the gray rings around the man's eyes caused by years of opium smoking. "Unfortunately for my daughter and me, I have already agreed to her marrying the son of a good and worthy neighbor."

Hồ's wife, Autumn Moon, came in with her face expressionless and refilled their teacups. She removed the empty bowls, for they'd finished eating the daughter-in-law's rice and dumplings.

"My client," Amiable Son then responded slowly, straightening his back with self-importance, "is none other than Nguyễn Trúc, Mandarin Second Class, and ruler of this prosperous Bình Định Province. Nguyễn Trúc has heard reports that your daughter is truly exceptional. He offers you 500 taels of silver if you break your arrangement with your neighbor and exchange betel cases and betrothal vows with him instead."

"Such a generous offer I could hardly refuse," Physician Hồ replied, pretending to laugh—trying to keep his fear firmly concealed behind his mask and determined not to lose face. *The mandarin is no one to fool with,* he thought. "Please tell the mandarin that this humble servant is deeply grateful for this exceptional honor, and greatly disappointed that he cannot honorably undo what is already done. Unfortunately, we parents have already exchanged our betel cases and our betrothal promises and, regrettably, signed the contract."

Physician Hồ rubbed his palms, which were sweating. He dropped his weight, opened his breathing, and let his anger fly to Java. His mind searched for ways to remain calm and relaxed. To his consternation, the negotiator was not so easily mollified. Amiable Son persisted. "Any such contract, of course you realize, his eminence Nguyễn Trúc can legally overrule as your magistrate."

Physician Hồ was taken aback. *Bitterness,* he thought, *is this a serious threat? This is dangerous; the demand is dishonorable.* His stomach muscles contracted. He suddenly wanted to kill the man before him. It was either give in to this ignominious pressure, or take an immeasurable risk. Prudence and fear both supported acquiescence. His thoughts shouted warnings of caution. Hồ Danh cleared his mind till it was empty and found some sense of rootedness. Like Genie spirits sitting on each shoulder, his sense of honor and pride argued with his desire for peace and tranquility. He refilled the cups slowly, and took a drink of tea, for time to think.

"I understand you," Physician Hồ said, hoping that he didn't. "But my word of honor is under the law of Heaven, and it is to my daughter as well as to my neighbor that I gave my support for this marriage. No true gentleman would bid me act differently."

"My dear friend," the broker said, his voice now as cold as ice, "are you sure that 'that' is your final position? Such persistence for a mere girl—for a girl you are giving away anyway—you would … disappoint … my client?"

Physician Hồ now was sure that he was asking for more trouble than he wanted. *Most men would give silver and jade as dowry to have a rich and powerful mandarin marry their daughter,* he thought. *But Nguyễn Trúc is reputed to be a misogynist. Several of his wives have died under mysterious circumstances. The rumors, for which I had some confirmation, were unpleasant. It was public record that the official ruled as a severe judge and it was reported that he commonly took bribes and dabbled in extortion. He is not the ideal son-in-law for a man of honor. But Nguyễn Trúc is not a man to trifle with. In this district he is all powerful.*

Physician Hồ knew that common sense argued for buckling under such clear pressure. *Besides, it is only a daughter; she is insignificant to the Cult of the Ancestors. It is her fate to leave her parents and join the family of her husband, as it is for all Việt women.* For a moment, Physician Hồ fixed his gaze on his ancestral altar. He conjured up the happy face of his smiling, beautiful child. *Oh Gods of Heaven and Earth, what to do? I love my daughter. My father, the Great Ancestor, and I would be dishonored if I gave in to a corrupt pervert, even a powerful one. But aiii, by the Gods there is danger.*

"Please tell his eminence, the magistrate, that I cannot help him, for my daughter is willful. She would rebel, and possibly even disobey me and kill herself. Then his eminence would have lost his silver and his flower, and discord with Heaven would prevail. Please beseech him to understand the position I am in, and apologize that I did not foresee such a gracious and propitious offer. And furthermore, please tell him that her reputation seems somewhat inflated. There are many uncut flowers that are equal or superior to my daughter, and that have far greater dowries."

The broker gave Physician Hồ a glassy stare with his mud-brown eyes. Amiable Son rose and stood as straight as he could, and refused to bow. "I will report to the magistrate what you have said." He said icily, "Good luck with your daughter." In a rustle of green and red silk, he left so abruptly as to be seriously discourteous.

❦   ❧

The next morning, Nhạc, Lữ, Huệ, and Jade River all rose early and went to a cousin's to help rethatch a roof. At the double hour of the Dragon, nine a.m., the mandarin's sheriff and ten deputies paid a visit to Physician Hồ. The constables carried clubs and whips. Each had a dagger hanging from his belt. The headman demanded to see the doctor immediately, and when the doctor emerged from his office, a patient peering from within, the sheriff ordered his men to seize the criminal. Hồ Danh thought to himself, *I should fight, I can take this rabble. But then there would only be more. What is the safest thing to do now to protect my family? Surrender, abide by the law? But Nguyễn Trúc cannot be trusted. His abuse of power is legend.*

Two burly men grabbed for the doctor's arms. Physician Hồ wasn't cowed by eleven men armed with short clubs and knives, but he was afraid, since these men were also supported by the full weight of the government.

He let the two men grab his arms, drew himself back, pulled his arms in—they, holding on, followed—and then extended his arms out, which sent the two burly men sprawling into the dust. Others charged, and Physician Hồ sidestepped one and then the second and then the third, giving each a fist or an elbow into the ribs or the head. The next two men didn't charge, and Hồ had to sidestep swinging clubs and fists. He entered close to the first attacker's body as the man brought his club down. Hồ Danh took the attacker's club wrist and pulled it down, lifting with his other hand, sending the man flying onto his face. He blocked the second man's club arm and pushed his palm up his chin, sending him splat on his back.

This would be almost fun, Hồ Danh thought, *if these men weren't officials.* Two more men approached, and while these two were jabbing and feinting at Hồ, a third drew near from behind and threw a large net over the physician and pulled him to the ground. The first four attackers were immediately upon him, and he was pinned.

They placed a heavy cangue onto his shoulders. The cangue was a portable stock. When the ladder-like cangue was closed and clamped around the doctor's neck and wrists, he could not use his hands to scratch or defend himself.

"Under what pretense am I arrested?" the doctor demanded of the head constable.

"You are accused of several charges, including the withholding of taxes, the selling of dummy medicines at exorbitant rates, the showing of disrespect to your seniors and the representative of Heaven, and now, resisting arrest and assaulting officers of the law. There are honorable men who accuse you."

With that, the headman raised his club and struck Hồ Danh repeatedly on the arms and legs. He carefully struck his elbows, knees, and shins, being careful not to maim him but to cause great pain and terror. *Oh bitterness,* thought Hồ Danh, *I was a fool to let all three sons leave me this morning, and not to carry my staff. The mandarin will never let me live. I curse him for a thousand lives.*

While Autumn Moon and Nhạc's wife, Spring Flower, watched in horror, the headman signaled his men. One of them started to whip the old man's back with a braided leather implement till his shirt was torn and the blood made rivulets down his legs. The other thugs tore apart the house, filling empty bags with jewelry, musical instruments, clothes, books, and other loot and breaking what they didn't want or couldn't carry. Wall hangings, ledgers, and books were torn apart and piled on the open hearth, covered with oil, and set ablaze. Tears trickled down Autumn Moon's rough brown cheeks. She watched her home torn apart and her husband whipped, and she silently swore to her husband's Ancestors, and then to her own father's Ancestors, that she would take revenge on Nguyễn Trúc.

While the constables wrecked the house, Physician Hồ regretted not killing every last one of them. Two porters supported either end of the cangue, and he was driven off amid the mandarin's officers of the peace. Autumn Moon, her face hard and her fists clenched, watched the constables march her husband away. Wiping her tears, she cried out in despair to Spring Flower and the Spirits, "What sins have either of us committed in some former life, that has caused Heaven to punish us so now in this life? Why have the Gods forsaken us?"

Chapter 5
Highlanders in the Greenwood
1770 – 1771

Nhạc, Lữ, Huệ, and Jade River laughed and joked as they returned home. Lữ said, "I thought I would pass out from blowing my wind when I saw how little our cousins had ready for the job."

Nhạc chimed in, "I looked around, hoping they had more volunteers than just us. *Where is everybody?* I almost said out loud." And they all laughed.

"No such luck," said Jade River. "We were their only coolies for the day! Now I can barely walk, I'm so sore." Her brothers all laughed, and she laughed with them.

Huệ said, "After we arrived, I said to myself, *There goes the whole day*."

Lữ added, "No wonder they were so glad to see us," to more laughter.

Autumn Moon waited for them before their house with a stone-cold face. Huệ was the first to see that something was wrong, and he reached over and gently tapped Lữ to get his attention. Lữ looked up and saw his mother and abruptly went silent before her.

"Your father was arrested on the order of Nguyễn Trúc," said Autumn Moon coldly. "He was severely beaten by the mandarin's soldiers. They tore up our books and broke our furniture. They dragged Father away in a cangue; he could barely walk."

The four Hồ siblings were dumbfounded. They just stared at their mother, whose eyes now silently teared.

After an awkward silence, Huệ asked, "Did Father resist?"

"Yes, he did, but there were eleven constables. After your father threw off four or five different men, he was overpowered from behind by a man with a net."

The three young sons hung their heads and wrung their hands in shame. Nhạc said indignantly, "How dishonorable to use a net."

Lữ cried out, shaking his fists, "Biting insects, if we had only been here! Instead, we were thatching a roof."

Huệ fell to his knees as if struck down. He spat out, "What can we do against official corruption? The mandarin is supposed to be like a father to us." Jade River was quivering, speechless, but she crossed the road to her mother and embraced her.

❧　❦

Autumn Moon pulled herself together. She hired a go-between to discover what the mandarin, Nguyễn Trúc, would accept in a settlement for the freedom of their patriarch.

Nothing short of 300 taels of silver, or the old man's daughter as maid of his side chamber, would do, finally came the reply. Autumn Moon sat with her sons and Jade River to discuss their dilemma.

They decided that in the short run, they owed everything to Physician Hồ Danh. So either Jade River should enter the official's household as a maid of the side chamber, a station below the status of extra wife or even concubine, or the family must produce the 300 taels of silver in a very short time.

They discussed the available options, but there were few. Nhạc said, "The only safe choice is to hand over Jade River to the mandarin."

Autumn Moon was torn. "Either way, Jade River must be sacrificed. It would be safer for your father if we give in to Nguyễn Trúc."

Huệ sat quietly at the beginning of their discussion. His heart was heavy. He loved his sister, and yet, he saw clearly only one way according to their customs, hard though it would be for Jade River and the family. At last he spoke. "Only one way will satisfy our desire to save our father and honor his decision. We should sell Jade River through a marriage broker to someone else, rather than surrender her to Nguyễn Trúc. Handing her over to Trúc, yes, that would be the safest choice," Huệ agreed, "but since Father already decided not to do that, it would be more obedient to honor his decision and for us to refuse the acquisition, even at obvious risk to ourselves."

Lữ spoke up, "If only we could ask Father. He said no to the mandarin once, but does he still want to challenge Nguyễn Trúc again?"

Nhạc added, "Father is now a prisoner of this biting insect. Lữ is right, the safest thing for Father is to let Trúc have our sister."

Autumn Moon spoke. She was now the head of the household, and there was no easy way through this dilemma. "We will resist. I feel that your father knew the danger he faced when he stood by Jade River and refused that dog's anus of an official the first time." As she said this, she could not look at her daughter. "Besides, as your father recognized, most any husband should be better than Nguyễn Trúc as a master."

So matchmakers were notified of Jade River's availability for the right price. After an uncomfortably long seven days with no successful inquiries, a female matchmaker finally showed up to introduce the family to a man with enough money: Scholar Mã, a rich merchant from Nha Trang.

Scholar Mã was older and overripe, as if he'd already lived life to its fullest several times. He wore diamonds on his fingers and perfume in his hair, and he obviously had the requisite capital. None of the attractive young candidates who inquired could produce even half the required amount. Lương Hoàng couldn't come close to such a princely sum.

While Autumn Moon and her sons received the ostentatiously dressed suitor, the daughter served tea and cakes with downcast eyes, as tradition demanded. Scholar Mã broke from the expected courtesies by addressing Jade River himself, asking her numerous questions, and then demanding that she demonstrate her skill at singing and playing the moon-shaped lute. To add insult to injury, he even asked to see examples of her sewing and embroidery, and her teeth.

After the examination, Scholar Mã said quite honestly that he was impressed and took his leave. The matchmaker was a hard bargainer, and after several days in which no other reasonable offers appeared, the family settled on Scholar Mã as the new husband of Jade River. She was to become his first wife, for the sum of 320 taels, ten of which went to the matchmaker.

Once the negotiations were finished, Scholar Mã and Jade River exchanged horoscopes and a wedding day was hastily agreed upon, as hastily as if a death in the family were imminent. Now that the lengthy formalities were dispensed with or abbreviated, the money could exchange hands.

The groom returned that same day, accompanied by hired musicians and retainers carrying the presents of the groom. Scholar Mã wore the traditional red silk tunic over black trousers. One of his servants carried the ceremonial gifts: a pair of gold earrings and a red lacquer box—overlaid with yellow dragons and phoenix designs—containing rice wine and sweet cakes to offer at the ancestral tablets of the bride's father. Though his knees were old and rickety, the groom kowtowed to the altar, presenting himself to the tablets representing the girl's father's forebears, and then kowtowed to her mother. It took all of Jade River's energy not to cry during these sacred rituals. After a long dinner for the men, the groom, tipsy but smiling, departed, saying, "It has been a great pleasure to get to know such a wonderful family. … And to have Jade River enter my household as my wife." The engagement ceremony was over, but instead of waiting several months, the wedding was to start the next day.

Jade River, alone in her room the night before her wedding, thought seriously for the first time of killing herself. *Oh, Hoàng, how could this happen to us right after our official engagement! Curse Nguyễn Trúc and the wicked demons. I worried that it was too good to be true that I should marry the one I love above all others. Some evil Genie must have become jealous of my happiness. Or was I very evil in a previous life, that now I have to pay for such a sin? Or do the Gods punish me for my independence? . . . How unfaithful I am, though, to my father. Think of the example of Buddha. He was a wealthy prince, and he forsook all of life's normal pleasures for the greatest pleasure of all, peace of mind, and tranquility of spirit.*

In spite of her best efforts, Jade River remained utterly depressed. She and her mother quietly packed her few things. When Jade River was alone again, she packed Hoàng's poem in a book and the golden bracelet with her other jewelry. She remembered his words, "Let us engage our troth in stone and bronze." Looking at this delicate commitment bracelet tore her heart and she broke down and sobbed.

Autumn Moon came into the room while Jade River was still sobbing. She stroked Jade River's hair and remained silent, letting her daughter cry as tears rolled silently down her own face.

અ   ઌ

The next day, the "auspicious" day chosen for the wedding to begin, Scholar Mã arrived in a carriage arrayed with flowers. A gong and flute ensemble marched before the coach in high ceremony. The rotund Scholar Mã presented to Autumn Moon a rented red silk tunic and trousers for Jade River to wear. A servant presented the groom's next red lacquer box, with packages of betel nuts and areca leaves for the bride's family altar. Autumn Moon went into the back room where Jade River waited and presented the rented tunic. Jade River forced herself to put on the elegant garment. She moved stiffly, as if preparing for her execution.

Nhạc and Lữ then performed the ritual of the candles. Nhạc held the red candles in the air while Lữ lit them and the group recited a prayer. Everyone watched the candles carefully, for if one should go out during the ritual, it would signify that the couple might not have a happy married life. Scholar Mã kowtowed to the altar, then to the bride's family, starting with the males, eldest first. Short the parents of the groom to be the officials, the groom made what should have been their toast. With the rice wine, he said, "I am honored to have Jade River join my house. Let me thank and honor the bride's parents and their Ancestors, and the lovely bride." And everyone drank.

Now the family sat down for a final meal together. Jade River's eyes moved slowly to find each member of her family. Her mother was quietly helping Spring Flower serve the meal. Nhạc was joking with Lữ, who laughed at his remark. Huệ bowed to his sister; he was also taking in and surveying the scene. Where Lương Hoàng often sat, there smiled her new husband, Scholar Mã, causing an involuntary shudder. Spring Flower returned to the stove, while Autumn Moon sat down at the head of the table.

My family all look so handsome, and so familiar, Jade River thought. *Had I married Lương Hoàng, I'd have that wonderful young man, and I'd have stayed right here in Tây Sơn. I don't know when we will be together again. If only the mandarin would let my father go before I have to depart. I so want to say goodbye to him. We never said goodbye.*

Huệ closely observed the strange Scholar Mã, and wasn't sure he liked what he saw. *His smile is so big, not relaxed, and he keeps holding up his cup for more wine. It is not a good sign that he wouldn't let any of us accompany our sister to his big house in Nha Trang to meet his parents and to present to them our engagement gifts. He explained that they are in bad health. But why did he make that point a part of the marriage contract?*

36

When it came time for Jade River to depart, it was Autumn Moon's turn to burst into tears. She murmured under her breath, "Great Buddha of Heaven protect us. My darling, this is not how I wanted to lose you."

Jade River could barely speak; her face was ashen with fear. "Mother," she said, "Father will soon be home. I can not permit my father—who, with you, gave me life—to wither away in a jail cell. We know this is the best that we can do. To honor and serve Father is my duty. This time of adversity is also the will of the Gods. Hopefully, some good will come of it."

Autumn Moon embraced her daughter and said, "Buddha protect you, my precious child. I don't know what we ever could have done in a former life that would call for such misfortunes to fall upon us now. Probably, our great happiness made some Genie jealous. Or Mandarin Trúc is just inexplicably evil."

Jade River could not suppress her tears. She had no desire to leave her handsome Hoàng, to whom she had first secretly and then openly promised her everlasting love, or to leave her village. She confided to her mother, who she might never see again, "I remember the way Hoàng looked on the day that his father informed him that the marriage was agreed upon. I had just had a touching conversation with my father as well. Hoàng and I were both suddenly so happy. Hoàng appeared and gave me a bouquet of roses and lotus blossoms. After watching him reluctantly depart, I ran to the stream to swim and to calm down."

"I hope you find happiness," said Autumn Moon. "Buddha and Lao Tzu and Quán Thế Âm protect you."

Jade River wiped her tears with her handkerchief. Moving to the front yard, she turned to her brothers and said, "Be good to each other. I will miss you all every day until we are reunited." She handed a scroll to Huệ and asked him to give it to his friend Hoàng.

Hoàng had kept away for fear that he would try to prevent her from obeying her mother and her own filial and virtuous duty. He had taken his bow and quiver, walked across the fields, and disappeared into the jungle of the western mountains that rose up just beyond the village. He hunted the man-eating wildcats and the tigers, to ease his loss.

Nhạc felt intense jealousy that his sister, even at their parting, should favor Huệ over himself, by giving Huệ a scroll. *Demons of Hell, aren't I the oldest,* he thought. *Don't I love my sister as much as Huệ? First Father began to favor Huệ for his good marks as a student. Didn't this scroll prove that Jade River now preferred Huệ also, mimicking our father? It is my shame and secret that I loathe Huệ's cleverness and good humor.*

Jade River felt her brother Nhạc's resentment. She went over to him and embraced him hard, catching him off guard. "Dearest Nhạc," she said locking eyes with her eldest brother, "I still depend most on you; don't forget that. Please take care of all the family for me. I will miss you terribly." And then she turned away.

Nhạc felt renewed. She had given him back his face. Suddenly he wondered, *How can I part from someone so important to me?*

Jade River saw Lữ hanging back, conflicted, and she went to him with yet another embrace. "Goodbye, my dearest Lữ," she said, smiling and looking directly at him. "Life will be so dull and different without you, and your jokes at the expense of our family. Who now will make me laugh?"

Lữ was grateful, but speechless. Huệ interrupted the awkward silence with, "Thank you for your words, little sister. We all hope you love your new husband and family, and that they are wonderful for you!"

"Goodbye youngest brother," she said. "Remember, after I leave, you and I must both mind our elders." And she embraced Huệ.

Jade River bowed low to all her family and then stepped into the red wedding palanquin that stood ready. The smiling groom now took a last bow and mounted the forward palanquin. Scholar Mã and Jade River departed with their bearers, musicians, and guards. The family stood in front of the house as if at a funeral, listening to the gay sounds as the flute and gong music faded away.

"Soon my husband will be free," said Autumn Moon. "Ah bitterness, why is it that throughout our region people are starving, while the rich and powerful throw innocent men in jail, so that in order to live we must barter off our loved ones?" *Control your tongue,* Autumn Moon thought. *You don't want to so enrage your sons that they charge off foolishly and immediately get killed. If you are weak, you don't try to kill a giant with the charge of a tiger, but with the bite of a snake. I should send Trúc teas laced with chicken's bane.*

❧   ❦

The gilded red palanquin carried Jade River into the village of Tây Sơn. Scholar Mã was full of good cheer, and he graciously asked Jade River to climb down and move into the back of a wagon with their luggage for the trip to Quy Nhơn. Scholar Mã mounted a horse, while a servant took the reins behind two mules, who would pull the wagon to Quy Nhơn.

That evening Scholar Mã and Jade River stayed at a cheap inn at the port of Quy Nhơn. He guided her to the inn door for refreshment. When Jade River came out of the ladies' washroom, they shared a simple meal of fish, rice, and vegetables in the dining room.

Scholar Mã was not a man of great ceremony. Though they would not be fully married until she'd met his parents and finished the second half of the ceremonies, he promptly tried to take her to bed that night. Jade River protested, "Scholar Mã, we must wait till we are fully married." The third time she said no, he slapped her face and ordered her to undress. She still refused silently.

Am I going to let this precious piece of fresh fruit escape me? Scholar Mã thought. He hit her again, and then ripped off her garments and dragged her to the bed, which his male body-servant had covered with a clean white sheet. Jade River was hopelessly confused and distressed.

Her body left a wine red stain on the sheet; her eyes dropped tears on the silken pillow.

ૐ   ૐ

After a week on board a junk carrying passengers and freight, they reached Sài Gòn. From there, they rode horses to an inn in the village of Biên Hòa, where they were greeted by a fat lady with a heavily painted face. A group of women with penciled eyebrows stood to one side. Several dandies, well dressed and groomed, sat drinking rice wine while they looked over the girls. Jade River's wildest fears were then fanned to flame.

The fat lady escorted them into a back room and took Jade River warmly in her arms. "Welcome to the Happy Valley Green Pavilion," she said, smiling critically at Jade River's beautiful face. "I am your new mother, Madame Camellia."

"But I don't understand," Jade River said, pulling away. "Husband, what does this mean?"

"Husband!" the fat lady snarled, and she turned on the man called Scholar Mã with a ferocious intensity. "Did you tamper with the goods and spoil my investment?" she demanded. Her eyes burned with rage and pain and her jowly face reddened. She looked him straight in the eyes, and could see his smug delight. "That was my silver invested, you lousy prick of a bumblebee. It's always my silver."

The fat lady turned to Jade River in a fury. "You strumpet," and slapped her across the face so hard it threw Jade River to the floor. "You rutting bitch," she hissed, "I'll teach you to mess with my man and play with his damned itch." The fat lady seized a whip hanging from the wall and flogged the young girl without mercy.

Jade River was horror-struck. The lash burned like fire. After a series of painful blows, Jade River drew a small penknife from out of her skirt. "Forgive me Father," she said aloud, "but life is surely much worse than death, and now I will regain my honor." Young Jade River plunged the knife into her heart.

ૐ   ૐ

The wound was not fatal—the instrument had been too small—but many times after that horrible day, Jade River wished it had ended her life. When she revived and the doctor had left, she came to the conclusion that the Gods had ordered that she should live, for whatever good purpose she couldn't guess. She must have behaved very wickedly in a former life. For her courage, she now commanded unusual respect throughout the house, and the customers very quickly discovered her. The bees swarmed; they jockeyed for the favor of her nectar.

Though reputed to be a virgin only available for her music, poetry, and songs, Jade River became one of the most sought-after ladies of the house, and a very busy entertainer. She swore that she'd kill herself if she was ever forced to submit again against her will, and the madam believed her. Jade River had lost all the people she loved. She expressed her grief and depression in her songs. The men still signed up and paid to spend their evenings with her, so beautiful was her appearance, so lovely her voice, and so plaintive her music on the lute. As well as there was the challenge of seducing her.

☙　❧

Though the Hồ family sent the money to the mandarin, Nguyễn Trúc was so angry to lose the girl he had requested that he ordered the doctor beaten again and tortured before he was released.

Physician Hồ was left for another week in a rank cellar, encumbered by the hardwood cangue. He could not eat or drink without the aid of a jailer, while his excrement and urine collected against the far wall and added to the stench that he sat in. Insects crawled on his body. As he waited for his release, a tormenter entered his cell with a variety of horrid instruments.

As the torturer set out his tools, Hồ Danh silently composed his death poem.

A man has many lives,

The forest has many paths.

If the void is a great elephant,

The world is but a speck of dust on his back.

The pleasures and pains of life,

are as transient

as a dandelion in the breeze.

The specialist spent several hours applying various screws and vises usually reserved for recalcitrant prisoners of war, and methodically broke the bones in one of Hồ Danh's hands and one of his feet. He ended the job by wrapping the damaged parts in rags and tying them with string, and departed.

Physician Hồ was sent home. The family, which had so looked forward to his release, were shocked by his tragic appearance. For a moment, Autumn Moon, Nhạc, Lữ, and Huệ just stared at the broken man with the bloody bandages, who was too tired and traumatized to speak. A lone bailiff, who accompanied the prisoner wagon, asked them to remove the patient. The sons moved forward and picked their father up. He was light as a feather. Carefully, they carried him into the house. Autumn Moon followed them inside, examined her beloved husband, and tried to make him comfortable in their bed. She excused herself, walked away from the house, and fell apart completely. She sobbed and screamed uncontrollably at the sky.

After seeing his three sons, Hồ Danh said to his wife, "Send for Jade River, so I can see her."

Autumn Moon looked down, then at her husband and quietly replied, "Jade River has been married off to a gentleman in Nha Trang, to raise the 300 taels needed to set you free."

"Oh no ... Oh no," Hồ Danh moaned, unable to say more.

ॐ   ॐ

Lương Hoàng came back from a trip to Nha Trang, where he had gone to check on Jade River. He had found that there was no Scholar Mã at the address they had been given. The wine shop he had found, according to its proprietor, was periodically the false address of a rather notorious flesh-peddler, whose identity remained a mystery to the owner of the tavern.

Autumn Moon and her sons had been scammed and had sold Jade River to a procurer for flower houses. These brothels offered little hope of a dignified or happy future for their "wind and rain" battered inmates. Physician Hồ could not bear this news on top of his dreadful wounds. He was so sick, cast down, and uncomfortable that he mostly smoked opium when he was conscious. His crushed foot and hand both grew gangrenous. The doctor who attended him amputated the foot and leg on one day, and the hand and arm on the next.

He died several days after his amputations. Some said that he died of a fever caused by his crushed extremities. Others thought it was from the opium. Autumn Moon said that her husband did not die of the amputations or the opium. He just quit; he died of a broken heart.

Hồ Danh's sons, Nhạc, Lữ, and Huệ, at their mother's urging, immediately began to plot their revenge. They had been in mourning since the day Hồ Danh came home. The same day that Physician Hồ's breathing stopped, they stayed up late to discuss their options. They invited the teacher of the four Hồ children, Scholar Trương Văn Hiến, to join them at this meeting.

Scholar Trương Văn Hiến, Autumn Moon, and Nhạc, sat on benches in the main room of the house. Lữ and Huệ sat on a rug. Nhạc began the meeting, "Thank you Scholar Trương for joining us at this dark time. To do nothing is unacceptable. I think I should immediately assassinate Nguyễn Trúc. I can't live with this shame, and I'm sure that I could easily kill him when he appears at the morning or afternoon tribunal."

"I agree," said Lữ. He looked carefully at each of his brothers, his mother, and their trusted teacher. "I want his blood. I volunteer to help you in the ambush."

"Nguyễn Trúc lives and works in the Quy Nhơn citadel. How will you both escape after the assassination, wherever it takes place?" Huệ asked with polite deference.

"I'm not sure yet, I can't imagine how," Nhạc admitted. "But at least I will try to escape."

Huệ said, "I wonder if there isn't a better alternative. Our revenge need not come this week, or this month. We can take our time. We need better opportunities.

We need allies who could fight with us against Nguyễn Trúc and his garrison." The youngest brother took a good breath for emphasis, "Why don't we become bandits? We could use some time to practice fighting and killing with weapons, and we could raise money to arm a band of followers. Then we could use the band as a rescue party when you both assassinate the mandarin. After the assassination, with our band, we could fight our way out of the citadel."

"Then we'll have to fight the Nguyễn Army!" Nhạc said, confused.

"That is true," Huệ said, "but so what? We can probably avoid troops indefinitely up in the hills—many bandits do. Doesn't such a plan offer more hope and promise than just a suicide attack? Even if you survive the assassination, the military would just hunt the four of us down like mere criminals, which we are not."

Scholar Trương held up his hand and said, "I agree with this idea of Huệ's. It would be useful also to make alliances with the hill tribes who hate the Nguyễn. Furthermore, at this time, my favorite astrologer, Mạc Đĩnh Chi, says that heavenly portents are favorable for a successful uprising against an unpopular government. Even without the seer's blessing, the Nguyễn, whom I despise, are vulnerable."

"It might just work," said Lữ, thinking it was a good idea, since he didn't really want to die.

Huệ added, "Why Nhạc, you might even become as famous someday as black-faced Sung Chiang of Liang Shan P'o. He defied the imperial troops of China over and over again." The comparison seemed both exciting and ludicrously optimistic, and everyone joined Huệ in grim, macabre laughter.

Why is that sapling Huệ so clever? Nhạc wondered silently. *I still haven't read that famous book.* But Nhạc asked aloud with real interest, "How long will we need to assemble a band that is strong enough?" He clenched his fist to hide the surge of old resentments he harbored against his little brother.

"I don't know," Huệ said. "We won't know until we start, and probably we will have to work at robbery for at least a year or two before we are strong and experienced enough to take on the troops of the citadel at Quy Nhơn. Maybe Nguyễn Trúc will let down his guard. We will have to study his movements."

Scholar Trương interjected, "This is a good idea; it is modest and realistic. You will be able to extort useful 'protection payments' from your neighbors and everyone you meet, and as your operation grows, so will your base of support, especially if you pay your local suppliers."

Autumn Moon finally spoke. "We must assassinate Trúc. Turning bandit will be hard, challenging, and irreversible. And we will lose the farm. But it gives you, my sons, a chance to survive the assassination and escape. We have the motivation"—and here she looked carefully at her three strapping young men—"the determination, and the talent. I would sacrifice all three of you to bring down this Nguyễn magistrate. I think we should do it."

No one spoke against her words. Nhạc informed his wife, Spring Flower, and consulted a second astrologer. Lữ prayed in the lotus position for the duration of an incense stick to burn in a Taoist temple. Huệ, who had found his father's original medical textbook hidden away, continued his old task of carefully making a second copy. The law and governmental exams would now be closed to him, and making the copy would help him learn the material, while the second manuscript would be valuable.

For months, the family prepared secretly to leave their sacred, ancestral farm. They kept quiet that Physician Hồ Danh had died. They told everyone that he was too sick for visitors. The Hồ brothers, Autumn Moon, Spring Flower, and Hoàng buried Physician Hồ's remains quietly, with a short service and no marker, between the graves of his parents. They harvested their rice, which they stored in portable baskets. They quietly sold off or slaughtered and smoked the hogs and chickens. Finally, they were ready to leave their house and lands, which they sold to one of the larger families in their village. Autumn Moon produced a jar hidden in a wall of her bedroom. It contained Hồ Danh's and her life savings of some jewelry and eighteen silver taels. Nhạc produced a sac with thirty-two more silver taels.

"Where did this come from?" Lữ asked in astonishment.

"A small bonus from the Provincial Treasury," the part-time tax collector said with a grin. "And separating this from the king's own hoard was no small feat, let me assure you." Nhạc looked from face to face to check his family for their reaction to the revelation of his larceny. His eyes found Huệ, who was looking stupefied.

Huệ's gaze changed rapidly to one of amazement and then to one of amusement, masking his disapproval. "By the Genie of the house," Huệ laughed, realizing the irony, "someone has jumped ahead and has been quietly practicing piracy on the sly." Huệ concealed his anger, thinking, *You committed a crime which only later by dint of what happened has become almost justified. Now, was that coincidence or karma? Did Nhạc's disloyalty to authority and law anger the Jade Emperor of Heaven and cause this disaster to the family?*

Lữ patted his older brother on the back. "You're not changing direction tonight; you're just emerging from the storm cellar."

Autumn Moon also hid her embarrassment and confusion. In spite of her anger at the local government, she knew full well that her number one son had siphoned off these silver bars before her husband had been wronged. Nhạc had recklessly endangered them all. Her strong sense of duty to the Lê Emperor and her respect for the Confucian ideal of the just king were disturbed by her eldest son's revelation. "You took serious risks, but we can use that money now," she said with ambivalence. She stooped over and picked up her *gánh*, or load—two baskets suspended at the ends of a stout bamboo shoulder pole.

The others shouldered their backpacks and *gánh*. With their ancestral tablets and good luck charms carefully packed away in the baskets hanging from their shoulder poles, they marched into the starlit night. Autumn Moon was despondent. She did not want to leave her house and rice fields. She began to fear the whole idea was absurd and suicidal. But she could see, proudly, that her boys were excited, and thought, *Each one of them seems filled with new unity and purpose. They have matured greatly in just a few months.*

"With ten thousand stars as our witness," Huệ said aloud, "we leave almost everything that we have behind, and begin a long trip of no return to avenge the murder of our father and the loss and ruin of our sister. Now we truly are like the great heroes of old in Liang Shan P'o, as recorded in the tales of *Shui Hu Chuan— The Margins of the Water.* May we all be as successful as the bandit, honest Sung Chiang, who cared for his neighbors and friends, and looked lightly on his gold and silver."

❧ ❦

And so they became "brothers of the green wood." They joined one of the ancient and universal fraternities of their world. The motto of this brotherhood was, "All good men of the four seas are righteous under Heaven," which is a classical Chinese euphemism for, "Rob from the rich, give to the poor." Since the Hồ brothers considered themselves to be quite poor at the time, they felt justified in robbing the rich and not at all compelled to give away much of anything.

Sensitive to public sentiment, they consciously refined their message. They came up with a recruiting slogan: "We seize the property of the rich and distribute it to the poor." Their profits and numbers steadily increased. They maintained their popularity and security by paying for their meals, and leaving good tips. Their suppliers became their eyes and ears.

The Hồ brother bandits robbed any rich person whom they dared to intimidate or overpower, and they soon acquired plenty of money and an arsenal of weapons— not to mention a local reputation. Since their father had been a master of boxing, the three brothers had already developed their personal weapons, which included various parts of the hands, wrists, elbows, knees, and feet.

Huệ suggested that they should invest a little of their wealth and advertise for recruits. They needed certain skills, such as a bow and arrow maker and a swordsmith. Nhạc, who was the natural leader of the band because of his position as eldest son and his physical prowess, agreed. They donated money to several temples and monasteries where they thought the priests and monks would be sympathetic, and tried to heed and serve the needs of the community. The Hồ family quietly indicated that they would accept any recruits who would swear allegiance to their leadership and serve with honor against Nguyễn tyranny.

On one occasion, the three Hồ brothers were walking to a market when they passed four men dressed as simple farmers. The four men turned swiftly, drew sharp knives, and seized Lữ and Huệ from behind. They held the knives to their throats and demanded their names.

Nhạc looked at Lữ, who could hardly move with his arms pinned. A razor-sharp blade rested on his throat. He looked at Huệ, who was likewise professionally trussed for slaughter. *Oh Quan Công, mighty warrior,* Nhạc thought, *deliver us from bounty hunters.*

"Tell me who you are quick or I'll shave your friend," the coarse-looking leader said.

Nhạc couldn't think of anything else to say, so he blurted out, "I'm Hồ Nhạc, and these are my servants. We've done you no ill, what do you want?"

"If this is true, what good luck. We've been looking for you," said the leader of this other gang. Nhạc immediately saw himself in the mandarin's dungeon, being shredded alive. After a terrible pause, the leader said, "The priest Nine Fingers told us to tell you that the white lotus grows ..."

"... on the back of a water buffalo," Nhạc answered. This was the password that he and Huệ had established with the head of the Eternal Springtime Taoist Monastery.

The fellow then said, still holding his knife to Lữ's throat, "We want to join forces . . . to fight Nguyễn Trúc."

"Then you are all most certainly welcome. Put away your weapons," answered Nhạc. The four sturdy men carefully relaxed their grips, and somewhat embarrassed, because of the crudeness of their introduction, eased their long knives back into their hemp belts. The leader of this cautious and lethal little band was called Snake. He and his brother, Midget, and their two companions, Night Hawk and Lover Boy, soon became trusted aides to Nhạc, and then his personal bodyguards.

అ   ❦

After a year, the group had grown to a hundred, including about thirty-five women. The women were responsible for cooking, sewing, repairing the tents and lean-tos, making arrows, and scores of other tasks. A few of them bore arms and practiced fighting, in the tradition of the ancient Trưng Sisters. The presence of female warriors in Nhạc's band was not a divisive issue. The Việt, at least within their own tribe, were tolerant of variations in nature, which made some men behave more like women and some women behave more like men. Vietnam had an honorable history of strong women providing leadership in resisting foreign domination, as fighters and even generals. In A.D. 40, the Trưng Sisters led one of the first national uprisings against a long Chinese occupation.

A terrible flood, followed by a drought and a poor harvest, made the Hồ brothers' recruiting much simpler. The mountain jungle became even more dangerous, however, as rival bands sprang up and challenged them. Many youths preferred becoming highwaymen to going hungry and trying to eat roots and locusts, or even worse, human flesh, which could be purchased in times of famine at most markets, and cost considerably less than the usual animal meats, vegetables, or rice.

The three brothers named their group the Tây Sơn Rebels. They fought off other bands when necessary, honing their martial skills. Each deadly fight with another band culled the weak from the group. Often the survivors of the other band joined the Hồ brothers. The band robbed wealthy travelers when possible, practiced regularly with their weapons, maintained discipline in their group, and generally prospered.

While Nhạc was the official leader, Autumn Moon continued as the authority figure of the group, and Huệ remained the tactician. Nhạc was required by custom and his own family tradition to weigh his mother's wise words like gold, and her wisdom and shrewdness served him and their cause well. Nguyễn Trúc had created a formidable enemy in Autumn Moon and her three sons.

Chapter 6
Lorient, France
1770

Stars melted away in the blue-gray light, and the black hills of Lanvaux slowly caught fire in blue-red streaks as the sky behind them turned from dark to light. The sun rose as a flaming God, the Sun King, behind the seaport of Lorient on the coast of Brittany. It was Anno Domini, in the year of our Lord, 1770.

Benoit Grannier walked down the cobbled streets, which were already full of workers quietly hurrying to start the day. Though only fourteen, Benoit was already a tall gangly lad, with curly red-brown hair and soft green eyes, unusual in a French boy, and perhaps revealing a Viking ancestor or two.

"Good morning, Master Quellenac," Benoit greeted the sword master, who nodded hello as he swung open the shutters of his ground-floor fencing studio. Benoit picked up the straw broom and attended to the floor. As he swept, his whole frame gently rocked, and he consciously loosened up his lanky, adolescent body. He finished dusting and polishing the front desk just in time to join the small morning class.

Twenty-one more boys had wandered in while Benoit was working, and now he took his place sitting with them on the floor. Barefoot, he brought the soles of his feet together, straightened his back, and pushed his knees to the floor, stretching his groin muscles.

He and the other boys all followed the brown-bearded Georges Quellenac through stretching and limbering, followed by attack and retreat drills.

The broad-built Quellenac said in a bored tone of voice, "Get your swords for the thrust and parry drills. Pair off and begin at your own speed."

Benoit faced off with one of the older boys, Gilles. They saluted and commenced the exercises. The room filled with the clashing of steel, practice rapiers tipped with wine corks and wadding. Benoit observed that Gilles was full of sleep.

"Keep this partner and commence fencing," said Master Quellenac. Benoit and his partner fought in earnest. *This boy always signals his intent with his body,* Benoit thought to himself. The two boys danced around each other, and every time the older boy lunged, Benoit struck his rapier against his opponent's sword, pushing it off the line of attack and flicking his cork-covered blade into the fellow's stomach. Gilles began to get angry, but the more angry he became, the more he signaled his moves. Benoit wanted to keep his opponent's spirits up, so he allowed the fellow to score a point periodically. But Gilles was already fit to be tied. "*Merde alors* [shit then]," Gilles swore, "wake up you cretin."

Master Quellenac could see how easily Benoit could handle his opponent. "Watch the body and not the blade, use the feint," he admonished Gilles, who now was crimson.

The class ended abruptly after an hour. Benoit helped one of the younger students with a question, thanked his instructor, and walked briskly out the front door. As he turned the corner he came upon Gilles and another older fellow and poor Grégoire, one of the smaller boys from the class. Grégoire was trapped between the two older boys. Gilles and his friend traded punches into the smaller boy's body.

"Ow, leave me be!" the young boy bawled.

"What's the matter?" asked Benoit, intruding himself. "What did Grégoire do to you?"

"Help me," said Grégoire. "I didn't do anything to them."

"Shut up," said Gilles angrily, and hit him again in the stomach. "He was fresh and ill-mannered, and he knows it. Doesn't respect his elders."

"Suit yourself," said Benoit, and he walked away. He consoled himself, *I shouldn't risk this trouble. I have to support the whole family.* Meanwhile, Grégoire tried to break free, but Gilles and his friend kept catching him, and while one bully held him, the other slugged him. Then they let him go so they could catch him again. The noise was awful. Benoit felt ashamed, which made him angry. He turned and trotted back. "Looks like a fight," Benoit intruded. "Let's make this fracas more even," and he walked right up to the taller Gilles. Gilles swung his fist at Benoit's face, but Benoit blocked the blow with his opposite arm and then right-fisted into the big boy's stomach.

"Ow," Gilles cried, throwing a wild punch. Benoit buried another fist in his gut, doubling him over. The other older boy just watched; he had already let go of Grégoire. Benoit jumped at the accomplice and let him have it with a volley of punches that left him writhing on the ground.

"Come on Grégoire," said Benoit, "let's not be late for school." They hurried down the cobbled streets to the school, the Abbey of St. Mathew. Grégoire was still upset.

"Damn those assholes, they beat me up for no reason."

"I'm sorry," said Benoit. "Are you all right?"

"I guess so, my stomach still hurts. Those cow turds—no reason at all."

"You'd better go wash your face," said Benoit.

"All right, thanks again," said Grégoire, and they entered the school building.

Benoit attended classes in literature and history before the morning recess, during which he and a few other scholarship boys helped clean the building.

I wish I could spend the recess playing ball games with the other boys, he thought. *But since Papa is dead, and I am the eldest, it falls on me to help Mama provide for the others. If I could work after school four days instead of three a week, we'd have that much more money, but then I'd never stay on top of my assignments.*

After the recess, Benoit greeted his best friend and cousin, Antoine Grannier, as they were entering the classroom. Benoit ducked as a pebble sailed past his head. He searched the back of the room, but not one of the older boys seemed to notice or call attention to themselves. Gilles was in the back corner, talking to his buddy from the fistfight. *Damn them and their stones,* thought Benoit. *They could really hurt me. I can't afford to have enemies.*

He sat at his desk and took out his workbook to check his graphs and equations, just as Father Sebastian plodded into the room. The boys all stood to attention and the old man with the bulbous eyes, shiny bald head, and long white beard waved for them to sit.

The class began with half an hour of review and discussion of coordinate geometry, advanced in the previous century by the Frenchmen René Descartes and Pierre de Fermat. Old Father Sebastian reviewed the homework problems. *Mechanics,* thought Benoit, *what does that have to do with chivalry, honor, or war?*

Honk! The old man blew his nose into an old mouchoir. "So much for Descartes for the moment. Today," said the priest, smiling broadly, "we are going to continue our study of physics and astronomy. I will introduce you to Sir Isaac Newton's mechanics."

The priest was a sight to behold, his once muscular frame now shrunken with age and his face ringed with beard and naked forehead. Beard and side-hair were yellow-tinged and frayed. Father Sebastian had a reverence for the doyens of science, which was unusual in a Catholic father. He shook a knobby finger at the room of boys and leaned over, peering through his spectacles, and orated.

"Copernicus, Kepler, and Galileo conspired in spirit—each facing excommunication—and they proved that the earth travels around the sun. To be more precise, Copernicus decided to side with Heraclides and Aristarchus, that it must be so. After the well born and brilliant alchemist Tycho Brahe ate too much dinner or poison at a banquet for Emperor Rudolf II of Denmark, and expired, Kepler finally gained access to Tycho Brahe's extensive collection of observations and calculations, which he used to prove the ancient Greek theory of heliocentricity. So there's a subsidiary lesson to this planetary discourse: For heaven's sake, don't ever overeat when dining out." The old man laughed hard with the boys at his own wit.

Benoit laughed along with his classmates. He loved the old wizard. *He is subtle sometimes,* Benoit thought. *In spite of his jokes, he is daring to teach us that the earth goes around the sun, and not the other way, as the Bible says in Joshua and Ecclesiastes and as it clearly appears to do. He keeps hinting at something else. If he insists that some of the teachings of the Bible are fallible, then other parts of it might reveal the flaws of human writers as well.*

Father Sebastian continued, "Sir Isaac Newton, unfortunately an Englishman, unlocked some of the most elusive secrets of the universe in his book, *The Mathematical Principles of Natural Philosophy*. Kepler and Newton translated the music of the spheres into the harmony of numbers. Building on Kepler, Galileo, and others, Newton, the Prometheus of modern science, gave the world the mechanics of the good Lord our maker, starting with the three principles of motion."

Father Sebastian searched the faces of his pupils as he pondered how to demonstrate his points. Benoit observed the teacher's rheumy eyes focus on Gilles, who had fallen asleep at his bench against the back wall. Benoit saw a special light come into the priest's eye. "Let me try to demonstrate the simplicity and power of this discovery," Father Sebastian chortled. He picked up his cane and walked over to the sleeping Gilles, whom he had heard was a bully.

"First: A body will remain in a state of rest or in a uniform motion in a straight line, unless acted on by an unbalanced force." As Benoit and his classmates began to chuckle in anticipation of an unrehearsed and extemporaneous demonstration, Father Sebastian slowly raised his cane above the unsuspecting Gilles. More students giggled. Sebastian smote the boy a blow against his side, knocking him to the floor. The boy yelled, but the priest demanded silence and continued with intense enthusiasm. "Second: A force is any action which can change the state of motion."

Father Sebastian proceeded to beat Gilles, who retreated from the blows by moving around the room. With poor Gilles cowering in the corner, the priest turned to the now very attentive class, and said in a full and theatrically slow voice, mimicking his own impersonations of Demosthenes to the Athenian assembly, "And Third: For every action, there is an equal and opposite reaction."

The priest swung his cane in an arc and banged Gilles on the shin. The boy yelped and doubled up, clutching his shin bone, and hopped up and down on the other leg. The priest grabbed the tall youngster, pushed him, hopping, to the doorway, and shoved him out of the room. His classmates laughed heartily—in appreciation, of course, of Newton's genius.

Mechanics, Benoit was thinking, *is going to be interesting after all. Gilles is having a rough day though; first me, then Father Sebastian.* Benoit smiled. *For all his talk of Christian love, Father Sebastian isn't gentle with those he dislikes.*

Father Sebastian raised his hands, demanding silence. "But give in not to temptation," he admonished. "Do not forget the love of Christ, only temper the insights of the Bible with the important new works of the secular non-saints. Or do I mean nonsense?" He smiled benignly as the sharper boys chuckled, and continued his lecture as if nothing out of the ordinary had been said. "Sir Isaac Newton became a living saint of science; he entered the realm of the Holy. Some English do! Now, don't go back to your cells in a panic, remember the Great Norman Conquest. Newton's ancestors, of course, were all Norman, and he discovered a secret of our blessed Lord Almighty with his Principle of Universal Gravitation.

"Every body in the universe attracts every other body with a mutual force that is directly proportional to the product of their masses and inversely proportional to the square of the distance between their centers." Father Sebastian looked over his boys to see if any were interested, or any still inattentive. He put the insight on the chalkboard:

$$F_{grav} = G \times \frac{M1M2}{D^2}$$

He makes it sound like the act of courting a girl, Benoit mused, and wanted to say this out loud, but didn't. Yet some of the boys were smiling.

Father Sebastian spoke with intensity. "G is the universal constant of gravitation, and the Lord has not yet revealed to anyone how to measure it. Some say he never will. I think it is about as possible as flying one of Leonardo Da Vinci's flying machines or visiting the moon. But I digress.

"This insight won't be as hard to remember as you might at first think." Father Sebastian paused to scratch his arms and to eye his charges. *My little scholars,* he thought, as he often did, *you are my only insurance against the vague and tempting promise of a heavenly immortality. Besides, how will the angels make everyone happy and free of hatred?*

Now the bulbous-eyed Sebastian loomed over Jean Plassy, a rich man's son and a philanderer of the class. "For instance, when a Lorient student meets a damsel at the Golden Valley Pub and Brothel, the directly proportional force of the product of the mutual attraction of their masses is a bastard, whose likelihood is inversely proportional to the square of the distance between their centers. Do you understand the prophylactic of this lesson of physics, my little Jean?"

"Yes Sir, I think I do, Sir!" the blushing boy said in a low voice.

"Good. I hope so. And remember, it was that great Roman scholar Epicus Fornicatus Ejaculatus who carved that famous doggerel into the ancient clay tablets of Izmir, 'Without sheath, no freedom for the bitch, no honor for the hound.' For tomorrow, read chapter one of Newton's *Mathematical Principals*, and do on your own all the problems he presents and solves in the chapter. There are four copies in the library. Class is dismissed."

The students clapped and hooted their approval of the priest's teaching. Benoit and Antoine both clapped and looked at each other and smiled in agreement with the class. In the hall, Benoit said, "Father Sebastian is a great science professor, a true philosophe, though he is a rare character as a Catholic priest."

"That's for certain," said Antoine. "The faculty here is divided over whether he will go to heaven or hell."

"I wouldn't want Saint Peter's job," said Benoit.

Benoit and Antoine went to the library to study before each returned to his own home for dinner. They were both day students at the school and often studied together. "Isn't it strange," said Antoine, "that in history and literature classes we learn why we hate the English and why they are the enemy, whereas in physics and mathematics classes we learn to respect them as members of the same brotherhood of science."

Benoit frowned, "Father Bartlette said that they're no longer true Christians, since they're Protestants and therefore heretics, and they will stop at nothing to increase their wealth and power."

Antoine laughed, "And we Catholics are different?" There was no argument there. "Yes," he went on, "it's queer that you can have it both ways. It's not rational, though, to call them the enemy all the time, and for the king to be constantly preparing for an expensive war when he can't house and feed his people. The famine and the food shortages cause the peasants to go hungry and more and more become homeless."

"Listen to you talk," said Benoit. "Every week you sound more and more like old Sebastian." Antoine didn't disagree; he looked pleased. The boys entered the library and sat down to study until the dinner hour, when they returned to their own families. The sun went down late in the spring, so people crowded the shops and avoided the horse-drawn carriages as they walked up and down the street. The tall stucco-and-brick apartment buildings and townhouses made the town seem dark against the bright evening sky.

Women and children leaned out on iron-wrought balconies, and Benoit walked in the street, away from the houses, in case someone dumped garbage or night soil out the front instead of the back of their apartment. The town reeked of uncollected garbage and rotting human waste.

Benoit climbed the two flights of stairs to the top floor of his old apartment building. Withdrawing a large metal key from his shoulder pouch, he unlocked the heavy wooden door. The living room was gloomy; a single oil lamp sputtered on the dining table.

"Benoit, help! Help me—Benwaaah. Ouch," cried Gabriel. One of Benoit's younger brothers, François, was overpowering an even younger brother, Gabriel, in a wrestling match.

Marie-Noelle ran in from the kitchen and called out, "*Bon soir* Benoit," and carefully presented her cheek to be kissed.

Benoit kissed Marie-Noelle on both cheeks, then pulled the two boys apart. He checked to make sure Gabriel was undamaged and in good spirits, let them both go, and Gabriel immediately charged back into François, who prudently let himself get knocked down in front of his biggest brother.

Benoit checked the baby, Isabelle. Her face lit up as she sighted Benoit, and when he picked up the three-year-old and hugged her, she laughed with pleasure. In all the family, the baby was the happiest and the easiest to please. She needed to be changed but didn't yet care. Benoit passed into the kitchen and kissed his mother, who barely straightened up from the coal stove, over which she directed her pot and skillet like the conductor of a symphony with two wooden spoons.

Céleste was a lean, middle-aged woman who worked small miracles to make ends meet. She earned money as a cook and a midwife when called by the neighbors or members of her church, and, when not busy with those tasks, as a seamstress. Benoit's father had been a lieutenant in the King's Navy, but had been killed in a sea battle against the English two years before, when Benoit was twelve. It had been a tragically unnecessary battle while the two countries were officially at peace.

Annette and Cécile came charging into the apartment with the five-year-old Georges-Louis, their baskets half full of vegetables, cheese, fresh butter, and garlic. On most days Benoit loved his eight brothers and sisters: Annette, Cécile, François, Marie-Noelle, Gabriel, Elisabet, Georges-Louis, and Isabelle.

Mama ladled out the beet and cabbage soup. It had scraps of beef from the bones she could afford. She gave just two ladlesful to the older children and one ladleful to the younger ones. They lined up before the stove like little refugees, dressed in their worn-out and patched-up hand-me-downs. At the long table, they took hands, and Mama gave their thanks to God. Next they all sang a doxology in four parts; beautiful voices created instant wealth. There was one fresh baguette, cut carefully into ten pieces—the bread of heaven.

"Benoit," said Annette, "will you join us after dinner in a round of charades?"

"No thanks, Annette, I must study tonight," he responded. After a noisy and cheerful dinner, Benoit returned to school to study in the light of the oil lamps at the school library.

Celeste wanted him to obtain a position as an apprentice in one of the professions. Benoit wanted to enter as a midshipman in the Naval Academy. He did well in school because he took his studies seriously, but he already knew in his mind that he wanted the seagoing life of the navy.

As he walked down the dimly lit streets, passing by the occasional candle wick lampion, his mind wandered through the career choices of sailor versus merchant, solicitor, or proprietor. *In the navy I won't be able to enjoy the comforts of family life for a long time,* he thought. *I've already helped to raise three brothers and five sisters. I like girls but I don't want to settle down anytime soon. I don't need more children in my life for a long time. The navy is a hard life, but I can't think of a better way for a man of small means to see the world. There is still so much out there to discover. And God forgive me, I have a small score to settle with the English before I rest.*

On his way home from the library, the butchers' stalls on Rue de la Coup were closed, but on the same street the pubs were all alight with adult activity, so Benoit stopped at the Siren's Call and went inside. He loved to hear the sailors talk and tell stories. As he entered, two of the painted women smiled at him, and he smiled back. *I wonder why so many men like to bed this kind of woman*, he thought. *Mother says many of them have the pox, and that, she says, means for a man rotting testicles.* He crossed himself. *God protect me from temptation and all forms of hell.*

Benoit purchased a small beer and sat at a table next to the gray-haired chanteyman, Barbarin, an old one-legged sailor who knew what seemed like an endless number of songs and song-fragments, thanks to his many years as a topman and gunner in the French navy. At the end of his ballad, the gray-bearded sailor greeted Benoit with a smile and a nod. Sunlight had creased his dark face like dried fruit. Benoit smiled and nodded back shyly. This little greeting from an old man made him feel important.

That night the old graybeard was reliving his own sea battles and losses and releasing some of his pain in song. He stared into his beer, and began to softly sing.

"The decks were sprinkled with blood.
The big guns so loudly did roar.
Then I did wish myself at home,
Along with my Annie on the shore."

Only a few of the women or sailors listened or paid any heed to the soused old man and his melancholy ballads, but he kept singing, verse after verse, song after song, many warning the young to avoid the courts of law in France, the press gangs of England, and the navy of either.

I hope Barbarin will cheer up, thought Benoit, *though I doubt there is anything I could say to help him. I think the singing is what helps. Like the poem we translated in Greek class, "Yet Apollo understands grief. Bring it to him in a song, and he will take it away."*

When the old man finished another ballad of the hardships of naval life, Benoit piped up, "That was beautiful." He asked, "If the navy paid better wages to sailors, it wouldn't need convict labor, would it?"

"But where will the revenue come from," said the old man, "if the rich and the aristocrats remain free of all taxes? Now that would be hard to change, lad."

Benoit had no idea, but he liked being talked to like an adult. Besides, the old man was probably wrong. *How could it be true that the rich don't pay taxes? Even his mother had to pay a window tax, ten sous per window every year. Luckily, their dark little apartment only had two, but still—three weeks of wages!*

Later in the evening, when Barbarin was singing with more energy, the leader of a group of young rowdies called out, "Old man, button up, because we don't like your noise." Barbarin looked at them, squinting his eyes in disgust, took a swig of his beer, and continued defiantly to sing, though in a softer voice.

The leader of the group made a face and a sign and the tattooed thugs rose up and encircled the old sailor. The leader upended Barbarin and his chair from behind, while the others laughed and egged him and each other on. They picked up the chanteyman and carried him outside, and threw him into a horse trough full of water while the toss-pots of the tavern guffawed or pretended not to notice. Some of the rowdies dunked the old man and held his head under the water. Benoit couldn't stand to watch any more. He checked for his father's knife, hidden under his shirt, then approached and asked them, "Please stop, he meant no harm." The toughs laughed all the more.

"Do you want to go for a swim too, boy?" said the leader.

"How do you know it's a boy?" said another.

"Well, cutie, do you know how to swim?" asked the leader.

Benoit looked around for allies, but no one from the crowd inside stepped out. Short of breath, Benoit suddenly had a vision of sorts. The painted ladies and cleaned-up sailors who chatted and laughed as they ignored the old man's plight were the gossips of old practicing their wickedness just before Noah's flood. He. imagined them all drowning.

Benoit wondered how many rowdies he could kill before they got him. He realized instantly that any force might bring on reprisals, which as the eldest child of a household he could hardly afford. Someday, if not today, by the grace of God, these fellows will get properly punished for their cowardice and meanness. But what could he do now? Master Quellenac always said, "Feign weakness to outwit a more powerful opponent."

He walked over to the leader, who'd just dunked Barbarin again, and falling to his knees and making himself defenseless, he said in a stentorian voice, "Please sir, let go of my father. He served his country well, and he's had the scurvy and the gout, and he is all I have in the world." The rowdies stopped their joking. The boy's words embarrassed a few of them.

"Run away, runt," the leader said with a scowl, "and let us have a bit of fun." He let Barbarin's head come up again for some air, and the old man exhaled and breathed in with horrible force. The thug said, "This will teach you to keep quiet," and dunked the old man again.

Don't force me to use my knife, you bastard, Benoit thought. "Oh, but please, sir, my father and I, we live alone and I take care of him. Sometimes he is in terrible pain from wounds he received fighting for his country in the wars. I'm sorry if he bothered you. I'll tell him he has to stop that. I'll tell him he can't go bothering people."

The leader could feel the support of his friends slip away. Men, now watching from the open pub doorway, were moving closer to catch the scene. The bartender, hearing the noise, had also come out to listen. He was always concerned for the reputation of his establishment, and now he was impressed by the boy's courage. He recognized Barbarin as one of his regulars.

"Let the boy's father up," the bartender ordered with authority, pushing the rogue away. Barbarin's gasping head surged up out of the water. Benoit helped his friend out of the trough, while the bartender continued, "You've had your fun, now it's time to quit." Several patrons of the pub stepped up behind the owner, baring their tattooed biceps. After a tense pause the chief rogue turned and strode away, and his buddies trailed after. Benoit exhaled with relief. The chanteyman was sitting on the side of the trough, gasping for air and dripping water. Though rumpled, battered, and soaked to the bone, old Barbarin, true to his seamanship, said, "Thank'ee, lad. Now let me buy you a drink."

"You're all wet, sir!" said Benoit, "Why don't you go home and change your clothes?"

"Nonsense." The old salt laughed. "What's a little water to an old tar? Besides, the night is warm, and I feel powerfully clear and refreshed, and baptized, but thirsty."

"As you like, if you're sure," said Benoit. "Are you all right?"

"Fine as on payday in a whorehouse," said Barbarin grinning. "Just a little damp. I guess you can just call me Pappy now." The old salt grinned and winked, and they both laughed. Waiting for their beers, Barbarin said conversationally, "Who is your real pap anyway, if you don't mind me asking?"

"Etienne-François Grannier, only he's dead, sir. He died two years ago in a fight at sea against the English off Gabon in Africa."

Now Benoit looked down at his feet, suddenly quiet. The old man understood he had touched on a sore subject, invoking pride and grief, so he changed the topic as two large beers arrived. "Those are on the house," said the bartender gruffly, by way of apology.

Old Barbarin looked doubtfully at the bartender, and barely accepted the apology, but smiled at Benoit and said, "I knew a sailor, lad, a Chinaman, who could lie almost as good as you do," and he clinked mugs and took a long drink. "He could get out of the worst trouble by lying, and when that didn't work he could spin around like a top and kick an opponent in the head with his foot. Now there's a trick you'll never see if you remain a wharf-rat in these parts, eh, lad?"

"Tell me more about China," Benoit said. "Do they really box with their feet?" The graybeard tried not to look too pleased, as he started to wonder which of his

China stories he should recount—or whether it was an occasion to make up a new one.

"Aye, there the men really box with their feet, but not the women, for they've had their toes cut off so they can't fight or run away from the men. Let me tell you about the time we were attacked by pirates just outside of Macao. I was a second mate in *L'Intrepide* at that point, and the day started out ordinary and all. …"

Benoit listened in wide-eyed amazement. He noted with pleasure that old Barbarin, committed to the tale, appeared to have forgotten his own sorrows and was absorbed in his story. Benoit listened in amazement, they drank their beers, and said warm goodnights. Walking home, Benoit wondered if he himself would be strong and lucky enough to thrive in the navy, living and fighting with men at sea. Something gnawed at him though. He missed his father, yet he only remembered a few scenes with the man. He remembered play wrestling—his dad was gentle but had scratchy whiskers—swimming in the ocean, ball-toss and a splicing lesson, but there weren't that many days together to remember.

Chapter 7
Merlier's Cliffs
1770

Benoit Grannier walked through the park with his friend Brigitte. The daughter of a successful shopkeeper, she was two years older than Benoit, reminiscent of Helen of Troy, and enjoyed the admiration of boys and men.

"Will you meet me tonight after dinner?" Benoit asked.

"No Benoit, I won't. Don't you understand, I'm older than you, and I am not one of those low-class girls."

Benoit looked at this buxom beauty and bit his lip. *How does a boy become a man if the girls are like her?* he thought. Benoit walked Brigitte to her parents' house and she disappeared within. Since it was a Saturday afternoon, he could spend the evening striding around the town with his companions or stay home and get ahead on schoolwork—a familiar choice.

After Benoit climbed the stairs to the family's apartment, his mother, Celeste, asked him to help her shift furniture so she could do the housecleaning. Benoit consented, but hurried to get the chore over with. As he approached the big bureau, he overlooked the small Venetian vase on it that usually stood proudly on the mantelpiece. The vase was of green handblown glass and it was encased in a spidery filament net of real gold. As Benoit pulled the bureau away from the wall, a leg caught a nail and it jolted. The impact sent the Venetian vase careening to the floor. Benoit shot his hand out for it but missed. The treasured family heirloom, his mother's favorite antique, shattered on the floor into a thousand shards. Benoit's mother looked aghast at her smashed Venetian vase. She looked at her son and cried, "How could you be so careless?" She stormed into her bedroom and slammed the door.

Benoit could hear her sobbing. *Shit, how could I be so dumb?* he thought. He swept up the broken glass, filled with self-loathing. He calculated quickly. It would take several years of working at the marine chandlery to buy such a vase from a shop. He had been saving his money for Naval Academy uniforms. *What a useless oaf I am.* He cringed in pain at the idea of causing his mother so much grief. Benoit swept up the mess and put the glass into the garbage, then swept up the rest of the room and left the house for a walk.

His feet took him to the town square, where a large crowd had gathered with picnics to watch the public hangings. He watched a thief standing on the gallows. *I wonder,* he thought, *if I couldn't sell myself to some rich thief or slave-trader and raise the gold I need for my mother in exchange for a quick ending to my miserable life.* Then his thoughts turned to his distraught mother. He hadn't meant to hurt her.

I'm no use, just careless and clumsy, he thought dismally, wishing he could simply cry. He watched with a certain grim envy as the poor thief on the scaffold fell through the trap door and dangled from the rope with a broken neck. *Now, there's one fellow who doesn't have to live with the shame of his mistakes,* he brooded.

Instead of going home for dinner, Benoit met Antoine and some friends. They wandered down to the shipyards where Benoit dared them to scale high walls. They practiced fencing with dowels and sticks while jumping about on logs and piles of lumber. Benoit fenced fearlessly, but accidently bruised several of his friends.

When he came in late that night, his mother was still up, sewing by the oil lamp.

Benoit," she said, "I'm sorry I got so upset. I realize it was an accident, and also, it was really my own fault."

"Mama, I'm so sorry I broke the vase. Please forgive me."

"Of course I do," she said, and she took him in her arms and hugged him. "But I want you to forgive yourself, too."

≈   ≈

After Mass with the whole family on Sunday, Benoit went to Marcel's Ship Chandlery and Dockyard, where he often worked for two hours after school. Though it was Sunday, he cleaned and stocked shelves until dinnertime. After dinner he couldn't concentrate on his schoolwork, so he went outside and practiced fencing drills.

On Monday he failed a history test for which he hadn't done the reading. The academic slump had not stopped by Friday, when Antoine invited him to go rock climbing on Saturday.

"No thanks," Benoit said. "I probably have to earn six *livres* to buy my mother another Venetian vase. Ask me again in a few years. I'm going to work at the chandlery all day on Saturdays."

"For Christ's sake," Antoine admonished, "breaking that vase wasn't the end of the world. Did you apologize to your mother"

"Let's not talk about it," said Benoit.

"Did you?"

"It's none of your business—yes I did."

"Then why don't you let yourself go on living?"

Benoit looked at his friend as if he were crazy. With that, Antoine walked off toward the library. Saturday morning Antoine came by early, but Benoit refused to go climbing. He went to the chandlery and stocked shelves instead. Sunday after Mass, Antoine tried again.

"Benoit, why go on punishing yourself?" demanded Antoine.

"Why shouldn't I make the replacement of the vase my priority? Mother loved it."

"Mister Viking bonehead, what is in the end more important to you, things or people?"

"People," Benoit admitted almost reluctantly, looking like a trapped cat.

"Then the best way to help your mother remains for you to take care of yourself, and not take each little mistake as a sign of total failure. Don't overreact to the less important things."

Benoit weighed these words of wisdom, and gazed at the huge white clouds in the clear blue sky. "You have a point. I'll go climbing."

        ❧   ❦

It was one of those perfect sunny days, a shocking blue sky dotted with anvil-shaped clouds floating in a cool October breeze—great balls of cotton pushed together by the wind or the invisible hand of God.

They packed fresh bread, Brie cheese, and scallions, and walked out the town road and across fields of fresh-cut wheat and barley, till they entered a heavily thinned forest of oak, beech, and birch. They followed the paths till they came to Merlier's Cliffs.

Both boys scampered up the goat path around the left to the top of the wall. They stood in silence, mesmerized by the beauty of the harbor, with farms and pastureland before the glistening ocean. Antoine brought out of his knapsack an iron ring attached to a long cord, which he tied around a tree so that the ring just dangled over the top of the wall. Benoit ran the rope till it was halfway through the ring; then he tossed both halves of the rope over the cliff so that the ends hung down equally from the ring.

They both descended the goat trail to the bottom of the face of the cliff. They had chosen to climb, with the protection of the rope, a piece of the wall known as Cluny's Crack—fifty feet of vertical rock. Benoit, as the belayer, tied himself to a tree stump so he couldn't be pulled off the ground by a fall as he held his end of the rope. Antoine, as the climber, tied the other end of the rope around his waist. The rope went from Antoine up the cliff face, through the ring, and back down to Benoit, who wrapped it around his back under his armpits.

Antoine began to climb and Benoit pulled in the slack to keep the rope as tight as possible. If Antoine fell, Benoit would twist his end of the rope around his body, the loose end across his chest, and Antoine would only fall as far as the existing slack and stretch in the rope.

After they had both climbed the Crack with the protection of the rope and the other as belayer, they climbed Hurdy Gurdy and then attempted Fauscheau's Folly. Antoine climbed first. He got most of the way up but then got stuck on the last long eight feet. The climb became a smooth-sided wall and the rock split into two columns, forming an open space called a chimney. The chimney crack was only about six inches wide. It was too wide for a foothold but too narrow to climb into and shinny up inside. This crack required a layback. He had to stick his hands in the crack, lean back against his hands, lift his feet up off their perch onto the flat opposing wall of rock, and then, feet pushing and hands holding on for dear life, he had to walk, hand over hand, up the crack, leaning hard away from the rock with just the friction of the flat bottoms of his boots supporting him below. He tried to keep his boots as close to his hands as possible to avoid falling.

After about nine feet, with his muscles bulging and his body shaking, his hand slipped and he fell, and yelled, "Falling!"

Benoit pulled the belay rope against his chest, and he stopped the fall after about six feet, the amount of stretch in the rope. Antoine bounced lightly against the wall, groping with arms and feet to find new holds. "Good catch," he said, hiding his disappointment. "Good reaction!"

"You almost made it," Benoit encouraged, his attention now absorbed by the challenge of the new route. After another attempt, and another fall, Antoine let Benoit lower him down.

They changed places. Benoit slowly worked his way up the vertical face with Antoine as the belayer anchored to the tree. *Save your strength,* he thought. *Lean out, use nothing but legs, use balance not strength.* He slowly but surely contorted his way up the vertical wall as he leaned away from the cracks and the fingerholds, which he quickly transferred to toeholds. *The rope is snug and strong. Antoine will catch me if he has to. Just keep moving.*

At the beginning of the layback, Benoit took a short rest and carefully looked over the place where Antoine had twice fallen. *The handhold is less secure there where the rock bulges,* he observed. *Maybe one could reach all the way above it to the better edge.*

Benoit was momentarily gripped by fear. *How did I ever get into this predicament? Keep the feet right under the hands.* "Here I go," he called to alert Antoine forty feet below, for Antoine held Benoit's life in his hands. Benoit drew a deep breath, exhaled hard, reached up, lifted his leg, placed his foot as close to his hand as possible, stepped onto the foot, and leaned away against his hands till he was airborne. His arms and legs were all perpendicular to the opposite wall and he was committed to the layback.

His body weight pressed his boots toward the rock while trying to pry his fingers loose. *Keep moving,* he thought, and he continued to climb-walk, foot, hand, foot, hand, leaning out away from the crack. He looked like a human spider going sideways up the vertical wall. His whole body straining at the hard part, the crux of the climb, he tried to keep going. He reached his hand way up. His hand started to slip, so he pulled with both arms and slipped the higher hand even higher, then he moved his feet and shot his other hand up above the first. It held. Then a foot, a hand, a foot, he inched his way up the last two feet and found a solid and reliable hold above from which to haul his whole body up and over the top, gasping with effort.

"Bravo," yelled Antoine, "that was terrific."

"Thank you," said Benoit. He sat down to catch his breath. His arms and chest stung with pain. His fingers were numb and motionless. He couldn't have tied his shoes at that moment to save his life. Benoit looked out and saw the whole valley of Lorient, the town, the port, and the tall ships, and clouds scudding across the blue sky, over the crystal green-blue sea. The sunlight sparkling on the myriad swells of the ocean held him in awe. His mind roamed free. He forgot himself in the beauty before him. Yet the colors reminded him of the Venetian vase, which dragged him away from the glory of his victory and back to his mistake and his mother's disappointment.

"I'm sorry I broke your vase, Mother," he said softly, "but someday, perhaps, I will be able to buy you another."

They couldn't leave until Antoine tried one more time. Copying Benoit's technique, he managed on the next try to move his body through the entire layback and over the top. As they swaggered triumphantly home, they remained silent through the woods. Benoit broke the silence. "I've been thinking of Father Sebastian and the physics class. The world doesn't appear round."

Antoine laughed and said, "Did Tycho Brahe really die from overeating?"

"No, not that. Father Sebastian never actually said that if some of the teachings of the Bible are fallible, than other parts of it might be flawed. Faith is so much more complicated if it is at the dictates of the Pope. Is challenging his authority really heretical? God forgive me if I am sinning for such thoughts."

Antoine took time to answer. "It is human to question authority. Even the Pope is a sinner. Under the robes and miter, he's just a man."

After climbing a fence and gaining the empty dirt road, Antoine went on, "It's a good thing the priesthood accepts sinners!" He paused. "Benoit, I want you to be the first to know, I have decided to take the vows and enter the priesthood."

"Congratulations, I guess. Sounds like a lot of religion. Is that what you really want?"

"I feel called to both scholarship and good works. Yes, I think it is my best option."

"God I hope so! And my sincere congratulations, it is a big decision."

After a short silence, Antoine asked, "Benoit, what are you going to do after graduation?"

"Mama is against it, but I'm going to try for an appointment to the Naval Academy as a midshipman."

"I'm sorry to hear that," said Antoine. "There are so many long wars, for such little reasons. You will spend your life fighting our neighbors, the English."

"Would you like an English Protestant as your king?"

"You have a point there."

"Do you think I must go to hell, if I become a soldier?" Benoit asked with the impish, irreverent look in his eye that often appeared when he discussed heresies.

"Not necessarily. At least, not according to the gospel of Father Sebastian," and they both laughed. "And it might all hinge on how much you can contribute to the coffer of my little parish." They laughed again. "You wait, dear Benoit. If I am frocked and have anything to do with it, no matter how many Englishmen you send to the bottom, I'll get you confessed and absolved in time so that even if you're as fat as a friar, I'll get you squeezed through the eye of a needle if need be to pass by Saint Peter."

"Very kind of you to say so," said Benoit, and smiled. "If you keep your sense of humor and a thimble full of humility, you will make a good priest."

"As long as you don't turn pirate or slaver, you should have a chance at Heaven through the navy."

"I hope that in the navy I help keep the English from overpowering France, fight a few Englishmen for Papa, and advance in good health to a decent pay grade."

"It may get rough," said Antoine cheerfully in a pompous old priest's voice. "With goals like that, you're going to need friends in the church—and you had better be a contributor of record approaching the tithe."

This caused Benoit to howl with laughter. "You're sounding more and more like a real churchman!"

When they reached the town, Benoit thanked his cousin for the climb with a handshake and a significant look, and took his leave, the big rope hanging from his shoulder diagonally across his body. His animal spirits had returned and he had a great deal of schoolwork to catch up on.

Chapter 8

Benoit and Sebastian

It was after class, and all the other students had rushed out as soon as they were dismissed. Benoit had stayed behind, his curiosity holding him back while the others began their recess. He asked, "Father Sebastian, what were you referring to when you said that the Church has skeletons in its closet?"

Father Sebastian's bulbous eyes peered cautiously at Benoit through thick glass lenses. "Did I say that? You must be mistaken."

"Just a few days ago," said Benoit, "you were describing the Inquisition, and you said at one point that certain leaders of the Catholic Church were perhaps over-zealous in their attempts at destroying all traces of the devil. Today you mentioned skeletons. Are the zealots connected to them?"

The old man frowned as he contemplated Benoit for a minute, then carefully walked to the door, looked about the hallway and shut it, so that neither the abbot, nor anyone else for that matter, would overhear their discussion. "I have to be much more careful about what I say," said the bearded baldpate, clearly disturbed. "I fear that I'm starting to ramble off the approved topics." Father Sebastian wrung his hands and clenched his jaw in thought, all the while staring at Benoit's open, inquisitive face.

"So, Benoit, can you keep a confidence? I mean a real confidence from every-one—absolutely everyone you ever communicate with?"

Benoit paused and thought a moment. It was hard not to share big concerns with either his cousin, his mother, or his confessor, but he had and could. "Yes, I can," he said.

"You swear a holy oath you will keep our conversation in strict confidence?"

Now Benoit was a little disturbed, but his curiosity remained great. "I swear a holy oath to secrecy," he said.

"Good," said Father Sebastian. He sat down, and pointed to the chair next to his desk. After Benoit took the seat, Sebastian lowered his voice. "I would like to tell the class that there was a dark side to the Inquisition, and that it isn't over yet. But the Pope has ruled that this subject is not a fitting one for public discussion. By his decree I am not allowed to speak of it." The priest paused, hoping he was done.

Young Benoit remained silent; he was not yet satisfied. Sebastian continued, "You see, Benoit, the story of the Inquisition has become political. You will hear different versions of the same events by different factions. I agree with the elements inside the Church who say that it went too far, much too far, that it became and continues to be a terrible blight on the record of the Church."

"But the Inquisition saved the Catholic Church from an outpouring of heretic doctrines: the Cathari, the Albigenses, and the Waldenses," said Benoit.

"Do you remember what the Cathari believed in?"

"They believed that the earth was ruled by Satan, and that many earthly things were evil. They condemned second marriages, and fornication, especially outside of the first marriage, and declared that Jesus was not the Lord reincarnate, but merely an angel or prophet whom the Lord sent down to earth to indicate the way to salvation. They also insisted that the human sufferings and death of the angel Jesus were mere illusions."

"All true," said the priest. "But the reason their bishops were so popular was that they were so upright, always looking after the poor and elderly, and there is some evidence in the Bible to support their interpretations of scripture. They condemned murder, war, and capital punishment. They criticized Catholic bishops for committing these crimes, and for using murder, war, and capital punishment to accumulate wealth and power—to steal."

Father Sebastian paused, still wondering about the wisdom of speaking his mind. "I think the Cathari were wrong and misguided on some issues, but they were peaceful, law abiding, and disciplined—in important ways, exemplary Christians. It still leaves the question of means unanswered. If you have a disagreement with your neighbor, does killing him prove that you are right and he is wrong?"

"That is a controversial question," said Benoit, unconsciously looking about to check that they were alone. "There used to be the Ordeal by Combat. The modern philosophes, such as Voltaire, say that all it proves is that one person is a better fighter than the other; it doesn't prove which contestant is right in any particular argument."

"That's right. My God, boy, what some people did in the name of God confounds the heavens!" Suddenly Sebastian looked unfocused, his face full of emotion. "The Inquisition started as a straightforward tribunal to enforce uniformity of belief within the Church, but somehow its mission changed to enforcing uniformity of belief within entire societies and to silencing any criticism of the Church. The so-called conservatives behind the uglier practices were really radicals. They reinterpreted the Bible as ordering all people to accept Christ as the Lord, or suffer terrible consequences. The Christians, who had once been persecuted, became the persecutors.

"In the 1400s, Konrad Von Marburg in Germany and Tomas de Torquemada in Spain each ordered tens of thousands of accused heretics to face either confiscation, or torture, or burning at the stake, and sometimes all three. There was no place in Europe where you could be safe from the greed and the evil of men who had insinuated themselves inside the Church when its power was at its pinnacle."

"Pope Paul IV mindlessly sent more thousands to the torturer and executioner. In the name of the Lord Jesus, he created a reign of terror in Rome, where no one was safe. In haste and credulity, he believed every accuser who denounced someone as a Protestant or a secret Jew. Each man or woman accused was tortured, sometimes to death. Of course, if tortured long enough, each one would finally name others just to stop the pain."

"At least that was over 300 years ago," said Benoit. "The Church has discontinued such practices, hasn't it?"

"Hmm … just a few years ago," said Sebastian, "a skilled woman in Lorient named Brigitte de Lac was found guilty of witchcraft and burned at the stake."

"She practiced no witchcraft?"

"Benoit, when a woman practices science or medicine, it's called witchcraft! She was a gifted herbalist and healer, and she had aroused jealousy with her extraordinary skill. What do you think of that?"

Benoit shuddered and said, "I have heard my mother complain about this. God forgive them for their brutality. I am ashamed to hear such stories, and wish such practices were abandoned."

"Amen," replied the father. "So do I, so do I. So beware of certainty my son. Thank God most churchmen are not like that," Sebastian went on, "and that is not, of course, how Christ instructed his followers to deal with their enemies, or the multitude of doubters." Sebastian displayed his tobacco-stained teeth in a smile. "Of course, the widespread confiscation of property meant that many Inquisitors became extremely wealthy. The doctrine of ruthless conformity was disgracefully profitable."

"How," asked Benoit, "can you separate greed from politics in the Church?"

"That is a problem," sighed the cleric. "No one has been able to do that. If you go back to the demands of Luther and the writing of Calvin, you will understand that they challenged the abuse of power and what they perceived as the corruption of Rome. But neither man advocated a system that had perfect checks and balances. Luther wanted all Church powers to be controlled by kings, and Calvin wanted all kings to be controlled by bodies of elected priests and wealthy elders, which he called presbyteries. Both men came up with an alternative to papal supremacy, but neither man came up with an obviously better solution. The Church needs a strong organizational structure in order to grow and prosper, but it shouldn't be at the whim of either tyrants or presbyteries drawn from the wealthy bourgeoisie. I never thought the wealthy could be trusted.

"There is an arrogance about Church dogma that disturbs me greatly," continued Sebastian, "but it is still perhaps the most sensible vehicle for the Word, and the Pope is our only direct connection with the blessed Saint Peter. It is my solemn hope that someday soon the Church will stop condemning what it can't or shouldn't control.

"Beware, Benoit, the Church is powerful, and it is led by men, some of who commit crimes and don't like to be criticized. Do you understand this?"

"Yes, Father."

"Good, now let's get about the business of the day. And remember, not a word of this conversation to anyone, especially your confessors."

"Yes, Father. I understand, and I appreciate your candor and taking me into your confidence."

Chapter 9
Pierre Pigneau
1770

Father Pierre Pigneau de Béhaine, Bishop of Adran and Vicar Apostolic of Cochinchina, arrived in Đại Việt in 1767 at the age of twenty-seven. He had been appointed by the Jesuit Society of Foreign Missions in Paris to take charge of the Cochinchina Seminary, which had been established by the esteemed Alexandre de Rhodes in Hà Tiên Province near the village of Tra Tien, not far from the Cambodian border. Why so many titles for such a young man? His title was somewhat inflated, since Vicar Apostolic means vicar of future growth—hopefully, a dioceses would be created through evangelism. (Apostolic refers to an apostle, meaning anyone sent on a mission to teach Christianity.)

Pierre was one of the older children in a family of nineteen brothers and sisters. Perhaps because he grew up in a large family, he had superior social skills. This was a man who knew how to get along with his superiors and subordinates.

His mother and several members of his family died of cholera, which he never discussed. He was known by friends and associates to be thoughtful, and a good listener, but a strict Jesuit.

His intelligence made up for his looks, as he was not much of a portrait. He had a square, owlish head, with round gimlet eyes, a straight, long, pointy nose and a small, narrow mouth. The little mouth sat in the middle of a sea of cheek, for the man surely ate plenty of animal fat, loved desserts, wine, and whiskey, and stored it all in his face and torso, connected by a short, almost nonexistent neck. He was such a strict disciplinarian regarding his religious and academic obligations that it seemed as if he permitted only gastronomic indulgences.

Though Pierre was not handsome, he was still attractive, due to his gregarious smile, his generous character, and his irrepressible optimism. In the sexual realm, he had little interest in women or they in him, and the ministry suited him in more ways than one. He appeared quite comfortable with celibacy.

Father Pierre had only been in Đại Việt for three years, but in that time, besides turning thirty, he'd learned to speak the language with some fluency. He'd also learned to read and write in *Quốc ngữ*, the Western system of writing the Vietnamese language using Roman letters and nine diacritical marks. *Quốc ngữ* was invented by Portuguese Jesuit missionaries like Francisco de Pina, Gaspar d'Amaral, and others, and improved upon by the famous French missionary Alexandre de Rhodes, who published in Rome the first Vietnamese Catechist and the first Vietnamese-Latin-Portuguese dictionary in 1651. Until Rhodes popularized *Quốc ngữ*, written phonetically in the twenty-six letter Roman alphabet, the Việt had always written in Chinese characters. Vietnamese had been primarily a spoken language. Việt scholars had developed *chữ Nôm*, which used Chinese and invented characters, called pictographs, to represent Vietnamese.

The Senior Vietnamese acolyte Paul Nghi came to the edge of the lesson shed. He had a plain, thin face, long black hair, and a thin mustache. He smiled and waved at Father Alain Artaud, the gracious elderly priest who had been Pierre's teacher and now, having passed the age when most missionaries retire, worked as his assistant and counselor. Paul Nghi waited politely while the gesticulating Father Pierre finished his speech concerning the conjugation of a Latin verb. Father Pierre wore a light gray hemp robe and displayed a large wooden crucifix around his neck. Sixteen Vietnamese of various ages listened attentively to their teacher from over the Western Ocean. "Now please conjugate the verb to love," Pierre said in Vietnamese. The class chanted in the foreign tongue, "*Amo, amas, amat, amamus, amatis, amant.*" The Việts knew this concept well, in the word *yêu.*

The idea of love was hardly new in the Sinic world. The precision of Latin grammar, however, was certainly alien. The Việts, like the Chinese, had a language ideally suited for poetry, free of verb tenses, conjugations, or noun declensions. When a Việt says, "I went to school yesterday," from the precise Latin perspective, he is really saying, "I go to school yesterday." Only the adverb "yesterday" determines tense.

The big French priest smiled. The hard, aspirant sounds of Latin were very difficult to the soft-spoken Việts. For Pierre, learning the soft, frog-like but sing-song, and bird-like sounds of the Việt language was not easy either.

Pierre started around the group, testing their vocabulary. He usually asked the slowest students the easiest questions, and prompted them when they hesitated. The students appeared eager to please and unafraid.

"Father Pierre," Paul Nghi interrupted, "there are Nguyễn soldiers approaching the mission." Pierre nodded dully, and looked at Father Alain Artaud for advice. They shrugged at each other. Artaud put down his quill, covered his inkwell, and stood slowly to meet with Pierre the armed Nguyễn soldiers, who strode fearlessly in their blue shirts into the compound without ceremony or protocol. The students of the seminary all came out of their classrooms and work rooms, and from their rice paddies and gardens, to see what the trouble was.

The captain of the soldiers did not bow. He demanded, "Are you the barbarian priests who worship impaling your king on a cross?"

Pierre answered, "We worship Jesus Christ, the son of God, who was crucified, rose again, and ascended into Heaven. We are perhaps whom you seek." He added, "Can we help you?"

"In the name of Nguyễn Dũng, magistrate of this district, you are both under arrest. Seize them."

A young acolyte wielding a hoe moved in front of his two teachers and protested the arrest. A soldier walked over, grabbed the hoe in one hand, and stabbed him through the heart with his short sword. Other soldiers seized the two dumbfounded priests, dragged them away from the students, and roughly tied their hands behind their backs. The two priests were marched into the village and placed in a prisoner's cart for transport to the provincial capital of Hà Tiên.

ॐ   ॐ

Two days later they arrived in the afternoon, and on the third day, they were taken before the magistrate, Nguyễn Dũng, a stern man with long side-whiskers and a black judge's cap. "Will anyone testify against the accused?" said Nguyễn Dũng, smiling coldly in his blue brocade robes and black gold cap. His jeweled nail cases, extending his fingers several inches, and his side-whiskers, showed him to be a learned man of wealth.

A hard-looking fellow stepped forward and declared, "I will testify against these barbarian spies." He gave his name and address, and said, "These foreigners have long been in communication with the King of Siam. They were selling military information to him for silver. These barbarian spies asked me to deliver letters, silver, and gold from them to emissaries of the King of Siam."

"What do you have to say for yourself?" asked Magistrate Nguyễn Dũng, fingering a side whisker.

"Your honor, thank you for letting this humble one speak," said Pierre carefully in Vietnamese. "We completely deny these charges as false and without reason. I would like to point out that there has been no proof given by the accuser to support them."

"You want us to have proof?" said Magistrate Dũng, dropping the side whisker. "You think I need proof about Christians? The torturer will tell me if you have sold secrets or not, then you'll have your proof. Take them to the jail. Give them each thirty lashes, and put them each in the cangue until they confess the truth."

The guards hustled the two Frenchmen away to the jail, down in the dungeon of the Hà Tiên citadel. The guards placed heavy wooden cangues over their heads and bound their hands roughly at each end of the rectangular structures. Pierre could walk, but his arms were tied in the outstretched position, so he looked like he was being crucified. These cangues weighed over forty pounds, so movement was difficult. Old Father Alain Artaud could barely move at all, and seemed disoriented.

Paul Nghi carefully followed the soldiers and the jailers into the dungeon. He went up to the head jailor. "Dear honorable sir," he said, "I salute you."

"Same to you," said the fat jailor, picking his teeth, "what's on your mind, skinny one?"

"There has been a terrible mix-up. My kind masters, these two barbarian priests, have been arrested instead of some other odious foreigners. I know you must torture them, but alas, I know they have no secrets to tell. I hope you will, out of kindness, not be too harsh on such learned and elderly men who have been so cruelly wronged, and make sure they are fed."

The jailor started to laugh, but Paul Nghi then reached into his sleeve and produced a small parcel, which he unwrapped. In it were two taels of silver, two one-and-one-third-ounce bars of the precious metal.

"I can probably go quite easy on them, and make sure they get fed so well that they gain weight." the jailor said, eyeing the little silver bars and looking around to be sure he wasn't overheard by anyone he would have to share them with.

"Good," said Paul, and held out the silver. The jailor's hand shot out like a snake and the silver disappeared into one of his large waist pouches. The jailer caned the bottom of their feet—not thirty lashes as prescribed, but only fifteen rather lightly, in honor of their devoted attendant with the silver bars.

The two men were left in their cangues as ordered by the court, and placed in a long stone cell full of other criminals. The stench of unwashed men, and the latrine, which consisted of a couple of buckets, was almost overwhelming. The prisoners were given food two times a day and were told to feed the cangue-bound priests, but when men volunteered to feed them, their food was stolen by a big, half-naked fellow with a face full of scars. The two priests began to starve in a forced fast.

At first, Pierre managed to keep positive about the whole experience. *Thank you Lord*, he prayed silently to himself, *for sending such a noble affliction as this cangue in this underworld, for I feel closer to you and the infinitely more painful suffering that you underwent on the cross of Pontius Pilate. However, I still have work to do here on earth in your name.*

The scar-faced giant took their food at dinnertime, and after dinner, he grabbed Pierre, turned him over roughly, so that the forty-pound cangue held him pinned to the ground, pulled down his pants, and sodomized him from behind, with the other prisoners looking on.

Pierre was blinded by pain, but even worse, he was mortally embarrassed. *Even Jesus*, he thought bitterly, *who was crucified, didn't have to suffer this indignity.* And he thought over and over, *At least the pederast will suffer in eternal hellfire for this.*

When scar-face was finished, another prisoner came forward to have a turn on the upturned rump, but a slight fellow with a big smile came forward and stopped him. The little fellow was very polite but firm, and the second man sat down in disappointment. The slight man helped Pierre by pulling up his pants, turning him over, and sitting him down again with his back to Father Artaud. He then deliberately untied their hands, so their outstretched arms could fall to their sides.

The next day, the short fellow with the big smile collected Pierre and Father Artaud's empty bowls, and after they were filled by a guard with the rice gruel, he placed them, along with his own bowl, next to the two poor priests, still collared up in their heavy cangues. They sat against each other in the middle of the floor, since other prisoners had taken all the choice spots against the stone walls.

The welcome stranger began to spoon feed Pierre. The big scar-face was now expecting the extra rations, so he came right over and grabbed the fellow's wrist in a vise-like grip, and carefully took the bowl of gruel out of the immobilized hand.

"It's all yours," said the little fellow as he surrendered his bowl with a deferential smile. Still smiling, he then placed his hand on top of scar-face's wrist and, with a sudden circular motion ending with a downward thrust, he twisted the other man's wrist against his own elbow in a way it was not designed to be twisted, and brought the oaf down to his knees. The slight man shattered the nose of the big man with his knee, and kicked him in the groin, doubling him up. Now his elbow came down crack on the big man's neck across the spine—and scar-face was dead. All the other prisoners watched in silence. They smiled and laughed and shook their fists in approval. They resumed slurping their soups, while the slight fellow rubbed his elbow and resumed feeding Pierre from one of the two remaining bowls of gruel.

"That was a fine performance," said Father Pierre in Vietnamese. "God forgive me if I do not to pray for the soul of that dead, heathen sodomite."

"Good, nor should you," laughed the man, "nor will I, ha ha ha. Please allow me to introduce myself," said the man. "I am the scholar and soldier Diệu Tri, at your service."

"It is a pleasure to meet you. My name is Father Pierre Pigneau, Bishop of Adran and Vicar Apostolic of Cochinchina," said Pierre, "and I thank you with all my heart for coming to our aid."

"Oh, it was nothing," said Diệu Tri, and then chuckled to himself. "I've said many times that I could easily kill for a little educated company." Then he laughed, cackling hard and loud at his own joke.

"Is Pierre your family name?"

"No, it is my given name. Pigneau is my family name."

"By heaven and earth, you barbarians have your names backwards!" And he roared at his own joke.

Recovering, he picked up the other bowl and fed it all to Father Alain, who said, "Thank you, blessed man, for this food and water—so appreciated. You are a gentleman and a scholar. My thirst was so great, the water tastes like wine to me."

Then Pierre said, "Honorable Uncle, how did it come to pass that a scholar such as yourself be sent to this God-forsaken dungeon?"

"I am so glad you asked," said the cheerful Diệu Tri. "I've been longing to talk to an educated person. Apparently my poems were too widely distributed and then considered to be too satirical for the tastes of the local powers-that-be. The poems became quite popular. For example, I wrote:

Before the world of power I'll fold my arms.
So many griefs I'll gladly spare myself!
Of present rights and wrongs I will not speak.
I've traveled through the realm of men and learned.
How many pitfalls lie along the road!

"I'm afraid the local magistrate took it quite personally. That's it. Not a long story, but an interesting one, isn't it? And these two educated barbarians, ha ha ha, if there is such a thing, what have they done to get into so much trouble?"

"The charge is treasonous communications with the Siamese, but I think the real issue is intolerance of the message of the Lord Jesus Christ."

"I'm not surprised at that," said the diminutive scholar, and chuckled again. "Here, let me help you." The fellow helped Pierre move the heavy cangue to a different spot on his bruised shoulders.

The next morning, when the guards returned with the first feeding of the day, Diệu Tri pointed out innocently that one of the prisoners had died. Without the slightest hesitation, the jailor and his men came in and carried out the body of the scar-faced man. Father Pierre felt much better after a few meals. Father Alain developed a fever. All Diệu Tri could do was to feed him water and watered gruel.

"How do we get out of this jail?" Pierre asked.

"With friends, money, and luck," rejoined the scholar smiling. "In such a case as yours, probably an enormous amount of all three." The door of the dungeon opened and the jailor called out someone's name. A prisoner stood up. He rushed over to Father Pierre, fell to his knees, and knocked his head to the floor. "Oh holy Father, forgive me for my cowardice. Forgive me for not defending you. I am ashamed, for I am a Christian. Now it is my turn to go to the killing field. Please bless me and pray for my soul." The man was shaking with fear and grief.

Father Pierre immediately thought of something revengeful to say to the coward kowtowing at his feet. *First, pull down your pants and offer your behind to all your cellmates as penance. Never mind, just roast in hell with the sodomite for all eternity.* Instead, he swallowed his resentment. He reminded himself, '*Judge not lest ye be judged,*' and made the sign of the cross with his head and intoned a short blessing in Latin. Then he laid his hand on the man's head and said in Vietnamese, "You are blessed, my child, and forgiven for all your sins by God Almighty. Go in peace to meet your maker and enjoy eternal life." The prisoner smiled with joy. He took Pierre's hand and kissed it, fell to his knees, and knocked his head to the ground three times. He stood and walked calmly to the jailor at the door of the cell.

"His execution today, yours or mine perhaps tomorrow," said Diệu Tri. "As far as I can see, that's where everyone in this waiting room ends up sooner or later."

Pierre suddenly understood where everyone went. The crowded cell never got more crowded, because as fast as they brought prisoners in, they took them out. He and Father Alain were in the cell for the condemned. As if in prayer, the entire jail cell was silent for a moment in honor of the brave prisoner leaving to be executed.

"How long have you been here?" Pierre asked Diệu Tri.

"I am not sure. Two years, five months, and sixteen days I think, if I've kept track correctly with my little marks on the wall."

"And why do they keep you alive?"

"Good question. Maybe they didn't put my name on their execution ledger," and he chuckled. "I think Magistrate Nguyễn Dũng is saving me in case he needs bargaining chips with my uncle Diệu Thái at the court in Sài Gòn. Uncle Thái is the Minister of Canals and Waterworks." Now the little fellow lowered his voice and grinned from ear to ear. "I would love to get a message to my good Uncle Diệu Thái and inform him of my condition. He is very well connected."

"Tell me," said Pierre, "I have heard that the King Nguyễn Đình rules only half the country, and that he is in a stalemate with Trịnh Sâm in the north. I've heard many stories of how the country fell into these two warring kingdoms, but the stories usually involve Genies helping the Trịnh or hindering the Nguyễn. How did the country really fracture?"

"Are you looking for military information to help the Siamese King?" the scholar asked with his penetrating eyes and mischievous smile.

"No," said Pierre smiling back, "but were I an agent, I would serve the King of France, who unfortunately, is far from here and not much interested in Đại Việt. As a Christian priest, I serve the greatest king of all, the God in heaven. He knows all. It is my ignorant self who would like to understand this country. Are Cochinchina and Đông Kinh separate countries that hate each other, or are they parts of one nation divided? It is quite confusing to a visitor."

"The answer to your question is simple and, at the same time, perhaps complicated. Đại Việt is one country with three regions: Đàng Ngoài or Đông Kinh in the North, Đàng Trong in the center, and Nam Kỳ in the south. What you have heard about is an old civil war that once ravaged our people. It has been going on for so long, people don't remember any more when it started. This war goes back, let me see, 100, no, no, no, about 150 years. To understand our interminable civil war, you must know what came before."

Diệu Tri looked around to see if any of the other prisoners were listening to his conversation. Instinctively, he dropped his voice. "Long ago, during the Han Dynasty, the Chinese conquered Đại Việt in a terrible war and renamed it An Nam, or Pacified South. But after a thousand years, under the leadership of Ngô Quyền, we drove them out, and we became Đại Việt, or Great Việt. The peasants still refer to their country as Đại Việt, or Nam Việt, while officials use Đại Việt in their official correspondences."

The evening meal was served. Diệu Tri and his recruited helpers got bowls of gruel for Pierre and Father Alain. Diệu Tri offered to feed Pierre.

"Thank you for your help. Why don't you feed Father Alain first, I'm sure he needs it."

"Certainly," said Diệu Tri, and he moved around to the other man for a while.

As he was feeding Father Alain with a soup spoon, he continued with Pierre. "I will tell you how the great civil war between the Nguyễn and the Trịnh families split the country into north and south. For 150 years, these two families have ruled, the Trịnh in the north and the Nguyễn in the south. For 150 years, they have tried to destroy each other and reunite the country.

"Several dynasties after the Great Expulsion of the Chinese by Ngô Quyền, to whom we will always burn incense and paper offerings, the Mongol fighters under Möngke Khan, a grandson of Genghis Khan, swarmed like locusts over China and then also our country. Aii-yah, we fear and despise the blood-drinking Mongols!" Diệu Tri handed the bowl and spoon to one of his recruits, walked to the buckets, spat and urinated into one of them, and returned. "Those northern monkeys pillaged and raped. We tasted again the bitterness of military defeat and occupation. Then Trần Hưng Đạo, another brilliant general, thrice defeated the Mongol blood-drinkers fighting for Kublai Khan, to our everlasting glory. The Trần Dynasty, which the great Trần Hưng Đạo served, lasted 175 years until the Chinese, under the Ming, reconquered our little country about 350 years ago. A brave Việt fighter named Lê Lợi raised an army of peasants and defeated the Ming cockroaches and started his own successful Lê Dynasty."

Pierre, in spite of the cangue on his shoulders, followed the story. He said, "That's amazing, that the Việts defeated the Chinese Mongols so many times. Isn't China fifty or a hundred times bigger than Đại Việt?"

Father Alain Artaud groaned and requested water. Diệu Tri took a bowl and filled it from one of the water buckets by the door, and slowly offered the water first to Father Artaud, and then to Pierre. Pierre drank thirstily. He was excited to talk to a Việt scholar. Up until that time, all the Việt scholars he had met had been cold, aloof, and reluctant to talk to him. Diệu Tri and he recognized in each other a level of education that made them naturally comfortable in each other's company, and they were both highly read, although in radically different histories and literatures. Their separate and shared bad experiences with the local government made them allies.

Diệu Tri helped the men change their sitting position. "Please forgive me," said Father Artaud, "I'm afraid I need to lie down." Now Pierre needed something else to lean against, or he would have to lie down too. Diệu Tri approached several men sitting against the wall and began speaking to them rapidly but politely. The men bowed and stood up, and helped Pierre up. Pierre asked them to help him use the latrine. They helped him over to the buckets, and then to the wall and sat him against it. His cangue was so long that it stuck out three feet on both sides of him, so three men had been displaced. Then with Diệu Tri, they helped old, white-haired Father Artaud over to the latrine buckets.

"Why were they suddenly so helpful?" Pierre asked. "What did you say to them?"

"I politely asked them for assistance, and informed them that I'd break their necks if they didn't," said Tri with a good laugh.

Diệu Tri showed Pierre how he could tilt the heavy cangue so that one end rested on the floor and Tri could support the other with his hands or hip while standing, and thus take the weight off Pierre's aching shoulders and neck. In this bizarre position, infinitely more comfortable than before, Pierre listened while Diệu Tri continued his story as if there had never been an interruption.

"Lê Lợi, may his temples always have incense and gold, defeated not one but two major Ming armies. Lê Lợi was yet another spectacular Việt general. The youngest of three sons, he started with a guerrilla band, which grew to an army of 350,000. His allies included the powerful Trịnh and Nguyễn families. Lê Lợi and his allies attacked the occupation forces of the Ming the day after the Tết New Year Festival started, while the Chinese were feasting. He defeated the Ming army using fake retreats, ambushes, and forged documents for confusion.

"After winning peace at home, Lê Lợi sent lavish gifts to the Emperor of China, attempting to win recognition as an official tributary—ha ha ha—that's a weak neighbor who regularly sends gifts. The Chinese Emperor's overwhelming military and political power could never safely be ignored, so precious tribute to the giant has become our wise and thoughtful tradition.

"Good times followed by bad times is another Việt tradition," and Diệu Tri laughed again at his own wisdom. "After the usual floods and droughts, followed by famine and plague, the peasants' misery became unbearable." Diệu Tri chuckled again. "As you might have noticed, desperate people have less to lose in an armed struggle than comfortable ones. So here, in this beautiful land, a group of peasants again challenged a king and his mandarins, out of a passion for survival and justice, ha ha ha.

"A hundred years after Lê Lợi kicks out the Ming, a lowborn son of an insignificant fisherman named Mạc rose to become Captain of the Imperial Lê Guard. This ambitious bodyguard, Mạc Đăng Dũng, led a coup that toppled the mature Lê Dynasty." Here Diệu Tri laughed again. "Mature as in, rotted through with dissipation and corruption—ha ha ha—very Vietnamese."

"Yes, Mạc Đăng Dũng, I've heard of him," Pierre said, adjusting his legs and moving his hips to straighten his back, "and that the Lê collapsed just before the first Portuguese missionaries arrived in 1527."

Diệu Tri continued, "With the fisherman Mạc in power, a prince of the Nguyễn clan, Nguyễn Kim, set up a government in exile in the mountains near the Laotian border. Poor Kim, hoping, I suppose, to merge with one of the rival feudal families, married one of his daughters to a fellow named Trịnh Gian. Dragon's breath, big mistake! Trịnh Gian poisoned his new father-in-law, Nguyễn Kim, organized some remnants of the Lê army, and defeated the forces of the fisherman Mạc, maybe 200 years ago.

"Trịnh Gian then made a slip of his own. He gave a post to a minor son of the father-in-law that he'd murdered, probably hoping himself to appease his angry wife and her clan. This minor son, Nguyễn Hoàng, carefully plotted his family's revenge. Nguyễn Hoàng, now the governor of a barely settled province near Phú Xuân, the Spring Capital, cut ties with the capital Thăng Long. He and his people were joined by peasants fleeing poverty caused by too many people, overcrowding, and Trịnh tyranny in the north. Nguyễn Hoàng's growing number of soldier-colonists pushed south until they emerged into the Mekong wilderness.

"Nguyễn Hoàng turned his southern outpost into an independent fief, and then fought off repeated attempts by the Trịnh clan in the north to dislodge him while he expanded it. These two feudal families scrambled in the power vacuum. Đại Cồ Việt was cleaved in two, north and south, in a feud over the Mandate of Heaven. The Nguyễn clan from the south and the Trịnh clan from the north, both potential national dynasties and each claiming the Mandate, began what became the interminable civil war."

Pierre interrupted, "What do you mean by the Mandate of Heaven?"

"There are so many Gods," answered Diệu Tri laughing. "Many Việts recognize the Great Spirit, the Ruler of Heaven and Earth, sometimes called the Jade Emperor of Heaven, and the ruler of myriad lesser spirits, and the God who orders the king to rule the country. The Jade Emperor of Heaven is very popular in Chinatown. The mandate is the legitimacy from the Great Spirit. It has very practical consequences. Once a leader has control of the king's throne, the imperial bureaucracy and the imperial seal, as well as the obedience of the army and the support of the peasantry, it becomes apparent to the priests and soothsayers, the nabobs, the feng shui crowd and even the Daoists that the new leader has the Mandate, ha ha ha. ... Where was I?"

"You just mentioned an interminable civil war."

"Yes, it's an interminable story, ha ha ha. After fifty or fifty-five years of fighting, the war exhausted both Nguyễn and the Trịnh. During the stalemate, the families reluctantly made peace by dividing the country quietly into two parts. The

truce was never very stable, since both kings claimed to be head of the whole country and the same people.

"After four generations, the Nguyễn and Trịnh Dynasties have shown the usual
decline. Political corruption, every official with his hand out, and such cow's wind
has pissed away the patience of the people—made them ungrateful. Which brings us
to this insect biting jail cell, ha ha ha."

"So that is the story," said Pierre with excitement. "The Nguyễn and Trịnh are
in a stalemate!"

"Now you understand the situation," said Tri, "but it doesn't help us escape,
does it?" and he laughed uproariously. Even Pierre had to laugh.

"And my apologies, the Siamese already know about it, ha ha ha."

"Hallelujah, your story explains the confusion, demystifies it," exclaimed
Pierre, as he once again moved his legs. "Could you support the other side? It hurts.
Then I could tilt the other way for a while."

⇢ ⇝

On the fortieth day in the dungeon, the jailor opened the door and called out,
"The barbarians from Tra Tien."

Pierre looked at his new friend, Diệu Tri, the slight scholar-soldier with the
wide eyes, and said, "Whatever they do to Alain Artaud and me, thank you for all
that you have done for us. Bless you, and may the Lord be with you."

Diệu Tri looked serious for a change. He bowed low and said, "Heaven and
Earth and the Ancestors protect you. And if they do, ai-yah, don't forget to come
back here and get me out of this government boarding house. The rates are fine, the
food is adequate, but the company, especially with you gone, will be seriously lack-
ing." Once more he laughed loudly, but it was forced. "My uncle's name again is
Diệu Thái, Minister of Canals and Waterworks."

The jailors approached Pierre and Father Artaud, unlocked the cangues and removed them. They helped Pierre to his feet. Father Artaud couldn't stand, so they
carried him out on a stretcher. The jailors took them up the stairs to the entrance of
the jail and turned them over to two waiting men: Senior Acolyte Paul Nghi, and the
Junior Acolyte Joseph Phạm!

"You are free," said the head jailor. "Your sentence has been shortened to forty
days and twenty-five lashes. Sorry about the extra ten," and he winked. The acolytes, with several other students from the seminary, greeted their two teachers.

Emotions were high. Everyone bowed to each other, but the bows were brief.
Paul Nghi gave Father Artaud some water from an animal skin flask, while other
students arrived with a hired palanquin carried by two porters. They lifted the semiconscious Alain Artaud into the chair and helped carry the palanquin, which carried
Father Artaud to the inn they were staying at.

Father Pierre breathed gratefully the fresh air of freedom, while he squinted in
the bright sunlight. As his eyes grew accustomed to the light, he studied the street

stalls, just enjoying the colors and people and activity. He passed an old woman clothed in blue with red trim, squatting by her mat covered with yellow, red, and green peppers and squashes. He enjoyed every smell and detail of color. The richness and beauty of the bustling town of Hà Tiên overwhelmed him with joy after the sensory deprivation of the dungeon. They found their inn, and carefully moved Father Artaud from the palanquin to his room and his bed mat. Alain Artaud was confused, and hot with fever again. Paul Nghi had already sent Joseph Phạm to find a doctor.

Pierre asked Paul Nghi, "How did you get us out?"

"Never mind."

"What is the matter?"

"It was expensive."

Pierre looked his student full in the eyes, and locked him in a commanding gaze. "Please tell me."

"We needed one hundred taels of silver, but we only had ten. We sold your gold altar crucifix, many of your personal things, many of our own belongings, half of the livestock, and many of our family altar accessories. We still were fifty short of the hundred we needed, so Peter Vũ sold himself into slavery for one hundred taels. He left the remainder to his parents."

"Damnation," cried Pierre. Anger and grief wiped out all the joy from the walk of freedom in the town. They walked in silence for several minutes, till Pierre spoke. "I thank you for all of these sacrifices. I'm sorry to hear about Peter, bless him. We will have to determine if we can find him, to buy out his contract."

It was the first time any of them had ever heard Father Pierre swear. That night, Alain Artaud, with another high fever and a rattle in his lungs, passed away. At last his body cooled down. In the morning they jury-rigged a stretcher from a canvas tarp and shoulder poles and carried the shrouded body back to the seminary for burial. All the students gathered, first to greet Father Pierre, followed immediately by the funeral service for Father Artaud and his burial.

Pierre spoke at length about his fine friend and teacher. He prayed aloud, "O God Almighty, creator of Heaven and Earth, please receive the soul of Father Alain Artaud, a kind, thoughtful and generous man. He was your faithful and loving servant. He spent almost thirty-five years here in Đại Việt, studying this land and teaching your heavenly gospel to its people."

෴   ෴

Only a few weeks had passed when a student ran back from the village and up to Pierre's outdoor study. "Father Pierre, the Siamese are invading!" he exclaimed. "Like locusts, they are destroying everything and everyone in their path, and many say that they are just two day's march from the village!"

"Ring the dinner bell," ordered Pierre, "and assemble everyone."

Pierre conferred with Paul and his elder students in front of all of the others. The Siamese were notorious for their scorched earth practice of conquest. Pierre and Paul decided to flee by the road to the coast, back to the seaport town of Hà Tiên. Everyone at the seminary must go. The road was crowded with families hurrying toward the town. A few hundred long-faced soldiers from the Nguyễn citadel moved in the opposite direction, in a noble but hopeless attempt to try and stop the Siamese.

In the port of Hà Tiên, none of the junk captains would agree to help Pierre unless he could pay cash. After numerous inquiries and begging, one particularly savvy Chinese owner-captain decided to honor a note on the Society of Foreign Missions in Paris, which had a large office in the Malaysian port of Malacca. He demanded as collateral all of them to become his property. If the Society failed to produce the extraordinary fee of twenty-five silver taels, he would own all the Việt seminarians and their teacher, to do with as he chose. All fifty-four members of the seminary, including Pierre, clambered aboard an old barnacle-encrusted junk, stinking of fish offal, and sailed away from the deadly Siamese army and the mobs of fearful peasants on the quayside. The captain had packed on board another hundred or so peasants who wanted to escape, so the fifty-foot junk was crammed with 170 souls. Half stood so half could sit or lie down.

Fortunately, and as expected, the Society of Foreign Missions had the twenty-five taels of silver in cash at its disposal. Pierre and his students were safe, although now they were at least temporarily marooned in Malacca. Father Pierre also had the funds at last to free Peter Vũ, but not the means to find him. The chances of finding someone sold into slavery were very small. Alas, the saintly Peter Vũ was never found.

Chapter 10
Quy Nhơn Citadel
1773 (three years later)

One wet morning during the rainy season, a man trotted up to the guardhouse of the Quy Nhơn Citadel, and while gasping for breath, demanded to see the officer of the watch. A tall soldier in a blue silk shirt emerged from the guardhouse. "What do you want?"

"Such bitterness, I am ruined. I've been robbed by four rough fellows. They took all the fruits and vegetables I was carrying to market, and all my money as well."

"Do roosters crow? We can't jump at every little story. Besides, they are surely gone by now."

"It's the second time. Those same four fellows robbed me last week as well," the man said with indignation, "but this time they recognized me, they let me keep my produce, and one of them apologized. He said, 'What is your name? Someday the Hồ family will repay you for your service.' Well, I told him I was Trần the Second Son, but that I wouldn't hold my breath. After they left me, I followed them into the jungle and discovered where their whole gang of thieves and knaves is camping."

"Weren't you scared of being caught?"

"Trần the Second Son is not afraid of death, and he despises thieves," he said with emotion and conviction.

The officer of the day immediately took the peasant to his commander, who took the fellow to see Magistrate Nguyễn Trúc. After the audience, the magistrate ordered the complainant out of the audience room to wait in the antechamber.

"What do you think?" asked Nguyễn Trúc.

The officer replied, "It's hard to tell, but in case it's true, we should prudently investigate. About ten scouts and one hundred soldiers should be able to handle whatever should arise, and with luck, we might even surprise the Hồ brother band. Remember last time we were just a few hours after they had moved."

"Aiyah, what a possible windfall. Do it," said Nguyễn Trúc. "I want them all, dead or alive, it doesn't matter."

A detachment of 110 men departed two hours later, in full battle dress, including many of the best fighters in the garrison.

❧   ❧

It was late in the afternoon when a group of peasants arrived proudly at the portcullis of the citadel with a captive. A large, wide-horned water buffalo pulled a heavy bamboo cage built on a cart. Its thick bars were set into timbers. This stout cage was a common device for transporting prisoners from a village to the military compound. The portcullis was up for the day, and the peasants rolled their prisoner cage into the large fortified square.

The officer of the watch asked, "And who might this ugly one be?"

A barefoot man in the black tunic of a farmer answered, "It is Chí Minh, who has robbed several people from the village of Xóm Mới while they travelled on the open road."

"Well done," the officer said, much impressed. "The court will convene as usual in the morning. Who will stay or return to testify?" Two men proudly slapped their thighs and bowed in affirmation. "Good," the officer said. "You must be here by the hour of the Dragon. But before you leave, sign this registry and roll this cage to the far side of the yard for me before leaving."

The men bowed and did as they were ordered, bowed again and left. The captain continued his rounds, checking his sentinels. As he left his watch, he reported the delivery of a prisoner in a tiger cage, and that the prisoner would remain in it overnight, as was customary with petty criminals.

The sun fell, the stars gradually came out without that old tattle-tale, the man in the moon, sitting under his tree. Sentinels marched above on the ramparts, and two more walked casually around the courtyard. An old, retired soldier, now a custodian, lit the oil lampions around the courtyard that rested on posts and hung from walls.

The Quy Nhơn Citadel was a fortress large enough for 5,000 men. In times of peace, 200 soldiers were garrisoned there.

The man in the cage lay still, but wasn't asleep. His name was Chí Minh but it wasn't. It was Hồ Nhạc. Nhạc opened his eyes halfway and rolled over as if still asleep. In the light of the lampions he counted the guards, two below; four, maybe, six above—two more than expected. They each carried a spear or bow and arrows, and a sword. *If the bowmen see me, I will enter the void,* he thought. *At least I'll be well rested when I die though. Remember Father's horrible death. Father, I will avenge your death tonight—or die trying to.*

Nhạc's mind raced through past events. He saw his father's crushed foot again in his hands, the old man's face gray and his eyes stricken with grief. He saw the doctor amputating his father's infected foot and hand. He remembered the feeling of security he had when his mother sang around the house, and when she put him to bed as a child. There was the horrible day when his father discovered that he had stolen sweets and lied about them, and his father whipped his backside black and blue. There was that funny horrible time when he and Lữ were playing with Huệ. While pretending to burn their brother at the stake, they lit a torch to terrify him. The faggots at his feet accidentally caught fire from the torch and they almost immolated their terrified little brother. *I should have been severely whipped, but Huệ, unbelievably, never told on us. I am still in his debt for that.* Nhạc pulled himself out of his reverie and turned his full attention to the guards. He studied them.

Nhạc slowly lifted the trapdoor that his men had cut into the floor planks of the cage. He took a short stick that had been wedged into the underside and used it to prop the trapdoor halfway open. Then he covered the door with his blanket, so one would see the lump of a body in the cage. He slipped down through the hole to the ground underneath the cage, where his two black-sooted daggers were concealed. He slid them out. Nhạc crept along the shadows of the walls till he reached the great gate. He studied the portcullis windlass spindle. To turn the spindle, work the pulleys, and winch the portcullis open, he would have to do the work of two or three.

He watched and waited, silent and still. If the two men in the courtyard didn't separate for a few moments, Huệ's plan might fail. The hours ticked away. The stars moved slowly and imperturbably across the moonless sky.

The new watch arrived. Passwords and greetings were exchanged. The old watch retired indoors. One of the soldiers of the new watch walked by saying, "I bet you a betel case that Little Blossom has the sweetest jade gate that has ever helped you into nirvana."

"That's a wager I'll accept," the other replied, "for I think Amber's gate is worth much more. Maybe I'm moon-struck, but I want to pay the fifty taels of silver to buy her contract. Besides, if I'm going to spend the money on her anyway, I might as well buy her."

"Sounds wonderful, but you'll have to feed her. Are you going to tell your wife though?"

The two fresh guards, one with spear, the other with bow, stayed together all the way around the yard. An hour went by and they didn't separate. In desperation, Nhạc decided to attack both at once. Doing so quietly would, regrettably, require luck as well as skill. It was uncanny and prescient that Huệ insisted that he hide two daggers under the cage. As they walked by the wall again, Nhạc stepped from his shadow and, copying their gait, he gently walked up to them from behind and tapped each on the inside shoulder with the bottoms of his fists, his daggers pointed up above his own face. The two guards spun around toward each other. As they saw Nhạc, Nhạc was driving his daggers from his chest straight into each man's throat. He continued his extension and sent the blades through their throats into bone. He finished the movement of his arms by making a circle, so that he pressed their two bare heads together. Then he lowered the two bodies to the ground like a father putting two children to bed. Their weapons fell, making sharp noises.

Someone should have heard the spear fall. Nhạc hurried to the main gate while sticking his bloody knives in his belt. No one raised the alarm yet. Now fear began to addle his brain and his breathing was heavy. He was suddenly terrified by the irrational idea that his brothers were playing a deadly trick on him, and that they wouldn't be outside to help him.

At the huge wooden gates, he knocked gently twice, and was relieved to hear three quiet knocks in response. He lifted the thick cross bar and pulled the gates open to the inside, first the left one and then the right. The hinges squealed and shuddered. The sentinels on the ramparts began to shout. Standing by the portcullis on the outside, to his relief, were his two brothers and six other archers with arrows notched in their bows.

A bell rang loud and long. Using the right gate to shield his back, Nhạc began the herculean effort to raise the iron-latticed grille. He strained to pull a hand lever of the windlass down, but it wouldn't budge. He was turning it in the wrong direction. He had the sense to try the other way. From outside, some of his men slid bamboo poles under the portcullis to lever it up. Slowly, they forced the spindle to move. The grille rose inch by inch and Nhạc groaned with effort.

The guards on the walls were now halfway across the courtyard. Five guards ran up to the great gate to see who was causing the disturbance, and they were only twenty paces away when the men outside let their arrows fly through the iron bars. All but one fell dead or wounded. The last kept running for Nhạc, his spear raised for a throw, but Huệ, who had kept his bow taut, let his arrow fly straight and true to the man's chest. This checked his motion, and the others, who now had redrawn their bows, pierced the brave soldier with more arrows. Lữ took note of his younger brother, thinking, *Should I tell Brute that Baby-Face saved his life?*

Nhạc strained at the levers of the windlass. The iron gate rose slowly. At a foot high, two of the smallest men in the band, lying by the bottom of the portcullis at the archers' feet, forced themselves under the grate and scurried to the left. They added their weight to the lever bars. Meanwhile, eighty-four or so remaining men were charging out of their barracks in an unorganized attack. The first wave charged madly for the gate, but just before they hurled their spears, the line of archers let fly a deadly hail through the lattice holes of the portcullis. Many of the iron-tipped shafts ripped into unarmored flesh. The portcullis began to move with ease as men rolled under and took up defensive positions on either side of the tired and straining Nhạc, while others added their strength to the spindle.

The next wave of royal Nguyễn troops scurried behind what little cover the courtyard provided, and climbed up to the parapets. By now Nhạc's own spear- and swordsmen had entered and were seeking the stairs to the parapet as well. Behind these forty peasant fighters came forty more carrying homemade pikes, knives tied to poles, hand scythes, and kitchen knives. They ran into the courtyard, murdered the wounded, and stripped the corpses of their priceless spears and swords.

The rebels maintained their assault, though some were armed only with cudgels. They drew the deadly fire of the awoken archers of the citadel. Many attackers were cut down. Another group of peasants appeared pushing an oxcart into the courtyard. The cart was built like a box, with narrow windows each two feet apart.

The eight Hồ bowmen jumped into it, pulled the door closed, and then while peasants pushed the cart deep into the courtyard to get closer to the main barracks, others protected these former farmers with crude but stout bamboo shields that stood five feet high.

The shield carriers screamed as they charged, making a terrifying sound. In a blood-curdling noise, the screams communicated their righteous anger, hatred, and determination for vengeance.

When the archers protected within the closed wagon began to cut down the remaining troops, the regular soldiers saw that the fight was lost and began to lay down their weapons and kneel face down on the ground. In this way, many of the remaining surrendered, including fat Nguyễn Trúc, the magistrate.

The attackers proceeded with an uncanny discipline for pirates. They stripped each soldier of his weapons, bound his hands behind his back, and marched him to the center of the courtyard to lie face down. After all the new prisoners were secured, the three tired but exhilarated brothers came together in the yard as the dawn light appeared. Nhạc gave first Lữ and then Huệ a great bear hug. Then Huệ and Nhạc broke their embrace enough to pull Lữ into their circle, and so still clutching bows and daggers, they held themselves together in a tangle of arms and weapons and laughed. All their pent-up anxieties fled to the Java. If they could find Nguyễn Trúc, nothing would stop their revenge, or keep them from finishing it.

They untangled, and immediately began to direct the mopping up action. As the sun rose, Nhạc, Lữ, and Huệ surveyed their fighters and scrutinized their captives. Three years they had spent hiding in the hills preparing for this showdown. Autumn Moon entered the citadel. She had come to be a witness to her sons' work and to her revenge. The three brothers were now searching methodically for the magistrate Nguyễn Trúc. They could not find him in any of the buildings or cellars. Could he have escaped?

Among the prisoners, a soldier identified Nguyễn Trúc in a blue cotton shirt trying to pass as a soldier. Trúc was betrayed by one of his own men. The pot-bellied Nguyễn Trúc, dressed as a common soldier, appeared serene and confident.

Trúc still didn't know who was attacking, but he had every reason to expect that his family could ransom his freedom for silver. Such ransoms were not uncommon with pirates and bandits. *This is a very powerful adversary,* he thought. *They must know that my ransom will bring a fortune.*

Nguyễn Trúc asked to speak with the leader of the outlaws. Nhạc, Lữ, and Huệ were quickly summoned by Snake and Midget. The three brothers approached the magistrate, who said. "This humble servant is Nguyễn Trúc, Mandarin Second Class and the personal representative of His Royal Majesty Nguyễn Đình. To whom do I owe the honor of this most unexpected and unprecedented visit?"

"I am Hồ Nhạc, this is Hồ Lữ, and that is Hồ Huệ," answered Nhạc. Trúc frowned in confusion and then his eyes opened wide in horror. The three brothers savored the transformation they watched in Trúc's demeanor. Lữ giggled demonically, and Trúc grew ashen. Nhạc kneed Trúc in the groin, and then struck him in the face.

"Ah bitterness," Trúc cried, and he shook with fear, fell to his knees and knocked his forehead to the dirt. He begged, "Mercy, mercy, please spare this old grandfather his miserable life."

"Do you remember Physician Hồ Danh?" said Nhạc coldly. "Show us now if you can die as bravely as he did."

"But I can make it worth your while to spare me. I have money, lots of money. I can make each of you rich if you will spare my life!" The Hồ brothers laughed, and so did their followers. Huệ said, "Do you remember what you did to our father, Hồ Danh? . . . We will refresh your memory."

Nhạc ordered Snake, Midget, Night Hawk, and Lover Boy to strip Nguyễn Trúc and tie him spread-eagled in the middle of the courtyard. Nguyễn Trúc now was tight-faced and white. "You won't get away with this," he shouted desperately. "There will be generations of reprisals. My family will find you, and you will wish you had never harmed a hair on my body."

As the three brothers waited for Snake and his men to finish, the thoughts of each turned to the future. Nhạc told himself, *I am about to satisfy my filial obligations and secure my place as the deserving leader of this band, even against my clever little brother. He is dangerous to me, but he is also very helpful.*

The youngest brother Huệ was thinking, *Our father will drink with us when we celebrate tonight. Nhạc did a splendid job. I think he was the strongest candidate in our group for this most challenging job, and he will prove useful for a long time to come. Unfortunately, now he'll want to be treated like a ruler. I hope he does not become unbearable. And now we must escape the wrath of King Nguyễn Đình, who is far more powerful and cunning than Trúc. Will we survive when there is a 1,000-tael bounty on each of our heads? We have stirred up a hornets' nest.*

Lữ was watching Trúc lying spread-eagled and the entire scene. His mind floated to his return to the Green Pavilion on Entertainment Street in Quy Nhơn that night and to the embrace and the administrations of his latest passion, Lily Blossom. *What a woman*, he thought, *and she loves me so much. Aye-yah, she can do the most wonderful things and will do anything.*

After all the buildings had been searched and the prisoners were assembled and bound, Nhạc took out of his belt pouch a short proclamation that Huệ had written. Nhạc spoke loudly to the prostrate prisoner and the assembly, "Nguyễn Trúc, you tortured, maimed, and caused the death of the good Physician Hồ Danh, who was our father, for refusing to hand over his daughter to you for one of your many wives.

There are those who swear that you beat and torture your women, and that you have killed at least two of them. You forced us to defile our sister, selling her quickly so that you could fatten your belly and your coffers by extortion and the abuse of your official power." Nhạc then listed a variety of crimes committed against members of his band, or to their acquaintances, announced the names of the victims and the witnesses as if in an official government tribunal, and then, "By the authority of the Righteous Under Heaven of the Tây Sơn, I condemn you, Nguyễn Trúc, to death in one of its severest forms," quoting a punishment from the Nguyễn penal code.

Huệ felt a twinge of concern for what was about to happen. He wondered, *Should we practice torture, even on the worst criminal, and not become tainted by the practice—a practice which we began our holy war by condemning?* The mandarin looked so vulnerable as he lay naked before them. *No,* he argued with himself and hardened his heart. *Justice requires revenge. I will watch, and I will help. This is the man who beat and maimed my father after stealing his wealth. I will, no matter how unpleasant it is, be responsible at least for crushing a hand and a foot.*

In fact, Huệ did very little. He watched, and he handed various instruments to his two older brothers. Autumn Moon sent for the magistrate's official court chair, and she sat, as on a throne, to witness their long-awaited revenge, while she drank Nguyễn Trúc's finest wine and mourned again her husband's horrible death and her daughter's sale to a pimp. She got drunk, and remembered her husband Hồ Danh when he was healthy, their long life together. Autumn Moon cried from the painful loss of her husband's body and companionship, of losing their home, fields, and ancestral graves—and the friends she had in the village. It saddened her that Nguyễn Trúc's screams for mercy could not bring her husband back or end her grief; revenge was satisfying, but very little was repaired. Buffeted by swings of emotion, she was also proud of her maturing sons.

Before the assembled crowd, Nhạc and Lữ went to work on Nguyễn Trúc with screws and kitchen knives. First they slowly crushed his hands and feet. Then they sawed off his genitals. After each major cut, they burned him to stop the bleeding. They cut out an eye. They removed his ears, nose, and lips. They purposely left his tongue. Finally, they cut open his stomach. Into the gapping cavity, they placed part of a nest of carnivorous jungle beetles. To Autumn Moon's grim satisfaction, Nguyễn Trúc kept begging and screaming for mercy throughout the whole long day and into the next night. Her heart was still broken, but she and her sons had fulfilled their duty, and the job was done.

Chapter 11
The Cotillion, Lorient
1773

They entered the candlelit ballroom as the black-suited butler announced, "Madame Céleste Grannier and Cadet Benoit Grannier." Benoit was vaguely aware that many eyes turned their way. He stood quietly erect, pleased to be able to display for the first time his new naval uniform. On each sleeve of his new jacket he wore insignia—a black bar with golden anchor and single gold strip with two blue bars, signifying an *aspirant* or midshipman in the *Marine Nationale*, the National Navy of France. The blue twill uniform was Benoit's first hand-tailored suit, and it made a great contrast from his usual duck trousers and work shirts, while it accentuated his strong back and height. Benoit smiled at his mother, who was as excited as he was nervous.

"You look great, Mama," he said, and he proudly kissed her on the cheek. Céleste Grannier had made a new dress for the graduation ball of the Abbey of Saint Mathew, which was being held at the Palace of the Duke of Lorient. She wore a green taffeta gown with small ruffles at the sleeves and hem, and with a fashionably displayed bosom. Her only jewelry were two simple gold rings in her ears, and a small diamond in a gold lace brooch at her neck on a gold chain.

The orchestra was playing a piece by François Couperin, and men were carefully walking glasses of punch or champagne to their companions. Benoit and his mother joined Antoine and his parents. Antoine wore a new but plain dark suit, suitable for a young man about to enter the Church.

"You'd better dance while you can," Benoit said to his cousin Antoine. They bowed and shook hands or kissed cheeks all around, and then the two young men ran off to get punch for the grown-ups.

"Look over there," said Antoine quietly, nodding his head.

"My God, is that Isabelle?"

"Isn't it too bad that you're going off to sea," said Antoine.

"Isn't it too bad you're becoming a priest," retorted Benoit.

The young woman in question, Isabelle Carpentier, had come of age. Her yellow chiffon dress, bunched at the hips and pulled low and taut at the bosom, left little doubt in the eye of the beholder about the quality of her lines. Isabelle's hair had been curled into ringlets, and the ringlets were so clean that they reflected light from the oil lamps and the candle chandeliers.

Benoit gave Antoine a funny look, and then said, "I should have apprenticed to a solicitor. Excuse me." He delivered a glass of champagne to his mother, and then boldly walked over to where Isabelle stood with her parents to compliment the ladies on their costumes.

The fencing master, Georges Quellenac, was also one of the local country dance teachers. As the Master of the Dance for the evening, he called for couples to form a cotillion, and Benoit was in a tactically favorable position to be the first man to ask the beauty Isabelle for the dance.

"Certainly," she said, and Benoit held out his right arm and led her into one of the forming squares.

For three years, Benoit and his peers had all attended the Duke and Duchess of Lorient's Dancing School, Master Quellenac presiding, every Friday night, which ensured that the young people knew the figures, style, and etiquette, and had some sense of each other as well.

The music began with a fanfare, and all the couples bowed to each other and to their neighbors in the square. Then to a lively reel, the dancers executed the first of the four-part dance by joining hands and slip-stepping to the left. After a *dos-à-dos* (back-to-back) with one's partner, all four ladies chained across the set and then chained back again to their partners. The first figures ended with an elegant, two-hand swing with one's partner with one arm behind the back, and a promenade around the set.

Benoit and Isabelle had no trouble dancing together. They spoke little. They did not behave like silly children, but more like good friends who were saying fare-well. When the fourth figure finally ended with a bow and a curtsy, Isabelle's eyes were moist. "Thank you for a lovely dance," said Benoit, his voice thick with emotion, and her remark to Benoit was barely audible.

Henri Millepapier was standing nearby and approached Isabelle for the next dance. Benoit, not having completely forgotten his manners, sought out his mother and asked her for a dance, for he was her escort.

"Please line up in contra lines," said the Master of the Dance, Quellenac, "in duple proper formation for *Trou dans le Mur*."

Hole in the Wall could be a very flirtatious dance, but Benoit danced it with his mother with a meticulous grace and smoothness, as if they were both floating in air and dancing to the music of the cherubs. They enjoyed and appreciated the presentation of each new couple that they danced with as they progressed down the line.

After a number of repetitions of the thirty-two-bar dance, Benoit began to clown about, pretending to make small mistakes, so that by the end of the dance he had his mother laughing, while ostentatiously reprimanding her naughty son.

Benoit thanked his mother and excused himself. He caught his old buxom friend Brigitte moving away from her last partner, and successfully detained her for the next dance, which moments later the Dancing Master announced would be the country dance Childgrove.

"Congratulations on your engagement to Richard Foncier," said Benoit, admiring once again the adorable and ample qualities of his older friend.

"Thank you very much," said Brigitte, "and good luck in the navy."

"In a few months I will be assigned to a ship, out of the seaport of Brest. But in three years, if all goes well, I'll be a commissioned officer."

"I hope you come back to us soon and all in one piece," she said, forcing a laugh to make light of a serious issue.

The orchestra commenced, interrupting all the small talk on the dance floor. As soon as the first strains of the music began, they were off, siding with each other, a simple move that required only forward and back. They moved forward on their toes till their right shoulders met in an intimate pairing, and then fell back to place. The dance got everyone aroused, because after the siding and back to back with partners and neighbors, one joined hands with the neighbor and executed a dynamic, two-hand turn once and a half around, before a slower, more erotic single turn with one's partner. By the end of the dance, both Brigitte and Benoit were too excited for words. They bowed and curtsied, thanked each other, and moved on, covering their stirred-up desires.

Benoit saw Louise, a shy and unpopular girl, sitting in a chair against the wall. Louise hadn't yet been asked to dance, so he headed over to her and politely asked the skinny wallflower for a dance. "Oh, no thank you," the bony-faced girl replied. "I don't want to dance right now."

"You seemed to think it was all right in dancing school," said Benoit, gently encouraging her, "and you dance well." The girl stood up hesitantly and allowed herself to be led onto the floor, her awkward motions giving away her fear of humiliation.

"Square sets for La Rousse Quadrille, announced the Dancing Master, and Benoit took Louise to the head of a forming square set. The tune had a frolicsome two-four rant-step rhythm with a rising, oom-pah base line by the cellos, and moments after the introduction began, the men spun away from their partners, balanced their right-hand lady, and swung her vigorously in a heavy, two-hand, peasant swing. Louise loved it. Everyone loved it, except the clerics, who clumped by the alcohol-laced punch, and a few of the old people at the card tables.

The men then careened home, checked their movement with a balance, and energetically swung their own partners. Everyone stopped and clapped at the end of the swing, except the first couple, who kept swinging! Louise and Benoit swung round and round so fast that her red hair flew out behind her. Louise's tight-lipped smile changed slowly into a real smile, which grew into a burning grin as she and Benoit moved faster and faster around to the intoxicating music. Suddenly the solo swing ended, and the pair had to promenade the inside of the square and bow to the other three couples. Dancers were laughing and pointing, because the first couples of each set were so dizzy that they could hardly stand up, much less walk on a designated path correctly, which was the humorous conceit of the dance. "Oh, that was marvelous," said Louise, now short of breath, when the dance had ended, and she gave Benoit a swift embrace.

"It was my pleasure. And thank you," said Benoit, "you danced that very well." And he almost added, *And you look beautiful when you smile,* but thought it better not to. Instead he said, "And you look beautiful tonight." Other men had made the same observation, and Louise had male partners for the rest of the evening.

Halfway through the evening, the master of the dance announced that members of his class would demonstrate a new dance from Vienna, a dance they called the Waltz. All the dancers moved to the side. Benoit and Isabelle found each other and walked with about ten other young couples out onto the floor. The music began, a lilting, one, two, three, in three-quarter time. Benoit presented his arm, and Isabelle moved into a new position resembling an embrace. Their bodies were just a foot away from each other. In a whirl of motion, they were floating around the room counterclockwise from the ceiling, while slowly spinning clockwise in the most intimate yet flowing and graceful motions that the crowd had ever seen on a dance floor.

Benoit and Isabelle smiled and gazed into each other's eyes. This would be their last dance together till only the Lord knew when. When the music ceased, a great noise erupted. Some people clapped, while others spoke rapidly to each other, shaking their heads and expressing their shock at the outrageous display of erotic informality, which was being imported from a place as obviously decadent and fallen as Vienna—not proper behavior.

George Quellenac, the part-Austrian dancing master, was not oblivious to the stir and controversy that the new dance had caused, and he was enjoying the fuss. He had not failed to find an accomplished and endowed partner. After a good pause for conversation, he called for square sets and let everyone settle into a familiar cotillion full of rights and lefts and allemandes—something far less demanding or challenging to the crowd than the newfangled Waltz step with its controversial intimacy.

Benoit looked over the many friends he had in the room, and felt uncomfortable about shipping out to sea. It was a bittersweet evening laden with a soft melancholy, even though he was enjoying himself. He was possessed by the spirit of the dance. He, and the music, and his partners, and the whole room were one. Many of the girls from dancing school had kissed him endearingly at one time or another. He was rarely refused a walk to the cemetery or the city gardens, but only the humblest and most unfortunate of creatures would want a naval midshipman for a husband, a man who would spend most of the next ten or twenty years out at sea.

Once, on a moonlit summer's night, Benoit had made love with Isabelle in a pile of hay under the stars. She knew he had just been accepted into the navy, and after the kisses ended and the awkward experiment in matrimonial love, with the protection of a store-bought linen sheath had ended, she began quietly to sob. Benoit didn't have to ask why. She had asked him to give up the navy for her, and after thinking it over for weeks, possibly the worst weeks of his whole life, he told her no. Yes, he would love to marry her, but no, he wouldn't give up a career in the navy for her. Soon after that night she stopped seeing him, and then suddenly she was going out with Henri Millepapier, who would apprentice to a solicitor.

"Please line up in three couple sets," said Quellenac, "for the Fandango."

Chapter 12
Nguyễn Đình's Retreat
1777 (four years later)

Paul Nghi signaled with his hand that he needed a private conversation. Father Pierre turned to his pupils. He pointed to an older student, John Ngô, and said in his fluent Vietnamese, "Please take over the drills."

Father Pierre was an imposing and animated spirit. At thirty-seven years of age, he stood taller and appeared heavier than his Vietnamese acolyte, Paul, and any of his students. He still looked a bit like a drunk bird because of his large eyelids, his pointy nose, and his thin mouth. His brown hair was now flecked through with gray and receded far up his shiny, bald forehead.

And yet Pierre still had a warm smile. He usually wore a kind and serious expression. Strangers would often smile back at him, and many students and acquaintances would tell him their problems. His Vietnamese students would confide in Father Pierre when they wouldn't talk to any other adults they knew.

Seven years earlier, Pierre Pigneau and his students had spent a year in self-imposed exile to the southwest in Malacca until the Nguyễn and Hồ forces in separate battles had fully repulsed the Siamese invasion. Pierre and his students then sailed back to Hà Tiên. The old site of huts and gardens had been burned. The whole area was still deserted. Pierre found some available land with buildings to rent near Kao Giang in Long Xuyên Province, also near the Cambodian border. In the next six years of peace, Pierre and Paul Nghi reestablished their missionary school.

☙　❧

Paul Nghi led Father Pierre over toward the mission rice paddies. Paul began to speak when they were between the students working in the shed, the paddies, and the large vegetable garden.

"The rumors we heard were all correct. I have just learned from a messenger from my cousin that King Nguyễn Đình himself, his royal entourage, and what appear to be the remnants of his mighty army, now only a few thousand men, are just a few miles outside of Long Xuyên. What's more, the Hồ brothers, and the Hissing Army of the Tây Sơn, are so close behind them that the Nguyễn rear guard is fighting as it retreats.

"My cousin's second wife, Chrysanthemum, serves Lady Purity, the widow of the fearless Nguyễn Phúc Luân. This brother of King Đình, Phúc Luân, is the one who supposedly committed suicide. They say he poisoned himself after his father King Nguyễn Vo overlooked him as the heir. Phúc Luân and the Lady Purity's son is the Royal Nephew Nguyễn Phúc Ánh, which makes the boy Ánh King Đình's nephew and, arguably, the heir to his throne. Chrysanthemum and Lady Purity are sure that King Đình is finished. They want to know if we can somehow rescue and hide the royal nephew, Prince Ánh, his mother, Lady Purity, and four servants."

Pierre was deeply troubled. He looked across the mission at its small huts, across the water-swamped paddies, and into the dark green tangle of jungle that they had laboriously cleared away. *I want to help the prince,* he thought, *but several of the cardinals in Rome will criticize me if I break with the official Church doctrine, which stands strongly against taking sides in the civil disputes of foreign peoples. You can always bet on the wrong horse.*

"We risk everything that we have worked and suffered for," Pierre said slowly. He knew that he had to decide almost immediately, with no one of greater authority to guide him.

Father Pierre remembered his arrival in Cochinchina ten years before, in 1767, his imprisonment, the beating, the rape, and then the extraordinary character Diệu Tri. *I don't know if I was able to help Diệu Tri, poor fellow. I sent money to the jailor on his behalf, and a letter to his uncle. That was the least I could do, and besides my prayers, all I could think of. I don't know if his uncle ever received the letter. If only the government here was allied with the Church, as in France. We Christians have no influence here yet.*

Now he was silent, at a loss for words. He stared out at the watery rice fields, searching for an answer to a very complicated question. Pierre didn't agree with the Church policy. It wasn't necessarily in the interest of the Church, and it certainly wasn't necessarily in the interest of France. *Could it be that it was an Italian papal policy aimed at least partly to hold France back? The English took sides in India, and now control large parts of the country.*

"We risk everything that we have," Pierre said again. "It isn't much, but the penalty for a misstep during this civil war could be death—and a wiping out of the Christians. We could gain much as well. Paul, what do you think?"

"We could do nothing and still all get killed. I like the idea of helping the son of Nguyễn Phúc Luân," said Paul. "He had my respect and loyalty."

Pierre asked aloud, "How can the prince escape his uncle's entourage unnoticed?"

Paul answered, "Someone dressed as an incense and food vendor could try to talk with his servants. But we still need a trick to get them away."

Pierre added, "When and if an opportunity appears, our agent could meet him in one of the village temples by the road, and then flee into the jungle."

"I could probably do that," Paul said. "I can navigate the jungle."

"Let's at least save these people from the slaughter if we can," Pierre decided. He picked the choice with the greatest risk and possible reward. "There will be six of them. They'll need to disguise themselves as peasants as soon as they are away from their guards. You had best take six sets of work clothes. Cover the clothes with vegetables, or even better, leave them exposed in a basket, and fill the other basket with vegetables. None of the soldiers will dare to openly buy the old clothes. We have incense, but you are on your own for other ancestral utensils to offer for sale."

"I will get these things together. I must go immediately."

"Prepare food for eight, I'm going to send someone else with you."

Pierre looked down at his senior acolyte. Paul Nghi was eight inches shorter than his teacher and was his best pupil. Pierre cared for him as he would have cared for a son. Paul was a gentle man of twenty-eight who read Chinese, Latin, and French. His face was plain and round, but well balanced.

Now Brother Nghi was proving very brave; their plan was almost reckless. *If Paul is caught by the Tây Sơn,* Pierre thought, *he will be treated as a member of the Nguyễn entourage.* Paul Nghi knelt and bowed his head. Father Pierre blessed his best student and made the sign of the cross. Then he helped Paul stand up and gave him a fatherly hug. The acolyte, dressed in farmer's homespun, turned around and went to gather the old clothes.

Paul called over the junior acolyte Joseph Phạm, explained the plan, and asked for his assistance. They took dry clothes right off the clothesline behind the main house, and stuffed a second basket with the produce set aside for the evening meal and cubes of sticky rice wrapped in bamboo leaves.

In the kitchen of the main house they found a box with all the cult of the ancestor utensils belonging to them and others in the mission. As Paul packed the utensils he said to Joseph, "These used to be kept on display and were used daily on altars in each man's cell, at least until two years ago. Do you remember when Father Pierre received the proclamation from Rome? Pope Benedict XIV had condemned the practice of ancestor worship as heathen sacrilege and counter to all the teachings and tenets of the Catholic Church."

Joseph cried, "My God, what a damned mistake—excuse me, Lord."

"Agreed," said Paul Nghi, "Grandfather Pope Benedict made our job almost impossible. I still remember the day that Father Pierre, full of embarrassment, reported on the Pope's Edict of Condemnation. Within a week, thirty-five students, half of the school, quit the mission and renounced their new faith as foreign and subversive. One student screamed at Father Pierre, broke his cross, and swore that the barbarians were devils who would be driven back into the sea where they came from, like so many poisonous snakes."

Joseph nodded and said, "Who could not be sympathetic with their anger? Nothing is more sacred to our people than our reverence of our Ancestors. Whether they are Confucian, Buddhist, Taoist, followers of a local deity, Christian, or other, what unifies our people against the Chinese or the Siamese is our filial piety and identity, which we preserve through the cult of the Ancestors. Without our unity, we would crumble before the might of the myriad of northerners."

"Yes, the Chinese hordes," said Paul crossing himself. "Pope Benedict was ill advised. We are the Việt, the people who worship their ancestors and who oppose foreign invaders and throw them out."

Joseph looked wistfully at one of the incense holders. "So why did you stay?"

Paul answered, "Maybe it was a mistake. For better or for worse, I have truly embraced the cult of Jesus, and the Pope is only another fallible priest, ever conscious and protective of his worldly powers. There has always been a need for priests in this world. He is only human. His bad decision, even though made in ignorance, could well undermine all our efforts to bring the word of love from Jesus of Nazareth to our people."

Joseph responded, "But Pierre is right, I hope, that the sacred teachings of Jesus will eventually overcome every obstacle. The questions are how and when."

Paul said to Joseph, "Please spread the word that I am going to help six refugees who are my own distant relatives, and thank the proper people for their clothing, which will hopefully be returned or replaced." Paul left Joseph Phạm to restock the supplies that they'd pilfered.

A large Việt peasant wearing a broad-brimmed straw sun hat approached Paul, who wondered, *What does this fellow want?*

"Here, let me help you with such a heavy load," offered the peasant.

"No thanks," said Paul. The big peasant picked up one of the baskets. Paul grabbed his arm very tight. The big peasant smiled broadly. Suddenly Paul realized that the peasant had hazel green eyes. It was Pierre Pigneau!

"Father Pierre, what are you doing in those old clothes, and what in heaven's name have you done to the color of your skin?"

"I'm going with you," Pierre answered.

"But this journey is going to be very dangerous," Paul exclaimed.

"You may stay behind if you like."

"But what if someone sees through your disguise?"

"You didn't."

"But we didn't talk very long."

"I'll just have to keep my distance and let you do all the talking. That will be the hardest part."

Pierre had stained his arms, legs, feet, neck, and face with a solution of oil and dye used in the French opera to darken skin. Paul realized that the disguise was quite thorough and he relented.

Everything had been carefully packed into four baskets. They were unarmed except for the *gánh* poles to carry the baskets, which they didn't know how to fight with, and small pocket knives. They bowed goodbye to Joseph Phạm, shouldered their loads, looked once at their home, then at each other, and then walked briskly off toward Long Xuyên wearing just light sandals on their feet.

On the road Pierre and Paul saw an endless stream of peasants fleeing before the two approaching armies. Men and women carried infants and children, or pushed carts full of belongings of every kind. Many of the grim-face men carried poles, axes, hoes, and flails, or roped threshing sticks, each unsure which side his neighbor would choose to fight on, and often unsure of his own position as well.

When Pierre and Paul reached Long Xuyên, they reached a ghost town. Chickens and pigs still wandered the yards and the street, but the people had all fled down the road or into the jungle. They passed a wizened old man sitting before the village *dinh*, the meeting house and temple to local and ancient Funan deities of the ancient Óc Eo Ancestors. The old man was enjoying the sun and a long pipe of tobacco. He was evidently in no mood to budge. Perhaps he thought that death would allow reincarnation and the joys of youth. A dog barked at their heels for a few yards, and then they were alone again.

Pierre was impressed by the avant-garde, the advance guard of the Nguyễn force when it arrived. He saw a column of soldiers that stretched down a long flat road and followed a narrow canal. The first soldiers, though tired and despondent, appeared orderly. Behind them came a line of war elephants, stubbornly slow but magnificently powerful, dressed in bright yellow harnesses and carrying basket litters under the large yellow parasols of the royal family. After five of these glorious war animals came another crowd of soldiers. They were not marching in lines, but there must have been several thousand of them.

Paul spotted his cousin's plump second wife, Chrysanthemum, walking by the side of the last hide-wrinkled elephant, and as she passed him he shouldered his *gánh* and took up beside her. Pierre wandered off casually to top off their water jars and skins. Elephants were drinking greedily from the nearest flooded rice fields.

A soldier started to shoo Paul away, but Chrysanthemum waved the guard back to his position. "Greetings, madam," he said in a loud voice. "How would you like to examine some fresh produce or some incense for prayer?"

"I would love to, kind sir." Then she dropped her voice, "Buddha protect us, thank Heaven and all the Gods that you are with us. I was afraid that I couldn't trust that canal boy." Paul noted that his cousin-in-law was in a state of suppressed terror.

Chrysanthemum looked closely at Paul. "Can you help us? We feel condemned, like the household of an ancient king that got buried alive when their dead lord was entombed."

"The boy delivered your message. The answer is yes, we can accommodate six of you. But besides some old clothes I brought in my basket, we have no plan for your escape but to wait for a chance for a temple visit. Here, look over these fruits. I have bananas, durians, guava, and jackfruit." Paul handed her a few pieces of each fruit and said, "We are being watched; why don't you pay me a few coins for some fruit and incense and take them."

Paul looked at the soldiers in front of the elephant of Prince Ánh and his mother. He counted twenty men. There would be that many behind the elephant as well, as the prince's bodyguard.

In front of them as they walked, one of the soldiers fainted from exhaustion. He hit the ground before anyone caught him. Three comrades dragged him to the side of the road out of the way of the elephant. Then these soldiers looked about. They made sure they had no chance of escaping into the jungle, and gave water to their comrade. An officer came over and drew his sword to cut the fallen soldier's throat. His friends forced him to stand, gave him more water to drink, and got him walking again. Paul realized that the soldiers were exhausted; the young woman by his side was exhausted. He also began to perceive just how perilous their position grew the longer he and Pierre stayed with the remnants of the Nguyễn.

The royal entourage stopped for a rest at Long Xuyên. Soldiers lay down on the sides of the road and slept. Garbed in light bamboo armor over brilliant yellow silks, the rotund King Đình, sporting a smooth double chin, climbed down from his elephant chair using a ladder. He questioned his favorite two generals and a few other officers, and then decided on a four-hour rest. King Đình ordered the mess to pass out enough dried fish and cooked rice to each man to last another two days.

There was no time to slaughter, prepare, and roast the pigs and chickens of the village. In fact, the last stand appeared to be imminent. The Tây Sơn avant-garde had chewed up over 3,000 soldiers sent to delay them during the last five days. Another 2,000 had deserted. Đình had only about 6,000 men left. He planned to use up the remainder of his men as necessary until he reached the Cambodian border. He and a small group would flee to Hà Tiên to the sea and then to the safety of Siam.

King Đình looked tired. He thought grimly to himself, *This trudge would not have been necessary if my general staff had somehow managed to preserve my navy. But they lost the navy in the last battle at the Sài Gòn River mouth. Incompetent admirals! Two hundred galleys and their 70,000 men, gone to the bottom. There is nothing left of my navy but the etching of names on so many ancestral tablets. How did the Tây Sơn accumulate so many fighting galleys? They captured them from the navy of the Trịnh of course, and wisely, didn't destroy them. They must have offered the sailors of these ships an amnesty if they agreed to fight for the Hồ—cunning devils.*

Paul Nghi decided it was time to move. He said to Chrysanthemum, "Tell her majesty that I strongly suggest that she and her son decide to immediately visit the local Buddhist temple. It is essential they bring no escort other than their four servants."

Chrysanthemum delivered the message and quickly returned with an assent from the royal widow. Paul shouldered his *gánh* and took off down the street as if on the important business of escaping the ensuing battle, which he was. He stopped at the public well, and from there he and Pierre watched Prince Ánh and his mother, Purity, descend from their elephant to their four favorite servants. The prince and the lady were quite used to the ladder. The elephant trainer stood with his hand gently on the elephant's trunk. The beast was tired, and anxious to search for water and then graze for food.

Pierre and Paul found the temple to Buddha at the other end of the village. They entered and searched it, and then took positions outside.

When Purity, an elegant lady with a high forehead and silver pins in her gray-streaked hair, spoke to the captain of her guard, he agreed to the visit, but of course with an escort. "I would rather that you all slept for the full three and a half hours," she said earnestly. "I will take my man Cho for protection. You and your men are about to fight a very important battle, and my security depends on your strength and your valor." Since he was about to collapse from exhaustion, he was too tired to argue with a direct order from the king's sister-in-law.

So Purity walked in her green silk tunic with her son and small entourage down the street to the temple. It was an old, square building of large clay brick and mortar, with ceramic shingles painted red. Two crude statues stood ready to strike any enemies on either side of the main entrance, and they glared out into the street. The wooden doors were left open, but they found the temple deserted. Then Paul emerged from a shadow and surprised them. "We are almost safe," he said.

A big peasant came in and said, "I believe the rear of the temple is unwatched. Please follow us."

"Perhaps we would be safer if we stay with our bodyguards and troops," said the young Prince Ánh apprehensively.

"Shush," ordered his mother sharply. "Proceed, gentlemen."

Pierre and Paul took them out a back door into an alley, and straight into the jungle. Before he turned to religion, and hunting men's souls, Paul Nghi had learned to hunt and forage and to find his way in the jungle. The trees grew tall and it was very dark in the shade of their bushy tops. Somewhere high overhead danced sunlight and butterflies, but down by the twisted trunks and the tangle of liana vines, snakes slithered and toads jumped from underfoot, while giant beetles scurried about and mosquitoes preyed on warm-blooded animals.

About an hour into the thick foliage, Pierre asked them all to strip off their valuable clothes and jewelry and put on the work clothes from Paul's basket. The party changed. They removed the jewelry and royal clothing, which they handed over to be meticulously concealed at the bottom of travel baskets under fake bottoms, since their detection would mean death, and they put on the old clothes. Pierre and Paul passed out balls of cold sticky rice and almonds wrapped in bamboo leaves.

At a brook the big peasant bid the ladies to wash off their makeup, and for all to smear their faces with wet mud. Then they used dirt to dry and powder their exposed skin. In this manner they hid their clear soft complexions and came to look almost like farmers. Their embroidered silk slippers still gave them away. To Pierre's careful scrutiny, they looked like wealthy amateur actors in an opera impersonating peasants.

Pierre looked closely at the boy Ánh, soon perhaps the surviving heir to the Nguyễn throne. This boy might change the outcome of the war and the success of the Church. Ánh was an awkward, unassuming boy of fifteen. He had high cheekbones, a long nose, wide-set eyes, and a small chin. Although he had the black hair and dark brown eyes of most of his people, he also had a smooth complexion. Pierre noticed that the boy was sluggish and depressed.

Since he wasn't eating, Pierre held a rice cube in a banana leaf out to the prince. The boy shook his head, indicating he wasn't hungry. Pierre thought, *This young boy prince needs to be cheered up.* He turned to Paul and said, "Isn't it time we formally introduced ourselves to our royal guests?" Paul nodded. They both approached the downcast prince and his mother in their peasant smocks. Pierre and Paul went down onto their knees. Pierre took off his hat. The royal party was shocked to see his brown hair, and learn that the big peasant guide was the barbarian priest they sought.

"Your highnesses," Pierre said, "please allow us to introduce ourselves. My companion and our guide is Mister Paul Nghi, currently of the Christian Seminary in Kao Giang, and I am Father Pierre Pigneau de Béhaine, the Bishop of Adran and Vicar Apostolic of Cochinchina, and a representative of his Majesty King Louis the XVI, the King of France." With that, the two men kowtowed carefully, heads to the earth, the correct three times. The prince, his mouth open, amazed at this peculiar spectacle of proper protocol in the middle of the jungle from a Western barbarian ambassador, dressed in sackcloth no less, was distracted from his misery and smiled. Here was correct homage from a barbarian priest to a disenfranchised prince in rags and powdered with dirt. It was a miracle—a small one perhaps, but still, unbelievable. If this could happen, Prince Ánh suddenly sensed, then almost anything could happen.

My life is not over yet, Ánh realized. He immediately became curious about these Western Ocean Christians, and his chances now of survival seemed significantly greater.

❧   ❦

Clouds had covered the sun. Paul confessed quietly to Pierre, "I am confused as to which way is which." Pierre handed him his small pocket compass. Paul smiled, and continued to lead the group to the west toward Kao Giang and the Cambodian border. They marched along in silence, as ordered by Pierre. Everyone was left alone with his or her own thoughts.

Prince Ánh's hopes had revived. He wanted to know immediately just how far he could trust this barbarian priest. The great potter's wheel had turned, and as chance would have it, these two leaders of different generations and different civilizations were left with a momentous decision, whether to become allies or not. Perhaps the decision was already made, and not by him, but by the Gods.

I need all the help I can get, Ánh thought. *I have little choice but to incur a debt of gratitude to this barbarian priest for my life. But I have done so only out of necessity, for their beliefs I have heard from my teachers are irreverent, even immoral and subversive. Did not their highest priest declare that the Cult of the Ancestors was a blasphemy? Oh Mighty Heaven and Earth, forgive me for my weakness, for needing these crucifixion worshippers from across the Western Ocean. My guardian spirits protect me.*

Pierre contemplated his new relationship and thought in prayer as well on the long hike through the jungle. *God Almighty,* he thought, *creator of all that is seen and unseen, creator of this spectacular jungle—help me to do what is right to serve thy greater purpose. What is the way to best serve thee? Should we harbor this young enemy of the new state or turn away from him, and hope somehow to win the confidence of the new dynasty, these Tây Sơn rebels? But aren't the Tây Sơn lawbreakers and usurpers of the general order? What would the cardinals of Rome say if I intentionally aided a peasant rebellion? Wouldn't they castigate me? Peasant rebellions are anathema in Rome. And won't the Church be safer in the long run of history supported by one of the great feudal families? Didn't Diệu Tri explain that these Nguyễn have a historical, legal, and spiritual claim to the throne?*

Picking the winning side is only part of the game; leading all sides to the love of Christ, that is the ultimate goal. An ally and a market for France are also important. Could the side that adopts the one true faith then lose the war? I fear, from experience and history, that immediate success is not guaranteed. But could the side of God really lose? Some battles, yes, but not the war. God's will remains always a mystery. But for the glory of the Church of France, don't the possible benefits outweigh the risks in this case?

What am I doing here? I am throwing the weight of the Church behind a powerless princeling, and possibly earning forever the wrath of the new Tây Sơn Dynasty. Are they a dynasty? Yes ... haven't they conquered the center, and now the south. The mighty Nguyễn are crushed. Or are they? Remember the dream of Pierre Poivre, and the writing of the great Dupleix. Both men saw that France has a role to play in the Far East. Both argued that the time had arrived to plant the flag of Mother France, and to build a church for the redemption of the heathen hordes, that Frenchmen and Christians should act boldly, even ruthlessly to guarantee that the Eastern Church is a French Catholic Church, and that the markets of East Asia become French markets.

The Church should look to France to save the East from an English Protestant swamp of godlessness and moral ambiguity. French Catholics should plant, and build and grow. France is the rowan shield and the iron sword for our Pope in Saint Peter's Cathedral in the city of Rome. Without a strong France against heretic enemies like the English, the Dutch, and the German Lutherans, the Roman Catholic Church will never be safe. Didn't Dupleix write that good French Catholics should not be overly constrained by a largely Italian and decadent papal court? Oh Jesus, who died for our sins and forgave us, forgive me if any innocents should be hurt while I endeavor to work and carry out the burden of service to you.

๛ ๙

They had started early in the day, so before nightfall they reached the mission at Kao Giang, even without the aid of road or path. Unfortunately, they'd had to traverse several large swamps. The royal beaded silk slippers no longer gave them away.

Wet up to the armpits and infested with leeches, Pierre and Paul brought their distinguished and royal guests into Father Pierre's Christian compound. Pierre showed them an empty hut with straw mat beds that they could use for the night, and invited them to join him for dinner in an hour. John Ngô showed them to the outhouse latrines and to a brook for washing. Paul Nghi found them a change of dry clothes.

Pierre and Paul also washed and changed. They were tired but confused—excited but sobered by the sheer audacity of their actions. The Tây Sơn brothers were expected to become the undisputed rulers of half the country, and they, a French priest and his Việt acolyte, were protecting this young Nguyễn prince, a direct male descendent of the Nguyễn kings. Their lives and works were forfeit if they were caught in such an act of treason to the new regime.

๛ ๙

In the morning Paul Nghi returned from the next village. One of his brothers was a river pilot who owned a flat-bottomed sampan on the Hậu Giang River. Paul's brother had agreed to convey the royal refugees down the river and along the coast to Hà Tiên for a triple fee.

Pierre kept the royal presence a secret from most of his students. The risks of a leak were simply too great. He did inform his three senior acolytes. These Việt students were exited. News had already reached the mission that the Tây Sơn had massacred the last of the Nguyễn at Long Xuyên. Over half of the troops had fled into the jungle in order to save themselves. The hundreds, who stayed and fought to the last man, would be venerated by all Việts for their courage and exemplary sacrifice to one of the most sacred of all filial obligations, duty to one's king. Their bravery and loyalty would be honored in poems, paintings, and songs.

The arrival of a Nguyễn prince, these three senior acolytes believed, was a small miracle that just added more proof that there was a Christian God, and that

Jesus had brought the dead to life, that he had risen from the dead, and ascended into heaven. Indeed, they treated the royal prince as if he were the next Messiah, which meant they viewed Father Pierre as a reincarnation of Elijah or John the Baptist.

The young prince called Father Pierre and these senior members of the mission together for a royal audience. Already Prince Ánh's spirits had revived. He even showed signs of being a shrewd, or at least a budding, leader. He accepted the kow-tows of the acolytes, their knees and heads pressed into the grass. Ánh said, "A time will come when I will not be powerless and unarmed, and dressed in sackcloth; and for saving my life and allowing my family line to fight on, you have my life-long gratitude. Hopefully, as your future king, I will always remember the service of the Christians at Kao Giang. Let the scribes and my royal Ancestors record that as long as the line of Phúc Luân survives, the Christians of Kao Giang will be remembered as faithful and loyal subjects."

He's amazingly self-possessed for a fifteen-year-old, Pierre thought, a little surprised. The royal refugees returned to their thatch hut, signaling that the audience was over.

❧ ❦

Ánh missed his teachers—strong males to talk to about his situation.

So, Ánh thought, adjusting and feeling again his cheap flaxen tunic, *I've been saved by one of those long-nosed barbarians who worships nailing people to a cross of timbers, of all things. Their head sorcerer condemned the Cult of the Ancestors—dragon's wind, what impudence. I studied the Classics with Nguyễn Binh Loan, who warned me that the Christians want to destroy us through the most insidious of devices. Loan liked to say, "If the people don't worship the ancestral father of each family and act with filial piety and obey the rites, why should they obey their king, or be loyal to your heavenly authority?"*

Master Loan also said, "How could society have order and harmony without all the rules of harmonious relationships as established since the beginning of time by the worship of the Ancestors? Who dares to challenge the perfect logic of the ethics of filial piety? What could be more natural and logical than to show respect for one's own parents, who gave each of us the miracle of life?"

Ánh wondered what had happened to his teacher, Nguyễn Binh Loan. Was he murdered by the Tây Sơn rebels, or did he escape abroad, or shave his head and enter a monastery?

Ánh resumed his meditation. *All the forms of filial piety were prescribed in the writing of Confucius. That is why we memorize his wisdom. His observations are like lights in the darkness. I can still recite from his Analects: Chapter One, Number Two applies to these Christians. "The sons and daughters who are fond of offending their superiors are indeed few. Those who bring confusion to our midst always begin by being fond of offending their superiors." And, "It is filial duty and frater-nal duty that are fundamental to manhood-at-its-best." As my teacher liked to say, the observations of Confucius have withstood the test of time. What could be more sacred than family ties? What could be more useful for protecting national unity than a strong central authority?*

Ánh considered Pierre and his students. How did they fit into his dreams? He wasn't sure. But their aid was certainly a gift from Heaven. *Is it also a sign from Heaven, am I the chosen one?*

❧   ❧

An armed deserter in a blue shirt, looking for a meal, confirmed to Father Pierre that the Tây Sơn troops under Hồ Nhạc and Huệ had annihilated the remnants of the Nguyễn force. And to add insult to injury, they had captured King Nguyễn Đình alive and were transporting him back to Sài Gòn for a ceremonious beheading.

Later that day, Pierre went into his chapel barn with Paul Nghi to further confer and possibly pray. "King Nguyễn Đình was a terrible ruler," Pierre started. "I have seen the hardships his people have suffered. Will the Tây Sơn prove to be any better?"

"Most unlikely," said Paul. "The reports, as you know, are that they are just as brutal and arbitrary. The best hope for creating a Christian kingdom here is for the Church to support someone who has a legitimate claim to the throne, but especially who is still young enough to learn new ideas. Someone whom we might even convert to the faith and so bring all his people to salvation."

"I quite agree," said Pierre.

Paul asked, "Do we dare make war to stop war? Will the Lord be merciful against a breach of his holy commandment, thou shalt not kill? Wasn't his first commandment, thou shalt have no other gods but me? Was the delivery of the young prince a sign, or was it an accident?"

Pierre responded, "Could it have been purely accidental that this Nguyễn prince was delivered into our care? I believe there are no pure accidents, so this turn of events might be an opportunity presented by the Lord. Hellfire and brimstone, all we lack is certainty. Therefore, I choose to take the appearance of this boy as a sign of God's will."

It is confusing," said Paul. "Won't this young prince plunge an already war-torn and devastated country back into years of more bloodshed and misery?"

Pierre replied, "Yet isn't there also the possibility that he will hear the word of the Lord and respond to it, now that I have his ear?"

"Another war means thousands more will die and perish in horrible deaths."

"That is unfortunately true," said Pierre, "but they are condemned to eternal suffering in hell without the succor of the holy sacraments. Ergo, even by increasing the bloodshed now, even by throwing the country back into another round of civil war, don't we act from a deeper compassion and a deeper understanding?"

"It is painful," said Paul. "But we might bring these people, in the next generation, or the next, into the everlasting light of heavenly peace."

"Amen," said Pierre. "Let us pray: Oh Lord, forgive us, for we are sinners, but we humbly serve thy cause and worship you through the work of thy Church, and we seek guidance in applying your word to our work. In the name of the Father, the Son, and the Holy Ghost,"

"Amen," they both intoned.

☙   ❧

That afternoon, Father Pierre and Paul Nghi found Prince Ánh and Lady Purity sitting on reed mats outside their assigned hut in the shade of a banyan tree. Pierre bowed deeply to the royal refugees. Lady Purity nodded with polite condescension, while Prince Ánh returned the bow. Pierre said in his excellent Vietnamese, "I'm sorry to be the bearer of bad news, but I'm afraid that King Đình and all his company are lost to the rebels."

"Please sit with us if you would," the young prince said with a twinkle in his eyes.

Then squatting, he duck-walked on his knees and ankles, imitating a *Qinna* wrestler's warmup. He glided over to his mother and gave her a kiss. He recited a line from a famous novel, *"Lạ gì bỉ sắc tư phong? Trời xanh quen thói má hồng đánh ghen."* ("Is it so strange that losses balance gains? Blue Heaven's wont to strike a rose from spite.")

Purity laughed, and so did Prince Ánh. Pierre was not particularly surprised, but it was awkward, so he said, "I take it that you were not inordinately close to your uncle, the king?"

The young prince answered, "Đình was a despicable coward. My father, the peerless Phúc Luân, was the eldest son of King Nguyễn Vo. In his old age, King Vo developed a fondness for his fifth wife, a beautiful and ambitious singing girl. She convinced him on his deathbed to proclaim her son, Little Đình, his heir. The entire court, including of course my mother and her friends, were scandalized. The timing, not to mention the choice, was totally improper and without precedent or merit. As soon as the king died, Little Đình, on his sweet mother's advice, put my father and mother and their servants under house arrest. My parents were locked into their separate compartments by the late king's bodyguard. In the morning, servants found my father's body cold ... from poison. The coroner—under the threat of torture, we have heard from a good source—announced it was a suicide."

Lady Purity had carefully watched her son through this discourse. Now she added, with a tone of bitterness, "I loved that man, Nguyễn Phúc Luân. Thus ended the life of a brave warrior, a great leader and poet, and a wonderful husband, and that is how began the rule of a tyrant and a profligate." Purity shuddered with hatred.

Ánh added with emotion, "Heaven has sent the Tây Sơn rebels as a scourge to punish my uncle for his fratricide, and to punish all those who bowed to his dishonorable usurpation. If Heaven will only help me now, we will right all wrongs." The boy then moved from cross-legged to kneeling, and spun around. He kowtowed deeply to the old banyan tree, touching his head to the earth. He repeated the kow-tow three times, as in a prayer to Heaven.

Purity smiled adoringly at her son. "You're right, my son, that Heaven is supporting the Tây Sơn today. But that in no way diminishes the validity of your hereditary claim to the throne of your country. Just as Heaven has helped you avenge your beloved father, Heaven will help you gain your rightful patrimony."

Father Pierre was smiling and thought, *Maybe they do believe in the one true God and but just don't realize it yet.*

Paul Nghi approached with a deep bow. "Your majesties," he said, "the boat is provisioned and ready for boarding. Father Pierre and I advise that you leave now, for we expect your enemies to search quite thoroughly for you."

"Are you sure this boatman is to be trusted?" asked the young prince.

"Hush, beggars should not be demanding guests," reprimanded his mother. "Thank you, sir, for you are taking risks for our protection. Our bags will eventually be packed and ready to go." Everyone laughed. Their luggage was ready, consisting of two half-filled sacks of royal travel garments gathered after disrobing.

Chapter 13
Vũ Chan, Madame Camellia, and the Jade Emperor
1777

When Madame Camellia had discovered that her man Scholar Mã had violated Jade River, the madam wanted to kill her lover, but instead, she had whipped Jade River. The unfortunate girl had stabbed herself. The wound was not fatal, but during the following year Madame Camellia did not require that Jade River have conjugal relations with her customers, so concerned was the Madame that Jade River would try again to kill herself. During this time Jade River entertained customers with her singing and playing of the lute. She was nevertheless sought after and hired for her musical talent and beauty alone.

One night, while she was playing and singing during a dinner party of businessmen and painted ladies, a handsome man introduced himself as Vũ Chan. He was attentive and kept returning every few nights. Mr. Vũ kept reappearing at events, and whenever they spoke together, Jade River was impressed by his earnest sincerity, and by the feelings expressed in the love poems he handed her with his tips of money. One night, Mr. Vũ Chan handed her some coins with a small note underneath them.

When she was alone in her room she opened the note. It read: *Miss Jade River, I salute you. I beg you to allow me to call you my darling. You deserve so much more than this life under the madam. I am guided by my heart. Elope with me, and I will make you a happy, wealthy, and respectable wife. With love and admiration, Vũ Chan.*

After a few more visits, she wrote him a desperate letter, which said: *I am a helpless water fern caught in the current of a river. It has been my misfortune to fall into this nest of birds of pleasure and mirth. Is it possible that you can restore me to my family and freedom? I believe my family could reward you with jade and silver. I am a virtuous woman of a good family, fallen into the hands of Scholar Mã and Madame Camellia through their subterfuge and deceit. If you are a man of honor, please help me to escape.*

At the next dinner party Mr. Vũ Chan attended, he handed her another tip with a small note underneath. Jade River excused herself to visit the ladies outhouse and water closet. She went to her bedroom. In privacy she read the note. It said: *My sweet young woman, I am no ordinary man, and you have called to the right person. Since you honor me with your confidence, I'll make it a point of honor to rescue you from your servitude.*

Here is my plan: You should escape with me tomorrow morning at the start of the hours of the Snake. Meet me by the copse of trees beyond the front courtyard, and I will have two horses for our escape. Your devoted servant, Vũ Chan.

Jade River studied this note. She thought to herself, *I must try this escape, though I do not know if I can trust this man. He appears trustworthy. Perhaps I will even be able to return to my family and find Lương Hoàng. Is Hoàng waiting for me to escape? This man Vũ appears to be a gentleman.*

Jade River picked up a brush and dipped it into the ink jar. She wrote: *Yes I will,* on a new piece of paper. She checked her makeup as expected with her hand mirror, and returned to the dinner to resume her lute playing and singing. Again Vũ Chan approached her with some coins, and while his body blocked the view of the other guests, she handed him her note with a smile of hope. He glanced down and said, smiling with excitement, "I would like to visit you again in a few days." .

܀   ܁

In the morning at nine a.m., she found Vũ Chan with his horses in the copse of trees. They bowed to each other, and with his help, she mounted the second horse. They rode down the road. Jade River could not believe her good fortune. She breathed deeply of the fresh air. Then someone stepped into the road, recognized her, and started yelling and raising an alarm.

Mr. Vũ led their horses down the road and into a forest on an old cart track. When he raced ahead, riding until he was out of sight, Jade River realized his behavior was unexpected—and suspicious. As she tried to find him on the cart road she was apprehended by a small posse of horse riders led by Scholar Mã. Mã led Jade River back to the Happy Valley Green Pavilion, and presented her to Madame Camellia, who said, "Trying to run off, you little bitch, I'll teach this slave who is her legal owner," and proceeded to whip Jade River till the blood ran freely from her back and thighs.

"Stop!" Jade River cried. "I do not want to die this way. I am worth more to you alive than dead. I was a fool to trust that con man. I will consent to kiss your customers, and learn to live with the shame of your trade."

"Now there is a sensible young girl," crowed Madame Camellia triumphantly, clutching her whip to her bosom like a dear friend. She turned to her attending slave, Fourth Daughter, and said, "Help this slave to clean up," and walked out.

Soon after, Jade River learned from her coworkers that Vũ Chan usually charged thirty silver *liang* or embossed coins for his contrived rescues, which always failed. He had trapped numerous other women before in the same way. It was a useful and common trick to help manage the more uppity slave girls.

A week later Vũ Chan came to the brothel and accosted Jade River in the public waiting room, "I hear that you claim I mislead you. You are a lying whore. I have come to teach you a lesson," and he pulled a whip out of his satchel.

"Don't you dare accuse me," Jade River answered in a firm voice. "I have all of your love poems, and I have the letters you wrote begging me to elope with you. I will prove in court that you broke the law." Mr. Vũ stopped short. He could tell from her hard, calm voice that Jade River was fearless and surprisingly knowledgeable for a girl. He looked around at the other girls and customers in the room, and they all stared at him in silent disgust. Without even raising his whip, he turned and walked out. He knew, and apparently she knew, that the local magistrate didn't take small bribes.

❧ ❧

The famous beauty who made such moving music was tutored by Madame Camellia in the arts of love. "Men are so simple," Camellia said smiling, "at least most of them are easily pleased. You only need a few tricks and techniques to make them pay for you over and over again. It is time for you to learn your new trade and become a professional. Supported by your music and poetry, you will be a sensation in the bed. Relax honey, let yourself enjoy it while you still have your looks."

Madame Camellia spoke the truth. The madam had allowed Jade River to just sing for two years for a reason. She auctioned off the first night rights to the famous virgin Jade River for fifty taels of silver. That she was no longer a virgin was no obstacle. The madam had one of her girls show Jade River how to fake both the pain and the stain: first a shriek of surprise, then a surreptitious squeeze of a bloody sponge.

Soon, Jade River had a new schedule, saying goodbye to one man in the morning, and greeting another man in the evening. Her jade was very expensive, which added to her desirability, for those who could afford it.

Jade River was often kept up late, but she was allowed to sleep in. She discovered, to some embarrassment, that she liked sex. Her ability to play and sing with great emotion improved. Throughout this shameful time she tried to avoid thoughts of Lương Hoàng; she believed that she no longer deserved his love. She convinced herself that she never wanted to see him again. Jade River no longer thought she should escape—in her shame, she banished the thought.

❧ ❧

The mountain tribes of the Central Highlands were of Cham, Mon-Khmer, and Malayo-Polynesian extraction. The main tribes of An Khê, the Gia Rai and Ê Đê, were resistant to Hồ Nhạc's entreaties that they join his fighters to defeat the Nguyễn. One day before his brothers, Nhạc said to their teacher, Trương Văn Hiến, "What can I do to win over these highlanders? They are great fighters. They control the mountain road to Pleiku, and their head man has said he would rather kill us than be coerced into supporting us." Scholar Trương Văn Hiến, dressed in rich silks covered in colored embroidery, pulled on his long gray chin whiskers as he contemplated the Gia Rai and Ê Đê—sturdy, brave, and dangerous but illiterate mountain people.

Trương Văn Hiến said, "There are several ways. The peasants have many strong beliefs. They expect their leaders to be descended from one of the great families. It is time for you all to change your name to Nguyễn, which will make you more plausible, and confuse the many real Nguyễn factions. This will give you credibility and invite new alliances.

"Furthermore, these highlanders are Taoists, they worship everything that moves or is stationary. But at the pinnacle of their Gods is the Jade Emperor of Heaven, a very popular deity introduced long ago by Chinese colonists."

Lữ said, "I've been to several of these Taoist temples. They are crowded with life-size papier-mâché statues, and the incense is so thick you can barely breathe."

Huệ laughed, "Maybe we should approach the Jade Emperor of Heaven, and ask him for his help in this endeavor?"

Trương Văn Hiến smiled, "We can't visit the Jade Emperor of Heaven, but we can arrange to have the Jade Emperor send us an official endorsement. We need to receive one of his famous celestial tablets of bronze. Let me explain how this could work. ..."

&⁊ ⁊&

A week later Nhạc, Lữ and Huệ went back up into the mountains to An Khê to pay their respects again at the food and wine stalls, during the evening of one of the region's many Taoist festivals. That day the festival celebrated the Jade Emperor of Heaven, and Kim Hua, the Goddess of Fertility. Men and women together found much to celebrate.

During the evening festivities in An Khê, there was a sudden eruption of fireworks from one of the mountaintops overlooking the town. Silence fell on all the revelers, as they gawked in delighted surprise at the unexpected fireworks display from high above. After the fireworks display finished, an orchestra of gongs and drums could be heard playing up on the hilltop, while a bonfire could be seen roaring, its flame blazing into the sky. Nhạc, Lữ, and Huệ were surprised and amazed, and they challenged each other and the townspeople around them to go with them to investigate these mysterious signs. A large group of townspeople followed the three brothers up the path to the top of the hill. Before the villagers could find the mysterious musicians or see the orchestra, they were met by a wizened old man in a high mandarin's official silk robes, who called out, "Nguyễn Nhạc, Nguyễn Nhạc, where are you?"

"I am here," said Hồ Nhạc, stepping bravely forward. "What do you want, your eminence?"

The wizened old man, wearing a black beaded skullcap, pulled out of the large sleeve of his silk robe a bronze tablet, which he held aloft with both hands, indicating that this tablet was inscribed with the word of a God. He reverently lowered the tablet, while villagers and townsfolk stood in silent apprehension. The old man turned over the tablet and read its message in a stentorian voice. "The Jade Emperor orders Nguyễn Nhạc to serve as the country's emperor." Then the old mandarin bowed to Nhạc and presented the tablet to him. The old mandarin fell to his knees and knocked his head to the earth five times, rose to his feet, and then walked solemnly into the dark forest, where he was swallowed up by the night. So impressive was this display that not a single villager dared to follow him.

Nhạc carefully read aloud the inscription on the tablet: "The Jade Emperor orders Nguyễn Nhạc to serve as the country's emperor"—exactly what the old mandarin had read—and then showed the tablet to the assembled crowd.

Nguyễn Lữ and Nguyễn Huệ, after being the last of the crowd to read the tablet for themselves, to see if it was true, bowed deeply to Nguyễn Nhạc, and the villagers followed their example, and all the crowd bowed deeply to Nguyễn Nhạc. Lữ and Huệ kept bowing, with their hands pressed together at their foreheads, till they had bowed five times, while the crowd followed suit. The younger brothers, sensing the crowd was with them, fell to their knees and kowtowed three times, and all the villagers followed, and knocked their heads to the earth three times to Nguyễn Nhạc.

Nhạc, full of emotion, bowed back to the crowd, and then fell to his own knees, and kowtowed with three head knocks to the people of An Khê. He then led them all in a processional down the hill, so they could bring the good news of their miracle to the rest of the town and to the other villages and tribes of the Central Highlands.

Going down the other side of the mountain were Snake, Midget, Night Hawk, and Lover Boy, with other members of the inner ring of Tây Sơn fighters, who had made up the mysterious orchestra of gongs and drums and produced the pyrotechnics. Walking with the musicians was the wizened old mandarin, none other than Scholar Trương Văn Hiến, still in heavy stage makeup to make him unrecognizable even to his friends.

The outcome of that evening's excitement and magic was that the elders of the town of An Khê decided within days to send tribute and fifty fighters with weapons to Nguyễn Nhạc, and they declared their allegiance to his martial ambitions. The Gia Rai and Ê Đê of An Khê would follow the anointed one.

Chapter 14
Chesapeake Bay
1781 (four years later)

In the light cast by a nautical oil lamp in the junior officers' cabin, one could barely see Lieutenant Benoit Grannier's features. In the dark one could mostly discern that he had a long, straight nose, and his clean-shaven jaw made him look younger than his twenty-five years. His red-brown hair was thick and curly, worn long and tied behind in a queue. Life at sea was hard work, and the aristocratic blood of his father had allowed him to become a lieutenant in the class-conscious French Navy.

Benoit closed the leatherbound volume of *Universal History* and placed it on his bunk. "Shades of Sebastian," he said to his bunkmate, Lieutenant Etienne Lalois, "Voltaire is either a great intellect, or a disciple of Satan. He wants us to study not only science, but especially English science, and tolerate all types of Protestants, and Muslims, and even idol worshipers. He goes even farther than Father Sebastian at Saint Matthew's."

Etienne smiled. "Sometimes books are like that; they make life richer and deeper, but more complicated."

"Voltaire writes, '*Ecrasez l'infame!*' (Crush the infamy!) And he isn't referring to Protestants or revolutionaries, but to Catholic bigots and purveyors of intolerance and superstition. And not to beat around the bush, he specifically mentions the Church! He attacks it as a dangerous force against intellectual and moral freedom. Does he have a good point, or is he a heretic bound for one of the nine rings of Hell?"

"Only a problem if you are a true believer," said Etienne. "Aren't we all candidates for Dante's Inferno? To which ring of Hell do you think he belongs?"

"The first or second, Limbo or Lust," replied Benoit. "Maybe these are the ideas which gave cause for Father Sebastian to joke that Voltaire was a mad Quaker? Old bald-pate Sebastian was obviously fond of Voltaire. He wanted us all to understand Voltaire's critique of the Catholic Church. To keep his position at the abbey, the old man swore all the boys in the room to secrecy, and he promised we would all burn in Hell if we ever reported that he taught from Voltaire's works."

Etienne asked, "Was he silly headed with fear, or did he tell you things that were, you know, really heretical?"

"Father Sebastian was probably in more danger than we were. There was the day he told me about the dark side of the Inquisition. Innocent people were tortured and killed. I felt honored that he would confide in me his critical thoughts. He insisted that it had been a terrible blight on the record of the Church. Old Sebastian was a fine instructor, though short of breath and slowing down. He awoke my skepticism towards the Church as an institution with his denunciations of its transgressions. Yet he supported the good works of the Church with real pride."

"So he did he hate the Church or not?"

"No he didn't," said Benoit. "Sebastian was complicated. The sarcastic and bitter edge to his wit and innuendo mystified me for a long time, till one day I learned from my cousin that bald-pate was discreetly having an affair with one of the other monks teaching at the school. He was a sodomite, leading a double life—which explained some of his odd behavior. This insight gave new meaning to Sebastian's frequent exclamation, 'God forgive us, for we are all sinners!' So maybe he's headed for the third level of ring seven.

"He also liked to say, 'Temper the insights of the Bible with secular works' after each foray into literature. So Sebastian was not so far away from Voltaire. But how do you decide what is divinely inspired and what is the work of the devil?"

"Beats me, mate," said Etienne. "Maybe you'll have to stow this stuff deep in the hold. We're on watch soon. I'll see you on deck, unless you are struck down by God or the Church before you get there." And he left the cabin.

Benoit pondered this and stared out into the little space where he and three other officers lived on board the *Ville de Paris*.

Benoit picked up his Bible and took an old letter from the inside of the jacket to read it again. It was from his cousin Antoine, who was serving God and having an adventure as a missionary on the other side of the earth in East Asia, in a place called Cochinchina. Antoine's mother had sent the letter to Benoit. It read:

September 4, 1778

Kao Giang, Cochinchina, Đại Việt

Dear Mama and Papa, Benoit, and all my beloved family:

Only one more month of this heat and then, God willing, the monsoon wind will make its semi-annual about-face. The Mission in Kao Giang is doing well enough, in spite of the Bishop Pierre Pigneau's frequent absences. Father Pierre keeps taking his three armed galleys in Hà Tiên to Sài Gòn to work a most complicated task. He is trying to convert Prince Nguyễn Ánh, his former student, to Christianity.

Meanwhile, Pierre is also continuing as tutor to the prince in European military science, a subject in which the bishop is surprisingly knowledgeable, reminiscent of Cardinal Richelieu. It seems to me that the prince's real interest in us is limited to military and scientific matters. Sometimes I wonder about the bishop's main interest as well. He seems to know the books of war as well as the books of the Gospel.

I study the Vietnamese language, but it is hard and it humbles me. Here at this mission, we have forty-one men enrolled, and twenty-six have already embraced the One True Faith. It is a constant joy to see the hope and gratitude in their eyes, as they explore the Good Book in Vietnamese. When we teach them to read Quốc ngữ, the new Vietnamese script in Roman letters, they are overjoyed at their new skill and the power it gives them. Half of them are reading pages of the Good Book now in Latin as well.

I cannot lie that there are hardships. There is too often a scarcity of food, since our taxes were raised and must be paid in rice, which we work so hard to grow. We have very few books for ourselves and our students. I remain anxious for our security, especially when Father Pierre is gone with all his Việt sailors and most of the Việt military guards assigned to him by the king, Nguyễn Ánh. Who knows if we can trust his soldiers, anyway? We are almost helpless should pirates or any of the various bands of marauders find us so poorly defended. I have no faith in the mandarin of this district. He communicates with Nguyễn Ánh, but people report that he has also sworn allegiance to the Tây Sơn government.

Our daily discomforts are actually minor when compared to the suffering of many of our neighbors, the peasants who live in and around Hà Tiên and Kao Giang. The poor here are as beaten down and unprotected as they are in France, and without the relief of the salvation offered by Christ, or the succor offered by his best followers. So you can imagine how important we feel, even when so far away from loved ones and all of the amenities of a great market town in France. It usually raises my spirits to be a light in the darkness.

I send my heartfelt prayers to you all. I also pray that the day will arrive shortly when I see French warships regularly patrolling the coast of this lush and beautiful country, bringing peace and prosperity to its new lambs of God. Many thanks, Benoit, for the money you sent. You are generous and not as dumb as you look. We have used your funds to support the programs of our mission, and a man in your profession can use friends in high holy places.

My love to you all.

Yours truly in the joy of Jesus Christ,

Antoine

Benoit carefully folded the letter and replaced it in his Bible. He lay on his bunk and thought about what he had read. A boy's voice came through the thin bulwark, "Fifteen minutes to eight bells." Pulled from his reverie, Benoit stored his well-worn volume of Voltaire and his Bible in a battered leather case. The case housed books with the voices of writers who were often his most articulate and thoughtful friends. He found his sea boots and jacket, and went from the officers' cabin on the middle gun-deck up two steep sets of stairs, through the rank smell of old sweat mixed with tar, pitch, and gunpowder, to the main deck and the fresh air. He had plenty of time still to relieve himself off the bowsprit head before he began his watch.

The French sailor in the crow's nest called out, "Sail to the northeast." Benoit Grannier cast his eyes out against the expanse of gray ocean. He stared beyond the headlands of Chesapeake Bay. With a spyglass he saw the ship, a French frigate, flying into the entrance of Lynnhaven Roads, where the French fleet, twenty-four great ships of the line, rested like huge nesting birds of prey.

The signal flags of the frigate drew the attention of all the commanders of ships near the outside of the fleet. Benoit handed Captain Albert Cresp de Sainte-Césaire his spyglass right in front of the Rear Admiral Le Compte François Joseph de Grasse. De Grasse was short and overweight with a thick white wig, his face tanned by a life at sea. Captain Albert Cresp was much younger and lean. He focused the glass till he could make out the signal flags, which read, "Enemy Fleet, Three Leagues, Battle Stations."

"*Sainte Marie de la mer*," the captain swore, "we could get trapped in the bay. We should slip anchors," he said to the admiral, who nodded. "Lieutenant Lalois, signal the fleet: 'Slip Anchors, Battle Stations. End of Message.' Bosun, sound the tocsin. All hands to make sail or battle stations," he cried.

The bosun blew his shrill whistle. A young midshipman began to beat a drum—the call to quarters. Another rang the large ship's bell. Benoit looked about, thinking, *Hopefully, action at last. Since I was a child, I've wanted to fight the English. My chance has finally come. God's blood, let us out of this harbor.* He looked at the lush green forests that came right up to the white sandy beaches of Maryland. *Such a beautiful country, but not if our ships get caught before they can move off from the rocky shore.*

The beating to quarters was hard to miss. Sublieutenant Guillaume de Martineau tamped out his pipe. Gunner Louis Boulanger rolled out of his hammock and pulled on his pants. The off watch stowed their hammocks, which swung above their guns, and made room for the rammer, the sponge screw, and the handspikes, next to the low racks of shot.

Six hundred men hustled as one busy but coordinated machine, to transform de Grasse's mammoth flagship, the 100-gun *Ville de Paris*, into its fighting trim. Sailors scurried up the ratlines to the topmasts. This was not a drill, as in the weary months before. Suddenly their lives depended on their speed and efficiency in changing the ship. All their training was preparation for this discipline of working and fighting together. The sailors climbed out on the foot ropes under each yardarm, and tore off the furling lines. The great canvas sails fell one by one, while sailors on deck heaved braces to backwind the yards and swing the bow off the wind. Lalois prepared the signal flags, ordering all captains to slip their anchor cables and beat to sea. Though it was hardly needed, the red and black "Depart in All Haste" flag sailed to the top of the admiral's mizzenmast amid the clatter and confusion.

Below decks, the gunners stashed their chess sets and playing cards and dice, preparing for battle. Luckily, there were not many whores servicing groups of men below decks that day. Sally Haymaker and her girlfriend Dockside Sue from

Lynnhaven were caught in the middle of the act of comforting the lonely, including Little Jacques, in hammocks on the second gun deck when the alarms began to ring. They charged three *derniers* for a poke, the cost of a few drinks, and ten *derniers*, or the cost of a few meals, for thirty minutes of their loving comfort.

Sally and Sue and their "husbands" quickly dressed. Sally borrowed duck pants and shirt and cap, so she could inconspicuously help out in the fight. The French were allies, weren't they? Sue made her way to the carpenter's room, where she knew that she'd be out of the way, and if there were casualties, she could be helpful to the surgeon in running the sick bay and operating room. These two were exceptional. All the other women took to the ever-present bumboats—small craft that carried passengers to and from land for a small fee.

The 100 gun *Ville de Paris* was but one of twenty-four French ships-of-the-line, each with between roughly 500 and 900 men living on board as crew. The floating city of ships awoke to the shouts of officers, sailors, gunners, and boys, all dashing to and fro hauling or carrying. The machines moved with the precision of giant clocks. Over thirty minutes the *Ville de Paris* and the other French ships metamorphosed into floating fortresses, cannons loaded and primed, as the English warships appeared and grew on the horizon.

Benoit identified men from his watch to see that they minded which crews they belonged on. His next job was to oversee the conversion of the captain's cabin to a gun room, and the launching of the longboats. He sent a group of his watch running to the hatchway to the captain's cabin, and he strode after them. *We can't afford any slip-ups now,* he thought.

With more than forty guns on each side, the *Ville de Paris* was capable of hurling over half a ton of cannonball, chain shot, and shrapnel in a single broadside—a fire-breathing dragon.

Benoit and sailors of the off watch dismantled the captain's cabin. The teak and mahogany walls were collapsed and carried below. The two sixteen-pounders were unlashed in his day cabin at the very stern of the ship. On deck, men lowered the longboats, some of which were laden with some of the admiral's and other officers' valuables, such as musical instruments, and the smaller livestock, such as lambs and piglets. Chicken coops were lowered over the side by rope. Sailors led bleating goats and sheep and squealing pigs to the side of the ship, roughly picked them up off their kicking legs, and unceremoniously threw them overboard. The screaming animals fell twenty-seven feet and plunged into the green water. Other sailors in the longboats then fished the stunned and terrified animals out of the chop. They set the longboats on cables to tow behind the ships, where they were usually safe from all but accidental cannon fire. Men tied buoy lines and buoys to the eighteen-inch-thick anchor cables made of hemp rope, and let them cascade into the water.

The forest of masts began to crack open canvas sails like popcorn. The canvas, forced open by the release of furling lines, the heaving of braces, and the hauling on halyards and clew garnets, and propelled by the wind, pushed the flotilla slowly backward and off the wind. The men swung the yards to catch the northwesterly breeze. The ships slowly reached toward the distant safety of the open sea.

Le Comte de Grasse had not expected the British fleet in the Chesapeake anywhere near so soon. He and General Washington were hoping to crush the British Army camped at Yorktown. De Grasse wondered in anger, *How did the British find out about our position so fast? Caught pissing with my pants down. I've dreaded making a mistake or bad luck like this all my life. Now my esteemed derriere is exposed. A mistake like this can ruin a good record—a record built over forty years, lost like water out the scuppers.*

∿ ∝

Rear Admiral Thomas Graves, of King George III's Royal Navy, was just as surprised to find an entire French fleet in Chesapeake Bay as the French were to see him. Graves had nineteen capitol ships. These ships-of-the-line each carried anywhere from 64 to 98 guns and, like the twenty-four French ships, were manned with anywhere from 500 to 900 men each to move and manipulate the big guns.

As Admiral Graves studied the French fleet before him, he felt the aching of his arthritis. No sailor wanted to make his men face a superior number of cannon. "God in heaven," he fumed to his lieutenant, "so unexpected! Where did all these ships come from? I was about to crush Washington once and for all."

The French fleet had sailed undetected across the Atlantic to a safe harbor in the West Indies. De Grasse had communicated through French Ambassador Anne-César de La Luzerne to Washington that he preferred to navigate the deep waters of the Chesapeake over the shallower waters of New York. A seasoned diplomat and strategist of the possible on a shoestring budget, Washington then decided to attack Cornwallis in Virginia with his entire force of 12,000, rather than Clinton in New York.

In Virginia, Washington finally had the chance that he had been waiting and lobbying for so patiently: a chance to use the ragtag Continental Army of the infant United States, in conjunction with an established, world-class navy, against the British.

Even as Captain Albert Cresp and Admiral de Grasse checked their escape route out of the bay on the ship's chart, they knew that the English fleet could bottle up the channel mouth, and with the wind behind them, they could hammer away at his ships while his ships barely had steerage off the rocky coast. It was a captain's nightmare to be caught on a lee shore.

Captain Albert Cresp turned to the admiral, with Benoit Grannier, who now stood by with the spyglass, waiting for the order to swing the yards, and said under his breath, all the while keeping a smile on his face, "If they press their advantage and attack us immediately, while we are against this coast close hauled and beating to open water, they can bottle the channel and rake us. They'll shoot up our deckmen and rigging before we can even turn a broadside." The admiral looked old as he squinted toward the menace in the distance. "This is bad. This will be close," he muttered as he studied the force of the wind on the water's surface. "What do you think, Albert?"

"It's close, sir, but they too have a light wind. We'll make it," the young captain answered. Benoit stood, listening in silence. His youthful face and his curly red-brown hair made a study of contrasts against the old admiral's wizened body and head of thick white wig hair. Benoit thought to himself, *I've waited since I was ten for a chance to battle the Brits. Off the wild coast of America is as good a place as any to try French gunners' powder and shot against pressed English farmhands.*

It is not so surprising that the untested Benoit Grannier did not fully appreciate that he and the whole French fleet were in grave danger, for the English admiral, Sir Thomas Graves, failed to see it as well.

The British were outnumbered, but they had many tactical advantages. In addition to the element of surprise, they had the wind behind them and they had the French stuck on a lee shore with the tide against them. Even worse, all the French ships were undermanned. What Graves did not know is that almost a quarter of the French crews, about 3,300 men, were ashore moving siege guns for Lafayette and Washington. The *Ville de Paris* was short 200 men. Some ships, like the 74-gun *Citoyen*, didn't have enough crew to man her upper deck guns.

Yet, almost inexplicably, Graves did not press his immediate and most critical advantage of position. Graves had firmly expected to find only a minor French fleet of eight ships under the command of Comte de Barras. Sir Thomas Graves also believed firmly in making war by the book. The book was a manual on tactics called *The Fighting Instructions*, written in 1653, 138 years earlier, under Oliver Cromwell. The official and now firmly traditional solution for organizing British fire power at sea was to line up the ships bow to stern, two cable lengths apart, and sail past the enemy's line.

Many battles had proven its effectiveness, and it was the established way that gentlemen fought one another at sea. Eighteen years earlier, during the Seven Years War against France, with this one tactic, the British Navy had destroyed much of the French Navy in a series of battles off the coasts of France and the colonies in the Americas, Africa, and Asia. Naval battles were deciding the political shape and religious outlook of the world. The English Admiral Edward Boscawen had captured Louisbourg at the mouth of the Saint Lawrence River. Boscawen, in a great sea battle off the coast of France that ended in Lagos Bay, managed to reduce Jean-Francois de la Clue-Sabran and the Toulon fleet just before it attacked England. Sir Edward Hawke then defeated the Brest fleet under the Comte de Conflans in the battle of Quiberon Bay. The English fleet blockaded the coast of France and managed to prevent France from relieving its surviving garrisons or from protecting its merchant trade around the world. Vice Admiral Thomas Pocock defeated Monsieur d'Ache and took Pondicherry in India. So Graves, with such precedents to respect, now expected to repeat history by "the book."

"Quite satisfactory," de Grasse said to Cresp. "The Limeys are waiting outside and forming into their expected line." And de Grasse walked toward his cabin. Captain Cresp handed the glass to Benoit, who noted how excited the captain had become. Benoit grinned boyishly and said, "This will be more exciting than a ball in Paris. But since they are going to wait outside for this little ballet, perhaps we should oblige them out there with a dance, a gavotte called *Un coup de pied dans ta gueule*" (a kick in your face).

"Like this?" said Lieutenant Etienne Lalois, and he attempted to execute the new dance step. Lalois pantomimed asking someone for a dance, started to waltz her around, then leapt up and kicked the imaginary partner in the head. Captain Cresp and Benoit both laughed. Their confidence was contagious; it lifted the spirits of the other men near the quarterdeck.

"All right my dancing master, we shall try not to keep them waiting long in the deep water," said the young captain, amused and annoyed by the clowning. "Check your weapons and your men. Make sure the weapons for boarding have been unlocked, no need to distribute."

Sir Thomas Graves's ships had furled all their mainsails and royals in anticipation of battle. They approached the bay using only their tops'ls. By the time Graves's nineteen ships, under such short sail and maintaining a perfect line formation, reached the mouth of the bay, all the twenty-four French ships were outside. The British came about sloppily, one ship at a time, the poor line losing its shape, and prepared for a proper engagement—that is, one between gentlemen and according to the rules of war. But the British were having signaling problems. Admirals Graves and Samuel Hood had different signaling systems, which had not been coordinated yet.

French tacticians had already plumbed the weakness of the "line ahead" strategy, and Admiral de Grasse well knew the success of the tactic depended on the enemy complying and forming its own line, and by forming it with fewer ships. The French had redesigned their own tactics after the devastating defeats of the Seven Years War to avoid all direct line confrontations at sea unless they, the French, clearly had a superior number of ships.

The French on this day had the superior numbers and were not intimidated by the British fleet. The French maneuvered their own ships into a line and engaged the Brits. With five more ships, the French had about 450 more cannon on their windward side than the Brits had on their leeward one, and because of the increasing wind, the British ships couldn't open their lower gun ports.

Before the heads of the two lines met, both French and British gunners waited tensely in the crowded below decks. Some finished stuffing wads into their ears or tying off the thick ropes that acted as springs to catch the heavy 24- and 32-pounders when they jumped back in lethal recoil.

Gunner Louis Boulanger could not stand up straight in the lower gun deck of the *Ville de Paris*. At five feet eleven inches, he was one inch taller than the floor of the upper gun deck, which was his ceiling. He was notably taller than the other five men on his gun crew. "Frenchies shoot better'n Limeys," he said to his friend Little Jacques, "cause Frenchies are mostly like you, inches shorter'n me. They can move about free-like in this cramp. If I were a four-foot-ten midget like you—just your luck anyway to be ashore yesterday on leave with your cock out in a hen house instead of kneeling here under the morning sun holystoning the deck. If I ain't talked back to that officer, de Martineau, damn his eyes, I'd still be on deck where I belongs, and my back wouldn't be all ripped up."

"You always did talk back too much to your superiors," said Little Jacques, grinning at his friend and still in fine spirits.

Louis's gun crew had been clocked as one of the fastest on the ship. They could load and fire three balls in three minutes and fifteen seconds. Louis tied large pieces of cloth around his head to keep the sweat from his eyes and to provide extra protection for his plugged ears. *Maybe I can kill this de Martineau aristocrat during the battle,* he thought. *I'd just as soon crush his skull as look at him.* Staring at the officer's fancy linen shirt and satin breaches with their silver buckles, he spat. With the fear of death in his throat, he began to make his peace with his maker, just in case. He remembered his mother and sisters. He blessed them, kissed his hand, and blew them a kiss. "To my poor old ma," he said. "She's got no such finery as that lieutenant, and she's all worn out, poor thing, but we love each other sober or drunk."

"Don't you worry," said Little Jacques, "we'll both get home. I'm past due to see my little wife."

Louis's mother and sisters all worked twelve hours a day in a rope factory in Rouen. They worked six days a week, and wore discarded clothes and sewed together rags. It seemed as if they were always hungry and sick. When Louis was an infant, his father died in a saltpeter accident on a road crew. His little brother hated working in the coal mines so much that he planned to join a gun crew, as Louis had. Louis thought to himself, *If this bulwarks here took a shot, and I use me knife, one cut in this aristocrat's pipe would look like—injury from flying debris. I'll just use me rigging knife.* He shuddered with fear, and he said under his breath to Little

Jacques, "Here we go again. The poor gin sots o' France and England mangles each other, while the satin-breached aristocrats encourage us like it's a lousy coq fight."

Jacques carefully looked around to see who might be listening. "Keep them thoughts to yourself, friend," he said with quiet vehemence. "At least we don't have to stand as targets on the quarterdeck." Louis also looked around. He felt no hatred for the English commoners whom he was fighting, but loathed instead his superiors who seemed responsible for the endless wars, and for his hard life.

He checked his earplugs. He'd lost most of the hearing in his left ear already, and the ear tended to bleed after about fifteen minutes of cannon fire, or after only eight or nine shots of his 32-pounder *Anique*. He could just make out the form of Sally in her disguise several guns down, and he waved at her. He'd enjoyed her charms the night before. "She's a good girl, and a cheap piece of ass," he said magnanimously to Little Jacques. Louis scratched the lice on his testicles, and joined his comrades on a rope that levered through a set of pulleys and swung the gun port open. He breathed in the fresh salt air with a relish. If he lived through the day, he'd sign up for the magnificent, cross-eyed Sally again, even if her rates doubled, as they probably would.

Chapter 15
The Battle of Chesapeake Bay
1781

The cannonade began at two p.m., and lasted three deadly hours. The heavy iron balls crashed into the oak planks and tore apart the men and machines in their way. Gunners hurled chain shot and shrapnel into the decks and rigging of the enemy. The French concentrated their fire above the British hulls. They tore up British rigging and sailors, as their own hulls and gunners were being reduced to splinters and limbs. Many of the deaths in this type of sea battle were slow ones, taking days or weeks, from infections in wounds caused by flying splinters.

Aboard the *Ville de Paris*, Benoit stared at wounded men groaning in agony on the deck. A young man right before him was severed in two by flying chain shot. A sailor near Benoit fell to the deck and began to shriek. He had just had his legs below the knees blown away and his life blood poured out onto the deck. Benoit ordered two sailors to apply tourniquets and carry the wretched man below decks to wait his turn for cauterizing and triage.

The carnage was a visit to hell. The stench of blood and vomit filled Benoit's nostrils and he wanted to retch. How could man, created in the Lord's own image, be so grotesque? This bloody hell was not the glorious battle he had imagined, or what he had wanted to be a part of. It reminded him of the outdoor butcher's stalls on *Rue de la Coup* in Lorient. In hindsight, life there wasn't so bad. He wished he was back in Lorient with Isabelle, Sebastian, his mother and siblings, and that his mother was young again. There he had played with Antoine and the other boys and heard the sailors talk at the Siren's Call Pub. For some reason, he remembered the one-legged Barbarin who sang:

"The decks were sprinkled with blood.
The big guns so loudly did roar.
Then I did wish myself safe at home,
And along with my Annie on the shore."

Oh God, the song was true. It warned me and I didn't get it. Benoit longed to hear that old melody again—not here, but back there in that pub, listening to the old Barbarin, rather than facing the cannon of the enemy, and possibly at any moment becoming a cripple or a corpse. He remembered the rowdies and confronting them: *Let him go, he served his country well,* he had said. *My father fought the Brits,* he thought, *and gave his life for his country, and so will I, if it's the Lord's will. At least I don't have a son who will never know me.* All this in a few seconds, then an explosion pulled his attention back into the battle.

Benoit could see that the French ships were allowed to sail as fast as they could, so they were able to form a proper line, though not in the usual order. The British failed for some reason to form a proper line, and the front of their line met the French line at an angle making a V, rather than parallel and all ships within range. Thus fighting only took place at the intersection of the two lines. This left the British attacking a superior force with only part of their inferior force.

Sir Thomas Graves gave the order to hoist the flag ordering "Bear Down," or for each ship to attack on its own, but one of his young midshipmen forgot to pull down the "Line Ahead" signal, and Graves and his officers failed to notice the error. The manual clearly stated that the "Line Ahead" order supersedes all other signals, so most of his well-disciplined captains, including Admiral Hood, stayed in line. This was disastrous for the British, because the front of their line had to take broadside after broadside. Lieutenant Lalois looked up from his spyglass and said to Captain Albert Cresp and Benoit, "Look there, we have disabled two of the British men-of-war."

The *Princessa* engaged the *Ville de Paris*. As the two ships pounded each other and shredded each others' rigging, grapeshot tore off the right arm and leg of Lieutenant Lalois. Lalois looked in horror at the stump where his arm had just been, as his body careened to the deck. The ballroom king was carried below; he would never waltz the ladies again.

The French returned the volley. When the smoke cleared, the *Princessa*'s quarterdeck was almost empty. Maimed and disfigured men lay bleeding about the deck. The English shot away the foretop bowline, which held the *Ville de Paris's* foretop mast in place, and clipped the mast itself. The huge fir timber threatened to crash down on the *marsouins*, the marines sharpshooting with musket from the foredeck. This would drop those shooting from the foretops and disable the gunners on the main deck.

Two brave topmen sprang into the precarious webbing and climbed up to retie the joint of the upper masts, but one was shot in the stomach and fell screaming into the water. The other caught a musket ball in the face. His foot caught in the rigging, and he dangled from the ratlines like an inverted scarecrow, scaring off those thinking to climb after. Other sailors held back at this sight, and Guillaume de Martineau, the officer of the top, was embarrassed to order anyone else aloft while the British musketmen stood so close.

Guillaume was on the spot. *Kiss-a-goose*, he thought. *I'm no hero, there's no heaven, and if I climb, I'll get shot. If I order one of my men to go and he isn't killed, what are the odds he'll retaliate the first chance he gets? That's why it's easier to be sailor than an officer. What the hell, he just won't live—and if his luck holds, I'll make sure he gets shot while on deck. So who will I choose? Who I choose dies. Who was the topman who spoke back to me the other day, Robere?*

Benoit remembered in an instant the story of how his father had fallen overboard and fed sharks off the coast of Senegal. He seized a short coil of rope from a belaying pin and slung it over his shoulder while Guillaume de Martineau scanned for Robere. Other sailors watched Benoit with apprehension. He could hear his mother's voice, as if just yesterday, saying again, *Be brave, but don't be a fool. Don't die a reckless hero.* Frightened by his own boldness, Benoit threw himself into the ratlines and scampered up the ropes awkwardly, his inexperience as a topman showing. He slipped and fell down a rung while a ball just missed his head. The musket fire from the *Princessa* made a halo around him. The French *marsouins* replied, letting loose a constant barrage of rifle and swivel gun fire, and some of the British sharpshooters fell into the foaming sea, while others twisted about wounded or looking for cover. Benoit reached up and hauled himself over and onto the top-mast platform. He hugged the floor, using the loose mast and a dead marine sharp-shooter as added cover. Crouching low, Benoit secured the mid-topmast to the first mast at the overlap with the extra rope, and then slumped down behind the body on the platform.

The *Princessa* sailed by, and the rifle fire stopped. Benoit grabbed a halyard and slid gracefully back to the deck below. Men from his ship cheered. Benoit was unharmed but for his hands. He burned them both on the slide down; in his haste and inexperience, he forgot to wear gloves or wrap his hands in his shirt.

ॐ   ॐ

The battle ended with the light. Admiral De Grasse spoke with Captain Cresp, who ordered Benoit to join them. The admiral, condescending to break protocol, said magnanimously, "Well done, Lieutenant, here is my purse in appreciation." But Benoit stood straight, saluted with a rope-burned hand and replied, "Thank you sir, but you need not reward me for doing my duty."

"That's nonsense, boy," laughed the old sea captain, and handed him the purse. "We needed someone to take the initiative. Now you can buy your gun crew a round, or whatever you wish." Benoit graciously accepted it, as he was expected to.

"Thank you, sir." He bowed his head and walked carefully through debris back to his post on the larboard watch. A sailor shook his head at this sorry display of brown-nosing, and the salts argued for days later in the fo'c'sle as to whether the lieutenant was a bootlicker, an idiot, or a romantic. After much debate, they decided it was even worse: He was all three, and no coward either.

ॐ   ॐ

Though the battle was over, the horror continued for the wounded and dying. The candles for the gunner's tapirs were extinguished, but oil and candle lamps burned for the surgeons and their loblolly boys. Their saws hacked and hewed into the night under the lamps. Intermittently, patients screamed in agony. During each amputation, the patients gulped rum or whiskey and clenched pieces of wood or leather between their teeth till they fainted from the pain.

The Royal British mug was finally bruised at sea. Sir Thomas decided to scuttle one of his great ships-of-the-line. He lost 336 men, and his chance for eminence in British history. De Grasse and his fleet escaped without losing a single ship. They suffered 230 casualties, most of whom died slowly from gangrene or infection. The surgeons knew no effective cure for infection except removing the limb, and that often just led to more infection.

Throughout the night, the screams of men under the saw, the moaning of dying men, and the hammer and saw of carpenters joined the usual creaks and hissings of a wooden ship at sea. The bodies were hand sewn into worn-out canvas, placed on a board, weighted with ballast rock, and slid over the side. Depending on the ship, they dropped down fifteen to thirty feet before hitting the water with a splash and disappearing into the black depths of the sea.

On board the French ships, the Catholic priests gave the last rite of Extreme Unction in Latin to the dying and the dead, guaranteeing that each soul had a valid passport with which to leave purgatory and enter heaven. The soul thus protected, each body in a canvas bag was dispatched. On the English ships, an Anglican minister or the captain said a prayer and blessing in English from the King James version of the Bible for the soul of each corpse, and to comfort the living left behind.

Benoit watched men slide the weighted bags over the side. He questioned seriously for the first time why his country was at war with England in the first place. *They're Protestants, we're Catholics,* he remembered. *They are heretics and infidels, while we are law-abiding, God-fearing Christians. But is it that simple? Antoine kept pointing out that we are all sinners. Both countries want wealth, power, and colonies, and isn't this butchery of men how the governments settle their differences, how they test their strength. When I told Antoine that I would join the navy, he had been disappointed. He told me he feared that that the navy was a terrible waste. God damn, maybe he was right? As I look at these men dropping into the water, I wonder.*

If we succeed in helping the Americans create a democratic republic, we will have checked the might and expansionist power of England while building up the rights of man. This misery and death will not be in vain. We live through hell to create heaven on earth.

At daylight, the British attacked again, finally in a proper line, but the French retreated far out to sea, taking the British fleet with them. Another irony of having lost the previous wars came out: The French ships were now newer and faster.

Benoit felt a boyish glee and manly French pride as he watched the English fall off behind. *In 1763,* he thought, *we lost all our colonies in North America, including Quebec and her enormous territory west of the Mississippi. We lost all our privileges in India to make military and political alliances, retaining only toothless trading rights, and we gave up some of our best-developed real estate in the Caribbean and Africa. But the English today aren't what they used to be. France is back!*

The British Navy had in fact grown complacent. For eighteen years, it had been in a building and refurbishing race with the French, but it suffered from profiteering by its suppliers. Vital supplies became overpriced due to government and supplier corruption. In the West, as in the East, decadence and malfeasance often followed success.

In France, King Louis XV had revamped his navy with determination. He founded an Academy of Naval Architecture, and proceeded to rebuild most of his fleet. Material and training expenses were neither skimped nor wasted. By 1781, the French ships were better designed and equipped and better manned than their English counterparts. (Although the effort paid off handsomely for the Americans, who became the principal beneficiaries of this arms buildup, it so strained the French economy that it contributed directly to the incubation of the French Revolution.)

While de Grasse and his barefoot salts led Graves and his Limeys on a wild goose chase, first letting the British catch up, then leaving them behind again, the second French fleet under Le Compte de Barras arrived at the Chesapeake with eight more ships-of-the-line and proceeded to unload more heavy artillery and reinforcements for the French and Continental forces under Lafayette and Washington, who were holding Cornwallis in the siege of Yorktown.

❧　☙

De Grasse led the British fleet in a large circle, and when the British finally sailed back to the mouth of the bay, Admiral Graves and his eighteen remaining ships discovered thirty-two fully manned French men-of-war waiting for them.

Sir Thomas Graves held a frosty meeting with his stone-faced commanders. Admiral Hood and his other captains were thoroughly disgusted. Since they had little chance now of a successful encounter using the traditional and the only "official" method of battle—or any other method for that matter—they sailed for New York for reinforcements. They could not return for months, well after Cornwallis, his supply lines cut, had surrendered his entire army of over 7,000 crack British troops to Washington and Lafayette. When Admiral Graves waited for the French to come out of the Chesapeake, he had no idea, as he smugly stared at the ships coming out to fight according to *His Majesty's Fighting Instructions,* that his multiple errors against this naval threat would prove so decisive that they probably cost Britain the thirteen colonies of North America.

On the deck of the *Ville de Paris* no one knew that the American War of Independence was almost over when the British ships fled. But everyone knew that the tide had turned for the new, democratic republic. Captain Albert Cresp de Sainte-Césaire ordered a shot of brandy for all hands, as well as the daily ration of tafia. Each seaman downed his shot below and brought on deck his mug of tafia, the rum and water drink served on French ships that was known on British ships as grog.

The officers assembled on the poop deck for champagne, and to view the British sailing off in the distance, followed and harassed by several fast French frigates.

Captain Cresp spoke again, "Lieutenant Grannier, that was a bold action, lad, splicing the mast. You're worthy of a new stripe. And if there is some small thing within my power that I can do for you, I will surely be of service to you."

"I do have a favor to ask of you," Benoit replied. "My cousin is a missionary in Asia, in Cochinchina. He says that he and the other missionaries are often without French protection. They have to rely on the Portuguese, the Spanish, or our enemies, the Dutch, and the English. These countries are all trading for profit out there, and we hardly show the flag. Well sir, we do have bases in India, and after this war, I would like to transfer there, and to get a position in the next expedition to Cochinchina."

Chapter 16
Quy Nhơn
1786 (five years later)

Nguyễn Huệ and Lương Hoàng noticed Nguyễn Nhạc riding by in the distance. Huệ placed an arrow on his longbow, slipped the notch onto the string, drew his arms apart, and released. The arrow made a low arc and sank deep into the center circle of a straw target. A second arrow followed the first, in the same long arc to the target forty paces across the field, and missed the target all together.

Huệ again drew the bow by holding it in his left hand and taking the arrow notched in the string in his right hand. He lifted his hands over his head and pointed the arrow into the sky above. As he gracefully lowered his left arm toward the target, he slowly pulled the arrow and bow string back toward his ear with his right hand. The bow bent tauter and tauter, till his bronze right shoulder blade stuck straight out of his back from the strain of the bow. The arrow fell gently from vertical till it lay almost parallel to the ground, his eye looking down the shaft, and the feather touched his cheek by the ear. *Thump-thing*, the huge bow sang again, and another arrow joined the cluster, like a flower arrangement around the middle of the target. Lương Hoàng was busy shooting at his own target.

Huệ suddenly said, "After all I've done for him, Elder Brother Nhạc sends Lữ north to conquer Thuận Hóa, risking the lives of our best troops in the hands of one who unfortunately is careless—no, incompetent. Harmony Province, what a great opportunity, the first ripe fruit tree on the road to Thăng Long. And who opened that road? Baby brother of course." *Thump-thing*, he sent another feathered missile into his bouquet. "After I engineered the taking of Quy Nhơn, who planned the defeat of the Nguyễn Army sent from their Spring Capital Phú Xuân? When the Trịnh General Hoàng Ngũ Phúc crossed the Sông Gianh River and fought through the Đồng Hới Wall, never before breached by the Trịnh, seized Phú Xuân and threatened our northern flank as a Nguyễn Army approached from the south, whose idea was it to shower Trịnh Sâm's General Phúc with gold and silk, and to make the alliance with him so that our northern flank was protected? Who then fooled Nguyễn Đình's General Tổng Phúc Hợp into moving up the Cài Gian River and then slaughtered Tổng and the entire Nguyễn Army at the ambush of the Cài Gian Gorge?"

Lương Hoàng laughed, "That was a great day. Our troops killed 50,000 of the enemy as they tried to maneuver their exposed boats to the shore. It was so stupid of Tổng Phúc Hợp to follow us up the river. It was your idea to have the troops move all those rocks and boulders to the edges of the gorge beforehand. Sometimes war appears to be so easy because victory seems so simple, so natural—especially when the Gods favor you with crazy ideas that work. It seemed like a terrible gamble at the time to spend so much energy and gold to move boulders to the edge of an empty river gorge in the middle of nowhere. I thought you had lost your mind. There was dissention, and we ordered the execution of many deserters. There is nothing like success to prove a difficult point."

Huệ smiled and said, "Sun Tzu wrote, 'In ancient times, those known as good warriors prevailed when it was easy to prevail.'"

Hoàng chuckled dryly and continued, "Heaven certainly turned against our new allies, the Trịnh. A plague broke out in their expeditionary force. They fell like stalks of rice at harvest. Even Hoàng Ngũ Phúc died, though bravely, refusing capture—bad karma."

Huệ shot another arrow and said, "But we have yet to face the might of the Trịnh. They still have Nguyễn Hữu Chỉnh, the savage eagle, who has never been defeated. If Eldest Brother Nhạc sends our troops under Lữ against Nguyễn Hữu Chỉnh, it will make me want to pull out my nails in anger. .... Brother Brute is almost crazy with jealousy at the respect I command with my troops. He sent Lữ to conquer the south. Lữ captured Gia Định and Sài Gòn, but he lost too many—over a quarter of our men."

Hoàng said, "Lữ's officers make fun of him behind his back and complain of nepotism. He let King Đình escape. Maybe that wasn't his fault, but then he let Đỗ Thanh Nhơn and a few thousand volunteers get the better of him and force his retreat—that was unfortunate! At least the campaign wasn't a total loss; they found enough rice in the Sài Gòn Citadel to fill a hundred junks and brought it all to Quy Nhơn with them. Nhạc threw that huge celebration, and proclaimed himself King of the Center."

Huệ interjected, "Now I have to kowtow to him at all formal events. Buddha give me patience."

Huệ then emptied his mind and relaxed his shoulders. He let his anger run through his fingers into the arrow. He took a deep breath, and drew his bow during the long exhalation. Huệ released his breath very slowly, allowing the anger poison to escape with his breath and move into his arrow. He released the arrow into his target. It split another arrow in two. He continued, "Who suggested we send a huge gift of silver, silk, and rhinoceros tusks to Trịnh Sâm, to demonstrate our allegiance? Then Trịnh Sâm makes Nhạc a Grand Duke of the North.

"Who, with the north secure again, then led our troops into Sài Gòn, destroyed the Nguyễn Army, and caught King Đình and all his family? I don't like slaughter, but sometimes it serves a higher purpose."

Hoàng said, "Didn't Confucius write that only just kings deserve to rule? And it is one of the world's great pleasures to destroy the corrupt and overfed with an army of rice-cutters, who yell and scream as they kill for the pleasure and joy of their revenge. They call us the Hissing Army. We do enjoy bringing justice and taking revenge for our people." Hoàng steadied his breathing. *Thwing*, his hardwood bow sang and another arrow sailed off.

Huệ responded, "How did Lữ and I let Prince Ánh escape? We didn't know for sure that he was there. That was a terrible mistake. Was it luck, or the will of Heaven? His gain was our loss. It didn't take Ánh long to raise another army and retake Sài Gòn, surrounded by his demonic French advisers."

Huệ examined his right hand and noticed that his fingers were red. The calluses were sore and it was time to stop. After Hoàng finished his last arrows, they inspected their handiwork. For both shooters, only a few of the arrows had missed the target completely. Huệ raised his hand and his guards trotted down the slope to where they stood. Silently the guards recovered all the precious iron-tipped arrows. Huệ called for their horses, and with the three bodyguards following discreetly behind, he and Hoàng rode out the western lane towards the hills of the central highlands.

"So then Brute throws another party, and proclaims himself Emperor Nguyễn Nhạc. Nhạc and I sailed south with 100 junks, took Sài Gòn again, but Prince Ánh escaped with that white devil barbarian sorcerer of his. There were Chinese pirates in Ánh's service, which seemed to surprise Nhạc. He thought he had all the Chinese pirates in our navy. Brute lost his temper. He directed our forces to destroy all the Chinese merchants of Cholon. They massacred over 10,000 innocent Chinese merchants and their families."

Hoàng added, "So stupid—such bad tactics. We were both embarrassed. The slaughter has made trade impossible. Although we broke several monopolies and stand to gain immediate profits for our own treasury, Việts don't particularly like to be traders, half our Chinese pirates deserted with their junks, and we injured our own future finances—less trade, less wealth, less tax revenue."

Huệ said, "Killing civilians by ethnicity is ugly work, and should always serve a strategic purpose. Ánh retook Sài Gòn, but I drove him back to Siam again. Then Chakkri kills the Siamese King, calls himself Rama I. I admire his boldness, but the bastard supports Ánh with 20,000 Siamese troops and 300 junks. Ánh, with his army and the Siamese troops, tore through the south, taking port after port under Chu Văn Tiếp, till I sank an arrow into Tiếp's chest and my Screaming Regiments stopped his advance. Then with my forces I destroyed the Siamese, and very few made it back to their wives and children.

"All this I've done for our father's memory, and for our Ancestors, and Nhạc then orders me to look after boat building and taxes while he orders Lữ to defeat Hữu Chỉnh and conquer the north. What a waste of good men! I should hang myself in protest. Nhạc is a sick turtle for being so afraid of me. I have always served him loyally, and kept myself in check—and this is what I get."

Hoàng looked pained. "It must be hard to be the older brother of a very talented tactician and leader."

Huệ and Hoàng rode their horses up a high round-topped hill for the view it offered. At the top of the hill they dismounted and stared at the light blue and gray sky. To the east, they could see Quy Nhơn, the harbor, and the placid South China Sea beyond, a deep blue blending with the horizon. Huệ stretched out his anger-filled body. Hoàng also stretched. Then as the sun set in a pool of red over the mountains, they faced the valley of the Hà Giao River, crawling with blue fishing boats with red eyes painted on their bows.

Huệ said, "How about *Sanchin*?" Hoàng nodded his assent. They began the karate *kata*. Moving with the intensity of a public demonstration, as if they were performing for the omniscient spirits of their Ancestors, they began to repeat the *kata* of three conflicts. *Sanchin* was the basic exercise of a boxer training in *Pang-gai-noon*, the half-hard, half-soft style of the Shaolin monks of southern China, which they both learned from Hồ Danh.

They rolled their shoulders over and tightened their backs and stomachs. With their arms in front of them as if they were holding firewood, they pressed their elbows down and pulled them together while tightening their buttocks and rolling their pelvises forward. Even as they tightened, they began to relax, sinking their taut, contracted bodies into the ground, straightening their backs. They became tree-like, sending their roots deep into the earth, so that like a tree, their musculature would withstand a punch, a kick, even a light stick attack. They held the position for a quarter of an incense stick, feeling their centers drop deeper and deeper, becoming rooted and immovable. They executed the kata fiercely in the four primary directions, performing circular blocks and deadly finger-tip strikes. They ended with horizontal circular blocks and open-palm thrusts. They held the last position at rigid attention while they brought their breathing under control. Huệ heard a bird's evening song. The clouds over Quy Nhơn were pale blue, white and pink, while the northeasterly wind was cool and salty-fresh.

Huệ's guards came closer to him as four horsemen rode up the hill; it was Huệ's chief rival, Võ Văn Nhậm, and three soldiers in the black farmers' shirts and red headbands of the Tây Sơn.

"*Không dám,*" (this slave salutes you) Võ Văn Nhậm said with a smile, using the habitual greeting.

"*Không dám,*" Huệ repeated the obligatory courtesy. "You're back from the north already?" Huệ said. "Don't tell me that you have already conquered the Trịnh and freed the Lê Emperor?"

"I have no such news with which to break your heart," Võ Văn Nhậm answered with a grimace. "But your oldest brother orders you back to court."

"Goodness, what's the matter?"

"I shouldn't say," answered Võ Văn Nhậm gravely. He leaned forward in his saddle and smiled. "But I do know that Lữ fell from his horse while jumping a brook, and broke his shoulder. He will not be travelling anywhere for a few months."

☙   ❧

Soon inside the citadel, Huệ briskly entered the south-facing reception hall. As he entered, Võ Văn Nhậm entered with him and joined a small group of mandarins standing over to the east side of the hall. Nhạc's cold expression, from his hard, flat face with his large ears, always made Huệ uncomfortable when Nhạc stared impassively at him from the throne. Huệ knelt to the ground and knocked his head three times against the floor. Nhạc watched as he sat on a black ebony throne inlaid with gold and pearls. Huệ's right hand burned slightly from the archery. He remembered the feeling of the arrow leaving the bow, and its sound: *thwinggg*.

"This humble one that I am salutes your highness," he said.

"Welcome, youngest brother, please make yourself comfortable." Nhạc said, but without ordering a second chair.

"To what do I owe the honor of your summons?" Huệ said, staying on his knees and sitting on his calves, to enjoy the mild pain of the stretching that the position demanded.

"Dear Youngest Brother, as you well know, I entrusted your Second Older Brother Lữ with the responsibility and honor of attacking the Spring Capital Phú Xuân. Lữ was earnestly carrying out my wishes when he lost the favor of the Gods and misfortune overtook him." Nhạc laughed at his own wit. "After a night of drinking, the clown fell off his horse."

At this point Nhạc dropped his voice. "His back is somewhat thrown out of line, his shoulder is broken, and his morale is shattered. Needless to say, he is very embarrassed and upset with himself, and he no longer can lead my troops into battle." Nhạc allowed for a significant pause while he continued to monitor his little brother's reaction. As Huệ's interest grew, he concealed his feelings behind a formal mask of solicitude. Nhạc continued, "You are my next choice for commander of the siege of the Spring Capital Phú Xuân. It would please me greatly if you would consider leaving the comfort of your wives and children and accept this position.

"I would be honored, Eldest Brother."

"Good. My heart is glad. Excuse my brevity, but time is short. Please join me now in the map room."

☙   ❧

Huệ was delighted, and it was clear at once that Nhạc was excited about something. His whole manner was buoyant.

"Youngest Brother, would you care for a cup of tea, and perhaps a light repast?"

"Very kind of you, Eldest Brother. Just tea would be perfect at this time of the morning."

Nhạc turned to Night Hawk, who stood armed with longbow and sword at attention inside the door, and said, "Please wait outside." Night Hawk bowed and departed, while Nhạc picked up a mallet and hit a matched pair of ancient bronze gongs, which filled the room with the richness and clarity of a perfect fifth. A lovely young maid entered with a porcelain tea set, placed it before Nhạc, poured three cups, drank from one, placed a small plate of morsels and cup by Huệ, bowed low. Nhạc and Huệ each drank their first cup of tea. The maid carefully refilled the two cups and departed. They drank and ate without speaking. Huệ waited in silence for his brother.

"I have some very good news, if it's true." Nhạc began. "Nguyễn Hữu Chỉnh has apparently defected over to our side. He has petitioned me through Lữ for permission to serve with our victorious armies."

Huệ suppressed the urge to shout for joy. Instead he smiled broadly and allowed himself to laugh. "This is good news," Huệ said simply, "if it is true, that the greatest general of the Trịnh Dynasty has changed colors. They call Chỉnh the Savage Eagle, and the Pirates' Bane. He led a fleet against the great pirate navy of Dong Fat Bing and destroyed it. … I hope it's not one of his tricks."

"I don't think so," said Nhạc. "He has surrendered himself to our camp. I've ordered Chỉnh to stay with our northern army, which you join tomorrow. After you interview Chỉnh, one of my aides will report back to me on what Chỉnh has to say to us."

"You will be obeyed, Eldest Brother."

"Here, Youngest Brother, are the documents and maps that you prepared for Lữ before his departure. Our latest report from Thăng Long [Hà Nội] indicates that the Trịnh court is still divided over the succession and will not interfere too quickly with our attack on Phú Xuân. We sent that fortune teller north, as you suggested. He delivered his gifts, and the prediction that Governor Phạm Ngô Cầu was about to gain great wealth, and could avoid catastrophe if he feasted his mandarins with food and wine while his troops fasted and prayed every day of the week. It happens to be the week before the expected arrival of our forces. You do have a flair for dirty tricks, little brother. The mandarins will be tied up with banquets and debauchery, while the troops grow weak and feeble."

Huệ bowed and looked carefully over the charts. He already knew how he would move the army; he had designed the plan that Nhạc had given Lữ to execute. Huệ wanted to know immediately whether he could advance past the Spring Capital, but thought it better not to ask. All Nhạc added was, "Once Harmony Province has fallen, there will be time for me to decide our next step. You are to wait there in Harmony Province until I join you."

"I understand," Huệ said simply. "It will be good to be back on top of my elephant Genghis." Then Huệ, looking his brother in the eye, smiled boyishly and said,

"Our father would be so proud of us, and of you especially. I'm sure that he will be with you and me when we defeat the Trịnh."

"Sometimes I feel his presence, though he should be reborn and among us already," Nhạc said, managing a smile, looking his brother straight in the eye, studying him openly. "Now you may go, and leave as soon as you can. But first, Mother of course would like a visit to wish you luck and to bless your campaign."

Huệ went to their mother, Autumn Moon. Like her sons, she had aged, but her lined face was less weathered than when she was a farmer, and it was still capable of expressing the greatest warmth. Her black lacquered teeth were still in place, thanks in part to the preservative powers of the lacquer. Still sharp at sixty, Autumn Moon loved her sons and especially enjoyed serving her youngest son tea. He understood the rites of tea, and conducted himself throughout their habitual interviews in the Hibiscus Garden with a most pleasing decorum.

Autumn Moon shrewdly recognized in her youngest son her husband's fascinating mind, and her most dangerous rival for influence and control over her eldest son, the king. Many times she had scolded Huệ for his impatience, and warned him to obey his elders or he would destroy their new patrimony. She had in fact been the major reason why he hadn't turned on his brothers long before. It was well known that one could ignore the advice of strong women only with great care, as there were many Genie who looked after them. A man could bring down the wrath of Heaven if he crossed his mother, and he should only dare to move against her with his father's explicit support.

Autumn Moon, in a pale green silk tunic embroidered with multicolored lotus blossoms, sat at her favorite mah jong table, surrounded by her maids. She sent them away for tea and dumplings and then ordered them to leave her alone with the prince.

"Youngest Son, you be careful, and don't let Genghis get ahead of the other elephants. You tell that trainer of his that I order him to keep you with the others or I'll have thumbscrews put on him and his nails pulled out."

Huệ laughed. "I'll do no such thing. And my trainer, Đông Ba, would deserve better treatment from you for his loyal service to me, even if I got trampled into goo in the next charge." Autumn Moon smiled. She enjoyed teasing and being teased by her youngest, but the smile didn't cover the concern evident in her sharp black eyes. She loved all three of her sons, while appreciating their differences. Nhạc was aggressive and strong; Lữ was funny and loyal; Huệ was brilliant and dangerously unpredictable.

"Is there any news from the search for Jade River?" she asked, changing the subject.

"Of course not, Mother, nothing yet, I'm sorry to say," Huệ said gently. "You would be informed immediately. After this next round of war, I hope we can redouble our search for her. I sometimes think she would help us keep peace in the family."

"Perhaps," said Autumn Moon. "You should be careful as you fight your way north not to exceed your orders."

Huệ took his leave of his mother after only a short visit. After giving orders to his household and aides, he took his lovely concubine, Blue Cloud (Thu Vân) for a stroll through the fortress arboretum. It was there that he loved to walk with his friends, and it was the only place in the palace where it was safe to share confidences. Huệ and Blue Cloud had a son and a daughter, and he had another son and daughter by his first wife, Green Willow.

Motherhood had treated Blue Cloud well. It had not diminished her beauty, but had made her more self-confident and self-assured. Her oval brow and delicate chin were part of her allure. It was this striking face that caught Huệ's attention at a brothel in Nha Trang, which he searched for his sister—one of scores of brothels he visited.

Blue Cloud twinkled as she said, "Your sons have both done well this week in their lessons with Scholar Trương Văn Hiến, who continues to lavish praises on little Cường's calligraphy. The girls, not to be confused with the boys, have been nothing but trouble and I have punished them both, first for insolence, and then for making me laugh too hard at myself."

Huệ roared with laughter. He always enjoyed those rare moments when he visited the sewing and needlepoint parties, where he could sit quietly and listen to his daughters take on the adult and matriarchal establishment which, due to their social preeminence and wealth, confined them to the women's quarters. His children could not work in the fields and play in the wild streams as other children did; in fact, as he and his sister once had. Their outdoor world consisted of an arboretum and a garden with an artificial pond inside the compound of the king's wives and concubines. Their confinement also served another purpose. Huệ's family was kept at the palace as hostages to ensure his good behavior and loyalty.

By now they were well into the garden. Blue Cloud led her master to a marble bench by an artificial pond full of carp and goldfish. They sat together in silence, listening to the wind in the banyan and banana trees. Huệ took his lovely concubine in his arms, and in the Vietnamese style of cuddling, he pressed his face into her hair and breathed deeply. Blue Cloud pressed her face against his strong shoulder and neck, and breathed with her husband as if they were one.

Blue Cloud then withdrew her head and began to speak. She was very serious and hushed. "Hồ Huệ, you must be very careful," and she looked around to make sure they were alone. "You remember that one of my maids secretly has a sister serving in Nhạc's household. Listen now, my maid has word that one of your brother's ministers—we're not sure who, but probably Võ Văn Nhậm; she thinks it was

his voice she heard through the screen—recently argued that you were too dangerous to the king's power to be allowed into the field any longer. Nhạc apparently
agreed, then changed his mind and insisted that you were still his most effective
general for defeating the Trịnh.

"Someone asked your brother Nhạc, 'What if your brother Huệ refuses to retire
from the field and command only paperwork?' Your brother answered, 'Don't worry, it would be very easy to eliminate the cadet should the need arise.'"

"I was afraid that such a day as this would arrive," Huệ said, and waited in case
there was more.

They were quiet and simply held hands for a long time, enjoying the gentle
breeze in the tangled banyan and a few banana trees with white and purple blossoms. Huệ considered the new information. *There is no way to verify it is true, but I
trust Blue Cloud. Her son is my heir.* Huệ said in anger, "So, for my outstanding
service and loyalty, my brother listens to serpents and snakes, and plans to retire me
from what I do best and turn me into a tax collector." And he thought, *There are
many questions that only the future will answer. One thing at a time. First, I must
say goodbye, and then seize Phú Xuân.*

With his mind cleared, he turned his attention back to Blue Cloud. Huệ smelled
again her perfume, a delicate rose petal fragrance, and he admired her clear brown
eyes and her smooth soft skin. They walked slowly to his room and held each other
for a long embrace in the silence. Then they undressed to the delicate bell tones of a
wind chime.

Huệ and Blue Cloud made love to each other very slowly, in case it was the last
time. They played together like two musicians in a duet. Where one led, the other
followed.

When Huệ moved faster, Blue Cloud kept up, in tune with the pace he set.
They played together till the moment of Blue Cloud's final, long chord—and the
crescendo at the end of the last movement.

Then all was still as they lay in the clouds and rain. Their bodies breathed heavily together. Their breathing slowly subsided, till the only music was the tinkling of
the wind chime. Huệ's mind returned to the earth. He started thinking of ways to get
his family away from his brother. "Blue Cloud," he said, "your father must take to
his bed and your mother must write to you that he is dying, and you must take my
wives and my entire household to say farewell to him, and help and support your
mother. Insist that you need Green Willow and Precious Stone and their children to
keep you and your children company. Do you understand? I must get you and my
family out of here."

Chapter 17
Saint-Louis, Senegal
1786

Benoit Grannier saw action against the British six times before the peace of 1783. De Grasse sailed his fleet to the West Indies and attacked British ports, merchantmen, and warships. They took Saint Christopher. Benoit was taken prisoner when De Grasse's ship was captured in the battle of Jamaica. He and the surviving sailors were exchanged and returned to France as part of the peace.

He and his fellow officers rejoiced at their new freedom and the war's end. Finally a great victory for France. If only they could have freed India from the intrusions of the British East India Company, which had turned parts of India into a veritable gold mine for the British. In the Treaty of Paris of 1783, which gave the Americans their independence, France renewed her pledge to avoid military alliances on the Indian continent. France relinquished her right to expand or compete in India, while the British retained these rights.

Benoit survived the ship and staff reductions following the peace. He spent two years under le Comte de Fleuris as a first lieutenant on board *La Resolution*. *La Resolution* was a smart, 32-gun frigate with 19 swivel guns mounted on the railings to fight off smaller pirate craft. Pirates often used galleys, which sat low in the water and could row directly into the wind. Galleys could attack when there was no wind at all. *La Resolution* hunted and fought pirates from the Mediterranean to the Indian Ocean, protecting French and European trade in gold, ivory, goods, and chattel, which usually meant slaves. Dangers abounded: the expected and the unexpected.

Le Comte de Fleuris was a demanding and stern commander with a long, equine face. He was respected by his men as a solid seaman. The men in the officers' dining cabin were an assortment of characters, and were so taciturn in the cramped confines of a ship that it took a while to break the ice. A few of the men were familiar. Benoit knew the Sublieutenant, Le Comte Guillaume de Martineau, from the 104-gun *Ville de Paris*. Benoit was more drawn to Sublieutenant André de Lagier, who was a singing and joke-telling Breton with sandy brown hair and an impish bent. On their second dinner together, Le Comte Guillaume de Martineau was discussing the stock market in France. "It's a great place to invest your money," said the black-bearded Guillaume, "if you can figure out what is a good company stock. It is so hard to know whom to trust. The sellers all say the right things. You have to do your own research."

"Sounds like good advice," said André de Lagier. "That reminds me of a story. In my village, there was a duck seller. He was very successful and contented being the only duck seller on the street and he sold his ducks for eight francs each. A new duck seller moved in across the street who stole all the business by offering his ducks for seven francs each. Then a price war ensued, back and forth, until the new duck seller was down to three francs for a duck. The original duck seller was beside himself with worry and frustration, but finally he put up a big sign that said, 'Two francs,' and then in small print at the bottom 'for half a duck.' And that, my friends, was the original canard." The tipsy men all laughed hard, and Guillaume seemed to enjoy the story. Ten minutes before the watches changed, the men all retired to prepare to go back to work on deck or below.

∾   ∾

Back in Saint-Louis, Guillaume de Martineau sat alone in his blue uniform at a table in Reynaud's Tavern, focused entirely on a beautiful woman with a rich and smoky voice singing in the corner as she played a guitar. When she finished her last song of the set, *Plaisir de l'Amour,* he rose and approached the performer, dropped a silver coin in her tip box, and smiled, saying, "Thank you for lovely singing. I wonder if you would care to join me at my table. I would like to buy you a drink."

The buxom brunette smiled and said, "I would be happy to. Let me freshen up and I'll join you." Guillaume stood when she arrived at his table. He pulled out a chair and helped her sit. She ordered a Sauvignon blanc and a small beer, the latter being safer than the local water.

Guillaume said, "Allow me to introduce myself—Le Comte Guillaume de Martineau. Thank you for such lovely music."

"You're welcome, it is my pleasure," she replied.

"And what is your name?"

"I am Margarita Bordechamp."

"Mademoiselle Bordechamp, where are you from originally?"

"I come from Marseilles. My father was a purser in a merchant ship. And you sir, where do you come from?"

"I grew up in Poitou, at the Chateau de Martineau."

"A real chateau, that's incredible," said Margarita. "What possessed you to choose the hard life of a naval officer?"

"I'm not interested in farming and animal husbandry, or religion, or academics. The navy life suits me fine. It combines adventure, service, and education, and it won't go on forever. What brought you to this backwater of Saint-Louis?"

"I came here with my husband, a naval officer, but he was a casualty in an encounter with pirates."

"I'm so sorry to hear that. What else can I say? That's terrible. Perhaps it's time for another glass of wine?" Margarita declined—she had more songs to sing—but she accepted an invitation from Guillaume to join him in attending a reception at the mansion of Admiral Pequinot and his wife in a few days time.

∾   ∾

For the admiral's reception, Guillaume hired a horse and buggy. He picked Margarita up from her cottage, and they entered the reception together, he in his blue dress uniform with white satin breaches, and she in a lovely purple dress and white pearl necklace. By the punch bowl, Admiral Pequinot said, "Martineau, who is the lovely lady accompanying you?"

"Sir, she is Margarita Bordechamp, widowed to the late Lieutenant Bordechamp. I found her singing in Reynaud's—great voice."

"Magnificent stays and stuns'l booms. Keep me posted on how she handles."

"I hope you're not going to pull rank on me over a new prize," replied Martineau, smiling at his wit. He bowed lightly to the smiling admiral, and took his drinks over to Margarita. Guillaume handed a glass of rum punch to her, as Benoit spotted them both.

Benoit had just refilled his own glass of punch. He crossed over and said with a friendly smile, "Good evening Martineau, please introduce me to your lady."

"Of course," said Guillaume, making an effort to be as cheerful. "Margarita Bordechamp, please meet Lieutenant Benoit Grannier. We sailed together on the *Ville de Paris* and now on *La Resolution*."

"Enchanted," said Margarita.

"The pleasure is mine," said Benoit, "especially after a month at sea on a frigate with 350 men."

Margarita offered a clear, lovely laugh at this pleasantry, causing heads to turn in the room. "The wheel turns. *Ça va*" (it goes). She acknowledged Guillaume. "You both are ashore now, with all the fruits of the land. Please excuse us Lieutenant Grannier, we must go now if we are to eat before I go to work. If you wish to hear songs from home, I start singing at seven at Reynaud's."

Guillaume interjected, "Let's say our farewells to Admiral Pequinot and his wife, and we will be off. Good evening Grannier." And they left him.

&? &

Benoit arrived at Reynaud's Tavern just before seven p.m. and jointed Guillaume and several other naval officers. They mostly listened as they ate and drank, while Margarita started by playing a violin impressively—a medley of jigs. She ended with a roaring rendition of the tune *En Passant par la Lorraine* (Passing through Lorraine). Then she laid down the fiddle and took up her guitar. She sang and played such songs as *Oh Dear Mother, Shall I Tell You?* and *Knight Guillaume and the Shepherd's Daughter*. She ended the set with everyone joining in on *Chevaliers de la Table Rond*. After a warm applause, she said, "Thank you for your attention and participation. Don't forget the importance of your patronage, and please put some coin in the tip jar. I'll be back in half an hour for more songs from home."

Margarita joined Guillaume and Benoit. "Well done," said Guillaume. "It is pleasant to hear the folk music of the common people."

"Thank you," responded Margarita. "I do favor old songs, and these are my family's, as I am one of the common people," and she laughed cheerfully. "And you, what did you think, Lieutenant Grannier?"

"Fabulous," said Benoit. "I sing some of the same songs. I learned *Knight Guillaume and the Shepherd's Daughter* from an old chanteyman in Lorient."

At the end of the evening, Margarita asked Benoit to come up and sing *Knight Guillaume,* which he did happily, and she sang along with him, harmonizing on the verses and taking back the lead when the shepherdess spoke. They sang together like lovebirds. Guillaume listened with disbelief, and watched his newest prize seized on the open seas before he'd brought her into port and boarded her. He had to look cheerful while twisting inside.

ॐ   ॐ

It was only a week later, on board *La Resolution* at a routine dinner in the officers' mess cabin, after the meal was eaten and the wine had gone round the table several times, that Benoit, André de Lagier, and Guillaume fell to debating.

"The institution of slavery," Guillaume interjected, stoking his beard, "is invaluable. It is thanks to slavery that we—and by 'we' I mean all of Western Christendom—are civilizing large parts of the world."

Benoit and André looked at each other and both smiled. They enjoyed gently needling their fellow officers with what they thought were heresies. Benoit now said, "I guess I can't fully agree. Perhaps good Christians should not support or permit the institution of slavery. I've heard many a preacher say one of the new characteristics of a civilized people will be their cessation of the buying and selling of humans like goods and chattel."

Guillaume raised his eyebrows and held them aloft. "My dear Grannier, let's not be too liberal. Plantations in the New World and the Far East need slavery in order to be profitable and to attract investment. Investment and trade bring the benefits of civilization—Christianity, and even prosperity—to parts of the world where these concepts didn't yet even exist."

André sat back and lit his pipe. He was going to let Benoit have all the fun this time, and make all the enemies. *There is a reason why you are not supposed to discuss politics or religion in the gun room. You have to get along with a group of men, day in and day out, in close quarters,* he thought.

Benoit responded, "You're probably right that slavery has played a part in development, but the economies of the world should work just fine with free labor. Destroying the market for slavery would reduce the black market in slaves, the attacks on free people, especially in Africa, to create slaves, and the subsequent brutalization of slave labor by many ruthless and piratical entrepreneurs."

Guillaume took some snuff on his sleeve from a silver box and inhaled sharply, and sneezed. "Why don't we free all the serfs, and give each illiterate one of them a vote as well? We could have rule by the illiterate mob. Which do you think is better, to be a free African native, probably a godforsaken, head-hunting cannibal headed for eternal damnation in the hereafter," and he smiled broadly, exposing a gold tooth, "or a Christian slave, adding to the economy of a Christian state, and possibly gaining eternal salvation?"

"In order to be Christian, you have to act Christian," argued Benoit. "Can a system which permits the breaking up of Christian families, or heathen ones, expect to have the blessing of the Christ, the God of Love, who commanded, Do onto others as you would have them do unto you?"

"It hardly matters whether or not you break up a heathen black family," replied Guillaume. "The blacks are an inferior race. It's not even clear that they have souls."

Benoit recognized the problem of this debate. Guillaume had a mind like ancient Egyptian mortar: mixed up, set, and out of date. Rather than repeat this well-known joke, Benoit rose and excused himself. "Thank you for the conversation," he said, "To be continued, I hope. I'd better change before our watch."

❧ ❦

Margarita lived in Saint-Louis, the French trading center in Senegal near the mouth of the Senegal River. She had a small, rundown cottage on the edge of town. Benoit was happy to remember her often when he was at sea. Her body was as voluptuous and glorious as her voice was clear and bright. She was a charming performer on the stage, and a loving one in bed. Her thick brown hair surrounded a face so well proportioned, it could have launched a flotilla, if not an armada. Perhaps she was more demanding than most women, and hard to please. She was a selective woman. Why is it that the less a woman falls in love with you, the harder it is to forget her? Men wanted to worship such beauty, and if they couldn't possess it, they often, like angry children, wanted to abuse it.

Benoit was twenty-nine, Margarita was thirty-three, and André was thirty-six. For Benoit, Margarita was his first serious woman since Isabelle Carpentier years before. He loved Margarita dearly, but without the commitment she desired. The day after his spectacular first night of loving with Margarita, Benoit had gone to Church and confessed, and said in penitence:

"Hail Mary, full of grace. Our Lord is with thee.

Blessed art thou among women, and blessed is the fruit of thy womb, Jesus.

Holy Mary, mother of God, pray for us sinners, now and at the hour of our death. Amen."

But he went right back and saw Margarita again the next night! They found great comfort in each other, and in music with which to rejoice. Benoit was with Margarita every time Guillaume tried to approach her. Guillaume took the hint and gave up trying to see her. Benoit move into her little cottage, and ate with her at Reynaud's before she sang, and he often joined her at the end for a few duets.

❧ ❦

Benoit had introduced André to Margarita, for André was his new best friend. André was also a good singer with the gift of harmony. The three of them discovered on their first evening at Reynaud's together that they shared many songs. After

Margarita sang a set by herself, they pleased the crowd as they traded songs until closing time. Benoit sang *Isabeau S'y Promène* (Isabeau Went a Strolling), André sang *Let's Have a Little Drink*, and Margarita brought the pub to silence with her rendition of *Plaisir d'Amour* (The Pleasure of Love), with her two friends making up simple but rich harmony parts.

Plaisir d'amour ne dure qu'un moment / Chagrin d'amour dure toute la vie. (The pleasure of love is but a moment long / The pain of love endures the whole life long.)

On the choruses, most of the customers in the room would join in. Before long Benoit and André performed regularly in the second half of Margarita's show, bringing variety to her set and enhancing her modest income. They swapped drinking songs and ballads and entertained the toss-pots for hours. Particularly popular was their rendition of *Knight Guillaume and the Shepherd's Daughter*. Benoit and Margarita soon taught all the verses to André, who diligently wrote them out and memorized them. The mug-lifters would usually stop their chatter for the famous ballad of rape and revenge. In their three-part harmony, Benoit usually sang the melody with his tenor voice. He would sing the first verse alone to introduce the song and melody.

"It's of a shepherd's daughter dear, keeping sheep all on the plain,
who should ride by, but knight Guill-i-aume, and he's got drunk by wine."

André and Margarita would come in immediately on the first chorus, letting the audience know their part: "With me rye, fal lai-doll, diddle-aye day."

Then Margarita's soprano and André's bass voices joined Benoit's, turning each verse into a musical banquet of chords:

"Well he has mounted off his stead, and quickly laid her down,
and when he'd has his will of her, he rose her up again,
With me rye, fal lai-doll, diddle-aye day."

Margarita had a rich low soprano voice, like smoke on the water. She would sing the melody solo on the verses of the shepherdess:

"Since you have had your will of me, pray tell to me your name.
So when our dear little babe is born, I might call him the same."

Most everyone in the room would join in for:

"With me rye, fa lai-doll, diddle-aye day."

André would take the lead next, with his bass voice singing the part of the poorly behaved Knight Guilliaume:

"Sometimes they call me Jacques he said, Sometimes they call me John,
But when I am at the king's high court, they call me Knight Guill-i-aume,
With me rye, fa lai-doll, diddle-aye day."

Then Benoit would return to the melody for the narration with André on the bass harmony:

"He put his foot all in the stirrup, and quickly he did ride.

She tied a handkerchief around her waist, and followed at the horse's side,

With me, rye, fa lai-doll, diddle-aye day."

৯ ৶

One night, when the trio started into this old ballad, the room hushed down to listen as usual. The drinkers sat back, some closed their eyes, and let the story transport them briefly to an older era. The three voices sang in harmony on the narrative verses, the next being:

"She's run till she's come to the river's brink, she's fell to her belly and swum,

And when she's reached the other side, she took to her heels and she's run

With me rye, fa lai-doll, diddle-aye day."

It sounded wonderful, but Benoit became aware of Margarita and André. They kept smiling at each other as they all sang their parts:

"She's run till she come to the king's high court, She knock-ed and she ringed.

None was so ready as the king himself, to let this fair maid in,

With me rye, fa lai-doll, diddle-aye day."

André smiled at Benoit, but Benoit did not return the smile. It pained Benoit that his once close friendship with André had been strained because of their mutual love for Margarita. Margarita took the lead, addressing Benoit as the king:

"Good morn to you kind sir, she said, Good morn to you said he.

Have you a knight all in your court, this day has rob-bed me?

With me rye, fa lai-doll, diddle-aye day."

Benoit, in his strong tenor, sang as the king, mocking the peasant girl with condescension:

"Well, has he robbed you of your gold, or any of your store,

or has he robbed you of your gold ring, you wear on your little finger?

With me rye, fa lai-doll, diddle-aye day."

Margarita retorted with a sweet, angelic innocence and a mock angry look and a smile at André:

"Well, he ain't robbed me of my gold, or any of my store,

but he's robbed me of my maidenhead, which grieves my heart full sore,

With me, rye, fa lai-doll, diddle-aye day."

And Benoit, while worried about where he stood with Margarita, took his second lead as the king:

"Well, if he be a married man, then hang-ed he shall be,

but if he is a single man, his body I will give to thee."

The audience showed their approval by singing louder on the chorus:

"With me rye, fa lai-doll, diddle-aye day."

The three-part narration returned, but now Benoit was keenly watching Margarita's behavior:

"The king has called his nobles all, by one and by two and by three.

143

Knight Guill-i-aume was the foremost man, but now behind comes he.
With me rye, fa lai-doll, diddle-aye day."
André, the bass, opined and sulked as Guill-i-aume:
"Oh curse-ed be the very day, that I got drunk by wine,
for to have a shepherd's daughter dear, to be a true lover of mine,
With me rye, fa lai-doll, diddle-aye day."
Margarita, as the shepherdess, triumphed over the man who took advantage of her (while Benoit was thinking she was expressing far too much warmth):
"If you think me a shepherd's daughter, then leave to me your lain.
If you make me lady of a thousand men, I will make you lord of ten,
With me rye, fa lai-doll, diddle-aye day."
While Benoit grieved inside over what he was witnessing, André and Margarita joined hands and smile at each other expressively, and the trio sang in harmony one more gorgeous time:
"So then these two to the church they went, and all small things were donned.
She appeared like a duke's daughter, and he like a squire's son
With me rye, fa lai-doll, diddle-aye day."

They received enthusiastic applause for the famous story well sung. André and Margarita embraced and kissed—all in the spirit of the song, of course. Benoit was crushed; it had been too good to last. One of Cupid's arrows had flown to Senegal.

The little spark that ignited between André and Margarita soon turned into a regular fire. Every time they ate dinner together and performed, Benoit saw his two friends grow closer and closer. He could no longer enjoy his songs or food or his best friends. Benoit moped, *How can I sing with them? I can't stand to see them together.* Margarita was looking for a man old enough to commit and to settle down. Even against their wills, André and Margarita fell in love, and it tore Benoit apart and soured the chords of the trio.

One night Margarita challenged Benoit, "Will you marry me and return with me to France to start a family?"

Benoit replied, "I care for you dearly, but no, I'm not ready to quit the navy, and I haven't yet been to the Far East." He added, "I will need another ten years to earn the pension we will want."

Margarita replied, "I will not wait as in the old ballads, seven years for you to sail away and then return. I am tired of waiting on shore. I want to return to France, not sail farther away from it."

They had enjoyed the time they had spent together, but they were on different time tables and paths. Margarita ended things with Benoit, who moved back to his boarding house. A week later she was with André.

ʕ   ʔ

After an awkward and painful couple of months, Benoit accepted the turn of events and managed to more or less forgive them both. He also acknowledged the bright side of it all: He had to admit that he was too early in his career to settle down with Margarita. Intellectually, he could view her love for André as less of a personal affront than as an act of nature. Benoit knew that Margarita, at thirty-two, was old for him. He soon became civil again to André on board *La Resolution*.

After several voyages and sea battles, and because of Benoit's good nature and strength, Benoit and André became reasonably friendly again. But the warmth and the laughter of the trio were gone. Benoit missed his best friends and loved being with Margarita, but he consoled himself that he still wasn't ready to settle down.

ॐ ॐ

Before Benoit reached his cabin, the ship's alarm bell rang out. The drummer boy beat to quarters as the pipe sounded. Benoit quickly took up his sword and pistols from his cubby, and hurried to the poop deck, wondering if this was another drill.

La Resolution had just entered the harbor of Cabo Lahoe off French Guinea. The smoldering nose of a charred hull of a recently burned sailing ship stuck out of the water. Over the small stockade by the little village flew a black flag, the signal for distress.

With all hands at battle stations, *La Resolution* carefully entered the harbor. A longboat left the shore, and from thirty yards, a Captain Pieterzoon respectfully asked in French if it could pull aside and come aboard. Le Comte de Fleuris gave the nod, and the bosun invited the longboat to pull up. The Dutch captain came aboard, and with melancholy touched his forehead in salute.

La Resolution had arrived just a day after the notorious pirate Bartlette Hawes. Hawes, commanding two three-masted privateers, had found six slavers sitting armed with just small-bore canon, like tethered ducks to be plucked at their anchors.

All but one of the slavers had agreed to parley, and to avoid a fight had ransomed their ships for ten pounds of gold each. Pieterzoon's schooner had tried to escape, was overtaken and boarded by the men of the pirate Bart's ship, *The Black Joke*. The pirates pressed three of the crew, robbed the rest of their valuables, and put them into lifeboats. This international assortment of sailors, still under the command of Pieterzoon, then watched the destruction of their ship and cargo.

Hawes ordered the female slaves out onto the deck and picked out the best looking for himself and his crew to play with. All the violated women but one were sent back into the hold. This last female was beheaded and butchered. Her pieces were thrown overboard, and the reason for this atrocity soon became apparent.

Hawes then ordered the plundered ship be set afire with lamp oil, although it carried 120 black African slaves chained two by two in the hold. For amusement, the pirates left the hatches unbolted and open. The slaves struggled out of the hold onto the deck in pairs. The surprise and excitement on their faces turned to dismay and wails as they realized that they had to choose between burning to death in the flames, or jumping into the sea and being torn apart by sharks attracted by the butchered woman's blood.

Just thirty yards away, the pirates aboard *The Black Joke* laughed and cheered at the gruesome deaths of the unfortunate black slaves. One of the pirates played a reel on an old fiddle while another danced a jig. As the flames began to engulf the ship, the mostly naked slaves, men, women, and children, jumped into water already boiling with feasting sharks.

La Resolution sent the longboat with Captain Pieterzoon and his men back to shore. Le Comte de Fleuris and Pieterzoon had determined that the pirates had probably headed south. De Fleuris, obeying his mandate from the King of France, immediately headed south, hoping to find Bartlette Hawes trawling for merchantmen.

Two days later, *La Resolution* caught *The Black Joke* and its escort, the *Hell's Revenge*, on a leeward shore. The French, approaching from the open sea to windward, forced an engagement. *La Resolution* and the *Black Joke* exchanged a broadside. The pirates were outgunned and at a serious firepower disadvantage. The *Black Joke* tried to escape, but *La Resolution,* with the weather gauge, stayed close and knocked out both masts of *The Black Joke* with its heavier cannons.

The *Hell's Revenge,* still full of determined men, decided to try and board *La Resolution.* It managed to sail into *La Resolution,* though taking a series of blistering shots, and tied in with grappling irons. It was an ugly situation, with sharpshooters on both sides firing from close range. After the first exchange of grapeshot and musket fire, Benoit saw pirates charge desperately onto the quarterdeck of *La Resolution.* Those who couldn't leap the distance used boarding planks or swung over on loosened sheets and braces that ran from the clews of the square-rigged sails. Suddenly, the Frenchmen were fighting at close quarter for their lives.

Benoit saw Guillaume fire four pistols, and the first four attackers to come near him fell with balls in their foreheads. Guillaume then retreated down a hatchway to reload his pistols.

Benoit stood his ground with a sword in his right hand and a loaded pistol in the other, and a second in his belt. The first man to attack him carried a sword, so Benoit parried him with his blade. The man was charging, so it was reasonable to parry, sidestep, and execute him with a cut to the back of the neck. The next assailant brandished a pistol, so Benoit shot him in the chest. Then another attacked him while two more swordsmen attacked André in tandem, and André couldn't get the better of either. When André finally managed to thrust through one of the two, the dying man twisted his body, robbing him of his sword. André tried to hold on but the motion sent him forward onto his hands and knees right before the other pirate. The pirate raised his arm to split open André's offered head with a cutlass.

Benoit saw that his friend and rival was in mortal peril. As the pirate raised his cutlass, André futilely raised his hand to protect himself. Benoit drew his second pistol and shot the pirate in the temple. Though dead, the pirate continued his killing swing, but Benoit lunged forward and caught the attacker's sword against his own.

Benoit looked about him. The attack was being repulsed successfully. He then looked down at André, who lay with the pirate's body on top of him. As he towered above André, he laughed at the cruelty of fate and said, "Aren't you lucky that I outdrew the devil today."

"Sure," André said, "but couldn't you have dropped him a little more to the left?" Benoit couldn't help but laugh. And André, now smiling weakly, added, "Now help me get this bloody corpse off me." André was still recovering, and he was unsteady on his feet. "Many thanks," he said again, and turned away to hide the emotion in his face.

❧   ❧

The surviving pirates were clapped in irons and tried at Saint-Louis. Most were found guilty of robbing from the king's estate and summarily hung, though a few who proved that they were pressed into a life of crime were given reprieves and pressed into the French Navy. Bart Hawes was sentenced to be hanged, drawn, and quartered.

The next morning, for his execution, Bart Hawes wore red satin breeches and a white silk shirt. Executions were a form of public entertainment and social control. Townspeople joined sailors to see the famous pirate meet his maker. He refused the absolution offered by a priest, and defiantly declared, "I'll see you all in hell."

The executioners stripped off Bart's clothes. He was suspended by his neck from a gallows, cut down while alive, and his limbs were pulled apart slowly by four teams of oxen. His sexual organs were amputated, his belly opened with a butcher's knife, and his entrails torn out. These pieces were burned before his still open and conscious eyes. For the finale, his heart was slowly pulled out, ending his agony and formally closing the spectacle.

The audience broke up after the show ended. Benoit and Guillaume and the other military officers retired to the Officer's Club for champagne and brandy before their midday meal, while André slipped away to join Margarita for a more private dinner.

Meanwhile, the executioners wired together Hawes's body, put it in a tight iron cage the shape of a body, and hung it at the harbor entrance for all passing sailors and passengers to see. The sun, rain, and birds slowly ate away his flesh. The King of France, like all the Western potentates, took extreme umbrage toward any piracy against his estate. The law was severe; his estate was equal to his body. Pirate captains were, by law, punished as assassins.

Chapter 18
Harmony Province
1786

Thuận Hóa, the Province of Harmony, in which stood the mighty Phú Xuân, the Spring Capital, in the middle of the country, was the most strongly garrisoned area of Annam (then called Đàng Trong). But Harmony Province fell into discord. The Trịnh governor had pursued his own interests. That is, he fulfilled his own physical and financial needs with such energy that little of his life-juice was saved for essential military preparations.

Huệ shuttled the Hissing Army by sea to the deepwater port of Đà Nẵng. Then the bulk of the army marched into the central highlands and through the Pass in the Clouds. Before the tempest of his fighters, the demoralized Trịnh forces quickly abandoned their fortresses by the pass.

Trịnh Khắc Khoan, the Second Commander of the Citadel in the Clouds, sent his wives and family north with a detachment of his personal guard. His first wife carried a letter from him to open upon her arrival, in which he expressed his deepest feelings of love for each wife and their children. Trịnh Khắc Khoan retired to his study. From a drawer of his desk he took a coil of red silk rope, which he fastened to a beam supporting the roof of his office. He lit an incense stick and prayed to his famous Ancestors for the last time. He climbed up on a chair and put the silk noose around his neck. Trịnh Khắc Khoan, hoping that his neck would break, jumped into the air as he kicked over the chair he had been standing on.

When his first wife opened the letter, she would read: *Even good men and brave soldiers cannot stop seasonal floods, or the rot of corruption. But every rotten forest finally falls to the fire. I die loyal to my lord, as Heaven and earth are my witness, the Tây Sơn are Heaven's fire to clean the filthy pigsty which my country has become. Oh Gods, be merciful to you all, my beloved wives and children. My dears, I love you all more than you will ever know. I have been ordered not to retreat, and I am a soldier who obeys his king to the end, even when that king shows great lack of judgment.*

Even in a regime noted for depravity and corruption, men of honor still remained. As their own troops ran out the north gate of the first fortress, at least two of the Trịnh's noblest officers hung themselves with silk chords. Their self-destruction was viewed by their own people as saving honor in the face of embarrassing failure.

Huệ sent his troops against the fortress of the Spring Capital simultaneously by land and by sea. He timed his naval attack and the landing of soldiers by sea to occur right after his land force arrived at the walls and moat of the Spring Capital. His junks and galleys moved up the coast easily, with the warm summer monsoon breezing up from the southwest. The land troops had to march through rain and cope with mud, but they sent their supplies mostly by ship. The Trịnh had counted on the mud to prevent any attack. At this time of year, August, the rivers were unusually high. Thanks to days of rain from a giant storm, the Perfume River had flooded over its banks. The large junks were able to navigate right up to the walls of the citadel. It appeared as if the Gods of wind and water were determined to help the Screaming Tây Sơn.

The Trịnh General Phạm Ngô Cán rallied his troops and ordered his lieutenant, Hoàng Đình Thể, to lead a counterattack. Hoàng Đình Thể moved with such speed and bravery that his troops began to repel the Hissing Army, at a great cost to the Hissing Army. Huệ knew that he was losing the momentum his plans required, and stayed up late the next night, searching his copy of Sun Tzu's *The Art of War* for a solution. He reviewed his favorite passages, including, "For the weak to control the strong, await a change," and "Cause division among the enemy." He prayed to his father for guidance, and wondered what that crafty old man would do if he were around.

My father, Huệ thought, *was often not the strongest in his many martial bouts, but he always found a way around his opponent's main strength. Father used to say, "If someone is stronger than you, always get off the line of their attack. Try to out-smart an opponent before you try to overpower him. Use the gentle way; yield to overcome strength. After the tiger has run by you, then you can stab." I need a new deception. Or even an old one.* By the time he had walked back to his tent, Huệ had an idea he remembered from *Two Men on a String,* a play by Feng Yi T'ing, which he'd seen at the opera. He ordered his scribe awakened. When the man arrived, Huệ dictated a series of documents.

After creating the false documents, Huệ ordered one of his agents to deliver them, with instructions, to one of his field spies who wore the red colors of the opposing Trịnh. The spy was to deliver the false evidence to General Phạm Ngô Cán that his brilliant Lieutenant Hoàng Đình Thể was in communication with Huệ and about to change sides. It was brazen. On one level, it was a silly argument. Its power lay only in that it was possible.

After these orders were carried out, Huệ waited two dismally long days, during which his forces continued to sustain heavy casualties. Huệ ordered his men to take a defensive position, which they held successfully for another two days of attacks. On the fifth day, Lieutenant Hoàng Đình Thể led a major attack, which Huệ's forces easily overwhelmed. The poison had worked!

General Cán had lost all confidence in his lieutenant and cut off the resupply effort to Thể, whose troops soon ran out of arrows, powder, and shot, as well as food and water. Hoàng Đình Thể, facing a desperate situation, decided to continue nonetheless. Historians, those learned scribes of eternity, would record Hoàng Đình

Thể's bravery and ultimate sacrifice for his king in the line of duty. Stern-faced, he mounted his elephant and encouraged his soldiers into a last suicidal attack. He saw his two sons both killed on the battlefield with his own eyes. When his attack was exhausted and he had no chance of escape, for he'd led his troops deep into the enemy's lines, he cut his own throat with his knife so that he couldn't be taken as a prisoner and humiliated. It was the defeat of such brilliant and brave men as Hoàng Đình Thể that made men fear and respect Nguyễn Huệ.

Huệ entered the citadel of the Spring Capital with his troops and there ensued a terrible bloodbath. Hundreds of surrendering soldiers were massacred without pity. General Cán, the man so easily duped, was captured, clapped in chains, and delivered as a trophy to Nhạc in Quy Nhơn for a humiliating execution. Of all the Việts who were captured alive, whether famous scholars, brave soldiers, or innocent women and children, none but the most attractive women escaped alive, and they did not exactly escape. A Spanish priest who traveled with the Hissing Army wrote back to Spain, "There was a carnage the like of which I could not begin to describe to you." For a while, Huệ lost control of his troops. He feared for his own life if he stood in the way of the mob. His great victory was thus tainted by one of the ugliest behaviors that humans are capable of—atrocities against the defeated.

Following the death of Hoàng Đình Thể, the citadel of the Spring Capital had surrendered after only a single day more of resistance, and the rest of the province, all the way up to the Sông Gianh River, followed suit. In a single week of fighting, Huệ had subdued the whole of Harmony Province.

Huệ inspected Phú Xuân, the Spring Capital of the Nguyễn kings, and set up his headquarters in the prime minister's chamber, leaving the emperor's rooms untouched and well-guarded. Some of the removable valuables had been carried off, but the palace was still filled with large statues, paintings, elaborate wood carvings, and furniture.

With two bodyguards standing at a respectful distance, he was examining a carved rhinoceros tusk from the Trần Dynasty when a guard announced Nguyễn Hữu Chỉnh, the Trịnh general known as the Savage Eagle, who had communicated his desire to defect. "Make sure he is unarmed, then show him in, and bring tea." Nguyễn Hữu Chỉnh appeared meticulously dressed in an expensive black silk shirt and trousers, which, along with his bald head and silver beard, made him look austere and commanding. Hữu Chỉnh entered and bowed low. He had gimlet black eyes and large ears that stuck straight out from his small head, as did his long white sidewhiskers. Huệ was standing and returned the bow respectfully.

"My humble salutations," said Chỉnh.

"My humble salutations," said Huệ. Ignoring the Chinese-style chairs, Huệ waved for Chỉnh to kneel with him Viet style on gold and red wool rugs, while an armed aid brought them tea. Several of Huệ's elite bodyguard stood watch by the doors to the room.

"Again, Nguyễn Huệ, you have lived up to your formidable reputation. The morale and discipline of your troops is high, their casualties low, their work efficient, and the campaign surprisingly successful."

"You are too kind, and I too undeserving of such high praise," Huệ said, "but I appreciate this honor nonetheless. It is not often that I can confer with a master of the arts of war. I would be most privileged if you would condescend to share with me any useful observations you might have made."

Chinh was shocked by this straightforwardness, which was rude. *Peasants,* he reminded himself, *are not civilized through higher education and southerners are the worst.* He merely responded, "My time here has been short, and what little I've seen of your officers and men has only impressed me."

"My venerable general, time is short, and for every mistake that I make, I might cause the deaths of a thousand of my men. The normal courtesies of civilization are the only casualties of war I tolerate in good conscience without remorse. Again, with all respect to your extraordinary experience and reputation, please feel free to share with me any helpful observations or opinions you might harbor."

"Spoken like a student of Mencius and Sun Tzu. This is an unexpected and abrupt but reasonable demand, and well put. You have the mark of a scholar as well as a soldier. As the senior advisor of Hoàng Ngũ Phúc, the deceased pillar of the Trịnh, and then as their most successful commander thereafter, I did develop an eye for both the immediate terrain and the distant cloud. Overall, I am in fact impressed with your men and officers. But I can certainly qualify such praise if you insist, and you will not be offended or hold it against me. First, I would not have sent so much of the army's vital supplies by sea. The dangers of storm and pirates are far too great at this time of year. Luck was with you. There should be better discipline in the disbursement of the mess. Once corruption of any sort sets in and is permitted, it grows like weeds in a garden and takes over." Huệ nodded silently in agreement.

Now the old weather-beaten general smiled as if sharing a private joke. "I cannot emphasize enough that the best armies don't loot or rape or murder unless ordered to do so. Such behavior should always serve a military purpose. Temporary detention and flogging is the only mild remedy that ever seems to enforce such strict discipline, and it does strengthen overall morale, but public torture and humiliation followed by decapitation is probably better on both counts. The military police corps should be enlarged and strengthened. After curfew, there should be no parties—not even without music after curfew, and overall discipline, especially punishments, as I have already stated, could be much firmer. Strong discipline, if applied fairly to all, would not seriously damage the presently excellent morale, and might improve it."

Huệ took a sip of tea. Nguyễn Hữu Chỉnh's enormous presence, the vitality of his eyes, and his penetrating knowledge of men reminded him at once of his own father and of the great masters themselves. "Your recommendations are extremely valuable," Huệ said. "I am impressed. In commanding armies I am still young and there is much to learn about the art of warfare from the wise. I am distressed by the massacre of prisoners and civilians. The soldiers of many regiments simply went berserk. I was not confident that I could stop the pillaging or the blood-letting.

Huệ continued, "It pleases me to hear that you think such behavior can so easily be controlled. I will publish an edict making future unauthorized killing punishable by flogging or death. We will return to a strict policy and flog or execute any soldier who disobeys a direct order." Huệ offered the famous general his boyish grin, to put the older man at ease, and added in a flattering tone, "These are useful observations and suggestions. Now please tell me about the situation in the north."

Hữu Chỉnh studied Huệ's face, looking for clues to his disposition. He guessed that his new master was only thirty. He wasn't far off: Huệ was thirty-two. Huệ could be one of his sons. Chỉnh took a deep breath, as he realized he was at another great watershed in his career. Chỉnh began, "The civil war has reached new heights of folly and ill-favor with Heaven. In Đông Kinh, a famine has broken out and discipline has broken down. I suspect you have heard this already."

"I have news occasionally, but please start from the beginning, or I should say, at the death of Trịnh Sâm," said Huệ.

"It would be a pleasure," and Chỉnh changed from kneeling to sitting cross-legged, his back straight but his arthritic knees more relaxed. Even as an old man of sixty, his body remained limber from yoga, T'ai chi, and weapons *kata*.

"The King of the North, Trịnh Sâm, had many weaknesses. He loved his wine and women, but the real trouble started when he fell madly in love with the singing girl Đặng Thị Nga. He made this beauty a wife, and was so unremitting in his attentions to her that he brought the demons of jealousy and hatred into his household. Đặng Thị Nga produced a son, Cán. King Sâm, on his deathbed, designated Cán, aged four, to be his heir-apparent, slighting his eldest son, Khải, by his honorable and highly respected First Wife. She was already jealous and now predictably angry.

"It gets worse," said Hữu Chỉnh grinning. "So many problems create opportunities. After the king's death, the court divided into two camps. Khải, supported by the *Tam Phúc*, the king's formidable Elite Guard composed of the best fighters of the eight favored districts, seized the palace, murdered the regent, and proclaimed himself king. Khải was unable, though, to control the Elite Guard, which began to terrorize the populace with robberies, extortion, and assassinations. They murdered any mandarins who spoke out or ruled against them in the tribunals. After two years of terror, rebellion broke out a few years ago. To add to the chaos, during the last two years, poor harvests made the price of rice shoot up dramatically. You know the old story—first starvation, then cannibalism. The revolts increased, and bandits roamed around robbing, raping, and killing. You see why my soldiers did not defend Quảng Nam; they didn't know who we were defending or why. As my troops retreated or fled north before your screaming cutthroats, it behooved me to offer you my sword and experience to more quickly bring peace and national reunification." Chỉnh sipped his tea and fell silent.

"I accept this story," Huệ said simply. "Your report confirms basically what I have already heard. But when would be the most propitious time to invade Thăng Long [Hà Nội] with 75,000 men?"

Chỉnh smiled, his teeth bright red from chewing betel nut, and bowed. "There is no time like the present for an invasion of Thăng Long." He paused, and his radiating eyes betrayed his excitement. There was something in the manner of the old man, including his confident intelligence, that reminded Huệ again of his own father. Chỉnh went on, "In a single campaign you have subjugated Thuận Hóa and sown terror throughout Bắc Hà, the domain and backbone of the Trịnh." Nguyễn Hữu Chỉnh studied Huệ intently. *Is Huệ as great as he appears to be? Is he the chosen one? Bet on the wrong horse . . . and you lose your head!* "In the art of warfare, three factors enter into play: the tactic, the speed, and the force. From their conjunction victory is born. Now there is nothing up north but incapable generals, undisciplined troops, and a government in full disorder. Why not exploit your success and their disarray, and continue your advance? Victory is almost certain. One must not ignore such an opportunity of timing and tactics, if one has the force."

"Bắc Hà doesn't lack for men of talent," interjected Huệ. "Don't you underestimate the Trịnh Army?"

"The north has many ardent flatterers. It has remaining alive only one general of stature and ability who could lead the Trịnh to victory in the field, and he is Nguyễn Hữu Chỉnh. And he quit them, for flattery is their main expertise. There is no one else to fear. You have no one currently in power there to worry about," Hữu Chỉnh said without any modesty.

Huệ smiled and chuckled. "Heh, heh, heh, you are right. The others do not worry me, only you." Chỉnh bowed slightly to acknowledge the compliment.

"I know that I have some talent in war, and many years of experience in command. My troops will die for me when I order them to, but I want to make you understand that the north, with the unexpected failure of Hoàng Đình Thể and my defection, is now deprived of superior leaders who could threaten you."

Huệ continued to scrutinize the famous general. He said, "The Lê Emperors have reigned for 358 years. If today we seize the throne, will the people of the north respect and follow us?"

"The north has the emperor, but also a king. You represent one of the significant revolutions in our history. Although the Trịnh kings and princes pretend to serve the Lê, the fact is, the Lê Emperor must serve the Trịnh. And the region does not willingly support the Trịnh clan any longer. If no one has yet come to the rescue of the Lê, it is only because no one was strong enough. Move today and all of Đông Kinh will soon march to your drumbeat."

Huệ was almost convinced, but he had saved his gravest objection till last. "What about my eldest brother, Nhạc, whom I once loved and respected? It was I who put him on the throne and made him king. Nhạc and his courtiers are afraid of me, and plot against me now. Nhạc ordered me to conquer Thuận Hóa, and not Bắc Hà. By overstepping my orders, won't I be committing a serious moral and political, if not tactical mistake?"

Chỉnh stroked the side-whiskers of his long white beard. He did not expect this question, even though he had thought it might exist. Chỉnh paused and said, "Didn't the Master Confucius himself write in the *Annals of Spring and Autumn*, 'Disobedience is a small thing in the face of the grandeur of a successful enterprise?' Sun Tzu wrote, 'When the laws of war indicate certain victory, it is surely appropriate to do battle, even if the government says there is to be no battle.' And furthermore, it is my view, and widely held, that a general in the field is hardly expected to conform exactly to the letter of his instructions. He must adjust to the unforeseen obstacle or opportunity."

Huệ smiled and said, "Sun Tzu also wrote, 'Advancing and retreating contrary to government orders is not for personal interest, but only to safeguard the lives of the people and accord with the true benefit of the government.'"

Hữu Chỉnh smiled, and finished the passage, saying, "'Such loyal employees are valuable to a nation.'"

Huệ saw the excitement in Hữu Chỉnh's eyes, mirroring his own, and he was allowed to see somewhat into the general's mind. Like two old friends, their minds were a pair of mirrors. Huệ bowed to his new advisor. The arrival of a tactician of stature who agreed with his own innermost thoughts was a sign of sorts from Heaven that his own arduous task would soon find respite. *My dear brother Nhạc*, Huệ thought, *please understand and forgive me for exceeding my orders—and be careful to mind your manners.*

Chapter 19
The Trio, Saint-Louis, Senegal
1786

La Resolution returned to Saint-Louis. Margarita was waiting at the quayside for André when Benoit and André walked down the gangplank to her welcome and to the solid land. To their sea-accustomed legs and minds, the land felt more like the rolling sea. They walked carefully, with wide stances, to counter their strong perception that the ground moved like sea swells.

Margarita's brown eyes and hair reflected the sunlight, while her body filled out a light green peasant dress. "André, I'm so glad that you're back safely." She threw her arms around him for a hug. "How was the cruise?"

André said, "Everything was dandy until we got in a fight with two ships under Bart Hawes. The pirates boarded us and it was close. Warbling Bennie saved my life."

"This man is so talented," she said, and threw her arms around Benoit, who stood near. Their reverie was interrupted when Guillaume approached smiling, and appeared to want an embrace from Margarita as well. After all, he had been in the fight.

Margarita was used to deflecting the forward advances of officers and sailors. She exclaimed, "Good to see you returned safely, Monsieur Le Compte," while she stepped back making a formal courtesy.

Guillaume understood the message and made a stiff bow back, and then walked on. André, after a quick consultation with Margarita, invited Benoit to join them that evening for a good dinner somewhere. Benoit gave them both a funny look, then started to pretend to die, as if the invitation was enough to kill him, which made everyone laugh a bit awkwardly. Then he agreed to join them.

That night, at the Cuckoo's Nest Inn, Benoit celebrated with André and Margarita, and after a cheerful dinner, they all sang together one of their favorite songs, *Ah! Vous dirai-je, Mamam?* Again, Benoit sang the tenor lead, André sang the bass, and Margarita sang the soprano harmony. They filled the air with rolling thirds, fourths, and fifths.

Ah! Vous dirai-je maman
Ce qui cause mon tourment?
Depuis que j'ai vu Lisandré
Me regarder d'un oeil tendre
Mon coeur dit `a chaque instant
Peut-on vivre sans amant?

As before, Benoit and André acted out the parts of the comic ballad with antic faces and gestures, to the amusement of their listeners. In this song André played the mother and Benoit played the daughter.

In English, they were singing:
Oh! Dear mother, Shall I say?,
Oh, dear mother, shall I say
What torments me night and day?
Since the time I met Lysander,
And I saw his glance so tender,
My heart tells me ev'ry day:
Without love, life can't be gay.

After that night, something broken was repaired. Once again they enjoyed the town as a trio. As they had before, they moved from pub to pub, singing and dancing in the streets like gypsies, and singing together in the pubs for free food, drinks, and tips.

❧   ❧

Benoit's magnanimity grew hard for André to bear. André began to feel guilty about his happiness and suggested to Margarita at one time that she could also sleep with Benoit occasionally. "That's a terrible idea," she replied crossly. "Then we'd all go crazy."

André was getting so emotionally intimate with Margarita that he was beginning to feel an unusual vulnerablility, and a loss of freedom and independence. Margarita sensed that when he offered to share her with Benoit, he was actually trying to keep an emotional distance between them. She said, "I'm sure that such promiscuity would drive Benoit crazy, even if we could handle it. It is natural for him to be possessive, and you should be too."

"I suppose you're right," responded André. "I just feel sorry for him sometimes. And he will be moving on before too long to his next assignment."

"And what if I get pregnant? Will you know whose child we are raising?

❧   ❧

One morning Benoit and André took their muskets and marched with a black Senegalese guide and six Wolof-speaking porters into the jungle on a three-day hunt for wild game. They came back with two antelope and a leopard on poles. They were in high spirits. They sang songs and told old jokes and reminisced, and paraded the animals to Margarita's doorway.

Margarita did not come to the door, though, when they knocked and yelled. They went in anyway to leave her a note. The main room was in disarray, with a broken vase and chairs knocked about. They found Margarita lying naked on her bed, tied up with a rope and a gag in her mouth. Her face and body were covered with dark welts and bruises. She was in a state of shock. They both spoke gently as they untied her.

Margarita trembled and cried as André held her, and Benoit gathered up some clothes for her to wear. André dressed her, while Benoit found drinking water and something for her to eat.

Benoit slipped back outside and paid the porters. He sent them to a butcher to skin and cut up the game. He quickly returned to sit with Margarita and André. When Margarita finally did find the words, she said, "Oh André, it was horrible. He was too strong, and he raped me. Oh André, I'm sorry, please don't leave me."

"Easy love, it's all right. I'm not going to leave you." André held Margarita in his strong arms, and she shook with anguish as the tears poured out. After she grew quiet again, André asked her, "Who was it?"

"I don't know. He wore a black hood over his entire head, like an executioner." Margarita then sobbed uncontrollably again.

When she finally calmed down, she described her attacker as a hairy man with smooth, light-skinned hands. He probably had a beard. She had fought, and for that she had welts across her face, arms, and legs. She only was able to scream a few times, but since she lived in her own cottage on the edge of town, apparently no one heard her.

The handkerchief that had been stuffed in her mouth had the Martineau crest embroidered on it, two lances crossed between four shields. It belonged to that man of the gimlet eyes, Guillaume de Martineau, so he was at least a suspect.

Since the night Benoit showed up at Reynaud's, Margarita had stopped seeing Guillaume. She had politely put him off. It was clear that he had not forgiven Benoit. The enmity grew mutual, and the trio had once made jokes during a performance in a bar about "snooty" aristocrats who expected others to do all the work. They suspected that this was his miserable revenge, and this crime was not the end of it; if it was Guillaume, he had probably left his own handkerchief to provoke a duel with pistols.

Benoit and André began to investigate. Three of Guillaume's poker crowd swore that Guillaume and they had all been together till one in the morning at the Black Queen Inn. The owner of the pub said that he'd seen Martineau arrive early, enter the private room in the back of the establishment, and leave through the front door at closing time.

The serving girl insisted he'd been there all the time, but she wouldn't swear it to God. She looked frightened. Benoit held up a purse full of copper coins and jingled it. He said, "Now no one will know what you tell us. We won't go to the police, on my word of honor as a gentleman. You may have this if you tell us what you're hiding."

The girl eyed the bag with hungry eyes. She took the purse, checked the quality of the coins, and weighed the bag in her hand. She did not make that much in six months. "He did go out," she said in a low voice. "I don't know how he left or returned, maybe the back window, but he was gone. Gone from the table for one, no, maybe two hours."

André and Benoit thanked the girl, gave her the bag of coins, and departed. They decided to accuse Guillaume and, hopefully, provoke him into challenging one of them to a duel. If he didn't, one of them would challenge Guillaume to a duel, but then he got to choose the weapons.

"Benoit, let's make a deal." André said.

"What deal?" said Benoit.

"If Guillaume should shoot one of us dead, let's agree right now that the other man will not challenge him ever to another pistol match. Someone has to take care of Margarita, and the obvious way to cut down Guillaume is with a sword."

"That makes good sense to me," Benoit replied. "It's a deal. But you must shake on it, your word of honor."

The two friends shook, and each one thought, *I'll find him first tomorrow.*

∾ ∾

That same night, on his way to his inn, Benoit was contemplating murder. *It's the only sure way—but I do not want to do it,* he thought, *even though the man is deserving of execution. Jesus, what a mess we're in.* Benoit stopped by the tavern where Guillaume usually dined, but couldn't find the man.

André found Guillaume walking down the street. "Monsieur Le Compte," André said.

"Yes sir," Guillaume answered smiling.

"Last night, someone violated Margarita," André said.

"Oh, that's terrible," Guillaume said in a cold, sarcastically neutral tone.

"We found something of yours in her room. Where were you last night?"

The alert Guillaume put his hand on the hilt of his pistol. "Is that an accusation?"

"Yes," said André.

"You had better be able to prove it."

"You can be sure that I will make every effort."

Guillaume smirked, and said, "Well, let me know when you get your courage up."

André squinted in disapproval. He had failed to provoke Guillaume into a challenge.

"It would be appropriate for you to fight someone who is prepared to fight back. Choose your weapon. How about tomorrow afternoon?" André had given the challenge, and given up the advantage of choosing the weapons.

"Good," smirked Guillaume, "Pistols, at four p.m., at the Negro graveyard," he said smiling, and strode off.

André stood for a while on the empty street. He noticed there were stars overhead. He marveled at the stars, maybe for the last time. He admired their beauty, and wondered in awe at the mysterious forces they represented. *God help me*, he prayed to the starlit night. *He is the best pistol shot on our ship.*

When Guillaume reached his inn, he found Benoit sitting in a bench by the entrance. Benoit also questioned Guillaume. They also exchanged views, and insults, and Guillaume informed Benoit that he had already met with André, and they would fight at four p.m. with pistols. "You are a base coward," Benoit said desperately.

"Calm yourself, Grannier," Guillaume smiled, "or you could get hurt." They stared coldly at each other, and both men refused to challenge the other. Now, more seriously than ever before, Benoit contemplated murder. *Unfortunately, it is not my way,* he admitted, and he left after Le Comte de Martineau retreated into his boarding house.

➻   ❧

Benoit was André's second. André chose a gun from a pair of Guillaume's pearl-handled dueling pistols, and followed the rules of the honor ritual. Benoit looked his talented friend square in the face, shook his hand, and gave him an embrace. "Shoot well and fast," is all he said.

The soldier André grimly nodded. Then he smiled broadly. "It's for a good cause. We will get our man in this life or the next."

André and Guillaume stood back to back in the late afternoon sun and waited. The surrounding jungle was quiet, as if attentive—at least aware of the presence of men. In nature, males often fight over females, but not usually to the death.

André was outwardly stoic in face of the odds. The two men walked ten paces, turned, and took aim. Guillaume fired first, then neither man moved. Slowly, André lowered his gun as his whole body collapsed. The ball had hit André right between the eyes.

Trying to stay calm, and his stomach already in knots, Benoit carefully walked over to make sure his friend was dead. It was hard to accept what was obviously true. He knew that he would fight Guillaume, and he wanted very much to fight him right on the spot. But he wanted Guillaume to challenge him so that he could choose swords, and he had agreed with André to wait for such an opportunity. He wondered, *How quickly can I force his challenge?*

André was indeed lifeless. Benoit faced Guillaume and said coolly, "What a pity that your fancy shooting should deprive us of satisfaction and justice."

"Are you accusing me of anything?" Guillaume said with a smirk.

"You are a beast. I accuse you of being the opposite of a gentleman—of being a snake, bringing evil into the garden, a beater of women, a rapist, and a coward."

Guillaume listened impassively, quite under control, waiting for his adversary to make the challenge. Benoit stood also under control, letting the insults stand without the challenge.

For a second Guillaume grew uncomfortable. He had just been severely insulted. But he refused to take the bait.

"The blood of one dear friend is enough for one day. Since you are young and arrogant, like your friend whom I have just disposed of, I will give you a day or two to cool off and get your wits about you." So saying, Guillaume turned away and walked over to his seconds. They vigorously shook his hand, helped him put on his jacket, and all three strode away.

∾   ∿

"Why didn't you both just murder the bastard?" Margarita screamed. "God damn it! André is dead. I've lost him. Will you be next? Will I lose you both?

"You don't have to fight him," she pleaded. "My revenge is not worth the risk of losing you too. And besides, then I would be with no one to protect me from this monster. Murder him or let him go. We don't even have proof that it was him."

Benoit decided to insult Guillaume so publically, and in front of so many officers and barmaids, that Guillaume would become a laughing stock of both men and women if he ignored it. The next day and evening, he searched for Guillaume all over town, but Guillaume had disappeared. It turned out he had taken a sudden leave from the navy and booked passage on a French corvette that had embarked that morning for France. He had told his captain that his father was dying, and received permission.

Margarita mourned for André, and so did Benoit. Margarita also suffered from the violent abuse she had received. She no longer felt safe in Saint-Louis or anywhere in Senegal. Benoit suffered from a sense of guilt that he had somehow allowed André to die in his place. They were both choked with anger at Guillaume, and when that anger finally came out, it was usually directed by each of them at the other. One night, Margarita screamed at Benoit, "Why did André have to duel Guillaume with pistols? You both knew he was the better shot. Why were you both so damned stupid?"

"Perhaps it was stupid, but it was to defend your honor," Benoit retorted, and he stormed out of her cottage, slamming the door as he went out.

André had promised that he would retire soon from the navy. He had planned to return to France to start a family. Benoit had made no such promise. Margarita was tempted to take up with Benoit again, but she knew that such a move was careless. She tried one more time: "Why don't you quit the service and marry me. We could live together in France. We could make some beautiful children."

"Margarita, I would love to marry you and return to France, but I won't. We could marry, but for many years you would have only my short visits home, like other naval officer's wives."

160

"Benoit, I can't live my life alone like that any longer," she said, with tears rolling down her cheeks. Margarita decided to go back to France. Benoit, though sad to leave her behind, decided he should take charge of his career. He requested, for a second time, a transfer to India. Somewhere out there, his cousin Antoine Grannier was practicing his faith and preaching the Gospel to the heathen of Cochinchina. He threw himself into his work as an officer in the king's navy. Someday he hoped to catch Guillaume. Someday he would find another woman and enjoy life again.

Chapter 20
Thái Đình Ky and Jade River
1786

Thái Đình Ky was an educated man of wealth with various business interests. He came to Biên Hòa to meet the talked-about singing girl. He reserved an evening and a night with Jade River, and they both enjoyed the encounter. They played the lute and sang old songs to each other, then traded amusing stories with some genuine laughter. Thái Đình Ky bedded her with amorous ardor, and then opened his purse and reserved her for a week. His lust turned to love, and Jade River responded to his wit and charms. During the weeks that flew by, they improvised linked verses, composed Tang style poems, drank tea while playing long games of chess, and performed lute duets. As long as the wealthy scholar kept producing his silver *liang*, the fat lady Madame Camellia kept harvesting the romance.

One evening Thái Đình Ky broke down and declared, "My darling, I must be direct: I love you like no other, and I would have you accept my devotion and consent to marry me."

"Well, Mister Thái Đình Ky," she said, "do you not already have a wife? Aren't you just playing with me?"

"Alas, I have a wife, as you have rightly guessed, but I hardly think of her during these months I've been with you."

Jade River responded thoughtfully, "I have enjoyed your company, but I have some serious misgivings. First, there is someone special that I've lost from a previous life. But also, I would agree to be your Second Wife my dear, but not without your First Wife's consent and support. How will my introduction into your family affect the harmony of your house? You must return to your wife and straighten out your domestic relationships. One might predict that we are better off to part ways, keeping our love safe from the possible disapproval of your wife."

"You do not need to fear my wife," Thái Đình Ky said quickly. "She is obedient, and follows the admonitions of Confucius to submit to her husband's will. She comes from a good family and knows her place. She is always generous with me, and considerate of others."

With such words of comfort, Ky overcame Jade River's reservations, and one morning, while on a long walk, they escaped the teahouse neighborhood, and Ky hid her in a distant farmer's house. Ky then approached Madame Camellia, demanding that she sell him Jade River's contract at a reasonable price, and with a good discount for all he had already spent. Madame Camellia was annoyed and impressed by the young man's business acumen; he had the goods, and therefore a strong negotiating position. She agreed to his purchase of her slave for 300 taels of silver, minus the 150 he had already spent. Ky claimed that he had business interests in the area, so he rented a house for his new mistress right there in Biên Hòa.

❧　❦

They lived in harmony and happiness for half a year. Jade River's happiness increased her beauty, and started to mend her heart. Then one day Ky's father suddenly showed up, and upon discovering that Ky had set up house with a former prostitute, the father scolded his son and dragged him and Jade River to the local Nguyễn magistrate. The father accused the prostitute of casting a spell over his son, endangering his marriage to his wealthy and powerful wife, and so requested that the magistrate send her back to the whorehouse where she belonged.

"Father, and your honor the magistrate," Thái Đình Ky pleaded, "I realize that this looks irresponsible, but please, I love this woman, and this is not her design. It was my idea that she leave the teahouse and live with me. I would rather die than make her suffer for my intervention in her life!"

"Nonsense," the old man said. "Son, you are an idiot, and she is a witch. You are under her spell. I look to the court for my revenge on her and justice for all!"

"Your honor the magistrate," begged Ky, "my father is not listening. This affair was all my doing, the woman is innocent of his charges. Furthermore, she is an educated lady who can read and write, and she writes lovely poetry in a beautiful hand. I sought her out because of her stellar reputation. After our first night together, I signed up and paid to spend the next two months with her. I waited patiently till she reciprocated my feelings. I bought her contract and set her free. I even lied to her and told her my wife would not object to the marriage."

"The plot thickens," said the magistrate, with a smile of intrigue on his face. "Call the prostitute in." Jade River came in with the bailiff and took an offered seat. The magistrate ordered, "Give the accused brush and ink. Young woman, show me your skill in poetry and write a verse. Is the young man lying and under a spell, or telling the truth about education and talent? At least we should get some amusement for our trouble."

Jade River was ashen with fear, but she sat at a desk, received a blank sheet of paper, took a deep breath, and brushed a verse. She wrote in her clean and confident calligraphy:

How to live in the world?
Learn a few things and live upon the earth.
How hard to please the world! It's no child's play.
When what you hear offends, turn a deaf ear.
Though anger churns inside, force lips to smile.
If fate so wills, where can you flee from fate?
Since you need men, you must submit to men.
Let them do what they please and bear no grudge—
By Heaven all's decided in the end.

Jade River handed her sheet of parchment to the magistrate. All waited in silence.

The magistrate sucked in his breath. "This is unbelievable. It is magnificent," he declared smiling. "Such poetry, such calligraphy!" He handed the parchment to the father. "Read it. It is a throwback to the height of T'ang. If this young man won't marry this talented girl, perhaps I will, ha ha ha. What say you, old man, how are your brains? Are you still against this woman as a mere gold-digging strumpet?"

"The woman has many attributes," Old Thái admitted somewhat grudgingly. Then he mumbled, "Perhaps she is a keeper after all." He looked at the judge and his eager son, and decided to keep his counsel to himself.

"Father," said Ky, "I wish to marry Jade River and bring her into our family." Jade River was now in a quandary. Mostly, she did not want to be sent back to the bawdy house to continue as a sex slave. Thái Đình Ky was a lovely man. And so she did not protest, and they were married with the father's blessing.

❧   ❧

Another half year, happier than the first, if that were possible, sped by in marital bliss, till one day Jade River confronted her husband. "My husband," she said carefully, "you have been a away a whole year from your primary house. You must return and make peace with your First Wife. I will never live under the same roof without her consent and approval."

"Oh my darling, you don't know my wife," warned Thái Đình Ky. "She might not ever approve."

"I know," said Jade River gravely. "I fear I will lose you forever, but we must make amends. At least I will have my freedom."

Thái Đình Ky accepted the truth of her words, made his preparations, and left for his primary home in Nha Trang. After the profile of the gentleman on his horse disappeared down the road, Jade River walked back into her empty little house and prayed to the Buddha and Quán Thế Âm, the Bodhisattva of Mercy, for the success of her first real husband's mission of reconciliation with his First Wife.

❧   ❧

Thái Đình Ky's First Wife was named Miss Hoạn. She was the daughter of a rich merchant trader who owned many ships. Her father also served as the Mayor of Phan Thiết. Miss Hoạn was a critical and proud woman who didn't like to be slighted. Her spies had kept her fully informed of her husband's infidelity and cowardly transgressions. She knew that her jealousy was not proper for a Việt wife, but in her anger, she made plans to revenge herself on her philandering husband, since he had doubly transgressed, first by whoring, and second, by not sharing his intimate news with her—a courtesy expected between husband and wife. When two of her henchmen first reported on her husband's affair before her maids, she had them beaten, saying that they had insulted her husband with lies. She then acted in public as if nothing was wrong, while she seethed secretly inside.

Thái Đình Ky finally came home and embraced his smiling wife, and he made excuses about his complex business affairs. They took up where they had left off, more or less, as if nothing were amiss. To Miss Hoạn's added fury, her husband still did not confess about the other woman he had plucked from a bawdy house, and even dignified with marriage, without bothering to inform her. Humiliated, her anger overflowed.

A year went by, and their intimacy was apparently restored. They shared news and confidences again, but still Ky made no confession about his other wife. After the year, Ky made noises that he needed to return to Biên Hòa to check up on his family's business affairs there, as before. Miss Hoạn acquiesced with stoicism. Ky decided to go to Biên Hòa by road, since he had relatives and businesses on the way that he could visit. Miss Hoạn sent some hired knaves to Biên Hòa by sea, which was much faster. These underlings found Jade River in her little house.

These thugs went down to the nearby river and found a woman washing laundry. They murdered the washer woman and carried her corpse with them back to the little house. They surprised the unsuspecting Jade River, bound her, drugged her into sleep, and dragged her to their cart. They put the corpse of the washer woman into the house, which included Ky's newest library of books, dowsed the rooms and books in lamp oil, and then burned the house down.

When Old Thái came to see the damage, he discovered the charred skeleton of a woman, what must have been the remains of his son's Second Wife in the burnt shell of their house. Her ashes were collected and given a proper burial with the traditional rites. When Thái Đình Ky arrived and he heard the tragic news, he gnashed his teeth and rolled on the ground weeping and moaning.

When Jade River woke up, she didn't know where she was. Jade River followed a grim housemaid to a stately room where she was presented to a richly dressed woman lounging on a Chinese couch as if it were a throne. The woman questioned Jade River at length, and required her to relate her life's story. When Jade River reached the end of her tale, where she was attacked in her cottage, and she could remember no more, Miss Hoạn shrieked, "Liar, these are all lies! You are my slave. I bought you fair and square, and your life before was of debauchery and ill-repute. Girls, seize this bitch and teach her her place—give her thirty strikes with the cane."

Some of the stronger female attendants grabbed Jade River, dragged her off, and beat her bloody with bamboo switches. One of the gentler maids took the bruised and bleeding Jade River under her wing, and produced medicines, ointments, and bandages for her open sores and cuts. The maiden quietly warned Jade River, "You must be the one she has been looking for. Be careful how you behave. Should you ever meet your man Thái Đình Ky in these rooms, that is Miss Hoạn's husband. Be careful and do not look or smile at him. Look away, or even my special ointments won't be able to help you."

"Bless you, mistress," said Jade River, alarmed with fear and new comprehension. "What sin did I commit in a former life to merit what I must suffer and bear witness to? How can I repay you for your brave kindness?"

"Please just pretend in public that I never spoke to you."

Jade River was given a coarse gray smock, and sent to work in the vegetable gardens and the horse stables. Her skin grew rough and tanned, her hands grew coarse and strong. Sometimes, she was called to attend and serve her mistress at meals, where she was forced to stand by and watch her mistress eat and drink with her friends. Occasionally Miss Hoạn ordered Jade River to play the lute for her guests. Jade River was heartbroken again. She knew that this woman was Ky's First Wife, and Miss Hoạn was making it impossible for Jade River to ever look at their husband in the face or to be his Second Wife.

ॐ   ॐ

Thái Đình Ky mourned for his beloved, deceased Second Wife in Biên Hòa, and he went daily to her grave with flowers to plant, until the rains came and his thoughts turned back to his extremely wealthy but difficult First Wife. He was too depressed to shop the flower houses, so he returned to Phan Thiết, and to his matrimonial bed. Near the end of their first meal and interview together, Miss Hoạn arranged to have Jade River appear to clear the table. Jade River saw her lover and husband and kept her face blank while she averted her eyes. Miss Hoạn had engineered that they meet not as husband and wife, but as master and slave.

"Meet your master and kowtow," Miss Hoạn said sweetly. Jade River kept her eyes cast to the floor in her embarrassment, as well as her fear for self-preservation. She went to her knees and knocked her head three times against the stone floor for her master and mistress.

Thái Đình Ky glanced at the slave, looked again, then looked more closely. An expression of pain and frustration filled his face as he recognized the woman he loved, and had lost, who died, but lived, but couldn't look him in the face. *Demons and Genie,* he swore silently, *my wife has caught us like flies in her web, and she will suck us dry! From what hell-hole did this woman hatch?* "Fill our wine cups," Miss Hoạn said sweetly to the slave Jade River. "Drink with me, dear husband, to the memory of your mother." After they had drunk several cups, Miss Hoạn said with authority, "Maid, fill our cups again, then take up the lute from the corner and play for us while we drink. No sad tunes. If my husband shows the least bit of sadness, I'll have you whipped!"

Jade River filled the cups, took up and tuned the lute, and with tears rolling down her cheeks, she played lively dance music, as Thái Đình Ky contorted his face to look cheerful. He needed time to think. He wanted to scold and whip his wife, but certain realities held him in check. The properties he managed, which provided his comfortable incomes, all belonged to his wife's father. The saying is often true, "The gong of the husband is not equal to the gong of the wife."

అా అ⊷

A few days later Miss Hoạn asked her husband to question the new maid about her past. Thái Đình Ky was most embarrassed and uncomfortable, as was Jade River. "No, please, I can't. Let me write my story," Jade River pleaded.

Miss Hoạn yawned. "If you have to, go do it. Get out of my sight now." Jade River withdrew, and returned later with her written account. Jade River gave the pages to a maid to take in to the mistress and disappeared.

Miss Hoạn read the story carefully to herself, and then out loud. Some aspect of it touched her hardened heart. "This girl might have married a gentleman and become a lady. Misfortune was her lot, and she has been blown about, poor thing."

"I agree," said Ky with a heavy heart. "So perhaps you could condescend to be kind to her."

"She asked to be allowed to serve Buddha within the Void's great gate," said Miss Hoạn smiling sweetly. "That is such an educated reference to one of his humble little temples. I can help and make this happen. There is room at our own courtyard temple. She could become a nun there and help tend their grounds and work in their medicinal gardens."

So it was agreed and Jade River became a novitiate at the Temple to the Goddess of Mercy, Guan Yin—Quán Thế Âm to the locals. It was a relief to Jade River to leave the house of Miss Hoạn and join the kind nuns in the temple. She threw off her gray smock of the house slave for the blue smock of a nun. Jade River discovered that she enjoyed the simple life of work and prayer. She even enjoyed growing her own food, while living, like the other nuns, on rice, beans, vegetables, water and tea.

అా అ⊷

One day Thái Đình Ky came into the temple, and he spoke to Jade River about how he could not forget her. He bade her remove herself from the family temple, since he feared his wife Miss Hoạn would not rest till Second Wife was in some way disposed off. Away from the compound, they could see each other again. A maid coughed, and Ky ran out. But the maid approached Jade River and said, "My mistress was here, hiding just behind that screen, and she overheard all. Perhaps you should not stay another night. I fear you are in danger."

Jade River decided to flee, but she had no money. In desperation, she took some valuable vessels of gold and silver from the altar to the Goddess, and departed that evening for the open road. She went to the wall of the courtyard, heaved herself up and over it, and walked into the darkness. She walked all night and half the day, till she came to a Buddhist temple. The prioress took pity on her and made her welcome. She made herself even more welcome by offering the gold and silver vessels to the monastery as gifts.

Weeks turned into months, the spring came, and a visiting pilgrim recognized that the vessels had belonged to the wealthy Miss Hoạn. The prioress confronted Jade River and learned the truth, then counseled that she should keep moving. "Buddha's gate is open to all, but you are in a danger I can't foretell. You should go, before flooding waters wet your feet." She arranged for Jade River to live with a farmer and his wife, the Bạcs, who greeted her with smiles and open arms.

Dame Bạc soon made it clear, though, that Jade River was a terrible burden and an unclean woman. She pushed the girl to marry a nephew, to clean up her life and reputation. Jade River reluctantly agreed to marry the nephew, Bạc Hạnh. He appeared in good clothes, bearing gifts, and he fell to his knees. He said, "My precious, I swear my devotion to you by all the Gods of hearth and home." The wedding dinner was lovely, but it was not her first, or second. After the dinner her new husband took her to bed, and after a week, he insisted they take a trip.

Bạc Hạnh took her to the port, where they boarded a sailing junk and sailed to the Sài Gòn River and up to Biên Hòa, while he used her as he wished. They rode horses and stopped in Biên Hòa, which seemed strange and disturbing. Bạc Hạnh grabbed Jade River and tied her hands and marched her to the Happy Valley Green Pavilion, still run by Madame Camellia and Scholar Mã. He sold Jade River with tears running down her cheeks to the fat lady for a healthy sum. "Welcome back, younger sister," said Madame Camellia, chortling with a smile. "Business will be good again! It looks like marriage didn't really suit you. You will look much better with some nice clothes and makeup. Don't cry silly girl; everyone will make money. Have a handkerchief."

Jade River rubbed her wrists where they had been bound. She hung her head, defeated. She thought to herself, *What have I done to deserve this? Oh Buddha, this is not what I wanted. I was happily married to Thái Đình Ky, a good man, and I was a free woman, and now I'm a courtesan slave again. While I was free, even with my shame and humiliation, I should have sought out my famous brothers in Quy Nhơn for their protection. Buddha forgive me, I was a fool to keep putting it off another season, but I felt so ashamed.*

Chapter 21

Thăng Long (Hà Nội)
1786

Blue Cloud asked King Nhạc in writing for permission to go with some of her sisters in marriage to see her father on his deathbed. The request was granted in writing. With that document, she took her family and Huệ's two wives, Green Willow and Precious Stone, and their children to the gate of the citadel. The guards stopped her and demanded her pass. She handed the head guard the letter of permission, signed by Nhạc. The guard read it carefully, and then waved the group to leave the fort. Blue Cloud was successful in moving Huệ's family to her parents' compound.

Hồ Huệ dispatched twenty of his bodyguards to find his wives and children at the family compound of Blue Cloud, and move them secretly north to the protection of Phú Xuân, the Spring Capital. He sent Hữu Chỉnh north as an advisor with the Hissing Army. His troops were to penetrate into the delta by the mouth of the Đại An, and to attack and seize the rice granaries by the river bank above Vi Hoàng.

General Trịnh Tú Quyên tried to stop Huệ's junk fleet in Nghệ An, but Huệ filled five junks with dummies, effigies with fake weapons, and sailed them in front of his fleet. The Trịnh forces fired so many arrows and guns at the leading five junks that they ran out of arrows and bullets. The Tây Sơn forces stormed ashore and took the fortifications. The Trịnh soldiers simply fled.

❧   ❧

They passed Thanh Hóa without meeting much resistance. The garrison of Vi Hoàng fled at their approach, and Huệ's troops captured immense piles of rice and provisions. They then set a huge fire to alert their chief and the naval forces of their accomplishment.

Huệ's junk fleet, armed with cannon and shot purchased from Dutch traders, and pushed by a favorable monsoon wind from the southwest, advanced rapidly toward the north, to the great joy of many Tonkinese peasants. Huệ landed his seaborne troops at Sơn Nam and began a rapid march, and threw his army against the fresh troops of General Trịnh Tú Quyên, whom his soldiers defeated in a violent battle. One could hear the cannon fire from many miles away.

Trịnh Tú Quyên was an elderly man with a long white beard, but of impeccable discipline and fierce loyalty to his king. As he watched his fleet of junks filled with expert spear and sword men splinter and sink under the pounding of the modern cannon of the Tây Sơn, he felt sure that his kingdom was lost. He thought sadly, *Even I argued against relying too heavily on the iron weapons of the foreign devils to defend ourselves. We chose to defend our land as our forefathers always have, with the weapons of our people, in manly combat.*

Trịnh Tú Quyên watched as Dutch cannonballs from the war junks flew like demons through the air. They indiscriminately tore apart the old and the young, the best and the least educated. Trịnh Tú Quyên understood that the cannon were creating a revolution of their own. "Foreign insects," he swore to one of his officers, "these new weapons act like Shiva the Destroyer. Against these foul weapons, the traditional skills of war, learned over years of study and apprenticeship, become irrelevant."

He saw another of his great junks slowly sinking, without rudder or mast. Its brave fighters were divided. Many were standing in stoic silence, while others were jumping into the water. *The world is changing,* he thought, *and the honorable ways have lost favor with the Gods. I am now in disgrace, such a bitter taste. I will not live to see another beautiful sunrise, or hold my wives, or comfort and protect my children.*

The Trịnh soldiers under General Ngô Cảnh Hoàn at Sơn Nam were very brave, but also outgunned and outnumbered. They lost after a terrible resistance and few escaped. General Ngô Cảnh Hoàn saw both of his sons die trying to protect him. To avoid the humiliation of capture, he jumped into the Thúy Ái River and forced himself to drown.

After this battle, Huệ made sure that prisoners were captured rather than murdered—including soldiers. The governor of Sơn Nam, when informed of the great military disaster, ran north with his troops. The Hissing Army hurried after. Huệ decided not to stop and rest at Sơn Nam after all.

High society in the capital of Thăng Long (Hà Nội) was not terribly upset by the fall of Harmony Province, which had only recently been conquered. It was considered of small consequence; it was only the fall of a new acquisition. But the fall of Nghệ An and then Thanh Hóa changed that blasé attitude. Then word came of Nguyễn Hữu Chỉnh's defection. After the surprise fall of General Trịnh Tú Quyên and General Ngô Cảnh Hoàn, the Trịnh began to worry. Huệ faced a second army commanded by another highly regarded general, Hoàng Phùng Cỏ.

Hoàng Phùng Cỏ was called out of retirement. He quickly raised fresh troops, which he sailed down the Red River to wait for the Tây Sơn Army. Believing the Tây Sơn were still far away, the troops bathed and dined, but were caught unprepared by the sudden arrival of Huệ's troops. Six of Cỏ's eight sons were killed in the terrible fighting. Cỏ and his surviving two sons escaped with very few of the new troops.

❧   ❦

King Trịnh Khải, the supreme ruler himself, personally led his third and last army out to meet the invaders in a final attempt to bar from them the road to the capital near the Van Xuân Lake. Trịnh Khải divided his troops into five battalions, spread across the city. He led one from on top of his elephant, holding a sword and a red flag, and charged into the approaching army. The Tây Sơn soldiers sent a great volley of fire arrows, which caused the Trịnh soldiers to flee. Realizing he was abandoned, King Trịnh Khải dropped his flag, turned his elephant around, and hurried his huge animal back to the citadel. The Tây Sơn entered the city gate without resistance.

❧　❦

The last battalion was dispersed by an irresistible assault led by Huệ's war elephants under the command of Bùi Spring Song (Thị Xuân). Khải's force, already divided in sections, disintegrated. The Trịnh soldiers ran out of the town into the rice fields and the forests.

King Trịnh Khải, the hope of the Trịnh Dynasty, fled toward Sơn Tây and the refuge of the mountains north of Thăng Long (Hà Nội). He was recognized and captured on the road by disgruntled local peasants, and faced with the threat of delivery to his enemies, he committed suicide by stabbing himself in the throat. And so the Trịnh Dynasty came to an abrupt end. It had lasted 240 years.

Huệ was beside himself with excitement. He wrote in a letter to his brother Nhạc: *We have taken Thăng Long more easily than expected. King Trịnh Khải had a powerful army, which he had divided into three. He had city walls for defenses, which he failed to make use of. These tactical errors possibly cost King Khải his army and his capital.* After Huệ reread the letter, he decided not to send it right away.

In just a month, Huệ's military operations had revealed the internal disaffection and dysfunction of the northern regime, and the lack of support that the Trịnh suffered in their countryside.

Nguyễn Hữu Chỉnh, the Savage Eagle, suggested to Huệ, "It would be astute politically, and it would reduce insurrection in the countryside, to publicize your generous intention to allow the Lê Emperor to continue as the Supreme Leader of the North." Huệ found this advice sophisticated and to his liking; he requested a ceremonial audience with the old emperor.

Huệ, surrounded by his troops, mounted his elephant and marched right into the ancient capital city of Thăng Long (Hà Nội). His banners proclaimed, "Long Live the Lê, Down with the Trịnh."

Nguyễn Hữu Chỉnh also advised, "To set up a completely new bureaucracy throughout the populous north would constitute an enormous task. It will be much easier to leave the old bureaucracy largely in place. To show your goodwill toward the conquered government, return Trịnh Khải's remains to the city. To win the hearts and minds of the conquered population, order a state funeral for Trịnh Khải." And so the body was ceremoniously interred with the greatest honors in the tomb of the Trịnh Ancestors.

Hữu Chỉnh also advised Huệ, "Insist that the emperor receive you in a solemn audience and in a public demonstration of the restoration of the monarchy. The next day, you should pay your respects to the Emperor Lê Hiển Tông, publically showing your support of his reign. You will appease many of those who might oppose you."

On the seventh day of the seventh lunar month, an auspicious day according to Huệ's astrologer, Huệ and his men of arms marched past the citizens of the city to the courtyard of the Kiến Thiện Palace. Thousands of flags and banners waved in the breeze, and the parade moved to the beat of drums and gongs. Huệ could not help but be truly excited. *I am only thirty-two, and Đông Kinh [Tonkin] is now my conquered fief.* As proud and as strong as a tiger, he came with his highest officers into the solemn Hall of Audiences. Huệ prostrated himself five times before the emperor and presented the alert and apprehensive old man with lists of all his soldiers and officers, suggesting by this act that the Lê Dynasty truly held power.

Huệ announced, "I have annihilated the Trịnh because they had usurped the authority of the Lê." The emperor's face, haloed by beaten gold signifying the rays of the sun, showed no emotion. Old Hiển Tông smiled benevolently and thought, *I have heard such double-talk and bullshit before—so much wind. I have reigned for forty-five years, always in the shadow of the Trịnh. Now I am seventy, and sick. The great farce will soon be over.*

The emperor said to Huệ, "Welcome, Nguyễn Huệ of Tây Sơn. May your sons be many. We have business to discuss. You may be seated."

Huệ said, "Thank you for your generous reception. I came today to assure you of my loyalty. I have intervened only to ensure the success of the legitimate authority of the Lê. I came to reunify our great country, and to punish these Trịnh who have abused you. Heaven, which protects you, permitted me to destroy their power and end their corruption."

The old emperor squinted his eyes, and barely moved a muscle of his bald head. He said, "It is the will of Heaven. But this victory that you have gained is due solely to your own merit."

"My only ambition has been to serve you," Huệ responded. "The protection of Heaven is manifest: The winds have been good to me in spite of the season and the floods that failed to stop me."

Emperor Hiển Tông smiled and hid his disgust. *I am trapped by this two-faced warlord. I was just a figurehead puppet for the Trịnh king, and now I have to work with the new strongman or be swept away.* Hiển Tông girded himself and said as loud as he could, "For his success militarily in the south, the center, and the north, I confer on Nguyễn Huệ the rank of general and grand duke."

Lê Hiển Tông ordered tea served, and made a few more polite remarks, after which Huệ and his staff took their leave. Huệ and his soldiers returned to the king's palace. Huệ said to Hữu Chỉnh, "I do not think that the emperor will be a problem to us. I am more worried about a feud between myself and my brother Nhạc. In fact, perhaps I am the problem. Now that I have worked so hard and won the north, I don't want to give it up."

Hữu Chinh replied smiling, "Old Hiển Tông knows who will fill his rice bowl. I would not expect too much trouble from him. Until you have your own administration, his support will prove invaluable. Only you can decide who will rule the north. Will it be you—or your brother? Which raises a critical question: If you turn command back over to your brother, will you and your family and your friends and allies be safe?"

"No, we will not," Huệ said, his bright eyes flashing. "I am afraid that now I cannot trust my brother any longer. That is a serious problem. And yet, I fear that the moment for my own coronation has not quite arrived."

"Nor does it have to be far off," said Hữu Chinh the Savage Eagle. "Be honest, who remains who can stop you?"

Huệ almost answered, *You haven't met my mother.* Instead he said, "You have a point. I must somehow quickly settle my differences with Nhạc, because there are so many other pressing problems. Every day I receive petitions from all parts of Đông Kinh begging for a campaign against pirates and lawlessness, demanding a return to law and order."

"Unfortunately for the Trịnh," Hữu Chinh added, "Bắc Hà and half of Đông Kinh have not recovered yet from the drought last year, and both need food aid and funds for security forces."

"No wonder so many become pirates, when there is so little to eat," replied Huệ.

Left alone in his new chambers in the royal palace, the intoxication of Huệ's recent victories wore off. The return to calm felt low and dull. His mind moved to disturbing thoughts that he couldn't dispel. *I believe the reports that Nhạc plans to put me out to pasture. There is no known reason why the maid would make up such a story. Also, it is time to look high and low again for our sister, Jade River. We should be able to find her, dead or alive.*

Huệ sat at the king's desk and carefully examined miscellaneous papers and trinkets. He found the king's gold seal! He coveted the office and what it stood for. In a significant decision, Huệ decided to make King Trịnh Khải's office his own. He sat and wrote lists and delegated responsibilities. He couldn't release or spare any troops until after he'd made some arrangement of peace or war with Nhạc, so they had to be fed, housed, and paid.

Huệ marveled at the bizarreness of the Imperial Court. He was actually disappointed that his own emperor would allow himself to be so docilely made a puppet. To further enhance the alliance, Lê Hiển Tông offered his daughter, the princess Gem Lake (Ngọc Hân), to Huệ as a bride. To Huệ's surprise, this woman, whom he

173

couldn't easily refuse, was gorgeous, and she carried herself with poise and dignity. This was the old man's last gesture, and as a tactical move for a man in his complex position, it demonstrated that he was not yet senile or without cunning. Lê Hiển Tông had been saving this beautiful girl for just such an emergency, so that her charms could serve the greater purpose of protecting his male heirs—and it also provided her with a suitably high husband.

After a rushed wedding ceremony, Lê Hiển Tông had Gem Lake well-placed in the household of the brash but powerful Tây Sơn general. The old emperor had little more to live for. A few days later, his poor health and heavy depression overcame him, and he died. He left his throne to his favorite grandson, Lê Chiêu Thống, who was healthy, ambitious, and only twenty.

On the day of the emperor's funeral, Huệ, dressed in Trịnh Khải's white mourning clothes, took the place of honor in the long funeral procession. Although the procession took several days, Huệ stayed with it only until the first river crossing. The ceremony and burial took place in Harmony Province, where the names of most of the ancient Lê survived as carvings in the thick walls of their mausoleums.

During the official ceremonies, Huệ saw a Lê mandarin laugh rudely at the mention of his new rule, showing his disdain for Huệ himself. The public rudeness was a trap of sorts. Huệ had to decide publicly how to deal with such a challenge to his claim of authority. He dared not seek advice of Hữu Chỉnh or others in public, lest he seem incapable. *Therefore,* he thought, *the choice is narrowed: Should this man who would try and undermine my authority die slowly or quickly?*

Toward the end of the ceremony, various priests chanted sacred burial prayers, lit incense, and sprinkled flower petals and paper figurines of soldiers, women, and animals on the casket.

Outside the burial temple, Huệ stood up and addressed the assembled crowd of dignitaries and soldiers. "May we remember with great respect and adulation for 10,000 generations the spirit of the great Emperor Lê Hiển Tông. May the reign of his line last forever.

"May he finally escape from the red dust of earth's toils and responsibilities, into the peace of pure tranquility in Heaven."

Huệ nodded to the captain of his bodyguard. Several soldiers seized the mandarin who had made the derisory noises, bound his hands behind his back, and dragged him before their leader. The audience was attentive and apprehensive.

Huệ continued to address the crowd. "Change has come suddenly to Đông Kinh. You must accept my rule with complete respect and obedience, and in return, I shall endeavor to serve Đông Kinh with all of my small abilities. I will not, however, tolerate any disrespect or disloyalty. My orders are to be feared and obeyed."

Huệ spoke to his head bodyguard, who strode over to the cowering Trịnh mandarin, already on his knees. The officer swung back his two-handed sword and neatly cleaved the mandarin's head from his shoulders. Blood spurted from the headless body.

Huệ waited while everyone considered the ugly scene and the message, which was clear: Insolence or resistance will not be tolerated.

Huệ then rose, and turned to leave. Rather than ride in a ceremonial palanquin, he chose to ride his war elephant back to the city. Even surrounded by his most elite soldiers, the ride left him high and exposed, so he could see the people of his new kingdom—and so they could see their new king.

Thousands of Trịnh administrators, policemen, and soldiers were allowed to remain in positions of power. But Huệ was determined by his behavior to show who was actually in charge, and to whom they had better owe their good manners and allegiance.

All the mandarins were summoned by an imperial edict. Little by little, they appeared at the court, paid their respect, and performed three kowtows, or headknocks, to Huệ in the late king's palace. Some either went into hiding, bravely resigned, or fled to the mountains to join fledgling opposition forces, rather than do a headknock to a commoner from the south.

Huệ's new wife, Princess Gem Lake, at first had opposed the accession of her nephew Lê Chiêu Thống. Her duty now was to her new master, who to her surprise appeared to be intelligent, educated, and polite. Gem Lake also felt the boy would be safer if he did not ascend to his throne. She finally consented, at the insistence of all her family, to Lê Chiêu Thống's coronation because her new husband approved of the choice.

જી ન્ફ

King Nhạc had declared himself Emperor eight years earlier, back in 1778. Now Emperor Nhạc was in the middle of a violent embrace with his third wife's second maid when his generals Võ Văn Nhậm and Lương Hoàng came to see him in the middle of the afternoon. A palace eunuch told them that the emperor could not be disturbed under any circumstances. The two soldiers looked at each other for a moment in exasperation. Hoàng said, "You must tell his majesty, at the first convenient moment, that General Nhậm and General Hoàng await to inform him of the fall of Thăng Long to an upstart, his brother Nguyễn Huệ!"

The eunuch sucked in his breath and lost his condescending coldness. His eyes widened with fear. He looked from man to man in disbelief. Not quite sure what to do, he bowed stiffly and disappeared behind the two bodyguards, the brothers Snake and Midget, into the personal chambers of the emperor. The two generals sat down at an old carved ebony table and began cheerlessly to play a game of chess that they hoped not to have time to finish.

Just minutes after the moaning of the wind and rain had obviously subsided, the eunuch Chen struck a bronze gong and entered the bed chamber with the Third Wife's first maid carrying a tray of light refreshments and hot tea. The Third Wife's second maid lay naked on the mat. The eunuch handed the naked Nhạc a note. The maid, with milky eyes, covered herself and carefully watched Nhạc read the note. She saw his heart sink like a coin in a carp pond. His mind fled away from their visit to the clouds and rain, where he had momentarily ruled supreme in the land.

Nhạc was furious at his youngest brother. He thought, *If only I had followed Võ Văn Nhậm's advice and removed my dangerous little brother when I had the chance—great Heavens, now what?*

He turned to the naked woman in his bed. "Well my precious, I hate to do this, but I must leave you abruptly and meet with my counselors."

"Business, war, and politics. Humph, what could be so very important that it can't wait another hour?" she said with pouting lips. Nhạc raised his hand and she quickly rolled over to protect her face. Nhạc slapped her hard on her bottom and she cried out.

"I'm sorry," she whimpered. "Excuse this slave her stupid outbursts." Nhạc decided immediately to teach this young slave her manners. "You are forbidden to speak," he hissed. He slapped her three more times on her buttocks with his hand. The emperor then left her crying silently on the pallet.

Nhạc washed his face in a basin of cold water and wiped himself with a towel. His mind felt more clear and relaxed due to the love making and the spanking. *It is so strange,* he thought, *how the yin and the yang, enjoying gentleness and roughness, complement each other.* The eunuch helped Nhạc into a gold silk tunic with embroidered blue dragons flying about on it.

After a twenty-minute game of *Xiangqui* (Chinese chess), right after Hoàng took one of Nhậm's elephants with a chariot, Nhạc entered the inner reception room. The two men rose and bowed deeply. Nhạc inclined his head in recognition. "Không dám," both men intoned. "Welcome my friends," Nhạc responded. "You bring news from the front?"

Hoàng began, "Your brother Huệ has taken Thăng Long. We have intimate details of his attack on the north, its capitulation, and then his successful marriage into the imperial family. Huệ has even asked his astrologer for a propitious date in which to coronate himself as king of the north."

Nhạc walked over to a window, instinctively putting his hand on his sword, which wasn't there; he was wearing only a silk robe. He turned to his generals. Venting his anger, he shouted, "By the Gods! I will punish that runt for his disobedience. Nhậm, you were right, we should have left him in the treasury, or removed him entirely as a possible source of competition."

Hoàng was shocked to hear this admission. He had only recently argued with Huệ not to break with his brother, saying that Nhạc would never stoop to evil against his own kin. *By the Mountain Genie,* Hoàng thought, *Huệ was right that*

Nhạc could not be trusted. Demons and Genie upon us, things are going to fall apart.

"Counselors, we have two more months of the southwesterly monsoon. I want you to gather your staff and present me tomorrow at this time with a full plan for the conquest of Thăng Long, including inventories of available troops, ships, arms, and supplies. General Nhậm, you can order the commissary to prepare immediately to collect enough supplies for a 200,000-man campaign to last up to six months. I want us to be ready to sail in two or three days!"

Hoàng decided he must protest. "Your highness, what Huệ has done is terrible, but a war will seriously deplete our armies. Will you even consider a negotiating posture?"

"I'll negotiate with that little know-it-all with the sharp edge of my sword," Nhạc said, and stormed out. *That you will,* Hoàng thought, *and he will show you the iron balls and grapeshot of his Dutch cannon. All that we have gained will be destroyed, and the people will suffer even more than they do already.*

ॐ ॐ

The Hissing Army of the Center moved north in a series of rapid forced marches, while Nhạc's imposing junk fleet pushed up the coast. Nhạc felt no joy, only dread for what he was about to attempt. He was pleased about only one thing: His mother, Autumn Moon, insisted on coming. Much worse though, as everyone knew, his little brother had never been defeated in battle.

"You and your brother shall not raise your swords against each other," Autumn Moon commanded. "You can always fight our enemies, but your brothers are not your enemies until they fail completely in their filial obligations and attack you."

"But Mother, he disobeyed me, and I'm the emperor. I am his king and commander."

Autumn Moon paused. She had hoped that she would never have this very conversation. The petite lady, white-haired and wrinkled like the skin of a dried prune, spoke slowly, with the confidence of a woman who loves all her children. "And who is your kingmaker? It wasn't me, or Lữ or Hoàng. It was your youngest brother Huệ who won the hardest battles, and devised the plans when we needed brains over brawn. Who gave you the plan to avenge the murder of your own father? If you allow Huệ to rule the north as a king in his own right, your dynasty will be more secure than if you insist on a test of forces. You will most likely lose the war, or it could go on for generations.

"I need all my sons to live in peace. I love you all. I do not want to be forced to take sides. Harmony is required if your children, who are my grandchildren, are to remain secure and have a future. Do you hear me? If you oppose your brother with force in such an evil struggle, one of you will certainly lose, and the winner will be militarily weakened and in less favor with the Gods and the Spirits and the people. If you attack your brother because of his success, your Ancestors will send you, like a leper, covered with blisters and lesions, away from this earthly paradise, I swear it."

"And you?" Nhạc said turning to his old friend Hoàng.

Hoàng did not know what to say. Ever since the news of Huệ's victory had arrived, he had dreaded this moment.

"I am torn between my two oldest friends," Hoàng said. "I love you, Nhạc, but I also love your brother Huệ. You have both been like brothers to me. Why can't you love each other? Suicide might be easier than joining with one of you against the other." Nhạc clenched his teeth. This was hard to hear from his old friend.

જ ✇

By the time that the Army of the Center reached the plains before Thăng Long (Hà Nội), Nhạc had cooled down considerably and had decided to allow a settlement. He was afraid of his mother's curse; he was more afraid of his brother, should he go to war. His generals reported that his troops had lost their zeal. They adored and feared Nguyễn Huệ. They had fought like demons against the entrenched regimes, but fighting their own kind, and in some cases, even their own relatives, held no interest. Desertion had grown to be a problem for the first time since Nhạc had first taken to the hills around Tây Sơn.

Võ Văn Nhậm suggested that war was now inevitable. Nhạc turned to his mother for guidance on his crumbling position. They decided to send Hoàng ahead in a diplomatic mission to sound out brother Huệ for some sort of face-saving concessions.

"My lord Buddha," Autumn Moon confided privately to Lương Hoàng, "what if Huệ decides now that he'll settle for nothing less than to be emperor of all? What if he wants the north, the center, and the south? Nhạc is not thinking or using his head. It is within his clever brother's power to get what he desires. Huệ is so much like his father, but so much more ruthless as well. Nevertheless, he will not attack or harm his mother. I know my sons."

"I pray to the Gods that you are right," replied Hoàng.

Possibly Nhạc had had similar thoughts, for when Autumn Moon suggested that she travel with Hoàng, in case he met strong and stubborn resistance, Nhạc agreed.

"In case he has any doubt as to which side I am on," she said gravely, "I want an armed escort of one hundred men of your personal regiment. I want him to see and feel the threat of his mother's wrath. I want to remind him of his father's agony, and of the anger of all our Ancestors."

Hoàng and Autumn Moon entered Thăng Long in search of Huệ. Meanwhile, Hồ Nhạc, jealous of his brother's victories and the loyalty he commanded with their troops, and fearful of his military genius, arrived with his own army before the walls of Thăng Long. Autumn Moon prayed to the Gods that Huệ could not refuse his mother.

Chapter 22
The Lê Dynasty and the Spoils of War
1786

When Nhạc reached the outskirts of Thăng Long (Hà Nội), the young Emperor Lê Chiêu Thống, with a few courtiers, tried to force an audience with him. Nhạc, through his minister of protocol, politely told the envoy of the twenty-year-old emperor that he, Lê Chiêu Thống, would have to wait, but King Nhạc sent his deepest regards and would see him before long.

Autumn Moon called on Nhạc and was received. She said, "You must consider allowing your brother to rule Đông Kinh."

Nhạc answered, "I refuse to enter the citadel. I absolutely refuse to acknowledge Huệ as King of Đông Kinh. I will only pardon "the cadet" for his breech of orders if he comes out to my field tent and greets me as his older brother and king, and kneels, and performs the kowtows to me and apologizes for exceeding his orders." Nhạc could not be swayed by his own mother to share his power.

Autumn Moon, Lữ, and Hoàng reentered Thăng Long to attempt to entice Huệ out to greet his older brother and king. Their entourage entered the reception hall of the late King Trịnh Khải. Now Youngest Son Huệ sat on a teak and ivory armchair before the gold throne. Huệ wore a tunic of green silk, and a black hat embroidered with a thin crown of beaten gold lace sat on his bushy black hair. As usual, he looked extremely well, and moved with graceful restraint.

Autumn Moon, in the traditional yellow silk of the Vietnamese kings and queens, washed her hands in a ceremonial bowl, drank a cup of wine offered by an old priest, and then advanced to a guest throne that had been set near her youngest son and sat down.

Lữ, Hoàng, and their guards stood on the left. On the right of Huệ stood Nguyễn Hữu Chỉnh and General Ngô Thì Nhậm, and all around were Huệ's personal guards.

Huệ rose from his armchair and kowtowed three times to his mother. After watching the exercise, she gave a shallow bow back without standing.

Rituals were well established for encounters between officials, even between kings. But this ceremony was very strange to Autumn Moon, even though she had treated her sons as kings since they were babes. Now her youngest boy had breached the code of filial piety by disobeying his eldest brother.

Autumn Moon had reached her sixtieth year. She was tired from the voyage north by sea, but she had limitless resources of energy for her sons, and right now they needed her. She smiled at her youngest and said honestly, "It is good to see you again, my son." Huệ bowed again.

Huệ then faced his square-faced brother Lữ, who bowed stiffly from the waist due to his back injury. Huệ returned the bow, recognizing his second eldest brother as an equal. Lữ, who had had several discussions with his older brother on the topic of eliminating their youngest brother, was now terrified that his "baby brother" would somehow know his mind and prove treacherous and murder him during the official visit. He kept his plain, flat face neutral, except for an occasional ingratiating smile.

After greeting his brother and mother, Huệ said, "Lương Hoàng, it is good to see you again. I hope you are well."

"Likewise, old friend," said Hoàng, and he bowed with sincerity. "I salute you. I'm afraid we have serious matters to discuss and negotiate."

"And we will," said Huệ. "Let me show you the guest rooms, where you can relax and wash. You are all invited in one hourglass to a light meal, and then we will talk." Huệ personally made sure his mother was comfortably installed in a wing of his own compound, and then joined her for tea.

Autumn Moon wore a yellow Chinese silk tunic covered with red cranes. She hugged her son, and then playfully twisted his ear till it hurt, and her anger was physically communicated. She asked in a commanding voice, "Are we going to reach an agreement?"

"Yes Mother," Huệ said, laughing, somewhat shocked at the anger she so easily communicated behind her play. "Honorable Lady, please stop, or I must spank you," he said, with a mischievous but nervous smile.

"Heavens," she said, "I never thought the world would come to this state of chaos and neglect, when disobedient sons threaten corporal punishment on the old bones of their venerable parents." They both laughed uneasily and sat on Chinese-style chairs. Chairs were extremely rare in Đại Việt. These were ornate rosewood chairs from China, made with four legs and a back to lean against. The chairs faced a rosewood table decorated with

pearl inlay. At the steward's signal, attending maids brought in tea and assorted spring rolls and dumplings.

The servants were sent away and mother and son began to negotiate. Would Huệ visit Nhạc in his tent? Yes. Would Nhạc recognize Huệ as the king of Đông Kinh? Autumn Moon put down her teacup and looked Huệ in the eyes. *No.*

"Your eldest brother, Nhạc, says he would rather fight you than reward your presumptuous behavior, after you betrayed his trust. He has decided. He will rule Đông Kinh, with Lê Chiêu Thống as the figurehead. You are to be given five provinces to rule: Quảng Nam, Quảng Trị, Quảng Bình, Hà Tĩnh, and Nghệ An."

Huệ said nothing, but he frowned in disappointment.

"Precious one, now listen to me, Nhạc will not let you be king of Đông Kinh. He demands that you visit his tent. He promises, though, that you will rule your domain as a king in your own right. But he will not be dictated to, and he will not wait long for an answer. I got your brother to agree that you will keep the Spring Capital."

"Mother," said Huệ, "Nhạc and Lữ have apparently discussed forcing me to retire from the field, and if I refused, my elimination."

"That's nonsense," said Autumn Moon. "You can't believe everything that is reported. And based on your behavior, they have reason to fear you. Even if half of this were true, your brother would reinstate you anyway to defeat the Nguyễn."

"And many of my soldiers and theirs would die under their command. Please excuse me, Mother, I need time to think."

Huệ took a long walk in the royal gardens to mull over his choices. He could handle his brother militarily, and part of him wanted to, but he also knew that it wasn't in the best interest of the country or the establishment of the Hồ Dynasty to begin with a civil war dividing the Hissing Army and the Hồ family itself.

If only my father were here, Huệ thought, *he would help me forge a sensible peace with my brother. He would probably even order Nhạc to let me rule the north, since I deserve to. Hữu Chỉnh would have me attack and destroy my brother. I'm sure I could, but I don't trust Chỉnh. He smells like a complete opportunist, even if a brilliant one. War between Nhạc and me makes our enemies stronger, including him. But I sense that Nhạc, although my brother, is a threat to me.*

During the walk in the royal gardens, Huệ decided to agree to Nhạc's disappointing terms. Huệ deeply loved and respected his mother. He could still remember a time when he idolized and loved both of his older brothers. Filial piety, that is, respect and obedience to one's parents, siblings, and ancestors, was the foundation of a Confucian society and of Vietnamese civilization.

He did not say very much to his mother, but she was greatly relieved for the moment. Huệ understood that Nhạc would divide the country into three kingdoms. Huệ would rule Quảng Nam to Nghệ An. Nhạc would rule both Đông Kinh through Lê Chiêu Thông and also continue to rule the south half of the center, while Lữ would get the Mekong Delta jungle. He would rule Sài Gòn and the underdeveloped south.

It wasn't a neat or efficient plan for the country as a whole, but one must make sacrifices if one is to preserve a large, and once close, but now powerful family.

In a foul mood, Huệ rode out of the city to greet his eldest brother, to kowtow with three head knocks, and to apologize for his indiscretion.

Nhạc realized that he would have to accept the apology. He did so reluctantly, for he did not trust his little brother. Nhạc thought to himself, *There will be an opportunity to assassinate my brother sometime in the near future.*

The twenty-year-old Lê Chiêu Thống, who was not to be easily put off, showed up again at Nhạc's camp while the two brothers were still conferring. The emperor's arrival could hardly have come at a more awkward but also more useful time. It forced the two brothers immediately to clarify and reestablish the old protocols.

Nhạc ordered his brother Huệ to go and receive the young emperor of Đại Việt at the entrance of Nhạc's tent. And when the emperor was introduced, Nhạc offered Lê Chiêu Thống the place of honor, the central seat that faced, like the front of the tent, to the south. He took for himself the seat to the emperor's left, the second place of importance. The seat to the right he offered to Huệ, and the next seat on the right to Lữ. Next to Nhạc on his left sat Autumn Moon, since she was the mother of King Nhạc.

Lê Chiêu Thống spoke in sweet and flattering tones, and offered to cede to Nhạc several prefectures to repay him for his troubles. Nhạc feigned disinterest. He said, "My forces came to Đông Kinh only to put an end to the encroachments of the Trịnh upon the royal authority of the Lê, but I do not want a particle of land. I ask only the emperor to govern with zeal and authority so that peace will reign in his domain. I will leave you one of my divisions, to form the new nucleus of your reestablished authority."

So, Huệ thought, *my brother will advance the Lê in order to hinder me. It is a clever argument to use with my followers. I wonder if he suspects that should he arrest me, my officers are ordered to kill him and rescue me if they can.*

Nhạc's solemn promises reassured the young Lê Emperor. Chiêu Thống and his more naive advisers even hoped for a while that Nhạc came north more to stop his brother than to advance his own hold over the north.

Nhạc immediately put such hopes to rest. He entered the city and ordered a series of banquets to honor the restoration of the Lê Dynasty in Đông Kinh under the protection of his beneficent royal power. Nhạc took possession of the king's palace and the king's seals, and had his brother Huệ move into one of the guesthouses.

❧ ☙

After a long meeting between Nhạc and Huệ and their military and political mandarins, the two brothers were left alone in the ministers' conference hall. Nhạc had some questions he did not want the group to hear that he needed to ask Huệ. Nhạc said to his younger brother, "The army is getting restless. They are mostly conscripts, and there are many requests concerning how soon can they return to their wives and families and tend to their rice fields."

"I am aware of the growing frustration. Desertions and executions are increasing in my own troops," said Huệ. "We should take the armies back to Quy Nhơn and Phú Xuân. We should leave some of our most professional soldiers and volunteers here under Hữu Chỉnh."

"But I don't trust Hữu Chỉnh," said Nhạc.

"Very wise, nor should you," said Huệ laughing. "He betrayed his own people up here, and he is now despised. Apparently, many call him 'the snake we let into our chicken coop.' However, it appears his life will be in serious danger if we leave him up here to rule."

Nhạc laughed at his brother's cleverness, and said, "So devious. Now this makes more sense. We will be safe and comfortable in our own palaces, while Chỉnh will have the difficult and dangerous task of organizing Thăng Long to take orders from our officials, whom they will despise."

"That's it," said Huệ, and added, "Let's make Hữu Chỉnh governor of Nghệ An also. He will be our point man in the entire north. You should command him to hunt down and kill the Trịnh generals who ran rather than surrender to us, starting with Hoàng Phùng Cơ. Phùng Cơ is a strong leader who could rally remnants of the Trịnh to retake the region."

"Yes, I have heard of him, and I agree. I will do this," said Nhạc.

"Elder brother," said Huệ, "it is time you share with me your thoughts on how to divide the rest of the country we now rule."

Nhạc looked hard at his brother. He considered such directness to be rude. How should he deal with such bold impudence? He drew out an ornate fan and opened it, giving him time to organize his thoughts." Lữ will get all of Sài Gòn and south of it; he has to get something. You will keep the Spring Capital Phú Xuân, and be king of all from the Sea Cloud Pass up through Nghệ An. I'll stay in Quy Nhơn and, though officially the emperor of all, I will rule only the six provinces from Bình Thuận in the south up through Quảng Nam. Youngest brother, can you live with this plan?"

"I have served you well, and I deserve more. At least let me keep all of Quảng Nam Province, as Mother said that you had agreed to yesterday. It means that I can secure both sides of the strategically vital Sea Cloud Pass!"

"We do not think this will be necessary. Let me think on what you suggest," said Nhạc, stalling for time. "I will probably oblige you, but let me discuss this idea again with my generals before it is final."

"Consider carefully," said Huệ. "Do not forget that most of our successful battles and campaigns were designed and led by me."

"Brother Huệ, how could I forget all you have done for our family."

჻ ჻

At the end of a month, the three brothers quit the old capital. Traversing Nghệ An, Nhạc decided to leave a garrison there under his officer Trần Quang Diệu and Huệ's new officer Nguyễn Hữu Chỉnh. Huệ, however, thinking that a man capable of treason once was capable of it again, ordered several of his most trusted men to keep a close watch on Hữu Chỉnh for any signs of independence.

Huệ received recompense for his outstanding service in the form of one hundred ounces of gold and five hundred ounces of silver. Huệ stared at the two bars of gold and the bucket of silver he now received, and compared it to the many Trịnh palaces full of treasure that he had captured, and the river of silver he gave up in tax collections. He exhaled, but the anger stayed in his stomach like food poisoning.

Nhạc noted that his little brother, the famous general, was very proud of his many military successes, and showed more than just vague desires for independence. It was therefore with great ambivalence that he proceeded to officially pass over control of even the provinces extending from the Pass in the Clouds (the Col des Nuages) north above Quảng Nam, which allowed Huệ to keep the Spring Capital Phú Xuân, and included all of Nghệ An and Thanh Hóa above it, with the title of King of the Center, Pacifier of the North. Nhạc, with General Võ Văn Nhậm and his other advisors, agreed to include only half of Quảng Nam Province. Then Nhạc changed his mind and rescinded his offer of even half of Quảng Nam Province, saying it made more sense to keep it together in his share.

To Lữ, he gave the provinces of the south called Cochinchina with the title of King, Ruler of the South. Nhạc took for himself all of Đông Kinh, the province of Quảng Nam, which he had just agreed to give all and then half of to Huệ, and all the lands from Quảng Nam to Bình Thuận, with Quy Nhơn as the capital. He gave himself the title of Emperor of Đại Việt and King of the North.

Nhạc, Lữ, and a few of their guards and closest advisors, excluding Hoàng, quietly examined ways to assassinate Huệ. But Huệ was too careful and well protected, and they did not see any opportunity. A few assassins were recruited, and directed to try to penetrate Huệ's organization. Nhạc and his regiments withdrew and moved by land and by sea back to Quy Nhơn, while Lữ sailed for Sài Gòn.

Huệ was furious that he didn't get all he'd been promised in the agreement with his mother, but he kept his fury to himself. He withdrew his army from Thăng Long back to the Spring Capital. He decided to take all his troops by ship, keeping his entire navy intact, and once at the Spring Capital, he continued to ponder his disappointment. *Wasn't it a betrayal?*

Huệ prayed to his father and grandfather, and asked them for advice. In his meditation, certain thoughts reappeared. *Is loyalty to a dishonored brother and a devoted mother greater than my loyalty to the spirit of my father or to the well-being of the state. And what about my dignity and honor? How wrong of Nhạc to betray the deal brokered by our mother—wrong and stupid.*

How can I serve either my Ancestors, my country, or myself by working for a man, even my own brother, who would plot murders of his kith and kin, and break his word as if he were a God, not accountable for his actions? I do not want the responsibility for putting such a man on the throne.

Huệ decided to change the new status quo. The division of the realm did not meet his expectations. His brother had agreed, through their mother, that all of Quảng Nam would be placed under his jurisdiction. Furthermore, Huệ did not like that his eldest brother took possession of almost all the gold, silver, and precious weapons and stones of the Trịnh treasury, which Huệ had captured. He concluded, *The moral obstacles are removed!*

❧ ⌘

Before attacking his elder brother, Huệ first set out to destroy Nhạc's moral and political advantage by undermining his reputation through a concerted rumor campaign. He ordered the publication and distribution of posters and pamphlets accusing his eldest brother of various misdeeds, and slandering him as the progenitor of reoccurring corruptions and scandals. In these broadsides, Nhạc was referred to as various kinds of animals: a cowardly hyena, a vicious dog, and a selfish pig. Huệ filled the country with a hundred negative stories. The uglier the story, the better; there was no attempt at truthfulness. One set of pamphlets accused Nhạc's troops of killing villagers they owed money to for services rendered, butchering their bodies, and selling them in markets as water buffalo and goat meat.

Nhạc was infuriated when his spies reported from whom these slanders probably originated and proliferated. Nhạc called together his generals and prepared to attack his brother. Huệ was equally well informed, but his army and navy were already on alert and standby. Huệ preempted Nhạc's move by launching his own army precipitously by sea. With the monsoon from the north, Quy Nhơn was just two days and nights away.

The armada, as planned, arrived just before dawn. The junks and galleys landed troops in every way possible. Some ships sailed up to the deepwater docks. Galleys rowed to shore till they grounded. More junks tied up to the junks at the piers, and the troops had special ramps prepared to move from ship to ship till they disembarked onto the pier.

Huệ and his army suddenly appeared with the light before the massive fortress at Quy Nhơn. His envoy delivered a short message to Nhạc, who was stunned and also trapped inside his fortress. In the note Huệ demanded Quảng Nam to Nghệ An and all of Đông Kinh. Huệ also wrote, *Your royal highness, brother Nhạc, now you can reciprocate and visit me in my tent, to apologize for reneging on part of your promise in Thăng Long. Agree or you will face immediate annihilation.*

This time Autumn Moon could not prevail upon Huệ to compromise. Hoàng and many other officers were miserable, having to choose one friend or the other, for what promised to be a most self-destructive showdown between two ferocious halves of the same army of national revolution. This great army had defeated the Nguyễn, and then annihilated the Trịnh, and now was threatening to destroy itself.

Huệ had so completely surprised Nhạc by his sudden move south, that Quy Nhơn was unprepared, and Huệ, with his 60,000 troops and inexhaustible supply lines, was in a much stronger position. Also, not all of Nhạc's troops had finished the march south. About half of the absent divisions had secretly been persuaded or coerced to join Huệ. They turned on the other half of Nhạc's missing forces and disarmed them. These soldier prisoners readily agreed to return to their farms and stay there.

❧ ⌘

"There is one other condition," said the white-haired Autumn Moon. "You will have to apologize for refusing to trust your brother's hospitality in Thăng Long.

"I will not," Nhạc yelled at his own mother and his trusted counselor Lương Hoàng.

"Oh, stop behaving like a child," Autumn Moon scolded. "Huệ was very blunt. He said to me, 'Nhạc should have kept his word on Quảng Nam. I no longer need him. He can only rule now if I permit it. If he is going to continue to reign, he is going to have to honor me with good manners and respect in all matters. He is lucky that I plan to leave him anything.'"

Nhạc responded angrily, "So, after I let him go free in Thăng Long, now it's fratricide in Quy Nhơn. I think we will have to test his patience and mettle, while we wait for my army and Lữ and his troops from the south to arrive."

Hoàng added, "He said that he will meet you in man-to-man combat, or fight you army-to-army here, unless you agree to the visit, the apologies, and also, to a sacred oath on your father's tablet to a partnership of defense against all foreign aggression for as long as your lines shall last."

Tears ran down Autumn Moon's weathered face. She could see and even feel her son Nhạc's agony. But he had overstepped. Nhạc sat crumpled on a chair, and stared at a writing table with his head in his palm.

"Dear Nhạc, my darling first born," Autumn Moon said, "now you have to live and harvest what you have sown. I warned you not to cheat your brother of Quảng Nam. Now you have given up the moral high ground, and this old bag of bones cannot bail you out, as I did in Thăng Long.

"This is what I see," said the clear-eyed grande dame grimly. "Huệ is hoping for a fight. He has changed the odds from one-to-two in Thăng Long to three-to-one in Quy Nhơn. He does not want to be ruler of only the north. He would prefer to rule all of Đại Việt. He will allow partition only out of filial respect for me. He warns, with good reason, that the country needs a united military and administration if it is to remain free of the Chinese hordes."

After a long pause, Nhạc lifted his head and said quietly to Lương Hoàng and Võ Văn Nhậm, "I want all the military reports we can muster on Huệ's forces and capabilities. I want a plan of defense to study by tomorrow morning at the second hour of the Snake [ten am]. I will honor you for all your efforts. You are all dismissed."

❧　☙

For only the second time, Nhạc did not follow the advice of his mother. Nhạc decided to fight. After all, he was the king, and the eldest son, and he had led his family since their father's death. He ordered the cease fire pennant pulled down as he sent troops out in a surprise strike. They skirmished with Huệ's pickets, overran them, and attacked Huệ's camp. Troops poured out of the citadel in a full-scale attack on the besieger's encampment. The surprise was quite successful, and Huệ's forces took heavy casualties as they fought to reorganize and counterattack. Huệ threw in his cavalry and his elephants, which sent the attackers back toward the castle. The two proudest Việt fighting forces of the past hundred years had never before fought such a tough opponent, and the bravery on both sides presaged a terrible siege. There was no joyful hissing on either side, only grim silence punctuated by death screams. Some of the fighters were as young as fifteen, but they fell even more easily than much older men, and the pile of corpses grew faster than young bamboo. The day was a disaster for both armies. Nhạc's forces retreated into the fortress and shut the gate. An awful siege commenced. Slowly Huệ's careful siege work began to pay off. His ditches and tunnels soon crept right up to the citadel walls, but at such an expense of blood.

                                               ꙮ   ꙮ

In the middle of a humid morning, an old hag approached Huệ as he walked through one of the nearby villages and instead of bowing, she shrieked, "You are doomed, you are cursed. You have betrayed your Ancestors with this cursed civil war and you have lost the Mandate of Heaven. Heaven will send us a more deserving king."

The woman drew a knife and attacked. Huệ stood motionless; he was completely stunned by the anger and bravery of this old woman. The swords of his guards leapt, one pierced her breast, and in the next instant her head fell. But it was she who'd won the encounter. This woman was old and her body had been racked by disease. She was angry and sought a meaningful death. That same week her story of martyrdom travelled from village to village, from one storyteller or newsmonger to the next. This old woman had seriously wounded the once invincible Huệ more than anyone else ever had.

                                               ꙮ   ꙮ

Huệ stood on a knoll overlooking the field before the Quy Nhơn Citadel. His heart was heavy, and a shiver ran through his body. He winced as he remembered the old peasant woman from the day before and her words. He had stood on that same knoll many times before, including once with his brothers, on the night they avenged their father's murder. *Mother said Nhạc had agreed to all of Quảng Nam, as well as Nghệ An. Then he said maybe, and he promised me only half of what I deemed was an acceptable reward. Then he went back on his word again and reduced that. Perhaps because he did not understand the moral basis for my capitulation, he failed to realize that his moral slip would be a major tactical error. Brother Nhạc, the sad part is that I no longer have any use for you in my plans; I have lost patience with your bombast and incompetence.*

Huệ looked at the tower his soldiers and thousands of peasants under forced labor had built, its base abutting the citadel wall itself. On top of this tower his soldiers had placed two Dutch cannon, archers, and riflemen, who hailed down arrows and shot on the exposed citadel ramparts from a slightly higher elevation. Thanks to this edifice, the siege would soon be over. Lữ had sent an army from Sài Gòn to help lift the siege, but Huệ's forces had shattered Lữ's off the port of Phú Yên.

Thousands of peasants and soldiers died constructing this tower, Huệ thought gloomily. *But this tower and these brave deaths will become the foundation on which I base my future and the future strength of a reunified country.*

Huệ's stomach contracted. These events would not have pleased his wise and demanding father. *Forgive me, Father, for not avoiding this fratricidal war,* he prayed. And then calling his guards, he mounted a horse and rode down to the area just out of cannon range. There, at the periphery of the no-man's-land, he saluted two more guards and entered the deep trench, most of which was covered, and which traversed the great field in diagonal lines, till he came to the back side of the tower.

Surrounded by one of his elite fighting units of twenty men, many of whom carried stout shields, he climbed the steps up the back of the huge tower, up to the room that had been built at the tower's summit. They passed a group of peasants carrying down buckets of human night soil, a wounded soldier, and two corpses. Huệ inspected the wounded boy. An arrow stuck through his shoulder.

If the shaft had been properly soaked in poison, the soldier would die if the shaft remained in the shoulder for as long as it would take to carry the boy out of the trenches. Huệ did not waste fighting men, and he had nothing more important on this routine inspection, so he ordered the men to put the poor boy down and to lift the young soldier to sitting. He asked his medic to give the boy a swig of the local *rượu* whiskey.

Huệ grabbed the arrow, front and back. Luckily, it had come all the way out the back side. He said, "Sư Mạnh, the small saw please," and the medic produced a fine toothed saw from a canvas shoulder bag. Huệ sawed through the wooden shaft. The young soldier stared in agonized amazement as the face of his commander-in-chief concentrated only inches away from his own. The young boy was determined not to scream, or to die, he was so grateful for this honor.

After the arrow was cut through, Huệ pulled the shaft smoothly through the wound from its tip extending out the boy's back. The boy fainted, and blood spilled out of both open wounds. The guard with the medical bag and another took over the job of bandaging the young soldier. They would turn him over to others to be taken to a medicine tent, to have someone clean his wounds with water, hot rocks, and dried mugwort cigars used to smudge and lightly cauterize the flesh. Huệ and his remaining guards continued on their way. Huệ said to his first bodyguard with a grimace, "Most of them die of the demon rot anyway."

The guard nodded and replied, "The demons jump into the open wound before the skin is healed again, and then eat out the flesh of their victims."

The second guard added, "The Gods are very cruel to the wounded of war," and he spat to ensure good luck and to keep lurking demons at a distance.

Huệ mounted to the top platform and observation room of his tower and studied the grim destruction, the pile of corpses visible on the fortress rampart below. Defenders were using piles of debris and shields for cover from Huệ's men shooting at them from above on the rampart. Huệ's men had two Dutch six-pounder cannons mounted behind the main wall. These guns rained pure destruction on the defenders in the castle, using barbarian-made grapeshot and cannonballs.

Three of the citadel's four walls were exposed to the tower. The fourth was protected by the inner keep. A drum inside the citadel roared with a syncopated cadence, and the defenders all held their fire. A flag of truce suddenly went up from a window inside the keep. Huệ spoke a few words and his drummer beat out their signal to cease fire. More drums responded along the trenches and through the great camp of the attackers.

Soon all the efforts of the attackers came to a halt. One of Huệ's men stood up and waved a truce flag. General Lương Hoàng stood up from behind a barricade only twenty-five yards away and spoke. "Hồ Nhạc wishes to speak with his brother."

"Hồ Huệ is on the tower, let Hồ Nhạc speak," came the reply. Hoàng stayed up on the wall. The friend of both brothers stood exposed to the eyes and barbs of both sides. Within minutes, Hoàng announced Hồ Nhạc.

Nhạc's head appeared above the wooden barricade. His flat square face looked haggard and pale. His voice rang out, "Where is my brother?" Huệ stood up on a plank, so his chest and head were fully exposed.

"I am here, Brother Nhạc, what do you want?"

Nhạc stood up next to Hoàng, exposing his whole body. He stared at his younger brother for a moment in silence, both united bizarrely in their fear of the archers and the treachery of the other.

Then Nhạc's stentorian voice boomed out. "What are brothers, if not the same flesh and blood? Do they not worship the same ancestral tablets? Do they not share in the same patrimony? How is it that you have the heart to seek the end of your own brother—your own father's son?

Huệ was doubly shocked; his brother's words pierced him like arrows. Huệ saw his brother not twenty-five yards away, wiping the tears from his eyes, and Huệ's eyes let loose their own stream of tears: tears of shame for his actions, tears of love for this bravery of his older brother. Huệ was caught. He had once loved his brother, though he knew he could never trust him again.

"Are you willing to compromise, my proud brother?" Huệ asked.

"Yes," came the barely audible reply.

"Then let's meet outside your main gate at the start of the next watch. The cease fire shall remain in effect."

"Agreed," said Nhạc, and both men retreated into the protection of their own barricades.

❧　❦

Huệ obtained what he had originally wanted, plus the giant jewel of Đông Kinh. The border between their two separate kingdoms was fixed in Annam, above Quy Nhơn but below Quảng Nam at the northern border of Quảng Ngãi Province. Huệ would rule Đông Kinh and half of Annam.

With the generous agreement and a stiff bow of filial acknowledgement, Huệ ordered his men to pack up and leave. He had to overcome great misgivings. He did not socialize or share rice or drink wine with his brother. There was no longer any pretense of trust between them.

Chapter 23
Departure from Pondicherry
1788 (three years later)

Benoit left Africa and sailed to India in 1785. He reached Pondicherry in 1786. There wasn't much going on, since France had given up the right to compete militarily with the British in India. It was two years later, however, that the first opportunity came to sail to Cochinchina in Đại Việt.

Benoit and Julian Girard, an older officer whom Benoit served under and had befriended, discussed over dinner and several bottles of wine one night a new expedition opportunity. "Grannier, should we join this Bishop Pigneau de Behain in his wild and unofficial military venture to Đại Việt?"

Benoit answered, "Peace is wonderful, but it's rather idle. We are enjoying co-existence with England, while we live a relaxed and circumscribed life here—to be blunt, Pondicherry has grown a bit dull. It is for civil engineers, not soldiers."

Julian added, "The rumors from Paris are that the French military might withdraw completely from India in order to avoid another war with England and to reduce the monstrous budget deficit."

Benoit nodded and said, "Fighting in a small, underfinanced army against a large, well-defended Asian kingdom is not perhaps the safest or easiest way to riches and fame, but the service to God, king, and pocketbook in a single effort makes the wild and risky ideas of Pierre Pigneau, bishop of whatever, seriously appealing. I feel marooned here in India during the doldrums of a dishonorable peace. The English are still a dangerous enemy, whose power keeps growing due to their imperialist policies and colonial interests. They should not go unchecked or unrivaled by any patriotic Frenchmen."

Julian raised his glass. "I'll have a glass with you for that noble sentiment."

ও ও

Both Benoit and Julian applied for and received official leaves of absence from the French Admiral at Pondicherry, which freed them up to sign on with Pierre Pigneau de Behain as mercenaries.

On a sunny, clear day in June 1788, Benoit reported for duty to the 38-gun frigate, *La Méduse (The Medusa),* under the command of Captain Henri Dayot. After dodging through the crowd of workers and vendors on the quay, Benoit walked up an enormous, moveable gangplank. The mainsail spars on all three masts had been rerigged as boom-cranes with block-and-tackle hoists. Sailors and Indian stevedores were hoisting huge pallets piled with stores from the quayside and lowering them into the hold. Young boys and men, mostly Indian but also Siamese, Chinese, and Islander, stood down on the quayside staring in awe at the tall, jury-rigged cranes and impressive weights that they lifted. Benoit climbed up to the quarterdeck where the new officers and sailors were signing in.

"Well, if it isn't my old shipmate Benoit Grannier!" a familiar voice spoke out. Benoit turned to face an officer smoking a cigar and sitting on the guardrail. It was Guillaume de Martineau.

Showing no surprise, Benoit answered, "Monsieur le Comte de Martineau, good morning. What a surprise to find you at last. How was France? Now where are you going to run to next?"

"Are you still in a stew about ancient rumors?" Guillaume asked, smiling magnanimously. "The woman you were concerned about was just a seaport Nancy. Haven't you heard of the statute of limitations?"

"No doubt your bravery and honor are famous throughout the homeland. Speaking of honor, would you care to settle an old score this morning with swords?" Benoit asked matter-of-factly, as if four years had been only four days.

"When you find the courage to make public your challenge," Guillaume retorted, "I'll find the wherewithal to put a ball through your hard head."

Benoit turned his back and walked over to the duty officer. All of his excitement about the voyage dissolved. Old memories came flooding back, and old grudges and promises. Could he let it all go? He would have to figure out a way to trap Guillaume. *If I can catch him in one of the bars tonight full of officers and women, that would still be the best place to insult him. Too bad I lost the advantage of surprise.*

The bald-headed duty officer introduced himself as Nicolas Tabarly, Sublieutenant. Tabarly smiled brightly, welcomed Benoit, assigned him his berth below decks in one of the officer's cubicles, and showed it to him. Tabarly then sent Benoit to the hold to help supervise the packing and securing of the cargo under the fore hatch.

"What rank is Monsieur de Martineau?" asked Benoit.

"Lieutenant, same as yourself," Tabarly answered. "Why do you ask?"

"We served together in Senegal."

"Well, isn't it a small world," said Tabarly laughing, "or at least, a small navy. Now, by God, you'll be glad to know that you'll both sail on *La Méduse* when the fleet leaves for Indochina."

"I'm looking forward to it."

❧   ❧

The next afternoon, Benoit attended a briefing with Father Pierre Pigneau, Captain Henri Dayot, Julian Girard, and most of their officers, and many others who were still trying to decide whether to join the expedition or not. They met in a warehouse not far from the harbor wharf. Father Pierre still had a round, chubby face with a thin mouth and now a double chin. His hazel brown eyes were wide-set, while his high forehead and balding crown made him look intelligent and commanding. At forty-nine, his face was weathered and lined, his body was corpulent, in spite of years of living on fish and vegetables, due to ample supplies of wine, whiskey, Việt fried doughnuts and crispy chicken. He would not have been attractive to the ladies, even if he had controlled his diet better, though for better or for worse, he had not allowed himself the slightest physical interest in women except for service to the Lord. His only allowed need for women was to fill nunneries and to staff orphanages and hospitals.

"Gentlemen," Pierre Pigneau, was saying, "it is an enormous task, but we can manage it. We have three frigates: *La Méduse*, 38 guns, 19 swivels; *La Dryade* and *La Castries*, each 32 guns, 15 swivels; and the corvette *Le Pandour* with 24 guns and 11 swivels. These four ships, on loan from the King of France, need stocks, including more powder and shot, and two need minor repairs. I think I know how to get what we need.

"Mostly we'll sell rice and silver in Macao, and use the capital we've raised. The main point is that there is no power in Đại Việt that can stand up to our naval force.

"We have 459 men signed up as of today, including some of the best officers, sailors, and gunners that Pondicherry and Chandernagore can spare." This statement produced a laugh, since it had been fairly easy to drum up bored, poorly paid naval officers and sailors to become soldiers of fortune. Many men were willing to take a leave of absence from those two sleepy trading posts after six uninspired years of peace with England. The French government was facing a debt crisis and famine in France, so it welcomed the reduction in payroll. "We are looking for about fifty more hands."

"France and India will hardly miss us," Captain Dayot said with a chuckle, his one gray eye gleaming. "Peace is a mixed blessing if you are in the military line of work." Dayot's white hair contrasted sharply with the black eye patch over his right eye socket. He was an imposing older man, armed with sword and pistol, as were the other officers present, since Pondicherry had its share of cutthroats and bandits.

Pierre continued, "As you all know, I have procured most of the funding for this expedition from King Nguyễn Ánh, from several of the French firms trading in India and the Mascarene Islands, the Foreign Mission Society of Paris, the French East India Company, and a small part from yourselves. We are not currently suffering from a lack of capital, so we will start the expedition reasonably well equipped."

"Tell them more about the Việt king we will be fighting for," said Captain Dayot.

"King Nguyễn Ánh and I met in the most unusual way," said Pierre nodding. "But to understand Ánh's claim to the throne, one has to understand the young king's position as a child in the civil war which has racked the country for 150 years. His story begins when the once invincible Lê Dynasty came to an end because of a peasant uprising led by a fisherman named Mạc Đăng Dung in the early 1500s. Just a few years after Mạc came to power, the first Christian missionaries arrived in Đại Việt in 1533 and began to preach the Word of the Lord. Unfortunately for France, these brave Christians were Portuguese, but at least, bless our Holy Mother, they were good Catholics. Their *Padroado Real,* or Royal Patronage Contract with the Pope, gave them and the Spanish exclusive rights to evangelize East Asia."

"The Portuguese are known to be brutes," Guillaume offered. "They do a good job making a colony produce profit. When Vasco de Gama returned from India for the first time, they say his cargo was worth sixty times the cost of his voyage."

"That's unbelievable! That's almost a 6,000 percent profit," exclaimed Dr. Michel Despiaux, a real medical man and ship's surgeon, who was contemplating the expedition.

Pierre nodded in agreement. "There can be big profits. Before the Dutch challenged them out here, the Portuguese had large parts of the Indian coastline under their control, ruled by their viceroy in Goa on the western coast."

"Vasco da Gama was ruthless," added Guillaume. "If he didn't execute his prisoners, he cut off their noses and ears to intimidate the natives."

"Unfortunately, this is also part of the story," said Father Pierre. "The Portuguese and then the Dutch had great success with their war galleons and flintlocks. They were just as ruthless as the Mongols who conquered China. Like the Mongols, if a city didn't succumb, they destroyed it, killing the men and raping the women. It encouraged the various tribes to obey their new European masters, and the law of the West, which initially was the law of powder and shot, and the whip and the leg iron."

Nicolas Tabarly whistled. His fat cheeks were now slightly flushed red from the gold-colored liquid in his water flask. "Madonna, no wonder the Dutch grew so rich—there was no one out here to stop them after they beat off the Portuguese."

"Till the English moved in," Benoit said flatly. "Now the English are using French tactics, worked out by Dupleix, such as forming sepoy regiments of native militia, to take over India. The South China Sea is becoming an English sea. If we let them control it alone, they'll monopolize the tea and spice trade, like first the Portuguese and then the Dutch. Isn't that why a place like Đại Việt could be so valuable to France?"

Pierre nodded with another smile, "That's right. You can invest in or support this effort for profit, for God, or for France, or for all three—take your pick."

Tabarly, scratching his bald head at the other end of the long table, asked, "Excuse me, Bishop Pigneau, but what's the difference between Đại Việt and Cochinchina?"

"Please call me Pierre, or Father if you prefer." Pierre paused and breathed before continuing his briefing. "Good question. Today, Cochinchina is the southern region, Annam is the central region, and Đông Kinh, also called Bắc Kỳ, is the northern region of Đại Việt." Pierre grinned, taking joy in his knowledge. "We calculate it was around 111 B.C., that the Han Chinese conquered Đại Việt when it was only the northern region, and renamed it Annam, or Pacified South. It took a thousand years, but the Việts finally overcame their overlords. After the Chinese were defeated around A.D. 938, Annam became Đại Việt, or Great Việt. Over hundreds of years, the Việt expanded south, taking the center from the Chams and Cochinchina from outposts of Khmers. So roughly 150 years ago, Mạc Đăng Dung toppled the Lê Dynasty. The Trịnh clan eventually defeated the usurper Mạc, but a big civil war broke out between the Nguyễn and the Trịnh clans. Neither side won, so after about fifty years of bloodshed they quit fighting. I was quite miserably stuck in a Nguyễn dungeon when a scholar named Diệu Tri explained all this for the first time to me. But that's a really good story for another day.

"Although it looked as if the unofficial truce between the Nguyễn and the Trịnh had become permanent, the Hồ brothers of the village of Tây Sơn have changed all that. Earlier in this decade the Hồ defeated the Nguyễn forces in the south half, and then the Trịnh in the north half. The whole country was once again united for several years under Hồ Nhạc and his brothers. In Cochinchina, the Nguyễn remnants rallied around Prince Nguyễn Ánh, whom I had helped escape from the Tây Sơn Army twelve years ago.

"I suggested to Nguyễn Ánh that he ask the King of France for help. After several years, he asked me to go to France to seek the king's support. He offered one of his favorite sons as a token to the King of France of his sincerity. That is why the young Prince Nguyễn Phúc Cảnh is travelling with me now. The boy went with me to Paris.

"It is my plan to uphold the interests of France and the Church by supporting Nguyễn Phúc Ánh, a rightful claimant to the title of Duke or King of Cochinchina, and a strong contender to the throne of all of Đại Việt. Ánh's grandfather, King Nguyễn Võ Vương, was a direct descendent of Nguyễn Hoàng. Võ Vương died about twenty-five years ago. Ánh's father, Nguyễn Phúc Luân, was the eldest son of Võ Vương by his First Wife. He has a completely legitimate claim to the throne."

"Wait a minute," interjected Tabarly, "I might be confused. Say that last part again please."

"I know that it's confusing," laughed Pierre. "King Võ Vương and his First Wife's first son was Ánh's father, Phúc Luân. But Võ Vương, instead of making his first son the heir as expected, changed his will on his deathbed. Just before his last breaths, he made his heir the son of a lesser but more favored woman; she wasn't a wife, just a concubine.

"The First Wife, her friends, and many palace officials were deeply distressed by this breach of custom and etiquette. Discomfort turned to horror when the new king, still a boy, put his older step-brother to death. Ánh's father expired mysteriously during his sleep. His family is quite sure he was murdered by poison by the new king, or more probably his mother.

"The new King Nguyễn Huệ Vương proceeded to be a worse tyrant and more corrupt ruler than his father. Mandarins discovered that they could raise taxes and pocket fortunes with impunity as long as they paid the imperial squeeze. After years of blistering hardship in the south, and the continuation of a trend toward decadence in the north as well, the sour mood of the peasants turned ugly. The country became a powder keg, and the Hồ brothers of Tây Sơn provided the flint."

Black-bearded Guillaume then spoke, "If the country is divided now into Nguyễn and Tây Sơn, but the Tây Sơn Army is run by mere peasants, should we have difficulty establishing ourselves?"

"I wish it would be easy," Pierre answered, "but the Hồ brothers are brilliant and their followers for the moment are ferocious and dedicated. The leadership is literate and well advised. The Tây Sơn peasant soldiers are some of the toughest, most valiant fighters I've ever encountered in life or history books. Most Việts, including their mandarins, are ancestor worshippers. They will fight till the death just to please the spirit of their great grandfathers, so that their progeny will worship them as ancestors in kind. Many are also Buddhists. They believe in the afterlife of reincarnation."

"Zounds, this sounds familiar. In a way, I worship my father too," piped in a dwarfish, bearded fellow named Baltasar Weber. "And my old mother, let's just say, she is in a manner of speaking an object of worship." Most at the table laughed.

Father Pierre waited patiently, and then continued, "The Buddhists expect to be reborn in forty days, and if they lived and died properly, they are reborn in a better life than the previous one. In the dungeon of the Hà Tiên Citadel, a scholar named Diệu Tri confirmed that the Việt literati worship someone called Confucius, which means the Great Sage. He wrote his famous books centuries before our savior Jesus Christ was born and we were blessed with the promise of salvation. Certain mandarins and Nguyễn Ánh never tire of reminding me that Confucius lived 500 years before Jesus Christ and is therefore his elder. Confucius emphasized a reverence for history and filial piety. He firmly espoused the virtues of propagating the cult of the ancestors and the cult of the emperor."

"We, too, heartily endorse the cult of propagation," said Guillaume smiling, and he produced a small chuckle throughout the room.

Pierre jumped back in. "Confucius did not promise immortality except through literature and history. To me, the cult of Confucius is godforsaken, pagan, and sterile, but it is not a useless vision. Although as a cult it is now an abomination, it nevertheless motivates the mandarins and scholars who study and follow the Great Sage and the Chinese Classics. Many of these mandarins are smart, hardworking, and loyal. I am honored to know and work with them.

"Confucianists believe in the atheistic doctrine of social harmony through filial piety and public service. They eschew thoughts of the supernatural. They remind me of those misguided Puritans in New England that you read about, mirthless slaves to work. In Đại Việt, even though they are partly in the tropics, as south as Senegal or Cuba, they defy the European notion that people of hotter climes are soft and lazy. The Confucian work ethic has seeped into the beliefs of the peasants, who are most industrious. Both the rich and the poor Việts are the kind of fighters that you would prefer to have on your side."

Baltasar said, "Oh, if only we were allowed to fight here in India. Here the pickings are easy,"

"On the other hand," continued Pierre, "the Việt peasants, mostly illiterate, are not often intellectuals and they are highly superstitious. To our great advantage, they are terrified of modern cannon and the demons which they believe inhabit them. Most of the peasants are either Buddhist or Taoist, and virtually all are animists as well. Whenever I questioned a peasant about his beliefs, I always heard the strangest hodgepodge of national and local deities. Many of them claim themselves as Christians because they think at first they can just add Christ to their altar of deities. They are deeply disappointed, even incredulous, when I explain that we believe there is only one God. This cultural polytheism is one of our biggest obstacles as apostles of Christ."

"What is a Buddhist?" Tabarly asked. Several officers rolled their eyes in contempt of the speaker from Savoy. How could he spend several years in India and not know that?

Pierre didn't mind. For one thing, he loved to show and share his knowledge. It made him feel keenly alive. "That is a tougher question than some might think," he said respectfully. "They have many sects, especially in China, but they all follow the Indian Prince Siddhartha Gautama of the Sakyas, a philosopher who turned ascetic, it is said, about 600 years before Christ, perhaps a hundred years before Confucius. The Buddha taught that man could only find true relief from suffering and the bitter cycle of reincarnation through meditation and self-denial. He insisted that he was a man, not a God, and he taught a philosophy, not a religion." Pierre laughed a big belly laugh. "That didn't stop it from growing to be one of the great religions of China and Đại Việt and all of East Asia," and he laughed even harder, to the astonishment of his audience."

"Everyone should follow Buddha," interjected Henri Dayot with a grin. "The Buddha recommends—self-denial! Gentlemen, that means no women, no tobacco, and no booze."

"That's right," said Pierre smiling, and continued, "As far as I can see, the Buddhist priests in Đại Việt do not usually participate in battles, but they can be dangerous in a fight. Most of them are trained boxers and martial artists with the staff. They have a powerful hold on their followers, who are known to be valiant and fight to the death when aroused. As I said before, they believe that they will be reborn in forty days into a higher social position, if they behave themselves, so they can afford to be brave for a cause that their priests support."

Tabarly remarked, "Forty was the number of years Moses spent in the desert," and wondered about the coincidence.

Baltasar added, "And Jesus spent forty days in the desert."

Guillaume said with a mischievous smile, "Yes, and it was forty days that Noah spent with his wife and the animals in the ark."

Pierre resumed, "Yes, and there was also Ali Baba and the forty thieves," which caused more guffaws. "I am not a numerologist. So back to Đại Việt. There are the Taoists, who seem to be everywhere. They appear to be obedient to their holy men, soothsayers, and astrologers, for their priests threaten that evil spirits will punish them if they don't obey."

"Reminiscent of the parish priests at home," Benoit observed with an impish smile.

"That is an improper remark, Grannier," Guillaume said in a low voice.

"I don't need any advice from the likes of ..."

"Gentlemen, please take care!" Pierre commanded. "I'm afraid in any case, Lieutenant Grannier, that to some extent you are right about some priests." Benoit was impressed by Pierre's diplomatic manner, his effectiveness at intervening, and his apparent freedom from either religiosity or dogma. And Benoit was not surprised by Guillaume's insolent tone.

Benoit asked, "Who are these brothers we will be fighting?" trying to divert his anger at Guillaume and be helpful.

"The Hồ brothers, Nhạc, Lữ, and Huệ—let me tell you the story of how they got started." Pierre looked at Benoit, who was noticeably tense. He looked at Guillaume, who seemed alert, coiled like a snake, as if he were trying to decide whether to goad the younger man into a duel. Pierre instinctively wanted to mollify these men, to lend them his patience, but he sensed that he could not easily heal the animosity between these two, whatever the cause.

"The Hồ brothers quietly collected a band of fighters in the highlands near the fortress city of Quy Nhơn. They captured the well-manned citadel using tactics reminiscent of the classical story of the wooden horse in the fall of Troy, if you remember your Virgil. Nhạc was locked into a stout bamboo cage by his supporters, who accused him of robbery and delivered him to the mandarin of the citadel. The cage appeared secure, and Nhạc was left within it overnight, as was customary, before his hearing at the morning tribunal. During the night, he quietly removed several of the bars, which were falsely fastened. He snuck over to the gates, killed three or four guards with a knife, and managed to open the gates and pull up the portcullis single-handedly. His ragtag fighters rushed in and captured the fort. The outsmarted governor was tried by the bandits, and publically tortured to death."

"They are right smart bastards, aren't they?" Guillaume said, his eyes taunting Benoit, whose muscles tightened as he wondered, *Is Guillaume trying to rile me here?*

Partly to diffuse the tension, Pierre retorted "They are as dangerous as any Burgundians I've ever heard told of, if you remember your stories of the Three Musketeers," and the men chuckled uneasily. "The Việts decapitate their prisoners," he added, "because it mortifies their living enemies. They have many strange beliefs, and one of them is that if your body is not buried with its head, your soul moves into a kind of purgatory and lives for eternity as a restless ghost.

Is that so different from what we are taught? Benoit wondered to himself. *Most priests say that we must pass through purgatory, especially if we fail to receive the last rites. The Church requires payment for priests to release such relatives from eternal purgatory, harvesting our beliefs with fees.*

Pierre continued, "Although most of the mandarinate is Confucian and do not believe in ghosts or spirits, there are many Buddhists and Taoists in the merchant class who believe in a plethora of spirits.

"The peasants are difficult, perhaps impossible to classify. They seem to borrow from every religion that confronts them. They are animists and idol worshippers. Every mountain and river, and every village, home, and tree has its own spirit. You must be careful where you spit or relieve yourself, but you can do it quite openly, as in India.

"The peasants fear losing their heads and becoming ghosts in purgatory, while in their ignorance, they of course do not know of the hellfire which truly awaits them. Someday though, thanks to our efforts, the people of this nation will know the Gospels, and they will enjoy the blessings of the sacraments and the mercy of our loving and forgiving God of redemption. But I digress.

"Practically, what matters here is that they fight like devils when motivated. In the Tây Sơn, also called the Hissing Army, recruits and draftees are trained in archery, sword, and spear. We can't lower our guard. We will have to help Nguyễn Ánh improve his own army's fighting abilities. We can also improve their fort design."

Father Pierre took questions from the men who had not yet signed on, and then dismissed the group to find their suppers.

Benoit felt his head twisting with questions and ideas regarding Father Pierre's discourse. Đại Việt was a most complicated place. This man Pierre was one of the most knowledgeable man he'd talked to in years. Pierre had a capacity to see and analyze. He was a God-fearing Christian priest, sacrificing his life so that he could help bring the Word of God and the blessing of eternal life to the heathen. And yet, Father Pierre was also a military tactician who knew almost as much about the fighting tactics and the modern gunnery of the French armed forces as any of the officers in the room.

This priest is surprisingly knowledgeable about the arts of war, Benoit thought. *He is like a Knight Templar in the Crusades, more Richelieu than Saint Francis, a soldier in the service of the Army of God.* The religious questions were many and profound, but more pressing was how was he going to make Guillaume lose his temper—how to push Guillaume into issuing a challenge?

☙ ❧

A week later, the frigates *La Méduse, La Dryade,* and *La Castries,* and the corvette *Le Pandour* left Pondicherry with a fanfare orchestrated by the Governor-General Monsieur de Conway. The ox-faced Conway ordered the military band to play and the fortress to fire a nine-round salute. Conway was glad to get rid of the bishop, who he felt was a hothead and an irresponsible dreamer, if not a God-cursed, radical liberal. He suspected the bishop of preaching republican doctrines. Father Pierre was furious at Conway, who had refused to release any of the troops agreed to in the Paris Treaty. A footnote in the treaty had stipulated that Conway could alter it as he alone advised.

Men turned the capstans of *La Méduse* and the other ships to weigh the heavy anchors. Sailors hauled up the jibs, the fore staysails, and the mainstaysails, to back wind the bow off the wind. After turning the ships' bows, sailors let fall their main tops'ls in order to catch the monsoon winds out of the southwest and glide to the harbor mouth. Small boats accompanied them, blowing horns and shooting off guns. The sun glittered off the wind-dappled water. At the mouth of the harbor, the sails dropped one after the other from the towering masts, and each ship, soon rigged tight as a violin, began to hum along through the chop, each ship a wind-powered leviathan. The warm breeze pushed the ships into the immense Bay of Bengal. They sailed off, becoming smaller and smaller, till they disappeared from sight.

Benoit no longer considered himself a young man at the age of twenty-six, when he finally set out for the shores of Đại Việt on board *La Méduse.* Had he stayed a land lubber in Lorient, he would have taken a trade and probably married, perhaps Isabelle, and started a family. But then he would have missed learning about North America, Africa, India, and whatever now lay ahead in Đại Việt and the islands of the South China Sea. Perhaps he would see and help Antoine. They might go to China or Japan together.

The shore of India moved away like a painted flat on wheels at the opera. Benoit noted its beauty without his usual enthusiasm for such things. During the week in Pondicherry, he had insulted Guillaume three times, and each time Guillaume laughed and said cheerfully that there must be some mistake, for he was sure that they'd never met before ... a case of mistaken identity. All the officers now knew that Benoit wanted to duel with Guillaume, but was unwilling to initiate a challenge for a duel with pistols.

Perhaps, Benoit thought, *I should just murder him and be done with it. If the good Lord sends me to hell for killing this man, hell can't be half as bad a place as they say it is.*

Benoit's reverie was disturbed by the passing promenade of the smartly dressed Guillaume, who walked by him without acknowledging his existence. The sight of his old enemy made Benoit remember and long for Margarita and André. He remembered them singing a rich harmony with him in a pub. He thought, *André is dead, and Margarita is God knows where. Hopefully, she's somewhere in France with some jack-in-the-box. No, that's small. I hope she is happy, with a good husband and wonderful children.*

He conjured up her face and her body and felt his old yearning. She was the only woman he had ever really loved. He was torn between someday returning to Lorient for a bride, or looking for Margarita in Marseilles or Paris. But that was not realistic. *Will I ever find an equal to her again?* he asked himself. *Accept that she is gone. Women like her don't stay unmarried.*

Guillaume passed by again. He was circumnavigating the three masts for exercise. *Did he, or did he not rape Margarita? Of course he did, and someday I'm going to fight him anyway for killing André. André, wherever you are, I shall try to avenge you and Margarita.*

Benoit stepped down the outdoor staircase to inspect the lower decks and the hold. *I'm ready*, he thought. *Now I just have to decide when and where to insult him, and as I did in Saint-Louis, keep watching my back.*

❦   ❧

It was not by mistake that right after their departure Father Pierre placed these two men on different watches. He saw their antagonism steaming under a veneer of cool gentility, even before he heard of Benoit's public challenges, an accusation of rape, Guillaume's declarations of innocence, and the facts of André de Lagier's death. Putting Benoit and Guillaume on different watches did separate the two men most but not all of the time, because of the watch system.

Out at sea, except when all hands were needed, every man worked four hours on, four hours off. Benoit, on the starboard watch, worked eight p.m. to twelve midnight, four to eight a.m., and twelve noon to four p.m. In the off hours the officers and crew rested and took their meals. They dogged the four to eight p.m. watch, meaning it was split in two: four to six p.m., and six to eight p.m. These short watches rotated the two groups to allow the men to take turns on alternate nights on the graveyard shift—midnight to four in the morning. It also rotated the sunrise watch, four to eight a.m., and the sunset watch, six to eight p.m. In good weather, sunrise and sunset were two of the greatest pleasures in a sailor's spartan day at sea. Even the roughest men were not immune to the extraordinary beauty of ever-changing light over an ever-changing sea—a palpable visual representation almost daily of the promised paradise of heaven. During one of the dog watches, if Benoit and Guillaume should walk by each other, one of them was on duty, which created a small buffer.

During the dog watches while out at sea, four to six p.m. and six to eight p.m., and thanks to the steady monsoon breeze from the west, the half of the crew who were off duty were allowed to relax, lounge, and sport on the main deck and the fo'c's'le head. The bishop, to everyone's pleasant surprise, encouraged boxing matches, wrestling, and both wooden and real sword practice. The officers occasionally organized a pistol shooting competition, which to Benoit's dismay, Guillaume invariably won. Benoit was the on-board champion of the sword. Both men coached others in their particular weapon during the long voyage.

The wigged French officers, even in their rudimentary toilette, appeared in stark contrast to their sailors, who looked more like pirates or convicts—which a few of them had been once or twice in their lives. The sailors, wearing short duck pants and old patchworked shirts, labored over the spars and rigging. A small detachment of marines were on board, as in a royal naval vessel, though on Bishop Pierre's vessels they helped with the work instead of standing guard all the time. They were available for police work if needed, but their main value was as sharp-shooters in a battle.

Benoit was pleased to recognize some of the seamen from previous ships. Louis Boulanger and Little Jacques from the Chesapeake days also worked on board *La Méduse*. Louis worked barefoot in an old pair of torn duck pants with a gold-painted earring in one ear. He was now close to retirement, for his teeth had gone bad and his rheumy eyes were starting to fail.

Louis still dreamed of revenge against the privileged class, and he had a new set of cat-o-nine-tail scabs on his back for responding to an order by Lieutenant Martineau too slowly. He still had many reasons to hate his superiors. He hated Guillaume, and every man on earth who abused power and privilege.

At six bells, six p.m., Louis and Little Jacques came off their two-hour dog watch and went below to the first gun deck to line up for a plate of hardtack, duff, and a mug of tafia. They sat on the clean gun deck floor, with their feet up against cannonball racks as footrests. They ate quietly; the rum and water helped the hardtack go down. Louis said, "I hate it that the officers enjoy the fresh meat. Every day they eat mutton, pork, or chicken from the livestock pens kept on the deck. They wash it down with bottles of good wines and champagnes."

Little Jacques chuckled, since they'd had this conversation many times already, *Perhaps Louis thought it somehow assuaged the envy.* "Yes," he agreed, "but they have to pay for it and carry it all in their own private stocks. And we like our rum. It is hard not to notice that all we get is salt beef and biscuit, with hard cheese twice a week. Don't forget there's mystery pudding or plum duff on Sunday."

"Look at this meat," said Louis. "Every day as the salt beef gets harder, the little brown maggots in the biscuit get longer."

"Those aren't maggots, my boy, those are raisins that dance," said Little Jacques on cue, and then, "But it ain't so bad, the maggots in the biscuit taste just like calves' foot jelly. It's only when the maggots take over that the biscuits taste like dust. When they squirm nice, we call it caviar."

Louis and Little Jacques washed down their meals, garnished with live insects and anima, with the last swigs of their pint of rum.

Despite Louis's complaints, life on board ships commanded by Father Pierre was far better than on most other ships of the day. Death due to flogging was unheard of, and keel-hauling, the old practice of dragging a sailor under the water along the keel of the ship against its barnacles, he forbade as barbarous. Scurvy was less common than usual. Father Pierre supplemented the sailors' monotonous diet of salt beef and biscuit during the first week after any port-of-call with fresh meats, fish, fruit, and produce.

& &

Benoit liked to walk the main deck during the day for part of his rest period. His eyes roamed the horizon and the endless dark swells of the Indian Ocean while his mind flew wherever it might. He'd had only one letter from his cousin Antoine in three years, which he took out of his pocket.

Antoine's earlier letters had spoken of persecutions against the missionaries, but had then reported that Đại Việt was so badly racked by civil war that the imprisonment and executions of Christians had mostly ceased.

His last letter to arrive came from the mission at Đà Nẵng, founded by the deceased Alexandre de Rhodes. Antoine had written, *Armies, pirates, and famines now ravage the cities and countryside of this ancient land. The civil war and famine take a worse toll in Christian lives than any of the persecutions did. When the Việt fight each other, they use javelin, pike, bow and arrow, sword, and musket. The fighting is brutal. I know that I should return to France now while I have the chance, but there remains so much of God's work here to be done.*

After reading the letter again, Benoit descended to his cabin cell and put it away, then returned to walking the deck. He reached up to a ratline and chinned up to it with fifteen pullups. *Got to stay in shape. Damn the navy, and the king,* Benoit thought, while he reflexively stretched out his tired forearms. Benoit's friend Julian Girard approached him. Julian, a quiet, but commanding fellow, now assigned as the new captain of *La Castries,* had been in the last gig to pull alongside for the officer's meeting. They exchanged greetings. After a pause, Benoit said, "It is frustrating. The French government has utterly failed to fulfill its treaty and agreement to move a large, well-provisioned force to Đại Việt's strategic coastland. France should have sent a host of troops and cannon, a force of consequence. How else are we to stop the English heretics from conquering China in the same efficient way that they are carving up India?"

"It is a problem," said Julian. "And who really is this Monseigneur Pierre Pigneau de Behain, Bishop of Adran and Vicar Apostolic of Cochinchina, who thinks 500 Frenchmen can save a pretender to the Đại Việt throne against a vastly superior force? Will our cannon make any difference?"

Benoit responded, "I suppose Việts have yet to deal with modern French gunnery, not to mention old-fashioned chain shot."

"But will we find gold, as so many sailors expect," said Julian, "and riches not to be imagined, or will we die horrible deaths at the hands of heathen cutthroats?"

"We will have to perform well," replied Benoit. "Father Pierre says that they are famous for killing with feints, ambushes, and booby-traps."

The ship came alive with orders and sailors moving. They watched the ship come into the wind and drop sails, to glide to a stop. Two captain's gigs pulled over to *La Méduse*. Their captains and lieutenants were coming aboard for the meeting. The officers on duty saluted each pair of officers as they climbed up the rope ladder. The task was made easier by a gentle ocean swell.

Benoit and Julian greeted a group of officers waiting to go below. The windward rail had been their windbreak to smoke cigars while they discussed the news. When the Frenchmen had left Pondicherry, they carried with them newspapers and magazines that were at least six months old. The latest paper they had was dated December 1787.

Commodore Henri Dayot appeared and said with authority, "Gentlemen, the bishop's meeting of the officers is about to start in the roundhouse cabin."

Chapter 24
The Warrior of the Chamber
1788

Lữ climbed out of his palanquin unsteadily and plodded past the gatekeeper of his palatial house in Quy Nhơn. He trudged past the noisy lounge of his guardhouse. His men were drinking and having their dinner, while a female performing troupe entertained them. The women, wearing Indian-style breast cups, underpants, and gauze saris, played traditional tunes, sang songs, and danced for the guards.

Tamarind Nectar, Lữ's favorite at the Paradise Flower Shop on Delight Street, had performed with her usual unbridled enthusiasm, but he had not been able to block out the difficult events of the past months. The first round had been somewhat embarrassing. She rubbed his back and his legs, which were unusually tired, and then he sat on a stool while she knelt at his feet to start the evening's fireworks with her mouth and tongue. Lữ had had too much to drink, and he finally stopped her because he was embarrassed at his lack of response, and he was also aware that she might choke.

He took out his pouch of implements and monk's remedies. He took a pill and let Tamarind Nectar apply a scented monk's lotion to his imperial pestle. The two medicines were both effective, and for the second endeavor Lữ discovered his ample strength. His courage returned in full and he elevated his beautiful but demanding new pet to the brink of the afterlife. After floating for just a few minutes on the clouds, Lữ's mind flew back to Sài Gòn, and the miserable retreat of his battalions after that turtle head Nguyễn Ánh approached the citadel there with a force twice as large as his own. The peasant farmers had rallied to the Nguyễn banner, the ungrateful scum.

"You wind-passing oxen," Nhạc had growled, "how could you fail to hold the citadel. Some excuse for a general you are, for allowing Nguyễn Ánh to retake Sài Gòn for the third time!" Lữ had never seen Nhạc so angry. There was little chance that Huệ would come back and dislodge the Nguyễn pretender now that he ruled all the north from the beautiful Spring Capital.

Lữ found that even his carnal games with Tamarind Nectar could not shake his sense of melancholy, and of course, added to his fatigue. He bid her goodnight, and although she hinted that it was too early, he returned home.

Back in his own compound, Lữ thought that he might be hungry, and he wondered, *Where shall I go? To my fourth wife, Golden Lotus? She's so hard to please. Or to Spring Bloom, my latest passion? Golden Lotus will be expecting me. She will be so angry if I don't come. What a beautiful wife she is. I do love Golden Lotus, but dragons and fireflies, she is so demanding, and I grow tired of her jealous repri-*

mands. She will probably try and scratch my face, but I've got to whip her soundly and show her who is the master and who is the slave.

Lǚ was tired and could hardly make up his mind. He decided to see his new concubine, Spring Bloom. She was his current favorite, and he wanted to show himself and his servants that he couldn't be intimidated by a shrill wife. He found Spring Bloom in her private room; her maid was fixing her hair.

Spring Bloom's eye shadow, liner, and rouge made her eyes stand out like those of a wild animal. Her round and pleasant face had a classical beauty by itself, but combined with her lustrous black hair and her feminine curves, she was most attractive and alluring. "Oh, it is so late, my master," Spring Bloom said. "I should be very cross with you."

"The business meeting of the Celestial Brotherhood Secret Society went on much longer than expected," square-faced Lǚ lied. Lǚ still had the rugged good looks of his family, though he sported a paunch in his belly. He was now thirty-four, and his hair was full and black. Spring Bloom had extraordinary luck to have become suddenly the favorite of such a famous and powerful man. All she had to do to ensure her success and the security of her parents and siblings was to maintain her position until either she got pregnant and delivered a male heir, or he asked her to become an official wife. Either way, their finances would be secure. She only had to avoid arousing too much enmity from the other six women of her master's household—his four wives and two concubines. It was well known that in the few years that Lǚ ruled the south, he had amassed a fortune.

❦   ❦

The quick-witted maid Aster came into her mistress's room to report to Fourth Wife Golden Lotus. Golden Lotus was a bony-faced beauty. Her face was V-shaped, with piercing brown eyes set deep into her angular cheek and forehead bones. Her red, brown, and blue silk tunic covered a petite and feminine body. Aster gave her a knowing look and said, "Our master has come home from his outing. I learned from the weaver's third son, one of the palanquin bearers, that our master spent the whole afternoon at the Eternal Paradise Flower Shop in the company of Tamarind Nectar."

"Aii-yah, that little whore," growled Golden Lotus.

"I'm so sorry, but that's not all the bad news, Master has gone to the chamber of that new cow, Blighted Bloom, and ordered his dinner."

"I hate him!" Golden Lotus said, and threw her sewing at the cat, who was alert to these moods and dodged it as usual.

"That dried turtle head, why must he ignore me?" and she burst into tears. Golden Lotus could cry whenever she wanted, though this time her tears were real and the droplets ruined her makeup.

It was turning out that her place in Lǚ's fickle heart was no different than the other women in his life, whom she had painstakingly worked to replace for the past two years. She would now become just another lonely and sex-starved extra woman in his stable.

Four maids entered carrying trays of hot and cold dishes and jars of wine. Lữ smiled at Spring Bloom and said, "I hoped that you would like to join me for a late dinner."

Spring Bloom blushed professionally, and averted her eyes coquettishly as if still a shy virgin. She rose and gave Lữ a passionate kiss, slipping her tongue inside his mouth and finding his. She then carefully poured his wine from her own hand, and began to knead his shoulders. She noticed how he rubbed at his own thigh muscles. She ordered her maids to bring pillows, helped him to recline, and rubbed his legs. Spring Bloom took her lute from off the wall and began to play some of the beautiful old melodies while Lữ ate. She let her clear sweet voice sing forth, and Lữ obviously enjoyed her sad songs. For a moment he forgot his own troubles as he listened to the sad tale of the woman who bathed in the Sông Giang but won the heart of the river Genie. Her clothes were found by the river, and her body was never seen again.

"Don't stop," Lữ said, popping another pork dumpling into his mouth. Spring Bloom adjusted her lute and began the old ballad of *Thsing Kou*.

"There stood, north of the river Nhị Hà, a certain village,
where dwelt a marvelously beautiful maiden, Thsing Kou.
A rich mandarin, who wished his son to marry her,
obtained permission, after the old custom,
to see his future daughter-in-law 'bared of all veils.'
The young maid came at her own father's command.
Throwing off with lofty gesture the last garment which covered her,
free of false shame. She kept her eyes lowered in modesty,
she showed her virginal body to her prospective father-in-law.
The mandarin was dazzled.
Never had he beheld so many assembled perfections.
Enchanted, he admired the long silken tresses,
the brilliant eyes, the dainty mouth, the dazzling teeth,
the firm breasts faultlessly modeled, the hips wide as those of a mature woman,
the gracefully formed legs—the fingers, above all, with their patrician nails,
and the tiny feet—so tiny that Thsing Kou, to keep a precarious balance,
had to lean on the shoulders of two serving women."

Spring Bloom realized as she sang that this story might not please her master. Was it not the story of a debauched mandarin whose escapades in flower houses destroyed his career and ruined his family? Even though she had only started the long ballad, she made up a false, happy ending. She improvised:

"The old mandarin realized what a 'source of felicity'
such a spouse would be for his son; and the marriage was agreed on.
The son was overjoyed by such beneficence."

She then sang another, of the valor of the Việt warrior Trần Hưng Đạo, who defeated three times the Chinese armies led by Kublai Khan. Her last song was a silly song about the wonder of wine and the joy of a bee going from flower to flower sampling nectar. Spring Bloom smiled and laughed, because it made her even more beautiful and because Lữ was just like the simple-minded bee.

By now Lữ had finished his dinner and was watching Spring Bloom sway and twist as her slim fingers danced against the fretboard. His heart sang at the idea that she was his for the evening, and for a few fleeting minutes of bliss.

Lữ reached under the table and took hold of Spring Bloom's foot. She tried to play one more tune while Lữ distracted her by stroking her arch. The maids quietly withdrew. Lữ was obviously now excited. They both got up and he caught her in his arms and helped her remove her garments. She untied his green silk robe and pulled it off. The monk's medicines were still in Lữ's system, so he was full of strength and passion, in spite of his tired condition and the large potbelly he now supported. To ensure his success though, he took from his little bag of utensils a silver clasp that he slipped over his horny elephant's trunk. The clasp had small carved fists that made little balls of pleasure that rode on top of his shaft of flame.

Golden Lotus was now lurking in the garden outside Spring Bloom's room, and she could hear her rival's most convincing screams of delight. "Oh, it's so big, it's so big," she heard the small voice moan.

That professional little strumpet, Golden Lotus thought bitterly, driving her own nails into the cold, clammy palms of her hands. *If she has a son, I swear by the spirit of this house, I will poison them both.*

Lữ finally had to stop, for he was winded. At any rate, Spring Bloom was well taken care of, and some women would have asked him to stop long since. Lữ simply wasn't as in the same shape as he used to be. He slowly withdrew, removed his silver clasp, entered her again, and finished with a final mighty gallop. Still out of breath, he rolled over pulling his sweat-covered body off hers. He was so tired that he closed his eyes and fell asleep.

He awoke an hour later with a start. *Dragon's wind,* he thought, *I'm spent, I don't feel well, the monk's medicine has worn off, and yet I promised Golden Lotus that I would sleep in her room tonight.* He rolled painfully off the raised mat and slowly stood up. His head ached from too much liquor. His body, especially his tongue, his stomach, and his head, now felt a craving for an old friend.

"You're so good to me," Spring Bloom murmured, "Please don't go." Lữ reached over and stoked her neck, then he pinched her hard on the ass, because he liked to hear his women cry out. While she was rubbing the spot on her behind and lecturing him not to do that again, Lữ dressed himself and left.

෴   ෴

When Lữ entered Golden Lotus's room, it was already past the hour of the Pig, two hours before midnight. Oil lamps kept the dark at bay. Golden Lotus was playing cards with two of her maids. Lữ entered and sent the maids to bring in wine, spring rolls, and sweetmeats. He graciously apologized, "Dearest Wife, I've been stuck at my desk all afternoon reviewing and signing papers for my demanding brother."

"You liar," Golden Lotus said, and threw her fan at him. "You can't fool me." In a most calculated fashion, she began to cry. "First you go to a dirty brothel, and then you go to that fat little acquisition of yours. And you promised never to lie to me?"

"Oh my pet," Lữ said whining like a child, "I just didn't want to hurt you. Sometimes I'm just like a little boy with too many toys."

"Go stick your head in a bucket of night soil," she said pouting, only half seriously now, acting the part of hurt little girl. The trick with Lữ was to punish him, but only in small amounts. She had already decided not to punish him too severely when he was obviously tired and drunk. Golden Lotus would get back at the new woman in her own time. "Now sit down next to me," Golden Lotus said in her sisterly voice, "and tell me what useful new tricks you learned from those mealy mouthed harlots."

Lữ did as he was told. "As for Spring Bloom," he lied confidentially, "I just like her singing. If I fool with her, it is just to be polite. Since she is one of my women, it is my responsibility to poke her occasionally. Neh, don't you understand?"

After several cups of wine, it appeared as if he was forgiven. Lữ asked her to prepare his pipe, for his legs and back were hurting him. Lotus suppressed her fury and disgust and sent Aster for the pipe, and from a little drawer near the table she took out the opium pellets. She hated him for coming to her for his smoke when his body was exhausted, and neglecting her own store of fragrant delights and unfulfilled desires. Lotus tapped down the opium and held the lit taper while he inhaled the heavenly smoke. His pains and soreness faded away like a morning fog burned away by the sun of Heaven.

"I feel much better," he remarked. "Let me have another pellet for this pipe."

"Nguyễn Lữ, where are your manners and good sense?" Golden Lotus reprimanded. "You have had more than enough for one evening." She sat down next to him, kissed him on the lips, and took his pouch of utensils from his belt. He was already staring ahead in a daze, but she popped one of the monk's magic pills into his mouth and then gave him wine to drink. Then she gave him a second pill and another glass of wine. She sent the maids away except for Aster, whom she bade play the lute. Then Golden Lotus began to massage the tops of Lũ's legs. The medicine slowly took the desired effect. Lũ began to pinch her and soon she had removed her own and Lũ's clothes. Lũ used the heel of his foot to play with her gate of Heaven, and she spread the monk's cream on his imperial appendage. Lũ noticed her impatience. Since Lũ needed time for the pills and the cream to work, he decided to tell her a story.

"A certain man died and the God Yen Lo Hoàng had him reincarnated as an ass. Later it was found out that according to his karma he had thirteen more years to live, so he was released into the world again. He was transformed once more into a man, but in the haste of returning him to earth before it was too late, the magic words were hurried and only partly effective, and the reproductive organ remained unchanged, and the man therefore came back to life with the organ of an ass. 'I shall return to the afterlife and have it changed,' he said to his wife. She, however, fearing that Yen Lo Hoàng would not release him but detain him forever, preferred him to remain. So you see that women prefer donkeys to nothing at all."

"Very amusing," lied Golden Lotus. She had heard this one several times before, and these stories of his were one of the things about Lũ that she'd learned to tolerate because he was both rich and well-connected.

The opium had gone far to relieve the pains in his body, and the aphrodisiacs were resurrecting his manhood. He put the silver fists on his imperial pestle when it was finally large enough to hold them. Then Lũ decided on one of his favorite games. He tied Golden Lotus down on the bed spread-eagle, her wrists and ankles securely fastened. This always helped him get excited enough. He then picked up his rawhide whip that he used to punish the members of his household, and cracked it first in the air, and then against the bed near Golden Lotus's beautiful and naked body.

"Stop it please," she murmured, "You're scaring me tonight. Please come to me." Lũ laid the whip down on her stomach so that it coiled on her breasts.

"Do you promise not to hurt Spring Bloom?" This demand Golden Lotus had not anticipated, and it scared her. She froze. Lũ raise his arm and brought the whip's lash down hard across her thighs and she screamed. "Do you promise not to hurt Spring Bloom?" he hissed.

"I promise," she gasped. Just below the pubis, one of her naked thighs oozed a trickle of blood.

"On your ancestral tablets?"

"Yes, yes, on my ancestral tablets."

Lũ cast away his whip and suddenly became gentle again. He carefully lay next to her and touched her face and breasts, and kissed her mouth. He had scared himself and he was confused as to what possessed him. His head was still foggy from the small dose of opium, while his body burned from the aphrodisiacs. He mounted his fourth wife somewhat clumsily, waited for her to respond with excitement, and then galloped off into the distance. Golden Lotus overcame her fear enough to marvel at his strength. *Lữ is a famous man,* she thought, *and he deserves his enormous reputation as a great warrior of the chamber.* He brought her to several peaks, till she finally could take no more and asked him to stop. He removed the clasp with the fists, and rode off again. He galloped against her as if out of control. It was painful for her, and for him. Halfway through this cataclysmic war between the Yin and the Yang, Lữ moaned. He slowly let the full weight of his body lie heavily on Golden Lotus and he rested in triumph. Soon he fell asleep on top of her.

Golden Lotus waited for Lữ to revive. When he didn't for several minutes, she tried to untie herself and couldn't. She waited for her own body to roll to a stop; the feeling of the warm man inside her was not unpleasant. He was rough, but he loved her. She tried to wake him. Then, as if awakening up from a dream, she realized that Lữ was too quiet. He wasn't moving. He wasn't breathing! Golden Lotus was still tied spread-eagle to the bed. She shrieked and screamed and screamed, "Aster, Aster, Aster, I need you!"

ෂ ෂ

Lữ was dead. The family announced that he had caught a deadly swamp fever—a malaria, but the members of the household knew otherwise. Lữ had succumbed, as had others before him, to one of the most peculiar diseases of the wealthy and decadent in advanced civilizations: death by drug and alcohol abuse and fornication.

Chapter 25
The Arrival
1788

It was about 1,825 nautical miles from Pondicherry to the five mouths of the Mekong River, sailing around the Malay Peninsula. The French sailors all settled into the routine of days on end, each much like the one before. The sailors washed, scrubbed, and flogged dry the deck each morning, and attended to repairing or refreshing much of the rigging and paintwork during the day. The steady monsoon breeze blew dependably from the west, promising a fine passage. The first leg was straight downwind. After which, the ships steered southeast through the Strait of Malacca to the settlement of Temasek (Singapore), then northeast, broad reaching with wind just abaft the beam, the wind coming slightly from the stern.

Moving at an average speed of six nautical miles per hour, it took *La Méduse* only fifteen days to sight the coast below Sài Gòn off Vịnh Binh Province. There was excitement on the day the crow's nest sighted the coast of Đại Việt. The first sight of Cochinchina made Benoit Grannier dismiss all his misgivings about his decision to soldier in the Far East as a mercenary.

"What do you think of our landfall?" said Father Pierre with a big grin.

"I can't wait to see my cousin Antoine," said Benoit, staring at the green shore. "It will be so good to see him again. Hopefully, we can make a difference here in the service of the Lord, and find adventure and some riches as well."

Father Pierre replied, "The opportunity is every bit as great as the danger."

"I hope so," said Benoit, and thought, *It is hard to live on a lieutenant's pay, especially since I had half sent directly to my mother and my siblings.*

The lush vegetation framed by sandy beaches made his heart pound in spite of the heat. The future here was unknown and fraught with danger, but for some reason he couldn't explain, Benoit liked tasting the bile of fear. The growing anticipation of war and possible death made every meal a blessing, something to be thankful for. *Besides, you only have to die once—perhaps there is a heaven for Christian soldiers.*

The gray-blue waters of the South China Sea turned colors as *La Méduse, La Dryade, La Castries,* and *Le Pandour* approached the wide mouth of the Nhà Bè River. The blue waters turned gradually more green then to a muddy brown. The land was flat, with the Annamite Cordillera, a distant mountain range, barely visible off to the north. *La Méduse* anchored off the village of Vũng Tàu, on the west side of the island also called Vũng Tàu, which means Anchorage for Boats.

Standing on the quarterdeck near the bishop were the Vietnamese passengers who had made the long trip to Paris with Bishop Pierre. "Passengers" was hardly the only word to describe these celebrities. They were publicized and scrutinized in the city of Paris, much the way the press had once capitalized on the Indians from North America brought to England by John Smith or to France by Samuel de Champlain.

Next to Pierre stood a ten-year-old Vietnamese boy in an ill-fitting and faded tunic. This young boy was Prince Nguyễn Phúc Cảnh, the son of Nguyễn Ánh and his First Wife, Pure Essence. Prince Cảnh had his father's wide cheekbones, short, flat nose, and large lips. He had accompanied Pierre to India and France to symbolize the trust that existed between Pierre and King Ánh, and to help secure military support from the King of France.

Cảnh had learned and grown much on that trip. He had become a playmate of Queen Marie-Antoinette's little son, Louis-Joseph. In Paris, he had been the toast of the town, the most celebrated oddity of the most important parlors, an "attractive savage," as one columnist wrote in *Le Journal de Paris*.

Taking off on his bizarre turban headdress, Marie-Antoinette's hairdresser had even created Le Prince Cảnh Hairdo for men or women, and for the extravagant, *Les Chignons de Cochinchine*. Both hairdos had become the fashion rage of the 1787 season in Paris, the undisputed fashion center of the Western world.

Pierre met Queen Marie-Antoinette on multiple occasions. Each time, she expressed genuine interest in his work in Đại Việt. Pierre admired her for her sweet, intelligent gentleness. On their parting, Marie-Antoinette, the thirty-two-year-old Queen of France, gave him a small bag of gold and said, "This gold is from me. Please take it to use in your work with the poor of Đại Việt. It is a token of my admiration of the young Prince Cahn and all that you are doing in the name of Christ."

❧ ❦

On November 21, 1787, Pierre Pigneau, representing Nguyễn Ánh, signed the Versailles Treaty with King Louis XVI, promising French military aid to Nguyễn Ánh in exchange for the island of Poulo Condore, the port of Đà Nẵng, to be renamed Tourane, and exclusive trading rights for France. Nguyễn Ánh was promised the use of four naval frigates carrying 1650 Kaffir troops and field artillery. However, there was a major caveat buried in the footnotes. The governor in Pondicherry, Thomas Conway, was given sole authority to implement the treaty at his discretion.

Nguyễn Thơ, Cảnh's cousin, a Catholic and a trusted mandarin of the first rank, stood in a well-weathered tunic next to the boy. Nguyễn Thơ was forty-five, a skinny man with crooked teeth and a ready smile. Cảnh's nurse and his bodyguard, stood behind them. Prince Cảnh tried to hide his excitement, but like most little boys he couldn't. "It's been so long, I forgot what the jungle really looks like," he said, trying to be properly circumspect but raising his voice in excitement.

"It looks just the same," his nurse, Orchid, said laughing. Trung Bình, Cảnh's valet and bodyguard, laughed as well, and then added under his breath, "Generous are the Gods and Genie for bringing us all across the Western oceans and safely home."

213

Orchid was a short, matronly woman in her forties. She looked at her handsome charge and thought, *My beloved child, our home is not the same though. It won't be a safe place for a child, especially one who might become the heir-apparent during a civil war. Buddha give me strength, and this child protection.*

Cousin Nguyễn Thơ remarked, "I said that if I ever saw my country again, and returned to make offerings at the graves of my Ancestors, that I would split four taels of silver between the Church of Notre Dame and the village Temple of the Dragon Kings near my grandparents' grave, and now I accept that obligation with an exhilarated heart." He felt tears begin to well up in his eyes, and he carefully fought off such an outward display of emotion. He wanted to shout and caper, but instead, he opened his breathing.

Bishop Pierre went ashore to the fishing village of Vũng Tàu with two long-boats full of armed marines and sailors. They found Father Lozier with many of his students from the Catholic mission and a crowd of villagers at the beach to greet them. There was a very happy reunion. Bishop Pierre ordered guards posted and pickets sent out. Men brought barrels ashore to fill with water, and with Father Lozier's blessings, they purchased what chickens and ducks and baskets of vegetables the villagers could spare.

The guard stayed ashore for the evening so that the bishop could dine with Father Lozier, exchange presents, and take his reports. Pierre revealed that he planned to proceed to Sài Gòn with just *La Méduse* and *La Castries*, leaving the other two ships to begin making detailed maps of the Vũng Gành Rái Bay.

During a break, Benoit asked, "Father Lozier, what news do you have about Antoine Grannier?"

"Do you know Father Grannier?" asked the priest.

"We grew up together," said Benoit, "and he is a first cousin!"

Father Lozier looked concerned. "I'm sorry, my friend, to have to report that Father Grannier is no longer with us; his soul has passed on. He was sent to an inland parish in Sơn Hà in the province of Quảng Ngãi, an area that was subsequently ravaged by famine and then the plague. Word came that no one from the Christian mission there survived. I'm terribly sorry."

Benoit nodded dumbly. "Oh no, this is terrible—such a wonderful young man. I never knew him as a grown-up. Please excuse me," was all he could say. Benoit carefully stood, pushed in his stool, and left the hut. He walked around the village twice. He made his way down to the beach, aware of the rolling surf and the brilliant canopy of stars above, sat down on the warm sand, and stared at the lapping moonlit waves.

Slowly and painfully, Benoit recalled Antoine in old memories. They had spent many years in school together, were playmates, study partners, saw each other on holidays, and learned to sail in small boats and rock climb together. They once capsized and almost drowned together. Each had seen the other fall down on his face, but then get up, shake it off, and try again. *Once, Antoine had hidden the rope in his knapsack, and, after a long hike to a distant cliff face, he turned to me and said, "Did you remember the rope?" He gave me such a fright, and then we laughed.*

He was kind and thoughtful, so he was more than a friend, he was a role model of a decent person. He never got into fights, like I did. May his soul rest in peace.

Where was that soul now: heaven, hell, purgatory, or the void? All these memories and questions made Benoit homesick and more lonely than usual. Finally, alone by the black water in the dark of the late evening, he cried for Antoine and for his loss of his oldest friend.

Chapter 26
Wind and Rain, Từ Hải the Bandit
1788

Madame Camellia pulled her embroidered red jacket over her ample bosom to indicate that she had something important to say. She informed Jade River before the noon meal that there would be a wealthy new client for the evening, Từ Hải, the local bandit chieftain. Từ Hải gallantly presented his fine-brushed card as the sun set. When he was introduced, Jade River was struck by his rugged good looks. He was bearded, broad-chested, and as tall as he was handsome. He left a sword in its scabbard and a stout spear against the wall outside her sitting room, along with his two bodyguards, and entered with a lute still strapped to his back.

Từ Hải was looking for himself at the popular courtesan, while Jade River was finally meeting one of the most notorious outlaws and fighters in her province. He lived a free man outside the law. Từ Hải was famous for sculling a longboat with a large oar on the rivers, streams, and lakes surrounding his mountain lair, always carrying a sword and a lute on his back.

"Men rave about your music and grace," said Từ Hải grinning, "so I had to see what all the fuss was about. Allow me to present to you an old song." Từ Hải swung his lute off his back and beckoned for a stool. He tuned the lute carefully, played a slow and then a lively air, and sang a song extolling the joys of tilling the earth, full of imagery and innuendo. Jade River was extremely pleased with his skill, his voice, and his appearance. She took her own lute from its rosewood stand, and she played a medley of tunes, followed by an old song of two ardent lovers who wait until they are old to be together.

Từ Hải clapped his hands with appreciation. He bowed his head low, and spoke gently, "I feel that two kindred souls have come together. Well met, fair maiden of the golden voice." He took up his lute again, and answered by singing a lovely arrangement of *The Four Pleasures*.

"Heaven and earth have granted me one gift:
The gift of joy to relish through my days.
By wine possessed, I can not turn down a cup.
To poetry enslaved, I must hone words.
That chessboard's ready, boasts a coach and horse.
This zither's kept its frets, still sings twing-twang."
Then Từ Hải changed the last line. He didn't sing,
Who's sleeping? Who's awake? Who's won? Who's lost?
Instead, he improvised:
"Let us not worry about small things, if you will sing with me."

"Well played, well sung, sir," Jade River said in a mellifluous and earnest voice. "May I offer you something to quench your thirst—wine or tea—and some meat or vegetable spring rolls?"

"I'll take water and wine, and what ever is easy for food," said Từ Hải, "but eat with me, instead of making a spectacle of my appetite." Jade River nodded to her maid, who departed for refreshments. Jade River was strangely excited. She carefully sang *The Zither*, with lute accompaniment.

"The zither on the wall has strings.
You, Master T'ao, put me to shame.
Neither can I play it myself—
but it does brighten my dull hours.
At times, I pour some liquor, too,
And then I pluck the strings with zest.
I've pledged to keep my heart as clean,
As limpid as an autumn sky.
If you love me, please often come
And be my 'guest in the west lodge.'"

"By the Gods," said Từ Hải, "the dandies who brag of your beauty and singing have undersold your worth, but they also whine and moan that not one has won your favor or your heart. As Nguyễn Du wrote:
"How often have you lucked upon a man?
Why bother with caged birds or fish in pots?
I carry Heaven over my head, and trample the earth under my feet."

Jade River laughed with delight and replied, "You speak elegantly, sir, but you over-praise me, which is suspect. I do not criticize those who pay to hear me sing. But I do hold my heart in reserve, and I strive daily 'to sift gold from brass.'"

"Come closer to me then," he said, "so you can see of what stuff I am made of. Look at my eyes, hear my voice, feel the aura of my Ancestors, and decide for yourself if I deserve your trust."

"You have a skill with words," she conceded with a playful smile, "and appear to have a large heart. If you really care for this weed, this lowly flower, can I look forward to seeing you more than just tonight?" she added, laughing and openly encouraging him.

Từ Hải laughed and nodded, "I will come again, for how often is it anyone so moves my soul? Unless I'm fooled, you can tell the difference between a hero and a pile of common dust. I can tell from what you say, you can see I am different from the crowd of bees."

The pair got along all evening like this, singing in verse and speaking in poetry, and the next, and then the next. In this warrior, Jade River saw the heart of a tiger and the soul of a swallow. In a fortnight, Từ Hải won Jade River's consent to marry him. He said in his straightforward way, "I would be honored if you would agree to marry me."

Jade River blushed and replied, "If you would take this widow of life, I would be honored and overjoyed."

Từ Hải declared, "I will build two thrones, so you can sit by my side as my queen."

He purchased the slave Jade River and set her free for one hundred silver taels. He took her in a parade of musicians and heavily armed men to his mountaintop lair, and married her at a feast with all his fighting men and their women. Jade River was in love with a great man, and a year sped by like a month or a week—the happiest days of her life. Finally, all the constellations of Heaven were in the right part of the sky.

ॐ   ॐ

Nguyễn military recruiters started stripping the villages under Từ Hải's control of all of their men aged fifteen to fifty. Từ Hải raised his banner, called his men together, and prepared for war to his south. Jade River begged, "Let me at least come with you, so we can stay together."

Từ Hải looked at his beautiful wife, musician, and lover and said, "I do not know where I will be sleeping each night. You can't come with me, for there will only be marching, discomfort, and fighting." He mustered his followers, and they grimly rode off wearing battle armor and carrying banners.

Jade River stayed in their mountain lair. She carefully bolted the doors at night. She tended the gardens, but the weeds ran wild. She thought fondly of her husband Từ Hải, but also of her parents, whom she had not seen now for so many years. Were they well, did they "have skin with scales and hair white like frost?" She even pined for her old love, Lương Hoàng, and his memory was the only shadow on her new and amazing marriage. Her love for Từ Hải burned brightly, and sustained her during this dark period.

ॐ   ॐ

After several months passed, Jade River was startled by the clang of gongs. She ran to a window to see hundreds of soldiers approaching her farm carrying colored flags. The armor-clad horsemen ringed the house. A man dismounted and many voices called out, "Where is our queen?" Jade River appeared at her door, stepped outside, and the soldiers, as a group, dismounted, laid down their arms, and kowtowed to Jade River. One man stayed on his horse. He dismounted last and approached. It was Từ Hải, and both king and queen kowtowed to each other, and then Jade River cried with delight, "Blessed are the Gods who answer prayers," and threw herself into Từ Hải's open arms.

Từ Hải laughed and said, "Remember what you said when we first met: 'When fish and water meet, it's love!' And you also said, 'To spot a hero took a heroine.'"

"The Nguyễn have retreated, and I am back. I hope you are as pleased to see me as I am to see you."

Jade River cried with joy and said, "I'm just a humble, clinging vine that by good luck may flourish in your shade."

After a week sped by, the happy couple gave a great feast to reward their troops. There was drumming, the clanging of gongs, and the music of flutes and strings. After several days of feasting, music, and singing, the soldiers and their women went back to their own farms or houseboats, and in the days that followed Jade River and Từ Hải were like watered flowers—"their love bloomed forth afresh."

☙ ❧

General Đỗ Thanh Nhơn led a Nguyễn Army into the area. General Đỗ came to Phan Thiết and sent messengers in blue shirts to Từ Hải bearing gifts: 200 pounds of the finest jade and gold, and two waiting maids for Jade River. They carried an invitation for Từ Hải to attend a meeting to discuss a truce, friendship, and an alliance. "I do not trust the Nguyễn under King Ánh," said Từ Hải to his wife. "Even though this new government is not necessarily as bad or corrupt as its predecessors. The only safe choice is to retreat or fight. No one has ever defeated Từ Hải and his mountain men. Why should I submit to their dressing me in a mandarin's robes?"

Jade River was a wonderful woman with a trusting heart. She answered, "We are like ferns that float on water. You should meet this general of the young Nguyễn King and hear him out. Find out if there is an honorable way to bring peace to this area. It would be honorable under Heaven to reduce the amount of fighting and bloodshed and casualties of your fighters and your peasants. If you can bring a cessation of hostilities, we could travel north and visit my family with great peace of mind."

Từ Hải said, "We are impregnable on our mountain, surrounded by our lakes and streams. It is my pleasure to stir Heaven and shake the earth. I come and go and bow my head to none. Why take the risk? You and I can travel north with ten or twenty men, visit your family, and return. We can hold out indefinitely."

"If you bring peace to the region, it would be a blessing. It would be easier for us to travel north, if we knew your mountain lair would not come under attack."

"But I fear we can not trust this man or his government. We do not know they will be honorable."

Jade River listened with care. "I wonder," she said simply, "if neither side ever takes the risk to make peace, are we doomed to eternal strife? We should swear allegiance to the king's throne, and travel up fortune's royal road. Our public goals and private needs will both be met. War is not good for women or children or grandparents."

Từ Hải decided to meet with Đỗ Thanh Nhơn, since he was growing older and he tired of his military life outside the law, with its constant vigilance. He took many of his men with him to the meeting, and he and his men were treated to a fine meal with wine.

While the music played loudly, Từ Hải's bodyguard outside the banquet hall were jumped and executed by men pretending to serve them food and wine. Đỗ Thanh Nhơn sprang his traps. Archers rushed into the main room through every door and window, and released a hail of deadly arrows. The Nguyễn host drew concealed bow and arrow, crossbow and spear, and fell upon Từ Hải and his men.

Từ Hải had never lost a battle, but now he watched as his followers and friends were cut down like grass as they tried to find their weapons, now removed from the antechamber. With arrows flying, Từ Hải swung his sword and killed many men before a dozen arrows, piercing him one at a time, killed him.

ও   ৫

Đỗ Thanh Nhơn and his army marched into the hills and attacked the mountain refuge and destroyed it. Jade River fled with other women and children into the jungle, but before long she was apprehended by a mangy group of bandits, the scavengers of war, who violated her person and then sold her back to the richest tea house in the area, the Happy Valley Green Pavilion in Biên Hòa.

Jade River was grief-stricken to lose her tiger of a man, Từ Hải, who had the soul of a swallow. He had become the pillar and foundation of her joyful new life. As she contemplated ways of ending her misery, she also wondered if she was too sad and aggrieved to care whether she lived or died. She was just a leaf in the wind. Madame Camellia was thrilled to harvest wind-blown leaves. She clapped together her chubby hands, smiled widely, showing all her black teeth, and warbled, "My beautiful daughter, fate has brought you back to my establishment. I am so delighted to see you."

Jade River became a fountain of tears. She wondered if she would ever forgive herself for the bad advice she had given her deceased beloved, and cried herself to sleep at night for weeks.

Chapter 27
The Meeting, Vũng Tàu
1788

On the third day anchored at Vũng Tàu, Pierre called a morning meeting of his senior officers in the great cabin of *La Méduse*. Benoit entered the roundhouse cabin and looked out the beautiful stern windows at small boats in the bay. Before the room filled, he moved to an empty place at the table. The captain's day cabin in the rear of the ship was full of light. On three sides the walls had windows paned with translucent glass. A narrow table ran from port to starboard. The room functioned as the captain's reception chamber, and his dining room. Two 12-pounder cannons faced the stern glass windows which, by their removal, doubled as gun ports. The cannon divided the room almost in half. The four hanging oil lamps were unlit.

"Gentlemen," Father Pierre the Bishop began, "Let us pray." All the officers bowed their heads toward the great slatted-pine sea table that hung on ropes next to the two cannon. "We thank God Almighty for his mercy and grace, for delivering us across the Indian Ocean to our destination on a great mission, *la mission civalitrice*." The French rolled out of his throat with a thick resonance. In contrast to English or German, Frenchmen spoke in musical phrases. Pierre articulated his words with pleasure and respect, almost as an erotic experience.

"May we succeed in our efforts to love one another, and to civilize and convert the heathen, and live up to the challenge and the blessings that our Lord, in his generosity, has provided. We serve him in his blessed name. In the name of the Father, the Son, and the Holy Ghost, bless you and keep you all, amen."

"Amen," the men chorused.

Father Pierre the Bishop had gained more weight in France. Twenty-four years in the Far East, twelve as counselor of Nguyễn Ánh, had taken its toll on his once robust complexion. His owlish face and beak nose gave him a professorial and slightly sinister appearance.

He looked about the room at the fourteen naval officers and hoped that his bold scheme would work. "The time has come for us to review the military situation. You each know what role you have agreed to play." He had each officer say his name, rank, and primary responsibility, and then (for not all of them had heard the whole story), he proceeded to review the military and political situation in the war that they were joining as mercenaries. *Fusils engagagés pour le Dieu* (hired guns for God) was the pet expression of Henri Dayot, the one-eyed captain he had chosen for his second-in-command, and the commodore of the small squadron.

"Our position is precarious but not impossible. As my father liked to say, there's both good news and bad news. The bad news is that the Hồ brothers now control Phú Xuân, the Spring Capital, and the city of Thăng Long, and two-thirds of the country. The good news is that we're still going to overpower them with our artillery. As I said in Pondicherry, with the support of our cannon well-served, King Ánh should defeat the Hồ of Tây Sơn and their peasant armies."

"Is it really possible that we can make a difference when there are so few of us?" asked Olivier Du Puymanel, the stocky, red-haired engineer.

"I have no doubt of it," Pierre answered. "According to Father Lozier—and mind you, these are merely estimates—the Tây Sơn are split into two forces. Each has a fleet of roughly sixty galleys, sixty-three war elephants, and about 100,000 foot soldiers, who, though poorly armed, have the bravery one expects from fanatics. They can muster another 50,000 to 100,000 farmers from the villages they control for a major conflict.

"Our employer, King Nguyễn Ánh, has assembled about fifty galleys, seventy war elephants and 30,000 soldiers. On paper, Ánh is much weaker, but he holds two aces. First, he has a hereditary claim to the throne that his people respect. Second, there is nothing in the country that can stand up to the fire power on our four ships. I have purchased twenty-six extra pieces of mounted field artillery, sixteen 12-pounders, and ten 6-pounders. Besides these field guns, we have muskets for 600 men. The Citadel of Sài Gòn should be safe from attack as soon as we have our field cannon in good positions."

"Do you think that the natives can learn how to shoot our guns?" Guillaume de Martineau asked, looking trim in his black goatee.

The bishop answered, "Pierre Poivre taught the Indian sepoys to shoot, didn't he? I've had Việt students learn to read and write Latin in just two or three years. I'm sure that the Việt are capable of learning whatever we can teach in warfare. I'm even sure that they possess knowledge they can teach us. Besides the archers of the Hồ brothers, we have to worry about the climate, especially the heat, the rain, the mud, the mosquitoes, and the water demons."

Benoit, dressed like all the others in his French naval officer's blue and red pants, but without the heavy jacket with epaulets and insignia, asked, "Why is the water so dangerous?"

"Only God knows," Father Pierre answered. "The Chinese say that there are evil spirits living in the water, and that they leave the water when you boil it."

"Do you believe this?" Guillaume asked.

"I don't know what to believe sometimes," Pierre answered. "Only the Lord knows why most water here makes Europeans miserably sick, while boiled water never seems to. Whether there are evil spirits in the water or not, exactly as in India or Africa, you are all ordered to boil your water and cook any food before you eat it. You train anyone who cooks for you to boil water and cool it, for drinking or to use for washing lettuce or greens."

Guillaume laughed. "If there's enough whiskey, wine, and beer, we'll be fine." Others, particularly his card partners, laughed too. Guillaume said, "How close are you to this king of the barnyard *Ane* (he substituted the French homophone meaning donkey) and what are his long-term chances? Are we going to eliminate him too, after we've destroyed the Tây Sơn?" Guillaume paused for effect and surveyed the room. "If we are so strong against these natives, why remain their servants when we could become their masters? If we play one against the other, why can't we handle the winner, following the India precedent? Isn't subjugation, in fact, a desired goal, so we may stay afloat, as it were, against the British?" Benoit stared at the aristocrat and almost forgot himself. He felt an enormous desire to challenge Guillaume to a duel right then on the bishop's behalf.

"Valid questions," Pierre grinned, hiding his dismay. "King Nguyễn Ánh and I are actually very close. I'll get to that later. I'm not planning to 'eliminate him.' Nor would it be advisable to try. There is much to learn about Đại Việt. First of all, this is not like India, where the whole country is fragmented into small, feudal satrapies. There, a European power with a few guns and some gold can start collecting warlords who are dependent on it for control of the field. In India, the government, the Moguls, are interlopers, Mussulmen who came down from Persia. The Indian population is predominantly Hindu. There are also a few Buddhists, and who knows how many minor sects. Each religion supports a different language, and people of the same religion from different cities often cannot understand each other. In short, the Indians are unorganized, disunited, and distrustful or hostile to their neighbors." He paused and took a sip of tea before continuing.

"In Đại Việt, there is one predominant people and culture. They speak one language. Until the Civil War of Succession began in 1620 between the Nguyễn and Trịnh families, the Việt had enjoyed some seven centuries of freedom from outsiders. Remember that the Chinese invaded during the Han Dynasty under Emperor Wu, in 111 B.C., but the Việt finally threw them out in the tenth century, a thousand years later."

Guillaume was leaning on an elbow. "Are you suggesting," he asked incredulously, "that France could not conquer this little satrapy of natives if it wanted to?"

"I think that France has more problems than are readily apparent," Pierre replied. "But even if we were a fully united people at home, the Việt have not been conquered for very long by anyone since they kicked out their Chinese overlords in 938 or so. At that time in France, the Vikings, the Magyars, the Burgundians, and other German tribes were carving up Charlemagne's empire of Western Christendom. Our beloved France was known then to the Romans as the northern barbarian tribes.

"The Việt have always disliked foreigners, and particularly occupational forces. They have a strong sense of national identity, even in their peasantry, of all places, and that phenomenon should be the envy of every true Frenchman."

"Aren't you siding with the natives here?" challenged Guillaume de Martineau. "Are you suggesting that peasants should be treated as if each one were equal somehow to the royal family or the aristocracy? And besides, many of the French nobility don't mistreat their peasants."

"Interesting issues," said Pierre, "but that's another discussion or two. No, I am just saying that a war with the Việts would be neither quick nor hold the promise of paying for itself in any reasonable amount of time. I would bet my money on the Vietnamese. France wants China, that is the big prize, and Đại Việt should prove an invaluable base from which to penetrate into China. But neither country, Đại Việt nor China, is intellectually weak, even if their guns and ballistic science are centuries behind Europe. Technical weakness does not mean military weakness.

"China sees Đại Việt as just a small satellite of its own dominant culture. It is easy for Westerners to underestimate the Chinese and their satellites. The Chinese call their country *Zhongguo*, which translates as Middle Kingdom. Middle refers to their central location between Heaven and Hell, or between the stars and the center of the earth. It is possible that the Romans had a similar notion in their word Mediterranean, which also means the middle of the earth. Nonetheless, the Chinese are proud and literate. They claim to have invented paper a century before the birth of our Lord Jesus Christ. Chinese philosophers calculated that the earth was round over a thousand years before Johannes Kepler did."

Then he laughed before expressing his next thought. "The Chinese are in some ways very like Frenchmen. They believe, for instance, that all other cultures and races in the world are inferior to theirs.

"Most Westerners who come out here underestimate the Chinese and the Việts. For centuries, the Chinese and their neighbors have chosen to disdain Western or any foreign technology. They will pay for their arrogance, but the discrepancy, which is prodigious, never had anything to do with lack of know-how or ability. They understood, correctly, that guns undermined their feudal institutions."

"They are astute on this point," said Guillaume. "We are having this problem in France right now, and also throughout Europe."

Pierre perused his audience. He held Benoit's and Guillaume's rapt attention. Some of the others looked politely bored by the subject of the native perspective, while most were thoughtfully grave. Many agreed quietly with Guillaume, that Bishop Pierre had apparently gone a bit native.

"Đại Việt is also called Nam Việt, which means Southern Việt. The Việt like to refer to their country as Nam Việt to irritate the Chinese envoys, for it refers also to an ancient kingdom that included two Chinese provinces, Guangdong and Guangxi, and a claim that Đại Việt theoretically has over those parts of southern China.

"It is hard to grasp, but the Chinese Empire claims to have been around longer than any other empire on earth. It is now much longer lived than the Roman Empire, one of the longest-lived empires in the West, which dissolved in 476, when Odoacer the Rugian defeated the Romans."

Dayot interjected, "One could argue that that is the year a Frenchman became the King of the Romans."

"Quite right," said Pierre. "The Chinese conquered the Việts before our Christian era even began, and before France was more than a wasteland of illiterate, warring tribes of heathen. But the Chinese were not successful here in Đại Việt in the long run. Though it is hard to imagine exactly how, the Việt, after a thousand years of subjugation, rose up and defeated a Chinese Army which was three times greater in size than its own force."

"That really is amazing," said the sun-tanned Julian Girard. "China is so vast compared to this little coastland of a country."

"You're right," Pierre said, his eyes now lit up with the fervor of his learned insight. "But one of the patterns of history in this area of the world is that outsiders have underestimated the cunning and determination of the diminutive Việt.

"Ngô Quyền is arguably the Charlemagne of Đại Việt. He defeated the Chinese on the Bạch Đằng River in 938 and destroyed an army of 300,000 with only 100,000 men. He used a classic Chinese strategy of feint and strike. He kept retreating before the Chinese, while his guerrilla tactics allowed his forces to ambush the enemy's supply lines and stragglers.

"The Chinese resorted to a naval attack with a galley fleet against the city of Thăng Long up the Bạch Đằng River. Ngô Quyền ordered his troops and an army of peasants to make large iron-tipped stakes, which they drove into the riverbed at low tide so that they were well beneath the water's surface at high tide. It was an incredible engineering feat. Ngô Quyền allowed half his fleet of galleys to be chased up the river as the tide was coming in. As the tide ran out, Ngô hurled his entire fleet of galleys against the Chinese, which though vastly superior, tried to retreat because the current was also against them.

"Oh my God, but that's brilliant," said the surgeon Michel Despiaux.

"That shows a lot of hard-assed organization and discipline," said Joachim Bohu.

"So you wait till we have signed up and sailed to tell us this new information," said Guillaume smiling.

"Hey, he never said it would be a picnic," said Olivier du Puymanel.

"The Việts are serious fighters," said Father Pierre. "The tide had certainly changed. The Chinese galleys rowed themselves full speed into the stakes, which were by now just below the water's surface. The huge stakes punctured the ships.

The galleys sank, or collided and jammed together. It was a slaughter. Few of the Chinese invasion force ever returned to China. The Chinese admiral, who was also the heir apparent, was captured and defiantly beheaded."

Benoit asked, "Is that why you had the extra copper armor plating nailed to the bows of all the ships in the yard at Pondicherry?"

"I thought that you had lost your reason," exclaimed Tabarly.

Pierre nodded. "The armor plating will allow us more freedom, particularly in ramming these galleys, and protect us some from being rammed. It's also a scientific experiment. I want to see if it will slow down the wood rot, which is endemic in these latitudes.

Commodore Dayot's cabin boy and two young midshipman quietly refilled tea and water glasses. "The extra port and bow swivel guns are to keep enemy galleys from boarding us, if possible. Our biggest problem will be their archers, who are not to be believed. They are more accurate at twenty-five paces than our musketmen. That reminds me, Henri, please make a note. We have to set up vertical shields by the swivels to give our gunners a modicum of protection from archers."

Henri Dayot nodded his assent, and then spoke with an uncanny relish. "With luck, none of us will feed their crocodiles, though many foreigners have. According to Bishop Pierre, those crocodiles have feasted on Cham, Khmer, Mongol, Chinese, and Siamese. General Ngô Quyền's victory at the Bạch Đằng was just the beginning of a long history of successes that have helped make the indigenous crocodile population some of the best-fed reptiles in the world." After a pause, Dayot, with his one eye gleaming, added, "And dinner tonight will be fresh, fat local crocodile." The whole room laughed.

"You should have told us about the crocodiles before we left India," quipped Olivier du Puymanel, the red-haired engineer.

Another nervous laugh ran around the room. Father Pierre continued, "This battle and subsequent victories established the supremacy of the Việt kings or emperors and their mandarins. All the would-be invaders of this country have understood that whoever controls the coast of Đại Việt can control the spice routes between China and India, and that is nothing to laugh at.

"Ghengis Khan was not indifferent to such an attractive area. In the thirteenth century, he and his horse-riding, blood-drinking Mongol fighters conquered all of China. After the Big Dragon of China was bent to his will, he sent 500,000 Chinese and Mongol fighters to conquer the Little Dragon. Đại Việt is one of the very few countries in the world to defeat the Chinese and Mongol hordes twice, first under Genghis Khan and then his grandson Kublai Khan. Unlike the Japanners, who also successfully repelled the Mongols, the Việt didn't have any typhoon storm do the fighting for them by sinking an entire invasion armada. A Portuguese priest reported that the Japanners believe they were rescued by a divine storm wind called a *kami-kaze*."

Tabarly said, slurring his speech, "How could the Mongols defeat all of China, and then lose to such a little country?" He was quietly drinking whiskey poured into his water cup from a concealed flask, and it was beginning to show.

"It doesn't appear to make sense, does it," Father Pierre the Bishop said gravely. "Evidently, many of the Mongols got terribly seasick on the sail down the coast, and their horses were terrified by the war elephants in their yellow harnesses. The art of using elephants for war is an art the Vietnamese learned from India that the Chinese were not prepared for.

"The Việt, under General Trần Hưng Đạo, continued to develop and refine their tactics of feint and strike. Trần Hưng Đạo, using these unmanly jungle tactics, avoided all direct confrontation, and relied instead on ambushes, ingenious and elaborate booby-traps, jungle heat, the rainy season, and tropical diseases to wear out their adversary. They also used simple weapons like caltrops to wreak havoc with the enemy's cavalry. Caltrops are known in the East as well as the West. Some of you know that they are small metal spikes, sharp at both ends, and bent around each other to make a lethal, four-pointed upturned nail on a tripod. One of the sharp points of the tetrahedron always points up when they are thrown on the ground, where they wound horses or foot soldiers.

"Trần Hưng Đạo also copied the mythic Ngô Quyền to an extraordinary degree. He resorted, in desperation I presume, to trying the old strategy of iron-tipped spikes submerged in the Bạch Đằng. History repeated itself. Because of the fast-ebbing tide at the river mouth, Trần Hưng Đạo sank and annihilated the whole Mongol fleet. The Mongols would have eventually succeeded perhaps, but the Việt were making the proposition too expensive. Then the Việt bought peace with a large tributary gift."

"Well, I'll be damned!" said Guillaume. "The Mongols evidently could not read Chinese history books as well as they could ride their horses and their women. Such a waste of horses. Could one of those oversized native spears stuck in the mud pierce our stout Bretton oak?"

"Probably they could," Pierre said seriously. "But we will use our own network of Christian and Nguyễn spies to stay informed about the weapons deployed by the Hồ brothers. Also, we will chart each river we navigate, to see if it is shallow enough to booby-trap with spikes. Furthermore, no one is ever to chase enemy galleys upriver in a rising tide. If you make and survive this mistake, you will be broken to maindeck waister with only half a seaman's pay.!

"The Hồ brothers," Pierre continued, "after seizing the Quy Nhơn Citadel with just a few hundred men, amassed a large force and marched upon the Nguyễn King at the Spring Capital. This known fratricide had no stomach for a fight and he invited his old enemy, the Trịnh up in Thăng Long, to come to his rescue."

Captain Dayot made a face and put his hands in the air. Then, in a high falsetto voice, he wailed, "My peasants don't like me. I know you're my worst enemy, but I have no friends to turn to. Could you please come to my rescue against these nasty peasants?"

The men round the table laughed as the old captain played the fool, bringing more levity to a long meeting at the expense of the cowardly Nguyễn King, whom no one cared a sous for anyway.

Pierre waited for the room to calm down, the rejoinders and mimics to end. Pierre respected Henri for his judgment as well as his wit, and wondered if he could really fight.

Pierre resumed, "The Trịnh sent word, yes, they would help out. And then they didn't. They double-crossed the Nguyễn King, who waited too long for the support from the Trịnh. He fled to Sài Gòn with his forces by galley fleet, and then overland till the Tây Sơn forces overtook him in a little place called Kao Giang.

"Kao Giang" Pierre slowed now to emphasize his own role, "is where my itinerant mission had just relocated after another round of persecutions by the Nguyễn authorities."

"Why were you persecuted?" asked Benoit.

"The charge was subversion," Pierre answered. "Christ teaches that all men and women are equal before God, that even the poorest female slave has a soul and can be a member of the Holy Roman Catholic Church. And worst of all," he said with added emphasis, "there's the eleventh commandment, a papal communiqué that says: Thou shalt not worship your great grandfather. Clearly, the Việt find that idea disrespectful, even undermining.

"Lieutenant Grannier, your cousin, Father Antoine, who died in a plague, was a great boon to me. He insisted on pointing out that what is surprising is that these Việts, so wildly superstitious, are basically so open and tolerant. He compared their tolerance favorably to how we treat heretics and abstainers from the one true faith in France. It is tragic that Antoine Grannier was taken from us, and that you managed to get all the way out here and just missed seeing your cousin, who was such a wonderful man of God.

"An important digression. Now, where was I? At Kao Giang, I had thirty-two students learning the Gospels in Vietnamese and in Latin. We had information that King Nguyễn Võ Vương's grandson, Prince Ánh, was in the entourage of the Nguyễn imperial procession, and his mother wished them to escape. So before the battle, we contacted his mother, the Lady Purity, the young prince, and their personal servants, and snuck them away and downriver on a sampan. We dressed them like fishmongers. My student and acolyte Paul Nghi and his brother poled the fishing boat right past the scrutiny of a group of Tây Sơn soldiers as the royals and their servants cleaned and folded dirty fishnets."

"The prince and his mother had a narrow escape. We heard that the Tây Sơn forces caught up with the remnants of the Nguyễn imperial procession. The Hồ forces killed all those who bravely fought, and captured King Nguyễn Đình and his family."

"That's dreadful," Nicolas Tabarly exclaimed, his bulbous nose gleaming in the amber light of the open gun ports and the oil lamps.

"I'm surprised, Nicolas, that you haven't already heard this whole story before," Guillaume interjected.

"Maybe snatches of it," Tabarly said, deflated, while clenching his fist. Tabarly wondered why Guillaume was being so unpleasant.

Guillaume asked with a grin, "What was the prince's mother like? Was she attractive and available?" trying to get another laugh from his peers.

"Lady Purity was and is an astonishing lady," Pierre said coldly, showing his irritation. "Perhaps someday I'll honor you with some of her story."

Guillaume is rude as well as dangerous, Benoit thought. *He has the devil inside him. I wonder how you become so evil. I would like to kill him today. Does that make me evil too? No, you must kill a rabid dog, even if the dog is only partly to blame for carrying a disease or a devil or whatever it is that makes him rabid and dangerous to others. Stow these thoughts; listen to the bishop.*

Pierre was back into his narration. "At any rate, I put them all on a junk that I'd hired, and we sailed to Phú Quốc Island in the Sea of Siam that we still use as a secret refuge. It was there I discovered that Ánh was an extremely quick student and already an ambitious young man, trained in the Chinese classics and using weapons at the age of sixteen. The Tây Sơn force took Ánh's uncle, King Nguyễn Đình, to the Spring Capital in chains and decapitated him. His family members were executed.

"Eight years later, in 1785, Hồ Huệ went north and pushed the Trịnh out of the Spring Capital. In four more weeks his peasant forces took Thăng Long. The Trịnh Dynasty was so corrupt and decadent that it just fell apart. The morale of Huệ's troops was excellent at that point. They were known as the Hissing Army because they screamed bloody murder and yelled for revenge when they attacked. The Tây Sơn Rebellion had accomplished a tremendous feat in a decade. They unified the kingdom after 150 years of civil war, and without the aid of a single one of the great Việt warlord families of power."

"Excuse me, Monsignor, but what right do we have now to take sides against the Hồ brothers?" asked Benoit.

"Excellent question," said Pierre, suddenly on the defensive. "Although Lữ ruled the south from Sài Gòn, Nhạc ruled the center from Quy Nhơn, and Huệ ruled the north from the Spring Capital, the Tây Sơn brothers are still considered by most Việt mandarins and scholars to be mere upstarts. They still lack legal legitimacy in their own culture, which they can only achieve by seriously improving the quality of government. They announced a program of land reform, but our spies report that it has lost all momentum. The Tây Sơn brothers apparently settled back to enjoy their new treasures, and according to the letters I have received, they soon started quarreling over fiefs, women, money, and protocol. Lữ died, apparently from an overdose of opium, to which he became addicted.

"After a quarrel over the spoils of victory, Huệ attacked his brother Nhạc and besieged Quy Nhơn, but the blood tie proved stronger than their greed and ambition. They made a truce and Huệ returned to his kingdom in the north."

Benoit could not hold back his next question. "Do you think that the peasants in France could unite behind such rebellious leaders and notions of redistribution of land?" The cabin became extremely quiet.

Pierre paused to organize his thoughts. "I'm afraid that peasants anywhere will become revolutionary if they are hungry, while their landlords grow rich through corruption and greed."

Captain Julian Girard then asked, "Monsignor, didn't you report earlier that the Tây Sơn revolutionaries are much stronger today in numbers than King Ánh?"

"Yes I did. King Ánh captured the old fortress of Sài Gòn in '82 with an assortment of allies of the Nguyễn Dynasty, which included Chinese pirates called the Black Flags, and Cambodian mercenaries. Nhạc and Huệ attacked by sea and destroyed Ánh's forces. To avenge themselves on the Black Flags, the Tây Sơn massacred 10,000 of the Chinese tradesmen and their families that lived in Chợ Lớn, the market outside of the citadel.

"Ánh returned with an army of Siamese soldiers loaned to him by the Siamese King, but Huệ and Lữ vanquished them. It was after this discouragement that I finally persuaded our proud friend Prince Ánh to seek and trust aid from France.

"I think, gentlemen, that the cannon and gunners of the Christian nation of France will stop this revolutionary tide in its tracks, and return the Nguyễn line and the rightful heir to the Golden Throne in the Spring Capital. He and his line will fall deeper in debt to the king and the people of France. King Ánh's heir, Prince Cảnh, includes Christianity in his studies, and you should remember that he is onboard now, and in my care.

"It is my dream to make this country safe for establishing the one true faith and for establishing trade with France. I hope and pray to finish the work which I began in my youth, to save these heathen from eternal damnation and to bring them into the light and joy of Christian brotherhood."

Guillaume looked down and admired his diamond rings, thinking, *Either we will all wind up dead, or, if we are lucky, with a little wealth and a few local wives.* "Well spoken, Bishop," said Guillaume smiling, "magnanimous and counter-revolutionary. The heathen will burn in everlasting hell if we don't help them." He decided not to say, *But do we really care for these smiling, two-faced, natives?* He finished, "What matters is that they provide us with markets for trade and wealth."

"Of course that is a major part of the picture," said Pierre, "especially for investors."

Benoit spoke up, "This task is a noble one, but the more I learn about it, the greater the risks appear. We are going to risk much for uncertain rewards. But for those of us who want to do God's work, bring civilization and salvation to the heathen, and to serve king and country, the gamble is a great opportunity."

Father Pierre jumped back in. "We do help these people if we teach them the word of our Lord, which offers eternal salvation. The risks are substantial, which I have never hidden or disqualified. The rewards are potentially prodigious as well, particularly if our trading company gets exclusive contracts."

"And before I forget, when we reach Sài Gòn, which Ánh has recaptured once again, I will present you to our ally and employer, now King Nguyễn Ánh. Though young, Ánh is no fool, and the king and his mandarins are exceedingly proud. All of you and your men are expected, as agreed, to behave well. And if you don't, as agreed, I'll lock you up till the next heathen junk sails for India. Should all go well, and we defeat the insurgents as I intend, the king will rule all of Đại Việt. You will, like it or not, have to obey court etiquette in the king's presence, including formal bows to him and his mandarins. If there is ever a state ceremony, there could be complications. Those of us who choose to attend will be expected to prostrate ourselves and kowtow, which means touching our head to the floor while on our knees, three times to the king—as do all his subjects, even his highest ministers and mandarins."

"I'll be damned if I'll fall to my knees and rub my nose in the dirt for any yellow-skinned idol-worshipper," Guillaume growled. "I'll fight his enemies, but I won't grovel and practice his heathen ways." Guillaume was expressing a feeling shared by most of the recruits, and Pierre knew that his French and Việt brothers would take a long time to respect each other. The formal kowtow, or head knock, was also repugnant to him, but a minor nuisance. And like most questions of prerogative and protocol, Pierre felt it should not hinder a great cause.

"You won't have to kowtow, I hope, because no one will be forced to attend official ceremonies that demand it." Father Pierre tried to forgive the sneer he detected in Guillaume's face and knew that he wanted more tolerance in himself for such men. *Some men will never overcome their fears and arrogance, or understand the joy of God's love, or have the strength to care for others,* he thought sadly, *but I need these soldiers and their skills. They can kill or subdue greater numbers of the heathen enemy faster than any other force under arms in the country, save for the Lord himself, armed with all the forces of nature.*

"I'll try to keep you away from his mandarins too, but a bow is no less important to them than a bow is in France. Every court has its protocols. They just execute their bows differently. It should not surprise you that, as in France, everyone here is socially inferior to the king and the royal family by custom and law."

Pierre then stood up, put his hands together as in prayer, and bent at the waist to demonstrate the simple Oriental form of respect that one shows to one's superiors, equals, friends, or strangers. "It is wise and Christian to bow to your inferiors, though you may just nod or ignore them as appropriate. A full, formal bow is simple and I want you all to bow back to me in this way right now."

Pierre bowed to his officers with the tips of his fingers pressed in the prayer position. There was a second of suspense . . . when one could tangibly feel the possibility of revolt. Henri Dayot, Benoit Grannier, and Julian Girard stood up straight to attention, clapped their fingers together with their thumbs to their chests, and began the bow with elegance, the whole room following these three. Even Guillaume stood up, and inclined his head a little, when he saw that the others accepted Pierre's leadership on the issue, but his eyes rolled with condescension and his puckered lips communicated his disapproval.

"Gentlemen," Pierre said with his natural authority as he stood up, "let us adjourn for the afternoon dinner. Thank you much, one and all, for your questions and comments, and even, I suppose, your humor."

Chapter 28
Nguyễn Huệ and the Chinese Invasion
1788

Trusted by both brothers, Lương Hoàng had become the messenger between Nhạc and Huệ. Lương Hoàng was no longer a star-struck boy. At thirty-seven years of age, he stood as strong and hard as seasoned teak. Hoàng was now visiting with Huệ. They sat on their horses and watched the games of the Hissing Army Northern Group in the open field below. The men were competing in archery, weapons *kata*, prearranged fight drills, boxing, and wrestling. There were also competitions in knife throw, javelin, rock hurdle, and a variety of track events. Every soldier competed as an individual, and as a member of a thirty-man unit. The men in the special musket regiment were also expected to compete in loading and firing their muskets. Each officer of the elephant corps had to perform battle tricks with his beast. The last day of events would be competition by the elite units, challenged by the best units of the regular forces. These games were used to choose which men would go into the special units that would spearhead the assault on the Chinese Army that had invaded the country.

After countless days of drill competitions, Huệ was tired of martial exercises and endless hours of logistical planning and preparations for war. He knew, though, that his presence was inspiring, so he sat on his horse, visible to the field, while he discussed his troubles with Hoàng. "We have only a thousand muskets," he confessed. "So I have a single musket regiment of a thousand men, which practices, but we don't have enough powder and shot for them to actually load and fire. That English trader, Roberts, promised a shipload of muskets, powder, and shot. We expected that ship five months ago. My informants tell me that the Chinese have 10,000 muskets, though mostly antiques. Although we have some ancient cannon in our junk fleet, the Chinese probably have many more. By the God of War Quan Công, imported guns are expensive!"

"Though the Nine Judges of Hell might disagree, that's true," said Lương Hoàng. "But on the other hand, you have twice as many muskets as your brother, and many more cannon. The Chinese buy their cannon mostly from the English and the Portuguese. Prince Ánh buys his from the French. You and Nhạc buy from the Dutch or the English, when those Western Ocean barbarians deliver."

Huệ continued, "These guns will ruin us. Life here will never be the same. With these guns, the West has brought moral decay and political unrest to the East. Warfare is losing its glory and honor. You no longer need a long apprenticeship for a trained eye, hand, and body. Now a general must study the low skills of merchants, traders, and money lenders and produce gold or silver or foreign exchange, or he can't afford to buy the best powder and shot for the newest muskets, cannon, and cursed grapeshot! No one seems to win if the other side has it. Even slaves or porters can load cannon with pig iron scrap and light the powder."

"Sad but true," said Lương Hoàng, "our best officers in both Tây Sơn armies are divided on the merits of the Western weapons."

Huệ replied, "We are not too proud. We will do what it takes." Huệ and Lương Hoàng sat on their horses near the knife throwing and the sword *kata*. Huệ had all his officers act as judges, and they also had to compete. Before him the best athlete-warriors in his army were running an obstacle course while carrying an array of weapons: spear, sword, and knives. Between sprints on the course, they had to throw the spears and the knives at specific targets, and finish with a complicated sword *kata*. They earned points for accuracy at each target, and they were timed as well and awarded points for speed and form. Huệ was thirty-six years old but still strong and flexible as hemp rope. He had already run the obstacle course himself, and only eighteen of the younger men had beaten his score.

His eyes followed the men running through the games as his mind struggled with logistics and politics. He confided to Lương Hoàng, "No matter how many Chinese we kill, the Chinese can always send another army. But nevertheless, we will drive them out of this beautiful land of the Gods, as we have six times before. And this time, I don't want Lê Chiêu Thông to escape. The young emperor has caused so much trouble. Domestic reforms must wait now till the Chinese are driven out of the country."

"I'm sorry," said Lương Hoàng, "that Nhạc ordered me to report back to him immediately on your activities. I fear I will miss the beginning of a historic campaign."

Huệ nodded in sympathy, and said, "It was the youngster Lê Chiêu Thông who reorganized the Trịnh remnants above Thăng Long, and made Trịnh Bồng their king. I sent Hữu Chỉnh north. With my troops, he handily defeated Trịnh Bồng, but then the taste of power was too great for the famous pirate-killer, the old turncoat. He won the support of Lê Chiêu Thông and declared himself King of Thăng Long. I was still busy besieging my brother and you inside Quy Nhơn, so I sent Vũ Mộng Duệ north. Mộng Duệ captured Hữu Chỉnh, and took his head."

Lương Hoàng smiled and said, "The eagle would fly and kill no more."

Huệ continued, "Vũ Mộng Duệ then decided that he would rule the north, so I rode north with some cavalry, and ordered his guards to let us into the citadel at the dark hour of the Tiger [four a.m.]. Vũ Mộng Duệ was so surprised when we marched into his bedroom and sent away his concubine. I valued and respected that man. Why couldn't he remain faithful to me? I keep remembering his death. It was the first time I ordered the execution of one of my old companions. But an example was needed, so I ordered Mộng Duệ cut into pieces and then fed to the ravens.

"That reminds me never to cross you," said Hoàng, "Now his unfaithful spirit will never rest."

"What is wrong with the constellations at my birth? In a month I lost my two best generals to greed and self-aggrandizement. Both men miscalculated, and both thought I would pulverize my army against the walls of Quy Nhơn."

This made Lương Hoàng chuckle. "No one thought that the siege would end so abruptly, or that Nhạc would capitulate and that you would accept his apology."

"Yes, it was surprising. I admitted that I was wrong to attack my brother."

"Now Nhạc sits morosely behind his walls in Quy Nhơn and gets fat," said Lương Hoàng. "He refused to join you in this most dangerous campaign against the Chinese, so once again, he hasn't kept his word and loses much face."

Hue nodded his head at Lương Hoàng and confided more. "Now I bite my nails and burn incense to the Gods and pray on my knees to the Bodhisattva Quán Thế Âm for success. When you see my brother, tell him I ask him one last time to join me with his troops to fight and expel the Chinese invaders. Remind him of his oath!"

"Eeyah, I will do that," said Lương Hoàng, looking wretched. "I would join you myself in a heartbeat, if allowed."

"Defeating the Chinese is just the first big step. To succeed in ruling the north, I still need support from the Tonkinese mandarins, which is why I called the old Lê scholars back into service, and put General Ngô Văn Sở and Trần Quang Đàn in charge together so they could watch each other. They had to send their families here to live in my palace before receiving their orders. I am reduced by circumstances to taking hostages. Neh, I do what's necessary."

"You are learning such tricks from your older brother. Unfortunately, hostages have their place," said Hoàng.

"I struck a deal with Prince Lê Duy Cận, a minor character if there ever was one, and made and acknowledged him Việt Emperor and the head of the official Lê cult, and then returned to the Spring Capital to plan my land, tax, and currency reforms. Then the real Việt Emperor, Lê Chiêu Thông, who had escaped my men in those rugged hills of Lạng Sơn, sent invitations to the Manchu Emperor Qianlong. Suddenly Đông Kinh was invaded by the Qing Expeditionary Corps, 200,000 trained fighters under Sun Shih-i. My Generals Ngô Văn Sở and Trần Quang Đàn retreated from Bắc Hà, and preserved their small force of 5,000 men. They moved our northern division to the mountains of Tam Điệp above Thanh Hóa. Am I going to reward them for their intelligence, or hang them for their cowardice?

"The Chinese, after occupying Thăng Long and Bắc Hà Prefecture, began to install an administrative apparatus, as if they planned to stay a long, long time. Lê Chiêu Thông was told what to say, and even had to date his edicts by the reign of

Emperor Qianlong, using their Chinese calendar, and report daily to Governor Soun Che-yi."

Lương Hoàng shook his head, "Lê Chiêu Thông was a fool, and now his own people of Đông Kinh despise him. His advisers should all be beheaded for not warning him that no leader of the Việt can invite in a foreign army and expect to keep the support of the populace. If we can defeat the northerners, Lê Chiêu Thông will need your protection to survive amid his own people."

Huệ laughed hard. "No disagreement there," he said. "The Lê rat has used the Chinese to avenge himself against the many mandarins who had agreed to work with us. These allies are now dead or in hiding, waiting for us to save them. And on top of all these misfortunes, the peasants have suffered a bad harvest and the worst typhoon season anyone can recall. My spies report that the people now hate the Lê as well as the Chinese. The Lê lost all their face when they invited the Chinese to occupy the land. It is the Tao. It is our essence and nature that our people hate foreign troops and foreign rulers. When you beseech Nhạc for military aid on my behalf, remind him that he will become a great hero to his people if he joins me in battle against our ancient foe to the north."

"That would be pushing my luck," said Lương Hoàng. "Don't count on your brother's help. I don't think Nhạc has any intention of marching to your aid. Demons and Genie, if you lose, Nhạc will be beside himself with regret that he didn't combine forces when he could have. I will gently let him know what you and I are thinking."

A cheer went up and they looked over to see a spear piercing the target in its bull's-eye. The young marksman under scrutiny then crawled under the ropes, scaled a high wooden wall, dropped down the other side, and threw a knife fifteen feet for another bull's-eye. After jumping several hurdles, traversing a rope, and pulling himself up and over another barricade, his second knife also found the mark. Now Huệ watched closely as the soldier drew his sword and displayed the Long Kata.

The sword danced around his head and body, and flew off in the four cardinal directions and the four oblique angles. The blade spun around like a juggler's baton, and at the end, he jumped over his own hand in an unusually strong 360-degree unaided forward flip, and swung the sword one last time so that it slid neatly into its scabbard. The bystanders clapped and yelled. The man had just passed with highest marks the test for the elite units, the nineteenth young man to beat Huệ's score.

Chapter 29
The Nhà Bè and Sài Gòn River
July 1788

After a week of provisioning and repairs at Vũng Tàu, *La Méduse* was ready to depart. The ship took aboard a Việt Catholic river man who had agreed to act as its guide while navigating up the Nhà Bè River. The longboats were hoisted back on deck with block and tackle swung on extra yards. Sailors scurried up the ratlines and into the rigging, and unfurled the sails. The ship slowly gained speed. *La Méduse* sped across the blue-green swells of the bay. Benoit, like most of the crew, stood on the deck and watched with great curiosity the variety of weathered junks, sampans, and rafts that crisscrossed the same waters at slower speeds.

One of the small junks sailed into a cove to the fishing village of Cần Giờ. The captain of the junk handed his report to the senior Tây Sơn officer, Trần Quang Diệu. Four well-armed French warships were not an auspicious sign. Then again, there were only four of them, so there was nothing yet to be afraid of.

So, Diệu thought, *that fat bishop who worships the vagabond storyteller is back. How do we persuade him to withdraw from the conflict? The Tây Sơn stand for economic reform and the development of internal and external trade. We are far more forward-looking than the Nguyễn. How can I send this barbarian holy man a message? Would he accept it, and who should deliver it? Perhaps we should attack these ships immediately. I have the troops and junks hidden in several places. I must consult Nhạc; it is his decision. I will take my galley to Quy Nhơn, speak to Nhạc in person, and manage to visit my wife Bùi Spring Song and distract her from her elephants.*

❧   ❧

Just outside the village of Cần Giờ, a farmer with lands overlooking the harbor talked to a burly fisherman. The waterman's family remained on the sampan that they had just sailed into the harbor. After thanking the fisherman and giving him a silver coin, and seeing him off, the peasant went to his bamboo house and made tiny inscriptions on small pieces of rice paper.

He placed the paper squares into capsules made of leather, and then went outside to his chicken coops. On the other side of his pig shed, he had a storage bin that he uncovered. It was filled with portable cages of carrier pigeons. He put one of the cages into a large wicker bag, covered it, and carried it into the jungle to a secluded spot.

Once deep in the forest, the farmer carefully secured the pigeon with a leather thong, tied a leather capsule to its leg, gave prayers to the Genie of the Wind and the Lord of Heaven, and let it go. The pigeon flew overhead in an ever-increasing circle as it gained altitude, and then veered northwest toward Sài Gòn. The man referred to as a farmer, for that is how he dressed, was wise enough not to depend on the Gods. He sent two more birds, at six-hour intervals, and each followed the one before.

Sài Gòn was somewhere to the north, sixty miles up the serpentine waterway. The jungle foliage made walls on both sides of the muddy river, with palm trees draped in creepers called liana vines. The liana hung like scraggily beard down to the water's surface. One pigeon was eaten by a hawk. A second, pausing to rest in a tree, was devoured by a snake. The third made it to Sài Gòn.

☙   ❧

The hot, humid days were suffocating, and time slowed down. The officers and crew of *La Méduse* were oppressed and exhausted by the heat of the summer monsoon out of the southwest. At a snail's pace, they maneuvered the ship up the winding river. A large landing party carefully approached two forts, which they discovered had been abandoned. One side or the other had spiked its antiquated, Chinese style cannon. The French engineers were shocked to see that the cannons were set in mortar. They could not be aimed! They were more decorative than deadly.

The officers and deck crew were fully armed, on the bishop's orders, in case of sudden attack by small boats. The gunners, their arms nearby in racks, were allowed to walk or congregate on the main deck when they were off watch and not eating or sleeping. It was so hot below decks that many of the sailors chose to sleep on deck, especially when the ship was anchored for the night.

When the river bent toward the southwest, directly into the warm southwesterly breeze, all hands had to pitch in to drop or furl sail. Sailors climbed down boarding nets to the six longboats that they had carefully lowered with booms and tackle. Once filled with rowers and rigged with warp lines, the longboats slowly pulled the 38-gun frigate upstream and directly into the wind.

☙   ❧

The bosun rang six bells. It was three in the afternoon, and the longboats were still ahead, pulling the ship into the summer monsoon. First Lieutenant Grannier was the watch officer on duty under Captain Henri Dayot. Benoit carefully watched Guillaume practice his fencing with the dwarfish Baltasar Weber; they practiced every day, at Guillaume's request. They were fairly well matched, and Benoit studied their fencing to keep abreast of his enemy's progress.

Louis Boulanger appeared on deck. As he walked past the two exercising officers, to report on cannon mount repairs to Benoit, Guillaume spanked Louis on his butt with the flat of his wooden sword for fun. Louis was surprised and cursed. Guillaume stopped the play and froze his smile. "What did you say, sailor, under your breath?" Louis looked terrified.

"I said, 'My God in heaven, that was a hard'un, which I don't deserve.'"

"You're lying," Guillaume said, curling his lips into a smile. "You said, 'Go to hell,' and I'll have you flogged for your insolence."

Louis's face turned ashen and twisted up in pain. "Oh please, not that again, merciful God, it'll kill me."

"It would serve you right if it did. ..."

"Gentlemen," Benoit commanded, "you'll put away this dispute this instant. Lieutenant de Martineau, I do not want to see you strike another sailor during your sword practice, or I'll forbid you to fence on the deck. Louis, come up here and report on the double."

As the officer of the watch, Benoit was at least temporarily in charge. Guillaume threw his wooden sword to Baltasar, picked up and tied on his real sword and pistol, and then walked over to the quarterdeck stair and climbed it carefully. He stopped within fist-striking distance of Benoit.

"You have just protected a common sailor who swore at me and then lied to my face."

"If you insist so, I shall be compelled to report that you harassed a member of my crew and picked a fight. You deserved as much," Benoit said coldly. "Now be off or I'll have the marines drag you to the brig for misconduct." It appeared as if Benoit had finally driven Guillaume into a fit whereby he would break down and issue the fatal challenge.

Even as Guillaume tried to control his anger, the words began to form on his lips. Guillaume could contain himself no longer. "You yellow-bellied whore's son," he hissed, "I'll teach you—anywhere you want—" but he was cut off by a cry from the crow's nest. "On deck, war galleys upstream!"

Guillaume pulled himself in, spun around, and lurched off the quarterdeck platform. Benoit ordered, "Sound the alarm; beat to quarters." The piper piped the alarm, and the longboats dropped their cables, spun around, and rowed hard to the protection of the ship. Bishop Pierre and Captain Dayot climbed up to the deck. Pierre took a look with Benoit's telescope and smiled confidently. "We will be officially met by our friends."

Dayot replied, "It's a big reception. How did they know so fast?"

"Birds," said Pierre, "most likely pigeons." He ordered Benoit, "Continue to prepare for any possible trouble, but announce that a number of galleys with the King Nguyễn Ánh pennant come down the river toward us. Prepare to meet our friends and allies. The off-watch officers should change into full dress."

"Oh shit, dress coats in this god-awful heat will be hell," Baltasar Weber murmured to Guillaume, "and for fucking heathen savages."

Chapter 30
The Twelfth Lunar Month
1788

Huệ was having trouble sleeping at night and he was grinding his teeth. He was taking every precaution he could think of before attacking the Chinese. First, he was waiting till they had become significantly unpopular with the peasants of the Thăng Long region, as he knew any foreigners would be, if allowed enough time.

To bring a sense of national purpose and political legitimacy to the campaign, he held a huge ceremony of sacrifice to Heaven and Earth on top of Bàn Sơn Hill, south of the Spring Capital. Troops surrounded the hilltop. In the inner audience were hundreds of Confucian mandarins and military commanders on one side, and Taoist priests and Buddhist monks, village elders, and feng shui geomancers on the other. During the rites, on the Solstice of December 21, 1788, replete with ancient music and magic fire, Huệ proclaimed himself Emperor Quang Trung. In defiance of his brother Nhạc, he changed the year count from Thái Đức 11 to Quang Trung 1. The new emperor issued a proclamation that began:

"Our country has not been governed by just one family. In ancient times, fate determined the change of dynasties. We have traversed the Đinh, the Lê, the Lý, the Trần, and the Lê again. Prosperity for the ruler, or his downfall, depended on the will of Heaven. Personal efforts counted for naught.

... I am a man of the people from the jungles of Tây Sơn. I own not a single piece of land, nor do I have any special talent that merits my becoming king. Only because the people, sick of constant fighting, have called on me to rescue them have I assembled a militia. My soldiers have tamped down thorns and cleared jungles to help my brother root out the Siamese, pacify the Khmer, occupy Phú Xuân, and seize Thăng Long."

And it ended:

"Oh, my people, continue to eschew unethical conduct in your work, in your careers! Mandarins, conduct your affairs properly, ensure that the people are well-served and happy. Maintain harmony and prosperity. See that worship takes place at ancestral shrines, and all will be well.

To mark an auspicious start to my regime, I hereby cut land and head taxes in half, and excuse them entirely for those villages that have been ravaged by warfare. I pardon all imprisoned civil servants of the former regime, except those who have been convicted of high treason. Those mandarins who fled with Lê Duy Kỳ are henceforth allowed to return to their native villages, and may abstain from government service if they so choose. Finally, people are free to dress in northern or southern style, whichever way they prefer."

ও৯   ৯৬

Huệ consulted his favorite fortune-teller, the Hermit of Sơn La, who said, "The Chinese are not conversant with our situation. They are unaware of our strengths and weaknesses. They are unfamiliar with our methods of attack and defense. 'The local snake will outwit the dragon that has lost its way.'"

Left alone in his private chambers in the Spring Capital, Huệ stared into space, thinking of his plans, even if he couldn't confide them yet even to his closest generals. He was so excited by his vision of success that he took a virgin scroll from the rack by his desk, dipped a brush into the water jar and across the ink plate, and began hastily to catch his own thoughts, as a jar catches water from a fountain. Huệ drafted an address he must soon give to his officers and advisors.

He wrote, *The Chinese come this time to sow oppression, but they will harvest a bitter sorrow. I have established my plans; in ten days, the whole thing will be over. Although their country is one hundred times greater than ours, I am afraid that after this defeat they will be too ashamed to return for vengeance, and too afraid of the cost. If the war must drag on, our people will suffer terrible deprivations and resist for 10,000 years. But there is another way. I plan a quick and brutal campaign. Then diplomacy will win us a peace. In a few years, after we have had time to rebuild, we will have nothing whatsoever to fear. With peace at last, I can turn to land and tax reforms. A man who owns his own land, and respects his government, will love and protect his country with his life.*

Huệ leaned his brush against a carved ebony brush stand in the shape of an elephant. He thought, *Battles I understand. Land reform will be much harder. Land reform will be a more dangerous campaign for me than repelling the Chinese.*

He called for a scribe and drafted a letter to the Chinese General Sun explaining that his efforts were to stop Trịnh tyranny over the Le, and beg for forgiveness and light punishment. General Sun took the bait, and ordered Hue to stay in Phu Xuan until decisions were made in the Chinese court in Beijing.

❧　❧

Huệ entered the room of his concubine, Blue Cloud. Her oval brow was knit in concentration, her delicate chin sat in her palm, as she studied at a table. Their nine-year-old son, Quang Toản, ran up to Huệ and held up his hands. Huệ picked the boy up and carried him against his chest while they immediately began to play their favorite game—roughhousing. The father tried to tickle the boy with his scratchy chin, while the boy tried to block the attacks with his head or his hands. Father called this game The Bull Against the Magic Hands Kata.

"Now what are you two pirates up to?" Blue Cloud said laughing. She was going over the accounts for the expenses of all the palace staff with the chief accountant, an aged eunuch whom she politely dismissed. As a lady of the house, she helped the First Wife, Green Willow, who directed all the domestic staff, set wages, and personally conducted the hiring and firing. Huệ whispered something to Quang Toản, who grinned like a little devil.

Huệ and Quang Toản slowly plowed into Blue Cloud, like a boarding party out at sea, and carefully toppled her out of her seat away from her desk, sprawling her out on the floor, while Quang Toản laughed.

"Help," she cried, "I'm being plundered," and she pulled her son down on top of her so that her son fell and Huệ pretended to be knocked down as well. By this time they were all giggling. A most unkingly sight, especially for an emperor, but of course, that was part of the fun. In private, Huệ liked to remind his family and friends that he and his brothers were basically peasants who could read, and only the second Việt dynasty to come into the world as peasants, the first being Mạc the fisherman.

When the giggling stopped, Blue Cloud said to the boy and man on top of her, "I am so honored by this unexpected visit. Why aren't you out checking the muster?" She pushed her thick black hair out of her face so that it fell behind her shoulder.

"We already beat the Chinese," Huệ said in mock seriousness. "We just got back."

"He's being silly, isn't he Ma?" little Quang Toản said, laughing loudly and looking from face to face to check for reaction and approval. "Father, you are teasing, tell the truth," the child said naughtily, and then giggled again. Huệ looked at his son. He saw that Thịnh possessed a delightful intensity and self-consciousness. Huệ cocked his head, rolled his eyes, and then screwed up his face into a ridiculous mask. The little boy, already excited, howled with pleasure. A bodyguard quickly peeked in to make sure everything was all right, then disappeared.

Huệ said, "Soldier, attention!" and little Thịnh jumped up and stood straight and still. "Prepare for punching kata." Thịnh bowed and dropped his little body into a wobbly but recognizable horse stance, with his arms extended down into tiny little fists. His ferocious stance couldn't have scared a rabbit. "Punching exercise, begin."

The little boy began to count and punch, "*Một, hai, ba, bốn, năm,*" and after each number, one to ten, he pulled back his blocking arm and sent his little punching fist into Huệ's stomach, which was barely hardened for the occasion. The little boy could not completely stop smiling, he was so pleased to be on display. "*Sáu, bảy, tám, chín, mười.*"

"*Tốt lắm* [very good]," Huệ then said. "Stand at ease." Huệ picked up his son and held him up against his chest again. "What else should I tell you? If you must know," he said to Blue Cloud, who seemed to enjoy all of this, "we're about to start marching north to meet our ships and then the Qing invasion force. I have to give a speech tomorrow to our officers. All my troops will assemble for it, and I thought that you could help me polish it up. You know that my literary style was never very good."

"We would love to hear your speech," Blue Cloud said gravely, honored that he would ask her opinion and by the face, or respect, her master was giving to her, but shaken at the thought that her man would fight a Chinese Army. Huệ took a scroll out of his waist pouch and unrolled it. He held it at arm's length because he was far-sighted. "I need an introductory sentence. I'm not sure how to start. I have, 'In the universe, each constellation is assigned a specific place, and on earth, each country has its own government. The Chinese do not belong to our racial stock, therefore their intentions must be completely different from ours.'"

"Your royal highness," Blue Cloud said laughing, "that is not—you're quite right—an auspicious literary beginning.

"Don't laugh, or I'll have you clapped in chains," Huệ said in deadpan, pretending to be serious. "These are the words of your emperor, and you must always show respect."

"Emperor, maybe, scholar-poet, maybe not."

"That remark will cost you three prostrations." After a pause he said, "Actually, I'm not good at this writing job."

"Why not something simple, like, 'The Qing have invaded our country, they are occupying Thăng Long, the capital. Are you not aware of the situation?'"

"I like that, I'll use it." Huệ said somewhat self-consciously. The role of emperor was still new to him. "Then I can proceed, 'In the universe, each constellation is assigned a specific place, and on earth, each country has its own government. The Chinese do not belong to our racial stock, therefore their intentions must be completely different from ours. From the Han Dynasty to the present day, how many times have they raided our country, massacred our population, emptied our treasuries? No one in our country could bear this humiliation, and everyone wished to drive the enemy beyond our borders. Under the Han, there were the Trưng Queens; under the Sung, there were Đinh Tiên Hoàng and Lê Đại Hành. Under the Yuan, there was Trần Hưng Đạo. Under the Ming, there was Lê Thái Tổ, the founder of the present dynasty.'"

"Oh, that is good," interrupted Blue Cloud. "The men will probably cheer throughout that part."

Huệ smiled and continued, "'These heroes could not sit silently and watch the enemy indulge in violence and cruelty toward the people. They had to comply with the aspirations of their people and raise the banner of justice. A single battle was often sufficient to overcome the Chinese and push them back into their own country. Throughout all these periods, Đại Việt and China were clearly separated. There were no incidents along the frontier areas while successive dynasties enjoyed long lives. Since the Đinh Dynasty 800 years ago, we no longer suffer as we did before when we were subject to Chinese domination. Is this an advantage or an inconvenience, a success or a failure? I let you be the judges of that. But the examples of previous dynasties provide an obvious pattern of conduct for the present occupation of Đông Kinh.'"

"Huệ," said Blue Cloud, "what do you mean that you can't write? That is very moving." Huệ bowed to her in gratitude, and continued.

"'Today the Qing have returned once again. They are determined to annex our country and to divide it into provinces and districts. How can they not be aware of what has happened to the Sung, the Ming, and the Yuan? For this reason I am assuming the leadership of the army to expel them. All of you are in complete possession of your intelligence and your capacities. Therefore you should help me achieve this great undertaking. Should you maintain the old vice of having two hearts, I shall immediately exterminate you, without exception. United and determined, and without any failure of duty, we will prevail over our enemies, for the honor of our Ancestors, and the safety and freedom of our children.'"

"That is good, and powerful," said Blue Cloud, "but must you be so threatening?" She stared at her master, as if she wanted to imprint his picture right then in her mind and never forget it. Then she rose and found his arms and the comfort of his strength. "It seems a little crude at the end," Blue Cloud said.

"Oh, I was afraid you'd say that," Huệ said in earnest. "It is crude, isn't it. I'm just a simple peasant, and the older I get, the more Confucianist I become in my heart. Besides, if we're going to repel 200,000 battle-hardened, Qing troops and their Lê and Trịnh lackeys, just between you and me, I can't afford to have a single man turn and run, no matter how much the poor devil wants to. Just between you and me, even I am a little afraid of the Chinese hordes. But don't despair, I know we can beat them if we pick good ground and an auspicious day and fight like devils."

Blue Cloud buried her face in Huệ's neck, taking him to her bosom. Huệ pulled his face to hers. "The speech has made me want to fight in your army," she said, and she kissed his neck.

Huệ squeezed her tight, ruffled the hair of his eldest son, and said to Blue Cloud, "I'll try to come see you late tonight," and left.

Blue Cloud wondered if the killing would ever cease in her short lifetime, or in a thousand generations. She looked at her little Prince Quang Toản as if he were all that she had left in the world. She sat and thought about the speech. She became more and more depressed, till her son called her back out of her fears. She turned to her young charge with renewed interest. "And who are the Trưng Queens, my young prince?" she quizzed, smiling cheerfully to hide her discomfort.

"Two sisters," Thịnh said, trying to concentrate, yet proud that he knew the answer. "The Chinese killed their daddies, who were mandarins."

"The Han Chinese killed their husbands, two generals who rose up against the Chinese—the daddies of their children. What did the Trưng Sisters do?"

The nine-year-old princeling began to twist his hands in his shirt, and screwed up his face trying to remember the lesson. "They led soldiers and pushed the Chinese out of our country. Then the Trưng Sisters ruled everyone, but the Chinese came back and beat them. The sisters didn't want to be captured, so they jumped in a river and died."

"*Tốt lắm* [very good]," Blue Cloud praised him. "Yes, they drowned. You know what? I just realized that your father forgot a very important person. He never mentioned Ngô Quyền. Do you remember him?"

"Oh yes, Ma," the child said importantly, his eyes brightening. "Ngô Quyền made men drive big spears into the Bạch Đằng and sank many Chinese boats."

"Good boy! What an astute young scholar. Here, give me a hug. Why don't you play outside for a while, young scholar, and I will finish checking the week's expense accounts."

Chapter 31
The Welcome
July 1788

Benoit, like the other officers, wore a blue broadcloth jacket embroidered in gold, a delicate cotton shirt, and white cotton breeches buckled above white stockings and black leather boots. As a group, the officers were sweating profusely. In their dress uniforms, they were uncomfortable and overdressed for the heavy, humid air of the Cochinchina tropics. The Bishop Pierre Pigneau wore a spartan gray robe with a silver cross on a chain around his neck and sandals rather than boots.

The nine-year-old Prince Cảnh appeared on deck in a new five-piece tunic, one that had been saved throughout the entire trip. In the three years he had been away, he had grown eight inches taller, and the tunic didn't quite fit. He wore a small silver crucifix around his neck. His Catholic cousin, the High Mandarin Nguyễn Thơ, smiling with all his crooked teeth, stood proudly by Cảnh's nurse and valet. All appeared in dress clothes that they had carefully preserved for this long-awaited moment.

"Won't your wife be glad to see you," the nurse said to the valet, and she laughed with excitement.

"Not nearly as happy as I will be to see her, and my three little ones, Buddha protect them," Nguyễn Thơ said with a smile.

The French officers were excited, curious, and a little nervous, not sure how they would be received. They were fully armed. The Việt travelers were very excited, but as was the custom of their reserved and careful people, they hid their emotions from strangers, particularly barbarians.

Now Louis Boulanger and little Jacques, like all the gunners, were at their battle stations, ramming their powder and checking their prime. Louis demanded, "Load powder but no shot, he says. Be alert, probably friends, maybe pirates pretendin' t'be friends. *Qu'est-ce qui se passe?*" (What's up here?)

"Easy old bugger," Jacques remonstrated. "He said plain and simple, ready for 10-gun salutes to friends, and to load shot if ruse it be. Oh, but if only I were up on top yard right now and could sees the silky, sneaky Orientals, like that grinning Negro Ali up there. Some gets all the luck."

The lead and largest galley, 130 feet long with 250 rowers and 100 archers, had a yellow dragon's head at its bow and a blue dragon's tail at the stern. The galley launched a longboat, which came to the ship's ladder.

A group of warriors wearing lamellar armor—lacquered, leather-platted breast-plates—climbed nimbly up the ladder and stood as a bodyguard for Nguyễn Thị Hiền, the Official Greeter, and General Võ Tánh. Nguyễn Thị Hiền was an elderly man with a small head, white hair, and beard. Similar to most Vietnamese, his teeth were dark red from chewing the betel leaf and the areca nut, which, when combined, were known to quench thirst, act as a stimulant, and supposedly had beneficial medicinal properties. He wore a fine full-length silk tunic embroidered with tigers and cranes. Nguyễn Thị Hiền had the long, uncut nails of a man of high class, which were protected by gold nail cases studded with diamonds. He was, in the Confucian vein, well educated in the use of paper and ink and above any manual labor other than painting, calligraphy, falconry, and concubinary. The Official Greeter carried a peacock-feather fan, another symbol of his high authority and academic achievements. Hidden in the same hand that carried the fan was a piece of scented sandalwood. He kept it close to his nose, for he couldn't stand the stench of unwashed barbarians.

The elegant old mandarin and his guards bowed deeply to the honored company. The returning Việts, Pierre, and his officers returned the bow with great formality. Hiền was pleased with this display of civility. General Võ Tánh was thinking, *This is disgusting. We don't need these long-nosed barbarians to help settle our internal affairs.*

The French officers were unanimous in assuming that the Việt official would be spellbound by the mighty warship with its cannon. They were quite mistaken. Hiền was not an expert seaman, or even particularly knowledgeable about naval warfare. Nor was he overly concerned about what he considered such trivia. His expertise was in the Chinese Classics, and he was an authority on ethics and the Book of Rites. In fact, he rarely had to deal with such uneducated rabble. The bishop was the only barbarian of the bunch who could comprehend a modicum of Chinese.

Nguyễn Thị Hiền thought to himself, *Butter-eaters; they stink of animal fat and months of rotting sweat. These long-nosed crucifixion worshippers smell worse than a Mung pigpen. We, on the other hand, are a civilized people. We study the Great Sage Confucius, the Chinese Classics, and many of us have sacred ancestral tombs in China and in Đại Việt. The Chinese invented paper, calligraphy, history, poetry, and literature. But most important,* he thought, as he stood amidst the stench of *La Méduse, the Chinese invented soap, deodorant, and perfume. Men and women learned to bathe in hot water and scent themselves several times a week, over a thousand years ago. Someday,* he thought, as he lifted his gaze to the dark rain clouds in the distance, *we will overcome the resistance of these barbarians and teach them to be clean and well mannered—to be, that is to say, civilized. But how,* he asked philosophically, *do you teach patience and manners to an arrogant but ignorant barbarian, who smells and acts more like a pig than an ape?*

The bishop and Cảnh's cousin Nguyễn Thơ had prepared a seat for the guest of honor, Nguyễn Thị Hiền, on the main deck, which faced south, and seats opposite for the bishop and Prince Cảnh, which faced north.

Mandarin Nguyễn Thơ said, "Nguyễn Hiền, please sit here in the place of honor."

Nguyễn Hiền replied, "Never mind, you may sit there."

"No, as my elder brother, I insist you take this seat," said Thơ. Only after these courtesies did Nguyễn Hiền finally agree to take the best seat. His guards stood behind him. Then Pierre and Prince Cảnh ceremoniously took their seats, with the other members of the traveling delegation behind them. Vietnamese civility required a well-mannered discourse involving introductions, greetings, and inquiries about parents, followed by what was really a very short message. After tea was served and the china service complimented, Nguyễn Hiền finally spoke his mind.

"We have come to welcome Bishop Pierre Pigneau and Prince Cảnh and all your party. We wish to escort the young prince and Father Pierre the Bishop to Sài Gòn without delay on board the king's own personal galley. His majesty has placed these other galleys under your command. They would be honored to help escort your ship up river, if the assistance would please you."

Pierre was delighted by this invitation. He wanted to keep his sailors on board, moving the ship north, and where they could always repair and refresh the rigging and also be kept out of trouble. After the meeting, the galleys took up stations fore and aft of *La Méduse*, while the sailors returned to the longboats to finish pulling *La Méduse* through the wind at the curve of the river. The rest of the crew were put back to work cleaning and repairing. The sailors were not given a rest, especially since in general they became more difficult to manage when not busy.

Pierre Pigneau de Béhaine, with the five Việts in his charge, went aboard the Nguyễn galley, *Dragon's Claw*, and glided stylishly upriver to Sài Gòn. Pierre left *La Méduse* to sail up the river at its own pace, escorted now by several war galleys.

Pierre had learned to enjoy regular bathing from his Việt students, so he was almost as relieved as the Việt passengers to get off his ship. He too looked forward to a hot bath. He left the galley, escorted by a group of the king's soldiers reassigned to the bishop as his personal bodyguard. As soon as they reached the city, the party divided up at the old citadel courtyard. Pierre and his own three servants were led by his new bodyguard to his new quarters. He found there that his previous major-domo, Old Goat, at King Ánh's request and expense, had rented a large brick-and-mortar house with a tile roof for his comfort. He was greeted by Old Goat and Paul Nghi, his pupil and friend. Old Goat, Paul Nghi, and Pierre bowed to one another perfectly.

"Brother Paul, it is so good to see you!" Pierre exclaimed as they embraced.

"Welcome back, Father Pierre, it is a blessing to see you here again." Pierre quickly learned that all was basically well with his favored student and the mission near Sài Gòn where Father Paul Nghi was the head.

Pierre took the much-anticipated hot bath in a wood-fired tub as a Việt gentleman or lady would, but without a bath attendant. He enjoyed the skill of a local masseur brought in by Old Goat, and then after, a light meal with Paul Nghi of fish, pork, vegetables, and rice with *Nước Mắm* sauce, a relish of chopped ginger, garlic, and parsley with soy and fermented fish sauce. The meal was served with tea by a doughty Việt matron renamed Sarah. After dinner, Pierre meditated in his private chapel for a few minutes before the figure of Jesus on the cross.

The figure of Jesus nailed to the cross had been carved by some anonymous Italian craftsman and then painted with oils. It was shockingly lifelike, and could easily inspire the admirer to thinking he or she was an onlooker, even a participant, in the crucifixion of Jesus. Father Pierre then silently read a confession in Latin in a well worn part of his prayer book.

Have mercy upon us, most merciful Father; in your compassion forgive us our sins, known and unknown, things done and left undone; and so uphold us by your spirit that we may live and serve you in newness of life, to the honor and glory of your name; through Jesus Christ our Lord.

Almighty God, you opened the way of eternal life to every race and nation by the promised gift of your Holy Spirit. Share abroad this gift through the world by the preaching of the Gospel, that it may reach to the ends of the earth; through Jesus Christ our Lord, who lives and reigns with you, in the unity of the Holy Spirit.

Feeling refreshed, Pierre went with his escort of soldiers to the king's palace in the citadel. Guards in blue pants and shirts with yellow belts were everywhere. Because he was expected, and because he had the rank of Mandarin First Class, Ambassador to the French Court, and Admiral Third Class of the Nguyễn Navy, he and his bodyguard moved with ease through the portcullis and the various checkpoints of guards.

Security, as usual, was strict, for dangers lurked everywhere for the young king. Great rewards awaited any assassin who could carry the king's head, or the head of any of his generals or advisors, to the enemy camp. King Ánh likewise offered substantial sums for any such service against the Tây Sơn brothers and their generals.

The personal guards of King Ánh were sharp-eyed soldiers with swords and halberds or longbows. The halberds were spears with a battle-ax and hook near the tip, and they were more than mere ceremonial devices. Their ax blades were kept, like the swords, as sharp as razors, and they could pierce or slice a swordsman before he closed within the range of his own weapon.

Thanks to Pierre's tutelage, there was also a detachment of musketmen assigned to the royal bodyguard. More than once before, when the main body of his forces had been overpowered by the numbers and determination of the Tây Sơn attackers, the musket detachment had helped King Ánh to escape.

After a long walk and climb into the citadel, Pierre was ushered into the royal study. He found King Ánh, now aged twenty-six, quietly studying a book of Chinese poetry. Pierre's own book, a translation of French and European military tactics, also sat on the desk, which pleased Pierre, though he wished there had been a copy of the Vietnamese Bible left out conspicuously in his honor as well.

King Ánh sat garbed in a bright yellow silk robe, with a dragon's head on his chest and claws down both sleeves and across his knees. The dragon had a stone in its mouth, and was gazing off into infinity, undauntable, afraid of nothing.

The king had a strong face, well proportioned with the high cheekbones of his people, and piercing brown eyes under almond-shaped lids. His face bore a remarkable resemblance to one of the most popular faces of the Buddha, found on many temple statues. King Ánh wore a red silk cap with beaten gold horns that suggested the rays of the sun, showing one and all that the king was a celestial being, and that he was destined to rule with the Mandate of Heaven. With his red silk slippers, King Ánh looked as his ancestors had looked for 900 years. His major concession to Western ideas was two hands with well-clipped fingernails. Since he had grown into manhood with Pierre as one of his teachers, he had accepted Pierre's advice on a variety of things, including the inutility of being physically handicapped by the ancient Chinese custom of growing one's nails long as a sign of rank and social station. Without such encumbrance, it was much easier to use a sword, a pistol, or a musket. But to Pierre's deep regret, it was always easier to teach Ánh technical and practical skills than to inject him with spiritual faith in the Lord Jesus Christ.

Pierre knelt before the king and bowed his head to the floor. He performed the kowtow, the ancient custom he hoped to help make obsolete, or transform into a ritual only for the one true God. *For mortal kings, the European bow does seem more dignified,* he thought. As Pierre stood up, feeling the pain in both knees, the king rose from his chair and greeted his old counselor with a firm handshake and an embrace, in the Western style, as he had learned from his Western tutor. They spoke in the king's native tongue, which Father Pierre the Bishop spoke now with fluency.

King Ánh said, "Bishop Pierre Pigneau, it is good to see you again old friend, after such a long voyage. I hope it was as successful as it appears."

"Thank you, your highness. It is good to see you in good health, and with more soldiers at your command. Please feel free to call me Father Pierre, as before. How is your mother, the Royal Ancestress?" Pierre politely asked.

"The Royal Ancestress is doing remarkably well," the king responded. She enjoys life immeasurably, especially eating. And how is your own mother, whom you hadn't seen for so many years?"

Pierre frowned. He said, "Twenty-five years has passed. The poor woman is not well. She lost her reason some time before I saw her. She is the victim of old age and many hardships. She brought nineteen good souls into the world, which made her tired and wore her out. Then, only God knows, I suppose that too many earthly concerns drove her mad. She is well cared for by a group of nuns, but her condition is pitiful and it confounds the mind, as so many maladies do, about the ways of God. The peace of everlasting life will be a great blessing for her."

"I am sorry," the young king said sincerely. "The Gods are much like humans. They are to be fully worshipped, but never wholly trusted. Each one of us has only one father and mother, and they are the world to us. Didn't you want to stay in your own country, surrounded by your own people, and care for your mother, and tend your father's grave, like a good Vietnamese would? "

"Yes, I did very much," Pierre said. "I realize that I leave something to be desired as a devoted son. But I feel called to serve the Lord, and I believe that my duty to him is to serve a larger family, far from my home and blood relatives. We are all one family going back to Adam and Eve, in the eyes of God."

After a short silence Ánh responded with a boyish grin, "Oh, I didn't realize that Adam and Eve were Chinese." Pierre bowed slightly, to acknowledge the wit. After a pause, Ánh asked, "What do you think of this poem?" pointing to a page of Chinese characters. "It is by one of our great generals, Ngô Tuan, whose penname became Lý Thường Kiệt. He defeated the Chinese and then the Chams during the reign of King Lý Nhân Tông (1077). Here is the original," which he then read aloud in Mandarin Chinese.

"The calligraphy is as strong as the cadence," said Pierre, who only spoke and read a little Chinese. "What does it mean?"

"I have translated this famous poem into Vietnamese myself. My translation is:
'The Southern emperor rules the Southern land.
Our destiny is writ in Heaven's Book.
How dare you bandits trespass on our soil? You shall meet your undoing at our hands.'
"There is no love lost between your people and the Chinese, is there?" said Pierre.

"There is no love lost between my people and any foreigners who do not show us respect and peaceful entreaties," Ánh said carefully, looking the bishop straight in the eye.

"I respect your prerogatives and sensitivities," said the bishop, and bowed.

One of King Ánh's favorite new wives, a beauty named Endless Joy, came in quietly with a maid and served tea and a dish of crabmeat and snails with bamboo shoots and vegetables. Ánh savored the young women's exquisite beauty above and below a veil of thin cotton. He noted one could make out through her chemise a tattoo that started below the stomach and went toward her groin.

"Would you like anything else?" she asked with an innocent smile, and withdrew. The men ate and drank slowly in the energy-filled silence. Father Pierre had a chance to practice his breathing, and to take in his surroundings. He had to act Vietnamese, or lose face before his protégé and ally. The stone wall to the left was a high interior wall of the castle. Pierre sat on a woven hemp mat on the floor, reclining on pillows. Ánh sat back in a large ebony chair of Chinese design that glistened with complicated inlays of gold plate, diamonds, and rubies. The room opened to the right through sliding rice-paper doors and windows into a sunlit courtyard and rock garden. Scroll racks, along with a few paintings and samples of calligraphy, lined the walls of the room.

It had taken years for Pierre to learn to relax at these moments, to enjoy the sunlight, and not feel uncomfortable sitting in silence on the floor with one of the principal actors of his life-long project. Pierre thought, *The great centers of power in the world are so conservative. They change so slowly. If there is progress, it does not grow like the bamboo, over several days, but like the oak, over several centuries. What I first thought was a repulsive cynicism in Việt scholars is often just a deep understanding that many of them have about the rate of improvement in the sorry affairs of men. Their Confucius wrote, "It is easier to move a mountain than to change a man's heart." Moses understood this. Perhaps, that is why he kept the Israelites in the desert for forty years: The minds of the young are more open.*

It will be near impossible to bring King Ánh to Jesus. Mathew wrote that a rich man asked Jesus what actions bring eternal life. Jesus said, "Follow the Ten Commandments," and, "If you want to be perfect, go, sell your possessions and give to the poor, and you will have treasure in heaven. Then come, follow me." And, Jesus said, "How hard it is for the rich to enter the kingdom of God! Indeed, it is easier for a camel to go through the eye of a needle than for a rich man to enter the kingdom of God." So, as I suspect did Moses in the dessert, I focus religious training on Cảnh, not his father.

After a suitably quiet interlude, the young man King Ánh spoke. "My venerable teacher, you left for India and France four years ago. There is so much to catch up on. We've had only the briefest correspondence. We are very curious about your voyage. And why do you arrive with such a small force to help us destroy the rebels? You would think that the French king, if he is as powerful as you say, would be sympathetic to another monarchy, especially against peasant upstarts?"

Father Pierre, now relaxed, took his time and responded, "I found that the French court was in trouble—living in a dream, and well above its means. They did take an interest in your cause, but the wars with heretic England, especially our victory over the English for the freedom of the English colonies in North America, have strained the French treasury to an uncomfortable and unsustainable degree. France is not stable. I saw with my own eyes that the peasants are suffering terrible deprivations in the countryside, and their condition is even worse for those in the cities. I cried when I saw their plight. There are terrible food shortages, work is scarce, and street crimes are common. The populace of the cities are preyed on by criminals, who are mostly men looking for work. Thieves are imprisoned, branded, and sometimes tortured on a machine called the wheel. These poor souls are sent to labor camps or the galleys to be chained to an oar even for stealing a loaf of bread or a handful of grain."

King Ánh thought, *My teacher would not concern himself always with the condition of the peasants, if he just accepted that all is karma; our position in this life was predetermined by our previous life.* But he said nothing, and did not stop to redirect the flow of information from West to East.

After Pierre had finished his travel summary, he ended with, "Please tell me what has happened here in my long absence."

The king offered his own report. "Our forces are growing stronger, and we have strengthened our relations with the peasantry with some of your ideas. So much has happened in the four years since you departed for your own country. I wrote to you about the major Tây Sơn victories and Lữ's death. The cause of death remains a mystery, but the rumors of debauchery are quite spectacular. A drunken orgy with multiple women in one day, followed by—"

"That's quite all right," Pierre said firmly. "There's no need to go into the details."

Ánh laughed. He was always amused at the prudishness of Father Pierre. For reasons he couldn't explain, sex and other subjects of the body made Pierre and most barbarians from the West extremely uncomfortable.

"After being chased out of the country, I returned from Siam and set up a military camp in Long Xuyên early last year. I gathered and raised troops. Nguyễn Văn Trường defected from the Tây Sơn, and brought with him 300 soldiers and fifteen warships. Sun Tzu inspired me to try political sabotage. I forged a letter from Nhạc to Lữ, ordering Lữ to execute General Phạm Văn Tham, and then let the letter fall into Tham's possession. Tham moved his forces toward Lữ under a white flag. Lữ assumed the flag meant Tham was already with me, so he took his troops and abandoned Gia Định. Tham then suspected the letter was true, so when I appeared, he surrendered Gia Định to me if I allowed him to switch sides, which I did. We won the battle without fighting!"

Ánh smiled, as he continued, "We were thrilled and delighted by the battle between Nhạc and Huệ. It's too bad that they reconciled their differences."

After listening to that story, Pierre asked, "How is the domestic front?"

"My peasants are restless and recalcitrant. We are forced to punish slackers severely to set an example. The times have not been good to them. The war has disrupted planting, and of course we need the peasants to work on all of our new fortification projects. Only when the rice critically needs attention are they allowed to work on their farms.

"Meanwhile, the dikes and canals are always threatening to fall apart and destroy our agricultural efforts, so we must insist that the peasants continue their responsibility to that task. The success of the Hồ brothers has demonstrated that the peasants will not forever put up with local corruption and extortion. Ordering the troops to work on all the public projects and to help the peasants, including their relatives, with their rice cultivation and harvest, as you suggested, has had an important impact on morale. The troops even have come to appreciate the plan, for it makes the populace identify with and support the army, thanks to the mutual aid and personal contacts. The soldiers train with their weapons in the afternoons, and return to the public works after their evening rice. Because they are on full alert though, they are allowed more sleep than the peasants."

Before leaving for France, Pierre had expressed his concern that sixteen hours of manual labor a day was too much to sustain. Six hours of sleep a night was not enough for physical laborers. For the sake of the harmony of their reunion, today he kept quiet.

Pierre and Ánh listened to each other with renewed respect as they discovered the variety of hardships each had encountered, King Ánh in the service of his prestigious line of Ancestors, and Father Pierre in the service of his merciful but demanding God and the Holy Roman Catholic Church.

❧ ❦

Lieutenant Skinny Minh and Phúc Du of the Nguyễn Royal Secret Police were reading over the list of Christians in the southern provinces. Minh had a tiny, pinched head with thick black hair and protruding ears, while his junior associate was rotund. Minh and Du were horrified, for the list was huge. There were tens of thousands of names, carefully collected by the Nguyễn bureaucracy with the help of the secret police. This list itself was secret, for the king did not intend that his foreign friends or his enemies know all of his government's activities. But the results were shocking. Christianity was spreading like an incurable plague throughout the masses.

"By the Nine Judges of Hell," Skinny Minh said gravely as he opened another new scroll, "if every French merchant isn't a priest in disguise, I'll be a turtle. Every village that a French trader spends over a month in suddenly develops a Christian community."

Phúc Du interjected, "The priests accompany the traders like lice on a dog. They are so conspicuous; you wonder why the authorities allow them in. It doesn't make any sense. These barbarian priests are obviously oily-mouthed and subversive."

Skinny Minh retorted, "Imagine preaching that all humans are equal in the eyes of the Gods. It defies the natural law of karma. And that there are only three Gods—what nonsense!

"Not only is it illegal," agreed Phúc Du, "it is subversive, and not only is it subversive, it's immoral. Why in the names of the holy Ancestors are the prohibitions against foreigners never enforced? Why doesn't the king enforce the legal proscriptions?"

Skinny Minh said, "But by my tablets, not all barbarians are bad. They have magnificent guns. They just don't have respect for authority. Long-noses utterly fail to grasp the value and need for filial piety as the basis of civil order. Could some dog-bone of a scholar explain to me what is going on with these numbers?"

Skinny Minh stopped his eyes at the name Bùi Moon Light (Bùi Ánh Nguyệt). *I wonder if she's related,* he thought, and checked his reference file. His dark brown eyes froze on the Bùi page of the ledger. *Moon Light is the daughter of Bùi Quang Dien, and the sister-in-law of the notorious Nguyễn General Trần Quang Diệu, who renounced his king and joined the Tây Sơn. There is more. His wife, Moon Light's sister Bùi Spring Song, is the gifted elephant trainer who also became a Tây Sơn general! Dragon's breath, this is spicy,* his mind raced. *How can this humble wretch that I am use this?*

After careful but agitated thought, Skinny Minh waited till Phúc Du left for the day, then wrote a memorandum to King Nguyễn Ánh. He walked through four different sentinel points and delivered it directly to the king, bypassing all his senior officers, and calling attention to the fact that he had the sense to do so.

❧　❧

Nguyễn Ánh stared at the fish in his pond. *Oh spirit of Confucius, what am I going to do about Bùi Moon Light? She is kin to an enemy, and she is a protégé of Father Villeseint, a barbarian, who of course is on good terms with my friend and ally the bishop. The bishop controls the cannon on the barbarian warships. Yet I must punish the traitor Moon Light's father, Bùi Quang Dien, and all his family to set an example. How do I punish the family of Bùi Quang Dien without hurting the relationship with the French?* He stared into the limpid water at the goldfish swimming above his catfish, and caught the reflection of red hibiscus at the pool's edge. Suddenly Ánh laughed so hard he shook himself. The fish moved away.

I'll marry her to a French barbarian. He chuckled. *Her family will be mortified, and the French will see the arrangement as a sign of my good intentions. Through such a present, I'll make one of the French officers bind himself to me. But how do I choose which one? I need to bring a few of these powerful foreign sea-devils into my house. What better way to tame a martial threat from abroad than through marital alliances? It worked for Ghengis, it worked for the Lý, the Trần, and the Lê, and it will work for the Nguyễn.*

Chapter 32
The Forced March Before Tết
January 1789

Hồ Huệ became Nguyễn Huệ as a young bandit to confuse his enemies. Now he became Emperor Quang Trung, which was intended to inspire his troops, impress the country, and send a message of warning to the Chinese Emperor: Beware, I am your spiritual, political, and military equal. A month before the great Tết and Chinese New Year holiday, after all the festival preparations had been scrupulously and extravagantly prepared, Huệ ordered his troops to very quietly celebrate the holiday early. After the early and subdued feasting, with no music or fireworks, he put into motion a secret forced march north.

Huệ met in his palace with only his closest advisors and generals at the second hour of the Dragon (eight a.m.). The mandarins all knelt and knocked their heads three times to the floor. Being on the other end of this ritual obeisance made Huệ feel triumphant—and oddly alone, even vulnerable. He watched his oldest friend, Lương Hoàng, his trusted Scholar-General Ngô Thì Nhậm and the other eminent men, like Scholar Trương Văn Hiến, whom he studied with as a boy, all on their knees, performing the kowtow. *Power isolates you,* Huệ noted sadly.

General Ngô Thì Nhậm was a virile scholar with a woman's name. As a child he had been given a female name to fool the demons and spirits, and obviously, the disguise succeeded.

"Welcome, my friends," said Huệ. "Make yourselves comfortable while you can." He paused while the group shifted to sit cross-legged. "The time has arrived for us to deal directly with the Qing Army that occupies Thăng Long. I have devised a surprise attack with the help of Ngô Thì Nhậm and Bùi Spring Song.

"Continue to gather all the troops that you can muster or impress, and in four days, today counting as day one, we will march rapidly to Vịnh. Do not discuss our true intention outside this room, tell your people we muster to attack Sài Gòn and the Nguyễn. Describe our last attack on Sài Gòn as if describing our plans for this new campaign. I mean to surprise the Qing during the New Year celebration, so not a word of our plans to your women, subordinates, priests, or to anyone, on pain of death. Our survival depends on this secrecy.

"You are to have your troops finish preparing the 34,000 sling-litters that I ordered three months ago. One hourglass before our departure, on my signal, a beating of the drums, order all the men to fetch their warm jackets and hats for a long march north, and form the line of march. After that order of our real destination, no soldier is allowed out of sight of the group, to prevent spies from escaping.

"We force march to Vịnh with no stops for sleep. You divide your troops into groups of three, so that all three in a group are about the same weight. After the first eight hours of marching, two men will carry the third man, who eats rice cakes and rests for most of four hours. Every four hours we stop for one quarter incense stick, for the men to relieve themselves by the side of the road. At every water hole, one regiment will stop and fill its water skins. Officers will be divided into three groups, and they will ride their horses and sleep in the wagons or on the elephants when their group rests. All deserters, troublemakers, and stragglers are to be decapitated immediately, and left by the roadside unburied, with their head on a spike. The only way home is to defeat the Chinese. Any comments or questions?"

Lương Hoàng spoke up, "This march should surprise the Chinese. Will the elephants be able to keep up with the pace of the three-men teams?"

Huệ pointed his finger at the only woman present, Bùi Spring Song, his general of the elephant brigade, and said, "General Bùi."

"The elephants will keep up with the army by staying in the rear," Bùi Spring Song said in a clear, high voice. "When the elephants need to sleep, they will sleep in small groups for about half an hour, eat some hay feed, and then they will simply catch up to the army before their next rest stop. They will drink at every opportunity. As you should know, they will require immense quantities of water. Their war baskets will start loaded with hay, and rice and bean cakes, but will be available for officers to rest and sleep in, or for stragglers you choose to preserve. Besides their need for water, they eat an enormous amount of grass, so they will be constantly foraging as they move north."

Scholar Trương Văn Hiến, who knew Huệ when a small boy, dared to speak. "How shall we act, if the army is too tired to fight, when we reach Thăng Long?"

"A good question, Teacher," said Huệ. "When the time comes to engage the Chinese, we will all meet again to determine if the troops are capable of fighting, or how much time they need to sleep. I hope and expect to give them a good meal and a full night's rest and a good morning meal before the attack. I am confident, because we are in accord with Sun Tzu, who wrote, 'In ancient times, good warriors prevailed, when it was easy to prevail.' We know our enemy, and they do not know us. He wrote, 'When you know that an opponent is vulnerable, then you attack the heart and take it.'

"Yesterday, I sent fifteen elite units north of this camp, who will act as scouts. They will interrupt and press or detain any persons, spies or not, attempting to travel north ahead of the Hissing Army and ruin our surprise party."

❧　❧

Four days later, Huệ started his army and navy toward Vịnh in Nghệ An Province, 270 miles to the north. They made the journey with the men marching day and night for five days and nights. Huệ's navy at the time was too small to move so many men and their stores, but it did transport his field artillery and supplies. Huệ and his officers moved almost 100,000 men in the forced march, supported by 100 elephants. Over 1,200 men were executed along the road to Vịnh for not keeping up or trying surreptitiously to dessert.

After a long night's sleep outside of Vịnh, the forced march began again. It was another 250 miles to Thăng Long.

An old farmer and his two sons from a village near Phú Bài below the Spring Capital Phú Xuân had been swept up in the impressments of all males aged fifteen through sixty that occurred right before the forced march. Their family name was Hải. The father was Hải Vân Đại and his sons were nicknamed Rice King and Daydreamer. Both sons were married and had their own children. During a short changeover for one quarter incense stick, in the morning light of day three, all three men were urinating into the grass by the road. Hải Vân Đại asked his adult son Rice King, "Did you sleep?"

"Yes I did, but I could sleep longer. Now it's Daydreamer's turn to be carried. It's tragic that he's so fat. It is pure wickedness that he has a sweet tooth."

"Always complaining," said the younger brother. "You missed some great scenery. We must have just walked by one hundred rice paddies, carrying your bulk and listening to you snore. Demons and Genie, I should have brought my earplugs."

Hải Vân Đại spoke solemnly, "There are others from our village here in this long line somewhere. My elder brother, Hành, should not have been taken, with his bad foot and ankle trouble. I am very worried about your Uncle Hành." They all hoisted up their duck trousers, returned to their sling-litter on the ground, and each took a packet of rice cake wrapped in green banana leaves out of their shoulder bags. These rice cakes were one of the tools of Vietnamese military mobility. They consisted of glutinous rice with mung beans and shallots, salted with soy and fish sauce. They ate the fistful of sticky rice cake in silence, chewing as fast as they could, while squatting or sitting on the ground with their tired legs outstretched. Horns blared, and each man took a measured swig from his own water skin.

An officer on horseback was moving down the line yelling, "Move out, move out now. Time is up. The Chinese are raping our women in Đông Kinh."

"Better us than them," said Rice King under his breath. The farmer Hải Vân Đại and his son Rice King picked up the empty sling-litter by the poles, which consisted of three killing spears bound together with twine into a carrying pole. The men each wore their newly issued short swords in their trouser waist ropes. They were better equipped than some, since they wore their own heavy work sandals on their feet.

The sling-litter of tent cloth was gathered at both ends, and then tied with rope to the shoulder pole made of the spears. It was Daydreamer's turn to try to sleep, so he carefully spread the cloth and sat on it. Holding his sword against his thigh, he brought his feet up, and twisting, put them on the sling-litter cloth. He then slowly lay down on his back. Rice King and his father lifted the litter pole up onto one of their sore shoulders—the right one first.

The horns blared again, and all the bearers started walking at once. Not to do so could get you whipped or killed. Rice King was in the rear bearer position now, looking as he walked at his reclining younger brother. "How can you sleep . . . when we are finally getting to see the north country? You will miss the women of Đông Kinh working in the paddies, winding mountain roads, views of unseen valleys below, even new fishing villages!"

"Rice King," remonstrated Hải Vân Đài quietly, "let your bother sleep if he can. If you both survive the professional Chinese soldiers, you can describe to him each rice paddy, each maiden, and every mountain pass vista that he slept through."

"I feel like a farting royal prince," said Daydreamer. "This is my palanquin, and you are my porters. Take me to see the Chinese Emperor. I have an invitation in gold paint. Do not wake me till we get there! Tell him I like pork dumplings and watercress spring rolls." Daydreamer of the Hải family, from the village outside of Phú Bài, relaxed and listened to the rhythm of the feet of his father and brother. "Father," Daydreamer asked, "are the Chinese soldiers much more dangerous than we are? Are we going to get slaughtered?"

"It is in the hands of the Gods," said old Hải, "but probably not." He looked with adoring eyes at his son. "My son, if you die, you shall be reborn—just like the Chinese. The Chinese soldiers are mostly just boys and men earning a stipend, and we are defending our own farms and families, and Nguyễn Huệ is a clever and ruthless general. The Gods are with us, as are the odds."

Daydreamer was soon fast asleep. Farmer Hải Vân Đài wondered if his sons would survive their first battle. He had already seen war. He had fought against the Nguyễn and the Trịnh after previous impressments. War wasn't all bad. He had stolen some fine jewelry from a great house during one campaign, which allowed him to buy land for his wife and their sons. He kept his eyes on the road ahead, to protect his feet and his sleeping son. In his peripheral vision he saw the corpse of a dead soldier wearing the farm clothes of his region. He looked up to see a head on a stake; it was the head of someone familiar. Hải Vân Đài squinted, since his old eyes weren't so good. The head came into focus. It belonged to his elder brother, Hành, who had had a bad ankle. "No!" Hải Vân Đài cried. "This is wrong."

He turned his head and found the corpse of his beloved older brother lying nearby—unburied! "By the Nine Demon Judges of Hell, this is a disgrace to our Ancestors."

As he trudged forward in front of his eldest son, carrying his youngest son, Hải Vân Đài's anger slowly increased. He didn't mind being pressed to fight the Chinese, the natural enemy, or being forced to march with little rest. But pressing the sick, and then executing them, was homicide, honorless murder. Not allowing proper burial was inexcusable and abominable. Tears for his brother Hành trickled down his face. He was stricken with layers of grief. In his heart, his new emperor had lost the Mandate of Heaven, and the loyalty of his clan forever.

∂   ∽

In five more days of forced march day and night, with only fifteen-minute relief breaks every four hours, two men carrying a third man sleeping on a sling-litter, Huệ's 100,000 exhausted troops joined Ngô Văn Sở's small army of 5,000 on Tam Diep Mountain. The men of the Hissing Army now had something in common with deep water Western sailors: They had learned to sleep in their hammocks on the off watch.

The two reinforced generals, Ngô Văn Sở and Trần Quang Đàn, attended the official public greetings in their brigandine leather armor and heavy cloth jackets with shoulder pads and pockets holding metal plates. After the ceremony ended, they entered Huệ's tent for an obligatory interview and possible punishment.

Ngô Văn Sở and Trần Quang Đàn kowtowed three times to their commander, Nguyễn Huệ. Then Ngô Văn Sở, the older of the two men, came swiftly to the point. "I am guilty of having retreated before the enemy. If I have displeased you in any way, please forgive me, and allow me immediately to hang myself."

Huệ smiled and said, "Again you have demonstrated your superior judgment and common sense. I once wrote a poem, some of which I'd like to share with you now:

'To mimic bamboo, Great men bend with the wind.

They choose to fight, when they can win.'

"But that is nothing. The sage Sun Tzu himself wrote, 'For the weak to control the strong, it is logically necessary to await a change.' And, 'The good warriors take their stand on ground where they cannot lose, and do not overlook conditions that make an opponent prone to defeat.' And, 'When you know you do not yet have the means to conquer, you guard your energy and wait.'"

The two wretched generals, as the meaning of these words sunk in, could not suppress their smiles of relief.

"You have used your judgment wisely," Huệ said. "I need your sound judgment and seasoned troops, and I thank you for not wasting them. I am weary, and we have had a long journey. I will hear your full report in the morning, at the beginning of the hour of the Snake [nine a.m.]. At that meeting, we will plan our attack, possibly for the same day, probably in the evening. Sharpen your weapons. Now use your 5,000 rested men to guard my army while it sleeps deeply, and stagger the guard so your men will also be able to fight whenever needed."

Ngô Văn Sở said "Yes sir, and thank you!"

"It shall be done," said Trần Quang Đàn. The two generals beamed with relief and pleasure. With a sense of adoration, they fell to their knees in gratitude and kowtowed again to their king and commander.

Huệ sent a letter by courier to the Chinese General Sun Shiyi. He claimed he was still in Phú Xuân, and carefully begged for mercy. He apologized for vanquishing the Trịnh, but insisted that he had immediately restored the Lê. Now there was just a big misunderstanding, but he would wait for the emperor's judgment.

Sun Shiyi wrote back that Hue should keep his troops garrisoned at Phú Xuân until the emperor's decision was received. Huệ sent an envoy, Đinh Văn Bánh, with a petition to General Sun Shiyi, requesting the Chinese to withdraw their troops from Thăng Long and suggesting reconciliation talks. The letter began, *Foreign forces have traditionally faced great difficulties when attacking Annam. I therefore suggest that you withdraw your troops to the frontier.* General Sun Shiyi was outraged by the cheek of this invitation, and ordered Đinh Văn Bánh immediately executed.

಄   ಄

The reign of Nguyễn Huệ as Emperor Quang Trung began on the Winter Solstice. After this holy day, all the people of Vietnam prepared to celebrate Tết, the beginning of the new lunar year, with banquets, offerings, fireworks, and dragon parades. All normal commercial activity stopped unless focused on the festival for the five days of Tết; it was the biggest holiday of the year in both China and Đại Việt.

The old year died on the Winter Solstice, and from its death, a new year sprang roughly forty days later—a cause for great celebration, for its rebirth was as miraculous as the daily rising of the sun or the perennial rising of the rice. In the Chinese calendar, the winter solstice must occur in the eleventh month. Tết, the Việt and Chinese New Year, usually falls on the second new moon after the solstice.

಄   ಄

Nguyễn Huệ allowed his troops twenty-four hours of rest and recovery. After this rest, his scouts completely surrounded and surprised the Chinese units busying themselves celebrating Tết at Sơn Nam. A few thousand fighters of Huệ's elite units quickly encircled and seized the forts that protected the capitol of Thăng Long.

Han Kao-tsu, a pigeon handler of the Qing Imperial Expeditionary Force, ran from the rampart as fast as he could. If he could release his pigeons, even without a message, an alarm would be sent to General Sun Shiyi. Tây Sơn troops had secured the front entrance and the black shirts were pouring into the fortress screaming an awful noise. Han Kao-tsu ducked into a side door of the inner keep, ran past Trịnh and Chinese guards looking carefully at him, until they recognized who he was and they lowered their weapons. Han Kao-tsu sprinted to the tower staircase, and bounded up the steps two at a time. He climbed four stories to the door to the roof and highest rampart. He swung the door open, and breathing heavily, walked over to his pigeon coops.

Kao-tsu opened the first cage top and looked with confusion and then horror. All his birds were dead—his pets and friends. He went to the next coop and the third—the same. All his pets were dead. *How did they all die*, he wondered? He was picking up a dead bird when he felt a blade stab his back.

🙞　🙜

Lu Yen-wu and his blue-shirted imperial soldiers of China were riding picket duty around the Thăng Long forts. At the end of their watch, they headed to the south fort, only to stop in disbelief. They could see black shirts pouring into the front gate. A few blue-shirted bodies fell from the outer ramparts.

"It's not possible, but these troops are Tây Sơn," Yen-wu exclaimed. "We must escape, follow me." He turned his horse and started to cantor away toward the capital. They cantered into a forest, but around a bend they stopped abruptly before a line of shields and bowmen. Lu Yen-wu was counting the bowmen before him when arrows came out of the trees on both sides of the road and struck some of his men. He yelled and ordered his men to charge the shields, which they did, but the archers shot their horses, and the survivors had to attack on foot. Not one made it to the line of shields. Lu Yen-wu was hit multiple times with arrows before he fell.

An officer in a general's cap, holding a bow, stepped out from the trees, followed by his archers. Lương Hoàng ordered his bowmen to hide again behind the foliage on guard. He ordered the shield men to drop their shields and hide the bodies in the forest. In short order, the ambush was reset.

🙞　🙜

When Huệ mobilized his troops to attack the main body of Chinese troops that were stretched along the Red River, he mounted his elephant before his assembled officers and troops, and read his proclamation, which had improved with rewriting.

The Chinese have invaded, and currently occupy Thăng Long. From north to south, Nam Việt is one country. The Chinese plan to annex it and divide it into provinces and districts. They are not of our race. They have different feelings, a different color to their skin. From the time of the Han Dynasty, they have several times raided our country, stolen our land, emptied our treasuries, and massacred our people. The situation is intolerable. I will immediately execute any one of you who retains the old vice of having two hearts. Those who love their country have no alternative but to fight and chase them out.

During the time of the Han, the Trưng Sisters fought the Chinese. Under the Sung, there were Đình Tiên Hoàng and Lê Đại Hành. Under the Yuan, the Mongols, there was Trần Hưng Đạo. Countering the Ming, there was Lê Thái Tổ, (Lê Lợi) the founder of the present dynasty. None of our leaders was content to sit with arms crossed, passively witnessing the cruelty of the Chinese. They all raised troops and chased the Chinese back across the border. A single battle was often sufficient for victory. I don't understand this time why the Chinese have not looked into the mirror of history. Let us live up to the glory of our forbearers. On to Thăng Long!

၏   ၆

During the evening of that fifth day of the New Year celebration, Huệ's scouts brought the Hissing Army to the Chinese Army, which was just outside Thăng Long, engaged in eating and drinking and setting off firecrackers and rockets. The Chinese had received various reports that Huệ and his army were still in the Spring Capital Phú Xuân, having their own feasts, and were preparing to move south against Nguyễn Ánh.

At midnight, Huệ ordered his elite fighting units to lead the attack. These groups each had twenty-one soldiers. In front of each group were ten strong soldiers carrying wooden plank shields. Since they needed both hands to carry the heavy shields, their knives were in their belts and their swords were slung in the small of their backs. The elite troops behind the shield-bearers carried longbows or cross-bows or muskets. The units charged into the enemy's poorly armed revelers, sitting at field tables of food and drink. Huệ, atop his elephant Genghis, held his elephant brigade in reserve and watched the attack on the surprised and intoxicated Chinese soldiers begin. The few sober bodyguards of various generals formed a ragged line of defense, but could not withstand the Tây Sơn archers and musketmen.

The second row of assault units charged into the enemy's party and attacked with arrow, spear, and sword. Huệ wished he could still lead the charge, but he and Lương Hoàng watched with satisfaction the performance of Huệ's well-trained troops.

A violent and pitiful massacre of Chinese soldiers ensued—but many of them fled like rabbits. Huệ gave his order to General Bùi Spring Song. She released her 200 elephants, followed by cavalry, to rampage into the camps of tents, shelters, and lean-tos. Three or four soldiers were mounted on each elephant, armed with fireballs and arrows that they hurled down on the disorganized Chinese troops. The uniforms of the Chinese soldiers caught fire from the exploding sulfur! The horses of the Chinese cavalry went berserk, and trampled to death many of the Chinese soldiers as they tried to avoid the elephants and the fireballs, which they had never encountered before.

The main fortifications of Ngọc Hồi were protected by cannon, which the Tây Sơn attacked by early morning daylight. But the wind was from the south, and the smoke from the cannon floated back into the ranks of the Chinese defenders, blinding them from seeing their attackers. The fortification walls at Ngọc Hồi were not high and were easily scaled. The defenders were overwhelmed by the bloody and determined onslaught of the Hissing Army.

When the Chinese finally managed a counterattack, Huệ committed his rifle regiment, who mowed down the first attackers with musket fire and then charged the enemy still standing with fixed bayonets. Several Qing generals perished in the ugly hand-to-hand fighting that ensued. Thanks to the timing of the surprise, and the tactic of the heavy shields, spear, and bow men followed by elephants, cavalry, and then muskets, the weapons of the more numerous Chinese could not stop the advance of the Tây Sơn, who screamed bloody murder as they killed.

The governor, General Sun Shiyi, learned of the disastrous defeat while the night was still dark. In haste, without putting on his armor nor even saddling his horse, he took off bareback shadowed by the light of countless fires, and he crossed the Red River followed by remnants of his cavalry. After a rumor spread through the Chinese soldiers that their general staff had fled, they panicked and ran. It looked like many thousands would escape across the river over the old bridge to a defendable position on higher ground. Thousands of soldiers converged on the famous wood bridge that traversed the Red River.

The bridge was not built to handle so many at once. It heaved a great sigh, wobbled back and forth, and then collapsed. Thousands fell with a roar with the collapsing bridge and drowned in their armor. Downstream, the shore became obstructed with Chinese cadavers. The young Việt Emperor, Lê Chiêu Thông, crossed the Red River by boat and found refuge in China with his empress and a handful of faithful Việt mandarins.

The Chinese soldiers were well trained, and those who crossed the Red River retreated to higher ground and dug in. From their elevation, they were able to stop the onslaught of the Hissing Army. But after five days of fighting, the Chinese had lost five generals and 30,000 men. The Chinese now defended a strong position, but lacked food, ammunition, and supplies. The Hissing Army allowed no respite. The Chinese Army had had enough; it retreated to the north.

Huệ had directed the entire campaign in person. His armor was black from gunpowder fumes. On the afternoon of the eleventh day of the new year, as his fortune teller had predicted, he entered Thăng Long. Most of his army followed the Chinese right to the gate of Ải Nam Quan at the border with China, but without any more unnecessary slaughter. Huệ ordered his generals to allow the Chinese a humane and dignified retreat, in the hope of lessening the wrath of the northern giant. Nevertheless, before the arrival of the Hissing Army, the Chinese inhabitants of the border region took off in panic and deserted their shops and houses. From Lạng Sởn to many miles to the north, one couldn't find a single inhabitant—even the noodle shops were deserted.

Governor Sun Shiyi departed in such haste that he left behind his seal of power and his secret instructions from Beijing. He had been ordered by Beijing, as Huệ had suspected, to turn Đông Kinh (Tonkin) once more into An Nam, a Chinese Protectorate. After consolidating power, he was to conquer the rest of the country, and then make the colony profitable again for China.

After the smoke had cleared and the dead were buried or burned, Huệ felt tired but elated. His excitement was muted by concerns. He realized that his third of the country needed time to rebuild. Controlling the south, there stood a threat to defeat—Nguyễn Ánh and his army, supported by French fighters and the dangerous Christian-devil priest.

ॐ   ॐ

After only a few days, Huệ wrote an effusive apology to the Chinese Emperor, and sent his Scholar-General Ngô Thì Nhậm, impersonating Huệ himself, to Beijing to deliver it, along with a rich cargo of gifts and the offer to release and return 800 captured Chinese soldiers, unless they chose to stay in Nam Việt, with the gift of a plot of land. In Thăng Long, after reestablishing guidelines for an administration for the Thăng Long to Bắc Hà area, using existing Trịnh administrators willing to kowtow in person to Quang Trưng or his portrait, Huệ and the main body of his troops moved back to the Spring Capital Phú Xuân.

The Chinese Emperor Qianlong stripped Governor Sun Shiyi of all his offices, titles, and salaries, but allowed him to keep his head. He immediately set in motion plans for the reconquest of Đại Cồ Việt. After the emissaries arrived from Đại Cồ Việt, the Chinese Emperor found the rich gifts and personal apology from Quang Trưng himself useful face-saving devices, and cooler heads prevailed. Emperor Qianlong even became friends with Ngô Thì Nhậm, who was pretending to be Nguyễn Huệ. Apparently Emperor Qianlong and his counselors were taken in. Emperor Qianlong recognized the domain of Quang Trưng with the old Chinese name of Annam, meaning Pacified South. With Pacified South, face was saved, but no one, of course, was fooled, at least as to who had really won the round. For the seventh time in 850 years, the Việt established through military force that the southern border of China stopped at the northern border of Vietnam.

Chapter 33
Pierre, Cảnh, and Ánh
1790

Pierre Pigneau was sitting in the study of his house in Sài Gòn when Old Goat came in with a sealed scroll in hand. "Father Pierre," the majordomo said, "excuse me for interrupting you, but a man came to the door and gave this scroll to the guards. He asked that they deliver it to you, and then he left without ceremony." Pierre untied the scroll and cut the wax seal, and examined it while Old Goat retired from the room. The scroll was from General Trần Quang Diệu of the Tây Sơn Army. It read:

Pierre Pigneau de Béhaine,

Bishop of Adran and Vicar Apostolic of Cochinchina,

Greetings and salutations. We salute you! We understand that you have influence wherever you go. Please give this information here your careful attention.

King Nguyễn Nhạc and his brother, King Nguyễn Huệ, whom I serve, are both in favor of relations and trade with foreign governments. They are both in favor of allowing Christianity to flourish in this great country of Đại Việt. You should relent in your support of Nguyễn Ánh, who is deeply conservative and who will not support openness and trade with foreigners, and who will betray you and turn on the Christians that he now pretends to tolerate.

The scroll went on to suggest that Pierre should withdraw from the civil war or change sides, and bring his French warships with him, for the future of France and the interests of the King of France would be served by the reform government of Nguyễn Nhạc, and not by the more conservative government of Nguyễn Ánh. The writer then suggested a place where a return message could be dropped, and Trần Quang Diệu would receive his response.

Pierre put the scroll aside and prepared to go visit Prince Cảnh for tutoring and Christian formation instruction. As he and his guards walked through the city of Sài Gòn, he decided he wouldn't even respond to this intriguing invitation. *Besides,* he thought, *there is no way to verify if what the writer stated is true. The Hồ brothers are masters of deception and intrigue. They are famous for telling their audience what it wants to hear. They do not keep their promises, even if what they say about Ánh is true.*

❧   ❦

The boy, Prince Nguyễn Phúc Cảnh, listened while Pierre discussed Jesus and read from the Holy Bible, which Alexandre de Rhodes had translated into Vietnamese. Little Prince Cảnh was ten now. He had the same wide cheeks and wide nose above large lips that his father had. Pierre was teaching the parable of the Good Samaritan. Pierre introduced the story by explaining that a legal scribe asked Jesus,

"How do I inherit eternal life?" Jesus told him you have to love your God with all your heart and soul and strength and mind, and love your neighbor as yourself. The scribe then asked, "But who is my neighbor?"

Pierre looked at Cảnh and said, "Jesus answered the scribe with this story:

'A certain man was going down from Jerusalem to Jericho, and he fell among robbers, who both stripped him and beat him, and departed, leaving him half dead. By chance a certain priest was going down that way. When he saw him, he passed by on the other side. In the same way a Levite also, when he came to the place and saw him, passed by on the other side. But a certain Samaritan, as he traveled, came where he was. When he saw him, he was moved with compassion, came to him, and bound up his wounds, pouring on oil and offering wine. He set him on his own animal, and brought him to an inn, and took care of him. On the next day, when he departed, he took out two denarii and gave them to the host, and said to him, 'Take care of him. Whatever you spend beyond that, I will repay you when I return.' Now which of these three do you think seemed to be a neighbor to him who fell among the robbers?

"The scribe said, 'He who showed mercy on him.'

"Then Jesus said to him, 'Go and do likewise.'"

Pierre then asked Cảnh, "Which of these characters would you want to be?"

"The Good Samaritan is the man of honor," answered Cảnh. "It is important to be honorable in all things." Prince Cảnh asked, "What is the big difference between the teaching of Confucius and the teaching of the Lord Jesus Christ? Wasn't the wisdom of the ancients inspired by God? Why can't you believe in Jesus *and* Confucius?"

Pierre looked at his clear-eyed young pupil and laughed. "That is a good question. Jesus was the greatest Lord and God, and Confucius was the greatest statesman and sage of China. But only Jesus died on the cross for the forgiveness of our sins, and only he offers us the promise of eternal life. The more I study Confucius, the more I respect him as a great scholar. He was the first to write, 'A sense of shame is the beginning of righteousness,' and, 'Oppressive rule is more cruel than a tiger.'"

Cảnh looked pleased, and said, "And he identified the five cardinal virtues." The boy held up his splayed hand and pointed to each finger. "Human kindness, rectitude, knowledge, wisdom, and sincerity."

"Very good," Pierre said. "But I thought this finger was rectitude?"

Cảnh giggled. "You are being very silly."

"Yes," Pierre said, "and if I recall, Confucius even preached the Golden Rule. Do you remember how he phrased it?

"Oh yes," the boy said brightly. "What you do not want yourself, do not extend to others. So is there such a big difference?"

"Now listen, Cảnh, if you are a mandarin, then what Confucius said seems wonderful. He called for rectitude, which in his day meant that the mandarins were the masters, and their wives, their servants, and their peasants were hardly more powerful than their slaves. He argued that harmony could only prevail if the legal masters were good masters, fair, just, and compassionate.

"Conditions were not so different in Jerusalem when our Lord Jesus disagreed with both the Hebrew and the Roman authorities. Jesus insisted that the rulers were servants of God, and servants of those whom they ruled. Jesus taught that women and slaves had souls, like their masters. They were their spiritual equals. Like their masters, the good ones who repented would be welcome in the heavenly kingdom. Jesus was something of a pacifist. He was against wars and bullies, but he was also a champion for the poor and infirm. Even women and slaves could attain forgiveness of sins and eternal life.

"Was he a master of Soft and Yielding Technique in warfare?"

"Yes, you could say that he practiced Soft and Yielding, or the Gentle Way."

"Are French Christians going to cause a revolution here in my country with the Gentle Way?" Cảnh asked.

This is an amazing young man, Pierre thought. *Through him, I might convert the whole country.* "I don't know," Pierre said. "Although many of my countrymen say they are Christians, by and large we are not a gentle but a warlike people. But someday surely a Việt leader will decide that the peasants here need more education and less taxation and forced labor. If you were a good farmer, you would treat your livestock carefully, so that they grow strong and multiply. A king must treat his people carefully, and not overwork them, especially on the royal construction projects."

"Do I have to, like the pope says, stop showing my gratitude or praying to the spirits of my dead Ancestors?"

Damn, I wonder who has been talking to this boy, Pierre wondered. *His father?* Pierre looked thoughtfully at the youngster, who was his main hope for creating a massive about-face toward Christianity throughout the country's bureaucracy in the miraculously short span of a single generation.

"The pope says that you shouldn't worship your ancestral spirits like Gods. 'Thou shalt have only one God' is one of the Ten Commandments. But I would never say that you shouldn't pray to your Ancestors or give thanks to them, or show them great honor and respect. We pray to many saints and martyrs in the Holy Catholic Church. I disagree with the pope! I firmly believe that one can believe in Jesus the Lord God, and pray to the spirits of your Ancestors with great reverence."

"Good," the young boy said solemnly. "Father Pierre, I want to be confirmed as a Christian."

Pierre smiled, "Alleluia, praise be the Lord," he said.

☙   ❧

Later that same day, Father Pierre, whose health was no longer robust, took a nap after lunch. Perhaps he was just aging rapidly, though he seemed terribly fatigued all the time, even for a man of fifty. His face and hands had a yellow pallor, and his stomach was growing larger, even though he was eating more carefully.

Father Pierre walked through the streets of Sài Gòn with a few of his guards after consulting a new physician, who recommended that he drink less wine and whiskey and eat less meat and more vegetables, especially salad greens, cabbages, and mushrooms.

Pierre's owlish, hawk-nosed face was now slightly bloated. He was ushered into Ánh's study for his appointment at two hourglasses after the midday, the second hour of the Goat. Pierre bowed, and Ánh waved to a servant, who brought closer a second armchair for the older man. Ánh's face was similar to Cảnh's, with the wide cheekbones predominating. The large brown pupils peered out of his almond-shaped lids. They were set wide apart and the flat nose was flared up and out at the base. "You're looking a bit tired," Ánh said warmly. "Have you been habituating the flower houses?"

"Only when I need to address one of my captains, or one of your generals," Pierre answered cheerfully.

The talk soon moved to the more serious topic of Nguyễn Huệ, self-declared Emperor Quang Trung, residing in the Spring Capital, victor over the Qing invaders, and who also controlled Thăng Long (Hà Nội) and all of Đông Kinh. Ánh said, "The Chinese invaded Đông Kinh, but Huệ's reinvigorated forces defeated them in just five days. Huệ's forces took only a light beating and survived intact. We have a terribly strong and capable adversary in that man. In fact, it could take us a long time to grow strong enough to challenge his Hissing Army for control of Đông Kinh."

Pierre smiled and said, "At least the Chinese are taken care of. That is a great blessing."

"Here is our latest report. His fleet of 120 galleys is apparently ready to move. He already has assembled over 200 elephants. In his army he has 100,000 soldiers in arms and more recruits from Đông Kinh than he knows what to do with. His brother, Nhạc, refused to leave Quy Nhơn, though he has been asked by Huệ to join the main force in a punitive war to reconquer Đại Việt's ancient northern territories from southern China."

"Do you believe that he will attack China?" asked Pierre.

"I don't know," Ánh said. "What do you think?"

"I think it's a ruse to throw us off. I bet he is building up his forces for a major thrust at us."

"That would be smarter of him, wouldn't it, so I agree. Rumors everywhere speak of unrest. Some think the brothers will fight each other again. One rumor suggests that the Chinese will attack again and come to the aid of the dispersed Trịnh remnants. Another suggests that the Christians are all secretly arming. Huệ is forcing the Christians of his domain to produce 10,000 pounds of copper for the casting of cannon. He has ordered the Chinese community around Thăng Long to give up their copper statues of Buddha—causing a big fuss. But what a clever way to produce copper. I think I will do the same. From the Buddhas alone his smiths produced eight more cannon for the citadel of the Spring Capital. Against a force the size I've described, I hardly know what to do. My generals are split into every conceivable faction. That's why I asked you to devise a strategy of your own."

"I am honored that you continue to seek my opinion, your highness," Pierre began using the language of the courtier. "With deep regret, I agree that Nguyễn Huệ is too strong and popular for a direct confrontation now. His forces have just defeated the Qing, and they are in peak condition. This opinion has been well expressed by Võ Tánh, and we both value his wisdom. What I would do is this: Instead of increasing rapidly the size of your force, I'd halt the recruitment, and even shrink your forces a little. Maintain as small an army as possible, only for defense, but organize and train it along European lines, for maximizing the effect of cannon and musket, and allow your peasants to breathe, eat, and sleep, and to be as productive and content as possible on their farms. Show the country that you can be judicious, fair, and strong. If your peasants can create a rice surplus, we can sell the surplus for ordnance.

"My engineers want to construct a shipyard to build and repair our Western-style ships, and an armory to make cannon. One of them, Captain Olivier du Puymanel, has plans to fortify this citadel. These ideas are excellent. They would keep all the French busy and eventually reduce your cost of Western weapons. We need time to grow stronger, and hopefully the Tây Sơn will grow weaker from the strain of their expensive mobilization. Let's see how well they can administer and manage all that they have won through military prowess."

Ánh listened carefully, and answered, "I will discuss all these ideas with my counselors." After several days of debate in the High Council, of which Pierre was already a member, Ánh accepted all of these recommendations. It annoyed many of Ánh's mandarins as it became clear again that Pierre Pigneau was not simply a member of the High Council of Mandarins, but he was emerging as one of its principal executives and tactical and technical advisors.

Chapter 34
Surprise in Sài Gòn
1790

Father Pierre, Henri Dayot, and Benoit Grannier were in a large room waiting for King Nguyễn Ánh, when a short mandarin with a small paunch came into the room wearing a big grin on his face. "Oh my God, is it possible?" said Pierre in Vietnamese. "Is it Diệu Tri?

"Yes it is, ha, ha, ha, returned from the dead. I bet you thought I was dead! I thought I was dead! And you left me there in that stinking dungeon with no one else to talk to. I should kill you, ha, ha, ha." The two men bowed low to each other, and then, much to the surprise of the others, they embraced in a bear hug.

"I heard a rumor that you were executed," said Pierre. "How did you escape?"

"It was my uncle, Diệu Thái. You remember, the Minister of Canals and Waterworks. You sent him a message about my incarceration, which he received, and he petitioned Nguyễn Đình to create a bail fee, which Đình agreed to, and then my good uncle paid it. A pardon soon followed. So you didn't actually abandon me, and if my left knee wasn't so stiff, I'd give you the three kowtows you deserve. But I like your barbarian hug. I learned it from a Russian."

"No need to kowtow," laughed Pierre. "It is good to see you not only survived, but have prospered. It appears from your fine tunic that you have been given a position."

"King Đình put me with my uncle at Canals and Waterworks. After Đình's luck ran out, I became a Buddhist monk for a little while, ha, ha, ha. Oh yes, thank you Buddha, that the hair grows back, ha, ha, ha. Nguyễn Ánh saved me from a life of vegetables and abstinence. I really missed sex, not that you'd understand, ha, ha, ha. I was reinstated as the Minister of Canals and Waterworks. Then I was promoted to be the Minister of Diplomatic Protocol and Foreigner Relations. Some say it is only a lateral transfer. You could say this mandarin has gone from managing a physical sewer system to a political one, ha, ha, ha."

Pierre introduced Diệu Tri to Dayot and Grannier, his two naval officers present, who were wondering what the jokes were about. Pierre summarized what had been said. "Congratulations," said Commodore Dayot cheerfully, "on your escape from incarceration and your promotion. We are the beneficiaries of your teachings to Father Pierre the Bishop."

"Isn't he wonderful? But I would almost have rather died than to be so in his debt, ha, ha, ha. You have travelled a long way from home, looking for trouble," said Diệu Tri smiling. "Welcome to Sài Gòn. You have come to the right place for some excitement. I hope your voyage from India was satisfactory." After some polite small talk about travel at sea, with Pierre acting as the translator, Diệu Tri, with a twinkle in his eye, said to Dayot and Grannier, "I bet you sailors could use a first rate house of pleasure. I would be delighted to escort you some night this week or next to one of my favorites. Bring your friends, there will be plenty of girls to go around, and it will give me a chance to know some Frenchmen besides this pious holy man, always asking sensitive political questions, heh, heh, heh." Pierre grimaced slightly, but he passed along the invitation. Henri and Benoit looked at each other and nodded. Dayot responded, "We would be delighted to take a night out on the town with you. I believe we are unscheduled tomorrow night. Do you object Father Pierre?"

"No, not completely, God forgive you, you fornicating sinners," he said smiling. "And God forgive me, we are all sinners. You sinners can do what you like on your time off. Just remember you are guests in this country." And then he gave their acceptance in Vietnamese.

"It will be a famous cultural exchange," boasted Diệu Tri, chuckling. "And it will go more smoothly if you visit a bathhouse just before we leave for dinner. And for the sake of prosperous cross-cultural exchanges, allow me humbly to suggest you put on freshly laundered clothes in honor of the ladies. They notice such things, and I have to keep my excellent reputation."

"It sounds like it will be for a good cause," said Benoit smiling.

Father Pierre dutifully translated the arrangements, and then continued, "Diệu Tri, we have so much to catch up on. Can you join me for dinner tonight?"

"It will be a pleasure," said Diệu Tri smiling. "As old cell mates we do have much to talk about. And because of my new position, I'll also be doing my job as Minister of Protocol, which entails helping the foreigners find their way around while we carefully watch them. I'll hit three ducks with one arrow, ha, ha, ha."

ဆ က

Benoit, scrubbed and bathed, was seated on a rug, leaning against a bolster pillow, listening to exotic, twangy lute music. He was in a well-appointed dining room at the Happy Valley Green Pavilion, a large house in a small town. Escorted by ten blue-shirted guards, they had ridden King Ánh's horses about forty-five minutes northeast of Sài Gòn. Diệu Tri was seated nearby, holding court, and more or less lost in the attentions of his favorite courtesan, Jasmine Nectar. Paul Nghi was on duty as the translator for Henri Dayot, Benoit, and Olivier du Puymanel. Jasmine Nectar kneeled behind Diệu Tri and quietly massaged his back. Three other courtesans served the barbarian customers their food and drink.

Benoit little noticed the three servers. He kept watching and listening to the Vietnamese lute player singing in the corner, whose Việt name was Ngọc Hà, which he did not know meant Jade River. The female musician was striking in a green and blue silk suit, and she was alternating between lively and slow songs. After each song, Benoit would ask Paul Nghi what the last song was about.

Regarding one sad sounding song, Paul Nghi said, "That song is called *The Rock of the Waiting Wife*. A woman waits for her husband to return from a journey for years, like a rock, her mind stays pure. She cries like autumn rain every day, so much that all around her the moss grows green. The faithful wife upholds the moral code."

"Please tell the musician I think she sang beautifully," said Benoit. Jade River listened to Paul Nghi's communication and bowed gently to Benoit to thank him for his praise. Her next song was upbeat and even Jade River allowed her lovely but solemn face to smile as she delivered its humor. "Monsieur Nghi, what was that one about?" asked Benoit.

Paul Nghi laughed and answered, "That song was called, *A House with a Hole in the Roof*. It is an old song, and one of my favorites. My mother used to sing it." Paul Nghi asked Jade River to sing it more slowly, and after each line, he gave his best attempt at a translation:

"Your leaky hut is exposed to sun and rain.
Watch Heaven gazing down—you know he cares for you!
For plenty of free water offer thanks!
Daylight streams in to make your mirror shine.
The Moon Goddess, Miss Phoebe, keeps you company at night.
The Goddess of the wind, Dame Zephyr, sweeps along your bed by day.
You call another luxury your own.
The elixir of dewdrops fills your tray. Your floor is wet."

Benoit chuckled quietly, and said to Jade River, "All good reasons not to fix the roof!" which Paul Nghi translated, causing Diệu Tri to laugh. Diệu Tri added, "Many men will sing this song when their wife says it is time to rethatch the roof."

Jade River responded with a smile, "There is a song for most sins in the world. We sing this song at the shrine to procrastination."

The men all agreed with this sentiment and drank "to procrastination." They enjoyed the evening: the food, the wine, the music, and the women. After the dinner, Diệu Tri arranged for each foreign guest to go off with one of the servers to her bedroom. Benoit asked Paul Nghi if he could go with the musician, Ngọc Hà, instead of the other remaining woman. Paul Nghi inquired and Jade River bowed and said, "If he can afford me, I will attend the barbarian sea captain." She carefully hung her lute on a peg in the wall, and took the tall young barbarian with the strange red-brown hair to her private boudoir.

Their conversation was limited, as they had no translator present to help them communicate. Jade River discovered that the barbarian had green eyes and hair on his arms and chest. She worried with some anxiety, *Does he know how to bathe? Apparently none of them do.* With genuine curiosity, they undressed each other. She asked Benoit with her hands to lie down on his stomach. Jade River straddled his back and massaged his shoulders. She pressed her nose against his naked back, and was pleased and relieved that he had bathed. *Thank the Gods that the worst reports are not true; some barbarians are learning to bathe.*

Jade River was also curious to know if the barbarian from across the Western Ocean knew how to make love to a civilized woman, even if a fallen one. Among the Việt educated elite, it was considered a good thing to know something about international relations.

જ ✦

General Trần Quang Diệu, the husband of General Bùi Spring Song, returned from an expedition into Laos to subdue hostile forces and require the tribute expected from Laos to the Lê Dynasty. Trần Quang Diệu gave Nguyễn Huệ his kowtows, and his report. Lê Duy Chỉ, one of the brothers of the Emperor Lê Chiêu Thống and the Princess Gem Lake, had tried to rouse the lords of Laos to fight against Nguyễn Huệ, now Emperor Quang Trưng. Duy Chỉ's small army was defeated and dispersed.

"The Laotian King escaped," said Diệu, "but we sacked his capital city. It was just a small town by our standards, but we brought back dozens of elephants, horses, bronze drums, and whatever of value we could find. We also had the help of a good local, and captured Lê Duy Chỉ and brought him back with us."

"You have done well," said Huệ. "I will have the usurper beheaded in short order."

Word of this conversation reached Gem Lake, who boldly approached her new husband. "Please spare my third brother's life. Do not behead him. He is young, and he was doing what he felt called to do by our code of filial piety. It was not a wise choice, but it showed bravery. I have spoken to my brother, and he gives his word he will never cross you again. He will become a monk, if you require it of him."

Huệ looked at his beautiful young Third Wife, and hesitated for a moment. "This young man, your brother, is guilty of high treason. But I will consider your request. Since you ask, I will not cut off his head, but confine him instead, till I think of something appropriate." Gem Lake fell to her knees and kowtowed, murmured her thanks, and quickly withdrew.

A few days later, Huệ called Trần Quang Diệu and ordered him to take Lê Duy Chỉ "to grope for shrimp." Soldiers marched Duy Chỉ down to the Perfume River. Behind a building, they tied the young man's hands and feet, placed him in a jute sack with a few heavy rocks, and rolled the sack in a baggage cart to a waiting sampan. The boatman used the sculling oar to row Diệu and two soldiers and their baggage out to the middle of the river. They dropped the sack containing Lê Duy Chỉ into the river.

Chapter 35
Macao
January 1790

Julian Girard, the captain of *La Méduse*, was in excellent health until he contracted dysentery, followed by the swamp fever malaria. His body was racked by diarrhea, and then by coldness, which turned to rigor, followed by severe fever and sweating for about five hours. The doctor, Michel Despiaux, gave the patient cinchona bark tea, to no avail. The fever would break, and two days later the cycle would occur all over again. This cycle continued for several weeks, until it killed him.

Once again Benoit lost a good friend. He also gained a position as the next captain of *La Méduse*. *La Méduse* was a fine ship, and Benoit was pleased to become captain of such a good sailing and fighting vessel. Its internal joints, the crutches and knees, were sound; it just needed new sails. It fell on Benoit's shoulders to sail off in search of munitions, supplies, and if possible, a fifth man-of-war or even a transport ship.

La Méduse left Sài Gòn in September of 1789, using the summer monsoon to carry it to Cavite, the Spanish port serving Manila and the Spanish Philippines—950 nautical miles away.

At Cavite in December, Benoit and the other officers were rowed ashore to present their credentials, to trade, and to look for women, whiskey, and newspapers. They would collect the news from other sailors in the bars and taverns.

Spaniards they met reported that King Louis XVI, unable to deal effectively with a severe famine and the growing deficit, had restored the defunct Parliament of Paris in September of 1788, and it had in turn called to order the Estates General to meet, as it had in 1614, in three separate orders.

The First Estate comprised the clergy, the Second Estate the nobility, and the Third Estate included everyone else, *id est*, the commoners, though it was represented only by men of wealth and commerce. The nobility, which dominated the Parliament of Paris, was trying to initiate reform by consolidating its control through its political domination of both the First and Second Estates.

"If you ask me," Nicolas Tabarly said, "calling the Estates General was a brilliant move. Now the king will get the elected dukes and counts to agree to desperately needed new taxes."

"My father, for one," Guillaume retorted, "worked hard to convince the king not to call the Estates General, to protect the privileges of higher birth. The republicans and constitutional monarchists are saying it's the king's authority which has grown too great. They say that the country needs reform from an over-centralized and top-heavy bureaucracy. Nonsense! The king can raise taxes if he needs to on his own authority. That is the tradition. The problem is that he keeps expropriating our seigneurial duties, and he keeps going to war, while alienating his own nobles with new proposed taxes to levy on them. In his profligacy, King Louis will be the end of us all."

Benoit, who had been listening, added to the discussion. "The nobility, it appears, are involved in a power play to relieve the king of some of his authority, arguably to make the state financially stronger, but they don't seem inclined to share that authority with any of the other groups in society."

According to the seven-month-old newspapers they found, a debate raged in France as to whether or not France needed an aristocracy any longer. An Abbey Sieyes had written a pamphlet arguing that France needed only the Third Estate, and declared that the nobility was a useless caste that could be abolished without loss. A writer and novelist named Jean-Jacques Rousseau had delineated in a pamphlet titled "The Social Contract" that the Third Estate was the only necessary element of society. It was identical to the nation, and the nation was sovereign, not the king. The Estates General had met as decreed in early May of 1789, but the more radical lawyers and businessmen of the Third Estate had boycotted the convention, insisting that all three chambers sit as one house, and that each deputy have one vote. It must have been unseasonably hot last winter in Paris, as the various factions considered compromise or violence.

During the two weeks in Cavite, on Manila Bay in the Philippines, three sailors and one officer took their leave from *La Méduse,* but Benoit nevertheless successfully traded King Ánh's silver, jade, and rice for an old ship, a weather-beaten corvette with 16 guns, which he rechristened *Le Saint-Esprit* (the Holy Spirit). He also acquired tobacco, sugar, and hemp for sale in Macao and for King Ánh's storerooms.

La Méduse and *Le Saint-Esprit* sailed in January for Macao, 800 miles to the northwest. Benoit avoided Guillaume most of the time by putting him on *Le Saint-Esprit* under Lieutenant Joachim Bluedot, whom he made the acting captain.

In Macao, Benoit and the other officers eagerly searched for sources of news. In the first tavern they entered, they crowded around an old coffee-stained newspaper. They were shocked at what they learned.

The headlines of the last few newspapers to reach Macao screamed that the king was responding to the revolutionaries by assembling over 18,000 soldiers at Versailles. On April 27, 1789, there was a riot at the Reveillon factory in Paris, and soldiers killed twenty-five rioting workers.

On June 13, several priests of the First Estate in Versailles outside of Paris sat with the Third Estate in protest. On the 17th, the Third Estate declared itself the National Assembly. King Louis XVI, siding with the nobles, closed the hall, but the merchants and lawyers found an indoor tennis court, a *jeu de courte-paume*, in which to continue meeting.

On June 20, the rebels issued the Oath of the Tennis Court, affirming the sovereign right of the new National Assembly to draft and ratify a new constitution. There the news abruptly ended. So the men in the taverns of Macao had a lot to speculate and argue about.

At a dinner in Macao with most of the officers of the gun room present, Guillaume was not shy. He said, "The king should order the army to arrest or shoot the lot of them. They have no legal basis for demanding nonexistent rights."

Tabarly agreed. "If the king doesn't stop the revolt quick, where will it end, where will it end—anarchy?"

"It will be chaos," said Jean Bluedot, "and who knows, civil war."

Benoit spoke up, "I'd give a gold piece to hear what has been happening. Whatever happens, there will have to be some major reforms to satisfy the demands of a frustrated public."

"With enough force, the mob will go back to their fields and factories," Guillaume said in disagreement. His eyes challenged Benoit, who chose to rest his case and attend his dinner. He was alone in this group in his enthusiasm for Montesquieu and republican reforms.

Joachim Bohu was tired of politics and changed the subject. "I discovered the sweetest whorehouse last night. Talk about celebrations."

Marine Captain La Fontaine said in deadpan, "I'll visit yours, if you visit mine," to hoots of laughter.

❧   ❧

Benoit had a terrible time arguing with the Portuguese authorities regarding his lack of export licenses. But after all was said and done, they were good Catholics and businessmen, and King Ánh's silver and jade were real enough to make their eyes shine and their hearts bend.

The governor-general signed the permits to buy powder and shot reluctantly, for both political and personal reasons. Only a year and a half earlier, he had offered King Ánh the service of fifty fully manned warships of the Portuguese Royal Navy to defeat the rebels and develop a most-privileged-nation treaty between Đại Cồ Việt and Portugal. Pierre, before leaving for France, had helped scuttle this alliance by sharing with Ánh the view that the Portuguese, like the Dutch in Indonesia, were brutal colonists who couldn't be trusted. Pierre insisted that the French were the more civilized barbarians.

When Bishop Pierre, in his campaign to win royal French aid, was frustrated by the French Governor of Pondicherry, General Thomas Conway, he almost accepted the offer of the Portuguese in desperation. But his patriotism to France was so great that in spite of the fact that King Louis XVI, through Conway, had reneged on some of his promises to help, Pierre still went out of his way to secure friendly terms with

Đại Cồ Việt for his motherland France. It was primarily on account of King Ánh's loyalty to his Western friend and the trust between them that Ánh turned down the tempting offer from the Portuguese.

Benoit soon spent the money and treasure entrusted to him, and purchased enough stores for both ships to return to Đại Việt loaded with munitions and supplies.

While his men were loading the stores, Benoit had a chance to explore Macao a little and mingle with the Portuguese officers. Most of them spoke French, and he, like most sailors, knew a little Portuguese. Benoit liked to walk through the European quarter in the early evening, enjoying the cool breeze from the northwest, or in the early morning when he could admire the Spanish-style houses with their white stucco walls and their red clay shingle roofs.

In the evenings he would hear people singing together in salons and pubs, which reminded him of André and Margarita, from his days in Senegal. André was still dead, Margarita was God knows where. Both still seemed irreplaceable, like Antoine.

Although Benoit tried not to dwell on the things he disliked, he was often uninspired by the regular company he kept. Most of the other officers were interested primarily in talking of and boasting about physical feats of manhood. Topics of currency concerned the quality of liquor, tobacco, horses, weapons, and women, although not always in that order. They scoffed at the reformers and republican thinking that were now fashionable in Paris. For most of the officers, their only goals were to magnify their wealth and the accumulation of manly conquests in one form or another. Vainglory and financial security were their missions in life. Only with Father Pierre, Dayot, and Girard before his death could Benoit analyze the news, discuss his readings of Voltaire, Montesquieu, and this new Rousseau, and share his curiosity and his excitement about new ideas, such as national sovereignty, manifest destiny, historical progress, and the natural sciences.

ও   ও

One luminous gray morning before the sun had appeared in the east, Benoit's wanderings took him into the Chinese quarter and through the entertainment district. He went past several blocks of garbage-strewn tenements, the quarters of coolies and cake sellers, which made him remember the slums of Lorient where he grew up. He watched a group of men collecting night soil, human feces and urine left in buckets placed by the side of the houses, and he realized that these Chinese streets were much cleaner than their counterparts in France. But he was struck by the similarities, as well as the disparities. On one street he passed a forlorn-looking cake seller, and purchased two cakes from yet another one, to her delight. "Please buy more," she pleaded. As Benoit left her, he was solicited by two beggars. There were too many mouths without enough wealth. The poor Chinese of Macao were living in overcrowded conditions. Like the wretches in a painting by Hieronymus Bosch, they held onto the great hayride of life with a slender straw instead of a rope.

Benoit watched a sick old woman tramp by in rags. The crone held out her hand, opened her almost toothless mouth, and pointed at her gums. It was unmistakable for "Help me, I'm starving." Benoit gave her a few coppers. Her face and arms were covered with colored wart-like growths: red, yellow, green, and brown. Benoit braced himself so as not to recoil and not to show his discomfort. She carried the smell of rotting flesh about her. He recalled that he had once seen another woman with a similar skin condition in Lorient begging outside a tavern.

The picture seemed incongruous with the luminescent blue-gray light of early morning. Returning his mind to a topic as old as civilization, he asked himself, *How do you lift the poor and the sick out of the mire? Even if you controlled all the armies of the world, could you afford to feed, house, educate, and succor all the poor? It might be impossible to feed everyone when they are multiplying like rabbits.*

Benoit marveled at the contrast between the beauty of blue and gray clouds over green trees and brightly painted buildings and the misery of the woman he quickly left behind him, only to pass more beggars, to whom he felt compelled to also give a few pennies.

If I'm a dreamer, what am I dreaming for? Am I a fool, as crazy as Don Quixote, jousting with wind mills? The Knight Errant of the Rueful Figure charged the windmill. It broke his lance and unhorsed him. Benoit laughed out loud. *Sancho Panza soon warned, "But your lordship, attacking so many armed men will be even worse than attacking windmills!" He should have listened to Sancho Panza. The men beat Quixote severely. Can you help the downtrodden, or must they help themselves? It is good Christian duty to try and help the sick and the destitute.*

Thomas Hobbes wrote that men are low and base, but John Locke argued that men are a creation of their environment. They can be nurtured and improved. Voltaire, as he presented both, seemed to side more with Hobbes. But he also wrote that to overcome ignorance, credulity, and priest craft, above all else it was necessary to weaken the Church and to strengthen the State. Father Sebastian once said, "Voltaire saw clearly the natural path between the Scylla and Charybdis of Hobbes and Locke. He demanded control of the masses, and freedom for the enlightened." At which point, old Sebastian would pull himself to attention and take a bow and then chuckle. Voltaire was a great observer, but a snob. But he was also a rich bourgeois in love with the aristocracy, and especially Plato's intellectual elite.

Montesquieu and Voltaire were both so impressed by the English philosophers, that one had to question the firmness of their allegiance to France. But the admiration of philosophes obviously went in both directions across the channel, Benoit mused. *Montesquieu's most dramatic idea, that a nation could govern itself best through a separation and a balance of powers, thanks to the efforts of the French, are now being tested in North America in the new United States. It is unlikely that Montesquieu would suggest such a political solution to the King of Đại Việt, for Montesquieu believed firmly that government varied according to climate and circumstances. He wrote that democracy would work only in small city-states. Despotism was well suited to large empires of lazy and illiterate masses in hot climates. If he is right, the United States, if it populates the continent, will prove to be too large for democracy. It will splinter through civil wars into rival states, even though her separation from England remains a major triumph for France. Is the victory of the American colonists a victory for mankind, or a victory for France? Is there even a difference? Maybe not; call it a victory for both.*

Benoit passed fancy inns with gambling and theatrical shows, which displayed gaudy signs in bright paint in both Chinese characters and Portuguese. There were the famous Green Pavilion houses, which offered food, entertainment, and women to the weary traveler. *How long has it been? There was that magnificent night outside Sài Gòn with the lute player, Ngọc Hà.* He was ready for another woman, but the fear of syphilis and other scourges helped his feet walk past.

Benoit was fascinated by all the different kinds of people in the city, and especially in the Chinese entertainment district, where many a European gentleman could be found making the rounds.

A portly old gentleman came stumbling out of one of the more well-to-do establishments, and began to sing to himself as he walked. Benoit was amused, until he noticed that a group of rough-looking Chinese men were also following the old man. Benoit continued to walk down the street. *It's none of my business,* he thought, echoing the wisdom of George Quellenac. *But if everyone in the world felt that way, what a shabby place it would be. Besides, "What is life, but a brief pause in death's anteroom?"* He decided to turn around and double back. The four men were walking casually behind the old European, who was leaving the busy part of the street for a quieter neighborhood that he apparently trusted, and which he planned to traverse to get to the European quarter.

The four thugs carried sticks and clubs, and were almost upon the old gent when Benoit, glad that he'd brought his sword, started to sing out in his cheerful tenor:

"Chevaliers de la table ronde, Goutons voir si le vin est bon.
Chevaliers de la table ronde, Goutons voir si le vin est bon.
Goutons voir, oui oui oui, Goutons voir, non non non,
Goutons voir si le vin est bon."

He was singing, "Knights of the Round Table, Taste to see if the wine is good."

The four miscreants let their weapons drop to their sides, and allowed Benoit, who was now walking as if completely drunk, catch up to them. He stopped singing, hailed good morning, and walked through them nodding and smiling to each. Each one gave a genuine smile back. Isn't it true that throughout the four seas all men are brothers? As soon as his back was to them he heard a footfall.

Benoit spun around to see a raised club. He rushed the assailant, grabbed the man's club arm, and arrested his forward motion. His other hand in a fist struck into the man's nose. Benoit grabbed both the assailant's arms and pulling down, kneed him in the stomach. He threw this body into the path of the next attacker, jumped backward, and drew his saber.

The next two men circled around him. One of the ruffians, his hair in a long queue, shoved his cudgel at Benoit's stomach. Benoit parried the staff downward with his sword and the man swung the other end with flashing speed at Benoit's head. Benoit's sword flew up to meet the attack. Benoit lunged forward and punched this man in the face so hard that the man fell backward off his feet.

The steel sword barely moved fast enough to catch the next staff, which entered his peripheral vision in full swing. The fourth man hit well both left and right, high and low. The fourth rogue seemed to have no trouble with Benoit's sudden strikes with the sword. Benoit tried to move so that he could also see the other attackers. Hitting with both ends of his staff, the fourth man came up again with a low cut. Benoit blocked down with his sword and bounced it off the stick and into the man's heart. He pulled it out and spun around.

Only one assailant remained standing, and he respectfully kept his distance. When he saw Benoit approach, the last ruffian turned and sprinted down an alley.

"Bravo, well done, my good fellow," rang out the old man in Portuguese.

The gray-haired gentleman had become considerably more sober watching this event. "Now all we need is a constable, and I can buy you a drink—Monsieur Stephano di Grandola, at your service."

"My name, sir, is Monsieur Benoit Grannier. I accept, quite happily," Benoit replied, messaging his fist. "I am ready for a bowl of coffee or tea. I often make a toast to my father after winning a fight, God rest his soul, and Georges Quellenec, the master with whom I had the honor to study the sword." Strolling up the street, they now could see two Chinese constables, whom they hailed.

Di Grandola was obviously a man of means. His blue velvet suit was well tailored and he sported diamonds and rubies on his fingers. His chin was round and recessed below bright red and puffy cheeks. "And who was your father, young man?"

"He was Lieutenant Etienne-François Grannier, French Navy. He died in a fight with the English off the coast of Africa when I was a boy."

"Bad news, life can be hard. But good fighting style tonight—this morning really. Your *paipai* would be proud of you," the old man said. He informed the two constables of the attack in Portuguese, and blessed them for their appearance. One of the constables spoke some Portuguese, and he insisted on taking down the names of the two barbarians, after tying up the two men who still showed signs of life. With the law satisfied for the moment, Benoit accepted the old man's offer of a drink, and escorted him to the Portuguese section and into a tavern.

"Damn good sword, my man," the old gentleman repeated in passable French. "I don't know why, but you can never find one of those heathen constables when you need one. I think they're all thick as thieves anyway, eh, don't you? Now I'm in a pretty fix. Oh God forgive me for being a lecherous old man. What will my wife say now, when the authorities want me to testify that I was caught by brigands on Comfort Street? If I could only keep my wick out of the hot, wet wax. Bought the theater tickets, that's what I'll say, but at this hour? She'll know better than to believe me. Thank God she's a Christian, and at least knows of forgiveness.

"I always tell her I'm at the club playing backgammon with Paulo. Paulo tells his wife the same. Good God, there will be a scene like Dante's Inferno. O Madonna, and if she ever forgives me, what will Father Lucio say? I'm lost. I'm a terrible sinner, and what's worse, I'm about to be caught and might have to repent."

All this was mildly entertaining to Benoit. The old Portuguese di Grandola continued, "Did you see the *San Pablo* come in yesterday?"

"I did," said Benoit, "but the ship's officers all went to the reception last night at the governor's."

"So did I, for a while anyway," the man with the wrinkled red cheeks said.

"So much the better. What's the news, sir?"

"These are strange and uncertain times. An officer reported that a mob in Paris went crazy and stormed the royal prison, *La Bastille*. The mob had help from uniformed soldiers, so they had weapons and cannon. *La Bastille* garrison surrendered, but the mob then murdered the commander and six or ten of the defending soldiers in cold blood. Then they attacked the City Hall and murdered the mayor, the poor souls! The regular army units outside the city didn't raise a finger, not a bloody little finger. Word is, the king didn't trust his own soldiers. He didn't dare use them. Then the king decided to disassemble the troops and recognize the new National Assembly! God's blood, King Louis has gone completely soft in the head."

"Or scared to use force against his own people," said Benoit, who felt dumbstruck. Benoit felt queasy; he wasn't sure which side he was on. In an instant he realized that his heart was mostly with the republican mob, though he disapproved entirely of the killings. He reined in his reactions so as not to give them away or be controversial. "What is the world coming to?" he said, shaking his head, although he felt a stirring of excitement. *Reform, always unachievable, was perhaps on its way. Without a Hercules as king, only fire or flood could clean the Augean Stables.*

The news was both awful and exciting. Benoit relished the idea that he might be the first to tell Le Comte de Martineau. Benoit allowed the gentleman di Grandola to order another round of coffees, with eggs and bacon and hot fresh bread. As they ate and drank, they discussed the other headlines from Paris and Lisbon—headlines from newspapers that were, again, over six months old—rehashing all they could recall of the upheaval in Paris.

Benoit said, "It might be too late, but if the French government can calm things down, they should balance the budget by instigating Calonne's reforms, especially the ideas of Maupeou and Necker. Their main ideas are simple enough. France has to start to tax the aristocracy and the wealthy as well as the poor."

"Good luck with that," said Stephano di Grandola. "It might snow in hell, too."

"If only I could sell this simple idea to King Louis XVI, think of all the good it would do. I would become as famous as Joan of Arc, and there would be vast fortunes of revenue to supply hospitals, soup kitchens, and orphanages, which at the present, for their absence, create the most grotesque scenes of poverty throughout France, juxtaposed against vistas of extraordinary wealth, just like Macao and Pondicherry—in fact, every city I've lived in."

Stephano di Grandola said thoughtfully, "It is a wonder that the peasants of France haven't revolted. But indeed, who would lead them—perhaps republican members of the French Army? But the officers of the army are paid handsomely, I have been told, which partly explains the huge deficit. And besides, many of them are aristocrats."

"Fair points," said Benoit. "Even I am the nephew of a minor count who lived well on his estates—not that I ever expected any help from that side of the family."

"Nor should you, you dog. But I'm still grateful to you even if you can't solve the problems of the King of France. For that, I forgive you."

After breakfast, Benoit escorted the old gentleman back to his big house, and bid him good morning.

Chapter 36
Lương Hoàng's Dream
June 1790

Lương Hoàng and his men, deep in Nguyễn territory, marched into the village of Biên Hòa, northeast of Sài Gòn, disguised as a wealthy merchant with his palanquin bearers and bodyguards. They went straight to the Happy Valley Green Pavilion. Hoàng still had his bushy hair and eyebrows, and his sharp nose and jaw, but the black hair was flecked with gray. By the orders of Nguyễn Nhạc and Nguyễn Huệ, he was becoming his country's leading authority on brothels, whores, and sex slaves, as he continued directing a lengthy, methodical search for Jade River, the sister of the new kings, even in Nguyễn-controlled territory. Jade River was now technically a princess, but it was her terrible fate, if she still lived, to suffer the intimate attentions of caterpillars and bumblebees. Ever since that dismal trip to Nha Trang, Hoàng had personally visited as many flower houses and pleasure boats as his other duties allowed for. After the fall of the Trịnh, Huệ asked him to organize a nationwide search.

As Hoàng approached the door, followed by his armed men, he thought, *This morning we will mark another brothel off the list. Do I really want to find her?* He asked himself again, as he did during every inspection. *What will she be like? Not the sweet virgin girl I remember, but then, neither am I the young man she might remember. Will she be disappointed that I took a beautiful wife, and then another? It was hard, visiting so many brothels. Dragon's breath, the guilt and the shame I felt on my first wedding day. And these feelings were just as strong at the second wedding. I forgive myself with—how many "husbands" has she had.*

The soldiers entered the front door of the large wood and thatch compound. It was the biggest establishment on the street. A well-powdered, bejeweled madam welcomed the soldiers with a lascivious twinkle in her eye. She clapped her chubby hands and called out, "Bring hot wine for these honored guests. Can I ..."

Hoàng interrupted her and commanded, "Assemble at once all the female staff before us in this room."

"Oh, but that's most irregular, honored guest. Some of the household are busy with clients, who, though not as worthy as yourself—"

"Enough, madam." In a well-worn script, Hoàng cut her off. "I am looking for a stolen woman for the Nguyễn King. I order every female member of the household into my presence for inspection. Fear and obey or die."

A guard drew his sword and approached her menacingly, but the woman fell quickly to her knees and began to knock her forehead politely onto the floor. "I will present the ladies of the house," she croaked loudly. "Girls," she ordered her servants, "call all the ladies to this room immediately, no excuses."

Hoàng's soldiers then explored the house and the grounds, and brought every apprehended female forward at sword point, as they had so often before. Embarrassed and insulted clients remained in various states of undress and excitement in the bedrooms, too afraid to come out. A few clients yelled angrily as they walked into the room, saw the soldiers with drawn swords, and fell mute and retreated.

Jade River was working in the garden when a soldier in the black tunic of a peasant approached her, and she wondered what military power approached and threatened her privacy. *Is it my shame to be exposed today?* she thought. *I was afraid that if I didn't kill myself, this would finally happen. And yet, I have always wanted so much to be free, to see my mother and father and my brothers, and to find out what happened to Hoàng. Should I run and hide? Isn't it funny how I've grown accustomed to my life here. As miserable as it is, it's what I'm used to. It certainly isn't all bad here. I've been encouraged to study music, dance, and poetry. As the wife of a merchant, I would be encouraged to have children and sew. But I would rule my own house and servants. I like children, but I'm too old.*

Jade River bowed her head in shame. *If I must leave, what will the future bring? Will I become a prisoner again as some man's third wife?* As she picked up her basket of fruits and vegetables, some intuition warned her that she would never see her garden again. She was no longer an unblemished fifteen-year-old, but at thirty-five she was a beautiful woman, a courtesan famous throughout the district for accepting only the richest and most handsome men. She required the longest and most expensive courtship in the region. When a man displeased her, she simply refused him and took the next paying customer in the queue to start the long, profitable process again.

Carrying her basket, half full of produce, she entered the main room of the inn, spotted the officer in a green silk tunic, and suspected that the officer in the fine robe was none other than her Lương Hoàng, whom she had so often dreamed of. Could the real Hoàng ever be as good as the man in her dreams? *I've known so many men to compare him to now,* she thought with trepidation, sadness, and a little amused embarrassment.

Lương Hoàng was studying each woman who entered, one at a time. When Jade River entered the room, he did not see her. When his eye did fall on her, she was looking down. He noted that she was shy, possibly the right age, and even from that angle he could tell she was attractive. He walked over to where she stood and said, "Mistress, what makes you so unhappy?" Jade River looked up and her clear brown eyes met his.

"I am unworthy of your interest, kind sir." Her voice was fuller, as was her face, but she still looked remarkably like Nhạc, Lữ, and Huệ's beautiful sister. She had lost the blush of youth, but had gained the mystery and power of age and experience.

"You remind me of someone I knew long ago," he said, unable to still his pulse.

"You must be mistaken," she said with a smile. "How could you make fun of me?"

Hoàng looked at her intently. She saw his frustration and she felt his discomfort. She was pleasantly surprised she could cause him pain, and it gave her strength.

Hoàng said, "I am like Wei Sheng, / I am ready to hug the pillar, / Under the bridge as the river rises." He stopped—and scrutinized her eyes. He had never once, in all the years he had searched for her, considered that her shame would prevent her from acknowledging him. He realized with a new foreboding that Jade River's sense of shame might be much worse than his own.

Tears filled her brown eyes, and she answered him with his own words written to her so many years ago. "Waiting for you to meet me, / Until I drown with the high tide." Her tears flowed. Pain was a double-edged sword.

Holding her eyes, Hoàng finished his heartfelt courting poem, "I must know, Will your warmth and beauty, Shine on my worthless self?"

With the whole room watching in stunned silence, Jade River slid gracefully to her knees and raised her hands high to begin a ritual kowtow. For the first time in years, Hoàng was stupid. He did not know what to do—or how to act. He stood frozen, and awkwardly watched the three exquisitely graceful prostrations, and as he watched, he knew with trepidation that he still wanted this beautiful woman, now an experienced and skilled courtesan. He would ask her a second time to marry him—if she would forgive him for his two wives and his four children.

Hoàng gently helped her to her feet. He smiled at her. Then Hoàng slid to his knees. His lieutenant barked a command, and everyone else in the room, including the soldiers guarding the exits, quickly dropped to their knees. Hoàng then performed the kowtow three times to the Princess Jade River, with the roomful of prostitutes, customers, and soldiers following his lead and kowtowing in fear, wonder, and confusion. Jade River stood amazed as the whole room of people knocked their heads to the floor before her. This was an unusual day at the brothel! She smiled in surprise. She enjoyed watching the fat madam Camellia on her knees, knocking her head on the floor.

Hoàng stood up, not sure how to contain himself. He brought his hands together and bowed from the waist three times. Jade River did not know how to respond. Throwing protocol to the wind, Hoàng embraced his one-time beloved and betrothed.

❧   ❦

Hoàng knew that he and Jade River would need some time to get reacquainted. He escorted her to Quy Nhơn to see her mother and brothers. Jade River blessed Hoàng daily for not pushing himself on her to any degree.

She rode alternately in the luxurious palanquin, or on horseback like one of the Trưng Sisters, to a river galley, which rowed them swiftly to an armed merchant-junk. During the trip to Quy Nhơn, the capitol of the center, she and Hoàng had long talks. Jade River learned of her father's horrible ending, and for the first time accurate renditions of the great triumphs and disasters of her famous brothers, and of Lữ's untimely and unnecessary death. Jade River remarked solemnly, "Bad karma. He must, like me, have done some terrible deed in a previous existence." As Hoàng described the horror of fraternal war, she saw that he too had suffered, and he suffered again with her as he recalled the bitter feud between his two friends—her brothers—after their glorious rise to power. When young children hurt each other, they rarely forgive, but the wounds quickly heal and their differences they soon forget. When adults hurt each other, although they might forgive, they rarely forget.

Lương Hoàng swore his men to secrecy. His discovery of Jade River had created an opportunity, and he decided, with Jade River, that they would surprise her brother Nhạc and her mother, Autumn Moon. So, unannounced, they entered the Quy Nhơn Citadel. They passed sentries at every gate and doorway.

Lương Hoàng sent one of his men ahead to ask Nhạc for an audience as soon as possible. Hoàng and Jade River were ushered into Nhạc's study, where they found Nhạc working at his desk. "Greetings and salutations," said Lương Hoàng, as he and Jade River dropped to their knees and kowtowed three times to the king.

"Welcome back, Lương Hoàng. What is so urgent, my good friend?" said Nhạc, not trying to hide his low spirits. Nhạc had hardly looked at the woman. Hoàng gestured for her to speak. Jade River said clearly but with emotion, "King Nguyễn Nhạc, I am your sister, Jade River. As if returned from the dead, I have been freed from bondage by our friend Lương Hoàng."

Nhạc's eyes widened, his back straightened, and he stared in surprise at the woman on her knees. He studied the beautiful woman and slowly recognized his sister. Nhạc rose and cautiously approached Jade River. "I can't believe my eyes," he cried. He offered her his hands, and helped her to stand up. After a good, hard look up close, he embraced his long-lost little sister. "Oh, Jade River," he confessed, "I have tried to take care of the family, but I have failed." Nhạc turned to bodyguard Snake, who stood by the door staring, with his bow fallen to his side. Nhạc said gently, "Snake, fetch my mother. Have her come here without telling her why."

Nhạc was telling his sister about his victories and defeats when Autumn Moon came in with her maid. She recognized an energy and animation in her eldest son, and with curiosity she scrutinized the strange woman, who seemed oddly familiar. As Autumn Moon approached the others, her old eyes slowly brought her only daughter into focus.

Jade River smiled wide with recognition at her mother and went to her knees. Autumn Moon would have none of that. She caught her daughter in her arms, and with surprising strength, pulled her back to her feet. After twenty years, she embraced her only daughter, while both women laughed and cried together. *Blessed woman, my husband's favorite child,* Autumn Moon thought. *Could her miraculous return somehow reunite my two favorite sons?*

இ ௸

Nhạc and Autumn Moon were overjoyed to see Jade River. Briefly Nhạc forgot his troubles with Huệ, and came at least temporarily out of a long period of depression. White-haired Autumn Moon laughed and laughed, and then cried and cried. She had been certain she would never see her daughter again. Her astrologer had also indicated as much, and she decided that very same day to forego his future services and find another.

Jade River's discovery was kept a state secret for two weeks, till the second day of the fourth lunar month. This day was the anniversary of Physician Hồ Danh's death, and in honor of their esteemed Ancestor, Huệ was visiting Quy Nhơn. It was dangerous for Huệ to do so, but he brought a large force by ship for his protection. And, there was business. He came also to discuss his plan to attack China, which was in fact his ruse for preparing to attack King Nguyễn Ánh. He wanted his brother to help him eradicate the Nguyễn threat, which was growing stronger in the south. Only a unified country could offer the chance of defending itself against the expansionist ambitions of the Chinese. It would make Nhạc's kingdom as large as Huệ's.

Nhạc's armed forces were mobilized and on full alert when Huệ's navy and marines poured into the great harbor. When Huệ and several hundred troops reached the citadel, Nhạc, with an army at attention, gave his brother all the protocol usually reserved for an envoy from the Sun King of China. Nhạc even invited Huệ to inspect Nhạc's troops, which Huệ did with a relish; he already knew personally many of the commanders. Huệ could feel that there was some excitement behind Nhạc's usually stolid demeanor. He knew something was up, and he feared some vile treachery was at hand. Special invitational cards announced a banquet for the evening, and Huệ was invited into Nhạc's personal chambers with only Hoàng and Autumn Moon and a few maids in attendance. *Nhạc is definitely excited about something,* Huệ thought guardedly, *and I'm not sure that it can be good for me.*

At the banquet table, Nhạc offered Huệ a seat opposite his own. After the guests were seated and the wine was poured, Huệ stood up. "I propose a toast," Huệ said, "to our noble Ancestors, especially the spirit of our father, that he always watch over us. To harmony in filial relations, that we may in the future always act in accord, and to our dear sister or her spirit, wherever she may be."

In his excitement, Nhạc almost choked while drinking. He said, "Thank you, Huệ, for your noble sentiments." He held up his goblet, and everyone drank a second sip of wine.

Huệ was now so suspicious he only pretended to drink the rice wine, in case it was poisoned. *Why is Nhạc so excited?* Huệ looked Lương Hoàng in the eye. Hoàng

288

was smiling. That was a good sign. *There is no danger, or Hoàng is not in on the plot.*

Huệ was still worried. He did not trust his brother. *Blue Cloud warned me that it would be like this,* he thought. *Think of something else. Remember that you decided not to wear arms today or bring a food taster, in honor of your father. Remember, only life is painful. Death is a once-in-a-lifetime adventure. After death is either only the commencement of another hard life, or peace. And if life continues even after death, so be it. What could be more interesting? My first wife, Green Willow, likes to say that I'll come back as a parakeet, because I like to sing so much.* He focused his attention on Autumn Moon, who was rhapsodizing about the weather. She looked so old now, with blue veins across her head and thinning white hair.

Nhạc made a sign to Autumn Moon, who whispered to one of her maids, who left. Huệ, who was still on edge, noticed both signals and wondered if his mother would actually help to plot his murder. *Relax, I trust my mother.*

Then the maid reentered with a handsome woman who looked strangely familiar. "Welcome, King Nguyễn Huệ," said Jade River with a lovely smile and a voice he recognized, "to Quy Nhơn, the capital of the center." Huệ froze. He carefully put down his wine goblet, as if, were he to spill any liquid, the image of his long lost sister would vanish before him. With the same care he rose. Although now past thirty-seven celestial cycles, his movements were still as strong as a tiger's, and as graceful as a crane's. Huệ, always fearless in the face of the conventions, caught his sister before she dropped to her knees, and lifted her off the ground and up into his arms. Everyone was grinning now like schoolchildren who'd hidden the teacher's brush and ink stick. The wary tiger, realizing finally why his brother was so excited, roared with laughter, and hugged his sister again and again. "I can't believe my eyes!" he cried. "Is it really our sister—my Rivulet of Jade?"

ɢ҂ ҂ɢ

The next few days passed all too quickly. Jade River's reappearance allowed the two brothers to bury their differences for a while and act again as a family. Huệ took long walks with his sister in the gardens. He wanted to get to know his sister as an adult, and find out about her last twenty years of life in a flower house. Although he was too polite to ask right away, Huệ wanted to know why she hadn't been able to escape. His concubine, Blue Cloud, said, "Time will tell. Perhaps she was so ashamed of her fallen state that she hoped to never rejoin her family. Tarnished women are often rejected by their families in our country. Remember my shame when you purchased my freedom. I tried to numb myself with opium, and nearly lost my freedom again."

Autumn Moon and Lương Hoàng prayed that all the cold winds of dissension in the family would dissipate. Jade River was still blinking and smiling at all the new members of the family that she didn't know. She had new sisters-in-law, and nephews and nieces galore. She had a new title, of which she was proud in the extreme: Aunt Jade River. The children meant a great deal to her. Although they some-times aggravated her self-pity, for she had often wanted her own children, they also cheered her heart, and helped her to forget her loneliness. She met and exchanged niceties with Hoàng's two wives. The first wife, Spring Bloom, was very kind, warm, and empathetic. The second wife, Red Lotus, was obviously somewhat jeal-ous of Jade River and fearful of being nudged into the wings of neglect and obscuri-ty, or worse.

The brothel in Biên Hòa had been backward compared to Quy Nhơn society. Jade River enjoyed all the educated people, fine clothes, jewelry, and artwork around her. They were precious and beautiful new acquaintances and things, even if they couldn't give her back the dreams of her youth.

To try to cheer herself up, she liked to remind herself—*it wasn't all bad. How many women are allowed to enjoy so many different lovers, like the men so often do? Of those, at least a few were truly exceptional—I miss Từ Hải every day.* Then she would laugh, or cry, depending on her mood. She once had been incapable of such thoughts. She had lost her innocence, but gained wisdom and knowledge. She never could have learned so much about the ways of men as a cloistered and pam-pered housewife. She had learned the secrets of men's appetites and something of their hearts as well. She was now thoroughly versed in tending the former, and she had broken a number of hearts along the way.

There were one or two men from Biên Hòa whom she was deeply fond of and whom she would never forget, as well as her two husbands: Từ Hải and Thái Đình Ky. But there was a scar in her heart too that would never heal. With her experience, she had also discovered self-hatred. Sex without love, sex as a business, was not al-ways pleasant. Sometimes it was like playing a lute out of tune—or eating old rice without salt. Sometimes it was kissing a fat Chinaman with dog's breath.

ର   ଚ

Before Huệ left for the Spring Capital Phú Xuân, from where he ruled half the center and all of the north, he arranged with Nhạc for his brother to hold a day of reckoning for Jade River. Agents were sent to Biên Hóa. By torturing the fat lady of the brothel, they found the notorious Scholar Mã, the worldly pimp, and these two rogues were presented to Jade River before Nhạc and Huệ and the adults of the fam-ily for trial and sentencing. Nhạc smiled broadly and said to Jade River, "As the high king, I am the supreme court of this land under Heaven. What would you, dear-est sister, have the court do with these scoundrels that have held you for almost twenty years in captivity, profiting from their deceit and your misfortune?"

Jade River looked coldly at the two wretches, Madame Camellia and Scholar Mã, brought before her. "These two have caused me and many other women great harm. They deserve no mercy, only death. Let all their property be sold and the pro-ceeds be divided up among their slaves."

"They shall die, penniless. Take them away," Nhạc ordered. Two guards escorted the fat, blubbering Madame Camellia and Scholar Mã away, as the pimp Mã yelled, "But I paid good cash for her. You put her for sale. You should have mercy and respect for a man of small business. By the Gods, I'm a taxpayer. …"

Next they brought in Thái Đình Ky and his first wife, Miss Hoạn, and the Farmer Bạc Hạnh and his wife. Jade River said, "Thái Đình Ky, I am deeply grateful to you for your warmth and love, and for releasing me from bondage. What I owe you is beyond measure. A poet wrote of the stars Shen and Shang, 'A morning star weds not an evening star.' I would come back to you if I could. Please accept my gratitude and accept my gift of a bolt of silk and your wife and father-in-law's entire estates."

Turning to Bạc Hạnh and his wife, all the warmth left Jade River's face. "But you, deceiving miscreants, I do not forgive for your transgressions. You are fiends disguised as people. Brother Nhạc, please send the Bạcs to the executioner." Farmer and Dame Bạc were speechless.

Nhạc was not speechless. He said, "Justice will be done, take them out."

The only one left to judge was Miss Hoạn, Thái Đình Ky's first wife. Jade River turned her gaze on her. "Miss Hoạn, it was so nice of you to show up today! It is so rare to find a woman with a heart of steel. It is unfortunate that no one ever taught you gentleness or kindness."

Miss Hoạn's face turned ashen, she bowed her head and said, "I have the weakness of a small-hearted woman, and a meager soul. I am completely guilty of a raging jealousy, for which I beg your mercy. It is human to be jealous. Recall, I let you tend the shrine, and after you fled, I did not pursue you. I admired you in my secret heart as my superior. Please, I beg you for mercy! What woman really wants to share her man?"

"Aren't you articulate today," said Jade River, taken off her guard. "You know just what to say. If I strike you down, as I desire, I'll look mean and revengeful. But there is some truth in what you say, and I will accept your careful apology and note with fairness your contriteness.

"Let this dreadful woman go penniless and serve her sweet husband Thái Đình Ky as his wife, servant, and slave. Her miserable life she may keep, but only if he allows it."

Miss Hoạn, with tears running, fell prostrate before the woman she had so abused, and blessed Jade River with all her heart. Miss Hoạn marveled that so much forgiveness could exist in a person so mistreated.

ॐ   ॐ

A few days later, following the proper custom, Hoàng's first wife, Spring Bloom, dutifully but stiffly approached Autumn Moon about Hoàng's wish still to marry his once beloved and betrothed Jade River. Autumn Moon, as intermediary, took the inquiry to her daughter.

Jade River was still conflicted. In some awkward moments, freedom can seem harder than bondage. The choices are often excruciatingly difficult. She longed for an innocent past that she knew could never be recreated, and now she had a strong impulse to become a nun and follow the inspiring teachings of Buddha. *If I stay single, simply as Auntie, for once in my life I will be no one's servant. I do not really want to be a second or third wife.* Jade River's heart was full of sadness while her mind was conflicted. She informed her mother, "I will need time to think over Hoàng's gracious offer."

Jade River's appearance gave the two brothers a semblance of a reconciliation. Autumn Moon gave a large sum to the temple of Quán Thế Âm, the Goddess of Mercy, and prayed for a miracle. Nhạc agreed to a joint campaign with Huệ to stop Nguyễn Ánh's seasonal movements northward and to try to eliminate his challenge. After a second week ended, Huệ forced himself to part from his sister, and with his entire entourage and bodyguard returned to the Spring Capital.

༄ ༈

Jade River was strolling alone in her favorite palace garden when Lương Hoàng found her and exchanged greetings. After all the proper pleasantries, Lương Hoàng said, "Excuse me for speaking to you directly, but it allows us both more privacy. I might be deployed soon for war to the south. Please tell me what your thoughts and feelings are now about my proposal that you join my house?"

Jade River smiled at her old betrothed, the handsome man with two wives and four children. The only general to advise both of her brothers, the two kings. "Dear Hoàng," she said with natural warmth, "I'm not sure what I want, and what I am capable of. I believe I still love you, but I'm not so sure that I love myself. I will not give you an answer until I've worked out some of these conflicts. I will need months, not days—I will need perhaps a retreat to a nunnery to contemplate the eightfold path to peace and tranquility."

This wasn't the whole truth, but it had a gentle ring to it. In all earnestness, she had made up her mind to move into a local Buddhist nunnery for at least a trial retreat. She would explore again the secrets of the life of spiritual purity and physical abstinence, as a way to explore and perhaps deepen her new-found independence, as well as to possibly heal her damaged self-respect. Only after this withdrawal and purification would she give him a final answer. She embraced Hoàng gently, kissed him quickly on the cheek, and withdrew from the garden.

Chapter 37
La Méduse at Sea
February 1790

La Méduse was flying southwest with the end of the dry season monsoon, the cool northeasterly filling her sails. Captain Benoit Grannier was in charge of bringing *La Méduse*, and *Le Saint-Esprit* back to Gành Rái Bay (the Bay of Saint-Jacques) at the mouth of the Sài Gòn River.

They sailed in early February, 1790, from Macao and hit the coast of Đại Việt at thirteen degrees longitude off Cape Varella and the Bay of Ben Goi in just six days. They had made the entire journey of two months, two weeks, and a day, without mishap—until now.

The lookout shouted, "Below deck, sails ahead!" The officer of the watch, Lieutenant Tabarly, spoke loudly into the speaking tube that ran down to the captain's great room, "Captain, there are sails ahead of us—many sails." Benoit dropped his pen, grabbed his glass, and climbed up the stair-ladder to the main deck.

The first mate, Joachim Bohu, was looking through the ship's spyglass to the south. "Have a look-see, captain," he said grimly, offering the glass to Benoit, "and tell me if I'm crazy."

Benoit adjusted his own glass, and growing clearer and clearer were not a few, but a fleet of war junks to the south, directly in their line of travel. Hundreds of warships, beyond count, of many different sizes, made a long line before them. "Lord Almighty," said Benoit. "Our friends don't have that many junks." Within the hour he could see the red flag of the Tây Sơn flying from the foremost junks, which were tacking slowly up the coast against the dry monsoon.

Nicholas Tabarly asked gruffly, "Aren't we going to sail out to sea and around these blood-drinking heathens?"

"Let's have a closer look at our enemies," Benoit replied. "We lack any secure knowledge concerning their naval capacity against us. And besides, it's possible that they've already retaken Sài Gòn for a third time, taken all our friends prisoner, or left them all dead. Lieutenant, has the off watch finished eating?"

"Yes sir."

"Pipe the current watch to an early meal." An hour later, with the enemy now only an hour away, Benoit ordered, "Tabarly, sound the alarm and beat to quarters. All hands prepare for battle." Tabarly passed the order to the nearest midshipman, who clanged the bell through the noise of creaking timbers. Another midshipman took up the ship's drum and began to beat out rhythms. Between the bell and the drum, the racket called all hands to quarters, even though most of the men were already loitering by their battle stations. Benoit went back to his cabin, took up and wrapped on his sword belt, stuck his pistols in his breeches belt, and climbed back up to the quarterdeck.

"Take in the stuns'l's and the stuns'l booms," Benoit ordered. He turned to Nguyễn Thơ, young Cảnh's crooked-toothed cousin, and round-faced Võ Tánh—the two Vietnamese officers of rank in his company—smiled, and said, "This could get a bit messy and dangerous. You'd best look to your weapons."

Father Nicolas Desangeles, a sunburnt Jesuit priest, translated the remark. Nguyễn Thơ looked perplexed. "You don't mean to advance against the entire Tây Sơn Navy with just two ships, do you?" Again the young Jesuit rapidly translated.

"Honestly, I haven't yet decided," Benoit replied. "But I won't say yet that it's impossible." General Võ Tánh said nothing, but he carefully listened to Father Desangeles, looked Benoit in the eyes, saw that Benoit was serious and not obviously intoxicated or joking, and then went below for his bow and arrows and his famous Chinese broadsword, named Pirate Slicer. Pirate Slicer was a weighted, single-edged sword with a blade as sharp as a fillet knife. A famous Chinese swordsmith had made this sword in the ancient style, by hammering the metal flat and then folding it in two, then hammering it flat again and folding it over on itself hundreds of times.

The war junks carried assorted old cannon, archers, and only a few musketmen. Like all sailing ships, they moved cumbersomely against the wind. Benoit had never before engaged in battle with a junk, much less with two or three hundred of them. *Be careful,* he thought, *don't let your curiosity get the best of you. Just look. Since they are downwind, we have the weather gauge.*

He remembered Father Pierre's advice. "Depend on your ship. It has speed and power against their old rice transports. They'll want to fight *nắm dây thắt lưng,* 'holding onto your belt,' with ship's ram, bow and arrow, and boarding. Stay clear. Fight from over a cable length. Just within the cannon's range lies our power."

Benoit felt the strong, steady breeze against the back of his neck, and saw his plan take shape. "Mr. Bohu, signal *Le Saint-Esprit* to follow us close, a half cable length behind, and to prepare for a starboard line of battle. Prepare all guns. Pass out small arms to every man who can manage them. Captain La Fontaine, get your marines with their rifles up onto the upper mast platforms."

Large cumulus clouds scudded across the clear blue sky. It was a joyous day for sailing God's great oceans, or for an action at sea. Benoit's mind reviewed questions and doubts. He retraced his reasoning for engaging the enemy. He wanted to know just how much better his ships were than these ancient-style junks, and how well armed they were with ordnance. *We can always outrun them if it becomes clear that we must,* he thought. *Just don't let them board. Caesar, we who are prepared to die, salute you. And God Almighty, protect us.*

The mates issued each man a sword or ax and a pistol—action at last! Each deck man also received a musket, which he loaded and primed and placed in racks near his station. Just before *La Méduse* came within 18-pounder range, Benoit ordered the helmsman to turn to the east, out to sea. The ship creaked and the spars whistled and sang as the men released tackles and heaved braces, swinging the yards on all three masts into a close reach.

Võ Tánh noted Grannier's calm and doubted the power of the barbarian ship. Watching the ship slice through the swells, and seeing Grannier studying the host of enemy ships, Võ Tánh wondered, *Why is he so relaxed? How can we fight and survive against so many?*

The Buddha-faced Tây Sơn Admiral Cảnh Dong was ecstatic at the idea of an exchange with two French warships, when the French were so hopelessly outnumbered. "The Genie of the Sea has taken all the wisdom away from the barbarians," Cảnh Dong said to his number two. "Didn't the stars just last night foretell of a big change of events? Were not two shooting stars seen to penetrate the walls of a triangle formed by the three great wandering stars?"

"Aii, maybe, but I admire such bravery," replied Number Two. "Luckily, there are so few of these long-nosed barbarians." Cảnh Dong cleared his throat and spat over the leeward rail. Below the poop deck of his three-masted junk, there was a bustle of activity. The admiral squinted against the sunlight as he searched the seas for other barbarian ships, but he could find none.

"This will not be the first time a Việt fleet has sunk a Western pirate," Cảnh Dong said to his number two with glee. "When the Portuguese supplied cannons to the Nguyễn, and the Dutch supplied them to the Trịnh over one hundred years ago, a Dutch squadron attacked the Nguyễn Navy and lost. Remember, one whole vessel was captured, and all the Dutchmen sold into slavery at premium prices. What fun! After a second victory against the Dutch, Nguyễn Phước Tấn annihilated the barbarian ships of the third attack under the Dutchman Van Vliet."

"Aii, I know," said Number Two smiling and nodding. "The barbarians were so angered that they sent a bigger fleet and raided the villages on the coast. The cowards captured sailors, fishermen, and peasants and beheaded them all. That was horrible and disgraceful."

The war junks were alive with activity as they prepared for action. Their crews loaded powder and shot into the few guns they had, while they tacked toward the wind under square-rigged batten sails. Benoit was struck by how well they sailed, not withstanding rumors to the contrary. The boom spars could turn sideways approaching a fore and aft rigged sail. Many of the junks sailed twenty-five degrees closer to the wind than *La Méduse* could.

Benoit could also make out a graver menace in the Tây Sơn fleet. Bobbing in the morass of ships were many smaller boats, junks with single, lateen-rigged masts and fore and aft lugsails, oceangoing sampans and proas. The Malaysian proa was the attack vessel favored by Arab, Malaysian, and Việt pirates. They were fast rowing and sailing boats. They were long and narrow, with a sharp, pointed bow and an equally pointed stern.

Benoit thought, *Today, roughly half the Nguyễn's Western Navy takes on roughly half the Tây Sơn Navy, so the odds are about right, or at least normal.* As they tacked upwind within range, Benoit ordered the helm to head east, turning his starboard broadside toward the fleet. "Open fire at will," he commanded Bohu, who yelled the same, and the nineteen guns on the starboard side reported with a deafening roar. The balls of the French frigate and the corvette caused immediate havoc and death. These gunners had spent many years perfecting their trade against the English. The war junks returned the fire, but their balls fell short. On one junk, one of the old cannons exploded, killing the gun crew and everyone near. The explosion ignited the oil pots set up for fire-arrows, and the deck of the old ship burst into flame.

La Méduse and *Le Saint-Esprit* sailed east, puncturing enemy hulls and occasionally splintering a mast. The proas moved forward to cut off the French. At first they were dispatched with the swivel guns, which fired down directly into their open holds, puncturing holes in their bottoms.

A few of the larger junks at the very end of the Tây Sơn fleet had sailed far enough north so as to stand firmly in the way of *La Méduse*. Benoit could not sail above them. His ship was cutting through the sea at a good clip, and there was still time to come about up into the wind and tack northwest. He couldn't out-point the enemy, but he could run away from them and then back out to open sea, and eventually run around them. But Benoit now committed his ships to a riskier action. He ordered his helmsman to sail under the challenging junks, essentially into the end of the fleet, through the eastern flank of the enemy.

Now five or six proas approached *La Méduse*, and Benoit knew that once their grapples took hold, his ship was in jeopardy. "Helmsman," he called, "hard to starboard, sail due south, 180. Mr. Bohu, signal *Le Saint-Esprit* to follow us through the enemy line." All hands hove to swing the yards to just past center.

The bow of the *La Méduse* swung south, the sailors heaved on the ropes simultaneously. They followed the rhythm of the boson's short whistle blasts, to synchronize their efforts. One of the ex-merchantmen chanted along with the whistle in a barely audible tone, "One" (heave), "two" (heave), "red white" (heave), "and blue" (heave). "Find" (heave), "the pier" (heave), "for girls" (heave), "and beer" (heave).

"Belay there," yelled a mate, and a sailor secured the brace on a pin. The helmsman turned *La Méduse* off the wind to 180 degrees south, and back toward the ships her men had just fired upon before. The Tây Sơn junk captains were surprised. *La Méduse* cut between the forward ships, firing both broadsides point blank at the slow-moving junks. Benoit could hear the yelling on the enemy ships, and screams as men fell shattered or dismembered by splinters, debris and chain shot.

Many of the Tây Sơn naval officers had once served as military mandarins to the Nguyễn or the Trịnh. None of the classical collections of rites, poems, or histories so assiduously studied by these Việt naval officers had prepared them to fight these barbarian war machines. Hell was breaking loose on the junks receiving cannonballs and grapeshot. These Western Ocean war machines were apparently manufactured with help from the Nine Demon Judges of Hell.

"Hold your fire," Benoit intoned and Bohu screamed, as the ship gained speed. *La Méduse* sped past the stern of two enormous junks. Iron-tipped arrows bit into the woodwork. A few carried oiled rags on fire, and sailors doused them with buckets of water and threw them overboard. The mizzen upper tops'l caught fire from a well-placed arrow, but a sailor extinguished the flames with the water from two of the fire buckets.

Arrows and bullets began to hit *La Méduse*, and a sailor staggered, wounded with an arrow through his shoulder. The man looked dismally about him for help. An ashen-faced officer yelled at him, "Carry yourself below, on the double."

"Help him below," Benoit ordered, and the bosun's mate gave the stricken man his arm. With the arrow sticking out of his shoulder front and back, the sailor and the bosun's mate disappeared down the main hatch.

They were almost through the far edge of the enemy fleet when the large junk commanded by the fat Admiral Cảnh Dong and fronted with a huge ram forced *La Méduse* into three proas. Benoit roared, "Open fire," which Bohu screamed again. The guns roared while the swivel guns blazed. Two proas were obliterated, but the third crashed into the side of the larger ship as the grappling irons landed and pulled taut.

The boarding party threw up grapples carrying a net ladder and scrambled up the side of the larger ship, protected by a hail of arrow and musket fire from their mates below. Benoit unloaded his pistols into two coming over the rail; his sailors cut down the rest with musket fire. Men hastened to reload the hot swivels. One gunner caught an arrow full in his chest and, shrieking, fell overboard, to where sharks were already feasting on men of the proas.

A fourth proa came along the other side, and with *La Méduse* dragging both hulls, its men stormed up the ship's wall on the grapple lines and boarding nets. The first wave fell to musket fire, but with no time to reload, each man drew his sword or swung his musket or ax.

Võ Tánh met the charge first, an inspiring sight as he sidestepped the first sword as if in a dance and decapitated his foe. He turned around and caught the second man, parrying his thrust and then slicing him in two at the middle. Võ Tánh was about to be overwhelmed when a group of gunners and marines fired their muskets cutting down three more. Võ Tánh was now fighting the last three for his life. Benoit rushed in and with two parries and a thrust skewered one. He turned just in time to block the cutlass of another. He dodged the next swing and pierced the opponent in the heart. Knowing that the attack had failed, the third man tried to escape. Võ Tánh caught him just as he was jumping with a sword thrust to the back. The man froze on the gunwale, while Võ Tánh instantly withdrew his blade and swung it behind while taking a pivot step. His arms made a graceful circle and the sword flashed as he stepped forward and took off the jumping man's head. It was as graceful as a ballet, but as bloody as a slaughterhouse.

With swords and axes deckmen hacked through the grappling ropes, and both proas fell off, sinking, the men in the water screaming and flailing their hands at the sharks.

The Tây Sơn Admiral Cảnh Dong was mortified by the spectacle of these two barbarian ships smashing some of the best ships of his fleet. The events of the battle seemed unreal to him; in fact, he'd never seen such rapid destruction from so small a force. It was as if nature were turned upside down, or he was caught in a nightmare, and not a real battle. *La Méduse* pushed out of the Tây Sơn fleet. *Le Saint-Esprit*, its bow almost touching *La Méduse's* stern, squeaked through too, as a prodigious junk with a ram just missed its stern. The guns of the junk might have damaged the stern of *Le Saint-Esprit*, but this large Tây Sơn junk had no cannon. Its archers had little to shoot at, since the main deck was protected by the rear poop cabin.

Le Saint-Esprit's two stern 16-pound chasers, peering out of the captain's cabin ports, were primed and loaded with grape. The gunners shot right into the quarterdeck of the junk, crossing the stern, killing the helmsman and all the officers assembled there. *Le Saint-Esprit* was rapidly pulling away in the stiff breeze, and in two minutes, it was out of arrow shot, but was able to send two balls crashing into the lower hull of the moving junk.

Benoit watched carefully as the danger fell away to windward behind *Le Saint-Esprit*. He picked up a gun rag and cleaned the blood off his blade. *That was riskier than I expected,* he chided himself. *Our advantage is mainly their present lack of cannon.*

᠊ᡣ   ᢟ᠊

As the two ships plowed south, leaving the junks and proas bobbing in their wakes, the men cheered with exhilaration and Benoit exhaled deeply. *That was much closer than I wanted,* he thought, *though it was great for the morale of the men, who have complained over and over that there hasn't been any action. The Tây Sơn guns are few and out of date, but they fought hard with what they had. Thank God the maneuver worked.*

As the enemy fleet fell farther and farther to stern, Benoit inspected the wounded in the sick bay. There were just a few, and the crew on deck went about setting the ship right. The corpses of the enemy boarders were tossed overboard, and the decks were washed with seawater. *Le Saint-Esprit* came up close to windward and reported two wounded. *La Méduse* had lost only two men.

ॐ ॐ

When all was in order, Benoit gathered his men on the main deck for a short service for the man lost overboard and the other slain on deck. Over the body of the second man, wrapped in a canvas shroud, he intoned, "Oh Lord, our comrade Jaques Menuisser was a good topman, companion, and musician, and a great addition in so many ways to our gallant company. The Lord giveth, and the Lord taketh away. Even as the vastness of the sea receives the body of this brave man, receive, oh Lord, the soul of our comrade. May he rest in everlasting peace, and the peace of the Lord be with him, and with us all."

Father Nicolas Desangeles then intoned the last rites and a short prayer in Latin. Four men raised one end of an eight-foot plank, and the canvas sack with the body of Jaques Menuisser, weighted with ballast rock, slid off and plunged into the murky gray South China Sea.

"Thank God we only lost two," Benoit said aloud. "Men, today you worked admirably, and I'm proud of you. Bosun, a tot of tafia all around. The off watch is dismissed."

Captain Grannier toured the ship and examined the damage, which was slight. He gave personal compliments or subtle suggestions to individual sailors and officers, like the director of an opera just performed. He returned to the surgeon's sick bay and inspected and complimented the wounded again. When the Tây Sơn fleet was far behind, Benoit went to his cabin to take off his weapons. After the excitement, he sat exhausted in his sea chair, grimly satisfied but lonely. He missed the time not long ago when, as just another petty officer, he could fraternize with the other officers daily in their gun room. *This was a great day* he thought. *It makes up for years of duller days. But the gun crews were slow under fire. Several starboard guns took one minute and forty seconds between broadsides. I want them under a minute. They will need more drilling.*

After the high came the low. *With whom can I celebrate our victories?* he opined. *Father Pierre and my fellow officers. I have no woman to share my victory. Must I abandon these men and Prince Ánh, and return to France and become a shopkeeper, just to find a wife? I feel so committed here. Other officers have taken native mistresses. Maybe I should find one as well.*

As the two French warships surfed away on the windswept crests, off in the distance, falling farther and farther away, were a handful of smoking wrecks and the hundreds of ships of the Tây Sơn fleet, reaching slowly west. Admiral Cảnh Dong slumped against the rail of the poop deck of the largest junk, starring off at the silhouettes of the two barbarian water dragons. He spat to leeward and said to his Number Two, "Are these foreign devils and their murderous cannons the big change which the stars foretold?"

Chapter 38
King Nguyễn Ánh's Banquet
1790

Benoit had not expected the honor of an invitation to dine with King Nguyễn Ánh. He was surprised and quite pleased, therefore, when he and Henri Dayot were invited to accompany Father Pierre to an imperial dinner. Accompanied by twenty of the fifty Vietnamese guards assigned to protect and serve the bishop, they walked through the crowded streets of Sài Gòn. The entourage passed cake sellers and peddlers, open-stall markets, and blocks of Việt and Chinese two- and three-story houses with storefronts open to the street, till they came to the royal square, which was bounded by the citadel and by three large temples. The largest temple was dedicated to Heaven and Earth. The other two were dedicated to Buddha and Confucius. All three temples were constructed of fine brick walls, wooden rafters, and tiled roofs.

The party crossed the drawbridge of the citadel and Senior Counselor Pierre Pigneau, Bishop of Adran and Vicar Apostolic of Cochinchina, presented his invitation to the captain of the gate guard. The old captain bowed very low and said, "Welcome back, Counselor to Sài Gòn. Permit this servant to escort you to his majesty's presence. Your officers must leave all their weapons here with my men." Dayot and Grannier relinquished their swords, knives, and pistols.

Father Pierre bowed to the men of his bodyguard, instructing in Vietnamese that they should remain in the main court. His bow was carefully measured, to show Vietnamese officers that he respected his soldiers, and yet refrained from treating them as full equals. Such egalitarian behavior displayed ostentatiously would irritate and excite the mandarins, while ignoring the correct protocols of degree would also annoy them. His men bowed back respectfully.

The Frenchmen followed the captain and three of the king's guards through the gate of the second wall, into the royal compound. They traversed several gardens, passed several guarded checkpoints, and passed through a large stone doorway to the reception hall.

The gate guards bowed to the guards of the reception hall, gave them the invitation, and departed. The evening was hot, sticky, and humid, and the Frenchmen were sweating in just their linen shirts, summer breeches, and new sandals. To allow for circulation, the great doors were open. Incense burned on altars to honor the royal Ancestors, and incidentally, to help keep away the mosquitoes.

They entered the reception hall. A number of Vietnamese mandarins dressed in light silk tunics or robes were already present. From the entrance to the hall, Pierre and his men bowed to the empty throne. He introduced his officers to several of the dignitaries, including Đỗ Thanh Nhơn, Ánh's commander-in-chief.

I wish to speak with your young captain," said Đỗ Thanh Nhơn to Pierre. "Would you mind translating for us both?"

"Not at all," said Pierre.

"Captain," said Commander Đỗ Thanh Nhơn, speaking to Benoit, "the king himself told us of your valor and the fearlessness of your orders in the—how shall we call it?—the encounter with the enemy off Quy Nhơn. General Võ Tánh was quite impressed by this first test of French guns and warships against a Vietnamese navy." Pierre translated this for Benoit, who listened carefully and turned slightly red.

"Please tell the General Võ Tánh that I was very impressed by the way he handled his sword," Benoit replied. Pierre translated.

"I'm not surprised," said Đỗ Thanh Nhơn. "He is a master among men with the sword. He said that your own swordplay was most impressive."

Benoit responded, "I'm also embarrassed that he had to use his sword at all."

"You need not be. As it says in one of the classical poems, 'To follow the path of the warrior, we must always be ready and willing to test our skill against our enemies.' If you would be so kind, I would like to hear your version of the battle, and of your tactics."

"I would be pleased to oblige, if Father Pierre will oblige us and continue to translate," said Benoit. With Pierre's approval, Benoit reviewed the engagement. "We found the Tây Sơn fleet blocking our sail south. We sailed east, testing our guns against theirs, till near the end of their fleet we were out-flanked, and I chose to sail between the main body and its eastern flank—allowing my ships to use both of their broadsides at once. We had to repel some borders from a pair of determined proas, and were dispatching these borders when Võ Tánh demonstrated his skill with his sword."

A gong sounded and everyone moved to their places and sat down on their knees in four straight lines, two lines facing two lines, with the most senior officers at the head, closest to the throne. Benoit noted that it wasn't an intimate dinner.

Father Pierre the Bishop walked calmly to the top of the forming lines and knelt just below Đỗ Thanh Nhơn and across from Phúc Hợp, the controller of the Exchequer, and Đoàn Thanh, the chairman of the Board of Rites.

Benoit and Henri knelt down behind Pierre, as instructed, their knees cracking as they knelt even though they had practiced. The gong sounded again. An orchestra in a corner of the hall began to play, filling the room with the sound of the five tones. The music of lute, zither, bells, and gongs gave formality to the occasion and an added sense of foreign, far away from home, elegance. King Ánh appeared from a side door and walked smoothly to the golden throne and sat down. The assembled congregation bowed their heads to the floor three times, and then knelt rigidly upright, all eyes forward and looking slightly down. It was a crime in an official ceremony to look directly at the king; one did not look directly at the face of the dragon. Ánh wore a dark blue robe with a bright yellow dragon embroidered on the front. From his black cloth helmet sprang flames of beaten gold.

King Ánh raised his hand and the music died away in a slow decrescendo, leaving the listeners suspended in silence that would have been timeless, but for the excruciating pain in Benoit's ankles. Ánh looked magnanimously about the room. "There is a time for work and a time for play," he said gravely, and then grinned hard and wide. "Tonight, I invite you all to dine with me, as we celebrate the Late Harvest Festival, and honor with gratitude Heaven and Earth, and the Goddess of Rice."

Ánh raised his hand, a gong sounded, and the company bowed their heads again to the floor. The king rose and left the dais. Then everyone rose and slowly paraded into the reception garden to discover low tables laden with food and drink, and surrounded by rugs and pillows for the company to sit on. The orchestra launched into a dance tune enlivened with drums, percussion sticks, and bells; the sobriety broke and everyone began talking and bowing to each other in the more relaxed atmosphere. Serving maids, dressed in Malaysian underwear and covered with transparent cotton gauze, appeared with jugs of wine and hot dishes. The Frenchmen sat cross-legged at one of the tables near the king's, and conversed with a few generals who politely asked, through the interpretation of Father Pierre about the four ships that the French officers commanded, and the most recent escapade with the Tây Sơn Navy.

Wives were not in attendance, but female dancers and singers appeared and performed to rounds of applause, and then sat down among the guests. The performers and the men they sat down with were obviously not strangers. Soon the Frenchmen found themselves sitting alone together.

King Ánh, no longer wearing the official robe and headdress of state, but a purple silk five-piece tunic, came over to the Frenchmen accompanied by two modestly dressed young women and made introductions. "This is Ngô Spring Blossom and Bùi Moon Light," he said smiling, "and since they are not artists or servants, but the daughters of good friends, and they are very curious about the West, I wondered if you would let them join you?"

Father Pierre was about to suggest another solution, so that his table could discuss military strategy and logistics, when his two officers said in emphatic French that even King Ánh could understand, *"Mais oui, bien sûr, absolument oui."*

Spring Blossom, overweight by Việt and voluptuous by French standards, was full of mischief. Her ordinary face was full and round. In contrast, Moon Light had high cheekbones and a finely proportioned and delicate mouth and chin. Next to a Frenchman, she was petite and her body slender. She was dressed in a light green tunic and pants with a blue silk shawl. Although small-boned, her feminine features were discernible more in her graceful moves than through her unisex five-piece tunic.

Father Pierre tried not to frown with disappointment. He was hoping he would talk strategy with General Đỗ Thanh Nhơn, but the general was totally absorbed with one of the singing girls, and it looked as if Father Pierre would be called upon by his officers to translate endearments and entreaties all night. Benoit said, "Monseigneur Pigneau, please ask Mademoiselle Moon Light why she wears a crucifix?" To their surprise, Moon Light answered in broken French. "Sir, I can explain myself. I am a student of Father Édouard Villeseint, and I experienced Holy Sacrament of Baptism two years in past."

"And how old were you then?" Benoit asked, with some curiosity.

"I was sixteen," she said, and met his gaze.

Father Pierre knew when he was being upstaged. He enjoyed his meal, favoring the fried pork dumplings and batter-dipped chicken, gruffly excused himself and tried to find one of the more serious-minded Việt generals to talk about military and security problems. But none seemed disposed to business that evening, so he took his leave of his two captains and went home to continue his translations of Confucius. He was in the middle of writing another book.

Bùi Moon Light smiled at Benoit and he smiled back. She noticed how Benoit's eyes twinkled, and thought his red-brown hair and green eyes appeared exceedingly odd. His face was not attractive to her; he wasn't Vietnamese. She remembered how she nearly screamed at the king, "But I don't want to marry an odorous, unwashed, barbarian from the Western Ocean tribes. I don't care if he is a Christian."

"Listen to me," King Nguyễn Ánh had snapped. "Your sister is the wife of a traitor and now they are both my sworn enemies. Your parents are completely disgraced. In fact, your whole clan is guilty by association and under suspicion. Do you want me to seize your disgraced father's land and property?"

"But when my parents married my sister to Trần Quang Diệu, he was still your general. My father didn't know that Diệu would join the Tây Sơn against the house of Nguyễn, any more than you did."

"But Diệu did turn traitor, and so did your sister," Ánh said flatly. "And your father is lucky to still have his head, much less his rice fields, after showing such poor judgment and giving his talented daughter to a traitor. She was the best elephant trainer in my entire army. To apologize for his immense stupidity, he gave you to me." Ánh took a breath and carefully softened his voice into a more mellifluous tone. "Now won't you try? We would appreciate your service." He asked graciously, hoping he wouldn't have to pretend to lose his temper and threaten to have her put in thumbscrews, or worse.

Moon Light felt trapped. The king's sudden gentleness was giving her great face, rather than a reason to rebel and inflict punishments on herself and her father. Hurting her father would be a grave sin, which the king was counting on to bring her around. "This slave will do as you command," she said, tears running from her eyes. "But I'm Việt," she said, falling apart, "and I don't want to worship the ancestral tablets of an uncivilized barbarian." Moon Light sat down and tried to control her flooding emotions. She couldn't look calm with tears running down her cheek.

"Don't worry about that," Ánh said with a cruel smile. "These barbarians don't have ancestral tablets."

"No ancestral tablets?" She looked up horrified. "How do they keep the dead from harming the living?"

"My daughter," Ánh said paternally, "you, not I, are the avowed Christian. You should be able to answer such a simple question better than I." It was like a tub of cold water poured on her head.

Suddenly Moon Light understood something she'd heard Father Villeseint say over and over: "You do not need protection from your ancestors. Tragically, they are all locked away in the dungeons of Hell. What you need is salvation. To be saved from the evils and slavery of sin, you need redemption through the sacrifice of God's only son, to be freed from the bondage of damnation. Absolution, the forgiveness of all sin, will be yours, God be praised, when you touch and accept Jesus in your heart and take the sacraments in the Church of Christ."

I didn't realize until right now, she thought, *how completely foreign this barbarian religion is. No wonder the priests will not accept the cult of ancestors if they don't have any ancestral tablets. But what then are their tombstones for? Of course, those are their tablets. They are just outdoors. They pray to their dead all the time in their own way. They are odd, putting their tablets out in the rain, but it is convenient, to double as grave markers. ... Backward barbarians, you should be able to worship God, as one, as three, or as myriad, and of course you appease the dead in order to protect the living. They say, but then forget, that God is beyond all understanding.*

All these thoughts ran through her mind. Moon Light could now see, under the moonlight, the torches, and the candles, that Benoit was certainly uncivilized and as she expected, odorous, but he was no ape. He had a powerful physique and an angular, though Western face. His eyes were wide and demon green beneath his thick shock of red-brown hair. He was not of a crude or sickly stock. She perceived a refined masculinity. She did not know that in his Norman blood ran the spirits of Norse pirate captains and German warrior chiefs, mixed with the musicality and grace and the delicate features of the Latin race. Although Moon Light could only sense some of this, she did know that he had a strong odor. *He must learn to bathe,* she thought practically.

"I've wanted to visit your country since my cousin Father Antoine first wrote about his missionary work here," Benoit was saying. Remembering his benevolent cousin, he realized that Antoine had visited Sài Gòn several times. "Did you ever meet Father Antoine Grannier?"

"No," she shook her head. "You are first Frenchman I really talk to besides Father Villeseint." Now she blushed, noticeably, and laughed. "He old, over fifty, and he take himself and his one God very serious." They both laughed, somewhat sacrilegiously, so Benoit crossed himself and then she did the same.

"You must be generous with the holy fathers," Benoit said. "Most of them make enormous sacrifices in order to pursue their good works. And, after all, they are only men."

Moon Light laughed. She liked this self-deprecating comment, and realized that there were in fact redeeming qualities about this sweat-smelling and oversized barbarian. She said, "Serious, I owe the great debt of gratitude to Father Villeseint. He teach me and many others about love of Christ, and equality of women and even children all before Jesus God. When I hear Christian men expected have just one wife, I am ecstatic very and pray for Christian husband." *A Vietnamese Christian,* she thought bitterly, as she looked down at Benoit's hands and thought how big and rough and hairy, like a giant's, they looked. "The Lord's Ten Commandments are sign from Heaven. He wisely repeat Confucius in most laws, with one big exception. I still no understand why he order, Thou shalt have no other Gods but me. Just like a man to be so selfish!"

They both laughed again. There was an edge to her humor. Benoit asked, "What did Confucius say on this matter?"

"The Great Master, he say, Thou shalt always honor and pay homage to emperor and to father and mother, for they are to man as God is to king."

"Which do you believe, Confucius or Jesus?" Benoit asked.

"They are both right," she said smiling. "You need both, one to balance the other, like the two baskets of shoulder pole." Her eyes challenged Benoit, and he caught his breath.

"That sounds so sensible, something Montesquieu might have written." *Wait,* he thought, *what in God's name is going on here? Am I helping to convert the heathen, or is the heathen converting me? I must concentrate more.* Benoit continued carefully, "When they reach opposite conclusions, they can't both be right. But perhaps what you believe depends on how you are brought up. I believe in the one true faith," he added solemnly. "I also love my parents, and I owe them for life itself, but they, like me, are sinners, and it was God, in the incarnation of his son Jesus, who died so that we might all make amends for our sins and gain eternal life."

"We like incarnation here too," said Moon Light smiling. "You have a wonderful God. He is generous and loving, and perfect Confucian the way he die so that world will worship his father." They laughed again, and she poured them both more wine from a jar on the table. "But like all men, he had shortcomings, very bad."

"What do you mean?"

Bùi Moon Light looked mischievous. "Jesus God really not is always so nice and loving. He love peoples, and animals, but of other Gods he very jealous, just like mens and womens. He want my peoples to abandon all wonderful Gods and spirits who inhabit and protect country. The commandment, Thou shalt have no other God but me, make Christian God one of biggest murderers of all time. He wars against the *Ma*—against all *Ma* of the waters, the trees, and mountains—and have us abandon even our own trilogy, the Heaven, the Earth, and the Dragon."

"And what are the *Ma*?"

"The *Ma* are the spirits; they are everywhere," she said smiling at his barbarian ignorance. "Every creature and object has its own spirit. Father Villeseint calls them, what is the word ... jenny ... ?"

"Genie?"

"Yes—jee-nee. Our priests can communicate with the Genies and they a powerful hand have in deciding our fortunes."

"And the Dragon?"

"Oh, there are many Dragons, mostly invisible, but they give people courage and imagination. The Great Dragon appear in Christian faith, only Father Villeseint call it Holy Ghost."

"Isn't that blasphemy?" blurted Benoit.

Moon Light's face frowned and she looked down. There followed an embarrassing silence.

"I'm sorry," Benoit said. "Tell me more about the Great Dragon."

Moon Light's anger was completely concealed behind her disciplined mask of calm. "Father Villeseint can never stop talking about Holy Ghost, the spirit of God, and he can never show it to you. It is spirit and imagination that can never be fully understood or described. It is really Great Dragon. It sounds same as Great Dragon."

Benoit was at a loss for words. As far as he was concerned, her description of the Great Dragon was an excellent description, even if a pagan one, of the Holy Ghost, which at any rate, he had never seen, and wasn't sure how to describe either. One priest called it Heaven's breath.

The evening wore on for Moon Light, but sped by for Benoit, till guests began to leave. Henri Dayot, who was talking in French and sign language to Ngô Spring Blossom, looked up and said, "If we don't get back soon, we will be the last to leave this party."

Before parting, Moon Light asked Benoit to visit her church on Sunday. Benoit rejoiced silently. He accepted with open enthusiasm.

Surrounded and led by their bodyguards, the two men teetered home, a little tipsy—but walking on the clouds.

As Benoit walked, he could think of nothing else but Moon Light. His mind kept reviewing her looks, her voice, her movements, her expressions, and her arguments. Returning to the river pier, the French bargemen stood up from their perches and saluted their captains. Benoit touched his forehead in respect. Lost in his own thoughts, the sailors rowed him out to *La Méduse,* anchored in the river. Benoit inspected the watch of six guards and retired to his quarters. After entering the captain's great cabin, he quickly undressed and crept into his alcove. His mind raced through the pictures of the evening, and always on the center of his stage was this mesmerizing woman Bùi Moon Light.

That night Benoit dreamed that he courted Moon Light at a ball in Paris, but she turned her attentions away from him. She danced continually with an older gentleman, who wore jewels and an expensive frock coat with an excessively lacy shirt. The old man had a devilish glint in his eye and a commanding presence. Upon inquiring, he discovered that the gentleman in question was none other than Voltaire himself, risen from the dead.

Chapter 39
Nguyễn Nhạc, Quy Nhơn
1790

Emperor Nguyễn Nhạc was arduously practicing his calligraphy. His desire was to become a worthy poet, like Li Po or Chu Văn An. His goal was to secretly take and try to pass even the lowest exam of his own mandarinate. He had decided to try and become a scholar, a man of letters, but since the effort took so much time and attention, it seemed an impossible task. He had already amassed a great fortune. Now, if only victory could be won or bought, he could settle down in retirement to a life of poetic and domestic pleasures—pleasures such as Perfume Shrine (Hương Miếu), one of his concubines.

He sat at his writing table, enjoying hot tea while listening to the rain. He had so enjoyed making love to Perfume Shrine. Now that he was bathed and refreshed, it was time for him to attempt another poem. He took a small ceramic pitcher and poured some water onto his gray ink stone. The ink stick had a pine tree articulated on one side, and on the other, three Chinese characters meaning: bold, swift, and strong. These characters were painted again in gold tempera on the top surface, with the brushmaker's red chop, or signature stamp, just underneath them.

Nhạc rubbed the stick into the wet stone, moving his wrist in circles, till the water turned a heavy jet. He placed the stick on the ink stone cover, to keep his table clean, and took up a calligraphy brush from a stand of brushes in a purple and crimson vase.

Now if the Gods are kind, he thought, *I will immortalize my splendid morning with Perfume Shrine, bless her writhing and cries of bliss, and capture the abandonment of our love with the strictest discipline of the highest art of civilized men, that of ink and brush.*

He breathed deeply, regulated his breathing, and searched the green and blue-gray vista out his studio window. His maid had slid open the oilpaper screens to reveal the view in Quy Nhơn of hills and the Cái River Valley to the north. On the top of a distant hill stood an ancient Cham tower, a phallic symbol and sentinel of ancient red brick protecting the valley and its history.

To the disgrace of my Ancestors, he thought, *why am I such a poet on the rattan bed? I can manage all the verse forms, the complex meters and every brushstroke. I can master the short cut off verse, and the long unlimited old style. Why then, when it comes to using these techniques on words instead of women, do I fall apart?* He gazed at the mist and rain, and then pulled a scroll out of the bamboo rack by the table. Working slowly around his long fingernails in their silver cases, he pulled apart the bow and untied the ribbon. He reread his favorite scroll, in the hand of the finest calligrapher of his court, of his favorite poems.

He read again the words of Lê Quát from the reign of King Trần Minh Tông, over 400 years old:

You'll ride your horse upon the long post road,
as I rejoin my mountain by the sea.
You, envoy from the South—I, nature's friend:
fame will be your reward, and leisure mine.

He read another favorite, *Love of Sleep*, an anonymous one perhaps as old, which began:

What do I love? I only love sleep,
Because sleep rests the body, calms the soul.
Inside the darkened net, new values rise.
Upon the rattan bed, old memories stir.
Porch with plum blossoms, garden with bamboos—
A hermit's joys, delights of woods and springs.
The wicker pillow props me at the back.
The jar of rosy liquor faces me.
Both gently carry me through the night....
By my north window I sing out wild songs.
In my west cottage I enjoy spring dreams.
    The poem ended,
At times I wander into Drunkenland—
Cushion of grass, screen of flowers, bed of earth:
I'm T'ao Yuan-ming beneath a setting moon
Still lighting half blind.
Or I'm that pillow-ridden Chou Lien-ch'i
Who heard the cuckoo cry in sleep.
Let them call me by any name they choose—
a slugabed, a loafer, or a God?

He held his brush distinctly vertical, and began to write. He let the words flow, imprecise but free, in easy brushstrokes:

Some men are great warriors,
others make laws, issue decrees.
While I witness the glory of the sun,
The power of the wind and rain.
The nape of your neck has the feel of silk,
and your breast the texture of jade. Am I dreaming by the river?
Across my window, the red horse runs by the stars of Heaven.
My Ancestors will bless us if you bear a son.

Nguyễn Nhạc frowned, as he noticed that there were many flaws in his attempt at a *lü-shih*, or regulated poem. This eight-line sonnet form of the Tang Dynasty had many rules—too many rules for his ability. He shook his head, thinking, *It's hopeless, this verse looks more like an old style poem, since none of the alternating lines rhyme. Each line has a different number of characters! As an old style, it's not so bad.*

A fly landed on his desk. He wished it away with his mind. When that didn't work, he caught it with his right hand, shook it in his hollow fist, threw it on the table, and then crushed it under his palm.

A gong sounded, and a eunuch entered the emperor's calligraphy studio. "Your highness, I salute you and wish you well. General Võ Văn Nhậm has come to see you and awaits your pleasure."

Nhạc frowned and looked once more at his sorry work. He would have to start over, maybe after bedding another member of his harem, in order to achieve the proper level of inner peace, poetic insight, and expostulation.

"Fine," said Nhạc, frowning, "send him right in." Nhạc carefully put his unfinished erotic poem away, and pulled out some long unread military reports, which he began to study for effect. There were lists of ships, stores, and men lost in the naval battle with only two barbarian warships! *Our best junks are no match against these warships from the West,* he thought morosely, *so we will try to not fight them, and the barbarians will eventually all return to their own lands.*

"This slave salutes you," said Võ Văn Nhậm, the frog-faced general with the large eyes and lips.

Võ Văn Nhậm kowtowed once on his knees, and then, with the permission of his king, sat cross-legged on the floor.

Nhạc was in a low humor. "There is so much paperwork," he said impatiently. "What is your business?"

"Your highness," said Võ Nhậm, and he chuckled, "as usual my business is your business. I have come to report on the culinary politics of the Spring Capital."

"Go on," said Nhạc, who was now listening attentively.

"One of your agents has managed to financially ensnare and corrupt one of the assistant cooks in the cadet's kitchen. In order now to avoid exposure and ruin, this cook has agreed to place any spice we should supply him with into either the cadet's food or drink. We agreed to 285 silver taels (500 ounces) as the price, and relocation and re-employment if necessary, if he survives the act. If he is killed or incarcerated, to pay his family."

"Excellent," said Nhạc. "Võ Nhậm, you bring good news. You have done well." Võ Nhậm gave an enormous smile; he was obviously pleased with himself.

Nhạc then changed the subject. "These two barbarian warships have just sunk six of our ships. What do you think we should do to rid ourselves of this threat?"

Võ Văn Nhậm was expecting this question. "There is no quick and easy solution to these barbarian ships. We can try to burn them at their anchorages at night, but they will be well protected. Perhaps we should discuss an alliance with one of their enemies. The French have many enemies, especially the English or the British, whatever they're called, who control much of India, and who keep sending trade delegations. The Portuguese are in Macao, the Dutch are in the southern islands of Indonesia, and the Spanish are in the Philippines. If Nguyễn Ánh can hire a French Navy, perhaps, we can hire our own long-noses to fight them! The English are of a splinter sect of Christians, and are their natural and traditional enemies."

"Perhaps you are right," said Nhạc gravely. "It will be difficult, but why can't we fight barbarians with other barbarians? According to my Spanish priest, the English might be too strong, and the Portuguese might be too weak, so we should start our discussions with the Spanish and the Dutch.

"Meanwhile, Huệ is the most immediate threat. All we have to do is decide on what ingredient we wish to use and in which food or beverage to use it."

"Why don't you go find my physician and bring him here. I wish to question him myself. No, I'll go with you. The walk will do me good, and I am done with calligraphy for the day."

Chapter 40
A Sunday in March
1790

Benoit arrived with four blue-shirted soldiers, members of his new bodyguard, at the Church of the Virgin Mary fifteen minutes early. The church was a modest Vietnamese temple made of wooden beams, lathe boards, and thatch. Most Viêts could not afford large houses made of the brick and mortar used in the wealthier temples and mansions. Visitors from the northern latitudes complained constantly about the humidity and the heat, while failing to observe that straw houses with dirt floors were a little less hot and damp than the brick and mortar constructions of wealthy northerners from China, because they often had better ventilation. Although Father Édouard Villeseint wanted the apparent luxury of a Chinese-style building for his church, it was a benefit that he couldn't afford one.

Benoit entered the straw-smelling lodge, crossed himself, and examined the room and the altar. A Vietnamese acolyte was setting out utensils for communion, while another was lighting oil lamps and candles. The main room was filled with benches, and light and air came in through the many sliding doors facing the street, which were open. Although most Viêt houses had no Western style windows, this church had windows on both the right and left walls, which were covered with waxed rice paper. They were dyed with light shades of blue, green, and red so as to soften the direct light when closed, and were highly suggestive, in a local fashion, of the simple stained glass windows one might find in a small parish church in the rustic countryside of France. Behind the sacraments table on the back wall stood a large wooden cross with a cut and scratched but serene-faced Jesus figure nailed to it.

Benoit walked out and strolled about the busy neighborhood with his guards to pass the time. When he came back, the benches were full of acolytes and congregants. Bùi Moon Light and a few other ladies and children sat to one side near the back, and Benoit sat across from them with the Viêt men.

Father Édouard Villeseint was a soft-spoken man who missed little around him. The prayers, readings, and communion he offered in Latin, and the sermon in Vietnamese. Because of that, Pierre missed the meaning of the sermon entirely. The father interrupted his introduction once, to repeat a welcome of all newcomers in French. He added, "There will, as usual, be a sermon in French at the five o'clock service, repeating the sermon this morning, which addressed forgiving one's enemies and one's oppressors, as did our Lord Jesus Christ."

A common antirevolutionary message, Benoit thought, *or is it? It is antirevolutionary if it is used to make peasants turn the other cheek to an abusive landlord. But it could be a liberating message, if one forgives in order to clear the mind, and then punishes, in order to gain freedom. A good soldier kills an opponent with-out hate, for a greater good—or maybe it's just a paying job.*

Benoit pondered the gulf that the Vietnamese language and culture presented, as he heard the strange singsong sounds of the father's voice and watched all the almond-skinned and almond-eyed people listening intently. He caught Moon Light looking at him and he smiled. She inclined her head to him slightly and then did not look that way again. *She has,* he thought, *the beauty of one of those paintings of the Huron or the Iroquois Indian princesses of the Saint Lawrence that I saw in a trav-elling exhibit from Paris.*

During the service, Father Villeseint led several short Gregorian chants in Lat-in, which many of the congregation knew and helped to sing. As they sang, Father Villeseint accompanied them on a violin, with which he was adequately proficient. He played the melody in double stops, creating a chordal drone in imitation of an organ or bagpipes.

A group of acolytes played the melody of a lovely traditional Việt love song on moon lutes and zithers while an offering plate was passed through the crowd and collected a bizarre variety of small coins, flowers, homemade trinkets, and several strings of cash and silver coins from the more well-to-do.

Benoit was surprised by how much he enjoyed the Việt folk music. *Some of it sounds like a slow Celtic air,* he decided. *What a marvelous coincidence.*

After the final prayer, Father Villeseint and his acolytes paraded out of the church in their white and red silk tunics and robes while the musicians plucked or bowed a lively Việt tune on their instruments.

Father Édouard Villeseint stood outside by the door of his thatched church bowing and shaking everyone's hand, conversing easily in Vietnamese. He was an-imated with a genuine energy and warmth, an attractive combination of outward-looking excitement and inward-looking grace and love of humanity. His white hair and beard framed a long thin face and tea-stained teeth. His bright eyes and gentle movements infused his actions with a sense of the holy.

Bùi Moon Light bowed to Father Villeseint and presented Benoit to him. "Holy Father, this is Captain Benoit Grannier, remember I tell you of him?" she said.

"Welcome to our little church, captain. The sight of French naval uniforms is a most comforting one, believe me," the old man said carefully while taking in and scrutinizing the new Frenchman with a penetrating look.

"Thank you, it is a pleasure to be here," Benoit said, smiling cheerfully. "That was a lovely service, Holy Father, though I didn't understand most of it. You do set quite an example here, doing the Lord's good work in this heat and humidity with your small Christian community, surrounded by idol worshippers and tropical jungle."

"So you noticed the humidity," Villeseint replied, softening a little. "You do get used to it after a while."

Benoit wondered if the father had as much power over his congregation as the priests at home had, and he hoped not. He wondered if he would roast in hell for failing to expurgate his critical views of the clergy. He said, "I would like to invite Mademoiselle Bùi to a small luncheon, and I rather hoped that you would care to join us."

Villeseint looked at Benoit with steel-gray eyes, as a hunter searches the jungle for danger, or a father searches a daughter's suitor for more information about him, in case he be a crook or man of casual morals. "That's terribly kind of you," Villeseint said politely, "but an old woman of my parish is dying and I must leave with her husband shortly for their hamlet. Why don't you try and drop by for the French service?"

Benoit made excuses about work, and after bowing goodbye, walked down the busy Sài Gòn street with Moon Light and her matronly servant woman, Papaya, looking at the variety of sights of this poorer part of the city and discussing where to eat. Two of his bodyguards walked before them, and two behind. Three-story buildings were lined on the ground floor with small shops, whose shutters opened onto the street. Tradesmen sat in their narrow stalls or right in the street, hunched over their tools, while others sat on the street patiently hoping a buyer would examine and purchase some of their meager wares. Many an old vendor had just a small grass mat and only a single item to sell. An old man greeted them energetically, and invited them to try his rice cakes wrapped in banana leaves. As they passed him he begged, "And cold tea, also cold tea!"

Moon Light and Papaya found a respectable looking noodle shop for Benoit and entered. The smiling proprietor was obsequiously friendly. As requested, he ushered them into one of the private rooms in the back of his little shop. Moon Light ordered tea, dumplings, soup, and the special of the day, braised fish and rice with *nước mắm pha*, or hot and sour fermented fish sauce. The waiter left and they sat in silence. The maid Papaya took a table next to theirs as chaperone.

Benoit said a short grace. Then his eyes met Moon Light's. He had no idea what she was thinking. "What did you think of the sermon?" Benoit asked.

"I hear this one before. Jesus sacrifice himself to give people salvation and endless life after death, very good story," Moon Light said somewhat distractedly. She had been thinking, *I wonder if my good reputation is now ruined since I have been seen in public with a barbarian. Maybe I should kill myself and thus restore all honor, or run to my brother-in-law and join the Tây Sơn. I could help destroy Nguyễn Ánh; that would give me some satisfaction.*

Benoit could tell that she was unhappy, but hadn't a clue as to why. *So much for the notion in so many songs that the natives are always happy,* he thought, somewhat amused at himself while noting her hostility with concern. "How did you meet Father Villeseint and come to embrace Christianity?"

"Oh Heaven, where will I to begin?" Moon Light said laughing, and she let her anxieties all fly to Java. She was one of the most beautiful women Benoit had ever laid eyes on. Her face was a portrait of balance and proportion, with her high cheekbones and forehead over a small mouth and a slender neck. She was, in fact, so beautiful that she scared some men. Her beauty gave her a power over them that men found disturbing.

"My Ancestors serve the Lê Emperor and then Nguyễn Kings. Only recently our clan fall out of favor, when my brother-in-law Trần Quang Diệu run off to serve the Tây Sơn rebels—aii, big troublemaker. He tell me before he leave that he sincerely believe that Tây Sơn will end all traditional corruptions, and that they will win anyway. Life much harder for my clan is since his defection and also defection my sister. What could she do, defy her husband?"

"What caused your brother-in-law to do such a thing? Was it the corruption?"

"There are reasons many. Maybe he follow his astrologer's advice urgent about horoscope. After King Ánh recapture Sài Gòn, the Tây Sơn attack Nguyễn Ánh eight years ago. Tây Sơn defeat Nguyễn Ánh Armies, very bad. Nguyễn Ánh order general retreat, but against advice of my outspoken brother-in-law Trần Quang Diệu. This become big embarrassment to Diệu, and also, I believe he very tempted by invitation from spies to join Tây Sơn, they were winning side. As Father Villeseint say, old barbarian wisdom, opportunism come not often back again."

"Opportunity rarely comes back again," Benoit corrected her.

"Opportunity rarely comes back again—oh please excuse my terrible French," she said.

"You speak French beautifully," said Benoit in earnest. "How did it come about that you found the father and took up his language and religion?"

There was a long pause while Moon Light arranged her thoughts.

"Like yin and yang, my father is Confucianist, my mother is Taoist, and they could never agree about anything religious other than this: One should practice always toleration and moderation. These main teaching come from both ancient philosophies, and it turn out also important main teachings of Christians. Christians are also like Buddhists, very sincere, almost fanatical."

"Which did you prefer, Confucianism or Taoism?"

"Why have preference when both so useful, but for different things. Confucius says, 'He who concentrate upon task and forget about reward may be called man at his best.' This is a lovely philosophy for civilized people. Confucius also say, 'Put loyalty and truthfulness first. Have no friends inferior to yourself.'"

Benoit asked, "What does that mean to you?"

"I agree with Lao Tzu, who said Confucius one bigshot, pompous, yes-man and snob," and they both laughed.

"Lao Tzu thought Confucius was a sycophant!" Benoit interjected.

"Sycophant," Bùi Moon Light repeated the new word. She continued, "Lao Tzu said, 'It is way of Heaven to show no favoritism. Way of Heaven is forever on the side of good man.' Confucius big reformer, Lao Tzu was not. He believed in the Tao, the natural way. Mother insisted he was revolutionary, but my uncle said he always support emperor. Lao Tzu said, 'There is nothing softer and weaker than water, and yet there is nothing better for attacking hard and strong things.' He liked *wu wei*, inaction, to solve all problems and always be harmonious."

"Inaction doesn't make any sense to me," Benoit suggested cautiously, while Moon Light took a bite of lunch. Moon Light finished chewing and responded, "Lao Tzu said to follow Tao, the natural way, rather than artificial, the forced or contrived way. *Wu wei*, inaction, therefore means don't take unnatural moves, only moves natural."

"If I understand it then, it's the same rule that good sailors discover," Benoit said in a flash of understanding. "We gauge the wind and the water, and chart our course within the realm of the possible, toward the wind perhaps, but never into it."

"That's good," she said. "I would like to go sail on a barbarian sailing dragon."

"I wouldn't be surprised if that could be arranged."

"Lao Tzu said support all things in their natural state."

Benoit could not prevent himself from making a face.

"What's wrong with that, why do you make a face?" She asked, "Do you see problems?"

"Well, you have to determine what is the natural state. The natural state, my teacher Father Sebastian always said, was change, and hopefully, progress. But part of nature is that man is never certain or constant. Even that Jesus is the son of God requires an act of faith, since he was born and died for our sins so many years before and we cannot see him. Does Lao Tzu tell you what the natural state is in various situations? What should you do when another man tries to kill you?"

"Oh yes, he explains. He is a most famous sage and poet." Moon Light took a book out of her woven shoulder bag. "I read to you some of his poem which I translate into French for Father Villeseint. This is from his greatest book, *Tao Te Ching*." Moon Light leafed through her book for a favorite poem, while Benoit watched the concentration in her face and drank in her beauty. She found one of the pages she wanted back at the beginning and looked up at him shyly. "These are not very good translations, but Father Villeseint make many correction." She cleared her throat and began: "Book One, Parts Two:

The whole world recognizes the beautiful as the beautiful,
    yet this is only the ugly;

the whole world recognizes the good as the good, yet this is only the bad.

Thus Something and Nothing produce each other;

The difficult and the easy complement each other;

The long and the short offset each other;

Note and sound harmonize with each other;

Before and after follow each other.

Therefore the sage keeps to the deed that consists in taking no action

and practices the teaching that uses no words.

Myriad creatures rise from it yet it claims no authority;

It gives them life yet claims no possession;

It benefits them yet exacts no gratitude;

It accomplishes its tasks yet lays claim to no merit.

It is because it lays claim to no merit

That its merit never deserts it."

"That is profound," Benoit said. "I'm not sure what it all means. And Papaya has fallen asleep. What does this writing mean to you?"

Moon Light looked at her elder maid, who was quietly sleeping with her head against the wall. She smiled and then chuckled. "Oh, I don't know. Much of life is unexpected, upside down. The Tao is the path. It is the truth, which is beyond understanding, like God."

"You make it sound like our Christian faith," said Benoit.

"Some, yes. But here, this part not so like Christian faith," replied Moon Light, and she read:

"Book One, Part Three:

Not to honor men of worth will keep the people from contention;

not to value goods which are hard to come by will keep them from theft;

not to display what is desirable will keep them from being unsettled of mind.

Therefore in governing the people, the sage empties their minds but fills their bellies, weakens their wills but strengthens their bones.

He always keeps them innocent of knowledge and free from desire,

and ensures that the clever never dare to act.

Do that which consists in taking no action, and order will prevail."

"My goodness," responded Benoit, "Lao Tzu was also a reactionary in this piece—an ultraconservative. 'The sage empties their minds but fills their bellies.' He's no revolutionary there. My God, he is another Hobbes."

"Excuse me, who?"

"Thomas Hobbes, an English Protestant who wrote a book called *The Leviathan*. He and Lao Tzu would have seen eye to eye. Hobbes wrote that men have no capacity for self-government, and that they needed a king of unlimited power in order to maintain order. He is famous for saying that life in the state of nature 'is solitary, poor, nasty, brutish, and short.' So like Lao Tzu, he felt that nature demanded an absolute monarchy."

"Excuse me, but it was Confucius who support idea of emperor. Lao Tzu, or his disciples, often support rebellion. When did Hobbes write this book?"

"Oh, I'm not sure, I think around 1650, when the English Protestants executed King Charles I."

"Are we not in the year of 1790 after Jesus, *Anno Domini?*

"Yes, *Anno Domini* 1790."

"But 1650 is less than 150 years ago."

"So?"

"Oh nothing, only *Tao Te Ching* is older much. Chinese record show that Lao Tzu served in Eastern Chou Dynasty maybe 500 years before birth of Lord Jesus." Moon Light laughed, showing her still white teeth. "Lao Tzu once met Confucius when Great Sage was still a young man, and Lao Tzu disliked him immensely. Lao Tzu was historian in charge of archives of Chou, Confucius ask him to instruct him in rites. Lao Tzu wrote later he think Confucius big fool and pompous, a big display of arrogance, ambition, and obsequious manners."

"Do you think that there are any shortcomings in the wisdom of this old man? I find this writing hard to follow. It seems incomprehensible, sometimes contradictory, and often cynical."

Somewhat offended, Bùi Moon Light said coldly, "Tao is still Tao. Truth, spirit, mystery, and magic are all mixed up. This is great strength of Tao. On other hand, the Taoist orders are no longer simple or small. Politics now important very. Adepts many practice magic, sometimes evil magic, sell potions, charge big fees for explaining portents and making protections from all normal household demons and local Genie."

"What sort of evil magic?"

"I tell you a true story. Once in city of Spring Capital a friend my father's, he has four wives. The fourth wife get jealous very when merchant spend any time with his other wives. Second Wife produce a son, and suddenly she become favorite. Well, Fourth Wife is jealous very. She seek out a Taoist magician with evil practices and purchase from him a number of spells. He make her two dolls, one of little boy, which he tells her to pound nails into and keep under her bed. The other was of man, and he tell she to paint his eyes red and drive nail through his feet."

"It sounds very similar to stories of Voodoo in Senegal." Benoit said.

"What?"

"Like a country I lived in in Africa—please go on."

"Soon little boy become sick, catch the fevers and die. The merchant is blind to Fourth Wife's intrigues, and couldn't leave her company anyhow. He stop paying attention to Second Wife, and she, knowing of hatred of Fourth Wife, grow very depressed and then lose her appetite, grow weak and die."

"How did anyone find out about the dolls, or the Taoist necromancer?"

"One of my mother's maids has a sister who work as a maid for Fourth Wife. This sister feel terrible, but what could anyone do?"

"Could your father have sent the maid to the magistrate?"

"Maybe, but merchant is so rich that he has mandarin on payment schedule."

"Sadly, the corruption of officials sounds familiar, a little like it is in France," Benoit said. "How did you learn so much about the Tao?"

"My mother and many of her relatives are Taoists. One of her brother is a Taoist scholar, and a cousin is a magician-priest and healer who practice massage, herbal medicine, and acupuncture. He is good person, though ugly as a frog, he is a masseur excellent. Oh, to feel his touch is visit to Heaven. I listen to them and their friends talk around the table after women finish eating their meal in kitchen. It is my uncle who begin teaching my brothers and I to read and write Chinese characters. Do you have brothers and sisters?" she asked.

All the while she spoke, Benoit admired the way her face and her eyes moved. "Yes, there are eleven of us. I have four brothers and six sisters."

"Six sisters! That is very bad karma for your mother—so sorry."

"My mother likes daughters. In the Christian world, daughters aren't such bad luck." A shadow darkened Benoit's brow, and Moon Light noted the change in his eyes. His expression turned inward as his eyes looked away.

"What is trouble?" she asked.

"Nothing really," he said, looking uncomfortable. "Only, I haven't spent much time thinking of my dear mother. After I left home, my mother, who was a widow, remarried out of loneliness, or hardship, I guess. I now have half-brothers and half-sisters whom I have never met. My poor mother was pregnant again when I last heard from her, and that was over a year ago. Her doctor told her that she must stop having children or lose her life. She decided, on a midwife's advice, to implant an Arab coil device to prevent another birth, but her priest told her that the Arab trick was evil, of the Devil, and that she must either become a celibate, or continue to procreate and have babies, or face excommunication and eternal damnation. And if that wasn't enough trouble, she wrote in her last letter that she fears her new husband has taken a young mistress. She feared that she would die of anger before she dies of old age."

Moon Light put both her hands around her teacup, and lowered her eyes toward the table. "Some problems exist everywhere," she said quietly. She appreciated, from her own collection of fears, how alert Benoit the barbarian was to dilemmas of her sex. "In this country here," she said, "men fall in love with women, and love you till you lose your beauty of youth. Then one day husband ask wife to visit some address and to meet some woman, and if she approve of her, to negotiate bride price or slave price of young girl who then replace you, First Wife, in heart of your husband. You get to make tea and serve it for just some new woman."

"Does that practice have anything to do with your becoming a Christian?"

"By Heaven and Earth, it does certainly," she said, as a smile burst again onto her face. "I became a Christian because I am a Taoist, and I practice *wu wei*, naturalness. What is natural most for the man is not always natural most for the woman." Again Moon Light smiled, hinting to her listener that there was something to laugh about in this crazy world. "Lao Tzu and Confucius both preached equal chance for prosperity for all men educated and civilized, but Jesus preached that rich or poor, freeman or slave, man or woman, we all equal are in the eyes of Heaven. Jesus is the savior that women in my country have been waiting for. Jesus is truly our deliverer," she said, and crossed herself.

Now Benoit grinned wide. "It looks as though we barbarian men are losing ground to men in the Orient. Maybe I should embrace one of your Oriental philosophies?" Moon Light suspected that she was being teased. She smiled pleasantly and kicked him in the shin under the table. "Ouch," he piped in surprise. He looked at her. She wore an expression of goodwill and mild, innocent reproach which was priceless, and made Benoit laugh so hard it woke up the maid Papaya at the next table.

After the leisurely lunch, Benoit, Moon Light and Papaya began a long stroll toward the flower garden of the Confucian Temple. Benoit paid off several deformed and aggressive beggars. The temple was a large, brick museum with many steps, pillars, and doors facing all four cardinal directions, and a huge red-tile pagoda roof.

On the way they met the Count Guillaume de Martineau on the street.

"Well Monsieur Grannier, aren't you lucky to have found such a delicate little doxy to replace the doxy you had in Pondicherry."

Benoit was caught off guard and almost exploded. For a brief moment, all he could think of was how to issue his challenge. *Hold yourself,* his mind ordered. *I must soon create the incident for a duel wherein he challenges me, or take up the pistol with a vengeance. The noise and smell of gunshot practice would be tedious and unpleasant.*

"Monsieur le Comte, I want you to check your language before my new acquaintance, Mademoiselle Bùi. You may address her in French and she will understand you perfectly clearly."

Guillaume looked surprised. He said, recovering, "Mademoiselle, I am delighted to make your acquaintance. I am always surprised at the facility with which your people pick up and practice our language."

"It is not very difficult, monsieur," Moon Light said coldly.

"You have a lovely accent," he said staring at her beautiful face. "I hope you will excuse my jest, that we become friends, and you will call me Guillaume?"

Benoit said, "Since we had news of the revolution in Paris, Guillaume has dropped his title of count. He's not the only royalist to do so, displaying the new partnership between cowardice and common sense."

The remark obviously made its mark. Guillaume's entire face and neck reddened in anger. Carefully, perceptibly, he dropped his weight into a fighting stance. Guillaume thought of drawing his pistol, but there were too many witnesses walking along the open street. He coiled to unleash his challenge, but then realized the great danger he was in. He was furious, and he was almost out of control with the desire to insult and challenge this man whom he had detested for so long, and who so often got the better of him in promotions, affairs of the heart, and friendships on board ship.

Yet he feared Benoit the swordsman, and after having seen Benoit destroy several opponents with his sword, he'd sworn never to risk a direct encounter armed with only that weapon. Once again he was in luck. There were no witnesses of any social import to this last exchange, just an Oriental doxie. But the time had come to dispose of Benoit, and to do it quickly. He drew his heels together, and declared, "My my my, it certainly is amusing being lectured on cowardice by your ilk. Mademoiselle, I can't wait to see you in more agreeable company. And beware of this man. He has mistreated many of the fair sex. I believe he even abused a woman in abandonment to his lust while living on the coast of Africa." Guillaume bowed, stood erect, and walked away.

Benoit exhaled slowly, releasing his anger with his breath. His fingers clenched, and he could feel his sword begging to attack. He carefully watched the other man walk off. He could sense Guillaume's fear, and he knew that his safety was threatened. Moon Light was shocked at how openly these barbarians showed their emotions. *You can read these men like they were children,* she thought. With a proprietary attitude toward her new responsibility that she hardly acknowledged herself, Moon Light knew that the long-nose whom she was ordered to court was in mortal danger of falling to an adder's bite.

What a pathetic wretch I am, she thought. *What sins have I committed in a past life? I must have murdered a government official or his sons. I might be condemned to marry a stinking barbarian, only to become a stinking barbarian's widow. I might as well contract leprosy, I would be an untouchable anyway!*

Chapter 41
Swordplay, Ánh, Benoit, and Pierre
1790

King Ánh was surprisingly frank and outspoken for a Việt, though still not open by French standards. Because he occasionally would condescend to speak his mind, his mandarins, who were often furious at his lack of circumspection and proper royal aloofness, in a rare moment would forget themselves and speak theirs.

Ánh especially liked to tease the foreigners, and his favorite game was to embarrass the Frenchmen with discussions of sex—a subject that French gentlemen were brought up to believe was strictly personal, even unholy. For instance, he liked to make fun of Father Pierre's prudishness by discussing the delights of his conjugal relations with his three wives and two concubines. Then there were always anecdotes, whether true or not, about the maids and the page boys. In fact, once Father Pierre the Bishop, in a pique wrote a stern memorandum to the king stating flatly that if he had to hear one more description of the biological process of fornication, he would leave with all his men and ships, and they would offer their services to the King of Siam and guarantee him military ascendency of the entire Indo-Chinese Peninsula for a hundred years.

❧   ❧

A pair of guards ushered Benoit Grannier into King Nguyễn Ánh's presence in his royal study. Benoit, with his long red-brown hair looked younger than twenty-seven years of age. He bowed low. "I understand that you sent for me, your highness." Pierre, who often acted as a personal scribe and translator for the king and his French visitors, sat at a smaller but elegant desk to the right. Father Pierre usually translated the words of the two men verbatim.

Ánh, the inscrutable Buddha-like man of twenty-eight years, looked up from his desk covered with scrolls, and put down his ink brush. He found distasteful large amounts of desk work; it made him tired and sleepy. He loved to exercise outdoors. He would not have minded changing places even with a barbarian such as Benoit, who that morning was actively supervising the construction of two new Western-style warships in the imperial dockyard on the river above Sài Gòn, or better yet, one of the joiners or adze-men. Ánh began, "General Võ Tánh tells me that you are more dangerous even than he himself in the use of the saber. Is this report true?"

"Goodness no," Benoit said laughing modestly. "In fact, I have asked Võ Tánh to instruct me in his techniques, and he has complimented me with a similar request, I suspect probably just to be polite."

"Is it not then true," Ánh went on, knowing modesty on the few rare occasions when he met it in a serious fighter, "that you are considered proficient in your Western style of swordplay?"

"To that I'll agree," Benoit said, wondering where this would lead.

"Would you show me the rudiments of your training?"

"I'd be honored," Benoit said. "When would you like a session?"

"How about right now?" King Nguyễn Ánh said.

"That will work, it will be a pleasure," Benoit said, somewhat concerned. Working with royalty took getting used to. He'd made an appointment with Olivier du Puymanel, the naval engineer, and the four royal Việt shipwrights for a meeting, which would abort without him.

"Come into my exercise room," the king said standing up. Benoit followed the king down the hall and his eyes studied the ferocious dragon embroidered on the king's yellow and purple silk tunic. The dragon was an important animal. It stood for, among other things, the king and his invincible moral and temporal authority as endowed by the Great Spirit of the Universe, the will of Heaven. The dragon had the head of a camel, the horns of a buck, and the eyes of a demon protruding from their sockets. This wild beast had the ears of a water buffalo, the neck and body of a snake, the scales of a carp, the claws of an eagle, and the paws of a tiger. The monster displayed a barbells, a slender whisker-like organ on each side of its mouth, and under its tongue supposedly lay hidden a precious stone. Its power was easily conveyed; one wouldn't want to disobey such a monster.

Việts believed there were real dragons that inhabited the magical landscape. They lived underground, in the water, and in the sky. Each dragon was capable of spitting either a stream of deadly vapor, or burning fire, or freezing water at will, or changing shapes. And every dragon was immortal. The dragon reminded Benoit, oddly enough, of old Father Sebastian. You wouldn't want to meet either with your lessons unprepared.

The royal exercise room was framed in natural woods and white panels and decorated with landscape scroll paintings. One wall displayed a full weapons rack. Half the floor was of a fine, hard wood, and the other half had canvas *ch'in-a* tumbling and wrestling mats filled with rice-stalk. The king removed his yellow and purple robe adorned with the imperial dragon.

Benoit removed his shirt, so both men faced each other barefoot and shirtless in their breeches.

"What is this?" the king asked, walking up to Benoit and touching his blond chest hair.

"It's just hair," said Benoit. "Where is yours?" and he and the king both laughed.

"I'm glad I don't have hair there," Ánh said cheerfully. "My wives might think I was descended from monkeys."

Benoit retorted, "In my country, the chest hair is a sign of greater manhood."

Ánh answered, "If only you had the extra wives for the extra manhood."

As Father Pierre translated this retort, his face turned red.

The hairy, sunburned barbarian looked much stronger than the smooth-skinned king, who was easily a foot shorter and forty pounds lighter.

Pierre sat on the floor and watched, staying almost invisible as he played the role of professional translator. He did not mind the interlude either. Pierre loved watching the human body in motion, male or female, in almost any dance or sport. He knew that Benoit was an expert swordsman and a good teacher.

Benoit first showed King Ánh the complete cycle of warm-up exercises. Anatomically, they were remarkably similar to a Vietnamese boxer's warm-up exercises. The exercises concentrated on stretching and strengthening the groin, the legs, the back, the arms, the wrists, knees, and ankles.

"Good," Benoit said, "let me show you five basic moves I like to practice. But we will need swords."

Ánh spoke to the guard standing silently inside the door, who handed back to Benoit his own sword. Ánh picked out a one-handed saber from his rack, and they went through a number of basic strike and parry exercises.

"Very impressive," Ánh said. "How do you teach sparring?"

Benoit set his sword against a wall, chose two wooden swords from the rack of practice weapons, and handed one to the king. Benoit showed him the basic strike, block, and thrust combinations. They played a form of percussive music, running through the combinations in rhythm, repeating each combination. Ánh had studied many weapons and both hard and soft styles of boxing, so he could easily see the value of the Etienne Quellenec style of French saber.

Benoit explained to the king the Parisian rules of sparring with swords, the point system again resembling that of some Oriental boxing styles. They sparred for a few minutes, with Benoit scoring only an occasional point. The king began to understand Võ Tánh's admiration for the barbarian. *This long-nose moves very fast,* he thought. *He is also trying to conceal his true ability.* Benoit realized that the king, like Võ Tánh, was very difficult to score a point on with a thrust. He asked the king why that was so.

"A straight attack is the easiest to defend against, especially with a soft or blending move," the king said, pleased to be consulted. "You move off the line of the attack to avoid blood. It's a simple rule, but the practice is hard. You can pivot your feet, or move them, but you must get your body off the line of attack." They went through some *Qinna* (ju-jitsu) exercises of avoiding the thrust of a full-front attack, and Pierre decided then and there to study more Việt soft style boxing and swordplay. They finished with a playful sparring session. King Ánh was no match for Benoit, but he kept his sense of humor and made a determined effort.

After the workout, King Ánh invited Benoit and Pierre to his bath. The two Frenchmen looked at each other. Father Pierre looked uncomfortable. "No thank you," he said firmly. "I've got some work to attend to."

"Who will be my translator, if I go with his highness?" Benoit asked.

"Oh, don't worry," Pierre said. "One of the female bath attendants speaks a little French adequately enough."

Ánh said, "Captain Grannier, before we leave our modest and temperate friend, I have a request. Could I persuade you to study our language?"

"I would be delighted to try, but I make no promises of my ability." Benoit answered.

"Good. I will ask my servant Bùi Moon Light to become your private instructor. I will of course cover her expenses."

"What a charming idea," Benoit said casually, concealing his feelings, which were soaring with excitement.

After the hot bath, which they took separately in wooden tubs in separate rooms, they each received a rub-down from the king's personal masseur or his assistant. Benoit lay naked on a table while the assistant, a very muscular fellow, searched his musculature for knots and pressure points. The man uncovered areas in the shoulder and lower back that were covered with large, hardened muscle, but also where Benoit stored much of his body tension. Repeatedly on the threshold of pain, ropes of hard muscle melted. When the massage ended, Benoit was so relaxed that he was ready for a nap. He dressed and a guard escorted him out of the compound. As Benoit walked through the citadel, he felt like a new man. With his four bodyguards, he went in search of Olivier du Puymanel and the shipwrights to offer his apologies and make his amends.

అ ❧

King Nguyễn Ánh entered his study to continue his attempt at balancing the budget, recently reported to him by his Financial Advisory Board. Father Pierre was still at his small desk finishing a letter from King Ánh to the Portuguese Governor of Macao.

"It is getting late, why don't you quit for the day?" the king said quietly.

"Oh, I'm about to go," Pierre said, "but I would like a few words with you before I go, if I may."

"Certainly, what's on your mind old counselor?"

"I'm still worried still about the condition of the peasants who are working on the new fortifications of the citadel. My officers tell me that the work continues no matter what the weather, and for such long hours that many of the laborers are sick, and several die every week from exhaustion."

There was a stiff silence while the young man who was king stared at the older man who was a barbarian Christian priest. Their wills met quietly in the silence in the middle of the room and clashed. Ánh thought in annoyance, *These barbarians know nothing about maintaining harmony, even between allies.* And Pierre thought, *Young Ánh will come around. He cares about his people and wants to win, as long as I don't force him into a corner.*

"What would you have me do?" Ánh asked with a touch of formal petulance.

"No major changes, I assure you. I'm as impatient as you are to make adequate preparations for a campaign north. But I feel that the ends can't always justify the means. I think you should shorten the hours, slow down the building, and increase the rations, or we will not seem to your people like much of an alternative government to the Tây Sơn rebels. We want and need the support of the people."

"Can you turn your generous feelings into a proposal?"

"Yes, more food and more rest. You could let the workers stop after sunset, and increase their rations."

"And how will I pay for the extra rations?"

Father Pierre had anticipated this question. "You could cancel or cut back the funeral parade for your second wife's father."

"Great Heaven, did you see the magnificent parade Nguyễn Hiền the Official Greeter and his clan put on for his mother's death? I'm afraid that you have learned little about our ways and values if you think I could ever ignore our esteemed Ancestors, especially our newest one. The people believe that new Ancestors are the most dangerous spirits in the netherworld. And just as important, you can not estimate the face I'd lose if I were not to order a parade with at least fifty musicians and sixty mourners. It's no more than any of my leading mandarins or the biggest landowners would do." The king thought the conversation was over, but Pierre was not through.

"You should take care of your workers. Either before or after your parade, you could proscribe all future funeral parades of more than ten hired mourners until the rebels are defeated and your workers are fed and housed properly. Or you could create a funeral tax."

"Yes," Ánh said, getting up from his chair, "and most likely alienate all the old families that have supported me, some only half-heartedly up until now. Maybe we should cut the Western ship-building! Good day." Ánh retreated deliberately through a doorway into his private office and closed the door.

Chapter 42
Typhoon
1790

In the marketplace of Cần Giờ, a storyteller listened to a fisherman he knew, who spoke quietly in his ear. The storyteller listened to the air and tasted it. He announced in a stentorian voice to his audience that the Mountain Genie, Sơn Tinh, and the Sea Genie, Thủy Tinh, have gone to war again over the beautiful daughter of King Văn Lang.

"You do well to tremble, my sons, when the typhoon breaks like a rice stalk the mightiest trees of the forest. It is time, my children, for everyone to seek higher ground and shelter." That warning abruptly concluded his program. He took up his long walking pole, adjusted his money pouch, and with his boy next to him carrying their bags on a shoulder pole, they joined a small the crowd moving northwestward toward Sài Gòn.

Henri Dayot's mercury barometer fell. One of the great Genies of the Earth, later named the Coriolis force, described part of the dynamics of waterwheels, and then later the earth's rotation as it acts upon the atmosphere above it. This great Genie causes the wind to curve to the right in the Northern Hemisphere, and to the left in the Southern Hemisphere. Coriolis force and earth's rotation, these are just new names for old Gods. Whatever you choose to call them, periodically the Gods fight and the wind spins out of control. Air and Water, the offspring of Heaven and Earth, go mad, terrorizing all living creatures in their path; a force as large as the Great Dragon and with the deadly speed of a spinning top.

The fishermen of Cần Giờ village saw that the waves of the bay had grown into ocean swells. They were the first to know. Usually the waves broke on the beach every five breaths, but now their frequency slowed, till they hit only every ten breaths. The fishermen did not go out that day, and they warned the storyteller, the long-bearded Father Lozier, and many others that they expected a typhoon. A rapid exodus from the village began, with fishermen loading carts and animals with all their worldly possessions.

Benoit was in Cần Giờ that morning on the king's business, with Bùi Moon Light as his translator and language teacher. They had gone to the harbor by one of the king's galleys, *Serpent*, to inspect the four French men-o-war and the new harbor fortifications designed by Olivier du Puymanel. Attached to Benoit now was a bodyguard of thirty blue-shirted soldiers. Assassination was a common practice in Đại Việt.

The French sailors at Cần Giờ prepared for the oncoming storm by securing the four ships with triple storm anchors fore and aft and removing the top masts. All the sailors and officers hurried ashore in the longboats, which they secured to trees, and then marched inland, alternating a fast walk and a trot. If the typhoon was a bad one, the whole village would be flooded. Twice in its long history, the buildings had been completely under water.

As the village began its evacuation, Benoit conferred with Admiral Nguyễn Văn Trương, the acting captain of the galley *Serpent*. Benoit wanted to fill the *Serpent* with indigents. Nguyễn Trương agreed to take fifty women with infants or the elderly on board. These people would have the greatest trouble marching far enough inland.

Benoit ordered twenty-five of his thirty bodyguards to go into the village and each bring back any two very old or young villagers who wished to travel up river in the *Serpent*. Benoit ran over to Father Lozier's school and invited the father and his forty students on board.

Thirty minutes later the galley pushed away from the dock. The main road leading away from the village was filled with a long string of refugees and it was littered with belongings picked up in haste and then cast away in desperation.

The drum of the galley began to boom, the oars dipped into the water, and the great longboat slowly pulled away from the village. The river was full of boats moving inland; the *Serpent* pushed through the throngs of smaller vessels with obscenities shouted from both sides. The clouds darkened. The rain began while the winds increased. As the tropical storm approached, the dark sky began to pour water onto the earth's surface. It rained up in Phan Thiết, and it rained down in Vịnh Loi. The storm was at least 200 miles in diameter.

In Sài Gòn, the streets were empty. Everyone took shelter from the downpour, except for several thousand peasants and a few guards who were mindlessly kept working on the new fortifications of the citadel.

After the rain came the Great Wind. The trees on the beach at the seaside village of Cần Giờ began to bend, and so did the bottom masts on the ships. Near the eye of the storm, the angry wind ripped trees out of the ground. Houses fell, masts broke, fishing boats scattered.

Many people were too old or sick to be moved from the coastal villages in the path of the tropical storm. These people moved into root cellars, if available. They were safe until the sea rose. Great waves crashed into buildings, which were soon several feet under water. Thousands of people were caught in cellars or on the roads and drowned.

A villager named Đoàn Hành was moving his whole family—wife, three children and grandparents—up the road when the waves caught them. They waded into an abandoned village and climbed up a bamboo fence to perch on a roof. A large wave knocked down his mother; she lost her footing and was swept away. The grandfather dove after his wife, but when he reached her, the next wave was upon them and they never came up again. The next wave hit the side of the house. The children were crying. The mother said, "We'll be all right, it is almost over." No one was holding the eldest son. He lost his grip on the thatch and fell into the swirl. As his mother screamed, the young boy bobbed up and down, and swam hard for the roof, but all the time the water carried him farther and farther away.

The husband and wife sat on the top of the roof clutching their two remaining toddlers in utter terror. The water continued to rise, and soon reached the bottom of the roof. Each wave seemed bigger than the one before it. After one very big one, the house began to collapse. The next huge wave toppled the hut, and the four innocents fell screaming into the churning water.

༄ ༅

The Great Wind found the boats of the French fleet. Most held fast with their triple anchors, but the three old lower masts of *Le Donnai*, Henri Dayot's ship, bent over and two broke. Then two stern anchor cables broke and the third began to drag in the water. The ship swung around in the water and hit the rocky shore. With the force of the waves, the rocks gouged large holes in its hull. The ship, vanquished by a force greater than the arts of man, heeled over on its side and sank to the shallow bottom, till only the starboard gunwale showed.

The Việts had seen these storms many times. The Mountain Genie and the Ocean Genie fought several times a year. The French were more unnerved. Had they incurred the wrath of the Lord? Even the irreligious of them turned to the Christian God for mercy and salvation, and begged—please, Lord Almighty, stop the wind and the rising water.

The galley *Serpent* with Benoit, Moon Light, and many grandparents and children rowed up river for three hours before the storm caught them. They had moved about fifteen miles when they were finally caught by the wind.

The pine trees on the shoreline of the river bent over and touched the ground. Banyan trees cracked and fell to the earth. The wind picked up leaves and debris and whole trees, and carried them away.

Admiral Nguyễn Văn Trương gave an order and the helmsman steered for the nearest shore with a mud flat beach, while the oarsmen kept rowing. In the front of the galley, Father Lozier ordered his young students to "hold on to each other," while the peasants in the middle and the stern of the boat didn't need to be told to huddle down and hold tight. Benoit and Moon Light sat and held onto the guardrail and to each other.

After a huge gust of wind, a great tree smashed into the water to the left of the galley. Then another tree hit the water near the shore on the right. Suddenly, from out of the sky, a tree trunk smashed into the middle of the galley, just missing Captain Trương. The tree trunk pierced the bottom of the boat. Water poured through the broken hull.

An old couple and some children were crushed. Benoit rushed over to look at the hole, and he checked the casualties for signs of life. A branch of the tree, just before it stopped moving, had caught and broken the leg of Captain Trương. The poor man was trapped under a limb as he lay on the bottom of the boat, which was rapidly filling with water.

Benoit began to analyze the situation. *The ship is still floating, the captain is about to drown. Can I save him quickly? Will helping the individual risk losing the whole group?* Moon Light and some soldiers tried to quiet the hysterical peasants. Captain Trương was pinned and in pain. Benoit ordered the rowers to begin rowing again immediately. He then ordered the officers of his bodyguard to try and free Trương. The soldiers could not budge the huge tree trunk. Poor Trương's head was just above the water.

Benoit took a spear and placed it between the planking and the tree limb, and tried to use the spear as a lever. The soldiers all fetched their spears and soon fifteen long shafts levered the bough until it moved. Other soldiers dragged the captain free. Benoit and the soldiers let the trunk fall into place again.

Captain Trương fainted from the pain of his broken leg. The galley was only thirty yards from shore when it finally began to sink. Benoit ordered the galley's longboat made ready for launching. He ordered that all the children and the unconscious captain be lifted into the boat, and picked eight oarsmen to row the children to shore. He handed his pistols to one of these men. To another of these men, he handed his sword and scabbard and boots.

"Moon Light, can you swim?" Benoit asked.

"No, no swim."

"Get into the longboat."

"No, there are only children in the boat."

Jesus, Benoit thought, *how many people here can't swim?* Benoit then asked Moon Light to organize all the people on the galley into two groups, swimmers and non-swimmers. He shouted, "Assign one swimmer and one non-swimmer to an oar."

With Moon Light translating, and both of them shouting over the wind, Benoit ordered the oarsmen to each take their heavy oar, one swimmer and one non-swimmer, and swim the oar to the shore. He ordered all these oarsmen with their oars and two more adults into the water. Some of the non-swimmers were so petrified that they had to be physically thrown in. Once in the water, holding onto the oar and kicking it to the shore was not too difficult, with the wind pushing in the same direction.

One hysterical woman refused to leave the sinking boat. She held onto the railing with all her might. She bit an oarsman. Benoit grabbed her under the chin, and bending her spine, he peeled her off the railing and threw her head first into the water. An oarsman jumped in after her. The hysterical woman was thrashing wildly in the water. She wouldn't grab the oar, and the oarsman was unwilling to tangle with her.

Since the boat was already swamped, Benoit ordered all those remaining to abandon ship. Moon Light was ash white. He ordered two swimmers to take the last oar and Moon Light, and help her swim to shore. "In you go," he said to his translator. He dropped the last oar and Moon Light over the gunwale with the two men following. Once on top of the oar, Moon Light was as fine as a wet duck.

Benoit stood momentarily alone on the deck of the *Serpent*, waist deep in water. The hysterical woman was drowning just ten feet away. The longboat was pulled up onto the shore and soldiers were helping the children climb out of it. Benoit, in just his shirt and breaches, dove in and swam over to the thrashing woman. The woman, no longer herself, tried to climb on top of Benoit and forced him under water with a vise-like grip around his neck.

Benoit let his body sink and pulled the woman down with him. Instinctively she let go. He grabbed her leg, climbed to her waist, spun her around, climbed up to grasp her hair with one hand, and kicked up for the air. At the surface, he kept a tight hold on her hair. She lay helpless on her back, but her face was out of the water, and he swam sidestroke and scissors-kick to the shore. Two soldiers helped them out of the water. No one else paid them any attention at all. Soldiers and villagers were moving as fast as they could to higher ground. For the first time, Moon Light lost her usual veneer of propriety and threw her arms around Benoit. Only the poor souls hit by the tree were lost; all the rest were saved for the moment. The *Serpent* would rise again.

At the Sài Gòn Citadel, the captain of the guards finally gave the laborers permission to leave. Some of them had already died from flying debris, while others had collapsed from exposure and exhaustion. The workers who could all ran for cover to the citadel to cower inside the outer wall. Four men were lifted into the air as they ran for the wall and disappeared into the maelstrom.

After the storm had passed, King Nguyễn Ánh dispatched several galleys down the river, and one soon returned with Benoit, Moon Light, and the crew of the *Serpent*.

❧   ❦

Only two days later, another kind of storm hit Sài Gòn, while Benoit was visiting Father Pierre. Among the thousands of peasant workers were a band of "friends of the Tây Sơn" who had planned long before to stage a revolt. They decided that now was the time to start their uprising. They attacked their few unsuspecting guards with picks, shovels, and knives and killed them. Hundreds of angry workers joined in spontaneously, and all the guards were either killed or forced to flee. The leaders started a march, shouting to all the workers, and incited them to follow and to riot.

The mob, more dangerous to Sài Gòn than the earlier tempest in the sky, charged across the outer courtyard and began to pour through the gate of the inner wall just as reinforcements of the King's Guard arrived from their barracks. After some bloody moments in which a few brave guards were overwhelmed, enough reinforcements arrived to push the marauders out of the inner courtyard and shut the portcullis. The mob then turned and began to attack the town. They searched out soldiers, officials and shopkeepers and clubbed them to death. Alarm bells were sounded to call the soldiers in the citadel and the soldiers of the barracks just outside of town to mobilize, but many officials and townsmen were mauled and murdered.

From the window on the second floor of Pierre's house, Benoit and Pierre watched the rioters move down their street. The mob broke into a variety store, dragged the old white-haired proprietor out onto the street, and bludgeoned him to death.

Father Pierre recognized some of the local peasants in the mob. "These are our children," he said sadly, "and look at what we have done to them."

"Look," said Benoit, "how some of them are pointing here to your house. It appears that the Tây Sơn brothers have sent agitators to ignite and direct this fire at individuals like you."

"The Tây Sơn might have provided the *agents provocateurs*, but they are hardly responsible for the anger and bitterness of the laborers," said Pierre. While Pierre was watching, he was conflicted with horror and with the curious fascination of a natural philosopher.

Benoit was of a far more practical mind. He moved quickly to the bishop's desk. He picked out a medicine bottle and emptied its contents into a drinking glass. He took his powder case and poured the gunpowder into the empty bottle. He then fashioned a small homemade bomb. He stopped the glass bottle with a rag, and dipped and held the rag for ten seconds in lamp oil. The crowd overwhelmed and killed the four soldiers who guarded the door of the bishop's house. The mob began to break down the front door, while members of the crowd yelled such things as "Down with Nguyễn Ánh" and "Kill the long-nosed barbarians." Pierre was surprised, and he realized that someone probably had directed the murderous crowd to him. He also suspected now that Tây Sơn agents were involved.

Benoit lit his jury-rigged bomb, held it high till the rag was almost burnt, and tossed it out the open window. The explosion made a loud noise and sent glass shards into a dozen or so horrified peasants. Benoit left the room, and from the top of the stairs he waited till the front door was broken down. The room below filled with rioters. At the sight of Benoit, they paused for a moment, till several at once rushed the stairs. The attackers carried poles, knives, sledgehammers, and rocks.

The first man on the stairs Benoit killed with a pistol shot. The next two he blocked using both his sword and pistol, and stabbed each man in turn through the chest. A rock caught him on the shoulder. Several more of the rioters wound up to hurl stones and Benoit jumped back into Pierre's bedroom. The rocks smashed against the wall at the top of the stairs as Father Pierre closed and bolted the door to his room. The rioters charged up the stairs and attacked the door with their heaviest implements. Frantically, Benoit moved furniture against the door. He reloaded his pistol, and shot through the door into a man on the other side. From the street came screams of agony. The rest of Father Pierre the Bishop's fifty-man bodyguard hacked its way through the crowd. They had arrived from their barracks just down the end of the street.

Pierre's soldiers burst through the open door of the house and slew every rag-tag laborer within. Pierre and Benoit listened, and after opening the door, watched the carnage with relief and disbelief. "These are our peasants," Pierre exclaimed to Benoit, "the backbone of our efforts. How did this happen? King Ánh has brought this on himself."

The storm passed and the riot ended, each following its course. When King Nguyễn Ánh heard about the attack on Pierre's house he was sorry, but when he heard about the sinking of *Le Donnai*, he was indignant. The other ships with their triple sets of anchors all weathered the storm. Why didn't *Le Donnai*? Several of the high mandarins insisted that the accident must have been due to barbarian negligence. Vietnamese law against negligence was strict. Ánh ordered the commander of the vessel, Commodore Henri Dayot, arrested and put in jail.

When Ánh's soldier's arrested Dayot, there was nearly a battle. It was prevented by Dayot, who ordered his men to hold their fire. Then he surrendered himself. The other French officers held a meeting that amounted to a council of war, and decided to demand that Dayot be released or there would be serious repercussions. The Nguyễn-French alliance was in jeopardy—even a crisis. Father Pierre the Bishop and Captain Benoit went straight from the meeting of the officers to the king's reception hall to ask for Dayot's immediate release.

"The mandarins were in grievous error," Pierre explained. "*Le Donnai* had been anchored properly, in fact, exactly like the other ships. There is variation in how anchors catch the bottom, which isn't uniform. Anchors in mud bottoms in a typhoon often do not hold perfectly. Furthermore, not all the anchor ropes are brand new." When these reasons did not move King Ánh, Pierre said, "I must warn you, my officers are outraged. They are fighting mad, and their ships are about to sail back to India in protest!" Actually, the French fleet was about to attack the citadel of Cần Giờ with their cannon to try and free Dayot if King Ánh refused their request. Ánh sensed the threat and the danger.

"These barbarians are hard to predict," Ánh complained to Võ Tánh. "They are so touchy and temperamental sometimes. Their loyalty to each other and to their honor is surprising. Who would have expected such good character from barbarians?

They view life as sacred, and worship a God of love and peace, but will fight and kill quickly for their honor for a single comrade! The contradiction seems absurd."

Võ Tánh replied, "Who understands Christian barbarians, by the Gods? They seem more dangerous than peaceful to me."

Ánh conceded, "Their argument about the variation of anchors and harbor bottoms makes sense though. We perhaps acted too quickly."

King Nguyễn Ánh ordered that Dayot be released with an official apology, and that two of his mandarins each be demoted two ranks, with the requisite cut in stipend, for their bad advice. These two acts ended the crisis.

❧ ☙

Two weeks later, Father Pierre met with Ánh and after the normal pleasantries, Ánh finally said, "Is there something on your mind?"

Pierre answered, "Yes, there is. I believe it is time to attack the Tây Sơn. It is time to harvest the rice or lose the crop." Pierre's officers had decided that the king was dragging his heels. Pierre said carefully, "Our Frenchmen are on the verge of quitting and returning to India. It is past the time that it seemed appropriate to them and me to start a campaign north against Quy Nhơn."

King Nguyễn Ánh listened quietly, held a meeting with his High Council of Mandarins, which included Pierre, and agreed to move. At the end of the meeting, Ánh said, "It is agreed. We will advance again at the start of the next dry season, until the rainy season begins. This is, in fact, what I was already planning. It was always my hope to eventually press forward during each dry season. My biggest reservation remains. I still firmly believe that the longer we wait, the weaker the Tây Sơn become."

"You are probably right about that," said Pierre, "but with our French naval forces still intact we are stronger than them now at sea. Like a blacksmith, we should strike while the iron is hot."

Henri Dayot announced nonetheless that he would leave Đại Việt on the next available ship, so Pierre took him to dinner to a fancy house of pleasure and offered him some succulent duck and an excellent red burgundy. "Henri," pleaded Pierre, "the king has apologized for your arrest. I need my captains to ensure the success of the naval campaign we are about to launch against the Tây Sơn. Please stay till the rainy season, and join in the first campaign. We are so close. It will help France and the Church if we, with God's help, can succeed here."

"God's blood, Father Pierre, it is hard to say no to you, but I don't trust Nguyễn Ánh, nor should you. It seems to me that all we can accomplish is to replace one tyrant with another. Is it worth all the bloodshed? But I'll give it till the rainy season and stay for this one campaign." Pierre's relief was offset by at least two concerns. He knew that they could wait no longer to make war with the help of the French mercenaries, since their patience had worn out. Second, he was running out of good burgundy.

Chapter 43
The Opera, Phú Xuân
1792 (two years later)

To celebrate her twenty-eighth birthday, Huệ's First Wife, Green Willow, asked Huệ to join her and his other two wives, Precious Stone and Gem Lake, and his concubine, Blue Cloud, for a dinner party followed by a performance of plays by some travelling opera singers.

The only other guest was Huệ's sister, Jade River, whom Green Willow included because she liked her, it was an appropriate thing to do, and everyone, especially Huệ, was fond of her. Each woman was invited to bring her personal maid as a server. So Green Willow's birthday banquet was for six: her husband Huệ, all three wives, the concubine, and Jade River. Their five maids served them.

Huệ's four women got along with each other reasonably well. Huệ was so careful in dividing his time among the four of them when he wasn't with his troops, who received by far the most of his time, that the others did not hate Blue Cloud for being the subtle favorite. Blue Cloud was very conscious and careful of the feelings of the other women. His only obvious preference was for Quang Toản, the son of Blue Cloud, over Cường, the son of Precious Stone, and Trứ, the son of Green Willow, but he tried not to parade that preference to anyone either. It was clear in his will and to his women that Quang Toản was the current heir.

When Huệ arrived at the Garden of Peace, an outdoor courtyard inside the women's quarters of the king's palace, he gave presents to his four women and his sister. He presented Green Willow with a large bouquet of lilies and a new necklace of pearls. The other three women and Jade River each received smaller bouquets as well, and a pair of gold earrings.

The meal was an exquisite display of the fruits of both land and sea. Huệ and his women chatted while the five maids brought in dishes of food and poured wine liberally. The small surprise of the evening was a lacquered duck, a favorite dish of Huệ's, and one that none of his women cared for. All four women and his sister abstained from eating animal flesh, but there were many beautifully arranged vegetable dishes, including dumplings, assorted spring rolls, fruits, and both raw and pickled vegetables.

Huệ's eldest sons, Cảnh Thịng, Cường, and Trứ, were not present, nor were any of the other six children Huệ had fathered with his women. At any rate, the children were a noisy bunch, and for such an elegant affair they were not included.

"How was your work today?" Green Willow asked her husband toward the end of the meal.

"Not too different from any other," said Huệ smiling warmly. "No fun surprises. There are always more military preparations, drills, laws, decrees, and appointments or promotions to check over and to sign. I met again with the special commit-tee of wealthy landlords to discuss my ideas of land reform and to hear theirs. No support from that group. I can't seem to persuade a single one of them of the value of tenants becoming landowners, at least, not at their expense. They're all afraid that one of their grandchildren might eventually have to till the land.

Jade River asked, "What did you propose to them?"

"I suggested that each landless, adult male peasant be allowed to buy up to eight *sao* [about one acre] at a nominal fee, say five ounces of silver per sao. It gets complicated. How many *sao* must a rich farmer offer at only five ounces of silver? In other words, how many peasants must he sell to below market? We are thinking up to 200 *sao* [about 25 acres], or twenty-five peasants. Any land purchased beyond 200 *sao* to the first twenty-five peasants must be at a price the seller agrees to. Does that sound reasonable?"

"Is such land reform really necessary?" asked Precious Stone. "Aren't you go-ing to alienate all the great families in the country with such an idea?"

"I'm afraid so, and I don't want to have to use force. But some relief for tenants would be helpful militarily. Sun Tzu once wrote, 'The leader of a contented people has little to fear in military matters, for a contented people will swarm to his banner in times of need and national defense.' And no amount of preparation can keep a dissatisfied people from abandoning you in your time of need either."

Jade River said, "It sounds reasonable enough to try. Is there any chance that these men of wealth will consider your proposal?"

"I really don't know the answer to that. If I can clear up the current military picture and unify the country, I will have a stronger position from which to encour-age or force concessions. We need to stay united to keep the Chinese at bay, and I anticipate attacks from Western powers in the future.

"Regarding the Chinese, Ngô Thì Nhậm talked me out of invading the south of China. We have sent an envoy to the emperor to ask for one of his daughters to join my household as wife, and for her wedding dowry, could he just hand over to me my real heart's desire, Guangxi and Guangdong Provinces." Precious Stone, Gem Lake, and Blue Cloud all looked at each other, and then to Green Willow for leader-ship.

Green Willow smiled apologetically, stiffened, and then relaxed. She said, "Men, they think they will never grow old. I knew about this little project, and was about to tell you all. My lord, I'm still not sure why you want southern China. Don't you still have problems in the south?"

Huệ sensed the awkwardness at the table and chuckled. "Perhaps it is ambi-tious! The situation is looking better to the south. My spies report that the French mercenaries are tired of fighting in our country, and they are all about to quit Nguyễn Ánh and sail home to India or France. I have moved my navy of galley ships upriver beyond the reach of the Western warships. It will be easy to wait them out. Meanwhile, I am discussing terms with the British Governor of India for the purchase of two of their warships, complete with officers as instructors for at least two years of service.

"And that, my darlings, is still a secret. I will be sorely disappointed if there is a leak from any of you here, and I will know where the leak came from!" Huệ looked at his women one at a time, smiling, to make his point. Then he turned to Jade River. "Younger Sister, how is life at the Monastery of the White Lotus? Are you behaving yourself?"

Jade River laughed. She was pleased to be included in such a private affair. "Brother, don't be naughty, but thank you for asking, I think. The abbess there is kind and the nuns always treat me well." She laughed again. "They probably know what happened to Madame Camellia and the Bạcs," which got all the table laughing. "I have found the simple life of physical work, study, and prayer useful, and I have been accepted by Sister Charity, the herbalist, as one of her apprentices. But I still haven't decided yet to commit myself to Buddha for the rest of my life. He is, in his own way, yet another demanding male master."

"We have noticed that you go to great lengths to get away from us—and father would be pleased with your study of medicine," Huệ said chuckling. "But I fear Hoàng will not be pleased if you remain in the cloister and reserve yourself just for Buddha."

"And besides," said Precious Stone, "being the third or fourth wife of 'a good man' isn't really as horrible as everyone says it is," and all the ladies and Huệ laughed, while Huệ also looked at each of them carefully. At this point, there was a relaxed lull in the conversation.

Huệ broke the silence and asked, "Green Willow, did I hear that you had a group of performers arranged for tonight?"

"We have a group from the Hà Nội Opera, and if it pleases you, we will call for them to begin."

"That would be excellent," said Huệ, and he smiled at Green Willow. "More time for my First Wife on her birthday after the show."

"Lotus Blossom," she called her maid, "call in the performers."

The performers soon appeared on the grass before the assembled party. There were musicians, acrobatic dancers, and actor-singers.

The master of ceremonies announced that the play for the evening would be *The Faithful Harlot*. The characters walked onstage in elaborate costumes and makeup, and they each introduced themselves and told a bit of the background to the play.

As the actors dramatized it, the Chinese maiden Su San was sold by her poor parents to a brothel, where she fell in love with a rich young scholar, Wang Chin-lung, who spent all his money for their pleasure together. Becoming penniless from his ardor, Wang was turned out by the brothel keeper, but was aided by the faithful Su San, who gave him money to journey to Nanking, the capital of the Qing Dynasty, to take the government examination and make his fortune.

Wang Chin-lung passed his examination! Blessed with promotions and wealth, Wang dropped his ties with Su San, the loyal brothel flower. Later, Su San was sold as a concubine to an unscrupulous and rich merchant named Shen Yen-lin, whose wife, Mistress P'i, regarded the younger woman as a threat to her position. The wife planned to murder Su San, but her husband unwittingly ate the poisoned noodles and died. Su San was accused of the murder, tried, and condemned. At that time it was customary to send prisoners convicted of grave offenses to a higher official for retrial. The action of the opera began with Su San and her guard on the road to Taiyuan, the capital of Shansi Province.

Su San: "Dear old uncle, please send a message to my beloved Wang Chin-lung."

The guard turned to the audience directly and said: "Still thinking of her lover! Gentlemen, look at this girl—she is still faithful to her man! This should teach you that if you go to a house of prostitution, you are sure to get your money's worth!"

By this time Green Willow had turned several shades of red. She had not actually reviewed the script for the show, and now she realized that the material might not be well received. To her great relief, she noticed that Jade River and Huệ both were laughing. Green Willow prayed to Quán Thế Âm, the Goddess of Mercy, that the play would not offend Jade River or Huệ.

"What do you think of that?" Huệ said in a low voice to his sister. "Do you usually get your money's worth?"

"No, that depends on the client. It all depends on how much you spend, and how much you get," she said smiling mischievously, and returned her attention to the lovely singing. Green Willow released her clenched fist and exhaled with relief that Jade River sounded cheerful and relaxed, and thought, *What a wonderful woman for an ex-prostitute.*

Back in the play, the guard heard Su San's unhappy story and agreed to help her present her petition to the high magistrate in Taiyuan, who turned out to be none other than her ex-lover Wang Chin-lung, the faithless one who had dumped her after accepting her money. Heartless Wang Chin-lung now had to review the case as the leader of a panel of three judges.

Wang Chin-lung was so upset to see the woman he deserted that he faltered and then fainted. When he recovered, Su San presented her petition. The other two judges soon understood that an intense emotional bond existed between the accused and the high magistrate, which caused them much amusement, all at the expense of their haughty superior.

Wang Chin-lung tried to stop Su San from explaining her whole story; he cut her off, but the other two judges now insisted on hearing her out. Jade River and Huệ both laughed hard, while Green Willow used her fan to cool her face and release nervous tension.

Su San explained how she supported her lover—a Master Wang—through his studies. After he finally passed his exams, he abandoned her. "Oh, that's terrible, that's disgusting," cried the other judges in the play.

Su San: "I persuaded my lover Wang to go to Nanking to compete in the government examination, but on the way he wrote that he met bandits who robbed him of every single cent."

Second Judge: "Oh, how tragic."

Wang Chin-lung: "Aye, really tragic, indeed!"

Third Judge: "How can you consider it tragic? It served him right—that frequenter of brothels."

Both Second and Third Judges laughed uproariously, as they had guessed the guiltiness of their superior, Wang Chin-lung. They proceeded to make insulting remarks against the character Wang, whom Su San with some loving innocence described roundly as a cad.

Su San declared that she gave him yet more silver for the trip to the capital—all she had left. Wang Chin-lung found the story unbearable, and he formally handed over the investigation to his two subordinate judges.

Mistress P'i, the unscrupulous wife of the rich merchant, and her paramour, Chao, entered and again accused Su San. The subordinate judges ordered Chao tortured so that they might know the truth, and he immediately confessed that he and his mistress murdered the merchant Shen Yen-lin with poisoned noodles meant for Su San.

They agreed to sign confessions and were sentenced to death. The magistrate they had bribed was brought forward, humiliated by the tribunal, and forced to confess. His life was spared, but he was dismissed from his high office and sent to the frontier to work at hard labor for the rest of his miserable life.

The subordinate judges awarded Su San money, flowers, and fine garments for her suffering, and then, feigning innocence, asked Magistrate Wang, since they must find her a place to live, whether or not he would be willing to marry her, or at least take her into his household.

Magistrate Wang was delighted by the proposal, for he could save face and he had come to realize that he still loved the beautiful courtesan that he had so mistreated. In one of the big songs of the show, *The Faithful Harlot*, Magistrate Wang Chin-lung sang for joy that he had come to his senses and declared his true love.

When the singing finally ended and the orchestra finished, everyone clapped madly for the excellent show. Green Willow felt a surge of relief. It could have been much worse. She looked at Jade River, who met her gaze with a warm smile and a laugh, so Green Willow smiled and laughed as well.

Blue Cloud and Jade River both smiled at Huệ to check his reaction to the end of the comedy, and he had fallen asleep in his chair. They smiled at each other, and their eyes communicated more amusement. Jade River reached over and nudged Huệ, but he didn't react. Blue Cloud nudged him again, and still no reaction. Jade River reached out and felt his forehead and then his wrist, and knew something was wrong. She put her hands on his face. Huệ wasn't breathing.

Calling for help, she and Green Willow moved Huệ to the floor. Jade River pushed on his chest and breathed into his mouth. Huệ did not respond to chest pumping. Jade River knew that her brother, the magnificent Huệ, the brilliant leader, was dead. She let out a wail, which was joined by the scream of Blue Cloud and the cries of his three wives, Green Willow, Precious Stone, and Gem Lake.

Huệ's bodyguards rushed forward from their stations around the stage and the courtyard. Green Willow, her face contorted with fear, turned to the captain of the guard and said, "Send for the doctors, Huệ isn't breathing! Arrest all persons in the kitchen, and lock down the palace. No one is to leave until we've conducted a thorough investigation."

Chapter 44
The Battle of Thị Nại, Quy Nhơn
1792

Nguyễn Huệ's death was kept secret, so not surprisingly, the entire palace knew of it. The news of Huệ's sudden demise flew on the wings of homing pigeons to Quy Nhơn and to Sài Gòn. Nhạc was not shocked by the news, and he did a poor job of pretending to be either surprised or disappointed. *The upstart got just what he deserved,* he thought, *thanks to the efforts of Võ Văn Nhậm, an inexperienced assistant cook, and a little lacquered duck laced with horse bane. Now no one can stop me from uniting our country under my banner.*

King Ánh was delighted by the news. He immediately shared the information with Father Pierre. "The enemy has lost its great strategist," Ánh declared. "What an unexpected boon. Father Pierre, what do you say we move quickly now on Quy Nhơn?"

"It is time," said Pierre. "Eastern and Western military historians and strategists agree that a weaker force must always try to choose the time and place of an inescapable confrontation."

King Ánh responded, "The Tây Sơn fighters will feel this apparent poisoning of Huệ is a terrible omen, and they will be fearful. We will launch an attack as soon as possible. I will call together the Council of Military Mandarins for early tomorrow morning to discuss and implement a plan of action."

❧　❦

While Ánh, Nhạc, and Huệ had been involved in a three-way arms race, the peasants throughout the country were being worked to the bone. Nhạc had amassed and built a great fleet of war junks and galleys at Thị Nại, the port of Quy Nhơn, and planned a campaign against Nguyễn Ánh. Now Ánh accepted that he should wait no longer, since the dry season approached. He committed his naval forces.

King Nguyễn Ánh was on board his own Vietnamese-built, Western-style frigate, *Le Prince de Cochinchine,* with Đỗ Thanh Nhơn, his commander-in-chief, as they approached the entrance to Thị Nại. It was five o'clock in the morning, or the hour of the Cat, and the wind was fresh from the southwest. King Ánh said to Đỗ Thanh Nhơn, "I have invested a great deal in the military theories of Father Pierre the Bishop. Now I shall see for myself what his sailors and ships can do."

As they watched the sky lighten and the stars fade, Đỗ Thanh Nhơn replied, "The outcome is in the hands of Heaven. What is there to fear? Didn't we turn back Hồ Huệ's campaign last year? He sent his navy to attack our coastline, while his army conquered Laos and Cambodia, and then attacked Sài Gòn from the west. The French warships stopped his navy, while the Siamese regiments made available to you by King Rama, helped our troops stop his army before it reached our capitol."

"Yes," said Ánh, "all I gave to the Siamese King for his support was my claim of jurisdiction over Cambodia, which I'm in no position to enforce now at any rate. My grandsons can worry about that. Someday we might win Cambodia back. Furthermore, my astrologer declared that this month was auspicious for me and all my family."

Henri Dayot commanded *Le Prince de Cochinchine*, while Grannier commanded *La Méduse*. Father Pierre had a fever and was trying to sleep in his large house back in Sài Gòn. Guillaume de Martineau was also on board *Le Prince de Cochinchine* as the first lieutenant. He watched *La Méduse* ahead, and he tried to make out Grannier. *His time is almost up,* he thought. *He will never quit. It's him or me, and the sooner he's gone, by whatever means, the safer I'll be. Just be patient. The opportunity will come soon.*

Grannier's ship entered the harbor just before sunrise. His mission was to cause confusion while the Nguyễn Army units seized the forts. The artillery brigades under Olivier du Puymannel could then set up field batteries along the hills by the forts overlooking the harbor.

The cannon of the forts were ineffective. They were ancient devices fixed in place so that their gunners couldn't aim them. Soon after sentinels sounded the alarm against *La Méduse* and most of the Tây Sơn men of the forts had rushed to the walls facing the harbor, Ánh's spies in the garrisons dispatched the remaining sentinels on the inland walls. Nguyễn Army units quietly trotted across the no man's land to the abandoned inland walls of each fort. Their *avant-garde* carried ladders, which they carefully placed on the massive walls and then climbed up the ladders and onto the parapet. These first soldiers rushed to open the gates. Nguyễn soldiers poured into the forts by ladder and gate. With the aid of archers and soldiers carrying Việt pikes or French muskets, the attackers cut down many Tây Sơn fighters before the remaining defenders fell on their knees in surrender.

On King Nguyễn Ánh's order, Dayot's *Le Prince de Cochinchine*, *Le Saint-Esprit*, and *La Castries* stopped at the mouth of the harbor and waited for the king's galleys to catch up. They were in clear sight and just minutes behind. Ánh expected Grannier's *La Méduse* to hit the anchored fleet with a broadside or two and then retreat. He was surprised, therefore, to see *La Méduse* sail straight into the fleet of anchored galleys and junks.

Rather than turn around and wait for the king's ship and his galley fleet, Benoit decided to take advantage of what was obviously a successful surprise attack and to press straight into the anchored enemy fleet with the 38 guns of *La Méduse* all blasting away. The ship sailed back and forth across the harbor firing upon dozens of ships. The number of galleys and junks that were able to respond slowly but steadily increased. Whenever a fully manned war galley or proa approached, the 19 swivel guns fired grapeshot and shredded the attackers.

King Ánh could barely believe his eyes. Was this brilliant or foolish? Grannier and his French and Việt sailors on board *La Méduse* simply amazed him. It was glorious, or horrible, to witness the firepower of *La Méduse*, depending on which side you were on. Ánh said to Đỗ Thanh Nhơn, "The last time Việts fought against Europeans with their own ships was decades ago when the Trịnh fought against some Portuguese traders, who turned tail and sailed off after the first exchange."

Đỗ Thanh Nhơn replied, "That was then. Thank the War God Quan Công that we are not fighting these French barbarians—that their Western warships are for us and not against us."

Fifteen minutes passed before the fifty Nguyễn galleys reached the harbor mouth. At that moment, *La Méduse* ran aground on an uncharted shoal. The tide was low and running in, but *La Méduse* could no longer maneuver. Stuck on the harbor bed, it was now firing all the guns that could be brought to bear as the Tây Sơn ships regrouped and threatened to overpower it with their sheer number of boats.

Dayot ordered Lieutenant de Martineau to signal the attack, and yelled for his crew to let the canvas out. *Le Prince de Cochinchine, Le Saint-Esprit,* and *La Castries* sailed into the fight with a kind of exhilaration particular to confident and professional soldiers. With the two French frigates and many of the Nguyễn galleys on either side, *Le Prince* advanced till it also struck bottom on the shoal. By now some Tây Sơn galleys had reached *La Méduse* and were boarding her. *Le Prince* stopped only twenty feet away.

Guillaume, on board *Le Prince*, could see Benoit fighting an enemy soldier on the deck of *La Méduse*. Guillaume aimed the musket he held ready, first at the Tây Sơn soldier. Then he moved his sights, aiming instead for below Benoit's heart, and pulled the trigger.

Benoit parried and thrust his sword into his opponent's throat just as the ball struck him down. The Nguyễn galleys swarmed around *La Méduse* beating off its attackers and throwing the Tây Sơn ships into utter confusion. After Benoit fell wounded, he remained conscious. First mate Joachim Bohu and Võ Tánh both saw him fall, and rushed to his side. Two sailors dragged him below while Bohu and Võ Tánh and Captain La Fontaine dispatched the remaining attackers coming up over the side.

Many of the Tây Sơn galleys and junks still stood at anchor, their crews waiting on shore for sampans and proas to ferry them to the warships. Olivier du Puymanel's shore batteries were now causing havoc throughout the harbor, destroying the docks where many Tây Sơn boats still stood tied to piers. The last of the mobilized Tây Sơn galleys and junks were soon sunk or subdued.

Below deck, surgeon Michel Despiaux, a thin, middle-aged gentleman with a mostly clean smock, was tying a tourniquet above an arrow wound when the sailors entered the sick bay with Captain Grannier.

"Well captain, nice of you to pay me a visit," Despiaux said, trying to sound cheerful.

"I'm sorry to add to your work," Benoit said.

"Here, have a drink on me," said the dour looking doctor magnanimously. Benoit took the rum between his lips and drank with purpose. The liquor burned his throat and sent pains into his head, exactly as it was supposed to. Benoit drank deeply again.

Despiaux and his loblolly boy cut away Benoit's shirt with a sharp razor. The ball had entered below the left floating rib under the heart and exited the other side. The doctor, trying to hide his unpleasant prognosis, poured alcohol over the wound, dampened it with a cloth, then probed with his finger to feel for the ball or any foreign matter. Having found no hard pieces in the wound, he said, "As long as the gangrene doesn't set in and you let yourself rest, you might survive this and even be able to hold a sword again."

The doctor took a red hot iron out of a coal brazier and cauterized both ends of the wound. The stench of burnt flesh filled the room; Benoit's body arced in pain and he fainted.

❧ ☙

"Great Heavens!" Ánh said to Đỗ Thanh Nhơn. "How bizarre. What was meant to be a harassing raid with this small force has turned into a major victory, thanks to the audacity of Grannier and Dayot and their crews, and the firepower of *La Méduse* and these other Western Ocean ships." He peered through the clouds of smoke at hundreds of ships burning, or sitting sunk or unmanned at their anchorages.

"The size of our victory is shocking," said Đỗ Thanh Nhơn.

"Before the Nine Judges, I'm a disgrace to my Ancestors," Ánh said laughing. "We have captured so many of Nhạc's ships that we haven't the men to move them all to Cần Giờ. I am not prepared for such a great victory."

"This does make up for their barbarian smell," said Đỗ Thanh Nhơn smiling. "It looks like we will have to burn what we can't take with us."

Ánh was known to be very cautious to preserve his resources. He was so concerned to retreat before the main body of Nhạc's army reached the port that he did burn most of the captured ships and supplies. For booty, he retained only twenty of the largest and best-armed junks and galleys. He ordered that the hundreds of other vessels be put to the torch. The contents of three of the harbor warehouses, full of rice, clothing, valuables, and money, were loaded onto ships. All the other warehouses, also full of military supplies including food and cloth, were simply burned. Henri Dayot and his officers did not like to see such great amounts of supplies go to waste, but Ánh would not listen to any plan for their removal. He absolutely refused to dally in Quy Nhơn with such a small force while the main body of Nhạc's Hissing Army approached.

By the dawn of the next day, as Nhạc's army entered the town unhindered, they found the port's warehouses all burned to the ground, and all that remained of its navy were burnt spars sticking out of the water or floating about. The Nguyễn ships, lying low in the water, rowed and sailed out of the harbor, with one less indigenous navy to worry about.

❧   ☙

The Nguyễn fleet returned to Cần Giờ in ten days at the speed of the slowest galleys. The cannons fired nine salutes and the bells sounded at the Nguyễn fort, alerting the town that the fleet had returned. The news spread quickly from tongue to tongue that the ships were returning. Wives, concubines, prostitutes, friends, and relatives of the mariners flocked from the town and campgrounds to the quayside for the sight of their loved ones.

Bùi Moon Light was waiting at the beach when the first longboats came ashore with some of the wounded. Guillaume de Martineau, in a scarlet jacket, walked deliberately over to Moon Light and bowed. "*Bonjour* Mademoiselle Bùi." He was all solemnity and graciousness.

"*Bonjour,*" Moon Light replied, worried and confused. There was concern in Guillaume's eyes, and he had color in his cheeks as he addressed her. "I'm sorry to report that Benoit did not fare well in the fray and comes home with a bit of a wound. I'm terribly sorry." He then bowed again politely and returned to the supervision of the wounded in his longboat.

Moon Light found her long-nosed barbarian. He lay semiconscious on a stretcher carried by his men. "Benoit, what happened?" she exclaimed, and took his hand. He did not answer, or recognize her or show any signs of hearing her. *Oh Quán Thế Âm, how can this be?* Moon Light thought, and her stomach suddenly went into knots. *God moves in mysterious ways. Is it his karma to suffer now? God help him. Is praying only to the Christian God enough?* A warehouse had been set up to serve as a hospital, and it was to this building that the wounded were removed. Moon Light was recognized by the sailors as the translator who accompanied the captain regularly, and was admitted into the warehouse with Captain Grannier. Benoit remained feverish and pale and unresponsive.

That day Father Pierre pressed Dr. Despiaux to see if there was any more that could be done for Captain Grannier, and Despiaux patiently said no, nothing that he was aware of, other than prayer. The doctor was frustrated that he didn't understand better what Benoit appeared to be dying of. Father Pierre was not as perturbed by this lack of knowledge. Pierre Pigneau always put his faith in the Lord, and prayer seemed to him not a last resort, but a logical part of the solution.

Father Pierre looked at Benoit, lying in a gray pallor. He took Benoit's hand in his own and prayed for his recovery. Moon Light looked at Father Pierre and asked, "How can I put faith in your God of love, when bad things happen to good people?"

Pierre nodded as if in full agreement. He answered, "When Job complained to the Lord about the unfairness of life, the Lord appeared to Job out of a whirlwind and demanded of Job, 'Is man wise enough to question the creator of the heavens and the earth?' Some things, my lady, will always defy our understanding."

Bùi Moon Light was confused. Why did she even care for a hairy barbarian? Did he just have bad karma? She prayed to the good Lord Jesus, and then, just to be sure, she prayed to Buddha, Quán Thế Âm the Goddess of Mercy, the Genie of the hospital, the Genie of the sea, the Genie of the town, and the Genie of the local woods. *When life is in the balance, no important local power should be overlooked or insulted,* she thought. She sang to him, all the songs she could remember.

The doctor inspected Benoit's wound every day and showed Moon Light how to change the dressing. Despiaux allowed Moon Light to apply tepid wet cloths to his forehead when the fever raged, and ordered his attendants to feed him soup and to hope. While alone with him, Moon Light sometimes quietly talked to Benoit, even though he was asleep. She begged his spirit not to wander off, and to let him wake up.

After five terrible days and nights, the fever mysteriously left Benoit's body. Pierre attributed the fever breaking to prayer and the intercession of God. Dr. Despiaux observed that something over time caused the swelling and infection of the wound to decrease; perhaps his salves helped. The grateful Moon Light thought, *For a while longer, the Gods and local Genie allow him to live. Thanks and praise to all the Gods and Genie, and thank you Jesus, Mary, and Joseph.*

The rainy season started, so King Nguyễn Ánh stopped his strictly seasonal campaign against the Tây Sơn. In disappointment and disgust, Henri Dayot and half of the remaining Frenchmen took their last payment in silver and returned to Pondicherry, taking with them the 32-gun frigate *La Castries.* The 24-gun *Le Pandour* had already departed fully manned with sailors at the end of the previous dry season.

Chapter 45
Quy Nhơn, Sài Gòn
1793

The doctors who rushed to help Huệ at the banquet of the lacquered duck quickly confirmed that he was dead. Among his valuables he had left three official scrolls in which he named and confirmed as his heir to the throne the boy Quang Toản, the son of his concubine Blue Cloud. He also appointed his companion Lương Hoàng as the regent of all his realm and protector of his family. And he had left a scroll for Lương Hoàng with one last order or request. Hoàng opened it and read, *Lương Hoàng, if I have passed on due to subterfuge, I ask you as a man of honor to be sure to avenge my death as soon as possible. I place my trust and confidence in you, my faithful friend, Huệ.*

In May, propelled by the summer monsoon, Nguyễn Ánh's Navy, still supported by *La Méduse* and *Le Prince de Cochinchine* and its new twin, *Western Dragon,* attacked and conquered Nha Trang, Diên Khánh, and Phú Yên. Soon, the Nguyễn forces had moved up to Quy Nhơn itself and besieged the great citadel and palace there.

Nhạc had sent messengers by boat to the Spring Capital to ask Lương Hoàng, the new regent of the child Quang Toản, for help.

Lương Hoàng arrived in Quy Nhơn with 28,000 soldiers, eighty elephants, and thirty war junks. *La Méduse* and *Le Prince de Cochinchine*, unfortunately, were not much use in a land battle away from the sea. Committing just his land forces, Lương Hoàng quickly sent the Nguyễn forces into flight, and marched proudly into the Quy Nhơn citadel as its liberator.

Nguyễn Nhạc and Lương Hoàng appeared on a rampart above the courtyard, and before a throng of assembled troops, Nhạc welcomed his old comrade, Lương Hoàng, now regent and general of the Northern Army. Nhạc presented Hoàng with a famous sword from the Ming Dynasty. The troops all cheered and shouted to show their approval. Nhạc withdrew with his bodyguard to the main reception hall to receive Hoàng, but when Hoàng entered, against the rules of his host, he brought his own bodyguard with him.

"Your guards are not to enter here," Nhạc remonstrated. "Show them out," he yelled to his own men.

"Greetings," said Lương Hoàng in a clear voice, and his men drew arrows on their bows. Loverboy put an arrow in his bow, but arrows immediately pierced him in the chest and throat. Snake, his brother Midget, and Night Hawk attacked the bowmen with their spears raised, but they were also cut down by more arrows and then finished off as Nhạc looked on in horror. Nhạc yelled for the hallway guards. They did not answer; none of his men remained alive in the hallway either.

"My old friend Hoàng, what is the meaning of this?" demanded Nhạc.

"My old friend Nhạc, as the regent of Quang Toản, the son and chosen heir of your brother Huệ, I relieve you of all of your titles and duties. You are now under house arrest."

"What right have you to arrest me, the King of the Center?" Nhạc demanded, playing for the sympathy of Hoàng's men.

"We have discovered that you were the director of your own brother's murder by poisoning."

"That's a terrible lie," Nhạc said. "Men, this man is a traitor to my family. I never would have even considered such a thing. You will all disgrace your Ancestors. ..."

I'm sorry," said Hoàng, in a strong but tired voice. "We discovered poison in the lacquer of a banquet duck, and we caught the man responsible. He confessed before an open tribunal to taking his orders from Võ Văn Nhậm, who commanded in your name. I sent agents to see General Nhậm. They were able to persuade the general to admit that he acted under your orders. With two accusers of murder, you are under house arrest."

"This is absurd. Of course I didn't poison my own brother. You won't get away with this!" Nhạc shrieked. "You are trying to take advantage of a tragic situation."

"Take him to his own chambers, search his room for exits, and then confine him to one of his rooms," Hoàng ordered.

Nhạc grabbed a spear from one of his slain guards and charged Hoàng. Hoàng sidestepped Nhạc's first vicious thrust, slid forward, took the spear in both hands, and with a shove of his hips and arms sent Nhạc sprawling into a forward roll.

Nhạc rolled out and sprang to his feet. He reached down to a corpse and picked up a sword. The captain of Lương Hoàng's bodyguard, Phước Tỉnh, brandishing his own blade, advanced on King Nhạc. Nhạc and the captain faced each other for a moment, until Nhạc began his attacks. He struck fast and furious, while Tỉnh parried, until he moved inside and caught Nhạc's arm as it came down.

Using his hip, the captain sent Nhạc into the air while still holding the handle of Nhạc's own sword. Hoàng's men quickly grabbed Nhạc and marched him off to confinement in one of his own private rooms.

Minutes later, Nhạc produced a concealed dagger and stabbed one of his guards. As he tried for a second soldier, who blocked the thrust, the other guards skewered Nhạc on their swords. That was the end of King Nguyễn Nhạc's raging tantrum and his life.

Informed by his captain, Hoàng inspected Nhạc's dead body. Hoàng gently closed Nhạc's eyes. He lovingly kissed Nhạc's forehead. Tears quickly came to Hoàng's eyes. Viewing the bloody scene, he said to his comrade Phước Tỉnh, "We have killed the last of the mighty Hồ brothers. Goodbye Hồ Nhạc. If man doesn't live by his principles and right conduct, he is no different than the savage beasts of the jungle. If we had failed to prove through Võ Văn Nhậm that you plotted your brother's murder, I would have reluctantly held you up again before the people as their king. I never wanted to rule, and I plan to hand the throne over to Quang Toản on the day he turns seventeen. But it is perhaps better this way, for since you were proved guilty, I would have personally slain you if needed to right the wrong. Great bitterness, so much gained and then lost."

With Nhạc's death by the soldiers of the regent, all of the three famous Hồ brothers of Tây Sơn were dead. Lương Hoàng—Nhạc, Lữ, and Huệ's neighbor and friend—was now the regent of Huệ's son Quang Toản. Lương Hoàng now ruled all of central and north Đại Việt.

For a fourth time, Autumn Moon went into mourning for one of her children. She was furious with Lương Hoàng, but respected that he had done his Confucian duty to her third son, Huệ. She also arranged with Lương Hoàng that she would live in Phú Xuân near Quang Toản. She moved her entire household north by junk to be close to her grandchild and Huệ's heir.

෨ ෩

Blue Cloud and Huệ's three wives, Green Willow, Precious Stone, and Gem Lake, approved of Lương Hoàng's arrest of their brother-in-law Nguyễn Nhạc. Nevertheless, they remained depressed and frightened by the loss of their husband the warrior-king. Blue Cloud wanted to put her feelings into poetry, but she wasn't confident in her writing ability, so she asked Gem Lake, who was renown locally for her poems, to help her. Together, they produced a poem, which they titled *Eulogy for Nguyễn Huệ*. Blue Cloud dictated the first draft in the first person. Gem Lake edited the poem and put her own name down as the sole author.

Eulogy for Nguyễn Huệ, by Lê Thị Ngọc Hân (Gem Lake)

Whenever the wind scatters flowers,
I seem to sense his heavenly scent wafting from afar,
And I hasten to dress up, and rush to greet him.
Alas, his lonely palace is woven with spiderwebs.

The more I try to recall his face, the more my heart is torn.
Where is it now, his dragon countenance?
Can anyone return from the Beyond
To give me tiding of him?

Death has separated us forever,
And this sad thought pierces my heart.
We were unable to live out our marriage in this life;
Can we, in another, once more burn fire and incense together?

Alas, springtime has passed, and the flower remains!
How can I disentangle the skein of my sadness?
I wanted to follow him to the tomb,
And hang myself from a post, or throw myself into the river.

But my two children are like eggs that have barely hatched,
And I could not abandon them to follow the call of my love.
Condemned, I must lead a miserable existence,
The body still alive, but the soul on the rim of evanescence.

I vividly remember the moment
When we swore to live and die together,
Of the times when he summoned me day and night
To manifest a love as durable as gold and stone.

Why now this silence?
And this solitude that no one else cares about?
My guitar is broken in the middle of a song,
Leaving me alone with my tiny orphans.

I look East: sailing ships appear
On the endless sea, under a cloudy sky.
I look West:
Nothing but lofty mountains and dense forests.

I look South: scattered wild ducks.
I look North: a whiteness flowing with mist.
Whichever way I turn my gaze,
I cannot make out the road that leads to his eternal abode.

&ea;   &ea;

Benoit recovered slowly from his wound. He spent long periods of his convalescence with Bùi Moon Light, learning more Vietnamese. By this time, he had an enormous respect for her patience as well as her intelligence.

Every morning Benoit spent working on Vietnamese with Moon Light. They sat or strolled through the king's gardens while conversing, building his vocabulary. He liked to say, "*Tôi nói tiếng Việt không được thạo lắm,*" (I don't speak Vietnamese very well) and "*Khó lắm*" (It is very hard).

During a discussion with Dr. Michel Despiaux, Benoit and the doctor figured out that from where Benoit had been standing on board *Le Donnai*, the musket ball that entered his stomach must have come from the direction of the main deck of *Le Prince*—from friendly fire—where incidentally, Benoit noted to himself, Guillaume and others had been stationed with muskets. He kept his eyes peeled for another ambush by Guillaume. He took to placing a loaded pistol by his bed at night. He also systematically questioned the men who had been on board *Le Prince* the day he was shot, one man at a time.

Before going back to his duties at the shipyard of Sài Gòn, every afternoon Benoit walked across the royal gardens to a field where he had set up a pistol range. There, for an hour a day, he practiced shooting four pistols of different sizes, while four of his guards helped load them and set up fresh targets. He already had the speed, and his aim and confidence were improving rapidly.

The king appointed an old scholar to teach Benoit the elements of Chinese calligraphy, which Benoit agreed to study. Benoit also asked if Moon Light could learn Chinese with him. The king asked, "Why would you do that?"

Benoit answered, "I think it will make my study easier and more interesting."

The young king shrugged and assented, saying, "It is not my advice. I agree with Confucius, who wrote, 'Educated women are nothing but trouble.'"

Moon Light was also teaching Benoit *Quốc ngữ*, the new European way of writing Vietnamese in Roman letters. As their studies lengthened, so did their relationship deepen. Benoit began to understand the complexity of Moon Light's position. Her father was a rich man who owned most of two villages and their surrounding farms. His eldest daughter, Bùi Spring Song, was a talented elephant trainer who married Trần Quang Diệu, who later marched north with a battalion of trained soldiers and joined the Tây Sơn. Bùi Spring Song also became a Tây Sơn general. The father, mortified by the eldest daughter and son-in-law, had offered his second and most beautiful daughter to the king as a gift. Now she was Ánh's slave. She would grow to be an old maid in the king's house unless Ánh either took her as another concubine or married or sold her off.

Benoit came to understand that this intelligent and beautiful woman belonged to the king, and the king had lent her as a servant to him. Benoit also knew now that he wanted her, and that he now had to decide, did he want to marry her—or just to bed her? *She would make a great mistress, and probably a good wife. But could you take a Việt wife home to your old Catholic mother and relatives? How would it affect my career in the French Navy? Would our children have a good future for themselves in France? After the battle of Thị Nại, all these questions seemed more and less important. Now I sound like a Taoist.*

I could take her as a mistress, he thought. *Many of the other officers keep Việt mistresses that they enjoy. But what's to become of these women after we have all left? Their own people will treat them as tainted whores, outcasts. Most of these women were tarts to begin with. But there's the hitch: Moon Light isn't and never has been a prostitute. She is an unmarried lady of twenty-one, and she should be married by now. Of course, I'm thirty, and so should I.*

It was clear that the king had put Moon Light at Benoit's disposal. What bothered him the most was the thought that politically she couldn't refuse even a cavalier advance from him without possibly incurring the wrath of the king. What kind of conquest or love affair would that be?

Benoit sought solace at one of the pleasure houses. There was a woman named Peach Blossom at the Yellow Gate of Heaven Pavilion who was particularly pleasing to him, and it had occurred to him on more than one occasion that she might make an easier wife than the more opinionated Moon Light. Peach Blossom could be his mistress, without damaging her status; his patronage would more likely raise it. His thinking about Moon Light became circular, or at least he kept coming back to the same points.

He wanted this woman Moon Light to the point where it was driving him crazy. Not only was she beautiful, charming and witty, she was friendly and available. *I could marry her and be very happy. But the marriage could set back, if not wreck my career in the French Navy. What career? King Louis the XVI is in prison, and his relatives and friends are being executed daily by the guillotine. The reformers appear to have gone mad with bloodlust. And my dear mother, when I do finally return to Lorient, she had no great respect for any of the colored races of the heathen. However, mother isn't the one getting married. The navy discourages this sort of formal relationship with individuals of native stock, but does not ban it. My chances of career advancement are unclear in the new Navy of the Republic. The Royal Navy has disappeared in the flames of revolution, along with the Régime Ancienne. And I am already a captain.*

I would spend little time in the future with my mother. Possibly she would grow more tolerant. My children, should God be so gracious, would be seen as half-breeds, but does that matter so much to me? Wouldn't it matter to them? Yet I could marry Moon Light . . . and probably be very happy. For now, my work is here. His thoughts went round and round, but they always reached the same dead end. *There is only one correct way to approach a lady of honor of any country—honorably.*

࿔ ࿔

A few days later Benoit decided. He wanted to marry Moon Light, and he would ask her directly, but privately. One morning, at the end of a lesson on grammar and pronunciation during which Benoit had trouble concentrating, since his mind was on something else, he decided to ask, "Moon Light, why aren't you married?"

Moon Light looked her dear long-nosed barbarian straight in the eye. By now she was scared that the fellow would never get his courage up. Then she realized that a lecture was out of order, so she averted her eyes and tried blushing shyly.

"I will marry when the king finds a husband for me."

"And when will that be?" Benoit persisted.

"There is no telling when."

You water buffalo, she thought impatiently, *when you finally get around to asking me.*

Benoit looked at Moon Light and knew that he wanted to marry this woman, to exchange the holy rings and tie the lifelong knot. His good Christian mother would just have to accept it, all questions of race and culture aside.

Benoit cleared his throat and pulled himself up straight at the writing table between them. "Moon Light, I understand that here in Đại Việt suitors should use intermediaries for good manners and politeness. But should I approach you in that way, you might not have any choice in the matter, but have to agree to whatever the king wants for himself. To avoid that, I must informally ask you on my own, Moon Light, would you desire and consent to be my wife? Would you consent freely?"

"Wife, first and only?" she said, as if to check that he wasn't teasing, as he so often did during the language lessons. "I would like, I would consent," she said smiling, afraid to show her emotion.

"But do you want to marry me?" Benoit demanded bluntly.

"Since you ask me directly," she said with a naughty smile, "how could I ever say no without making you lose a big amount of face?"

Benoit looked carefully at her winsome smile. "I see that I have put you in a compromising position," he said, with a deadpan delivery. "Since I've made a social blunder, let's forget all about it and pretend I never brought it up. Of course, I was only joking. I would never do anything purposely to embarrass you."

"Well that's good," she said with mock concern. "I was afraid for a moment that you had the bad manners to be serious."

"Oh, how could you have thought that? That would be so unlike me."

"Yes, of course, you always are so proper," she said.

A long silence ensued. Benoit decided to hold his tongue and call her bluff. He returned his eyes to his language work, and reached for his brush.

"Not so fast," Moon Light blurted, not quite sure where the conversation had gone. "I would like, very like, to marry you. It was king's idea first. I was unhappy very. Then your idea. Now it is my idea, I do. You are still one big hairy barbarian, but—I love you anyway." Benoit gave her a beaming smile, then they both smiled, somewhat embarrassed and amused by what had just transpired. Benoit stood up, raised her to her feet, and kissed her very gently on the lips. Moon Light's body froze in stiffness, and then slowly softened and relaxed. She overcame her shyness and responded. They embraced and she kissed him back.

❧   ❧

Benoit and Moon Light walked through the gardens in silence, enjoying the brightly colored flowers and the groves of young planted trees.

"There is a problem," Moon Light said.

"What is that."

"I do not want to immediately become a widow of a long-nosed barbarian."

"So?"

"Before you approach King Ánh, I want you somehow to eliminate snake in the tall grass Martineau. He lies waiting to bite you again."

Chapter 46
Jade River and the Regent
1793

The Regent Lương Hoàng rose when Jade River entered his private reception room in the Spring Capital Phú Xuân. She carefully kowtowed on her knees to the regent, although she sensed his embarrassment, and then he offered her one of the ornate Chinese chairs. "I salute you," she said. "If you don't mind, I would prefer the floor," and she knelt on one of the rich rugs. Hoàng knelt down facing her, and simply enjoyed her beautiful face for a moment while a serving maid placed tea before them and left.

Jade River wore a long five-piece tunic of fine white silk over white pantaloons. She was still in mourning for her two brothers, Huệ and Nhạc. As she looked on her old sweetheart, Hoàng, she could see in the manly lines and scars on his face hints of the long history of her powerful and famous family. Now her brothers were all dead, and the power they once wielded had been given by her brother Huệ to Hoàng, to rule as regent until Quang Toản was no longer a child.

"I was about to go inspect the naval yard," said Hoàng. "Would you care to accompany me?"

"Thank you, no," said Jade River. "I have come here today to discuss your kind invitation to make me your third wife."

"Yes," said Hoàng, and he braced himself, still unable to tell what this extraordinary woman would do.

"Excuse me for not using a go-between," she said. "I know it is proper. But I thought it better not to, for matters of state, to make sure we understand each other, and for our privacy."

"That makes sense," said Hoàng. "Please continue."

"Hoàng, I have some issues and a question. I am pulled apart by this decision. Selfishly, I wish to enter the White Lotus Monastery and take the vows of the nuns. You are a great man, but my youth is spent, and I feel unclean. I have had enough of lying in the red dust, enough for several lifetimes.

"There is more. I am disgusted that my own brothers Nhạc and Huệ, whom I loved, would actually come to mortal blows, and fight their armies against each other over mere treasure and power. Such bad behavior must be some kind of disease of success. How could my brothers be so engrossed in the trappings of material wealth, as to forget the important things in life—filial piety, respect for parents, family and neighbors, and to work for spiritual and political harmony?

"Finally, my mother insists that before I withdraw from society, I receive your blessing and permission to do so. She also wants your reassurance, and your guarantee that you will hand over the rule of our land to her grandson, my nephew, even if I should choose not to enter your household."

Hoàng's heart sank and he felt stepped on. He was insulted, on at least two counts. "Power makes everyone behave strangely," he said bitterly. "I thought that you might accept my offer now that I am the regent. And after a lifetime of service, does Autumn Moon not trust my loyalty, especially to Huệ? Does she really think that I arrested my old friend Nhạc out of personal ambition? That is so insulting."

Jade River smiled. She immediately understood and felt for her old friend. "Hoàng, I trust you completely. It is Mother who is so worried. She is old and she has irrational fears without cause. She is angry at you for arresting Nhạc without consulting her, even though she grudgingly admits you were honor-bound to do what you did. She is a little crazy; she blames Huệ for falling out with Nhạc."

"I am sorry," he said, and then paused and cleared his throat, "that you don't wish to marry me, but I think I understand. I will hand over the throne to Quang Toản, or any of his brothers or cousins, for that matter, whether you stay with me and join my family or not. You may tell your mother, since you are apparently the go-between and not she, that she can make someone else the regent today or tomorrow if she doesn't trust me."

"She trusts no one," Jade River said seriously, and then smiling, "but she trusts you more than anyone else. She is so depressed over losing all her sons that she is on the verge of some sort of breakdown. I will continue to attend her until she no longer needs me."

"Jade River, I must ask you, or I will regret it for the rest of my life: Are you sure you would rather take the vows than live at court as a wife and a queen? I could declare you First Wife if that is the problem. I could enforce our engagement vows by decree."

"That is very generous of you," Jade River replied. She met his gaze, and understood his longing for a dream in the past that was never fulfilled. *It was a beautiful dream. We were so young and innocent.*

"Queen of my own country and people—and married to my first love—that is an interesting temptation." But she did not stop and rethink about such wealth and power for very long.

"I am mostly content with my decision to follow the path of Buddha. The great teacher once said, 'You must give up worldly things in order to achieve nirvana.' He described nirvana as the peace of Heaven on earth—no small thing. I believe in the wisdom of Buddha, in the Eightfold Path, and that fewer material things, attachments, and responsibilities mean greater spiritual growth. There is a teacher of the healing arts at the monastery, and she will only teach those who have taken all the vows.

"Our marriage would threaten the harmony of your lovely household. For us to marry, your Second Wife might have to be sent away, or she might demand a divorce. I would not want either on my conscience. I love your wives like the sisters that I never had. You love them as women, friends, and the mothers of your children. Their children are the only children that I have, and I love them also. And I have seen enough now of politics and military power to want as little to do with them as possible."

Hoàng had not understood until that moment how disappointed he would feel. His stomach went sour and he silently wept without tears. Jade River was sensitive to his grief, in spite of his stoicism, and she shared his disappointment, even though it wasn't hers exactly. *Hoàng's love is much greater than I expected. I am sorely tempted by his deep emotion. Oh, to be held and loved again by a powerful man who really cares. Do I dare walk away from this—such temptation.*

"Hoàng, it would be a privilege and joy to receive so much love from you. But would you ever care for me again as much as you do at this very moment? If you could love me greatly, wouldn't I destroy all the harmony that exists between you and Spring Bloom and Red Lotus, the women you have already married? I should not do that to them. We women live in a very proscribed, custom-bound society. Only in the monastery will I be allowed to follow a spiritual and intellectual path unfettered by strict social conventions."

Hoàng looked deflated and miserable. He wondered in desperation, *If I send my wives away or have them killed, would she come around to me? No, these thoughts are evil and mad. Honor her desire for peace and harmony.* "Oh Heaven and Earth," he said, "I love you, and the idea that we will be reunited. But you are right, I also love my wives and children."

"Dear Hoàng, what is life but foolish dreams and imperfect choices? You have wonderful wives, beautiful children, and now you are the commander-in-chief of all the Tây Sơn Army. You even have a mission. There are still Nguyễn forces to defeat and barbarian fighters and their priests to repel. My love for you is deep like the ocean. It has become pure. Let's keep our love as pure as the white lotus, which grows in the mud of the swamp. I will pray for your military success, and for you— long life and happiness with your lovely wives and children."

At this point Jade River arose, as did Lương Hoàng. She embraced him carefully once, with strength and feeling. She pressed her body against his, and left him, still silently crying, in the privacy of his inner room. As regent, he was the acting King of Đại Việt, and yet all he felt was failure and loss.

Chapter 47
Conflict in Sài Gòn
July 1793

Moon Light reported to King Nguyễn Ánh that Benoit had finally asked her to marry him. Ánh was pleased, for Benoit was quite useful for a barbarian. He was smart and courteous without ever being obsequious, and a successful fighting captain. Moon Light explained that she had told Benoit that he must get rid of Guillaume de Martineau. Ánh was angered by this, but when she explained why, he understood. The Việt patriarchal system had its own safety net, the extended family. Widows were not treated well in Việt society, and widows of foreigners were outcasts, often even to their own families.

By the next day Ánh had decided to have Guillaume eliminated through assassination. He called Skinny Minh and set the wheels in motion for a common late-night robbery and incident to take place.

Meanwhile, Benoit spent the afternoon at the pistol range, trying to relax and cope with a gnawing fear of impending doom, and trying to decide whether to duel with Guillaume or murder him. He had promised André that he wouldn't face Guillaume in a pistol match. Since Moon Light was pushing him to do something, and he wasn't exactly sure why, he had to deal with irritation at her as well. *Why is she forcing a confrontation?* At the beginning of the crimson and blue sunset, he took a long walk upon the citadel ramparts overlooking the city.

Benoit analyzed the choices again. *I could murder Guillaume on his way home from a pleasure house, or challenge him to a pistol fight.* The gray clouds swept to the northeast with the summer monsoon. *The only problem is that Guillaume is still the better shot. The same old choice: private dishonor or public death?* As the sun sank beneath the plains and distant hills, the heavens darkened with a canvas of color: orange, yellow, purple, and blue. Dark but familiar rain clouds rolled in from the southwest on the steady breeze. As Benoit walked home, the daily late afternoon rain began in earnest.

Benoit Grannier asked Henri Dayot and Olivier du Puymanel to be his seconds. Benoit took them to dinner at a favorite restaurant, and then they visited the Golden Vessel, the bar and brothel adopted by Guillaume and his cronies. Dayot, du Puymanel, and Benoit were all armed as usual when they entered the Golden Vessel. Benoit found the black-bearded Guillaume at his habitual poker table with Baltasar Weber, Nicolas Tabarly, and Jean Bluedot.

Neither Guillaume nor any of his friends stood up as Benoit and the other senior officers approached. Military protocol among the French mercenaries was always quite relaxed, so the breach went almost unnoticed.

"Monsieur de Martineau, I must have a word with you."

Guillaume smirked. "Speak, brave gallant."

Benoit pulled up an empty chair and sat at the table. His two companions did the same. A waitress hurried over and Guillaume asked for three more wine cups. After the cups had arrived, Guillaume poured his visitors each a dram from his jar, and then toasted Louis the XVI, the former King of France. "May he survive his imprisonment and be restored to the throne!" Everyone drank.

"To what do I owe the honor of this visit?" Guillaume asked.

"There's a sailor from *Le Prince* who claims to have seen you shooting a musket towards me when I received a ball in the gut from the direction of that ship."

Guillaume's face froze. He looked up—there were no guards at the door, no one in the room was paying any attention. Without a trace of emotion, he quietly put his hand on the stock of his pistol.

"Put your hands on the table," Benoit ordered quietly, "or I will shoot you in the stomach. Now all of you put your hands on the table."

Guillaume and his three friends casually put their hands on the table.

"Martineau, I accuse you of cowardice, rape, and murder, and now attempted murder. I invite you to choose your weapons!"

Martineau smiled broadly. His worst fears of an arrest were unfounded. Perhaps there wasn't really a witness. His enemy would regret his generosity.

"Pistols, walking ten paces."

"Just so that one of us is sure to die, why not pistol and sword?"

"Fine," Guillaume scoffed with a smile, "pistol and sword."

"Tomorrow at nine a.m., in the field past the woods at the north end of this street?"

"That will suit perfectly."

"You bring the pistols, your own sword, and your seconds. Are those arrangements satisfactory?"

"Quite." With that, Benoit turned and left. His two seconds watched the men at his back, and then also retreated. No one else in the tavern knew of the challenge or the acceptance. Although illegal by French law, in the French custom, it would be a private affair between consenting adults.

❧ ❧

That night Benoit slept as usual in his room at Father Pierre's house. The next morning, he was up early. He drank some clear soup and then began to stretch out and exercise. His bullet wound was almost healed. At least he could run slowly, though in pain. After a light breakfast of tea and sticky rice prepared by his cook and valet, he took a long walk.

For an hour, Benoit prepared for the duel the way he always readied for a sword fight. He went through the entire set of fencer's warm-ups, stretching and limbering the entire body while awakening the mind. He added the boxer's exercises he had learned from Võ Tánh and other Việt fighters.

As Benoit walked to meet his seconds in the sunlight, he remembered Plato's definition of courage. "Courage," wrote the Greek philosopher, "is the virtue of fleeing from an inevitable danger." Plato was never renowned for his fighting ability. The advice did have a Confucian ring to it. *Here I am,* thought Benoit, *heading for revenge or disaster. Has man evolved positively or negatively since the time of the ancients? Quellenac was a firm believer in the code of chivalry. To die fighting for one's honor was no shame. Quellenac also warned that dueling over petty squabbles was a waste of talent. He often said, "Gentlemen are not hotheads. Remember your Shakespeare: 'Discretion is the better part of valor.' Which means, donkey heads, you duel not to solve every problem, but as a last resort."*

Nevertheless, Benoit felt alert and organized, and found himself breaking into the old ballad about Knight Guillaume and the shepherd's daughter. He changed the last verse, and instead of singing of a happy marriage between the rapist and the enterprising and forgiving peasant girl, he made up a new rhyming couplet.

Knight Guillaume said I'd rather die,

Than a peasant girl to wed,

So the king he then made good his word,

And he took off Knight Guillaume's head.

With me rai, fal lai-dall, diddle-aye day.

Benoit met his seconds outside the Golden Valley Inn at 8:45 a.m. Olivier du Puymanel warmly shook his hand, and the one-eyed old gent, Henri Dayot, embraced Benoit with a Russian bear hug. The three men walked along a path to the field. Guillaume, the dwarfish Baltasar Weber, and Nicolas Tabarly arrived shortly behind them. Though it was warm under the tropical sun, they were in luck in that the daily downpour had not yet begun. The pine, banyan, and rubber trees rustled softly in the tireless monsoon breeze.

Guillaume's seconds, Weber and Tabarly, loaded Guillaume's two pearl-handled dueling pistols in front of Benoit's two friends. They were the same weapons Guillaume used when he had killed André de Lagier many years before. Benoit remembered André, and his laugh, and their rivalry for Margarita.

Both men wore clean white shirts and their best officer's white knickers and swords in scabbards. The two men stood back to back. Dayot reminded them that they couldn't turn till he said ten. He counted, "*Un, deux, trois, quatre, cinq,*" as the men stepped farther and farther away, "*six, sept, huit, neuf, dix.*" Both men turned smoothly and aimed fast. Benoit spun around to his right to face Guillaume.

In the instant that Guillaume fired, Benoit stepped just slightly to the left with his front foot, sank his weight, twisted his hips, and then pivoted on the ball of his front foot, turning his head to look behind himself.

Benoit remained standing, his whole spine straight. He had used a *Qinna* sword move. With a twist of his hips, he had whipped his head off the line of fire. Benoit slowly turned his head back and faced Guillaume, who yelled, "Grannier, you have broken the rules of the pistol duel."

Henri Dayot responded, "No, it is not a pistol duel; it is a duel of pistol and sword." Benoit slowly aimed his pistol and jerked his arm up. Guillaume dodged the shot in an awkward way, but Benoit hadn't really fired. Benoit aimed again at Guillaume's head for a moment longer, casually pointed his gun at a nearby stump and fired it off.

Benoit tossed his pistol to the ground and drew his sword. Guillaume's eyes widened. He drew his blade as well and the two men approached each other with dreadful care. They stood facing each other and waited for the longest time, neither man wanting to make the first move. Benoit breathed deeply. He allowed his opponent to tighten with fear.

Guillaume attacked first. They exchanged strikes back and forth as they warmed up. With a burst of energy Guillaume struck left, right, left, creating an opening, which he jabbed for with a lunge. Benoit blocked. He felt the shock of the steel blades through his arm and into his healing lower chest wound, which ripped open. A long fight would be extremely dangerous to Benoit. A blood-red stain spread across his shirt as the wound began to bleed.

Benoit struck right again, but it was a feint. He pulled the move, entered with his left side, grabbed Guillaume's sword wrist with his left hand, and twisted out. Benoit struck with his sword, forcing Guillaume's left hand to grab Benoit's sword hand. He fell for an old trick. Benoit kicked Guillaume in the crotch with his right boot. It felt good; he connected with the hard tip of his leather shoe. Guillaume doubled up in pain. Benoit followed with a right punch to his face using the handguard of his saber as a steel fist.

To the four solemn witnesses, the sword fight up till now had been a kind of ballet. It had an elegant ritual quality. Guillaume did not fall far from the punch, for Benoit still held his sword wrist fast. Benoit pierced Guillaume in the heart, saying sharply, "For André," and then in the throat, "for Margarita," and in the heart again, saying quietly, "for justice."

It was over. The duel had become an execution, but not the one expected. Benoit backed away from Guillaume, as Weber and Tabarly cautiously moved in and watched with horror as their friend lost all signs of life.

Henri Dayot shook Benoit's hand with sincere congratulations and joy. Benoit viewed the corpse on the ground with a profound sense of relief. He carefully wiped the blood off his sword with a rag offered by Dayot. Finally, the rape of Margarita and André's killing were honorably avenged. He had something to celebrate, and someone to celebrate it with. *This news should please Moon Light.*

Chapter 48
The Red Dress
1793

Moon Light and Benoit announced their engagement to their family, friends, and superiors. King Nguyễn Ánh and Pierre Pigneau each gave his blessing. Father Édouard Villeseint was the only one who asked a lot of questions and tried to be difficult. He was somewhat reluctant to endorse the arrangement. He gruffly challenged Benoit, "Will she be happy if she sails with you away from her people to France? Will she make friends in France, where the people are so disapproving of mixed marriages?"

"I have discussed these matters with Moon Light," Benoit answered truthfully. "You may discuss them with her yourself."

Moon Light said, "Father Villeseint, you must understand that this marriage is what I want."

"But do you love this man?" challenged Father Villeseint.

"Yes Father, I do love this man. Let me confess to you, with the confidentiality of confession, Benoit asked me in private—no intermediary—so I could defy the king—say no if I choose to."

"Do you know that your interracial marriage will be frowned upon by many in France, as well your own country?"

"Yes."

Father Villeseint was taken by surprise, but he heard her, and he admitted to himself that he did not approve of interracial marriages. In the end, he agreed to marry them in his little church. Father Pierre the Bishop attended, and so did Olivier du Puymanel and most of the remaining officers. Captain Henri Dayot agreed to be the best man, while Endless Joy, Ánh's favorite wife, played the matron of honor.

Benoit was "happy very" to be getting married that day. After putting on his best uniform, he walked with Henri Dayot and his bodyguard to the church. He said to Henri, "I wish my mother and all my brothers and sisters were here—all eight of them. I sent them an invitation and announcement, but it hasn't even arrived home yet."

"You will just have to bring your bride home to meet them all," said Dayot with a chuckle.

"Oh Lord," said Benoit, "I hope my mother understands, or at least is forgiving. She will probably be horrified."

"And she will recover and soften," responded Dayot, "after she meets and gets to know this extraordinary woman."

Bùi Moon Light, in a crimson tunic, rode to the church with her mother in a red bridal palanquin, with musicians playing to delight the onlookers and the Gods.

Moon Light said to her mother, "At least Benoit formally presented betel leaves and areca nuts in proper red boxes to you and Father.

"Yes," Madame Bùi replied, "but since he is a Western Ocean barbarian, it is so sad we couldn't reciprocate to his parents. Our lord, King Nguyễn Ánh, must be pleased that your father is so upset underneath his mask of composure."

"Ánh must be pleased," said Moon Light. "Father was so surprised and shocked when I confided to him and you that I really want to marry Benoit. I remember you burst into tears. I didn't mean to upset you."

"He's awfully nice for a barbarian," said Madame Bùi, wiping her eyes. "Buddha and Heaven protect you both. I keep reminding myself, it is normal for parents to lose their daughter! We do, however, prefer our own kind. I'm sure you understand."

"Mother, I keep telling you, French barbarians are not all as bad as people say! Benoit will never marry a second wife. He can't; his church forbids it! My children will always be his only legal children. These are good ideas for our country."

"It is normal for you to move to the next village, not to disappear across the Western Ocean."

On Moon Light's side of the aisle (for it was decidedly a Christian wedding) sat her subdued father and mother, much to King Ánh's silent satisfaction. Nguyễn Ánh attended with his First Wife, Pure Essence, and several of his wives and concubines who were friends of Moon Light's. They all wore new red tunics to signify that they were the bridesmaids. They wore dresses identical to that of the bride to fulfill an old Western custom. In old Europe, the bridesmaids dressed like the bride to confuse local demons, who might, from jealousy, wish to spoil the happiness of the bride.

There were other precautions. Because of the presence of the king and his women, the church was surrounded by a hundred of the king's bodyguards, and the guards of Pierre and Benoit stood on alert as well. A thousand more soldiers created a second perimeter around the neighborhood of the church.

If only I had a pump organ, Father Villeseint thought as he watched his spartan church fill up with important people. *Then I could show them the sound of the glory of God from Johann Sebastian Bach.* Nevertheless, three naval officers played a Telemann trio sonata on flute and two violins. It was excellent music for amateurs.

Moon Light admired her oversized, hairy groom, and thought to herself, *I didn't dare tell my parents the truth, that Benoit approached me in private and he allowed me the freedom and privacy to say either yes or no.*

He plans to take me away from the country of my Ancestors. I have agreed to go by ship and live with him in France. For our wedding present, Nguyễn Ánh has offered to make Benoit a Mandarin of the Second Rank, and given him a raise in salary. Benoit says he can't wait to take me to his country, but I can wait. I have no real desire to leave this beautiful land of the Gods to go to the other side of the world, to a land like the north of China with ice and snow, which they say is so cold it can kill you.

It was three years now since Benoit and Moon Light had met at the king's Late Harvest Festival banquet and discussed the differences between Confucius, Jesus, and Lao Tzu. Moon Light was now twenty-one and she looked young next to Benoit at thirty-six. Her long black hair, coiled in rings and held fast by silver hairpins, framed her graceful and delicate face. She now wore the pearl necklace and earrings Benoit had presented her as wedding gifts, and the ceremonial red silk wedding dress of her people, as red was the color of good luck. She couldn't have chosen white, like a French woman, as white was worn for mourning in Đại Việt.

"Who gives this woman away?" asked Father Édouard Villeseint, in French and then Vietnamese. Moon Light's mother poked her father, who stood up stiffly and quietly said, "I do."

"Who gives this man away?"

Father Pierre the Bishop stood up, and though frail, for he was recovering from another round of dysentery, he smiled and said, "I do." The French officers all chuckled, and they chanted as a group, "And so do we," causing some laughter.

Benoit looked into the eyes of his beautiful bride and hoped with all his might that he was doing the right thing. *I wish my family could share this day with us,* he thought. *I hope my mother is still alive when we finally see the shores of France, and God only knows when our work here will be done.* Father Villeseint proceeded with the vows. He said each vow in Vietnamese and French, and Benoit and Moon Light each answered twice, in both languages. "*Tôi đồng ý,* I do."

"I now pronounce you man and wife," said Villeseint, who finally smiled and beamed with support, a convert of sorts. "You may now kiss the bride." And Benoit did, short and sweet.

ॐ ॐ

After the ceremony, King Nguyễn Ánh threw a reception under many tents in the king's palace garden, near an artificial pond. To the astonishment of all, five wild cranes landed on the lake in the middle of the festivities, and for half an hour they swam around the lake before taking off again. The sacred birds left unharmed, and the Vietnamese were impressed at the message from Heaven. The landing of such wonderful birds was an auspicious sign. It must mean five healthy sons, or fifty years of happiness, or both, agreed some of the older women.

There was a sumptuous meal, followed by toasts with Father Paul Nghi acting as the official translator. The Việt were not accustomed to including their wives at a banquet at which there were toasts and jokes. At first only the Frenchmen stood up to speak. Henri Dayot said, "I've sailed with Benoit for a good many years." Paul Nghi repeated each sentence in Vietnamese for the comfort and inclusion of the Việt guests. Dayot continued, "He is a fine friend and navigator. Now he is navigating a new life. Now that he has wisely married a Vietnamese princess, he becomes a prince. Drink a glass with me," he said holding up his wine. "I give you both joy, my sincere congratulations and best wishes."

King Nguyễn Ánh rose for the occasion. King Ánh said, "Moon Light is like a daughter to me. Captain Grannier had made his mark here as a fine sailor, fighter, and leader of fighting men. I hope that this union will bring these two the happiness they deserve, and bring our two countries closer, into a new era of trust and benevolence." Moon Light's father could not bring himself to speak, but Võ Tánh stood up and praised the courage and talents of the newly formed couple. "Captain Grannier is a man of talent, a master swordsman, and Moon Light, obviously, is a tamer of wild barbarians," which got a good laugh twice, first in Vietnamese, then in French.

ॐ   ॐ

Benoit and Moon Light left the party after eating and drinking and making the rounds to see their guests. Amid cheers, drums and gongs, and falling rice and confetti, they entered one of the king's own palanquins. Fireworks exploded as they were carried away by eight royal porters to the house of Pierre and Benoit. Servants had made the wedding chamber ready with the traditional red curtains.

Moon Light was afraid of what was about to happen. She had come to care for Benoit, but she had heard that men were often rough and barbaric on their wedding night. Something of this, Benoit was able to sense. He embraced and kissed her for a long time. They then removed their house slippers and lay on the bed. Slowly and delicately, Benoit let Moon Light cuddle next to his body, and then without rushing, they undressed each other and began to touch.

Benoit's gentle hands on her breasts and thighs stirred them both with excitement. When they finally made love, it didn't take very long. Moon Light was surprised and confused, and she had to suppress a laugh. It was neither as bad nor as good as she had heard tell. Evidently, there was a lot to learn.

They lay quietly, and before long, Benoit touched her and explored her again with his fingers. Moon Light shuddered with excitement. When Benoit entered her a second time, she was prepared and welcoming. Even though he was a hairy barbarian, he was clean and he was still a man. Their intimacy was both an aphrodisiac and an antidote to loneliness. Benoit felt the joy of homecoming while in a foreign land. When all the complications of this marriage came into his mind, he pushed them aside for another time. He felt complete with this magnificent woman, and a deep sense of peace.

Moon Light moaned softly. Benoit carefully followed the rhythm of her breathing. He changed his pace according to and following her need, until she felt the earth move and her voice pierced the room with cries of pleasure. High above them in the purple light of sunset, a hawk sailed slowly above the clouds and rain.

Chapter 49
Monkey Business in Phú Xuân
1795 (two years later)

Three years had passed since Jade River lost her brother Huệ during the opera, at the birthday dinner for his first wife Green Willow, and over two years since her brother Nhạc was killed. Jade River lived with her mother, Autumn Moon, in her mother's mansion inside the magnificent Imperial Citadel of Phú Xuân, the Spring Capital. The two women worked daily to comfort each other.

Jade River grew closer to Lương Hoàng, but much closer to his two lovely but nervous wives, Spring Bloom and Red Lotus, due largely to the daily routine that she developed. Jade River spent her mornings helping the Buddhist nuns at the City Temple of the White Lotus. The nuns there instructed her in the secrets of *Dhyana*, the art of meditation, and healing with herbal medicines. Jade River then joined her mother, Autumn Moon, for a light lunch, followed by either a game of cards such as Chinese blackjack or poker, or mahjong, or an outing for fresh air in the early afternoon, sometimes by galley on the Perfume River.

Jade River also visited her favorite nephew, Prince Quang Toản, his mother, the concubine Blue Cloud, and Huệ's widows, Green Willow, Precious Stone, and Gem Lake. When the prince was available, she and Quang Toản would take turns reading to each other and copying the calligraphy of famous poems.

They were sometimes a bit naughty and read popular fiction. Educated people were not supposed to be too interested in this delightful and sometimes satirical lowbrow material. In this vein, they recently finished the famous adventure book, *Sun Wukong, The Monkey King's Journey to the West*, by some discreetly anonymous author. Prince Quang Toản enjoyed the book so much that he said a few days after they finished it, "Let's look up and reread our favorite parts of *Monkey*."

Jade River looked around conspiratorially at their tutor, the elderly scholar Trương Văn Hiến, and said, "Don't tell anyone, but I would enjoy that." The old scholar shrugged, as if he didn't care. Jade River and Quang Toản sat together on Chinese chairs at a long desk. Quang Toản was a handsome sixteen, and had been learning Chinese already for about eight years, so he was able to take turns with Jade River reading aloud. Quang Toản moved his eyes along the Chinese characters while Jade River read, and then they traded. Each of them read the manuscript, with the help of Trương Văn Hiến sitting on Quang Toản's left, while Jade River sat on his right. It was slow going, because after reading each sentence in Chinese, Quang Toản or Jade River would try to repeat the sentence in Vietnamese. Then Trương Văn Hiến would approve or make amendments and corrections.

"Let's start in chapter three," said Quang Toản, "after Monkey has slain the Demon of Havoc and seized his sword, but he didn't like the feel of his new weapon. In order to arm his monkey followers, he used his magic to steal an arsenal of weapons. How did Monkey King get so much power?"

Jade River chuckled, "From diligent study of course. Remember, he studied for twenty years with the great sage, the Patriarch Subodhi, who reluctantly revealed many magic secrets to Monkey, including the secret of immortality."

"Do not mention to your mother," said Trương Văn Hiến, "that I helped you re-read any of this infamous comedy, or that I suggested that we reread the part when Monkey upsets the natural order of Heaven and menaces the Ten Judges of Hell and defeats an army from Heaven, but is finally captured by Lao Tzu's magic snare!"

Jade River laughed and added, "And we won't mention, Scholar Trương Văn Hiến, that you have been enjoying this book as much as we have!" The old scholar bowed in silent agreement.

He smiled, and said, "Now Quang Toản, where exactly should we start?"

"After the four old monkeys tell their king to ask the Dragon of the Eastern Sea for a magic weapon to match his new powers. The Dragon's fish soldiers and fish generals bring out many heavy weapons, but Monkey says they are all too light."

Jade River laughed and added, "It was the Dragon Mother who suggested he try the discarded iron beam that was once used to pound flat the Milky Way. She said no one could lift it, but Monkey was able to lift it at once, and transformed the old metal beam from twenty feet long and weighing 13,500 pounds, down to just a four-foot-long walking staff."

"Ah yes," said Trương Văn Hiến, "the story is coming back. Monkey appreciates the ancient magic weapon, but then rudely demands new clothes to show off the new weapon—such impertinence. More dragons are summoned and arrive to give Monkey his cloud stepping shoes and impenetrable jerkin of yellow-gold chain mail and a red-gold cap with a phoenix plume. At last he was handsomely armed and extremely well dressed—for a monkey."

Studying the pages before him on the desk, Quang Toản said, "I will start right here," and pointed with his finger under the characters for Jade River to follow along. They took turns reading:

"The Dragon King was delighted (with all these gifts) and brought them in to see Monkey and offer their gifts. Monkey put the things on and, with his wishing-staff in his hand, strode out. "Dirty old sneaks," he called out to the dragons as he passed. In great indignation they consulted together about reporting him to the powers above.

The four old monkeys and all the rest were waiting for their king beside the bridge. Suddenly they saw him spring out of the waves, without a drop of water on him, all shining and golden, and run up the bridge. They all knelt down, crying "Great King, what splendors!" With the spring wind full in his face, Monkey mounted the throne and set up the iron staff in front of him. The monkeys all rushed at the treasure and tried to lift it. As well might a dragonfly try to shake an ironwood tree; they could not move it an inch. "Father," they cried, "you're the on-ly one who could lift a thing as heavy as that." "There's nothing but has its master," said Monkey, lifting it with one hand. "This iron lay in the Sea Treasury for I don't know how many hundred thousand years, and only recently began to shine. The Dragon King thought it was nothing but black iron and said it was used to flatten out the Milky Way. None of them could lift it, and they asked me to go and take it for myself. When I first saw it, it was twenty-four feet long. I thought, that was a bit too big, so I gradually made it smaller and smaller. Now just you watch while I change it again." He cried, "Smaller, smaller, smaller!" and immediately it became exactly like an embroidery needle, and could comfortably be worn behind the ear.

"Take it out and do another trick with it," the monkeys begged. He took it from behind his ear and set it upright on the palm of his hand, crying "Larger, larger!" It at once became twenty feet long, whereupon he carried it up on the bridge, employed a cosmic magic, and bent at the waist, crying "Tall!" At which he at once became a hundred thousand feet high. His head was on a level with the highest mountains, his waist with the ridges, his eyes blazed like lightning, his mouth was like a blood-bowl, his teeth like sword-blades. The iron staff in his hand reached up to the thirty-third Heaven, and down to the eighteenth pit of Hell. Tigers, panthers, wolves, all the evil spirits of the hill and the demons of the seventy-two caves did homage to him in awe and trembling. Presently, he withdrew his cosmic manifestation, and the staff again became an embroidery needle. He put it behind his ear and came back to the cave.

Prince Quang Toản interjected, "I kept practicing these commands, but my weapons never grew bigger or smaller."

"Of course not," said Trương Văn Hiến. "It's all rubbish, even if entertaining."

"One coolie's rubbish is another coolie's gold," said Jade River. "There is energy and imagination in these ancient stories."

Trương Văn Hiến smiled with condescension. He retorted with another proverb: "The miracle is not to fly in the air, or to walk on the water, but to walk on the earth."

ॐ   ॐ

Sometimes they would write skits in Vietnamese about Monkey, and perform them for the other children, Blue Cloud, Spring Bloom, Red Lotus, and women of the court. Quang Toản and his Aunt Jade River concocted a puppet show emphasizing parts of chapter twenty-eight, which they translated into Vietnamese with Trương Văn Hiến. Jade River hired professional marionette puppeteers from the city to provide the stage and the string puppets, and to control them, while reading out the amateur script.

Quang Toản approached his Aunt Jade River, who was conversing backstage with the puppeteers about the show the two of them had written and translated. It was just an incense stick before show time. Quang Toản said, "Have you seen my two brothers, Nguyễn Trứ and Cường?"

"No," replied Jade River, "I expected them to be with you." Quang Toản turned about, scanned the crowd again, and walked briskly through the assembled audience of mostly children and maids, including many of their sisters, little brothers, and cousins. He questioned the guard at the meeting hall entrance, who suggested the boys were probably in one of the adjacent courtyards. Quang Toản walked quickly through the first courtyard, into the next. He heard his bothers before he saw them. Trứ and Cường were rolling on the ground, arms locked, wrestling in earnest with each other, and Trứ appeared to have the better of the smaller Cường. Quang Toản pulled his half-brother Trứ off of his smaller half-brother Cường by his hair.

Quang Toản said, "Don't you want to see the puppet show Aunt Jade River and I have adapted about the Monkey King? You're about to miss the beginning."

"Fine," said Trứ, neatening his hair, "I am done here. I was just teaching younger brother some manners." Cường said nothing, but he straightened his tunic and gave Quang Toản a small bow of gratitude. Trứ and Cường followed their half-brother, their dead father Huệ's heir, into the hall set up with a puppet stage and benches full of their siblings, cousins, mothers, and servants.

Nguyễn Trứ confided to Quang Toản, "Cường and I are now reading this book with Trương Văn Hiến. We struggle with all the Chinese characters though."

Cường teased, "We have not gotten to chapter twenty-eight yet, so this show will give away the ending."

Trứ admonished, "We have acted out the whole story with Quang Toản anyway, so we shall be able to compare what we learned from him with the words of the storybook."

Quang Toản smiled and said, "It was hard in play to enact so many magic transformations. That is why the card game *Monkey Magic* is so interesting; we can play one transformation card against another with the roll of the dice."

Jade River came from behind the puppet stage and approached. "Quang Toản, the puppeteers are ready if you are."

"I have rounded up the usual suspects," Quang Toản said smiling. "Thanks for waiting, let's start!"

Jade River walked to the front and addressed the room of children, maids, and mothers. "It is good to see so many shining faces. Please accept our humble offering for your entertainment," and she sat down with the teenage brothers as three puppets on strings came onto the stage: Sun Wukong the Monkey King, now a lowly servant to Tripitaka, the Buddhist monk, and Tripitaka's other disciple, Pigsy, the always hungry pig with super powers. With his magic powers, Pigsy usually gets his snack. The bodies and hands of the puppeteers were blocked from view by curtains at the back and sides of the narrow stage, and across the top and bottom of the proscenium in front—making a picture frame of curtain around the stage.

The puppet and puppeteer of Tripitaka started the prologue. "Welcome honored guests. Let me set the scene for you. Sun Wukong was a monkey born from a stone, who learned the magic secrets of the Tao from a famous teacher. Monkey mastered the seventy-two polymorphic transformations into animals or objects. He learned the secret of attaining immortality, and he gained a position in Heaven as a caretaker of the horse barn. When someone explained to Monkey that his position was not exalted, that cleaning up horse excrement was actually not highly rated, he grew angry and complained to the Jade Emperor of Heaven himself, who made Monkey the protector of the Peach Orchard to shut the complaining monkey up. Monkey took advantage of his new position to steal and eat many of the best peaches of the orchard. They were to die for, and Monkey almost did.

"When Monkey learned that he wasn't invited to the Peach Banquet of the Jade Emperor's wife, the Queen of Heaven. Monkey transformed himself into an exact copy of one of the invited guests, the Red-Legged Immortal. He arrived at the banquet early, and stole many of the finest delicacies and meats, got seriously drunk, and then more or less trashed the banquet hall. He stumbled into the laboratory of Lao Tzu and drank up his new batch of magic elixir of eternal life, which was forbidden to all the lesser immortals, and then flew back down to earth making childish and vile noises and hand gestures."

The children in the audience laughed with glee.

"The Jade Emperor of Heaven was furious. He sent his best fighters to capture Monkey, but they could not overcome him in battle. Then an army of spirits failed to capture him. So Lao Tzu came down and captured Monkey in his magic snare."

Now the string puppet of Pigsy took over the narration. "The Jade Emperor ordered the Demon King Mahabali to have Monkey executed at the field of execution, but no blade could harm Monkey, and no fire could burn him. Monkey challenged Buddha to a flying contest, which the uppity little ape lost. For punishment, the God Buddha buried Monkey under a mountain, where he was trapped for the next five hundred years.

"But Guanyin, whom we know as Quán Thế Âm, the Bodhisattva of Mercy, took pity on Monkey, who for once said all the right things. Women can be so softhearted. Monkey was sorry, he repented, he promised to embrace the true faith, do good works, and always pay his rent on time. Guanyin said, 'Wait till I go to the land of T'ang and find my scripture-seeker. If you serve and protect him in his mission to go to India, and bring back the scriptures of the living Buddha to China, you will be delivered and forgiven.'"

"We know all this," whispered Cường. "This is just review."

Trứ whispered back, "Patience donkey, have patience." Quang Toản put his finger up to his lips to signal his half-brothers to be silent.

The string puppet of Monkey took up the narration. "The blessed Bodhisattva Guanyin found Tripitaka, the chosen scripture-seeker, who freed Monkey. They joined Pigsy, and the monster ogre Sandy, and a minor sea dragon impersonating a horse. Protected by these bodyguards, Tripitaka travelled for thirteen dangerous and harrowing years across mountains, gorges, rivers, and oceans. After many adventures and battles, the monk on his white dragon horse and his three ugly, wind-breaking disciples, finally reached the mountain palace of the holy Buddha of India.

"We hurried to the Great Hall and informed the Tathagata, the Most Honored One, which is Sakyamuni Buddha himself, that the priest from the court of China had arrived at the mountain to fetch scriptures."

The puppet Pigsy had quietly left the stage, and now the Monkey puppet left, while the Buddha puppet floated in, supported by his strings, and said to Tripitaka, "I have three Baskets of Scripture that can save mankind from its torments and afflictions. One contains the Law, which tells of Heaven, one contains the Discourses, which speak of Earth, one contains the Scriptures, which save the dead. They are the path to perfection, the gate that leads to the True Good. But the people of China are foolish and boisterous; they would mock my mysteries, and not understand the hidden meanings. My disciple Ananda, take these four pilgrims to the Treasury, and give them just thirty-five sections from each basket. That will be enough for the lazy and ungrateful Chinese. It will be a boon there forever."

The adults in the audience roared with laughter.

Buddha floated out, while a puppet disciple, Ananda, entered the stage. Ananda waved his hands about and said, "Look at all these magnificent and precious scrolls of wisdom. Having come here from China, you have no doubt brought a few little gifts for us. If you will kindly hand them over, you shall have your scriptures at once."

The Tripitaka puppet held his hands out in supplication and said, "During my long thirteen-year journey, I have never once found it necessary to lay out gifts of any kind."

"Splendid," said the disciple, "so we're supposed to spend our days handing over scriptures gratis! Not a very bright outlook for our heirs—lives of deprivation!"

At this point Trứ and Cường and their siblings roared again with laughter. Quang Toản and Jade River looked quietly at each other in triumph.

The Monkey puppet shouted, "Come along master! We'll tell Buddha about this and make him come and give us the scriptures himself!" There was more laughter from the children and adults in the audience.

"No need to shout," soothed Ananda. "Come here and fetch your scriptures."

The Pigsy puppet came out and narrated, "We collected box after box of scrolls, packed them away into bundles, and loaded them on the back of our sea dragon disguised as a horse. More bundles were put in backpacks for Sandy and me to carry. No one cared about our comfort. We rushed back to the Great Hall, kow-towed to Buddha, and skedaddled out of there before they changed their minds. We hadn't gone far when Dipankara, the Buddha of the Past, and the White-Haired He-roic Bodhisattva decided to intervene and prevent a great fraud on our pilgrims from the East. They sent a powerful whirlwind of swirling demon hands, which seized the scriptures and carried them off. Monkey was about to slay the White-Haired Heroic Bodhisattva, who flung down a box of scriptures so that they broke open, and sud-denly Monkey and the others could see that the scriptures had no writing—the parchments were blank!"

The Tripitaka puppet burst into crying, and said, "I must say, it's hard luck on the people of China. What is the purpose of taking them these blank books?"

The Monkey puppet said, "Master, I know what is at the bottom of this. It is all because we refused to give Ananda his commission fee. This is how he has re-venged himself on us. We must take our case to the Buddha."

The Buddha puppet came out on the stage, and the Monkey puppet shouted at the Buddha, "After all the trouble we had getting here from China, Ananda has made a fraudulent delivery of goods."

"You needn't shout," said the Buddha smiling. "I quite expected that he would ask for a commission. As a matter of fact, scriptures ought not to be given on too easy terms or received gratis. Many times I have reprimanded my disciples for sell-ing far too cheap. No wonder they gave you blank copies when they saw you did not intend to make any payment at all. As a matter of fact, it is such blank scrolls as these that are the true scriptures. But I quite see that the people of China are too foolish and ignorant to believe this, so there is nothing for it but to give them copies with some writing on them." The Buddha exited, floating on his strings.

The Ananda puppet appeared again and said, "Welcome back to the Treasury. Are you sure you don't have any little present for me?" More giggles ran through the audience of boys and girls and women.

Tripitaka said, "I have only one valuable possession. This my golden begging bowl, which the Emperor of China gave to me with his own hand, that I might use it to beg with on the road. If you will put up with so small a trifle, it is yours. And I expect that if I return to China with the scriptures, that you may count upon being suitably rewarded."

The Pigsy puppet spoke as narrator, "Ananda took the bowl with a faint smile. But all the divinities in attendance—down to the last kitchen-boy God—slapped one another on the back and roared with laughter, saying, 'Well, of all the shameless acts! He made the scripture-seeker pay him a commission!' Ananda handed over 5,048 scrolls, and they all had writing on them."

The Monkey puppet came forward, and addressed the audience, "And if you do not know how they returned to the East and handed over the scriptures, you must listen to what is told in the next chapter." The puppets all bowed, and the room of mostly children yelled, stamped, and clapped their approval.

Trứ and Cường both bowed low to Quang Toản. Quang Toản returned the bow and began to describe his efforts. Cường quietly kneeled behind Quang Toản, who was talking importantly. Trứ pushed his older half-brother, who fell over the back of Cường down on his hands and knees. Trứ fell down on top of both of them to show his appreciation.

❧   ❧

Jade River usually took her evening meal with Spring Bloom and Red Lotus. Frequently, Regent Lương Hoàng would join them. One evening Lương Hoàng's First Wife Spring Bloom dared to broach a subject long on their minds, while her husband was present. "Jade River," she said gently, "my honorable husband still wants you to marry him. You did once pledge yourself and promise him under Heaven that you would marry him. We wonder if you shouldn't fulfill your pledge before Heaven."

"Oh Spring Bloom," answered Jade River with a laugh, "you're putting me on the spot. Yes, we pledged our troth in stone and bronze, but that was in another age, twenty-five years ago. I was sixteen, and I was being disobedient to my parents, and a disgrace to my Ancestors. Look at how I was punished for my indiscretion. I spent so many years in the brothel, and two times I was a married woman! For all these years I was exposed to 'the wind and rain,' as you know. I blush to think what sort of fresh, virginal bride I could never be."

Lương Hoàng then spoke up. "You did make an oath, and so did I, before Heaven and Earth. So much time and life have passed, but sworn pledges are meant to be unbreakable!"

"I know you still love me," said Jade River, "and I still love you! But after so many years of bees and butterflies, what I most feel is a deep shame. I cannot wear the dress again of a virtuous bride. And I'm happy to be finished with being a dutiful wife." This last remark broke the tension and actually got the other women laughing. It was a scandalous thing to say out loud.

Lương Hoàng did not give up. He pressed, "You allowed yourself to be sold into marriage because you were a dutiful and virtuous daughter. There should be no shame in sordid mishaps after such noble sacrifice. Red dust and dirt could never stain your honor or stain your Ancestors. Your heart is still pure. Please consider a new idea. You could become my wife, without consummation if preferred. It would give you important rights and protections. You could still follow your mending heart, remain clean, and become a cloistered nun if that will make you whole."

Jade River answered, "I could never marry you if it would disturb the sweet harmony you have with your two wives, whom I now love as sisters that I never had."

Red Lotus finally broke her silence, "Dear Sister," she said smiling shyly, "Spring Bloom and I welcome you to marry our husband, and join our family. This we entreat, whether you join our conjugal bliss—or retreat into your spiritual community. We welcome you; you are already like a sister to both of us."

Jade River was stunned. She would never, not in a thousand years, have expected to hear such welcoming words from the once cold and fearful second wife. *Perhaps there is a God of love among the throng of spirits after all.* She consulted with Autumn Moon, who approved the marriage, as she had done many years before. The fragile old woman cried and said, "I want only the best for all my children," and then cried some more.

❧ ❧

The wedding was private and intimate. Only immediate family and a few servants were invited. Prince Quang Toản was excited for Aunt Jade River, but he didn't fully understand what was going on. "Auntie," he said, "now you are Third Wife, you can be my third mother!"

At the end of their wedding dinner, Jade River retired with Lương Hoàng to his private sitting room. They both sipped cups of wine. Lương Hoàng made a request. "For old time's sake, would you take my lute and sing for me some of your beautiful songs?" Jade River smiled. Her music she would share when requested. Her maid took a lute from its pegs on the wall, and Jade River carefully tuned each string. She played a dance tune, sang a sad love song, and then another, while Lương Hoàng kept his eyes on her lovely face and bathed his heart in her rich voice and the beauty of the five-tone scale. Then Hoàng took the lute and played for her. They traded songs and tunes and poems, and even played a half game of chess, till midnight, the second hour of the Rat.

Before leaving Lương Hoàng, Jade River knelt to the floor and the new Third Wife kowtowed to her third husband. She said, "If ever I feel clean again, it will be because of your love and affection. You are a gentleman and a good soul. My self-respect returns to me in some small portion tonight." Jade River kissed her old betrothed good night quickly on the lips, and retired to her own room still in her mother's mansion. After that bittersweet wedding night, heartwarming and heart-breaking, she never played the lute again for any man.

❧ ❧

A month later, in the courtyard just inside the main gate of the palace, with the regent's bodyguard standing at attention around the perimeter, Jade River said goodbye to her husband Lương Hoàng, and her new sisters, his wives Spring Bloom and Red Lotus. She hugged them each one at a time. When she hugged Spring Bloom, she said, "Take good care of our husband," and laughed. When she hugged Red Lotus she said, "You look so beautiful today, but somehow bigger."

Red Lotus smiled wide. "I am bigger. I am with child again, and you are the first to notice. I am doubly blessed. It has been a gift from Heaven to meet you."

"I give you all my love," said Jade River warmly, "and also to your children."

Jade River hugged Blue Cloud and her son Quang Toản, who said earnestly, "Auntie, you can still come back to visit."

Jade River smiled sadly. She then gave her naughty look. "Here," she said, "this is for you," and laughing, she took a package from her shoulder bag and placed it in his hand. Quang Toản ripped off the paper wrapping and found *The Monkey King's Journey to the West*.

Quang Toản did not try to hide his delight. "It won't be leaving after all! I will treasure it. As it entertains me, it will remind me of you and how we read it so slowly at first. How can you give it away though?"

"I have been through it enough times for this lifetime," she said with a smile. "There is always the next life."

Toản threw his arms around his aunt one more time, and said, "It is thanks to your patience with my education that I will be like Monkey, with great powers equal to the Taoist Gods."

Jade River laughed. "You remember to always be more careful than Monkey," she said playfully. "Remember, he was imprisoned by Buddha under a mountain for 500 years." She hugged her young protégé, who had learned much of Buddhist and Taoist folklore and the virtue of cooperation through the many stories and folk tales in the novel.

Finally, Jade River hugged her mother, Autumn Moon. The white-haired mother of the three famous warriors and two emperors of the Tây Sơn rebellion said through her tears, "May the Buddha protect you. Serve him well. May you attain in your lifetime the peace and happiness we all crave and aspire to. Don't forget to write and visit this old bag of bones." Autumn Moon handed Jade River a heavy package in a sack with handles.

"What is this," asked Jade River?

"This is for you, my child. It is a copy of your father's medical notebook and texts, which was made by your brother Huệ, and is in his calligraphy. Perhaps it will help you in your studies."

"May the Buddha bless you! This is so thoughtful; I am honored. Thank you Mother, I will cherish this."

Jade River kissed her mother, both of them in tears. The daughter and only surviving child smiled, then bowed low from the waist three times. Lương Hoàng, Spring Bloom, and Red Lotus bowed low in return. Jade River waved goodbye to her assembled family, and stepped into her palanquin. Lương Hoàng nodded to an officer, who barked an order. The porters raised the poles to their shoulders. On Lương Hoàng's hand gesture, they started to move. The newest and third wife of the regent was escorted by twenty-one mounted soldiers of Hoàng's royal bodyguard.

The entourage marched off toward the hills and the distant White Lotus Monastery, where Jade River would start her new life with a shaved head as a novitiate.

Lương Hoàng, Spring Bloom, and Red Lotus stood in honor, and patiently watched the palanquin disappear around the bend in the road. Lương Hoàng embraced and kissed both of his wives in turn, to reassure them that life was satisfactory—he also loved his first and second wives, the two who remained.

ॐ   ॐ

In 1795 and 1796, most of the French officers and sailors who were still left in Đại Việt finally quit the country in frustration and disgust. Olivier Du Puymanel and the other engineers in this group had designed and supervised the building of many strong, defendable forts. King Nguyễn Ánh was too cautious for these French mercenaries. They felt he was timid and deceitful, that he was dragging out the war. Many also wanted to return to France to look after their families and interests during the political upheaval of the French Revolution. Some had lost relatives to the guillotine during the Reign of Terror of 1793–1794, when an estimated 30,000 aristocrats and their attendants were executed or murdered. The guillotined included King Louis XVI and his innocent Austrian Queen, Marie Antoinette.

The departing Frenchmen took the 38-gun *La Méduse* and the 32-gun *La Dryade* with them, for they had been on loan from the King of France. They left the 32-gun *Le Prince de Cochinchine*, its new copy, the 32-gun *Western Dragon*, and the 16-gun *Le Saint-Esprit*, which all belonged to Nguyễn Ánh.

France was now governed by the First French Republic. Revolutionary France fell into the War of the First Coalition. France had to fight against the monarchist, antirevolutionary governments of Europe, including the Hapsburgs of Austria, the Kingdoms of Prussia, Great Britain, and Spain, and the Holy Roman Empire, also known as the Kingdom of Germany, which now included much of the Netherlands. A young artillery officer named Napoleon Bonaparte rose to prominence. He led many successful campaigns against these enemies of revolutionary France.

Benoit Grannier was one of only four French officers who stayed on to assist Father Pierre and King Nguyễn Ánh. Benoit and Bùi Moon Light were married for better or for worse, and raising healthy, mixed-race children. Benoit had a high position at court and in the war, and their bilingual children were widely accepted by the polytheistic Việt culture.

Chapter 50
Father Pierre the Bishop in Quy Nhơn
November 1799 (six years later)

Father Édouard Villeseint, holding a cane in one hand, beckoned to Benoit with his free hand to enter the tent of Father Pierre Pigneau the Bishop. Benoit handed his arms to a guard, as a servant carried outside a bedpan smelling of liquid excrement and blood. They were all encamped before the walls of Quy Nhơn, and were in the third month of an ugly siege.

Benoit entered the sick tent and tried to focus on his old friend while his eyes adjusted to the dim light. Father Paul Nghi was sitting by the bed, watching his teacher suffer. They had been together since Pierre's arrival in 1767. Paul Nghi had studied and worked with Pierre Pigneau for thirty-two years.

Benoit walked up to Father Pierre and took the old man's hand and kissed it. Father Pierre's eyes were yellow and rheumy—his skin was a dark yellow. This man had been like a father to Benoit for the last ten years. They had shared Pierre's house in Sài Gòn. Benoit smiled at Paul Nghi, who looked wretched, and he looked back at Pierre. Suddenly Benoit found himself holding back tears. "Hello, Father," he said. "How are you today?"

"He is not to talk," said Dr. Despiaux, but the gray, owl-faced Pierre held up his shaking hand for silence.

"Paul and Benoit, come closer," he said in a barely audible voice. "I feel better today than I have in years. I believe that my suffering and toils on this good earth are soon over. But I have no major regrets. The best is yet to come. May the good Lord, in his mercy, forgive me for what I have left undone.

"I am content to leave this world. I love my friends, my students, my work, and my adopted country. I have the respect of mandarins, soldiers, and peasants, and I have a great friendship with you both, and with the king and prince, and many others," he said, politely waving to Father Villeseint and Dr. Despiaux, "but I do not regret my passing on. I leave my vanities and my afflictions. Death generously offers me rest and peace, the welcome end to all of my desires. My precious work, God's work, I leave in your capable hands." The two younger men both nodded in acceptance.

At this point the emaciated old man blanched in pain. His intestines leaked like a sieve. His belly was bloated with fluids. He shut his eyes and tried again to breathe normally. Then he opened his yellow-stained eyes and looked at Benoit again. He smiled, warmed by his faith and inner fire. His eyes shifted to Paul. After working for so many years together, he loved these two men like sons: the Vietnamese priest and the French naval officer.

Benoit and Paul watched their dying mentor struggle to breathe. The man was too weak to feed himself, but his eyes slowly focused, first on Benoit, and then on Paul, still flickering with life.

"I await death now with just a little impatience. If I could still be useful on this earth, I would not refuse any work. I would submit myself to more ordeals, which I have always found wherever I work, among the corridors of wealth or the hovels of the poor. But if God calls me now, I have fulfilled many of my personal vows to him. Although I fear his terrible judgment, I also have confidence in his mercy and grace."

Father Pierre, for the last month, had eaten very little. For nourishment, in the last week all he could manage was to suck on a small cloth that had been soaked in a soup of mashed rice and vegetable broth. Now, near the end, his insides could handle only water and herb tea.

"Father Villeseint, I am ready for the last rites."

Father Édouard Villeseint looked with concern at his old friend. He had administered the last rites the day before, all of them: Penance, Anointing of the Sick, and the Viaticum, or Final Eucharist. Father Pierre did not appear to remember any of this, but it didn't really matter. Villeseint said again to Pierre, "Now you may confess your sins, so that you may place your trust in God's mercy with a quiet conscience." Pierre rolled his wrist to signal to skip this part in public.

Villeseint read in Latin for the second time, "James 5:14. Is any among you sick? Let him call for the elders of the Church, and let them pray over him, anointing him with oil in the name of the Lord; and the prayer of the faithful will save the sick man, and the Lord will raise him up; and if he has committed sins, he will be forgiven."

Father Édouard Villeseint blessed again some wine and bread from a sideboard, and administered the bread and the wine, saying in Latin, "Our Lord Jesus said, here is my body, eat this in remembrance of me. ... Here is the blood of Christ, the cup of salvation, drink this in remembrance of me." Pierre Pigneau struggled to chew and swallow the wine-soaked crumb of bread.

Father Villeseint recited from John, 11:25–26, still speaking in Latin, "Jesus said, I am the resurrection and the life. He that believeth in me, though he were dead, yet shall he live. And who so ever liveth and believeth in me shall never die."

Father Villeseint then blessed his old friend, "May the peace of our Lord, which passes all understanding, bless you and keep you in eternal life and salvation. In the name of the Father, the Son, and the Holy Ghost, Amen."

After the rites were finished, Father Pierre asked for his crucifix. It was around his neck. He took it in his shaking hands and said, "Precious cross, which inspired me all my life, and which now is my consolation and my hope, permit me to embrace you one more time. My God, you have been vilified in Europe. The French revolutionaries have thrown you out of their temples, but they will return to you. Now come to Đại Việt. I have wanted you to be known to these people, more ignorant than evil, and to plant you in the realm, as well as on the throne itself, but my sins have prevented me from being the final instrument of so great a work. Plant the Gospel here yourself, Lord, through us, your disciples. Oh my savior, raise your temples over the debris caused by the work of the devil. Reign with peace and love in these eastern lands."

Father Pierre pressed the crucifix against his face, which was now wet with his own tears. Benoit, tears running down his face as well, took the old priest's hand and kissed it again.

"A million thanks, Father Pierre," he said, "for so many opportunities to serve the Lord, and for bringing us to this land of beauty and magic. I am blessed to know and work for you." Father Pierre the Bishop smiled, and made the sign of the cross over Benoit. King Ánh and Prince Cảnh were ushered in, so Benoit politely withdrew.

It was the last day in which Father Pierre recognized anyone or spoke rationally. He lingered in delirium and pain for three more days, alleviated occasionally by the smoking of opium, and died quietly in his sleep.

It became widely known later that the King Nguyễn Ánh wept openly during his last meeting with his trusted barbarian advisor. The death was kept a secret so as to not raise the spirits of the enemy. Ánh ordered the body moved secretly in a well-armed galley bearing the king's own banners, to *Le Prince de Cochinchine* for transport to Sài Gòn.

Chapter 51
Victors and Vanquished
1799

A month later, in Sài Gòn, Pierre Pigneau de Béhaine, Bishop of Adran and Vicar Apostolic of Cochinchina, was buried as if he himself was of the Nguyễn royal family. His coffin was honored by a great procession led by King Nguyễn Ánh and the Crown Prince Cảnh, and which started at the hour of the Water Buffalo, two hours after midnight, in the cool of the night. The great procession included all the mandarins of the court, the king's whole regiment of 12,000 soldiers, and 40,000 hired mourners, both Christian and pagan. Father Pierre would have been greatly honored, and absolutely horrified at the expense. More than 200 paper lanterns of different forms and thousands of torches lit the march honoring the dead.

The coffin was wrapped in a fine tapestry, and supported by eighty honored pallbearers, including the Mandarin Diệu Tri. They all walked under a huge travelling canopy that was decorated with gold paint.

The 12,000 soldiers marched in full battle dress in two lines of three. Behind them came the modern artillery brigade, with field cannon with trunnions on wheeled carriages and limbers pulled by horses, and 120 war elephants carrying their battle platforms and harnesses.

Thousands of musicians among the 40,000 mourners played ceremonial music on reed horns, trumpets, tambourines, and drums. Soldiers shot off their rifles using powder and wad, while others set off firecrackers and rockets burst into the sky, illuminating the darkness with lights and colors. A hundred ushers passed out thousands of memorial booklets that included the texts of the eulogies that were about to be read, but few would be able to hear.

At the burial site, the king himself joined the ceremony, and to the astonishment of his mandarins, he was accompanied by his mother the frail Lady Purity, his brothers, his wives and concubines, his children, and most of the important women of the court. They all paid homage to the Esteemed Barbarian Advisor.

The king had ordered a fine tomb constructed for his mentor and friend. Father Édouard Villeseint and other Christian priests said prayers and gave the last benediction, and the word of the Lord—but not the last word.

The coffin was placed into the earth and the priests began to throw handfuls of dirt into the ditch next to the new temple. The king stopped them and asked them to step aside, for his other priests had their own prayers to offer. About one hundred Buddhist and Taoist monks came forward and offered chants and incense. The Buddhists were Theravadins. They were divided into chanters and the preparers of offerings.

The chanters could be heard saying such things as, "Even the gorgeous royal chariots wear out; and indeed this body too wears out. But the teaching of Goodness does not age; and so Goodness makes that known to the good ones. ... Reverend sirs, we humbly beg to present this *mataka* food and these various gifts to the Sangha [the Buddhist community of monks, nuns, novices, and laity]. May the Sangha receive this food and these gifts of ours in order that benefits and happiness may come to us to the end of time. ... The Fully Enlightened Peerless One, with the Sublime Doctrine and the Noble Order, do I respectfully salute, and shall speak concisely of things contained in the Abhidhamma [the manual of scriptures]. The categories of Abhidhamma are fourfold in all: consciousness, mental states, matter, and Nirvana. ... There are two realities—apparent and ultimate. Apparent reality is ordinary conventional truth. Ultimate reality is abstract truth. ... Physical happiness should be differentiated from mental pleasure. So should physical pain be differentiated from mental displeasure. ... All forms of physical pain and happiness are the inevitable results of our own karma."

The nonchanters brought forward cattle, pigs and goats, and vats of wine. They slaughtered the animals next to the grave, making a significant and bloody sacrifice to the spirit of the departed and to his Ancestors. Fathers Édouard Villeseint and Paul Nghi were aghast by this pagan spectacle, but they dared not protest.

Benoit was not surprised. His wife, Moon Light, reminded him that the king was doing well by Father Pierre the Bishop in his own way. To his people, his behavior was an obligation of such a high funeral, and the sacrifices would all end up feeding the members of the processional, who were working up a great appetite and were not paid much money for their contracted work.

Again the king openly cried, and so did Prince Cảnh. What surprised the mandarins the most was the appearance of the king's five war banners. These yellow and blue banners, purportedly full of magic, always accompanied the king on the battlefield. During the parade, his famous banners were carried on both sides of the coffin by members of the king's own bodyguard. Most of the mandarins were astonished at this extraordinary sign of honor.

The Military Mandarin General Võ Tánh was not surprised. General Võ Tánh read the king's official eulogy, written personally by King Nguyễn Ánh. Võ Tánh's strong voice rang out: "The king has written the following words:

I had a sage and intimate confidant sharing all my secrets, who in spite of distances of thousands and thousands of miles, came to my country and served me faithfully, even when my fortunes were extremely low. Why must it be that he dies under my banners now, at the moment when we are more united than ever? A premature death separates us suddenly. I speak of Pierre Pigneau, decorated by the dignity of the office of his Church, and by the title of Plenipotentiary by the King of France. I will always have the memory of his spirit and of his virtues, but I want to give witness today of my affection. I must because of his rare qualities. In France, he passed for an above-average man, but he was just one of many bishops of his faith. Here he will always be remembered as the most illustrious foreigner to ever pass before the throne of Đại Việt.

"Since my childhood, I have had the honor of knowing this precious friend, whose character and disposition found themselves so agreeable to mine. When I first mounted the throne of my Ancestors, he was right by my side. He was for me a rich treasure, where I was able to find the greatest counsel when I had the greatest need for guidance. ...

"When I was in grave danger, it was he who came to my rescue with help. In times of distress, he furnished me with the means he alone knew how to find. The wisdom of his councils and the truth, which burned in his conversation, were qualities which brought us closer and closer together. We were such friends and so familiar, that when my affairs called me out of the palace, our horses walked side by side. ...

"Since the day where, by the happiest of chances, we met, nothing has ever come between us, nor caused an instant of displeasure."

All these generous words and displays of admiration brought tears to Benoit's eyes. He cried and he laughed. *Now, don't overdo it,* he thought. But he also knew the king spoke the truth. This was the king's way, to be extravagant with his friends. Benoit looked across at Queen Pure Essence and her ladies, other wives and concubines—silent and respectful. Moon Light, who was sitting by his side, looked solemn, beautiful, pregnant, and tired. Their children, Pierre and Marie-Noelle, were asleep safely in their house. Moon Light looked with concern at her husband, who cried in public, and she was embarrassed. *I will never understand these barbarians,* she thought. *One moment he is a tiger, the next, a child.*

Võ Tánh continued, "I will read the official epitaph that is carved into a wooden plaque in Chinese characters that will be placed on the front of Pierre Pigneau's tomb. It reads, 'Bishop Pierre Pigneau de Béhaine, was born in France. ... He aided us in our hour of difficulty. He voyaged quickly to France and India, and he returned with a fighting force he had personally recruited. Over twenty years, he assisted me in the command of my armies and the administration of my country. ...

The restoration of our country is due in large part to the inexhaustible efforts of this great master. ... He died bravely of disease at the age of fifty-seven before the walls of Quy Nhơn. I hereby declare him Principal Accomplice to My Reign.'"

Benoit was very proud that night, and pleased with the honor paid to his mentor and employer. As the rockets burst in the dark sky into a thousand glittering stars, he remembered the robust Father Pierre and missed him. He thought of Lorient, and his distant and almost forgotten mother and siblings, and sent them a blessing.

God, let me and my loved ones return to Lorient before I die, he prayed. *I want to return to France in triumph, with my wife and children—grandchildren for my mother, and nieces and nephews for my brothers and sisters, and with some gold in my strongbox. It would be so good to see them again. They will all be adults now, and not the young people I once knew. Now I have trouble remembering their faces: Annette, Cécile, François, Elisabet, Georges Louis, and Isabelle. Gabriel and Marie-Noelle have already passed away, bless their souls.*

At the end of the ceremony, Benoit and Moon Light, with his entire bodyguard, slowly followed the crowd away from the handsome new tomb. They walked side by side like a French couple, but did not hold hands, like Vietnamese. In fact, the other women of Moon Light's social standing rode to their homes in closed palanquins.

Moon Light thought, *Without Father Pierre, the few remaining barbarian sailors and advisors will all depart, and soon my husband will too, and I will leave this lush green land of Gods and Genies and my Ancestors forever. But in France, according to barbarian custom, I will not have to live with and be a slave to my mother-in-law. I will be the mistress of my own house, and I will run my own family and household. But then, aiii, when my son marries, I cannot expect his wife to take care of me! And the graves of my Ancestors and my relatives will be far away and across the oceans. Benoit has promised, we will build a Việt bathtub for bathing.*

Benoit's mind moved to Father Pierre, and the business that was not finished in Đại Việt. He spoke to Moon Light, "It seems almost a certainty that Bishop Pierre's dream of planting the Gospel of Christ securely in Đại Việt will come to pass in our own lifetimes. My cousin Antoine would have been so pleased, bless his soul."

Moon Light responded, "This war has raged back and forth every day of my entire life. When will it end?"

"The Tây Sơn Army, and perhaps Lương Hoàng himself, defend the Citadel of Quy Nhơn, but they are surrounded. We expect the citadel to fall in weeks, not months."

Moon Light said, "Peace will be so welcome. When Nguyễn Ánh defeats the Tây Sơn, it will be largely thanks to Father Pierre, and to you and your associates."

"You are probably right, as usual," said Benoit smiling. "His thanks will also have to go to the King of Siam and his armies and navies. It has been a long war. I too welcome peace. My ten years in the war here have sped by like a year of childhood. I hope we soon sail to France, even if just for a visit. I will introduce you to my family, and I will show you and our little Pierre and Marie-Noelle a very different world!"

Moon Light replied, "I can wait. I have heard about snow. And political turmoil and regicide, and a general disdain for the children of mixed marriages by people who don't bathe—the same people who do not protect the living from the dead."

"You have heard well. But France is also a land of milk and honey, where on every city street you can walk about and purchase fresh baked baguettes of bread, rich butter and fragrant cheeses, sweet fruit pastries and the richest red and freshest white wines. There are magnificent temples, called cathedrals, to our Lord God Jesus Christ. When it snows, our children will learn to play with sleds and skates." Moon Light smiled politely and looked extremely skeptical. Benoit laughed and gave her an embrace. "Thinking of all this food, we'll have to bring with us a keg of your favorite *Nước Mắm* fish sauce."

❧　❦

Jade River rode her mule, Full Moon Angel, through the high pass that separated her monastery from several neighboring villages to the north. Jade River had ridden out in the early morning to check on invalids, the sick and the dying, in the closest of these three villages. She had set a broken arm, washed and cleaned numerous wounds, applied poultices, and helped the village midwife deliver a baby safe and sound. She used massage therapy and acupuncture for a headache, and a few other aches and pains. She had also instructed each patient on the proper herbs and diet indicated for their conditions. She gave an old man ginko bilboba for better energy and mental performance, and silybum, or milk thistle, for his liver. The old man liked the attention and the care, and he paid her handsomely in silver and vegetables.

Jade River looked up constantly from the path before the mule. The mountains marched endlessly and magnificently to the north and the south. She let her mind wander and meditate, and when she felt rested, she sang some of her old ballads from her years as an entertainer. She sang *The Rock of the Waiting Wife*, and then to lighten her heart, she sang *A House with a Hole in the Roof*:

"Your leaky hut is exposed to sun and rain.

Watch Heaven gazing down—you know he cares for you!

For plenty of free water offer thanks!

Daylight streams in to make your mirror shine.

The Moon Goddess, Miss Phoebe, keeps you company at night.

The Goddess of the wind, Dame Zephry, sweeps along your bed by day.

You call another luxury your own.

The elixir of dewdrops fills your tray.

Your floor is wet."

The song was an old friend; she let the laughter ripple through her body. Full Moon Angel knew the way home. As the sun was setting with colors glorious enough for a queen, they entered the stone archway to the old monastery and rode by the neat rows of plants in the extensive herb garden. Jade River put the mule in her paddock, and the stable girl filled the mule's containers with hay, grain, and water. Jade River entered the small hospital

building, and checked on a few of her neediest patients. In the dorm building, Jade River cleaned herself in the washroom. She studied her face quickly in the mirror. She didn't care for the look of her shaved head very much, but it was a cost of admission to this new group of nuns. Jade River didn't shave it every week, so she now had a light shadow of fur on the top of her head. She would have to shave it again soon.

Back in her little room, Jade River changed into a clean smock over dry underpants and a triangular *yếm* bodice. She approached the top of the bureau, and in a small incense burner in the shape of a Buddha lit an incense stick. She addressed the ancestral tablets on the bureau that her mother had given her, copies of the originals kept by Autumn Moon.

Jade River took a long, cleansing breath, as she opened her arms up to Heaven and out toward the earth. She exhaled deeply as she slowly drew her extended arms and hands together. She clapped her hands twice and gently shook them as she slowly exhaled. In the quiet of her cell, she put her hands together in prayer and thanksgiving, brought them to her forehead, and bringing them down to her chest, she bowed three times to the tablets of her father Hồ Danh, and her brothers Nhạc, Lữ, and Huệ. *Thank you Father*, she prayed, *for your love and devotion, and your medical book that helps me and others so often, including today. Mother and Lương Hoàng, and our extended family—I hope you are all both well and prosperous.*

Jade River picked up her small journal of prayers and fanned the pages from start to finish, thereby offering all of the words moved in the air as prayers to the Gods. The movement in the air was enough to register their offering. She sent her love to many, without emotionally dwelling on them for more than a few seconds. Jade River kissed the cover of the book and put it down by the tablets. She found her fellow Buddhist sisters in the dining room at two long tables.

After polite and cheerful greetings, she sat at one of the tables of nuns she worked and lived with. Some were her teachers, others her peers, and a few were her students. A lovely bell sounded and she joined the other women in a chant to give thanks for the food.

"First, let us reflect on our own work and the effort of those who brought us this food.

Our second reflection, let us be aware of the quality of our deeds as we receive this meal.

Our third reflection, what is most essential is the practice of mindfulness, which helps us to transcend greed, anger, and delusion.

Our fourth reflection, we appreciate this food which sustains the good health of our body and mind.

Our fifth reflection, in order to continue our practice for all beings we accept this offering."

After a brief silence—the women started to help themselves to the dishes of food on the table. Jade River filled her plate from the dishes that passed: rice, beans, vegetables, and fruit—good *đồ ăn chay*, vegetarian food.

"What did you find on your travels today?" the abbess said warmly to Jade River.

"It was a beautiful day to go over the pass. The sky and the mountains were transcendent. My patients were diverse and mostly well behaved," Jade River said, chuckling with an easy smile. "I like this work of tending the sick. It is honorable work, and it is never dull. And to come home to such a family of learned sisters is a blessing. I treasure all that I have learned here about medicine, tranquility, and the long, perhaps endless path to becoming a bodhisattva."

A new friend of Jade River's with a freshly shaved head said in mock seriousness, "Unfortunately, not everyone here reached nirvana this afternoon. I spent half the day doing laundry. But it does sound like *you* had a wonderful day." The women at the table joined in the friendly laughter.

Epilogue
1801, and 1802 to 1825

The Regent Lương Hoàng was not in the Quy Nhơn Citadel when it was finally taken in 1799. The Tây Sơn forces under Regent Lương Hoàng retook Quy Nhơn in 1801. Two Nguyễn generals, Võ Tánh and Ngô Tông Chủ, were left to defend the citadel when the ever-cautious Nguyễn Ánh moved the bulk of his army back to Sài Gòn for the rainy season. The new siege of the citadel was long and ugly. The Nguyễn garrison, now on the inside, defended the citadel till they had no more food or water. As the defenders surrendered, both Võ Tánh and Ngô Tông Chủ, following the highest standards of Vietnamese military protocol and to prevent their persons from being insulted, each committed suicide in their respective studies by hanging. Nguyễn Ánh had been extremely lucky to have had such faithful, competent, and honorable generals.

In 1801, Nguyễn Ánh's Christian son and heir, Prince Nguyễn Phuoc Cảnh, at the age of twenty-one, died suddenly of either smallpox, measles, or typhoid fever. French missionaries reported to Paris that Prince Cảnh was probably poisoned.

In 1802, the Nguyễn Navy, with the help of Benoit Grannier and the three other remaining French advisors, finally destroyed the last fleet of the Tây Sơn Navy, and then supported another siege of Quy Nhơn. During the siege, the Nguyễn Navy sailed north and took the Spring Capital Phú Xuân and then Thăng Long (Hà Nội).

During the fall of Thăng Long, many soldiers of the Hissing Army fled the city. In despair, Autumn Moon, the mother of Nhạc, Lữ, Huệ, and Jade River, swallowed opium that evening and died quietly in her sleep.

Many of the soldiers who remained, surrendered. The Tây Sơn Regent Lương Hoàng committed suicide in his study by hanging from a silk cord to avoid capture.

Huệ's son and chosen heir, the young Prince Quang Toản, tried to flee with his mother, Blue Cloud, but they were caught. Though Nguyễn Ánh was not known for cruelty, he wanted to frighten his enemies and avenge his clan for its many casualties and defeats. In August of 1802, with a reluctant Benoit Grannier as one of many witnesses, all the surviving members of the Hồ (Nguyễn) family of Tây Sơn and their leading generals, and their entire families, were assembled at the Spring Capital and executed. The skeleton of Huệ was exhumed and placed in a basket. The corpses of Huệ's wives and concubines were also put in a pile for abuse. Soldiers of Nguyễn Ánh's Army were ordered to urinate on Huệ's remains in the presence of the young Prince Quang Toản.

The young Nguyễn Quang Toản was dramatically tied between four elephants and slowly torn apart. The parts were then fed to wild ravens. Without burial, Quang Toản's poor soul would never rest.

The only Hồ family member to escape was Jade River. She had quietly disappeared inside a remote Buddhist monastery under an assumed name, where she could pray to the spirits of her Ancestors and family, and study and practice medicine and Buddhism.

Benoit Grannier and Bùi Moon Light lived in Đại Việt with one other French officer and his Việt wife until 1825. The Granniers eventually had six children.

ॐ   ॐ

Policy and politics did not evolve in Đại Việt as Bishop Pierre Pigneau de Béhaine had hoped. The death of Ánh's Christian son, Prince Cảnh, of mysterious circumstances in 1801 was a grave setback to Pierre's master plan.

In 1802, after complete victory over the Tây Sơn, Ánh took the name of Emperor Gia Long, and the Chinese Emperor accepted a peace offering from the new Đại Việt Emperor in the form of tribute, and declared that his southern vassal would henceforth be called Việt Nam, meaning the Việt to the South. With this change of name, the Chinese Emperor signaled that he allowed to expire any Chinese claim over Nam Việt, or Southern Việt, a name that still invoked an old territorial claim by both sides to the borderlands of the other.

Over time, Nguyễn Ánh grew disenchanted with his foreign policy, and therefore with his French advisors. Nguyễn Ánh had come to admire the isolationist policy of Japan, which he decided to try and imitate. By the time Nguyễn Ánh died in 1820, he had made up his mind to turn away from France and the West, and to try to rid his country of Christianity. His toleration of Christianity had been, perhaps, mostly expedience, and out of respect for the memory of his close friend and advisor Pierre Pigneau de Béhaine. It appears that when the Catholic Prince Cảnh died abruptly, either Nguyễn Ánh felt betrayed by the Christian God and no longer felt obliged to honor his old friend Pierre Pigneau, or someone, and possibly the king himself, interfered more deviously by having the Catholic heir poisoned.

Near his own death in 1820, Nguyễn Ánh chose as his heir his fourth son, Nguyễn Phúc Đảm, who became known as Emperor Minh Mạng. Đảm was devoutly conservative, Confucianist, anti-Christian, anti-foreign, and against trade with the Europeans. As Emperor Minh Mạng, Đảm passed a number of edicts against foreigners and foreign religions, he turned his back coldly on the Granniers, who in February of 1825, while clearly out of favor and unwelcome, departed with their six children for the "anonymity" of a retirement in France in the countryside around Lorient. Or as likely, in Lorient they became fascinating celebrities. Benoit was sixty-eight, Moon Light was fifty-three.

ॐ   ॐ

Benoit was disappointed, but not surprised. He had debated many times with Nguyễn Ánh and watched him turn slowly and deliberately to his conservative counselors. They promoted the Japanese model for managing barbarians as promising the greatest security for his young and vulnerable dynasty. The silver lining of this falling out was that Benoit was free to return to his beloved Lorient in France, and see his adult siblings and their families. He had, in fact, achieved the main personal goals of his life. He had traveled the world, become wealthy as a fighting sea captain, married a wonderful woman later in his career with whom he could enjoy intimacy and family life, and had learned exotic new philosophical and religious ideas.

He might never know with certainty the right course of action between the arguments of Hobbs and Montesquieu, but having acquired some knowledge of the teachings of Buddha, Lao Tzu, and Confucius, he had a broader framework with which to help sort the wheat from the chaff. Benoit might not be able to fix any of the world's problems in his lifetime, but as a Christian interested in social justice, he felt compelled to try his lance against monsters and windmills. Meanwhile, he understood that as a Taoist, he could relax and enjoy some time off in his retirement. The Tao, the natural Way, like his one and only God, was truly beyond understanding. Life's disappointments and failures might be self-inflicted, but they also might be caused by angry or jealous spirits, or immutable karma.

Benoit saw an ironic incongruity in his political fall from favor with Nguyễn Ánh and subsequent return to France. In Nam Việt, he and Bishop Pierre and their compatriots helped an aristocratic family fight off a merchant-led peasant revolt. Now he returned to a France, upturned by a successful merchant-led revolt against the aristocracy he still belonged to. He had once been keenly concerned about the shortcomings of his Catholic Church. Now, thanks to his love and respect for Bishop Pierre Pigneau, Fathers Paul Nghi and Antoine Grannier, and other outstanding Christians, he felt gratitude to God for the blessings of his life. He now also respected the part of the Church that promoted good works by good people, whether Christian or Pagan, even if success in the short run was not guaranteed.

Bishop Pierre Pigneau de Béhaine, one of the great Christian missionaries, military advisors, and deal makers of this period of Vietnamese history, was perhaps in the end just an instrument of his cunning student Nguyễn Ánh. However, the bishop's work continued. In the Socialist Republic of Vietnam today, with a Communist government, one sees active Catholic churches throughout the entire country.

Nguyễn Ánh was clever, patient, and perhaps brilliant, but not necessarily wise or gifted with foresight. With the obvious advantage of historical hindsight, his choice of Minh Mạng as heir was probably a mistake and arguably had disastrous results. It slammed the diplomatic door shut against all the Western powers just as the imperialist impulse of those powers was growing prodigiously.

If the Việts, like the Siamese, had granted special diplomatic status and trading rights to all the imperialist powers, the Western powers would have more than likely each fought to protect Vietnam from being colonized by any of the others. Siam, for example, maintained its independence by allowing all barbarians limited access and trade.

Once Vietnam was shut tight like an oyster in a bed of starfish, it was only a matter of time before one imperialist nation or another sailed back as conqueror and imperialist colonizer to pry it open.

Minh Mạng passed laws prohibiting any proselytizing by all Western religions. French and Việt missionaries were warned to desist from preaching. A few were then arrested, tried, and executed, all according to carefully publicized laws.

These priests became holy martyrs to the expanding Christian communities. The missionaries felt compelled by persecutions and executions to lobby in Paris for a French invasion to protect the Holy Church of Vietnam and its members. France, having finally recovered in the 1850s from two revolutions, was in an arms and an empire-building race with Britain, Germany, and the other European world powers. Emperor Tự Đức, a son of Minh Mạng, killed even more French missionaries. France under Napoleon III did not refuse an invitation by the Society of Foreign Missions to intervene, and invaded Vietnam in 1858 at Đà Nẵng (Tourane).

The Vietnamese fought gallantly with their arrows and spears, and their sixty-year-old cannon and shot. With far superior armaments, it still took the French almost a year to take the city and its surroundings, and over fifty years to conquer the whole country and subdue all the pockets of resistance up in the mountains. That resistance, which lasted about fifty-five years, is comprised of a series of heroic but tragic stories. These histories include the life and death of Phan Đình Phùng and Hoàng Hoa Thám. Phan Đình Phùng, a mandarin of the highest grade, led the Hương Khê Uprising from 1885 to 1896 in Hà Tĩnh Province. And Hoàng Hoa Thám, or Đề Thám "the tiger," the Vietnamese leader of the Yên Thế Insurrection, held out against French control in northern Vietnam for twenty-five years, from 1887 to 1913.

The French colonists carried out an extensive "land reform" program. They used taxes and other legal maneuvers to throw hundreds of thousands of peasants off their ancient and ancestral plots of land, and forced these new landless workers to work for slave wages on large, French-corporation-owned plantations and mines.

According to the historian Martin Murray, these firms sent ninety-five percent of their profits out of Vietnam back to shareholders in France, so the Vietnamese as a whole did not benefit from the vast development projects, and many peasants were pushed off their farmlands. This servitude to the French colonists was not the future that either Bishop Pierre Pigneau de Béhaine, King Nguyễn Ánh, nor the Hồ brothers, Nhạc, Lữ, and Huệ, had anticipated or worked so hard for. However, as the French eventually discovered, one should never underestimate the ability of the Vietnamese to overthrow a foreign invader.

the end

Author's Note

Like the miner who finds precious stones buried in the earth, I have culled various archives for published histories and literature in English and French for the preponderance of my working material. My second task has been that of the jeweler, to provide settings for the selected gems of the historical record, the venerable "stories recorded in old books."

Though many of the characters are based on real figures, much of this historical fiction was created by the storyteller. The text is therefore neither reliable, nor purposely misleading. I tried not to rearrange the sequence of historical events, based on the sources I found. The outline and timeline of this story is not invented, but revealed.

King Nguyễn Ánh's official eulogy and the epitaph on Bishop Pierre's tomb quoted in Chapter 48 are direct translations from the historical record. There are many other direct historical excerpts, and I have tried to list all the major ones in the endnotes, even when the translation from French into English is my own.

The following main characters were completely fictional: Physician Hồ and his wife, Autumn Moon, Jade River, and Lương Hoàng. Jade River and Lương Hoàng were deliberately based on similar characters in *The Tale of Kiều* by Nguyễn Du. Nguyễn Du wrote this epic poem during the Tây Sơn Rebellion period. The poem became extremely famous in Vietnam as a recitation piece.

In earlier drafts, I spelled Nguyễn as Nwin because the common name of Nguyễn, is pronounced Nwin, according to my language tutor, Huỳnh Sanh Thông, the talented but now deceased scholar at Yale University and translator of *The Tale of Kiều* into English.

Benoit Grannier is a fictional character, based only in outline on a real naval officer named Philippe Vannier, who was one of the four officers who remained after most of the French mariners quit. The real Vannier did have several spectacular naval victories over the Tây Sơn. Vannier did marry a Vietnamese woman, they had six children, and they returned to France in 1825 after Christianity was banned in Vietnam. The rest of my story of Benoit Grannier is made up, though some of the battles and action scenes were mentioned in Alexis Faure's biography of Pierre Pigneau, which was a major source for material about the Bishop of Adran and Vicar Apostolic of Cochinchina, including his imprisonment.

Like many others who enjoy historical fiction, I am interested in what is fact and what is fiction. All the anecdotes and briefings on earlier Vietnamese history are from source materials or history books. The endnotes are a reasonable guide for which parts of the current story have sources, but not all the sources are historical.

Acknowledgements and Gratitude

Many people have read and commented on this work and helped me to improve it, and I give them all my thanks. Back in the 1980s: Elly Lindsay, Elizabeth Lindsay, Marney Morrison, Ray Farinato, Leigh Cromey, Jean Webb, Liz Wiltsee, Huỳnh Sanh Thông, and Eric Swenson. My language tutor and consultant, the erudite Huỳnh Sanh Thông, who passed away in 2008, was a lecturer at Yale in Vietnamese Studies and the director of Yale's Southeast Asian Refugee Project. Around 1986, he read an earlier draft of this book. To my great relief, he found my portrayals of Vietnamese acceptable and enjoyable. He said, "It is a good book, and well written. But it is too much like James Michener, and not enough like James Clavell." I was relieved and delighted. I never forgot his help or advice, and I hope he would be charmed by the changes. Eric Swenson was the senior editor at WW Norton. He admonished, the book was good, it just needed a little more work. Ten years invested, I put the manuscript away for twenty-two years.

From 2010 to 2016, I received help from the following: Professor Emeritus Beatrice "Betsy" Bartlett, Kimanh Nguyen, Quang Phu Van (senior lecturer at Yale in Vietnamese Studies), Karen Van (Van Thanh Truc), Louise Harter, Ray Farinato, Sandra Greer, Professors Peter Perdue, George Dutton and Michele Thompson, historian Jonathan Dull, June Burton, Steven Beck, Francis Braunlich, Wilhemina "Billie" Lance, Austin Lindsay, Iva Hilton, Richard Pershan, Claudia Chapman, Jack Merrill, Vincent Gulisano, Patrick Rossiter, Neil Olsen, Marney Morrison and George Lindsay, Jr.

Special thanks go to Sheldon Campbell, Anne Cherry, Elly Lindsay, Marney Morrison, Jean Webb, and Kathleen Schomaker for volunteering their editorial skill and time. Sheldon Campbell went beyond all expectation, and twice he reviewed every page of the manuscript with his critical and authoritative eye, demanding rewrites and even new chapters. Kathleen Schomaker then helped review and evaluate myriad copyedits by the talented professional copyeditor Beth Adelman, and a smaller round of copyedits by the skilled proofreader Catherine Lindsay. Kiều Nguyễn Hồng Ân corrected many diacritical marks for Vietnamese names and words.

Peter Perdue teaches Chinese history at Yale University, as did Betsy Bartlett before she retired. While I was an undergraduate at Yale College, I studied Chinese and Vietnamese history and the Cold War with Michael Hunt, Milton Osborne, and Gaddis Smith, and modern American history with John Blum.

During my three weeks in Vietnam in 2010, many people answered questions, especially, the historians Mai Khắc Ung and Nguyễn Quang Khánh.

In spite of the help of all of the terrific people mentioned above, the problems and weaknesses of this manuscript remain due to my own inadequacies, deficiencies, and pure stubbornness.

About the Author

David Lindsay, Jr. is a writer, blogger, accountant, dance caller and folk music performer living in Hamden, Connecticut. He conceived of *The Tây Sơn Rebellion* after studying American-East Asian Relations at Yale, where he earned a BA in history in the spring of 1976, with a thesis titled *The Cold War and the American War in Vietnam.* He graduated a year after the American War in Vietnam ended.

David first drafted *The Tây Sơn Rebellion* writing part time over ten years between 1978 and 1988. Failing to find a publisher, he went off to business school, where he earned an MBA from the University of Washington in 1991. He also got married, had three children, and worked in information technology and bookkeeping and accounting with companies and nonprofits for the next nineteen years. In 2010, a tennis ball hit him on the head, and he went back to working on this book.

There is more about *The Tây Sơn Rebellion* and David's journal of his three weeks in Vietnam in 2010—about visiting many of the sites in the book—at his *On Vietnam Blog* located at *TheTaysonRebellion.com.*

David also blogs at *InconvenientNews.Wordpress.com* focused on the United States, and *InconvenientNewsWorldwide.Wordpress.com*, focused on the world. Both cover politics and foreign policy, the environment (climate change and population growth), the drug wars, and the arts.

In a previous life, before business school, David studied *Uechi-ryu* (Okinawan) karate for over twelve years, earning his *Nidan*, or second degree black belt. He studied *Uechi-ryu* under Adam Versenyi, Robert Moore, and Frank Gorman, and (Japanese) aikido for over ten years, stopping at *Ik-kyu*, right before testing for first degree black belt, under John Harabushi, Ray Farinato, and John Kaluzynski.

David enjoyed and studied folk music and dance at Pinewoods Camp, run by the Country Dance and Song Society. Early teachers included May Gadd, Genevieve "Jenny" Shimer, Arthur Cornelius, Eric Leber, and John Langstaff. David started calling contras, squares, and English Country dances in New Haven in 1976. With the Fiddleheads dance band, he started a dance series which became the New Haven Country Dancers. In 1977 he founded the New Haven Morris and Sword Team. He co-founded Take Joy: A Celebration of the Winter Solstice, featuring morris and sword, and also performed with the morris team in a similar show in Stratford CT called Yulefest directed by Henry Chapin. Following Chapin, David wrote and directed four of their productions. At the YMCA Indian Guides, he was known as David Dances with Bells On.

There is book purchasing and other information at TheTaysonRebellion.com, also called DavidLindsayJr.com. For promotions or bulk purchases, contact: footmad.cbpress @gmail.com.

End Notes

Page

ii   Map of Provinces of Vietnam. https://en.wikipedia.org/wiki/Provinces_of_Vietnam

Prologue: Historical Background of Vietnam

2   "The Chinese remained eager to reconquer their old colony to the south." China itself was conquered by the Mongols. The Mongols, as the rulers of China, invaded Đại Cồ Việt in the thirteenth and fifteenth centuries, but to their surprise and dismay, they were defeated both times by a determined and united people. Following the great expulsion of the Chinese in A.D. 937, these epic battles established Vietnam as a vital regional power and set an example of courage for the Eastern world, as a David who had thrice defeated Goliath, or as the Monkey King, who defeated the armies of Heaven repeatedly.

Chapter 1. Tây Sơn, a Village in Đại Việt, 1770

5   "He was a *kung-fu*, or master …" Chinese boxing is known in the West by many names, such as karate, meaning empty hand, Chinese fist, and kung-fu. Kung-fu translates as master or expert, because it originally meant one who works with great time and effort.

Chapter 2. The Tết Thanh Minh Festival, 1770

12   "… *if Merciful Heaven hadn't given her a nose, you couldn't tell her front from her behind.*" Robert Van Gulick, from the Judge Dee mysteries (historial fiction), Charles Scribner's & Sons, New York

16   "The market of Tây Sơn is a fine market!" Clotilde Chivas-Baron, *Stories and Legends of Annam*, Andrew Melrose, 1920, "The Market of Phù-Cam," pp.57-59, traditional piece. Translated from the French, E.M. Smith-Dampier, *Contes et Legends de l'Annam*.

17   "The story of the Rival Genie." Chivas-Baron, pp.99-104.

19   "I walked you home from the Temple of Lao Tzu." Also called Lao Zi or Laozi.

Chapter 3. The Boxing Match, 1770

22   "…the Mountain, using both his hands, twisted the challenger's wrist to the outside." Sensei Ray Farinato confirmed that this move is called Kotegaishi, in aikido.

22   "… stood beside his opponent and applied the auger pin." The auger pin is a basic pin in modern aikido, where it is called the Kotegaeshi pin. It is described in *Aikido and the Dynamic Sphere*, A. Westrook and O. Ratti, Charles Tuttle, Rutland VT 1970, p. 216-218.

22   "… trained, especially in *Qinna*, the art of seizing" Donne Draeger and Robert Smith, *Comprehensive Fighting Arts*. Qinna was called *Ch'in-na; Ts'o-ku shu* now *Cuogushu*.

Chapter 5. Highlanders in the Greenwood, 1770-1771

40   "As the torturer set out his tools, Hồ Danh silently composed his death poem: *A man has many lives* …" this poem, like Lương Hoàng's, is not historical, but by David Lindsay

44   "We seize the property of the rich and distribute it to the poor." George Dutton, *The Tây Sơn Uprising*, University of Hawai'i Press, Honolulu, 2006.

45   "In A.D. 40, the Trưng Sisters led one of the first national uprisings against a long Chinese occupation." Several writers have suggested that if the sisters had not resisted the Chinese successfully when they did, leading an army of 80,000 fighters and retaking sixty-five citadels, there might not be a Vietnamese nation today. WomenInWorldHistory.com and Library of Congress Country Studies, www.workmall.com.

Chapter 6. Lorient, France, 1770

49   "Kepler finally gained access to Tycho Brahe's extensive collection of observations …" From a lecture by Prof. Peter J. Brancazio in a class covering his book *The Nature of Physics,* Brooklyn College, CUNY, Macmillan Publishing, NY, ~1976.

54   "The decks were sprinkled with blood" *Polly on the Shore*, from the album, *Days of Forty-nine*, by Jeff Warner and Jeff Davis, Minstrel JD-206, Jackson Heights, New York. Also, the Frank Warner Collection of American Music.

54   "Yet Apollo understands grief. Bring it to him in a song, and he will take it away." Mary Renault, *The King Must Die* (historical fiction)

61   Photo of a "layback", compliments of climber and photographer Graham Nash.

Chapter 9. Pierre Pigneau, 1770

68   Chapter from Alexis Faure, *Les Français en Cochinchine au XVIIIe siècle. Mgr. Pigneau de Béhaine Evêque d'Adran,* Paris, Augustin. Challamel, Librairie Colonial,1891, Yale Library.

68   "*Quốc ngữ* was invented by Portuguese Jesuit missionaries ... Alexandre de Rhodes." He published the first Vietnamese catechism and the first Vietnamese-Latin-Portuguese dictionary in Rome in 1651.

68   "Until Rhodes popularized *Quốc ngữ* ... Việt scholars had developed *Chữ Nôm*" The famous Việt poem *Tale of Kiều* was written by Ngyen Du in *Chữ Nôm*.

73   "Before the world of power" By Nguyễn Binh Khiem (1491-1585), Huỳnh Sanh Thông, translator, *The Heritage of Vietnamese Poetry*, Yale Press, New Haven, 1979, p.51, #135.

74   Đại Việt is one country with three regions: "Đàng Ngoài or Đông Kinh" (Tonkin) in the North, Đàng Trong (Annam) in the center, and Nam Kỳ (Cochinchina) in the south.

75   "Lê Lợi raised an army of peasants ..." and started the Lê Dynasty in 1428.

75   "Isn't China fifty or a hundred times bigger than Đại Việt?" According to one source, modern Vietnam is 125,622 square miles and modern China is 3,600,927 square miles, or about 29 times larger than Vietnam.

Chapter 11. The Cotillion, Lorient, 1773

91   "... a new dance from Vienna, a dance they called the waltz." Improbable, but possible. See https://en.wikipedia.org/wiki/Waltz. Master Quellenac could be part Austrian.

Chapter 12. Nguyễn Đình's Retreat, 1777

Nguyễn pronounced Win (or Wean). There are fourteen common surnames in Vietnam which cover 90% of population. Nguyễn is the most common at 39% of 90%, or 35% of total.

103   "It is filial duty" said Confucius, Kuo LianYang, *Tai Chi Chuan Theory and Practice*, 1999

105   "Blue Heaven's wont to strike a rose from spite." Huỳnh Sanh Thông, translator. *Nguyễn Du, The Tale of Kiều,* a bilingual edition, Yale University Press, New Haven and London, 1983, p. 3. Kiều is pronounced gee-yew.

Chapter 13. Vũ Chan, Madame Camellia, and the Jade Emperor, 1777

107   This scene with Vũ Chan is from Nguyễn Du, *The Tale of Kiều,* p. 57-65.

109   The main tribes of An Khê, the Gia Rai and Ê Đê, in English are the Jarai and Ede.

109   The story of the Jade Emperor from George Dutton, *The Tây Sơn Uprising, Society and Rebellion in Eighteenth-Century Vietnam,* University of Hawai'i Press, 2006, p.72.

Chapter 14. Chesapeake Bay, 1781

Transforming the ship. Having raised two sons and a daughter, I cannot help but remark to youngsters of all ages that these great ships were the original Transformer machines.

115   "to transform de Grasse's mammoth flagship, the 100-gun Ville de Paris" A.B.C.Whipple, *Fighting Sail*, The Seafarers Series, Time-Life Books, Alexandria, Virginia, 1978, p. 47-53.

115   "100 gun" Jonathan Dull, author of *The French Navy and American Independence,* Princeton University Press, 1976, corrected minor and major facts in this and the next chapter.

118   "Graves (believed in) making war by the book" Whipple, A.B.C., *Fighting Sail*, p. 47-53.

118 "British Navy had destroyed much of the French Navy" The British also won on land. Vice Admiral Charles Watson defeated France's Indian ally, Suraja Dowla, the King of Bengal, in the battle of Plassey.

Chapter 15. The Battle of Chesapeake Bay, 1781

126 "Graves ... discovered thirty-two ... French men-of-war" Whipple, *Fighting Sail,* p. 47-53.

Chapter 16. Quy Nhơn, 1786

128 "Nguyễn Army sent from their Spring Capital Phú Xuân". Phú Xuân means Abundant Spring. It is sometimes called the Spring Capital or Citadel, or Spring Palace.

129 "Sun Tzu wrote, 'In ancient times ... '" Sun Tzu, *The Art of War,* translated by Thomas Cleary, Shambhala, 2005, p.61.

131 *"Pang-gai-noon,* the half-hard, half-soft style of the Shaolin monks of Southern China ..." George Mattson, *Uechiryu Karate Do*, Peabody Publishing Co., Newton MA, 1974.

133 "We sent that fortune teller north" Thomas J. Barnes, *Tay Son, Rebellion in 18th Century Vietnam*, Xlibris, Bloomington, Indiana, 2000, p.83.

Chapter 17. Saint-Louis, Senegal, 1786

137 "That reminds me ... a duck seller." Online Etymologic Dictionary—the original canard.

142 "It's of a shepherd's daughter dear" Traditional English song, *Knight William*, from The Young Tradition, their music CD titled, *So Cheerfully Round.*

145 "Hawes ... ordered the ... ship be set afire" Susanne Everett, *The Slaves*, Putnam, 1978.

147 "Hawes was sentenced to be hanged, drawn and quartered." Bart Hawe's death. 98% sure it was, *The Slaves,* by Susanne Everett, Putnam, 1978.

155 *"Ah! Vous dirai-je maman" Favorite French Folk Songs,* Alan Mills, Oak Publications, London/New York, 1963, p.9.

Chapter 18. Harmony Province, 1786

148 "Annam (then called Đàng Trong)" George Dutton gave very helpful feedback, including, I had misspelled Tây Sơn. He also wrote: "The labels Annam and Tonkin or Thang Long/Hanoi are all more formal and often later-used terms that are not contemporary to the era. They more likely used 'Dang Trong' and 'Dang Ngoai' or 'Bac Ha' for some of the regions, and 'Thang Long' might have been used, but equally likely would have been 'Ke Cho'—literally, market of the people, which was the more commonly used vernacular term." I chose often to keep the more modern names, as just easier.

150 "A Spanish priest ... wrote ... 'There was a carnage.'" Dutton, *The Tây Sơn Uprising.*

153 "In the art of warfare, three factors enter into play ..." Barnes, *Tay Son,* p.85.

154 Confucius reference can be found many places: Kuo LianYang, *Tai Chi Chuan.*

154 'When the laws of war indicate certain victory ...' Sun Tzu, *The Art of War*, p.137.

Chapter 20. Thái Đình Ky and Jade River, 1786

163 *How to Live in the World*, by Nguyễn Cong Tru, *The Heritage of Vietnamese Poetry*, Yale University Press, 1979, p.13, #234.

167 "The saying is often true, the gong of the husband is not equal to the gong of the wife." *Women's Social Status in the Lê Period of Vietnam, 1428-1788*, Yu Insun Seoul National University, p.6.

168 "Dame Bạc soon made it clear, though, that Jade River was a terrible burden," . . . Bạc Hạnh said, "My precious, I swear my devotion to you" *Tale of Kiều*, pp. 107-111.

Chapter 21. Thăng Long (Hà Nội), 1786

169 "General Trịnh Tú Quyên tried to stop Huệ ... in Nghệ An." Barnes, Thomas J. *Vietnam, When the Tanks were Elephants*, Xlibris, Bloomington, Indiana, 2005, p.140.

170 "Ngô Cảnh Hoàn saw both of his sons die" Barnes, *Vietnam*, p.140.

171 "The Tây Sơn entered the city gate without resistance." Barnes, *Vietnam*, p.142.

Chapter 22. The Lê Dynasty and the Spoils of War, 1786
182 "… the snake we let into our chicken coop." Based on Barnes, *Tây Sơn,* pp.103-104.
183 "Huệ, how could I forget all you have done for our family?" Barnes, *Tây Sơn.*

Chapter 24. The Warrior of the Chamber, 1788
207 "Spring Bloom …. began the old ballad of Thsing Kou." Chivas-Baron, p.255.
210 "… the God Yen Lo Hoàng had him reincarnated as an ass…." Source is lost.

Chapter 26. Wind and Rain, Từ Hải the Bandit, 1788
216 Chapter 26 is based on Nguyễn Du, *The Tale of Kiều,* pp.113-129.
216 "… singing a lovely arrangement of *The Four Pleasures.*" Poem by Nguyễn Công Trứ, translation by Huỳnh Sanh Thông, *Vietnamese Poetry,* p.92, #231.
217 "She carefully sang *The Zither*" by Cao Ba Quat. Huỳnh, *Vietnamese Poetry,* p.94, #236.
218 "When fish and water meet, it's love!' *Nguyễn Du, The Tale of Kiều,* p.117.
219 "their love bloomed forth afresh." Nguyễn Du, *The Tale of Kiều,* p.119
219 "I come and go and bow my head to none." "We should swear allegiance …" Ibid, p.127.

Chapter 30. The Twelfth Lunar Month, 1788
240 "The new emperor issued a proclamation" Barnes, *Vietnam,* pp.219-220.
241 "The local snake will outwit the dragon that has lost its way." Ibid, p.227.
243 "The Qing have invaded our country …" This speech by Huệ is historical. Trương Buu Lam, *Patterns of Vietnamese Response to Foreign Intervention, 1858-1900.* pp.63-64.

Chapter 31. The Welcome, July 1789
249 "Have mercy upon us" *Common Prayer Book,* St. Mary's Catholic Church, p.393.
251 "The Southern emperor rules" Huỳnh, *Vietnamese Poetry,* p.3, #2.
253 "Nguyễn Văn Trường defected from the Tây Sơn …" parag. from Barnes, *Vietnam,* p.314.

Chapter 32. The Forced March Before Tết, January 1789
256 I learned of the forced march while in Vietnam, 2010, from Barbara Dawson, of Barbara's Kiwi Connection Café in Quy Nhon.
261 "Tết, the Việt and Chinese New Year, usually falls on the second new moon after the solstice." A changing Western date between January 21 and February 20.
257 'good warriors prevailed, when it was easy to prevail.' Sun Tzu, pp.58-61.
260 "The good warriors take their stand on ground where they cannot lose," Ibid, pp.58, 61.
261 "Huệ sent an envoy … to General Sun Shiyi," Dutton, p.49, Barnes, *Vietnam,* p.223
262 "*The Chinese have invaded,* …" Ibid. p.225, Barnes with alterations.
263 "The uniforms of the Chinese soldiers caught fire from … sulfur" Barnes, *Vietnam,* p.227.
265 "For the seventh time in 850 years, the Việt established through military force that the southern border of China stopped at the northern border of Vietnam." (David Lindsay) 1. A.D. 938, Ngô Quyen. 2. 1076, Song Dynasty Invasion, Cao River. 3. 1258, Mongols attack under Möngke Khan. 4. 1285, Trần Hung Dao defeats 500,000 Mongols of Kublai Khan. 5. 1288, the third Mongol Invasion, Bạch Đằng River repeat. 6. 1418 to 1426, Lê Lợi defeats 300,000 Ming troops with army and charging elephants.

Chapter 33. Pierre, Cảnh, and Ánh, 1790
270 "Show the country that you can be judicious" Faure, *Pierre Pigneau,* p.214.

Chapter 34. Surprise in Sài Gòn, 1790
273 "song is called *The Rock of the Waiting Wife.*" Huỳnh, *Vietnamese Poetry,* p.104, #263.
273 "Your leaky hut is exposed to sun and rain." Huỳnh, *Vietnamese Poetry,* p. 183, #409, with minor additions by David Lindsay. (Also repeated page 386 in this book.)
274 "…take Lê Duy Chi 'to grope for shrimp." Scene from Barnes, *Vietnam,* pp.239-242.

Chapter 35. Macao, January 1790

276 "The nobility, it appears, are involved in a power play" RR Palmer and Joel Colten, *A History of the Modern World to 1815*, 4th ed. Alfred Knopf, pp. 318-322.

279 "Voltaire was ... in love with the aristocracy, and especially Plato's intellectual elite." Ibid.

280 "What is life, but a brief pause in death's anteroom?" Alexander Dumas, *The Count of Monte Cristo*.

280 "*Chevaliers de la table ronde*" Mills, *Favorite French Folk Songs*, p.76.

Chapter 36. Lương Hoàng's Dream, June 1790

287 "When adults hurt each other, ... might forgive, they rarely forget." James Clavell, *Taipan*.

Chapter 37. *La Méduse* at Sea, February 1790

295 "One hundred years ago, a Dutch squadron attacked the Nguyễn Navy," Joseph Buttinger, *The Smaller Dragon: A Political History of Vietnam*. Praeger, New York, 1958, pp.248.

Chapter 39. Nguyễn Nhạc, Quy Nhơn, 1790

309 "You'll ride your horse ..." by Lê Quát, Huỳnh, *Vietnamese Poetry*, p.70, #161.

309 "Love of Sleep" Anonymous, Huỳnh, *Vietnamese Poetry*, p.71, #163.

309 "Some men are great warriors . . ." Nhạc's poem by David Lindsay.

Chapter 40. A Sunday in March, 1790

316 "Lao Tzu ... said Confucius one bigshot, pompous, yes-man and snob" Adapted from *Lao Tzu, Tao Te Ching*. Translated by D.C Lau, Penguin Books, New York, 1981, p.8.

316 "Lao Tzu said, 'It is way of Heaven to show no favoritism.'" *Lao Tzu, Tao Te Ching*.

317 "Do that which consists in taking no action, and order will prevail." Ibid., pp.58-59.

Chapter 42. Typhoon, 1790

334 "King Nguyễn Ánh ordered that Dayot be released" Faure, *Pigneau de Béhaine*.

Chapter 43. The Opera, Phú Xuân, 1792

336 "We are thinking up to 200 *sao* ..." ~25 acres. *sao*: One *sao* equals about one-eighth acre, or one acre equals roughly eight *sao*, a traditional unit of land area in Vietnam. The *sao* varies somewhat from province to province. It is equal to 360 square meters (430.6 square yards) in many places. http://www.unc.edu/~rowlett/units/dictS.html.

336 "Ngô Thì Nhậm talked me out of invading ... China." Barnes, *Vietnam* pp.250, 261.

337 *The Faithful Harlot*, Su San and Wang Chin-lung. Source lost, but a famous opera. A version can be found in A.C. Scott, *The Classical Theatre of China*.

Chapter 45. Quy Nhơn, Sài Gòn, 1793

347 "[The Tây Sơn] sent the Nguyễn forces into flight, and marched ... into the Quy Nhơn." Lê Thanh Khoi, *Le Vietnam: Histoire et Civilisation*. Edition de Minuit, Paris, 1955, p.~318.

349 "Eulogy for Nguyễn Huệ," from Barnes, *Vietnam*, p. 262. A friend of the late Thomas Barnes, Dr. Andre Van Chau, thinks Barnes left no footnotes. Chau says that this poem is historical, and was translated into English by the late scholar Nguyễn Ngọc Bích. The original poem is much longer, and the authorship is not certain. (Thomas Barnes's footnotes might be useful if they could be found.)

Chapter 46. Jade River and the Regent, 1793

357 "what is life but foolish dreams and imperfect choices?" Bette Bao Lord, *Spring Moon*, Avon/Hearst, New York 1982, Harper & Row, 1981.

Chapter 49. Monkey Business in Phú Xuân, 1795

366 One element of this chapter is based on the *Tale of Kiều*, i.e., Kiều entered a monastery.

367 "The four old monkeys and all the rest were waiting for their king" Wu Ch'êng-ên, *Monkey,* (or, *Sun Wukong, The Monkey King's Journey to the West)* translated from the Chinese by Aurthur Waley, Grove Press, New York, 1943, pp.37-38.
367 "Milky way" is usually called Silver River in China, Vietnam and Korea. Wikipedia
372 "… how they returned to the East and handed over the scriptures" Ibid. pp.283-289.

Chapter 50. Father Pierre the Bishop in Quy Nhơn, November 1799
379 "It was the last day in which Father Pierre recognized anyone or spoke" Georges Taboulet, *La Geste franciase en Indochine*, Paris, 1955, pgs. 230-232, possibly includes some of Pierre's own words as reported by witnesses.

Chapter 51. Victors and Vanquished, 1799
381 "General Võ Tánh read the king's official eulogy, written personally by King Ánh." Nguyễn Ánh's speech, translated by Trương Buu Lam, also in French in Alexis Faure.
381 "Even the gorgeous royal chariots wear out" www.buddhanet.net/funeral.htm.
381 "Abhidhamma," Narada Maha Thera, *A Manual of Abhidhamma,* Buddhist Missionary Society, Kuala Lumpur, Malasia, 1956-1987, pp. 16, 21, 97, and 177.
382 "the official epitaph [on] Pierre Pigneau's tomb." Trương Buu Lam and Georges Taboulet.
385 "First, let us reflect on our own work" *Gokan-no-ge,* the "Five Reflections" is from Mahayana Buddhism: Zen in Japanese tradition, Ch'an in Chinese, Thiền in Vietnamese. http://buddhism.about.com/od/becomingabuddhist/a/mealchants.htm

Epilogue, 1801, and 1802 to 1825
387 "Nguyễn Navy sailed north and took … Thăng Long." Dutton, p.56.
387 "Nguyễn Quang Toản … tied between four elephants and … torn apart." Buttinger, p.~267.
390 "these firms sent ninety-five percent of their profits out of Vietnam." Martin J. Murray, *The Devolopment of Capitalism in Colonial Indochina (1870-1940)*, Univ. of California Press, Berkeley, CA, 1980.

Bibliography (Abbreviated)

History and Biography

Buttinger, Joseph. The *Smaller Dragon, A Political History of Vietnam*, Praeger, 1958.
Dull, Jonathan. *The French Navy and American Independence,* Princeton University Press, 1976.
Dutton, George. *The Tây Sơn Uprising, Society and Rebellion in Eighteenth-Century Vietnam,* University of Hawai'i Press, 2006.
Everett, Susanne. *The Slaves,* Putnam, 1978.
Faure, Alexis. *Les Français en Cochinchine au XVIIIe siècle. Mgr. Pigneau de Béhaine Évêque d'Adran,.* Challamel, Librairie Colonial, Paris, Augustin, 1891, at Yale Library.
FitzGerald, Francis. *Fire in the Lake*, Little Brown & Co., 1972.
Fraser, Antonia. *Marie Antoinette,* Knopf Doubleday and Random House Audio, 2002.
Lao Tzu. *Tao Te Ching,* translated by D.C. Lau, Penguin Books, NY, 1963-1981.

Le Thanh Khoi. *Le Viet-Nam, histoire et civilisation*, Editions de Minuit, Paris, 1955.

Lindsay, Jr., David. *The Cold War and the American War in Vietnam*, BA thesis for the Department of History, Yale University, 1976, unpublished.

Narada Maha Thera. *A Manual of Abidhamma*, Buddhist Missionary Society, Kuala Lumpur, Malasia, 1956-1987.

Nien Cheng. *Life and Death in Shanghai*, Grove Press, 1986, Penguin, 1988.

Palmer, R.R., and Colton, Joel. *A History of the Modern World to 1815*, A.A.Knopf, 1950, 1971.

Sun Tzu. *The Art of War*, translated by Thomas Cleary, Shambhala, 2005.

Taboulet, Georges. *La Geste franciase en Indochine*, Adrien Maisonneuve, Paris, 1955.

Trương Buu Lam. *Patterns of Vietnamese Response to Foreign Intervention, 1858-1900*. Yale University Press, New Haven, CT, 1967.

Trương Buu Lam. *Resistance, Rebellion, Revolution: Popular Movements in Vietnamese History*, Institute of Southeast Asian Studies, Singapore, 1984.

Whipple, A.B.C. *Fighting Sail*, The Seafarers Series, Time-Life Books, Alexandria, VA 1978.

Vietnamese Poetry

Huỳnh Sanh Thông, translator. *The Heritage of Vietnamese Poetry*, Yale University Press, New Haven, 1979.

Huỳnh Sanh Thông, translator. *Nguyễn Du, The Tale of Kiều*, a bilingual edition, Yale University Press, New Haven and London, 1983.

Folklore, Historical Fiction, and Literature

Barnes, Thomas J. *Tay Son, Rebellion in 18th Century Vietnam*, Xlibris, Bloomington, Indiana, 2000, first edition.

Barnes, Thomas J. *Vietnam, When the Tanks were Elephants*, Xlibris, Bloomington, Indiana, 2005, second edition. (This book is a rewrite of *Tay Son*.)

Chivas-Baron, Clotilde. *Stories and Legends of Annam*, Andrew Melrose, 1920. Translated from the French, *Contes et Legends de l'Annam*, by E.M. Smith-Dampier.

Mills, Alan. *Favorite French Folk Songs*, Oak Publications, New York, 1963.

Nguyen, Kien. *Le Colonial*, Little Brown & Co., New York, 2004.

Shi Nai-an. *Shui Hu Chuan (Water Margin), All Men are Brothers*, translated by Pearl Buck, 1933.

Wu Ch'êng-ên. *Monkey,* (or, *Sun Wukong, The Monkey King's Journey to the West*), translated from the Chinese by Aurthur Waley, Grove Press, NY, 1943, 1970.

The following books added general knowledge and inspiration

Buck, Pearl. *This Good Earth, The Pavillion of Women, Dragon Seed, Imperial Woman*

Cao Xueqin. *The Dream of the Red Chamber*, 1791.

Cervantes Saavedra, Miguel de. *Don Quixote of La Mancha*, 1605, 1615.

Chen, Pauline. *The Red Chamber*, Knopf, Random House Audible, 2012.

Clavell, James. *Shogun, Tai-Pan, Noble House.*

Dickens, Charles. *A Tale of Two Cities*, 1859.

Dumas, Alexander. *The Count of Monte Christo*, 1844.

Forester, C.S. The Horatio Hornblower series.

Hugo, Victor. *Les Misérables*, 1862.

Lord, Bette Bao, *Spring Moon*, Avon/Hearst, NY 1982, Harper & Row, 1981.

Michener, James. *Hawaii, Chesapeake.*

Mistry, Rohinton. *A Fine Balance* (a novel about India). McClelland and Stewart, 1995.

O'Brien, Patrick. The Aubrey-Maturin series, WW Norton & Co., New York.

Van Gulik, Robert. The Judge Dee Mysteries series, Charles Scribner's & Sons, New York

Lists of Main Characters

The Tây Sơn (8)
The Hồ family: the three brothers, one sister, two parents
Hồ Nhạc, eldest brother, changes his name to Nguyễn Nhạc
Hồ Lữ (Lữ pronounced Loo), middle brother, changes his name to Nguyễn Lữ
Hồ Huệ (pronounced Whey), youngest brother, changes his name to Nguyễn Huệ
Jade River (Ngọc Hà), sister of the Hồ brothers
Hồ Danh or Physician Hồ, their father (Hồ Van Phúc in history)
Autumn Moon (Thu Nguyệt), their mother
Lương Hoàng, a neighbor who loves Jade River
Nguyễn Quang Toản, Son of Huệ and Blue Cloud (Thu Vân)

The French (6)
Benoit Grannier, naval officer
Pierre Pigneau de Béhaine, Bishop of Adran and Vicar Apostolic of Cochinchina
Guillaume de Martineau, naval officer

André de Lagier, naval officer, folk singer
Antoine Grannier, Benoit's cousin
Margarita Bordechampe, singing girl, widow and harbor nancy

The Nguyễn (3)
Nguyễn Ánh or Nguyễn Phúc Ánh, the prince, son of Nguyễn Phúc Luân
Nguyễn Phúc Cảnh, son of Nguyễn Ánh and his First Wife Pure Essence
Bùi Moon Light (Bùi Ánh Nguyệt), sister of Bùi Spring Song (Bùi Thị Xuân), a female Tây Sơn general

Supernumeraries, in alphabetical order (lesser characters and walk ons)
Alain Artaud, Father, teacher, then assistant to Pierre Pigneau
Bạc Hạnh, the nephew of farmer and dame Bạc
Baltasar Weber, dwarfish friend of Guillaume de Martineau
Blue Cloud, (Thu Vân), concubine of Nguyễn Huệ, found in a brothel (Tây Sơn)
Bùi Quang Dien, the father of Bùi Moon Light and Bùi Spring Song (Thị Xuân)
Bùi Spring Song (Bùi Thị Xuân), Tây Sơn female general of the elephant brigades, Bùi Moon Light's sister and the daughter of Bùi Quang Dien
Cảnh Dong, Tây Sơn admiral who fights *La Méduse*
Captain La Fontaine, marine
Celeste Grannier, Benoit's mother. Benoit's eight siblings are Annette, Cécile, François, Marie-Noelle, Gabriel, Elisabet, Georges-Louis, and Isabelle
Chrysanthemum, Paul Nghi's relative who serves Lady Purity (Nguyễn Ánh's mother)
Confucius, philosopher, founder of Confucianism, historical reference only
Đặng Thị Nga, singing girl, mother of Cán with King Trịnh Sâm, Đặng Thị Huệ in history
Diệu Tri, Nguyễn scholar and soldier in prison with Father Pierre the Bishop
Đỗ Thanh Nhơn , Nguyễn Ánh's commander-in-chief
Đoàn Thanh, Chairman of the Board of Rites under the Nguyễn.
Édouard Villeseint, Father
Emperor Quianlong of China
Endless Joy, Nguyễn Ánh's favorite wife
Etienne Lalois, Lieutenant, Battle of the ChesapeakeFather Lozier, Vũng Tàu, Vietnam
Georges Quellenac, sword master and dancing master, Lorient, France
Gem Lake (Ngọc Hân), daughter of Emperor Lê Hiển Tông, given to Huệ, becomes his third wife, Lê Thị Ngọc Hân
Green Willow, Nguyễn Huệ's First Wife (Tây Sơn)
Hải Vân Đài, peasant conscript on the forced march, father of Rice King and Daydreamer
Hải Vân Hành, Hải Vân Đài's elder brother, also a conscript
Henri Dayot, captain, becomes commodore
Hoàng Đình Thể, a Trịnh Army lieutenant, ordered to attack Huệ by Phạm Ngô Lam
Hoàng Phùng Cỏ, general, called out of retirement by King Trịnh Khải
Jean Bluedot, lieutenant on *La Méduse*
Joachim Bohu, first mate on *La Méduse*
John Ngô, Vietnamese Christian
Joseph Phạm, Vietnamese Christian, Junior Acolyte

Julian Girard, naval officer, captain of *La Castries*

Kiều, a given name for a girl, pronounced Gee-yew

King Trịnh Sâm, fell in love with singing girl, Đặng Thị Nga

King Trịnh Khải, son of King Trịnh Sâm

Kin Hua, the Goddess of Fertility

Lady Purity, Nguyễn Ánh's mother, wife of Nguyễn Phúc Luân

Lao Tzu (now Laozi), philosopher and founder of Taoism, historical reference only

Lê Chiêu Thống, grandson/heir of Emperor Lê Hiển Tông, nephew of Gem Lake

Le Comte François Joseph de Grasse, French rear admiral

Lê Duy Chỉ, brother of Lê Chiêu Thống, the sons of Lê Hiển Tông

Lê Hiển Tông, the Lê Emperor, father of Gem Lake, Lê Chiêu Thống, and Duy Chỉ

Madame Camellia, the madam of the Happy Valley Green Pavilion of Biên Hòa

Michel Despiaux, Doctor

Minh Mạng, Emperor, son of Nguyễn Ánh, born Nguyễn Phúc Đảm

Miss Hoạn, First Wife of Thái Đình Ky in Phan Thiết

Ngô Spring Blossom, at Nguyễn Ánh's banquet, Bùi Moon Light's female associate

Ngô Thì Nhậm, general who served Huệ, sent to China impersonating Huệ

Ngô Văn Sở and Trần Quang Đàn, generals sent by Huệ to rule Đông Kinh after Vũ
    Mộng Duệ

Nguyễn Binh Loan, Ánh's tutor

Nguyễn Quang Toản, Son of Huệ and Blue Cloud (Thu Vân) (Tây Sơn), King Cảnh
    Thịnh (first reign name)

Nguyễn Cường, Huệ's son with Precious Stone, his second wife

Nguyễn Đình, King of Cochinchina before Nguyễn Ánh

Nguyễn Dũng, district magistrate of Cochinchina

Nguyễn Hữu Chỉnh, "the Savage Eagle," the Trịnh's greatest contemporary general

Nguyễn Phúc Cảnh, first son of Nguyễn Ánh

Nguyễn Phúc Luân, Nguyễn Ánh's father, married to Lady Purity

Nguyễn Thị Hiền, mandarin of diplomacy, official greeter

Nguyễn Thơ, Phúc Cảnh's first cousin

Nguyễn Trứ, son of Green Willow and Nguyễn Huệ

Nguyễn Trúc, mandarin of Bình Định Province, including Quy Nhơn and Tây Sơn

Nguyễn Văn Trương, acting Nguyễn captain of the galley *Serpent*

Nguyễn Võ Vương, King, Nguyễn Ánh's grandfather

Nicolas Desangeles, Father, Portuguese

Nicolas Tabarly, Sublieutenant, bald-headed

Olivier du Puymanel, engineer, red-haired

Old Goat, Pierre Pigneau's major domo

Orchid, Nguyễn Phúc Cảnh's nurse, Trưng Bình, his valet and bodyguard

Paul Nghi, Senior Acolyte to Father Pierre Pigneau the Bishop

Papaya, maid servant to Bùi Moon Light

Perfume Shrine (Hương Miếu), one of Nhạc's inspiring concubines

Phạm Ngô Cán, Trịnh general, the spy was to deliver the false evidence to him

Phúc Hop, Nguyễn Ánh's controller of the exchequer

Phước Tinh, friend of Lương Hoàng (Tây Sơn)

Precious Stone, Huệ's Second Wife (Tây Sơn)

Pure Essence, Nguyễn Ánh's First Wife
Quách Nu Xấu Xí, Quách Ugly Female (or Tidbit)
Quách Văn Thọ, patient of Physician Hồ, his wife was Quách Nu Xấu Xí
Quan Công (the God of War)
Quán Thế Âm, the Bodhisattva or Goddess of Mercy (Chinese: Guanyin, QuanYin,
    Kuanyin; Sanskrit: Avalokiteśvara, also the Mercy Goddess)
Quang Toản, son of Huệ and Blue Cloud (Tây Sơn), becomes King Cảnh Thịnh
Quang Trung, Emperor, formerly Hồ Huệ, becomes Nguyễn Huệ
Red Lotus, Lương Hoàng's Second Wife
Rice King and Daydreamer, the two sons of Hải Vân Đại, Tây Sơn conscripts
Scholar Mã, procurer of flowers, or flesh-peddler and boyfriend of Madam Camellia
Skinny Minh, Nguyễn secret police agent
Snake, Midget, Night Hawk and Lover Boy, Nhạc's first bodyguard
Spring Bloom, Lương Hoàng's First Wife
Spring Flower (Xuân Hoa), Nhạc's First Wife
Sun Shiyi, Governor, leads Qing invasion of Đại Việt
Thái Đình Ky, suiter of Jade River, then first husband, but married to Miss Hoạn
Trần Quang Diệu, Bùi Spring Song's husband, was a Nguyễn General, both defect-
    ed to the Tây Sơn, Trần Quang Diệu was Bùi Moon Light's brother-in-law
Trịnh Cán, son of King Trịnh Sâm and Đặng Thị Nga, was made heir over first son
    Khải
Trịnh Tú Quyên, Trịnh general, defended Thăng Long (Hà Nội)
Trưng Binh, Nguyễn Phúc Cảnh's valet and bodyguard
Trương Văn Hiến, scholar and tutor of the Hồ children, then their political advisor
Từ Hải, bandit leader, suitor of Jade River, then her second husband
Võ Tánh, Nguyễn general and famous sword master
Võ Văn Nhậm, Nhạc's general, frog-like face, considered Huệ dangerous
Vũ Chan, con artist, suitor of Jade River
Vũ Mộng Duệ, General sent by Huệ to subdue Nguyễn Hữu Chỉnh

Important places
Phú Xuân, the Spring Capital (now Huế)
Thăng Long is an early name for Hà Nội